Krampus Kristmas

2020

An Anthology of Fright and Melancholy

By

David V. Stewart

TABLE OF CONTENTS

THE WASTING DESERT

-To Lucita, my love-

I have entrusted this letter to Darala, your servant, whom I have sent back on a secure ship to Balta. May it find you and our son well, healthy, and happy.

Tomorrow we begin our expedition in earnest by entering the Wasting Desert. Our journey to Progenosus, though fraught with danger, was but the first step. Our guide, who is of that race called often "Dark Elves," has already proved himself of great worth in that first step, detecting and dispatching with ease a group of assassins, hired no doubt by Palimo, who still seeks my ruin, if not both of ours. Give my thanks to your uncle for finding and recommending the elf. I will owe him a share of the profits, such as I can dispense.

The elf assures us the trek across the desert will take no more than a week, and that he can find the hidden paths through to the outposts of the great eastern empire of the Draesenith. His payment is queer – he wants only modest dispensation, but he also intends for us to cart back some largish object that he assures us is not guarded and of no worth to the Draesenith. He also assures me that the Draesenith will not stop us at the border. He is a mage, apparently, though like his payment, his magic is strange, but I have seen him demonstrate the ability to deceive the minds of others (which he used to save the lives of your servant and myself).

He brought a companion with him that asks no payment save for a share of the profits after we return. I suspect he is a Draesen himself, though I have never seen a real one to compare, and he seems to match the drawings in your book. If he is any indication, you need not fear that I stray while on this trip (not that you ever need fear, my fidelity belongs only to you); the Draesenith are far too orcish for any man to be long tempted.

I have faith that our expedition will be successful. If it is, I believe we can finally purchase a title and return to Datalia – our families be damned. Pray to Denarthal for me, and remember the silver I left for you to offer at the temple. One piece per day, as interest for my life. I pray to all the gods that you and our son are secure, and that you are able to continue to keep him so. Trust me that when we have our title, he need no longer fear.

Your devoted,
Alastan

Alastan reached the top of the ridge and looked out upon the desert. An endless sheet of hardpan stretched out below him, cracked open by scrubby bushes and succulents grey in the early sun. Through it all ran a trace of a rutted wagon-road, fading along with the shrubs. He could see in the distance the dunes, ever-shifting in white streaked with dirty red. He looked back and could see, far in the distance, the grove of palms and other dry-weather trees that lay nestled in the canyon, which at a distance looked like a crack in the great grey tooth that was the rain-shadowed Darus Mountains.

"Get a good look. It will be some time before we are back in the land of men." Mondal walked past Alastan, his eyes faintly luminescent in the shade of his white hood and his expression moot. The dark elf led by a heavy chain one of the barsils, its great scaled flank heavy with water, causing it to waddle with its grasping reptilian feet. It's load bounced back and forth; pots clanked against each other in the rhythm of its steps. The beast turned a reptilian eye to Alastan as it passed, then rumbled a greeting softly.

"I have no expectation for a short journey," Alastan said. "Still, it would be best this excursion go as quickly as possible. There is much business afoot in the strand and I am loathe to be in absence."

"Business? Running from vendettas is hardly a business. If so, I should be quite rich." Mondal said. He turned back, and in the early sun, his unknowable flashed iridescent yellow. He reached into his hood, scratched at one of his long ears, and then drew a linen scarf around his face.

"I call it a job," Datero said, following behind Mondal and leading another barsil. "Keeps the nasty bits impersonal."

Alastan ventured one last glance at the grove, and the village within it, then fell into step with Datero as they moved down the ridge.

"That I can understand," Mondal said. "I've had that job – to be a living dagger." He growled softly. "I do not care much for it."

"Neither do I," Datero said. "Which is why I'm here and not back in Datalia." He turned around and looked back. The gigantic Thokar, his skin grey no matter the light, was looking back the way they had come, tall and still as a gnarled tree. "Hey, Thokar! Stop waiting for him! If he falls behind, it's his own fault."

"We paid good money for that barsil," Alastan said. "And I think we shall need the water before the end, even if we find its master of little use."

"It's my understanding Bartolo did most of the paying," Datero said. "Pity the fool doesn't trust us to cut him in after everything is said and done. He's not suited to this business, methinks."

"He trusts you enough not to murder him," Mondal said. "It would be a simple thing, out here."

Thokar frowned as he jogged back toward Datero and Alastan. "He's riding it."

"Tell him to get off his ass," Datero said. He looked up at Thokar, who towered over him. "That ass could use a walk. Too many years in a chair, and not enough in the saddle."

"He's in the saddle now," Alastan said.

"You know what I mean."

Alastan smiled at Datero. "I'll go make him walk."

*

It was a quick transition from the scrubby brushlands to the full desert, and by midday, the sun beat down on them with a heartless fury. Bartolo had a healthy ring of wet cloth in his shirt around his neck, and both Alastan and Datero held their large hats close to their face. Even Thokar, as well-traveled as he was, looked uncomfortable. Only Mondal seemed un-phased by the desert, and though he was draped in pale cloth, it, as well as his face, was dry of sweat.

"Drat this," Bartolo said, dabbing at his large neck and brushing moisture from his beard. "This had better be worth it."

"It will," Alastan said. "Trust me."

"I still don't see why we can't ride the barsils. We have saddles, after all."

"Once they are lighter of water and we are heavier of foot, we can," Thokar said.

"It will happen all too soon," Mondal said.

"What's that up there?" Datero said, pointing uphill toward a dead tree surrounded by stones. "Is that the first sign?"

"Yes," Mondal said. "Let us pause there and have a drink."

"Let's not bother going all the way up there," Bartolo said.

"We must unless you want to get lost," Mondal said.

Bartolo grumbled but followed the dark elf up the hill to where the dead tree stood. Its bark was deep-ridged and twisted up from the cracked earth to a cluster of dead branches. In the branches sat a vulture with closed eyes. A hot wind stirred loos feathers around its bald neck, but otherwise, it was still.

"Is it dead too?" Alastan asked. As he spoke, the vulture opened its eyes and regarded them, then tucked its head back under a wing.

"Is what dead?" Mondal said.

"The vulture – nevermind," Alastan said.

"The vulture is alive," Mondal said. "What else is dead?"

"I said nevermind," Alastan said. "I'm too thirsty for your riddles."

Mondal looked at Thokar, who shrugged.

"I think he means the tree," Thokar said. "It does *appear* dead."

"It's not?" Datero said. He touched the tree with his hand, pushing against it, then let himself down to the ground and leaned his back against it. "At least it provides a fraction of shade."

"It's quite alive," Thokar said. "This whole area is, though it may not look it. The flows of the prim are strong here, beneath the surface of what you see. Did you consider how a tree like this would get all the way out into the desert?"

"A bird could have carried the seed," Bartolo said. "Or nut, or whatever."

"Undoubtedly, but what fed it?"

"An underground spring which has gone dry, of course. It's quite simple."

Thokar sighed, his deep voice rumbling.

"Nevertheless, it is the first sign," Mondal said. "We will trace the flow from here to the first oasis."

"Why don't we travel at night, when it's not so hot?" Datero said. He opened one of the waterskins and drank deeply from it.

"You never travel the Wasting Desert at night."

"And why is that?" Bartolo said. He wiped his mouth with his sleeve.

"Pray to whatever gods listen that you do not have to find out," Mondal said.

Bartolo threw his hands in the air. "*This* is our guide? That wasn't an answer!"

"It's as much of an answer as you deserve," Mondal said. "And can handle. I judge your spine to be as soft as your belly. I dislike upsetting people unnecessarily."

"*And* he insults his employer!" Bartolo said. "The things I put up with for you, Alastan."

"The things you put up with always make you money," Alastan said. "I'll contract a competent rude man over a kind but incompetent one. And I think you already owe me for that decision."

"Owe you?" Bartolo said. "You know as well as I do Palimo sent those men after us. Nobody would have attacked us had-"

"There are men following us," Alastan said. He was looking out behind them.

Mondal and Thokar stepped up to look out over the yellow-grey waste, and they could perceive far to the west a row of black dots on the pale sands.

"Men sent by Palimo?" Mondal said. "Or does he employ other races?"

"I don't know," Alastan said. "Why?"

"Few Draesen know the way across the Talamask. Even fewer of the other races know," Thokar said.

"I don't think they shall survive to trouble us," Mondal said. "Unless they have employed someone from the empire, as Thokar suggests."

"What do we do?" Alastan said.

"Don't say I have to get my armor on in this bloody heat," Datero said.

"No," Mondal said. "They will get lost on their own."

Thokar turned and looked at the vulture. He raised his great arm and gestured toward the dots in the distance. "Those men are likely to die soon, should you need a meal."

The vulture picked its head up and looked to where Thokar pointed. He flapped his wings and then took off. A short ways off, he started to glide over a thermal on the sandy desert floor, floating up into the sky.

"I'll be damned," Bartolo said. "I think he might have actually understood you."

"Why would he not?" Thokar said.

Bartolo forced a false laugh and threw his hands down.

*

The sun was hugging the horizon behind them as the cluster of stone and greenery appeared in a low place. It stood out bright against the rust-colored sands of the wide valley, sharp and shining among the dull and featureless expanse.

"Is that it?" Alastan said, mopping sweat from his brow.

"I believe so," Mondal said.

"Our guide *believes* so," Bartolo said between pants. "You *have* been this way before, haven't you?"

"No," Mondal said.

"What?"

"I've never been this way before," Mondal said. He turned back and gazed impassively at him. "You seem agitated."

"You think!?" Bartolo said. "I'm not looking forward to dying out here!"

"You don't understand the nature of this desert," Thokar said. "There are several oases, but where they are is not always set."

"How is that possible?" Bartolo said.

"This desert is filled with the flows of the prim spilling from the Fay Lands. It is a mirror of sorts to the wastes in the north. Being subject to such chaos, and being uninhabited by beings such as ourselves, things are not fixed and are subject to changes. Only the oases hold firm."

"What does the desert being uninhabited have to do with it?" Alastan said.

"There is much you have to learn," Thokar said. "Without the dreamers, there is no dream, eh?"

"I don't understand," Alastan said.

"It's not meant to be understood," Bartolo said. "These men are charlatans, using old tricks of rhetoric to make you think they have expertise when they, in fact, have none."

"Neither of us is a man," Mondal said.

"And do not count your own ignorance as proof against anything, merchant," Thokar said with a deep chuckle. "Here is the oasis."

They crested a ridge of crumbled rock and fine iron sand to find the Oasis a few dozen yards ahead of them. Palm fronds waved in the reddening light, growing from stunted trunks crammed into cracks in the sharp rock. As they went down the hill, shifting sand tricked their feet, making them slip on occasion over a treacherous spot, and they would have to fling out their hands and arms to stop themselves from rolling down the slope. The barsils, by contrast, had no trouble negotiating the terrain, their long-toed feet gripping slippery rock and spreading their immense weight over smooth sand equally well.

They reached the basin and walked around the encircling walls of rock in a slow arc before they found an opening large enough for the barsils to get through with their wide-stanced crawl. There was a space of soft sand and soil past the wall of rock, and as they passed into it, it was apparent that the rocks were not natural. They were the remnant of some structure made by tools, though not made of bricks or stacked stone, but rather solid rock growing from the ground and shaped with precision. The remnants of windows and doorways opened up around them into empty, roofless cells filled with scrubby plants.

"Where is the water?" Bartolo said. He leaned up against a wall and took his hat off, revealing a red pate of thinning hair, which he mopped with a handkerchief. "Isn't an oasis supposed to have water?"

"There are shrubs here," Alastan said. "That means there is water."

"But where? Isn't there supposed to be a pool, or pond... or *something*?"

"There's bound to be a well at least," Datero said, already working on unburdening one of the barsils. As he worked on one of the knots, he looked around with a curious expression.

"This is not that sort of Oasis," Mondal said. "Rather, it is a safe place among the shifting paths of the fay."

"Are we in the Fay Lands?" Alastan said.

"Not quite," Thokar said. "More the spillover from the Fay Lands. The true Fay is far too perilous to cross in this manner. Since no people have remained here in the long ages, it shifts its nature like the Fay, but far slower and with much less profundity."

"Fay lands," Bartolo said with a scoff. "So much myth."

Thokar gave him a deep, rumbling grunt of irritation.

"Don't lose your temper and skin the poor man," Mondal said. He leapt onto one of the stone formations and looked over it out into the desert.

"I am little used to the manners of the Divine Strand," Thokar said. "There is more faith in the North. And more politeness."

"There's no point in being polite to fools," Bartolo said. "Especially a fool who bases his standard of manners on the savages of the Petty Kingdoms." He scoffed and turned away.

"Patience, Thokar," Mondal said.

"This shall be a long trip in more ways than one," Datero said. He sighed. "I'll go look for a well. Whoever cut this stone surely needed one."

"Let me know if you find one," Alastan said. "If not, this is why we brought the barsils."

"Drinking lizard juice is not a contingency I wish to explore," Bartolo said. "Please do find a well." He wiped his face again, then slid down the rock to the dirt. Groaning, he pulled his hat down against the last of the light.

*

Alastan woke from a nightmare with a sudden urge to relieve himself. To his surprise, the gulley had grown very cold, and he could see his breath in front of him. He took the wool blanket off and crept carefully past the rest of the party, sleeping soundly. He noticed a radiant heat from a small pile of glowing stones as he passed by Thokar, and make a note to himself to sleep near the big half-orc the next night. Alastan ducked under some green fronds that hemmed in what was once a small room and began to urinate in a corner.

"Spilling a lot of water there, Alastan."

Alastan jumped back with surprise and saw Mondal sitting at the top of a tall boulder above him, his eyes shining so brightly their details were lost in an impassive wall of pale blue. The ancient dark elf's passionless gaze left Alastan feeling even colder, and he shivered.

"Are you still holding watch? Why haven't you woken someone else?" Alastan said.

"Sleep is not as necessary so close to the Fay Lands, where the flows of the prim are so easy to touch and drink," Mondal said. "Only in the mundane world is the escape of sleep a true necessity."

"Huh," Alastan said with a nod. He looked up at a field of stars that were unfamiliar to him. "What time is it?"

"I don't know."

"Well, the moon has set," Alastan said. "It's a few days out from full, so it must be close to morning, yes?"

Mondal shrugged. "Perhaps. What does it matter?"

"I figured since I was up, I would take watch."

"I told you that I don't need to sleep."

"Everyone needs sleep, Mondal."

"What is there to dream when we are already treading on the edge of dreams? Besides, an enemy approaches. Best not take to sleep now." He nodded outward.

Alastan looked back at the camp for a brief moment, then climbed up the rock to where Mondal sat with a crossbow across his lap.

"Where?"

"Yonder." Mondal said, pointing out to the long and level plains beyond. In the distance, Alastan saw a pale white light, like that of the moon or stars, shifting over the ground.

"I see some lights."

"The spirits of the lost. They pursue a man."

"If you say so. I should have brought my spyglass."

"To relieve yourself? That would be an odd choice of tools."

Alastan chuckled in spite of his rising anxiety as he watched the lights. "He must know where these waypoints are in the desert."

"It is more likely that he is following us, considering how long it has taken to arrive," Mondal said.

"He couldn't have followed. That's not the way we came here."

"It is."

"No, we came over a tall ridge, remember?"

"Yes." Mondal pointed to his right. "There is the old gate where we entered. This is the side of this hold-fortress we first spied."

"The landscape changed?"

"During the night, it seems much is subject to change," Mondal said. "It makes sense, no? Our companions over there are dreaming, after all."

"This place is the same. At least, I think it's the same."

"Now you see."

"How, though?" Alastan said.

"It was built long ago by your empire, by beings of very permanent, mundane persuasions. Their outposts remain, even though the world has changed, because they were built to stand against the shifting thoughts of the Fay, when it was a greater thing than it has become."

Alastan was silent a moment, then said, "And what shall we do with this visitor?"

Mondal patted his crossbow. "I'm a fairly good shot, but I also have ways to close the distance without being noticed."

"I don't know that he's an enemy."

"Don't you?"

"I haven't spoken to him."

"How could he be anything else? Who else would be seeking you besides an enemy? Do you have a kingdom to inherit?"

"No, but still."

Mondal's voice croaked softly in a low tone, then he said, "I thought men were prone to logic. And you are a merchant, yes?"

"I am, but a murderer I am not."

"I am a murderer," Mondal said.

"Not on my behalf. There is only one way into this hollow. Let's prepare a defense."

"Very well, Alastan, but beware. When the spirits draw near, we may have more to risk than a single assassin."

"That reminds me," Alastan said, climbing down from the rock, "It's just one man?"

"Yes."

"Yesterday, there were three. What happened to the other two?"

"I suppose we shall be asking him," Mondal said. "Go wake the others. I will watch the approach and shoot if required."

Alastan nodded. "Only if it is necessary."

*

Alastan watched the man as he steadily got closer, running and stumbling over rocks in the sandy stretch of land before the oasis. Behind him were phantoms, which through Alastan's spyglass looked to be of vaguely human shape but with indistinct faces and limbs. Because they provided the majority of light and were behind the running man, Alastan could make out no details on the man except that he wore some sort of simple, bulky cloth armor.

"That's close enough!" Alastan called as the man approached the walls. "Unless you want to die." Alastan drew his head down to aim his crossbow. Thokar, who stood upon a nearby boulder, lit up the crystal of his staff with bright green light and held it forward, illuminating the face of a harried and frightened man wearing a gambeson dyed grey and cut in the generous style of the Structania military.

"Let me in!" the man cried, falling forward onto his hands and getting up again just as quickly, heaving with steaming breath. The shades that followed a few yards behind him closed the distance, and their features increased in clarity. They had thin and angular faces with shining dead eyes and gaping grey mouths. The ghostly shapes wore strange clothes and reached forward with their long, fog-wrapped hands. Alastan lowered his crossbow as he began to hear their voices. They were loud and yet indistinct, crying without words, or in a simple language, he could not understand. All he knew was that they sounded afraid, desperate, and furious.

The running man found some extra reserve of energy and doubled his speed as he approached the tumbled stone barrier.

"Stop!" Alastan said, but the man ran forward with his hands out and plowed into the rock wall. He scratched upward with his hands and feet, trying desperately to climb up and away from the spirits. Behind him, his pursuers faded in detail, turning blurry and misty as their approach slowed. They then spread out, with some drifting away from the walls of the oasis, like waves being drawn back into the ocean.

Alastan sighed and dropped his crossbow. He hopped down to a lower boulder and lay down on his belly, reaching a hand down. The man, who was frantic and almost crying, did not notice the hand, but continued trying to claw down the rock.

"Open your eyes, man!" Alastan said.

The man snapped his head around and saw the dangling hand. He jumped up and grabbed hold of Alastan's arm with both of his hands, nearly pulling Alastan off of the rock. Datero ran from the open gate and scrambled up to Alastan, gripping his friend's clothes to keep him from falling away. The stranger clawed and scrambled up over Alastan, then tumbled down eight feet over the uneven stone to the soft floor of the oasis, where he gasped with closed eyes.

"What about those ghosts?" Bartolo said. "How will we keep them out!?"

"They cannot enter here," Mondal said, jumping lithely down from the wall to examine the gasping stranger. Alastan rolled over, rubbing his arm, and looked out to the desert to see the white figures backing up and moving away from each other, thinning to a collection of foggy clusters amid the black night.

"Already they are wandering away," Thokar said, taking a heavy few steps down from where he stood to the floor of the ancient fortress, illuminating the stranger with his staff. Mondal quickly disarmed the man, taking his sword and finding several hidden knives.

"No, they aren't!" Bartolo said. He fired his crossbow into one of the phantoms. The bolt flew through and the spirit seemed to shimmer a moment in place, gaining a face before fading back into mist and moving on. Bartolo squatted down and, placing his foot in the stirrup of his crossbow, attempted to span it with great effort.

"I said they cannot enter here," Mondal shouted. "Stop wasting ammunition."

Bartolo strained and managed to get the bowstring into the machine slot. When he looked up, the spirits were already more distant and had lost much detail. He loaded a fresh bolt and sat back on a rock with a grunt, his dark, wondering eyes darting between the pale lights in the desert.

"Our visitor looks like he has seen much," Mondal said, turning his attention back to the man who was stretched out on the dusty floor, gasping with his eyes tightly shut. The dark elf drew a long dagger and squatted down beside the man.

"You're alright now," Alastan said. "You're safe, for the time being."

"Safe from the spirits, you mean," Datero said. "Safe from me? Not so much."

"Quiet," Alastan said. "That's not going to help." He slapped the stranger on the face lightly. "Come on, come out of it."

"Leave him be for a few moments," Thokar said. "The Phantoms of the Wasting Desert are no small thing to endure. No tales return that lack for horror."

"You think the other two are out there still?" Datero said.

"In one form or another, yes," Thokar said. "The phantoms are those who have become lost here, neither part of the Fay nor the mundane world. At least, that is what the Draesenith believe."

"Alright, well, let's keep watch, then," Alastan said, rubbing his neck. "Tomorrow will be a long day."

*

Alastan shook his head to chase away the temptation of sleep as the stranger stirred. Light was growing, drowning out the stars and bringing up the oasis's details in a flat, colorless light. Alastan shuffled over to the would-be assassin to see his lips moving, but his voice was so soft and strained he couldn't make out any words.

"He's waking," Alastan said, glancing over to see Datero shaking off his own drowsiness.

Datero yawned and stood up, fumbling his unsheathed sword, which he had laid across his knees. He pushed himself to his feet and swung his sword in a circle, then walked stiffly toward the man on the oasis floor.

In the grey of dawn, the stranger's face looked ashen-grey, the dust in his beard and uncovered hair chasing away any hint of color that might have humanized the man. He breathed heavily and quickly. His arms and shoulders seem to shake against invisible bonds. Finally, pale blue eyes opened.

"A Northman," Datero said, pointing his sword at the man.

The man's eyes closed, and a teardrop escaped from one. His breathing slowed.

"Who hired you, assassin?" Datero said. "And where did you come from?"

The man was silent.

Datero took a step closer, brandishing his sword, then flinched in surprise when he noticed Mondal standing beside him. Almost gently, the elf pushed Datero's sword downward toward the sand.

"Our employer doesn't wish to spill unnecessary blood," Mondal said softly.

"Nonsense. I say kill him," Bartolo said. The fat merchant had woken up and was sitting up in his bedroll, trying to pull a knife that hung on his nearby bag, but was finding his sizeable belly to be a significant hindrance to reaching it.

"You are not my employer," Mondal said.

"Oh, yes, I am!"

"No," Mondal said. "I am removing you as my employer due to your incompetence."

"What? You can't do that."

"I can," Mondal said. "Alastan is my employer now."

"Fine, I guess I don't have to pay you."

"Yes, you do," Mondal said.

Bartolo looked at the elf, agape, then he stood up and pulled his knife free of his pack. "Well, what do you intend to do with him, eh?"

Mondal looked at Alastan, who shrugged.

"I guess we could leave him here," Datero said. "He doesn't seem like he's getting up."

"That would damn him," Thokar said. He was standing near the doorway to one of the roofless rooms, leaning on his staff. "This place is a wasteland in more ways than one."

"He deserves it. He's an assassin!" Bartolo said.

Thokar shook his head and knelt beside the man. He placed one of his large, ashen hands on the man's forehead, then spoke softly. The man's eyes opened again.

"Come back to yourself. We will need to travel far," Thokar said.

The man took a deep breath. "Are they here?"

"No, but they are close."

"They want me."

"What of your companions?"

The man closed his eyes, and his body trembled. "Gone. All gone."

"Can you walk?" Alastan said. "Our baggage is rather important. We can't afford to leave any behind so that we can strap you to one of the barsils."

"If it means I can escape the… those things, then I can walk," the man said.

"Then let's get to it," Alastan said. He extended a hand toward the man. "I am Alastan."

"I know," the man said, gripping Alastan's forearm and pulling himself up. "I am Haggin, for what it is worth."

"A Northman indeed," Datero said. "What sends you so far south and east?"

"Work," Haggin said, leaning on a nearby rock on uneasy legs.

"For whom?"

Haggin looked blank-faced at him for a few moments.

"If it is anyone important, he won't be able to tell us," Alastan said.

"He bloody well better," Bartolo said. "If we're going to spare his life, we might as well know who has a price on our head. Or probably *your* head, Alastan."

"You misunderstand, my friend," Alastan said. "He will be *unable* to speak the name. The high guilds bind their members to an oath with magic."

Thokar grumbled. "Many things may be unmade along our path. If you can speak the name, you should, for your own sake."

"My own sake?" Haggin said. "So I can be hunted by man and ghost alike?"

"I think all hunts will be given up," Thokar said with a grin, "when we reach the end of the Fay Waste."

"The guild would not rest… would never accept failure and betrayal."

"Then kill yourself now," Mondal said. "We will bury your body."

Haggin narrowed his eyes. "No. I will survive as I always have."

"Then get moving," Mondal said. He stepped away from the group and toward the gate of the ring of rocks.

"He's just going to slip a dagger in our backs," Bartolo said.

"How easy do you think it will be to return?" Alastan said. "I think for you, Haggin, this is a one-way trip, whatever happens, but like you said, you can survive."

*

Bartolo was hunched forward in the saddle of his barsil, sweat dripping – practically streaming – off of his nose. The beast seemed to bear the burden without issue, but that was probably only because so much of their water was already gone.

The rest of the party, save for Mondal, had stripped their upper bodies to skin or shirtsleeves once the heat of the day began its assault. Mondal wore his full armor, a set of strange, dark mail, but didn't sweat. Whatever substance dark elves were made of, they apparently did not suffer the effects of the elements in the same fashion as mortals.

Thokar, his dark skin glistening over taught muscles revealed by his thin inner tunic, walked beside Bartolo's mount. Silently, he stepped back and put an empty flask below Bartolo's face, catching a few drops of sweat.

"If you refuse common sense, at least preserve some moisture," he said.

Bartolo frowned at him and took a heavy breath. "You would drink my sweat?"

"If I needed to," Thokar said. "Pride yields to need, merchant. Always."

"I should charge you, then," Bartolo said.

"He just doesn't want us to see his fat, pasty body," Datero said. Or he'd have the sense to ditch the jacket."

"And perhaps I should insist that *you* do not charge *me,* bodyguard!"

"Relax, Barty," Datero said. "They'll be plenty of gold to go around once we get back."

"Easy to trust the future when you have nothing at risk."

Datero laughed. "Look around you! You think I have no risk?" He drew his sword and swung it about himself. "And who is going to be doing the fighting, eh? Your lizard?"

"Ideally, nobody," Thokar said. "Besides, that sword will be of little use out here."

"Yes, but on the other side are the Draesen."

It was Thokar's turn to chuckle. "Little man, they will laugh at you. Would you believe I am considered quite small?"

"So, you are one!" Bartolo said. "I knew it. I said as much to Alastan." He turned in his saddle to where Alastan walked. "I was right! He's *not* a half-orc!" He looked at Thokar again with an appraising eye. "But why are you not the guide, eh?"

"Because I have never been this way," Thokar said.

"Gods, what mess have I gotten myself into?" Bartolo said.

"Keep your mind on the prize," Alastan said. "Within five years, you will be the richest man in the strand."

"I trust you'll be the one taking care of our new pets."

"I will, unless I'm dead. Surely you can stand to feed them if that is the case."

Bartolo wiped his nose. "Bah. I hate spiders."

"They're more like eight-legged dogs, if that makes you feel better," Alastan said, grinning.

*

"Just in time," Mondal said, giving Alastan a strange half-smile.

The sun was sinking quickly into the sands behind them, covering the dull landscape with a wash of colors. Grey and tan became pink and orange. There were even hues among these that were somehow outside of regular sight: blues and strange greens that reflected off the sheer faces of cut stone that ringed in the next oasis.

Haggin began to run, then sprint, toward the stones.

"Don't let him!" Bartolo said, urging his barsil forward. He whipped the reigns harshly. The beast seemed to ignore his commands and continued its steady plod.

"They are coming!" Haggin shouted back. "I can hear them. Run!"

Alastan looked back and saw nothing but the setting sun. If there was life in the sands, it was invisible to him.

"I see nothing," he said.

"I would trust him," Mondal said. "But we need not panic just yet. Undoubtedly, the lost ones follow us, but we are safe as long as the light lingers."

Haggin slowed far in front of them and stopped, kneeling in apparent exhaustion. He got up after a few seconds and began to walk. Slowly, the rest of them started to close the distance with Haggin, but after a few minutes, Alastan noticed that the oasis did not seem to be getting any closer.

"What sorcery is this," he said. "Why is it still so far away?"

"It is like that sometimes," Mondal said. "Distance and direction are not always what they seem, nor does time always flow smoothly."

"I feel it in the air," Thokar said, breathing on the crystal on his staff, giving it green-hued life.

"I feel it in the soil," Mondal said. "There is a finger of ancient magic here."

"Pity the dead chase us. There could be a pathway to another realm."

"Somehow, I think the exploration of it would not leave you happy. This place was always of chaos. Who knows where you might end up?"

Thokar nodded. "True. I feel that the Fay itself runs through here. It is trying to pull us back, like a riptide. Am I wrong?"

"You are not wrong."

"I do not wish to interrupt the wizards, mortal that I am," Datero said. "But darkness is indeed falling. Don't you think we should panic yet?"

Mondal shrugged. "You can if you like. You will not reach the walls any quicker."

Datero drew his sword. "You said it's useless. Can't you enchant it, or something?"

"Yes," Mondal said. "But not here. Just keep your mind fixed on our endpoint, and we shall reach it."

"They are behind us," Alastan said. The rest of them looked back them to see, amid the failing light of the west, a pale mist of white, swirling over rocks and the sand. Within the mist, spots glowed – eyes, perhaps – and the spots rocked onward, growing in size.

"Do not focus on them," Mondal said. "Focus on the oasis."

"What if they reach us?" Alastan said.

"Heed my words. Focus on the *oasis.*"

They marched onward. Soon they could see the procession of lights in their peripheral vision, beginning to enclose them. As the light of the sun fled from the desert, the mists gained the shape of men, but only loosely. The wind picked up at their backs, and it seemed that it bore in its currents whispers of words unknown to any of them.

"Now is the time to panic," Mondal said. "We are almost there. We must run. Do not fight!"

Thokar mounted his barsil and flicked the reins. It raised its hips and began its strange run. Bartolo's mount followed suit of its own accord. They were all running, and as they ran, they caught up to Haggin, who ran with pure desperation toward the purple stone ahead of him.

They reached the outer mounds of the ruins together. The spirits of the desert were no longer wandering but pressing forward, spreading out in a line as if to surround them. Thokar jumped down from his saddle and planted his glowing staff in the ground just in front of the ruins of what was once a gate.

He gave a shout. It had no words, or the words were of some primal language the men could not understand, but it had an effect. A great halo of light sprang forth from the staff, radiating outward into the desert night. The spirits disappeared for a few seconds. They began to return to luminescence but were no longer evenly spaced. They circled for a bit before turning their uncertain faces back toward the party.

Thokar repeated his spell, and once again, the spirits were banished. Once again, they returned.

"Get inside," he said. He pulled his staff from the earth and pulled his barsil through the gateway and into an empty courtyard. He stood beside Alastan, looking out at the desert for a while, watching the white beings swirl and move away, each one slowly fading to a pale phantom.

"There were more this time," Alastan said. "Maybe our guest really *is* being followed."

"Undoubtedly, but we were bound to attract attention as we went along," Thokar said.

They walked into the inner courtyard. It was, to Alastan's surprise, filled with growing plants. A quick search revealed a well, but it was totally dry. Thokar even enchanted a piece of glass to glow and dropped it down, only to watch it bounce and shatter on something hard at the bottom.

"There must be water here," Bartolo said. "Look at all the shrubs. Even more than the last place."

"They are not fed by water," Mondal said. "No wonder it was so hard to reach. I am surprised this place still stands, to be honest. I suppose it is a testament to the will of your people, to make something so permanent here."

The dark elf's eyes were glowing brightly of their own accord. He sat down on a rock and removed one of his gloves. He touched the leaves of a nearby fern lightly and smiled to himself.

"I am thankful for it," Thokar set. "Let us finish making camp and rest while we can."

"There's got to be water!" Bartolo said. He was leaning against a wall, wiping his forehead. Even in the light of the stars, he looked red and hot. He opened one of his water skins and twisted it, dripping a few drops into his mouth.

"Looks like it's lizard juice for you," Datero said. He sad down near Thokar, who had conjured a magic fire of blue amid a pile of stones.

"And for you!"

"I've managed my own supply," Datero said with a smile.

"Bah!" said Bartolo. He threw himself down on the dirt and covered his face with his hat, as if he was going to nod off in protest.

"What feeds the plants, magic?" Alastan said, taking his seat near Thokar. He opened up a small leather bag and began eating the dried meat inside.

"Yes. The prim," Thokar said. "The remains of the primal flow of creation. Always it comes from the Fay Lands and out, to us. Here it is strong, like it supposedly was in ancient days, when it could be harnessed and used to fashion reality itself."

Alastan smiled. "You really are a wizard, though you don't look it."

Thokar raised a dark eyebrow at him. "Thank you?"

"I remember this place," Mondal said. His eyes looked outward, focused on nothing. He pointed toward where his gaze lingered. "There was a watchtower there. This whole place was a fortified garrison for the human empire. There were many rooms for many officers. I was young when I was here with my father, and they were eager for the magic goods we could make. There was a whole village outside, but it is gone now. I cannot remember the names of any of the men I met here, nor do I remember what the sweet-natured women who cooked for us were called. Their faces are fleeting, but I remember the building. So much focus here on this stone. Your race is capable of such everlasting creation..."

Mondal bowed his head and sighed. "This whole area was plains and sparse woodlands. Forest deeper in."

"What happened?" Alastan said.

Mondal shrugged. "It was always a place of chaos, as I said."

"Something bothering you?"

"Many things, but nothing that you need concern yourself with. I will take the watch tonight."

"Surely even *you* need sleep."

"I am sleeping now, Alastan. Let me have my eyes on the world that is, at least. Otherwise, I fear I will despair."

"I will sleep for a while," Thokar said, "but I will join you before dawn. The prim will refresh me quickly."

"And what do we need to watch for?" Bartolo said from beneath his hat. "We already have the assassin with us."

Alastan glanced over at Haggin, who sat by himself, staring through the ruined fortress gate to the endless desert beyond.

"One of them, yes," Alastan said.

Haggin turned toward him with wide eyes. "Don't let them in here." His voice dropped to a harsh whisper. "Gods! Slay them on sight. You must."

Bartolo sat up. "He's losing his wits."

"I will kill them if I can," Mondal said.

"What happened out there?" Alastan said.

Haggin silently shook his head and turned away from the plain.

*

Alastan woke sometime in the night. A dream made of fractured images of his past mixed up with memories that seemed false in a strange landscape still echoed through his vision in the dark, fading to half-remembrance as he took several deep breaths and sat up.

Mondal and Thokar stood together on a heap of stone, gazing out at the desert. There was no moon in the sky, and Alastan wondered to himself if there had been a moon that night at all. He knew there should have been, though he had trouble remembering the phase in his tiredness.

He pulled the blankets off of himself to find that it had become deathly cold. Bartolo was wrapped in a pile of cloth by the remains of the magical fire. Even Haggin had slept, though his hands were fists that gripped the pack he used as a pillow. Alastan got up and began packing.

"Already up?" Thokar said from where he stood.

"I don't want to lose any daylight. Who knows how long it will take to reach the next resting place?"

Thokar nodded. "You should rouse the others, then."

"I'll give them a few minutes. I think they'll need it."

Alastan woke the others just as the sky was lightening. Mondal led them out of the gate as dawn was still growing behind the mountains in the east. The ghostly beings were there, milling about in a massive horde. Mondal seemed unconcerned, but Haggin had to be practically dragged forward; Bartolo insisted they leave him behind, but at the thought of being left alone, the would-be assassin relented and went along.

The sun soon banished the strange beings, and Mondal took them south. Once again, the day wore away, almost too quickly, and they still found themselves in the desert. Near sunset, they, at last, happened upon the Oasis. It was once a structure, but its form was now unrecognizable to them. A large circular wall, now reduced to piles of broken stone, hemmed in squat square buildings, long since open to the sky. Each of these went a few steps into the earth. In the center was what once was a pyramidal structure, but it too had collapsed long before.

Bartolo was nearly mad with thirst, but once again, there was no water in the oasis. He refused to drink the liquid secretions extracted from the glands of the barsil, found just behind its hind legs. Instead, he promised to pay Datero an aural to trade him for real water.

"How's it taste?" Alastan asked his friend as Datero gulped down the lizard's secretion.

"Sour," Datero said. "But it's wet. That's what matters. I think you'll find out soon enough."

"You're probably right."

When the sun finally set, Haggin began to get hysterical.

"They're coming! They know where we are!" He screamed. "They're coming to get me. Please, give me a weapon."

"I'm compassionate, but no fool," Alastan said.

Haggin sat on the steps of the central structure and looked out into the desert in all directions. The walls were not high enough to give the illusion of shelter, and as the gloom deepened, the specters once again began to appear. Their numbers grew as the sky turned black, filling the whole stretch of dry plain to the west with ghastly light.

"What sort of place is this?" Alastan asked Mondal. "I've never seen anything like it."

"Part of the Draesenith empire, once," Mondal said. "That was long ago, from when the grey warlords sought to conquer all the world."

"Now they are content to decay," Thokar said. "This was one of their ziggurats." He pointed to the pyramid. "Here, they interred the dead in the belief their spirits would return to repossess their bodies."

"Did they return?" Alastan said.

Mondal grumbled. "Yes."

Thokar looked at the dark elf and nodded. "I'll take his word for it. They no longer believe in the return of the spirit, but once, they worshipped a being who promised such to them."

"This is a dangerous place to remain," Mondal said. "Like the other place, it is thin here. Very thin."

"It's intentional," Thokar said. "To allow the spirit easier access to the body. I wonder if the lost ones will search for the bodies here."

"Any dead body interred here would be long gone to dust, judging by the state of things," Datero said.

"You do not know the power of the Draesenith in their height," Thokar said. "They had methods of preserving the body for ages."

"Gods, let them lie," Alastan said.

Thokar nodded. "Forever, yes, I will pray that as well."

"Why do they come?" Alastan said, nodding to the gathering phantoms beyond the crumbled encircling wall. "More every night."

Thokar glanced at Haggin, who was whispering to himself.

Alastan caught the gesture. "You think I acted rashly?"

"I cannot fault your compassion," Thokar said. "But there is something he has not, or perhaps *cannot*, tell us." He pointed one of his great fingers to the desert. "These are not aimless souls, nor are they the beings of the Fay that get lost from time to time. They have a purpose, however weak they are."

"We should leave the raver," Mondal said. "It would satiate them, I think."

"Have you seen anything like this?" Thokar said.

Mondal's eyes grew brighter for a few seconds. He frowned. "Not quite like this. Leaving the assassin is the prudent choice. You cannot trust him, and as long as he is with us, he is a burden to us."

"What if I turn him loose and give him a sword?" Alastan asked.

Mondal's face was passionless. "You cannot trust him."

"Remember that his oath is to his guild," Thokar said. "If the oath was bonded with true power, he will be unable to resist it, no matter how honorable he might wish to be."

Alastan shook his head. "I can't just leave somebody to die out here. To turn into one of those things."

Mondal's voice dropped to a whisper. "If he dies on this holy ground, he might not suffer that fate. I don't think it will satiate the spirits, though, if I were to end him here. They will still follow."

"No," Alastan said. "We'll continue to carry him. Besides, I might still be able to learn which guild he works for. That will be vital information for my survival when we return with the queen spinners."

"I will defer to you, for now," Mondal said. "But if I judge it to be necessary..." He looked at his fingers and rubbed them together, his eyes narrowing.

"Fine," Alastan said.

His thoughts wandered back to Lucita and his son. He prayed silently for their safety, but not to his patron god of Denarthal, with whom one must make pacts, but to Verbus, the god of death, words, and time.

You know the lines of men's lives. Let not my family's be cut before my own.

He repeated it three times. Even in prayer, he could not avoid attempting to make a covenant of some kind.

"Your gods are strange," Mondal said. Alastan looked up to see the dark elf's flat, fathomless eyes of light fixed on him as if he could hear the prayer.

"Can we stay here tonight?"

"We have no option but to stay here," Mondal said.

Alastan looked over at Thokar, who was busy making his magical fire in a pile of stones. Haggin was huddled very close to it, staring at the pile expectantly.

"Is there any way to fight them?" Alastan said.

Thokar looked up from his incantation, and the fire began to die away. His deep voice rolled out with a soft, rhythmic cadence. "Certainly, but not, I think, for any of you. Maybe Mondal. I don't know his full powers."

"I'm too wicked to send off the souls of the dead," Mondal said. He stared at the sky as if pondering for a moment. "I can, at best, hide us for a time."

"I can temporarily repel them as before," Thokar said. "And I have a few illusion tricks, but I doubt they will work on ghosts. I admire your attempt at strategy, Alastan, but you should probably leave that to your guides. You should get some sleep."

"It'll be hard to sleep," Alastan said. "My dreams are not right of late."

"As expected. Tomorrow will be hard. Rest."

*

The sun caught them by surprise. Alastan woke to find it warm upon his face, though the ground around him remained cold as a winter field. Thokar was asleep nearby – the first time he had seen him sleep past dawn since they struck out from Structania.

Alastan sat up and saw that everyone was else around him was also asleep, except for the assassin. Haggin sat upon his haunches atop a sandstone pillar, gazing out into the endless desert, a large cloth wrapped around his head against the new sun.

"Did nobody watch?" Alastan said aloud.

Haggin turned his face to look at him. "Everyone slept."

"Not you?"

"Not me."

"We need to get moving," Alastan said, standing up briskly.

"We're safer here. They're afraid to come in. Afraid of what's in the tomb." He turned his head and nodded to the fallen ziggurat.

"I suppose *they* told you that."Alastan frowned as he lightly kicked Datero in the rib.

"What is it?" Datero said. "Oh Grim's bones, it's already daylight."

"I can hear them talking, yes," the assassin went on. "They remember things. Things that the Eastern Men did – why they built this place, and why they abandoned it."

Datero scoffed. "They abandoned it because they lost the war with the old empire. Were you listening last night, or not?"

Haggin smiled sardonically. "Oh, they left these outposts behind well before that. Those shades out there – they were there. Most of them aren't human, but they can't really remember what human is, either."

"I see a night of rest has straightened the wits of our would-be assassin," Datero said. He was already up and kicking Bartolo in the legs. The fat man rolled over and growled wordlessly.

"I think he's right," Thokar said. The conversation had apparently roused him, but he moved slowly, reigniting his magical fire and rummaging in his bags.

"Glad to see I don't have to kick you awake as I prefer not to wake sleeping giants," Alastan said. "But we shan't have time for breakfast."

"I'm not making breakfast," Thokar said. He removed his satchel of herbs and unrolled it on a flat rock.

"And what made you sleep so long? You said that out here, a little sleep goes a long way."

"I was lost in dreams – memories of the people that once labored here. I did not realize it, so forgive me for not waking early. And yes, the assassin is right. This place predates the old war with the empire by at least a few centuries. I mentioned my people once worshipped a dark god. This tomb is from that era. We would be wise to move on quickly, for the magic of the pact they made with... *it* still lingers, and their spirits are waiting, perhaps..." Thokar shook his large head and sighed. "The light of day is a welcome sight to my mind. Let me brew this potion, then we must be away to the next oasis, if one exists."

"A magic potion?" Datero said.

Thokar chuckled, but did not look up from his work. "I suppose it *is* magic, at that. Something to keep Mondal and me from sleep." He looked around and frowned. "Where is he?"

Alastan realized suddenly that the dark elf was absent, but his things were still lying on the ground, including a messy bedroll.

"He must have gotten up when I was rousing the others and went to scout our next passage," Alastan said.

Thokar frowned but nodded as he poured a meager amount of pale brown spirits into a small pot. "Go look for him, please. But stay clear of the ziggurat."

"I will," Alastan said. He went back to his pack and quickly belted on his sword.

"You going to hack the ghosts to pieces?" sneered Bartolo, who half leaned on a rock chewing a piece of dried meat, his face somehow already red.

"I'd take it easy on that meat if I were you. You'll need water to flush out the salt."

"And starve?"

"A little hunger is more tolerable to me than thirst, but suit yourself," Alastan said. "And I keep my sword with me because... Well, I feel better with it on."

"And I feel better with a full stomach. Especially if I'm to die out here." The merchant spat something out. "Go on and fetch our guide."

Alastan pulled his hat on and stepped out into the tumbled ruins.

One lap around the decaying once-fortress revealed no sign of the dark elf, so Alastan reversed his path, stepping up onto tall rocks, broken pillars, and piles of bricks to see further and checking quickly some of the more easily viewed underground rooms. There were a great many of these, most of them long since collapsed into little more than pits. A few cellars, however, seemed to have survived the fury of the sands, and into these he peered quickly and with great trepidation, expecting in his stomach something other than the elf.

Below ground level, it was cool, almost cold, and there was an eerie silence. Alastan realized the constant blowing of the wind across the loose dirt above had filled his ears without ceasing for days. Its absence sent chills across the back of his arms and neck. The cellars, however, were all either empty or otherwise filled with debris. Shadows of calm blue greeted him, with occasional yellow sun motes from a broken portal or crack. The underground rooms, filled with potsherds and what once might have been the wood of crates and barrels, seemed to sit waiting as if they had a sleeping consciousness of their own.

Only one of these rooms did Alastan leave unexplored, for it went further underground via a stairway, black as tar in the artificial night. He made up his mind to brave the darkness, *with* Thokar, only if he could not find Mondal, then went on his way.

Always as he walked, with the sun seemingly frozen in the east, the fallen ziggurat was on his left. Always it seemed engulfed by shadows. At one angle, Alastan could see a shadow larger and darker than the rest – a doorway, or some other hole left by the falling building.

Thokar's advice rang in his ears, but the time spent in the ruins was beginning to feel over-long, and he made up his mind to simply peek through the portal, not actually enter the Draesen tomb.

As he picked his way between two fallen rows of roofless columns, he came upon Mondal, stepping up out of the shadows of the Ziggurat.

"There you are!" Alastan shouted, his feet sliding over a thin layer of dust as he flinched and stopped himself. He realized Mondal had one of his swords drawn, a large basket-hilted weapon of strange make.

"Did Thokar not warn you to steer clear of this crypt?" Mondal said as he approached, his voice as placid and unknowable as ever.

"He did, but I thought I might just look – and I was right. You *were* in there."

"You should heed the advice of a Draesen regarding their burial places." Mondal sheathed his weapon. Still in shadow, his eyes glowed brightly in a strange hue of green, obscuring his pupils. As Alastan fell into step beside him, the magic seemed to drain, and pale eyes of yellow regarded him.

"*You* didn't heed the advice," said Alastan.

"It is not so dangerous to me."

"Why, though?"

"I wanted to see something for myself," Mondal said. "Most of the inner crypt is still intact, untouched by this shifting Fay Waste."

Alastan laughed. "What was it? A crypt?"

Mondal smiled, a rare gesture, and looked at Alastan warmly. "Are you sure you wish to know, human? You have been given to bad dreams since we started this journey, not just last night."

Alastan scoffed. "How would you know that?"

"How, indeed?"

"You read minds?"

"I read the telegraphed emotions of humans," Mondal said. "So, I ask again – do you wish to know?"

Alastan shrugged. "Well, now you've built it up, I have to know. I won't be able to sleep until you tell me."

"Assuming you'll be able to sleep after I tell you."

"This is like what we did in the army, trying to rile each other up during dinner round the campfire. Just tell me."

"There are Draesen down there."

"Dead ones?"

Mondal narrowed his eyes. "In a manner of speaking. Were you to look upon their bodies, as I did, you might think them alive, but they are inanimate."

"Gods, how?"

"One of the secrets of their ancient religion," Mondal said. "One passed to them by their god. I shall tell you more, if you like, in Thokar's presence."

"Oh, there's more!" Alastan said. "Now you can't leave me just thinking about *that*."

Mondal chuckled softly. It was almost imperceptible among the ever-blowing wind, but Alastan detected a certain sardonism in the elf's tone. As he stepped into the shadows of the hollow, his pupils and irises were once again obscured by an inner light.

"Gods, that smells foul," Alastan said, approaching Thokar.

"You've been in the tombs, eh?" Thokar said. "Did you find out more?"

"A little," said Mondal. "The human wants me to tell him. Should I?"

"Knowledge is power, but comes at a price, since ignorance is bliss," Thokar said, taking the small pot off of the fire and blowing acrid grey smoke from it.

"So I've heard," Alastan said. "Unfortunately, once you reveal a man's ignorance, he won't be content until he either eliminates the ignorance or kills the messenger."

"Oh my," Mondal said. "I suppose I'd better tell him."

Thokar laughed. "I have a draught of dreamless sleep here. In case you and I need it."

"Our employer here might need it. He confided in me that he's been having bad dreams this whole time."

Thokar looked at Alastan and blew air out of his nostrils in a snorting sound. "You should have told me."

Alastan sat down, smiling to himself. "Now I simply *have* to know."

"There are indeed Draesen buried here," Mondal went on. "In the old way. The clothes have rotted, but the body remains. Beautiful, some of them, like statues."

"Interesting that they stay that way for this long, even without the spirit returning," Thokar said.

"What?" Alastan said.

"You see, my people were obsessed with immortality, once," Thokar said. "Supposedly, they – or perhaps it is just one Draesen, Katach the Conqueror – made a pact with a dragon god. My race would serve her against her ancient enemies. In return, she would grant immortality to all who performed a certain secret rite she gifted to Katach, who was high priest in addition to being emperor. The nature of this rite has been obscured by time, but it involves the spirit returning to re-animate the flesh of the dead."

"A lich?"

"No," Thokar said. "I have fought a lich, did you know that? No, a lich is something of a different horror – a being without a soul, but with a mind. For the elite of the Draesenith Empire, immortality was being bound within a preserved corpse."

They were silent for a few moments, then Alastan pinched his nose. "That smells bloody awful, you now."

"It tastes bad, too," Thokar said with a smile. "But it works." He looked at Mondal. "So their corpses remain."

"They are each locked away within a casket. And I mean locked, with bar and bolt. Unfortunately, time has worn on the steel, though the body within is immaculate, and the iron has gone red or to dust."

"Hmn," Thokar said. "Interesting. Perhaps at some point, they feared the ritual working."

"Did it ever work?"

"Supposedly, it worked on Katach," Thokar said. "Do you know the tale? He went back to the dream, body and soul, when he donned the Crown of Sight, a pure artifact he did not understand. His supposedly immortal body was drawn back into the chaos of creation."

"Undoubtedly, it was Diorgesh who desired it for herself," Mondal said. "Good that she did not receive it. May she lay locked for all eternity."

Thokar, seeing Alastan's confusion, said, "Diorgesh is the Unbinder, a dragon-god of the first beings to move beyond the twisting impermanence of the dream – that thing which remains as the Fay Lands to our north – but it, or she, was imprisoned by the gods. That is who my people worshipped, but I did not grow up there, and there has apparently been a great iconoclasm since then. She may be forgotten, now."

"I worry, Thokar," Mondal said. "This place is on the edge. The way to the mist realm was sealed in that crypt, but it is thin, and all that the Draesenith built is rotting away to nothing. Everything but their bodies. A spirit could find its way in."

"Let us be gone, then, and be thankful, for if they find a body, they are likely never to find their way out of this wilderness."

"It depends on which spirit finds the bodies," Mondal said with raised eyebrows. "Below, they wait."

Thokar began pouring the potion into a few small flasks. "I had not considered that. Let us be away quickly, then."

"We go towards the foothills next."

*

Mondal led them steadily along what once might have been a road which wound its way steadily between two rocky ridges partially engulfed by sand dunes, their tops still standing against the whistling wind, rounded and banded with colors of red, black, and light yellow.

The path was a bare track of flat earth, cracked but otherwise bereft of feature or any remnant of a cobble. It was wide enough for the barsils to waddle comfortably, and they moved quickly. An occasional milestone stuck up from the dirt like a shriveled piece of fruit, dark and worn amongst the colorless Wasting Desert.

Bartolo rode hunched over his mount, the writhing shoulders of the great lizard seeming to keep him awake against his will. By midday, he began to cough and sputter, and the company had to halt to allow him to vomit. His body seemed to rebel against the act and was unwilling to give up the paltry moisture in his stomach.

Reluctantly, Datero gave the merchant his own water, which he had saved away. He received no thanks for his sacrifice, but it did succeed in stopping the nausea and allowed them to continue.

"Somehow, I doubt he'll pay me for the privilege of drinking lizard water," Datero said aside to Alastan.

"We'll extract some tonight. Next time, just give Barty the barsil drink."

"It's got a very particular flavor."

"He won't notice when he's sick."

As the sun began to cast long shadows behind them, the track started to climb. They left the dunes behind for a short stretch and wandered through a high desert filled with strange, alien shrubs that stood before a spire of mottled stone which stood like a massive monolith above the gentle slopes of brown.

"I've heard of these succulents," Bartolo said, seeing the clusters of fat, spiny shrubs dotted with nettled flowers. "You can extract water from them."

"Perhaps in the more mundane desert to the west," Thokar said. "But these plants are fed by the Fay. We cannot count them to be fit to eat."

"Well, we can at least cut one open and see," Bartolo said. He dismounted and used his knife to cut part of one of the strange plants. Inside was nothing but a strangely wet kind of sand. He put some of it in his mouth, only to spit it out and dry heave once again.

Thokar took the plant from him and dipped a finger inside. It did indeed look like sand. He gave it a quick taste, then spat it out harshly. "Salt and... Soap, I think."

"Guess it's lizard juice after all," Datero said.

"Gods, I need some water!" Bartolo said, then rubbed his tongue on his sleeve.

"You've had the last of it," Datero said. "Anyone else secret some away?"

The rest of them stood there, silent.

"If they did, would they share it? No! I knew I shouldn't have come."

"I told you not to," Alastan said.

"Either way, you're going to cheat me!"

"He could have killed you at any time," Haggin said cooly. "Grim knows I would have."

"We should keep moving," Mondal said. "We can milk the barsils when we reach the oasis. Not far now. Hold your belly until then, human, and you will yet survive."

Bartolo, however, seemed unable to climb back atop his mount, and in the end had to be helped by Datero and Mondal. He slouched in the saddle even worse than before, occasionally coughing and sputtering, then cursing vainly between each fit.

As the sky finally darkened, the feeling of being watched set in, well before there were any visual signs of the shades. Soon, though, their ethereal pursuers were present once again. Unlike the day previous, they were close to the oasis when the darkness set in, and they reached the cluster of rocks before any ghostly whisps could fully materialize around them.

"Yes, I remember this place," Mondal said, leading them down a gentle slope, past a large pile of boulders, and into what looked like a tall crack in the spire of rock. "So much has changed, but the rock remains," he went on, his eyes blazing and flickering with the magic of memories centuries gone. Within the crack, some thirty feet high, opened a true cavern that seemed to howl softly with the movement of air within. Mondal placed his hand on the mottled, many-colored stone, touching it gently like it was a beast alive. "Whoever dreamt this rock... He, or she, still remains in the world that is."

"I don't understand," Alastan said.

Mondal smiled inwardly. "Once, there was nothing that was fixed, mortal. We were beings of spirit, and the world was spirit, but things changed. We grew fixed. Though thousands of years separate us, we are of the same stuff, in the end. Of both worlds, in different degrees – the mundane and the spiritual. That is the power and the curse of our existence."

Thokar stepped up beside Mondal and lit his staff with a breath of magic. Tears gathered the pale light of bauble perched on top, running slowly to Mondal's chin, though he smiled.

"Are you alright?" Alastan said.

"I realize I miss my brother and father."

"Not an uncommon feeling," Alastan said.

"Likely true," Mondal said. "Come. We can shelter inside."

They followed Mondal into the caverns, guided by Thokar's light. It was an immense space, tall enough for the barsils to walk through with no difficulty, though they plodded with what seemed like trepidation.

A little way in, Thokar bent over with his light and revealed a vast mirror on the floor, running the length of the cavern, reflecting perfectly the glittering stone above them. The mage bent down and touched it, and the image trembled.

"Water!" Bartolo cried. He was still riding his barsil, and he fell awkwardly to the sandy floor of the cavern, then began scrambling toward Thokar on hands and knees.

"No!" said the Draesen. "Do not drink it! It is a hot spring, and there could be hidden life in it."

"I don't care if it's hot, and don't care what stupid thing is living in it. It's wet!"

"We must boil it first," Thokar said. "It's the only way to make it safe."

"I'm dying here!" Bartolo said. He bent over the rocks and began scooping the water into his mouth with his bare hand. He grunted at the taste but continued trying to shovel it into his gullet. He burped. "Boiling water that's already hot? How stupid do you think I am?"

"Don't answer him," Datero said.

Thokar reached for the merchant with one of his immense arms. Despite his demeanor and round shape, Bartolo was quick, and rolled away, then scrambled quickly to another place where he could reach down into the pool.

"Listen to the mage, you fool!" Datero said. He stepped toward Bartolo, but the merchant, his eyes gleaming, drew a dagger from his belt. He waved it impotently at Datero. The bodyguard threw up his hands and stepped away, shaking his head.

"You're trying to kill me! Or torture me," Bartolo rasped. "I'm nobody's fool!"

"Fine, drink it," Datero said.

Bartolo bent down quickly and began scooping the water into his mouth again, this time with two hands. Again, he grunted in between swallows. He stopped to burp but continued soon after.

"I guess we shall see what lives in this pool," Thokar said with a sigh.

"The minerals will make it an unquenching draught," Mondal said. The elf, his eyes brighter than ever, bent down and waved his hand over the pool. A soft light spread out in the water, making the whole caver glow softly. "I had almost forgotten how to do that."

With the light, Bartolo finally stopped. They could see the pool for what it was now – a healthy hot spring but teeming with strange life, none of it familiar to them. What looked like barnacles and other mollusks clustered in cracks deep in the far side of the pool, from which a rippling flow of heat ran, not disturbing the tranquility of the surface.

Bartolo burped again. "Ha! Life indeed. I can hardly drink… Whatever those worms and snails are. Hideous."

"That is not what I meant."

"Well, I'm willing to wait for some water to boil," Alastan said. "We can feed some to the mounts as well. Now, where's my cookpot?"

*

Thokar made a magical fire, which was well, because a real fire, even had they possessed wood or dung, would have filled the cavern with smoke. On the pile of rocks, he patiently boiled the water a pot at a time and then left it to cool on the floor. Eventually, he filled every heat-resistant vessel they had.

Having relit the pool with some fleeting form of magic, Mondal stripped and began bathing in the spring, saying that it was once an attractive spot for such a purpose. Alastan and Datero, their skin dry, chaffed, and itchy from days of sweat soaking their clothes and drying to a salty crust at night, followed suit. The water was a perfect temperature, hot and invigorating without scalding.

Alastan had brought along a large wedge of tallow soap, which they used to clean themselves beside the spring. Even the assassin Haggin had ceased his nervous twitching to bathe himself, and it was this act that inadvertently exposed his allegiance. He had a small tattoo of a clover in blue ink on his right breast, along with a small dagger on his left. Alastan took note of this silently. The guild of clovers was infamous in the Divine Strand's western countries but had not moved into Datalia and Structania - or at least, it was not yet common knowledge that it had.

Thokar, when he was done boiling the water, washed himself in a shallow inlet of the pool. It was the first time they had seen him without his traveling clothes, and he indeed lived up to the reputation of his race. His frame was massive and heavy with muscle. His skin, hairless, was dotted with battle scars and small orcish tattoos – prayers to the war god Alatesh that the orc clans wrote in thanks of mended injuries.

Bartolo did not bathe. Instead, he flopped down on a sack for a pillow and fell promptly asleep.

"Truly, this is an oasis," Alastan said to Datero and Mondal. "The first real Oasis. One for the spirit."

"Perhaps not for him," Mondal said, nodding to Bartolo.

"He thirsts for different things," Datero said. "A hot bath is best for a man like that when he's spent the day counting money, and even then, he'll only really enjoy it with a wench present to scrub his skin."

"Humans *do* understand pleasure," Mondal said.

*

The sickness began in the early morning, just before sunrise.

Bartolo woke the entire party, groaning and coughing as he stumbled toward the entrance to the cavern. Haggin, who had leapt up screaming at the echoing wails from Bartolo, was the first to recover his wits and restrain the red-faced merchant before he could stagger out into the sand.

He was partly successful, for as he wrapped his arms around him, Bartolo lost his bowls. Haggin released him in revulsion, and Bartolo staggered into the pale moonlight to begin vomiting. As he did so, the gully began to glow with clusters of longing spirits.

It was Alastan who risked himself, running from the cave entrance to handle the soiled and vomiting Bartolo. The spirits took notice and began to emit a droning, keening sound that deafened Alastan to the wind of the night and the shouts of the his companions. Outside the ramp down to the cave, the shades clustered like swirling fog, and Alastan could even in some places discern eyes, glowing with their own colored light, not unlike the eyes of Mondal.

He ignored the smell and the incomprehensible whining breath of the ghosts and pulled Bartolo back to the entrance of the cave. He had to fight against the combination of desperate flailing and deadweight of Bartolo, but somehow managed the effort, though he found himself covered with sickly bodily fluids for it.

While Alastan and Thokar tried to calm the distressed Bartolo, Haggin stripped himself naked and went to the very threshold of the cavern.

"I am here!" he shouted to the fog. "If you want my body, you must come and take it from me. Come!"

"Quiet, idiot!" Datero said, drawing his sword. "Or all I'll make it so that you never shout again."

"No!" Alastan said, ignoring Bartolo and moving to restrain Datero. Datero flinched as Alastan grabbed hold of his sword arm. "Gods, let me go!" he said, shaking off Alastan. "You smell like death!"

"Do not kill him in cold blood. We are better than that."

"Those sorts of questions are left to men who survive, Alastan. He's begging those spirits to come in and kill us!"

"No, they cannot," Mondal said. "Not unless they can step into the oasis and become flesh once again." The dark elf watched the heavy-breathing Haggin as he raved to the mist. "Or perhaps they can - or some can. If they do, we could slay them... or would that be in cold blood as well?"

"Don't entertain such things," Datero said. "Let's be rid of this assassin at last."

"You should be the one to do it, then," Mondal said.

"Well," Datero said. "He's an assassin!"

"So am I," Mondal said. His face was set in its usual impassive state.

Datero remained silent, staring at him.

Alastan broke the silence. "Leave Haggin be. We have another man we must consider anyway."

Just inside the cavern, Bartolo had stopped his heaving and lay on the sandy floor breathing slowly, unresponsive to Thokar.

"I suppose we have tested my prediction," Thokar said, shaking his head.

"What can we do for him?" Alastan said. "Do you have potions or magic for something like this?"

"Potions? No. There is medicine for such afflictions, but it doesn't always work, like anything in the World-That-Is. I lack the ingredients anyway."

"And I suppose we cannot gather them."

"Not here. I'm afraid we'll have to let this pass."

"Will he survive it? I've seen outbreaks of this sort of sickness in Datalia. It can kill a man within a day."

Thokar held his palms up. "Prayer is all we give him for now, I think. If it was a wound, I could force it closed, but it's life - an unwelcome sort of life - inside of him. He will have to kill it himself. And you should bathe quickly."

Alastan took a quick whiff of his shirt and nearly retched himself. It truly smelled deadly, like rotten eggs but mixed up with bile and feces. Like the assassin, he immediately stripped himself naked and began to draw water from the hot spring. Somehow, though the sickness was born from the water, Alastan thought he would defile the place by bringing Bartolo's waste into the serene water.

*

Barolo had gone as pale as the sands.

His eyes, dry but clear, gazed out into the desert beyond the shadows of the rock spire, as if he could see the wandering army of shades they had attracted from the outset of their journey. From where he lay, only the side of his face could be seen by the party, and one cheek muscle slowly twitched. The blanket that lay over his stripped body had been wetted against a fever and had begun to smell of body odor and mildew, which added to the other foul smells that clouded around the merchant.

"We must move soon," Mondal said quietly. He leaned against a rock and had again donned his mail for reasons he would not communicate. "Otherwise, I fear we will not meet the next waypoint before sunset."

"Can't we stay here a day?" Alastan said. "We have water, with effort, and we still have food."

"You are certainly the leader now, so I will leave that judgment to you, but I will tell you I have a deep unease in remaining in one place."

"The spirits can't enter here, can they?"

"Not for now, but perhaps they could find a way in. Best to be ahead of them, especially now that we have gathered so many."

"Then we will stay awhile and trust what has worked so far. Bartolo will be recovered enough to travel soon enough."

"Fair enough," Mondal said. "But I fear there may be more than shades out there. The necropolis has been in my dreams today, like it has yours."

The statement gave Alastan pause. "I thought you took Thokar's potion."

"It didn't seem necessary. But no matter, I was glad for the dreams. Something was waiting in there. Or something was searching. I will not feel at ease until we have left this desert, and that dead fortress, behind us. And at the same time, I want to solve the mystery of the place, and the presence that I felt."

"Why?"

"I dare not indulge it," Mondal said, closing his eyes. "No, we should get to the Draesen lands as quickly as possible."

"We'll give Bartolo a day, at least."

"I think he will be dead in a day, Alastan. If it were me, I would leave him behind. He's slowed us tremendously up to this point, and it will be even worse now that he's sick, even if he gets better."

"I am not you. I won't leave someone that can be saved. If I have to, I'll tie him to a barsil and carry him out."

"You may have to."

*

The sun was drowning in a haze outside the cavern, its colors all ashen and red even above the horizon, for a gale had picked up during the day and started blowing all the loose sand of the hills around them into a great grey storm. In the shadow of the cavern, the whistling of the wind as it picked up the sands and thrust them into the cracks of the stone spire had turned into a sound like rain, save for the fact that it was more constant and unsettlingly high in pitch.

Bartolo lay breathing heavily on his back. The constant attempts to feed him clean water had been only partially successful. He had continued to periodically vomit or lose his bowels, and despite the fat around his face, he was starting to look withered.

"It was just as well, then," Datero said, sitting cross-legged next to Alastan and watching the storm with half-lidded eyes. "I doubt even Mondal could find his way in that."

"We could have been out ahead of it," Mondal said. He was lying on his bedroll, his eyes closed. Nearby, Thokar lay fast asleep. "But perhaps you are right. I am anxious, though."

"You don't look it," Datero said.

"I would hope not."

"Well, you'll get to sleep tonight, I suppose," Alastan said.

"I don't intend to," Mondal replied. "I will keep watch and hope the spirits do not find a way across this narrow veil."

"I can feel them congregating already," Haggin said. He, too, lay in his bedroll. "I thought I'd be rid of them, but it's always night in my dreams. I can hear them when I close my eyes – a thousand voices of pain and anguish. And a few that are more easily understood."

"Your compatriots," Mondal said.

"Yes," Haggin said. "No point concealing it. I'm sure it is them."

"What happened to them?" Alastan asked.

"I didn't see." The assassin's face went pale, and he swallowed slowly. "I ran. They cried out, and I ran. I ran until I thought I would die, then ran some more. I didn't want to believe it, but I hear them. They're calling out to me, but they don't know my name, nor do I know theirs, or I would beg for them to stop. We were bound by an oath never to tell each other anything outside the job, you see. Not even our real names. It's part of the guild's rules, and they use a sorcerer to make it real."

"Is Haggin your real name?"

"Yes, not that you would – or should – believe me. But I was somehow able to break my oath in the desert and abandon my fellows."

"I am not surprised," Mondal said. "What is bound in the World-That-Is can be unbound in the Fay Lands and its wastes – even body and soul. Pity you didn't learn their names. One of the only ways to hold power over a ghost is to know its true name."

"Now you know mine," the assassin said. "Haggin Rona Balemaro. If they get me, banish me. Release me. Kill me. I don't want to wander here, forgetting everything." He suddenly reached up and squeezed his head with his hands. "They are coming for me. I can almost feel their ghostly hands on my shoulders."

"Did one of the spirits touch you out there?"

"I don't know," Haggin said. "I was too scared to know what was happening exactly, but I swear I could feel them. Not on my skin. Bah! I don't want to think about it!"

The assassin flinched as Thokar stepped past him silently, his eyes on the stormy sunset. "If you can hear your friends, then these voices really are spirits. Curious. I thought for a while they might be some of the beings of the Fay to our north."

"Are ghosts better or worse than the... what did you call them?"

"There are several types. The Watchers are the most... human, I suppose, but I've never dealt with them. A friend did, once. Ghosts..." Thokar shrugged. "I would prefer not to find out."

"They hunger," Haggin said.

"Indeed," said Mondal.

The sun eventually set, but rather than giving up its red glory to the darkness of the night, the sandstorm became a new light of its own, swirling grey-white and blue, a sea of dead spirits empowered by the magic of the waste and now hungering for life. The keening returned and grew, adding to the fury of the wind and the rage of the sands against the fortress of rock. Alastan and Datero, who had both intended to sleep, found that such a task was impossible.

It was too loud and, worse than that, when they plugged their ears with candle wax, they found that while the sound of the sandstorm died down, the ghosts were no less silent. Like Haggin, they could hear voices, a great din of dead men, dead elves, dead Draesen, and perhaps other races, their tongues different but in death united into one state. And though the words were seemingly incomprehensible, they could understand the emotion behind them – one of longing, but also terror.

Sometime in the night – it was impossible to gauge the passage of time properly – the glow of the horde of spirits began to dim. Their eyes, which had been so clear, began to fade, and the light started to roll back. And yet, the storm blew on, swirling and chaotic.

While the party watched the scene with curiosity, Bartolo sat up, his eyes wide. A sound came from his throat: creaking and gurgling. All eyes fell on him. Alastan drew close and heard the merchant say with great effort, "We have to... get out of here."

"What?" Alastan said, and not because he did not hear. He turned to Datero "He says we have to leave."

"Now," Bartolo whispered. He took a deep breath. "Now. I've seen-" He began to cough again. Thokar gave him a little water, but he began to retch again.

"We should obey him," Mondal said. "The spirits are leaving."

"They're afraid," Datero said. "I heard them. You could too, yes?"

Mondal nodded.

Bartolo was shaking his head and shivering. "...coming... coming for... who... living!" he then collapsed on his bedroll, and they could get nothing else out of him.

They sat in silence for a while. Datero was the first to break it."I'm not usually the one to say this, but I think we should listen to our boss, Alastan."

"He's delirious," Alastan said. "Those spirits could be trying to lure us out or something. We don't know their intelligence."

"All they know is that the living are here and that they want to be alive, too," Mondal said. "We must leave this place."

"Yes, but what do we do with Bartolo, leave him?" Alastan said. "I already said I won't do that."

"We'll tie him to one of the mounts," Datero said.

"He won't sit in the saddle," Alastan said.

"We can make a litter out of our tents. Drag him along."

"There are rocks now. It is not all soft sand."

"We'll make it rigid," Thokar said. "I will carry him out of here until we are on level ground again."

"And I believe you could," Datero said. "But it won't do. I'll help you. The man is fat enough to tire out even a giant like you, especially when he's dead weight."

They worked quickly, repacking their things and strapping them to the great lizard mounts' load frames in a haphazard fashion. They discarded what they thought they might not immediately need: cookware, empty jars and bags once filled with foodstuffs, and clothes for cold weather. They made a litter for Bartolo from several poles from the cargo harnesses and material from a tent. He groaned as they laid him on it.

"Gods help me!"

"Keep praying," Datero said as he straightened the man. "Just keep praying."

"Alastan! Where is Alastan!"

"I'm here," Alastan said, kneeling beside the sick man.

"The deeds to my properties," Bartolo said with some effort. "They are in the treasure house of the Brothers Farhartha, in the capital. Under the name..." He scrunched up his face as if trying to remember. "Bartolo Taravas. Not even my accountant knows, or he'd cheat me out of them. Take this ring-" at this, he pulled a heavy gold ring with a strange geometric design on the crown from his finger and pushed it into Alastan's hands. "Get those deeds to my family. Or Verbus help me, I'll curse you."

"Relax," Alastan said. "You'll be better soon. We'll get you out of here."

"You idiot," Bartolo said. "Bah! I'm the idiot, coming on this fool expedition. I could never trust any man, and now I have to trust you, a filthy Datalian!"

"You need not trust just yet," Alastan said.

"Swear to me!"

"Bart-"

"I said, swear to me!" Bartolo sputtered out.

"I swear I'll get the deeds for your wife."

"And my share of the profits."

"That, too. But it's not going to come to that."

Bartolo took a heavy breath. "I can feel them coming for me, Alastan. They're coming." With that, he fell back into the cloth of the litter and closed his eyes.

Datero and Thokar worked hard, carrying Bartolo out of the cave and up the rocky slope to the higher, more easily tread ground. They were sweating in the cold by the time they could put him down. The Barsils, being lizards, had no issue with the rocks but were not happy about leaving the warmth of the hot springs behind.

In the wide desert, it was night. The moon was a sliver, but the stars were bright for lack of light as the ghosts retreated to fill the distant points with a gentle glowing haze. They could see everything around them clearly, but a little ways off in any direction, the land became too dark to see.

"Which way?" Alastan said to Mondal.

Mondal was standing silently, turning his head this way and that. "The danger does not come from the west," he said.

"What do you mean?"

"I thought the ghosts feared the returned Draesen, but they fill the west in a line, and... whatever they fear," he seemed to sniff the air. "It's in the east."

"Yes, that way," Haggin said, nodding in the direction the dark elf was staring. "They're afraid of it. Can you hear them crying out to each other?"

"No," Alastan said. "Now, which way do we go?"

"Not east," Mondal said. "We'll have to go north. We cannot retreat, or the spirits will be on us. Yes, there is another place to the north. We shall have to feel our way."

Mondal once again led them. The terrain seemed to have shifted in the storm, and where before there was hard-baked soil and the strange succulent plants, now there were piles of sand, like snowdrifts against the rocks. The remains of the road were still there, however, standing in defiance of the desert.

They went as quickly as they dared, sometimes jogging, sometimes walking swiftly, along the track. In front of them, the spirits wandered but seemed to flee before them.

"Do they fear us, too?" Datero said.

"No," Thokar said. "They fear what follows us. I can sense something behind us – some ripple in the prim. We are walking through an ocean of it, so it is beyond me to make sense of it, but there is definitely something behind us."

"Something that can use magic," Datero said.

"Or something that is born of it."

*

"Why aren't we running?" Haggin said. He stood a few paces in front of the party, his empty hands twitching and steam rising from his quick breaths. The moon had gone down in the west, and only Thokar's crystal staff gave off any comfort of light. The stars were hazy and dim.

"It's the barsils," Alastan said. "They're reptiles, and they're getting cold."

"Can we warm them up?" Datero said. "Thokar?"

"I know of no way to do that," the Draesen replied.

"The hungering ones will come upon us soon," Haggin said.

"Is that what they are called?" Mondal said, tilting his head.

"Yes," Alastan said. "Yes, I believe it. I can remember the voices in fear of them... but what are they?"

"I don't want to find out," Datero said. "If it's hungering and coming after us, it can't be good. So how do we get these lizards to move?"

"We need the sun to warm them up," Alastan said. "Or something. Can we light a fire, Thokar? Something to hold near to them, to keep them warm? We have no fuel, but we do have you."

Thokar rubbed his face. "Perhaps. I could potentially put the fire on our weapons or on our other equipment that won't burn."

Thokar set to work, lighting small magical blue fires on the ends of swords and spears. Reluctantly, Alastan gave Haggin his sword back and a spear, which they lit with a long flame. They held the weapons close to the animals, near their great central trunks. Thokar and Mondal had the constant job of re-invigorating these magical fires with their minds or a whispered spell. It seemed to help a little, but only in that the slowing of the reptiles was delayed. Eventually, they would move only a little way at a time, then pause and breathe slowly.

"I cannot keep this up forever, even in this prim-rich place," Thokar said.

"What do we do?" Alastan said. "We cannot abandon our tack, our trade goods, and our last source of water."

"Then we must fight who is following us," Mondal said. "I don't recommend it. The barsils can be replaced. Our supplies can be replenished. We can find a way to make gold in the lands beyond, but we must be alive for that. We still have potable water from the spring we can carry. We are close to the end of this accursed place if we can go just two more days."

Alastan sighed. "I guess it's my call. Take what you can carry – enough water for yourself for two days, and every ounce of gold. Anything too bulky, throw onto the litter with Bartolo. We're going to have to drag him."

"Sweet Althius, you're serious?" Datero said. "He's as good as dead. Just leave him with the beasts."

"I'm loathe to leave our poor animals here, but a man is another story. We're taking him with us, and that's that."

Despite Datero's protestations, he was the first to pick up half of Bartolo's litter. The barsils were cut free, their burdens of magical trade goods left in the dirt.

"Farewell, my scaly friends," Alastan said aloud. "May you find your way out to greener pastures." He doubted his blessing would do anything, but he took the time to pat his own beast on its long, horned head one last time.

Relieved of their saddles and packs, they sluggishly moved a little way off and began to very slowly dig themselves into the loose dirt.

The party continued on, faster now, exerting themselves dragging Bartolo with the waterskins around their shoulders and stacked on the litter. The night, it seemed, would never end. Before them, the shades grew more distant. *The Hungering Ones* were gaining on them.

"It is too late," Mondal said at length. "They come, and we are too distant from the Oasis. We must face them, whatever they are."

Alastan, who was dragging Bartolo, dropped his pole. His sweat was chill in the night air, his skin crusted dust.

"I suppose there's nothing for it," Alastan said. "Ah, but now I regret leaving our animals."

"The way out is forward," Mondal said. "We cannot undo our decision."

Alastan nodded. He loosened his sword and took up his spear. "Here, by these boulders. At least we won't have to expose our backs."

"Now you know why I donned my mail," Mondal said.

Thokar busied himself by creating a bright magical fire on a few nearby rocks. It lit the area around them enough to see clearly. In front of the line of boulders he began to trace lines in the dirt, eventually making a large arc around them. Meanwhile, Datero roused Bartolo enough to shove a sword into his hand, but the man was paler than ever and closed his eyes, oblivious to the danger.

"I will attempt to conceal us," Thokar said.

"And I will muffle our sound and presence," Mondal said.

"Good thinking," Alastan said, "but I think it will do no good. Whatever has chased us has done so presumably without having seen or heard us."

"That sense toward us may not be keen enough close up," Mondal. "We should take every advantage." The dark elf leaned against a boulder and closed his eyes, his lips moving soundlessly. A seeming barrier went up in a shallow arc, making the fire ripple as though looking through water.

Before they saw anything, they heard them. It was the sound of shuffling footsteps and plodding, stomping boots, but the cadence was irregular and unpredictable.

"Courage," Alastan whispered. "Do not run, for there is nowhere to run to until our foe is dead."

They came into the edge of the firelight, slowing as they approached the flames. They were huge, even gigantic, each taller than Thokar and more massive, and there were six of them. They were Draesen, or at least were once of the Draesen race, for their bodies looked impossibly damaged. Skin was missing, peeled away by injury or worn away by the passage of wind-blown sand, revealing grey, weathered muscles and bleached bone. Their eyes were sunken and dull but held within them a strangely even inner light, though it was far paler than the light in Mondal's eyes.

Tarnished armor hung from their broken bodies like rags of woven rust, and any jack that lay beneath the mail was long since turned to strands of thread. Only hideous, pot-marked skin remained, and with revolution, the party noticed that some of the male monsters, four of the group, had lost their manhood to some trauma or the passage of time. The females fared little better, their breasts long since coiled into wrinkled sacks or torn from their chests.

In their huge arms they carried weapons to match their girth, but these were worn beyond belief, the keen edges of swords long gone to weathered, jagged teeth. Hilts were bare of wrapping, and no wood survived for ax hafts. Instead, a few of them carried iron bars like clubs. Their boots were rotten, but iron sabatons remained hanging over bony white feet.

They spoke to each other a strange language in an awkward manner, for their voices were like breaking straw or pebbles grinding under wagon wheels.

They could not see the party, nor seem to hear their breathing, if their senses worked at all. They walked curiously around the fire, close to Haggin, who stood the furthest forward, talking to themselves.

"They hunger not for our body, but for our souls," Mondal whispered. "That is why the spirits fear them."

One of them, a female, turned its head suddenly and stared in the direction of Haggin, though she didn't seem to truly see him.

"Let them come in close, then take that female out," Alastan whispered. His sweaty hands gripped his spear tightly. "Now!"

The shambling creature cried out as Alastan stabbed it in the neck, sending his spearpoint into its skull and out the other side. Haggin just as quickly thrust his spear through her heart. The creature turned its head to look at Alastan, apparently unaffected by the spear in its brain. It reached out quickly and grabbed Alastan's shirt. He screamed as it pulled on him with inhuman strength.

He dug his heels in, pushing desperately against the ice-cold hand, then suddenly fell backward. The hand remained gripping his shirt, its fingers twitching and writhing. Mondal had severed the arm with a single stroke. He had both his swords out now and was slashing through the undead horror, hacking desiccated flesh away from brittle bone. Datero attempted the same with his arming sword, slashing at the creature's legs, but his attacks were less effective – there was something about Mondal's twin swords beyond the steel that made them.

The other reborn Draesen, at first puzzled, lurched forward with a unified cry of anger as the spells dropped, and they understood what was happening to their companion.

The fire burst open and exploded out. Shards of blue-hot flame leapt onto the monsters, searing flesh and giving off a nauseous smell, but it apparently caused them no pain.

"To me!" Alastan said, leaping up and moving to Haggin, who had released his spear and drawn his sword. "Do not let them surround you!"

All of them had experienced war before, and while they were not themselves a military unit, the party was able to quickly fall into a fighting formation. They moved together, hacking at the first Draesen and driving him to the ground, but they could not stop another from moving around behind and swinging its club wildly at their heads. Thokar dropped back and began sending bolts of flaming magic at them. They had a little effect, enough to slow down four of them so that Alastan, Datero, and Haggin could break down their target. It was a good thing that the swords of the arisen attackers were so ancient, for had they been new both Alastan and Datero would have died. They took several blows while cutting away at legs and arms.

Meanwhile, Mondal moved quickly around the monsters from the flank, his swords slashing at exposed flesh and turning away the clumsy strikes of the Draesen with their broken weapons.

Nothing, it seemed, could kill them. It became evident that whatever life was in them was not of their flesh, but some other magic or device. Their hearts did not beat, nor did their brains house thought. All the party could do was follow Mondal's lead and disable them by separating arms and legs and breaking bones.

There were four, then three. Then there were two, and the party pressed the attack. Swords began to chip. Datero shattered his somehow and had to continue with his dagger, hiding behind his shield as best he could. Finally, there was one Draesen, injured and burned. He shambled away from the light and stopped, locking eyes with Mondal.

The elf spoke to him, and the ancient Draesen spoke back, throwing his rusted and sand-blasted sword into the dirt. Alastan raised a hand to signal a halt to the others.

The Draesen turned his large bony face toward them, stopping on Thokar. He snorted and spoke again in his dry creaking voice. Thokar spoke a few words back. At last, the monster looked at Mondal, and spoke what sounded like a few sentences.

Mondal said one last thing to him, then rushed forward. The Draesen made no attempt to resist the attack, and Mondal cut his head off with a one powerful swing. The body collapsed onto the fire, and the flames began to sear the flesh. Thokar extinguished the fire before the oily stench of burning flesh could grow strong.

All around them lay the remains of the attackers, in some cases twitching. One of the Draesen still had an arm and was trying to crawl away. Mondal hacked its head off, then kicked the skull away.

"What was that?" Alastan said, kneeling to catch his breath and nurse a painful bruise on his ribs. "What did you say to him?"

Mondal sheathed his swords, then knelt and picked up the colossal head of the last Draesen. The eyes were motionless, but were still aglow. The elf stared at it. "I promised I would carry his skull out of the desert and then obliterate it, so his spirit could be free of this place."

"The old tales were true," Thokar said. He leaned on his staff, exhausted. He too was bleeding in several places. "My ancestors did indeed have some method of attaining immortality, and this was it—an eternity trapped in a preserved mortal body.

"These were not the bodies from the necropolis," he went on. "That last one said they had been wandering here for years, and they lost count of all time. They would have to have died in the Second Dominion, perhaps the beginning of the Third at the latest, for they built those complexes before the withdraw of the empire."

"Before the desert was here," Mondal said.

"And who knows how long it took them to return."

"So, they've been wandering here for a thousand years?" Alastan said. "Trapped in a desert that you cannot escape, always hungering for what you cannot have. What a wretched destiny."

"Are you really going to carry that with us?" Datero said, watching Mondal stuff the head into a sack.

"I made a promise."

"Are we going to carry the other heads? They look heavy."

"I hadn't planned on it," Mondal said. "They weren't part of the bargain. Besides, we only need one head to keep away the others."

"Others?"

"They are but one group," Mondal said. "They have rivals, but they will have difficulty sensing us in the presence of the arisen. The ghosts, too, will fear us."

"I'd hate to leave anyone like this," Alastan said. "Trapped in a... severed head."

"Perhaps they deserved their punishment."

Alastan shook his head. "A thousand years is enough."

"We could take one with us for the journey home," Mondal said. "To keep the spirits away. Then we can destroy it in Structania. That would be a mercy."

"Alright," Alastan said. "Take another. The others let us break apart and burn as best we can."

"Morning is coming soon." It was Haggin, who, though bloodied, wore a slight smile. "We've survived."

"Not all of us," Datero said. "Barty's nearly gone."

"We'll drag him as long as he breathes," Alastan said.

"We'll need to move quickly," said Mondal. "I fear we will lose him soon, and then his spirit may be condemned to wander here, rather than… going wherever it is mortals go. If he expires in an oasis, he might find his way out of here."

"You're right, of course. Let's throw the heads on the litters and huff it. Damn, but I wish I hadn't turned the barsils loose. We can't go back for them?"

"I doubt we would find them," Mondal said.

Alastan looked at the glowing remains of the fire and nodded.

It took three of them to drag the unconscious Bartolo, and all six gigantic Draesen heads through the dirt, but somehow they managed it.

The sun rose, and their sweaty labor increased. Exhausted and thirsty, they reached the oasis, which was the bare remains of a town, where only a dried well and a cluster of stone foundations remained. It was, however, calm there, and real. There were even a few green shrubs and a few small creatures living within them, persisting against all odds.

There they smashed four of the still-living Draesen heads and burned them in magical fire. The reek that it gave off was overpowering, and Bartolo alone did not react. He breathed still but remained unconscious, and nothing seemed to rouse him.

"Stubborn bastard refuses to die," Datero said. "Just like him."

"He may live yet, he's so stubborn," Alastan said.

They spent the rest of the day and the night there, where their wounds were healed by Thokar's magic and a fair bit of his strange medicine. They were, however, out of food after dinner and low on water, having had to drink a great deal of their remaining stores to replenish themselves from the effort of carrying Bartolo. The well was not totally dry, but they could only fish a small amount out of it at a time, for they had abandoned their cookware.

As they sat around the fire, eating their last morsels, Mondal said again, "We may have to leave him. We must be gone from this desert, or we shall run out of water."

"I won' leave him," Alastan said.

"Then I may leave you," Mondal said. "Others, too."

In the end, Alastan did not have to make the decision he feared. Haggin, who slept all night soundly, woke just before sunset to find Bartolo mumbling. Before he could get anything out of the merchant, he had laid his head down and died.

They dug him a shallow grave, placed his body in it, and marked the spot with a stone that Thokar etched with magic – runes to guard against thieves. They took his valuables, though it was unlucky, for they had left all their trade goods with the barsils. True to his reputation, Bartolo had a large stash of gold and tradeable gems secreted throughout his body.

"We'll pay his widow back," Alastan said.

"I expect you'll pay mine, too, if I go," Datero said.

"Of course."

"What about you? I gathered you wrote a letter to somebody before we set out. Who is your next of kin? Just in case."

"My son, I suppose, and his mother. Her name is Lucita, and she is in hiding in Balta," Alastan said. "I meant not to tell anyone. We are not wed, you know."

Datero laughed. "Hiding scandals from me? You know better than that. In fact… No, I don't believe you. There's more to it, eh? She's someone important's daughter, and you're in it hot, or you've got debts in Datalia."

Alastan gave his friend a curious look.

"You don't have to tell me now. I'll find Lucita if you die, and give her your share of profits if any."

"Thank you. We might as well say a final blessing for our late employer."

"Who does he follow? Denarthal? Of course, he does." Datero laughed. "Why do I ask? We should pray to Verbus instead."

"Pray to the Dreamer himself," Thokar said from nearby.

"He doesn't do anything," Datero said.

"It's him who created your soul," Thokar said. "I would not anger him."

"Alright, I'll add a prayer for him."

"I'll say my own," Mondal said. "For the Draesen we have put to rest, too. Perhaps they can escape the curse that is upon them. They bought immortality with more than misery."

"Supposedly, they pledged to serve the Unbinder, Diorgesh," Thokar said. "Who will unbind such a pact, if not the wyrm herself?"

"I do not have the answers, just prayers," Mondal said.

*

It was the following day that they, at last, arrived at the end of the first stage of their journey. The desert thinned and turned to dry brushland. Birds and other animals appeared, and finally, their waterskins wrung dry, they came upon a muddy creek and drank their fill, but only after boiling the water.

The assassin caught a rabbit, and they split it for supper. It tasted all of sage and bitter herbs, but hunger proved the more pungent seasoning, and though it was a small meal for each of them, they felt immense pleasure in it.

"It's a bit like coming up for air," Datero said, eating his share of the meat off the bone, "When you've been diving." He chuckled. "I don't know if elves and orcs dive for pearls."

"We have another dive ahead of us," Thokar said. "To our west lies the Draesenith Empire, and who can say what challenges await us there?"

"Indeed," Alastan said. "And it is there we shall have to find not only our way to our goal but also find the funding to achieve it."

"I'm sure there is plenty of work for men like us," Mondal said. "Even if we are a bit undersized."

Gen Y Chronicles

Nostalgia Chronicles: Gen Y

It's a hot day, and it isn't helped by the thirty-five pounds of books in your backpack. You walk steadily away from the chaos that is the end of the school day; the swarms of cars and kids move steadily behind you, and the quiet of the deserted streets sets in, interrupted only by the occasional quip from one of your walking companions.

One by one, the friends of mutual direction peel off, and you're by yourself, walking through the empty suburbs to your house. There's never enough trees, and you begin to accumulate a layer of sweat under your jean shorts and T-shirt.

Finally, you get home. You pad across the empty driveway and stop by the mailbox. It's mostly junk, except for the Software-of-the-Month Club CD. You open your front door and feel immediate relief from the AC, which has been dutifully running, though nobody has been home all day. You toss the CD-ROM on the keyboard of your PC and head to the darkened living room.

The curtains are shut against the sun and the blinds are closed in the adjoining kitchen. You ignore the stack of dishes in the sink. You plop your backpack down at the kitchen table. There's a mountain of pointless homework inside that you know sooner or later you'll have to do. You're a bit burned out on the boring parts of life, though, so you let it stay safely sealed away in the protective denim of your Jansport. Besides, if you aren't done with it by the time your mom gets home, you can probably do that instead of the dishes.

You grab a coke from the fridge and head over to the couch. You sigh as you finally sit down, barely noticing the familiar smells of your house – mostly canned Pledge. You pull off your nearly worn-out sneakers and take off your socks, then rub your feet on the thick brown carpet. You look over again at the kitchen table. The cat has already decided to lay down on your bag. It would be a pity to disturb her. Homework will have to wait.

It's like a cocoon inside – there might as well be nothing outside those windows.

You get up and turn on the TV, then flip over to the video input. You open up your PlayStation, same as always, just to make sure your disc is still in there. You slam the lid closed and hit the power button.

You are greeted by that familiar sound which first gave you goosebumps back when you got the console for Christmas from your father. The rumble of it distorts the speaker on your big TV. The cat leaps up from her nap, disturbed by the sound as usual.

You pick up your controller and sit down on the carpet, putting a couch cushion behind your back and head as you lean into the sofa. The menu music starts up, and you listen to it all the way through, imagining you are watching a group of recorder and lute players from some other world. When it ends, you let it play again.

As you stare at the menu, you have an impulse not to play. You know you are at the end of the game, but something inside is telling you not to finish. You load up your game, wondering if there is a sidequest or two you could finish up for some special items, or if you could make some gil and get geared up before the final boss, which you know will be tough.

You smile to yourself. Maybe you'll finish today after all, or tonight after everyone else goes to sleep.

Iron and Clay: A Doomer Tale

Jim was the smartest kid in Glenns Ferry, Idaho.

He aced every math exam, always tested well in science and English, and got exemplary marks in history.

He was otherwise a normal, well-liked kid that played football and soccer throughout high school. Though he was never the star athlete, sports kept him active and grounded and provided him a good set of friends off the field and year-round. All of them knew he was the smartest of the group, but he never made a big deal out of it, preferring to go with the flow and help with homework only when asked.

If the gang was going to do something stupid, he was going to do it, too. Glenns Ferry was a small town, and the gang of gangly white boys mostly got away with their stunts; when they got caught, discipline tended to be handled by fathers, not the law. Luckily, they all preferred pizza and video games to things like cow tipping or drinking a majority of the time..

Jim had a beautiful girlfriend named Courtney he managed to land as a junior, after months of flirting and months trying to get up the courage to ask her out. They loved each other as much as kids could love each other, which is a lot, but as Mormons, they avoided having sex and routinely talked about getting married sometime in the future. Jim's catholic friends teased him about it, but they were all virgins just like him.

All throughout his schooling, everyone told Jim he was destined for greatness. He was going to work for NASA, or find the cure to cancer. After talking to his math teachers, he became attached to the idea of becoming an aeronautical engineer. Designing machines that flew – even to space – began to occupy his mind as much as video games. He began taking math and science much more seriously, even driving up to Boise State to take an early seminar in differential equations prior to his senior year.

He also took up programing with a few of his friends, and they produced a functional, though ugly, computer role-playing game for an English assignment that landed them in the local papers.

As he approached graduation, he was offered a spot in the prestigious Massachusetts Institute of Technology and was ecstatic about it. Accepting a spot meant postponing his mission trip, but after talking it over with his parents, he took the leap. As a fresh-faced 18 year-old kid, he packed his bags and went to Cambridge, Massachusetts, enrolling as an engineering student.

MIT was the first place that Jim ever felt that he wasn't special. In fact, he quickly realized that he was in the bottom half of the pack in his math skills, but he adjusted to the challenge quickly. At the same time, he had trouble finding friends. Everyone was so… different from him. They all came from big cities, many weren't even from America, and it seemed like all he ran into were graduate students who couldn't be bothered to talk to him, even when he had labs with them.

It was lonely, and so Jim concentrated on his studies, calling his girlfriend every night until she left for her own mission trip and he had to subside on postcards sent once every-other week. He stayed in Cambridge for Christmas after talking to his parents: a plane ticket was just going to cost too much, and his loans were already pretty large.

Eventually, though, he did find a group of friends toward the end of his first year, and they filled in his social needs like his old friends. They were from smaller towns, too, and had done a few of the things he used to do, though none of them had been spelunking. He told them he would take them sometime, but the opportunity never arose. They were always too busy with studying, programming, or gaming.

He flew home that summer to find town much the same as when he had left. Most of his friends weren't there – they were either on their mission trips, or else had joined the military.

Early in the fall semester, Jim's girlfriend broke up with him via telephone. Apparently, she just didn't think it would work out with him living out of state for school. Jim was heartbroken, but his friends were there to cheer him up. They even got him to talk to a girl at a bar and he managed to get her phone number. They went on a date, but nothing more than that – still, it was enough to remind Jim that other women existed.

Jim and his friends found distractions in a few new hobbies they found together – things they could play indoors during their downtime, like Magic the Gathering and Dungeons and Dragons. William, the best looking and perhaps smartest of the friends, often mused that he could design better systems, but he never bothered to make his own game. He, like Jim, was too busy with schoolwork, and was content to play 3rd Edition D&D despite his gripes.

Jim made it through the semester. His marks suffered initially, but he passed all of his classes without much trouble in the end. One of his friends, Reggie, got academically disqualified. They all said they'd keep in touch, but Jim only talked to him once during the spring semester. After that, he was mostly a memory.

Things rolled on like that.

In their third year, Will left MIT to attend a state school near his hometown, feeling convicted that his destiny was to be a fantasy author. He emailed Jim frequently at first, but then the communications dropped off. Eventually, all of his freshmen year friends fell away by either leaving school or graduating.

At the end of his Junior year, Jim got a wedding invitation from his ex-girlfriend, whose family was still close with Jim's. He took out a loan and attended a special seminar on thermoacoustic materials in Japan to avoid going home for the summer and being subjected to the wedding.

It was the loneliest few weeks of his life, and he did nothing besides attend the lectures in English and hide in his Osaka hotel room. His friends would ask him about the experience after the fact, and he would play it up, but he always knew that although he had flown to Japan and spent weeks there, he had never really *been* there.

Jim finished his undergraduate degree with high marks and was faced with the choice to pursue a graduate degree or look for a job... or go on a mission. He had racked up huge amounts of debt from his degree, and wondered if payment could be postponed for a religious obligation. He had already been accepted to several schools when a headhunter for Boeing of all places found him and asked him to interview for a job. He interviewed for the job in Los Angeles, but the actual job was in Seattle.

Once again, his parents told him to pursue his dreams, so Jim packed his meager possessions, sold his car, and flew to Seattle, where he moved into a tiny but expensive apartment.

The job was in quality control of plane body components, which was tedious work, but had the potential to lead to what Jim really wanted work in – design. He got a few hints from his higher ups that he would land a design job if he had the master's degree after all, so he started taking classes for his MS at night.

He had never been busier. He never made any friends in Seattle, except for work acquaintances who would never invite him out on the weekends because he didn't drink. He didn't date, or even consider dating. His first set of neighbors might as well have been non-existent. He only saw them leaving on weekends, but they never said a word to him. They eventually moved out and were replaced by a couple that smoked pot relentlessly, making the entire complex reek in the hallways, and it even stunk up Jim's apartment, until they got arrested for dealing. After that they were replaced by a family of Asian immigrants who said nothing to him, but always eyed him suspiciously and argued loudly in the hall in their home language.

At the end of two years, he got a call from General Electric, who wanted him for a design job in their aerospace program. He had to move yet again – this time to Cincinnati. It was a fast move and he had to give most of his furniture to charity, but what he could fit in his old used pickup he took with him to his new city.

The job turned out to be more quality control, along with a lower salary than what he had been told. He could barely cover rent in the apartment he had found ahead of his move. It seemed like all of his money was going to rent and to pay down his student loans, which were growing now that he had to pay back the tuition from his MS. He slogged it out for a few years, not even bothering to buy furniture for his apartment, then was finally given the design job he had wanted. It was enough to get his head above water and start saving for a house, but the work didn't satisfy him the way he thought it would. He was working on engine components, which though challenging and technical, was not working on planes or spaceships.

Then he got another call from Boeing. They had his dream job waiting for him in Los Angeles: aerospace design.

He moved once again, this time to El Segundo, excited to, after a decade, finally get to have what everyone told him was his destined dream job.

The rent in the Los Angeles area was more than he had ever experienced, more even than Seattle. He paid almost three thousand dollars a month for a small two-bedroom apartment, but he was making such good money it didn't bother him too much. He could still pay his loans and have a little left over, though he was worried he would never own a home when all the houses in town were over a million dollars.

For the first time since arriving in college, Jim felt like he had time to really think, time to spend with other people.

The thing was, the other people around him were nothing like him. They weren't Mormon... most of them weren't even Christian. They were from different towns, different states, different countries – but nobody was from Idaho or, it seemed, Los Angeles. His best friend at work was a Muslim named Amir – the only person he had met in what seemed like years he could talk about God with, but the conversations were hard, so they mostly talked about games.

Jim got into his first serious relationship since high school with a Jewish woman named Darlene he met through a mutual at work. They got along great, he thought, but the relationship ended after two years, quite abruptly. Darlene thought they were too different, that he was too rigid. Of course, their final argument had come up over religion, when he mentioned off-hand that he would want to raise their children as Mormons.

This wasn't what offended her; apparently, she didn't want children at all.

Jim was surprised at how well he took it. He barely felt sad – just disappointed.

At the age of thirty, he was starting to see all of his friends from home on Facebook with children, their kids re-living the youth he had experienced so many years ago in the 80s and 90s. They were doing the same things – fishing, playing Nintendo, even camping.

He realized that in every city he had made, at best, temporary friends that left shadows in his life in the form of facebook profiles. He saw their posts from time to time, but all the response he could muster was hitting a like button; he nothing to say to them, except for Will. Will always was posting about his game designs. He was shipping home-made table-top RPGs and was building a video game in his free time, and Jim felt slightly jealous that Will had moved back to his hometown and gotten a job at a pizza parlor instead of finishing at MIT.

In the time since college, Jim's only real hobby had been gaming, and it had been forced to the margins of his workaday life.

Not knowing what else to do as a single thirty-year-old, Jim started using online dating apps to try to find a partner – someone like him. He found himself in another relationship rather quickly. Her name was Sara, and she was from a small town just like him, though she came from Texas. She wasn't Mormon. She was a Baptist, but of course it had been years at this point since Jim had gone to church (he never did complete his mission), so he considered it close enough.

They got married quickly by Los Angeles standards, which was two years later.

They pooled their resources together and put a down payment on a town house, which was a steal at 850,000 dollars. With both of their student loans and the mortgage to cover every month, they decided to put off having children for a few years.

A few years came and went, and Jim came home early from his design job one day to surprise Sara with a birthday present, only to find her entertaining another man. A divorce quickly followed. When everything was settled, including alimony, Jim silently counted himself lucky that he hadn't had children with Sara.

He was back to living in a one-bedroom apartment, but in Inglewood rather than South Bay, and he was poorer than ever, still driving his beat-up truck.

One night, Jim got an itch. He picked up his phone and called his friend Will. He was surprised when Will picked up (he had apparently kept the same cell number since college).

"Will, this is Jim, from MIT."

"What's up dude?" Will said in the same ever-positive voice he had back in college.

"Not much."

"Living the dream down in LA?"

Jim looked around at his sparsely furnished apartment. The most expensive things he owned, indeed the only things he valued, were his computer and his television. "Yeah, I guess."

"Designing spaceships? That was what we all wanted back in the day. We should have been making model planes instead of working on Everquest hacks."

"Not quite planes just yet. It's mostly little things..." Jim realized he couldn't remember what project he was currently working on. The blank in his mind startled him slightly.

"It's in the industry, though, right?"

"Yeah, but it's kind of tedious. It's really tedious, actually. Doesn't matter though, it's good work. What are you doing these days?"

"You know what I'm up to; you chat with me about it all the time. You never post about *you*, though."

"Sara and I got a divorce."

"Yeah, that sucks, man. LA is a fun place, though, yeah? Especially single I reckon."

Jim laughed. "Maybe for some people. It's busy. Always a million things to do, but I never have the time or the money, or know the right people to do any of them."

"There's millions of people there."

"Yeah, I know, but… It's hard to find similar minds out here." Jim chuckled. "Everybody is from somewhere else and nobody wants to know you. You know, at my last place I only met my neighbor one time? It was when I was clearing my stuff out. He wanted to know if there was a room for rent. He didn't realize Sara and I were married. Just thought we were roommates."

"I felt that way in College. It was hard, being alone all the time. If it wasn't for you and the other guys, I'd have probably offed myself. That's real grim, I know, and I'm past it now, but that's what it was like. Everybody is a stranger that couldn't care less if you died. Especially the teachers. Anyway, thanks for being my friend is what I guess I'm saying. It mattered."

"You're welcome." Jim was silent for a few moments, then said. "How did you manage it? Just walking away from your dream?"

"Shit, man, it wasn't a dream. I was the smart kid, I was supposed to go to a big name college and get a job for NASA – that was what my parents wanted. I didn't want to design spaceships, I wanted to fly them. I wanted to go on adventures. I wish I'd joined the navy or something."

"How about now, though?"

"Life's good. I do some things I don't like so I can do other things I do like – that's what I say if I'm being honest. I don't tell my employees that I don't care about the pizza business."

"Employees? Did you buy the place?"

"Naw, I took out a loan and opened my own restaurant, then a few more here and in Tulare – that's the next town over. Couple franchises. Easy business to manage. As close to a kit as you can get. Scales up nice. I might add one up the road a bit. Lots of little towns between here and Fresno."

"If you don't mind me asking, how much do you make?"

"Who cares, dude? I do as little as possible to pay down my mortgage and spend my time doing things that matter."

"Just humor me, please."

Will laughed at him. "Fine. I made eighty-five grand last year from the franchises. Not a ton, but plenty to live on, since my mortgage is small, and I don't have to work that much to keep it going. I hire managers to do all the real work."

"Damn," Jim said. "Not bad."

"How about you?"

"I get about a hundred thirty-five."

"Doing better than me."

"You wouldn't say that if you were here with me." Jim felt tears welling up in his eyes. "I got nothing, man. Nothing. I don't even have a dog. I live in a shit part of town… and I don't know how to walk away from this."

"Just go home."

"There's no engineering jobs at home."

"So? Just hit up your parents until you find something to do."

"I'm thirty-six."

"So?"

"My parents aren't taking in a thirty-six year old in who just felt like quitting his super-high paying job."

"Then come crash on my couch. I'll even give you a job. Visalia isn't that far away."

Jim laughed. "I have student loans and alimony."

"How much in savings?"

"Nothing."

"They can't squeeze a turnip, then. Let 'em try. I'll pay you under the table."

"I can't. It's too much. I have to have this job… I…"

"Don't listen to me, man. I'm just a guy who likes to make games."

"Is that fun?"

"Oh yeah. It's hard work, but I love it. I'm finally getting to play some of them with my kids, too, which is awesome."

"I didn't know you had kids."

"Yeah, I got married like right after I got back. Sherry - she actually hated me in high school, but that's a whole 'nother story. Four kids, so far. I never post about them, so it makes sense you wouldn't know."

"Yeah. Listen, I should go. Thanks for chatting with me."

"No problem. I'll call you tomorrow."

Will hung up and Jim sat in his darkened apartment for a few minutes, just listening to the cars passing by outside and the neighbors arguing in Spanish.

He imagined another life – one where he ignored everyone's advice, went on his mission trip, and married Courtney. He came back to reality when his phone buzzed. It was Will, texting him his address in central California.

Jim stood up and looked around his barren apartment. After some thought, he realized that everything he cared about would fit in the trunk of his car: his computer, his old gamebooks, his TV, and most of his clothes.

With a half-smile, he unplugged his monitor and keyboard, and started packing them into a duffel bag.

It would be best to be out before the traffic on the 405 going north got bad.

New Thing, Old Thing

It's raining again.

Like it did yesterday. The forecast says it will rain tomorrow... maybe the day after that.

You walk home in the rain, stopping to buy a soda at the corner store like usual. You pocket the change. Maybe you'll start saving your pocket money tomorrow, but today would be worse without that bottle of Dr. Pepper. Your hands are numb by the time you get home, since the soda was cold, and the rain was colder.

You shut the door on the rain and listen to it's rumble on the roof in the otherwise silent house. You take off your shoes. They're soaked, just like yesterday. You lay your socks out on the tile floor to dry next to the ones from yesterday, which you never picked up. You roll up your wet jeans and throw your backpack by your chair, then boot up your computer.

You open up your messaging program – AOL, even though you don't have AOL. Maybe it's better than ICQ... I mean, everyone is using it. But you don't like it as much, plus there are a few friends that you lost on the way, like Andrew who switched schools in the 8th grade.

It's a new thing. A good thing. But you don't like it as much as old thing.

You forget about your homework and boot up a game: Quake II. You try out a harder difficulty on a few maps. It's definitely fun, but after a while you close it and open up Doom. It familiar and just right, but you admit Quake II is still pretty good.

It's a new thing. A good thing. But you don't like it as much as old thing. But it's raining. There's not much else to do.

Your friend pops up on AOL IM. He had planned to camp out for tickets to the new Star Wars movie, but it's been raining, so he's staying home. You decide to go to the movie together after opening day, since standing around in the rain sucks.

It's raining again when you decide to go see it, just like last week. You meet up with your friend at the bookstore outside the theater, where you always go to kill time before standing in line, especially when it's raining or hot. You look through the books, going through the genres you don't usually read. Maybe you'll choose something new this time... but in the end, you spend your money on another horror book, even though you haven't liked the last few horror books you've bought.

It's a new thing, but it's never as good as old thing.

You look through the CDs – maybe they'll have something new, but it's always the same thing as last time. The only things added are the newer bands from the radio, who get their songs played every hour. They're okay but not as good as the stuff you used to hear.

Finally, you cross the rainy courtyard and throw a coin into the fountain, like usual. You cross into the carpeted foyer, then get in a line just forming outside one of the ten theaters in the multiplex showing Star Wars. You talk about expectations and how great Dark Forces II was, until it's time to go in.

You find your usual seats in the first row up from the floor, right in the middle, where you can kick your feet up on the rail while watching. You and your friend pull out your smuggled snacks, like usual, and watch the endless parade of slides, then previews before the movie.

The movie's wild, but something's not right.

Your friend who works at the theater nods to you as you leave.

"Pretty awesome, huh?"

You hesitate. "Yeah..."

It's a new thing, but definitely not as good as old thing.

...

Prom is coming up. Everyone is going.

Instead of asking out the girl you have a crush on, you ask out the most attractive girl in your class who doesn't have a date and is in your league, because you think the girl that you actually want to ask is too good to say yes.

It's a fun night. The girl seems to like you. You like all the same things and laugh at each other's jokes. And she's pretty, too. You find out she like Type O Negative and Pantera. Rad.

But she's not the girl you really like, so the next week you just go on and pretend to be friends when she wants to be more. And you spend your idle minutes in school fantasizing about the girl you like but don't talk to.

...

It's raining again today, harder than yesterday. You're soaked by the time you get back to your dorm room. You throw your messenger bag down on the thin, torn-up blue carpet. Your bag is what everyone uses, but it makes your shoulder hurt. Your old backpack was better.

How many people have walked on that carpet, slept on this bunk, looked out this window?

You boot up your PC. You ought to get on your homework since finals are coming up, but decide to play a quick game of Warcraft III first. It's pretty slick, but after one game, you decide to open up Starcraft. Warcraft III is definitely a great game, though.

It's a new thing, but you don't like it as much as old thing.

You watched the newest Star Wars film recently. It felt good. Not as good as the old ones, but good.

You decide to pop in your Phantom Menace DVD while you play. Your roommate comes in a few minutes later, just as Obi-Wan and Qui-Gon are swimming down to the underwater city.

"This crap?"

"Yeah," you say. "It's got some cool scenes."

"Sucks compared to the old ones."

"Maybe. I don't know; I was in the mood."

"Not playing EQ?"

"Not in the mood, I guess. I thought you were going out with Jessica this afternoon."

He smiles at you. "I broke up with her, actually. Didn't feel right, you know? I shouldn't be with someone if it doesn't feel right."

"I get it." You think about Michelle, who you dated this year, but it didn't work out. She never made you feel the way you did about-

"Well, whatever, there's like fifteen thousand girls here, ya know?"

Yeah, but never the right one.

...

Finally, some rain.

You open up your apartment window and wait for the familiar smells to come in. You boot up your computer and log into WoW. It's fun. More fun than you've had in a long time, and it helps you to forget about your job for a while, but you miss your friends from EQ. Most of them didn't make the switch, or didn't roll on your server. The new game is good enough to make up for it, though.

It's a new thing. A good thing, but it doesn't make you feel quite like old thing.

Guild chat is buzzing about the new Star Wars movie. You tell them not to give any spoilers, as you were planning to watch it later, once the rest of your friends were done with work.

That night, you drive through the rain to the theater, the sound drowned out by the drone of an old Type O album. You go to the bookstore to wait for a text from your friends. You look through the stacks, counting off the books you've read from the meager fantasy section. You smile as you find a copy of The Hobbit.

It's an old thing, a good thing, and new things never make you feel quite as happy.

Your friend texts you that she's already inside. You step out into the rainy courtyard. You remember to throw a coin into the fountain on your way to the theater.

You find your seat, and your friend already as popcorn for you. She gives you a slight smile, which you return awkwardly.

The movie is good, but it's a new thing, so it's not as good as old thing. While you watch the credits, you chat with your friend, and she mentions she plays World of Warcraft.

For a moment, you wonder if there is something there. Maybe?

But then, you don't feel the same way about her that you did about the girls you knew before, so you to make up your mind to just relax, enjoy the conversation, and take her for a beer afterward.

...

Your phone buzzes, and you pull it out to check it. You wipe an errant raindrop from your screen as you slip into the car. Someone added you on Facebook. For a brief moment, you remember MySpace, then remember ICQ. New thing, pretty much the same as old thing.

"Who's that?" asks your girlfriend, seeing you open up the app.

"Some girl I went to high school with, I think."

"Man, she looks rough."

You stare at her profile picture for a few moments and frown.

It's her, isn't it? It has to be. You double-check her details. Sure enough, it's her. She's just...

"I had a crush on her, once."

"Oh boy, you've either really stepped it up, or you're secretly into ugly-cute." Your girlfriend laughs. "We should get a pug."

"She didn't always look that way," you say. "She was really cute."

"Some people age like milk. Facebook is weird like that. You see everybody time-warped forward. Like a perpetual 20-year high school reunion, only without the option to not show up because you just lost your job."

"Yeah."

"Hey, you declined the friend request!"

"We haven't even seen each other in years and years. She's probably one of those people that just adds everyone from high school and only vaguely remembers me."

"You never know, she might be trying to reconnect with you because she's been thinking about you all this time. Your chance to fix unrequited love."

She says it a little sarcastically, but you feel the truth of the statement.

"I think it's better to remember her as she was. Or, as I thought she was. We never talked much, anyway. I didn't really know her."

"Suit yourself. It's not like she's competition to me."

You smile. "She's really not."

"What did you think of the movie? Pretty wild, huh?"

"Total and complete trash."

"Better than the prequels, though, right?"

"It's probably the Star Wars movie my fifteen-year-old self would have made, if you gave him a hundred million dollars and let him go wild. It's a new thing, but it's trying to be the old thing way too hard, and it sucks."

"Can't you just enjoy explosions and bad acting for a few hours?"

You laugh. "I enjoyed who I got to watch it with."

"Thanks. You look kind of morose, though."

"Just thinking about the bookstore that used to be here."

"I'm sure some other company will put one in."

"Yeah, but it won't be the same." You pocket your phone. "Oh well, let's head home."

Jimmy Turns 35

Jimmy, who was "James" only on his tax documents, was looking forward to his thirty-fifth birthday. Like always, he had carefully managed his money over the year to provide for all the things he wanted and to have a bit extra to buy himself something special for his birthday. This year, it was a doozy. He had seen it coming all year and had taken extra care to stow away even more of his pizza delivery tips (which were more than usual), actively cutting back on his consumption of alcohol and pot.

What had Jimmy's mind wandering so much when he was washing dishes between deliveries? It was the dawn of a new console generation, which was as exciting a time as he could think of. His father had managed to buy him a PS2 the day it came out, and he had stood in line overnight for the Wii and the PS3 (he had bought an Xbox 360 as well, but there wasn't quite the same hype around that console – though it was his favorite at the time). By the time the PS4 and Xbox One (the "bone," he called it) had come, the prospect of waiting in line was moot. He had pre-ordered his consoles, along with the launch titles, but it was no less exciting to pick up the box at store opening, go home, and enjoy the sight and smell of the unboxing.

Usually, he took the day off work so he could properly enjoy the experience. This time, he wouldn't, because the launch was on his birthday and he knew his friends at work would want to come party with him. He couldn't very well call in *sick* and then have his managers come over for beers, and of course, to enjoy the new PS5.

The PS5... The console wars were never a big deal for Jimmy. He never had to choose. He always bought both, but the question this year was which one he would get *first.* He supposed, as he was packing up his uniform and counting out his cash for his manager, that he could have done some extra saving to buy both right away, but that would have been too much. The point of life was to enjoy it. Too much asceticism would ruin the overall experience, no matter how cool the Xbox Series X (*man, they love that letter even though the 90s were more than 20 years ago*) was.

But the PS5 was the better choice. Sony always had better exclusives, timed exclusives, and, well, it just *looked* cooler, too. Microsoft had bought the mighty Bethesda, but there were definitely no cool games coming from that camp until 2021.

"You're short a dollar," Roberto said. "But don't worry about it."

"Thanks. You gonna come by tomorrow for my birthday? I'll have a PS5. There'll be girls there, too, I guess."

Roberto laughed. "You bet. I can't believe you put down the cash to buy it already."

"And some games, too. It's not all about streaming Netflix. I'll pick it up before work, then have it all updated by the time I get home."

"Cool."

Jimmy smiled. "Remember when you used to be able to just plug in a console and have it turn on and work? No patches, none of that?"

"No," Roberto said. "I didn't have any videogames growing up until my brother got an Xbox 360."

"Oh yeah. Well, it was a thing. I remember me and my dad pulling out the PS2 and plugging it in, then realizing there was no pack-in game."

"What?"

"Consoles used to ship with a free game. My dad didn't buy a separate game, not realizing. We had run out to the store and get one."

"Oh yeah, I knew that. Alright, see you tomorrow."

"Later, bud."

Jimmy got in his car, a dinged-up ford focus he had owned since he was an undergrad, slight anticipation already tingling the back of his neck. While he was driving home, he got a call from Rosa, his girlfriend.

"Hey babe, what's up?"

"You're off of work?"

"Yup, just headed home now."

"So, it's your birthday tomorrow." Jimmy smiled at the way her voice went up.

"Sure is, the big three-five. Once you get past twenty-one, I guess birthdays only matter every five or ten years."

"I'm wondering if you might want your present at midnight."

Jimmy laughed. "I'd love it."

"I'll be over in a little bit, then. I have to finish up a few things here while we close. Split tips the cooks and all that."

"Cool."

"You want anything to eat? Jose owes me a favor."

"Not pizza," Jimmy laughed.

"How 'bout that chicken ranch sandwich?"

"Oh, man, I'd love that. Happy birthday to me!"

"That's not your present, though. I got something special for you."

"Alright, can't wait."

Jimmy hung up and smiled. He turned his stereo up, hearing one of his favorite Zep tunes come on his Spotify stream.

*

Jimmy opened up the door of his second-story apartment. It was dark inside except for the light from his refrigerator's ice maker. He flipped on the lights and saw his familiar home. He breathed a satisfied sigh as his cat mewed at him. Her bowl was empty again. He gave her a few pets as he refilled it, then he opened up the fridge, grabbed a bottle of Moosehead, and plopped down on the worn leather couch.

Usually, he took a shower since he always came home reeking of the pizzeria, but he decided to skip that, knowing that Rosa would smell like her restaurant, and the two would cancel each other out. He picked up his bottle opener from where it eternally rested on his coffee table, opened up the beer, and took a grateful sip. It was so cold it was almost, but not quite, painful, killing any malty aftertaste that might threaten to ruin the experience.

Out of habit, he picked up his PlayStation controller and turned on his PS4 Pro, waiting for his TV to catch up.

"Hey, this might be the last night I play this," he said aloud. He felt a slight sadness as he said this, running his hands over the handles of his well-greased favorite controller.

He thought for a few moments, then loaded up Skyrim to just do some relaxed exploring. There was no point logging into multiplayer games. With the PS5 launching on the next day, those games would soon be ghost towns, at least for the more serious players. Best to just enjoy a few hours doing whatever.

He was halfway through a cave that he had randomly come across, but apparently never cleared, when Rosa walked in the door, carrying a few take-out boxes in a large plastic bag. He went back out to the menus and followed her to the small square table that sat in what amounted to his dining room, which was the space between his small kitchen and his comfortable living room.

"Thanks for dinner," he said, helping Rosa to set out the food. "Do you ever get tired of the restaurant food?"

"It's a big menu, so it's a little harder to get bored of it compared to pizza."

Jimmy laughed. "Hey, we have an expansive menu. We have stuffed crust, thin-crust-"

"Regular crust-"

"Yeah, of course. And wings. And then you have all the toppings. That's like an infinite number of menu items."

"No, it's all pizza. Pizza with anchovies just tastes like fishy pizza. Pizza with hot peppers just tastes like hot pizza. Not like the difference between tacos and a chicken sandwich."

"I guess you're right. I'm a creature of comfort, though."

"I noticed," Rosa said, raising her eyebrows at him, a slightly perturbed look on her face.

Jimmy ignored it. "Have an okay night?"

"As good as we can. Pretty busy considering we just opened the main dining room again."

"Yeah, I bet eating outside in the cold was getting old."

"We have those lamp heaters. It's pretty comfortable. Kind of has a cold beach ambiance."

Jimmy shrugged and bit into his sandwich. He washed it down with a guzzle of beer.

"So, I've been thinking," Rosa said.

"Yeah?"

"You've been working at that pizza place a long time, right?"

"It's a good job. Especially this year."

"Yeah, but you've had it forever. Haven't you ever been offered the manager position?"

"Of course. Bunch of times. Every time it opens up the owners try to get me in as at least an AM."

"Why don't you take it?"

"It's a pay cut. I make a ton on tips, especially now. A two-dollar an hour raise isn't going to cut it."

"Yeah, but you could learn the business."

"I already know the business, babe."

"But you aren't *running* it."

Jimmy laughed. "So? I don't *want* to run the business. That's more work for not much more money."

"You could open your own place."

"And work eighty hours a week and still probably lose my ass? No, thanks."

Rosa grumbled softly. "I just want you to do well, is all. Don't you want more than this?"

"You're one to talk. You're a waitress. Where's *your* restaurant?"

"I'm a woman, Jimmy."

"So?"

"It's different. I'm supposed to be..." Rosa shook her head in frustration. "Doing different things."

"Like what? Popping out kids? You hate kids."

"I don't."

"You were just complaining about babysitting your niece."

"Fine, just forget I said anything."

"Alright, I will."

"It's your birthday. I shouldn't have nagged you. I'm sorry."

"It's fine. I do what I do by intention, Rosa. It's no big deal. But I'll ask you something. We have fun, right?"

"Of course, we have fun."

Jimmy tilted his head. "I like a fun life. My friends – my college friends, specifically – they don't have fun. They're grinding their asses into the ground at jobs they hate, falling ass-backward into debt with mortgages and car payments, falling into bed without even seeing their kids. They're miserable, chasing some bullshit American Dream our retarded boomer teachers sold us on, which we'll never have. But us? We have fun."

"You're right. We do have fun. Sorry for the heavy mood again."

"No big deal, babe. So what did you get me?"

Rosa glanced at the clock. "I guess it's been your birthday for about five minutes."

Jimmy smiled. "So, yeah? What is it?"

"You'll have to bang me first if you want me to give it to you," she said with a smile.

"No problem," Jimmy said, raising his eyebrows. He left the remains of his sandwich on the table and followed Rosa into his single bedroom.

*

After their routine fornication, Rosa rose from the bed and retrieved something from the closet.

"I snuck in before work and stashed it," she said. She returned, holding an electric guitar, which she handed to Jimmy on the bed. It was an old Fender Mustang in white, but it had numerous chips on the body, and the logo on the headstock was worn off in a few places.

"Whoa!" he said, running his hands over the instrument and flipping the switches. "This is a Japanese model. From the 90s?"

"That's what the guy said. You like it? I got a good deal on it."

"Babe, this is awesome."

"I remember you telling me about how you used to play, and how much fun you had with your friends back in the day."

"Good times." He strummed the strings and winced at the tuning. "I'll have to find an amp to play it."

"He had one of those, too. A little one. I left it in the closet."

"Cool. This is a really great present, thanks." He started tuning the guitar to the A string, thinking that one might be the closest to concert pitch.

"I'm so glad you like it. But now you'll have to play something for me."

Jimmy laughed. "I can't remember anything. But I'm sure I'll figure something out."

"No Nirvana."

"Hey, you liked that live album."

"Sure. I'm thirsty. You want a beer?"

"Yeah, that'd be nice."

Jimmy smiled as he examined the guitar and continued trying to tune it. He didn't even glance at Rosa walking naked to the kitchen.

*

Jimmy smiled as he ran his hands over the box, taking in the lettering and the image of the console on the front. This was a moment that came rarely, and he enjoyed savoring it, the way a cigar aficionado smells his Churchill before he lights it. He was reminded of at least a half dozen other box openings, stretching back to his childhood. Always, it was during a big event, like Christmas, but since Jimmy's birthday was in November, he had gotten a few on launch day as a surprise.

As he opened the box, he was assaulted with a particular plastic smell. It was a scent that couldn't be duplicated; it could only be found again and enjoyed briefly, because it faded like the smell of a new car. It reminded him most vividly of opening his Super Nintendo all those years ago, also on his birthday, and instantly forgetting the smell of cake. It was the smell of something new, exciting, uncharted.

The black and white console, looking like some alien ship, waited for his hands, and he gently pulled it free and felt its weight. It was bigger and heavier than anything he had owned thus far, save for his PC. He ran his hands over it as he pulled off a few pieces of protective plastic, noting where it was smooth and where it had a slight texture. It almost felt made to be held.

It occurred to Jimmy at that moment that he was alone with this experience for the first time. His apartment was empty except for himself and the cat. He thought Rosa might have been there otherwise, but she was roped into working a split shift and had left early. Quickly, he took out his phone and snapped a selfie of himself holding it, which he sent to Rosa with the accompanying message, *I know you like em big, but damn!*

He went to plug it in and hook it up to his television, and found that it didn't fit. His shelves were not tall enough, nor was there room around his TV to fit the thing. Shrugging, he put the console on the carpet in front of the TV and was immediately filled with a certain nostalgia for Saturdays spent on the living room carpet, his Nintendo or Playstation sitting on the floor where he and his brother could easily swap out games.

Jimmy plugged it in, including his controllers, and booted it up. The TV flashed with a loading screen, then the ambient menu music kicked in. He sighed and sat down in his easy chair, then proceeded to go about setting up his profile and logging into his account.

After a few minutes, things were finally ready. There was a system update (of course), which he started downloading while he opened up one of his new games. It was Demon's Souls, a game from the PS3 era that had spawned a whole genre of titles that were noteworthy for their difficulty – at least for games journalists.

That, too, had a patch, so he set the system to running and went to the fridge. It was early, but he still had a few hours before he needed to go to work. He opened up his fridge and pulled out a Moosehead, popped it open, and started making himself a small lunch.

When he was done with the sandwich, but only half done with his beer, he sat back down to play.

He couldn't suppress a smile as he launched *Demon's Souls* and started playing.

After a few minutes, though, he found himself frowning.

It was the game he remembered. It was better to be sure, but it was still the same game. It looked better, he supposed, but he couldn't help but feel that something was missing from the experience. He didn't feel like he was playing a sudden jump in technological power.

As he played (and died, due to focusing on his feelings), he recalled similar sentiments with the previous PlayStation. Sure, it looked better, but not *that* much better. It wasn't like the first time he booted up a Super Nintendo game, or when his dad brought home the Playstation, and he and his brother were able to fight each other in full 3D. It wasn't like loading up Final Fantasy X and seeing things with sudden detail he didn't know existed. It wasn't even like plugging in the Wii and seeing a strangely amazing little hand move wherever he pointed in the blurry menus.

He was playing Demon's Souls. It was a good game.

"How much has changed, really?" he said to himself as he died yet again.

His mind answered him. *Nothing.*

Jimmy looked around his apartment: at the fridge he didn't own, at the table he bought in college, at the shelves he built when he moved in almost ten years prior.

"Is that bad, though?" he said aloud.

He looked down to find his cat rubbing herself on his leg. She, too, had been with him for a long time. He picked her up and scratched her behind the ears. She drooled slightly, enjoying it, and he laughed.

"Yeah, it's okay. Nothing to complain about."

*

The small size of Jimmy's apartment made the crowd look bigger than it was, spilling out onto the patio where Roberto and a few of Jimmy's work friends shared a joint and told raunchy jokes. Inside, a mixture of music that would have seemed eclectic to anyone that wasn't a teen in the late 90s blared. The apartment below Jimmy's was vacant, and his next-door neighbor, a college student named Tanya, was over at the party. She was an attractive blonde and highly extraverted, so nobody seemed to mind when she drank beer but didn't bring any or didn't pitch in for the bowl she smoked.

The PS5 was seemingly only interesting as an overlarge black and white sculpture on the brown carpet. There wasn't much to show to his friends at a party, and they ended up playing Street Fighter II and some SNK fighters instead of taking any time to marvel at the new PS5 games. It didn't matter to Jimmy much, though. He'd have plenty of time on his day off to dig into the new system.

Around ten, James, his best friend from college, showed up. They shared a first name, barely, but that was the apparent extent of their commonalities. James came in, wearing a full suit and tie. He was clean-shaven and had short, neat hair, and he brought a bottle of wine rather than beer.

"James, there you are!" Jimmy said. "Why are you dressed like that?"

"I had a late meeting with a client and didn't have time to go home and change. Trial starts tomorrow, and the team had to go over a few things with them."

"Whoa, you have a trial tomorrow, and you're showing up to my party? I'm surprised. Perhaps I should say honored?"

"I'm not actually arguing it, so it's no big deal," James said with a smile. "Lawyers do more things besides go to court. I have tomorrow off, so it's fine to let loose a bit. I've also noticed something about suits – you never really look overdressed. You just make everyone else look like a slob."

"Thanks," Jimmy said, looking down at his black t-shirt. "Well, I still appreciate you coming."

"I wouldn't miss it. I brought some wine. Figured you'd have beer to spare, so why not something different?"

"Cool, man." Jimmy took the wine and looked at the label. He didn't recognize anything about it, other than it was from California. "Why don't we have a glass? I haven't had wine in…"

"Probably since the last time you and I hung out."

"So, awhile," Jimmy laughed and spent a few seconds rummaging in his kitchen drawers until he found his corkscrew, then opened the wine. He poured two glasses into tumblers, as he didn't have any real wine glasses. "It's good," he said, taking a sip.

"Got the new Playstation, eh?" James said, seeing the space-ship like box sitting out next to the TV. "I guess you wanted everyone to know?"

"Yeah, buddy! You know me. You gonna get one?"

"Yeah, I'm sure once they, you know, are available just to purchase, and it has a few killer titles. I'm not into the whole pre-registering for pre-ordering a new console or randomly hoping that a retailer decides to put more units up. It's not like I have a whole lot of time to play, anyway."

"Lawyering keeping you busy?"

"More than I like, I guess, but I figure I'll have more free time soon."

"Dropping the suit life and coming back to work with me at the pizzeria?"

James laughed. "No. I think I'm getting a divorce." He gave Jimmy a funny look, with one eyebrow raised.

"What? You're kidding."

"Nope. I said, *I think*. Not sure, yet. If I do, I think I'm going to have to file, not her."

"I thought you and Jen were like…" Jimmy paused and took a big swig of the wine. "Anyway, I feel like I'm about to start talking out of my ass. What are you supposed to say to something like that? Sorry?"

Jimmy pursed his lips and took a sip of wine. "I don't know, man. Frankly, it'll be a relief."

"You got me kind of morbidly curious, but I think I'd be a dick if I asked."

"You will be, but you're going to ask anyway, and I'm not going to care."

Jimmy rubbed his neck. "Here, let me show you what my girlfriend got me for my birthday. It's in my bedroom."

"Listen, I'm sure your girlfriend got you a nice electrostim device, and we're good friends, but just because I'm getting a divorce doesn't mean we should take this relationship to the next level," James said with a chuckle.

James followed Jimmy down the little hall to the bedroom, where Tanya was sitting on the bed with one of the guys from the pizza place, laughing.

"Hey guys, there's a good bottle of wine we just opened," Jimmy said. "Like really good. This guy brought it."

"Alright, I'll have a glass," Tanya said and got up, her doting companion for the moment following her.

Jimmy closed the door and opened his closet, digging out the guitar.

"She's a looker," James said.

"Lives next door, would you believe it?"

"I would. How old is she?"

"Twenty, I think."

James whistled.

"You whistling at her, or this?" Jimmy said, holding up the Fender.

James's eyes lit up. "Whoa, cool." He took the guitar from Jimmy and played a few quiet chords on it.

"Yeah, it's just like what Kurt Cobain had."

"Naw, he had some kind of mashup between this and a Jaguar, if I remember. But it's close and pretty damn cool." James sat down on the bed and began awkwardly playing through a few scales. "Man. Takes me back to that shitty band we had back when."

"Shitty, yeah, but we could have been good if we had kept going."

"Sure."

"So, what happened between you and Jen?" Jimmy said. "Since I'm inevitably going to be a dick for asking."

James laughed as he tried to play a Metallica riff and failed. "In short, it turns out she's awful, and living with her is pure misery."

"Well, shit. That's like ripping a band-aid off."

"I've done a lot of reflecting on it," James said. "We went to counseling after she told me that she was considering divorce. The counselor helped me realize just what an insufferable bitch I married."

"Dude," Jimmy said. "That's so weird to hear you talk like that."

James shrugged, then smiled as he started playing the chords to a song Jimmy couldn't quite place. "It's true. Like, I've done a ridiculous amount to try and please her and make her happy. Her saying out of the blue that she's considering a divorce because she doesn't *feel* the same about me was like a kick in the balls. The relationship was so one-sided it isn't even fucking funny. Remember this?"

"Sounds familiar," Jimmy said, listening to the chords.

"It should. We wrote it," James laughed. "Anyway, counseling, strangely, made it super clear. I live where she wanted us to live. I worked the job she wanted me to take. I paid her way through graduate school for a useless degree because that was something she wanted to do. She's a university counselor; you know that? That's her career, telling confused freshmen what classes they have to sign up for and helping them pile thousands of dollars worth of loans onto their own naïve heads. Shit!" James took his hands off the strings and made a fist. "It truly makes me fucking sick when I think about it. *She* makes me fucking sick."

"Damn, dude."

"She wouldn't quit that job or even go part-time to have kids, and now I'm fucking grateful. No way I'd want my kids with that harpy of a mother for them."

Jimmy stood quietly, listening to the song. When James paused, he said, "Wow. I had kind of always looked at you two as the standard – kind of envious, like maybe the whole family life thing would work. I look around here and... Well, there's not much to say about it. I'm a little blitzed to hear this about Jen."

"She's nice enough if you only see her here and there, but *man* can she nag. It is impossible for me to get home and just turn on a game before she starts bitching at me about some little thing, like where I left my laundry, or why I spent money on a game without talking to her. I make all the money! Meanwhile, she has all the free time and does nothing with it. Her dumb 'career' doesn't even cover her costs. That's why I think she didn't bother to file, by the way. Besides just being too lazy for it, she'd be losing out on a lot of money and comfort. In fact, I think she was trying to set up a side guy to mooch off of once she could leave. I know her phone passcode, but she doesn't know that I know. Well, fuck that. I'll file on her ass. Hell, I just made up my mind! It's my day off tomorrow; I'm fucking filing the papers.

"Sorry, man. Saying this shit is like vomiting," James said. "Painful, but oh so pleasing when you're done, and of course you can't stop until you're empty. I can't talk to anyone about this crap besides you, Jimmy. Everyone is too judge-y. Too focused on making me a good guy."

"You are a good guy, James. Better than me."

James laughed. "That's a gaff. It's *you* I envy."

"Just because I'm not divorced?"

"Because you aren't a lawyer." James shook his head with a smile. "It's a shit career, even when you're doing alright at it. I mean, do you know how much I wish I could just go home after a few hours and have a beer? Maybe finish an RPG once a year?"

Jimmy shrugged. "I definitely set my life up for that. It's true."

"You know she hasn't had sex with me since before the whole COVID thing? And even then, it was like being drip-fed methadone. You'd think working remotely would have just made it happen, but no. There are a million little other things, like the fact that she skips shaving, and won't shut the fuck up about Donald Trump." James leapt up and cackled. "Yeah, FUCK that bitch."

He played a loud chord on the guitar and stopped.

"It's fine, man," Jimmy said. "You're always welcome to vent to me. You know I'm in your corner one-hundred percent."

"I appreciate that. I'll remember it when my mom is upset with me. Divorce is a big no-no with my family. Anyway, how are you and Rosa doing? You guys are always together, it seems."

"Great. She should be getting off work now."

"Thinking of marriage?"

Jimmy laughed. "After that tirade, you're going to ask if I'm going to pop the question to my girlfriend?"

"Sounds weird, yeah? It's not marriage that's the problem, Jimmy. It's who I picked. Real bad judgment on my part. Counseling confirmed that to me. You'd kind of have to be there, but it's the person, not the institution. If one person in the relationship doesn't care, you're in trouble. And this guitar? I don't know her that well, but this girl gets you."

"Even though she didn't buy me a game?"

"Especially so. I would have bought you one, but I know you. You'd have already bought all the good ones you wanted, so why bother with that? She bought you something your *soul* needs instead. This thing."

"You think so?"

"You were just telling me how good it would have been had we kept going."

Jimmy was quiet for a minute as James handed the guitar back. "You ever think about starting something like that back up, James?"

"I fantasize about it, yeah, but I can never see a path through to that. Plus, we're getting old now."

"Too old to rock'n'roll, too young to die." Jimmy frowned as he sat down with the guitar and started playing one of his old songs.

"That was a good one," James said, smiling.

"I think about it a lot, man. You know, I got mad at my girlfriend last night. She was kind of pressuring me to do more with my life. Take a manager job somewhere, open a franchise or something."

"Familiar to me," James said. "But then she gives you the guitar, so what is it?"

"I think she sees something I don't want to."

"Maybe you get excited about games because you feel like that's all that's worth bothering with."

"That's not it," Jimmy said. He started awkwardly fingerpicking a song, then stopped. "I think I'm afraid of failing."

James shrugged and finished his wine. He smiled and laughed. "I'm failing right now. My marriage is failing as we speak. I have half a mind to go take that blonde girl, what's her name?"

"Tanya."

"Take her back to her apartment. But I'm not gonna. It's what I want, but *not* what I want."

"What do you want? The second want."

"I want something worth having. I want a wife who gives a shit about me, who values what I do. A family... A reason to continue on this world."

Jimmy finished his wine. "That's kind of dark."

James shrugged again and peeked out the bedroom door at the people in the kitchen. "It's dark, but it's also true. Doesn't mean I'm considering suicide, trust me. It just means I know what I got - it ain't it."

"But how do you get a reason?"

"You're asking *me?*"

"I guess it's just an open-ended question. Looks like Rosa just got here."

"You started smiling," James said. "That's a good sign."

"I love her," Jimmy said, frowning slightly.

"Yeah, well, what are you gonna do?"

"How do I know she won't be like Jen? I mean, how do I know that we won't end up like you and Jen."

"There are no guarantees in life. I think she won't end up like Jen simply because she actually gives a shit about you. Beyond that?" James shrugged.

"Jen cared about you, once."

"Not in the way I cared about her. It was a dependent relationship the whole time."

"Yeah, anyway, we should probably party a little, yeah?"

"Hell yeah."

Rosa's voice echoed down the hall. "Jimmy! I got something for you! I hope you like chocolate!"

"You know I do!" Jimmy said.

*

"I've been doing some thinking about what you said," Jimmy said, then blew on his coffee. The little breakfast shop was almost empty, so he could hardly take more than a few sips before the waitress topped the cup off with more boiling-hot black glory.

"Hangover cleared your head?" Rosa said, sipping on a soda.

Jimmy laughed. "No, I don't think so. Advil is helping, though."

"Which thing were you thinking about?"

"Getting a better job."

Rosa gave him a smile that didn't meet her sad eyes. "I didn't want you to feel pressured. I don't want to be that kind of girl. I guess I was just feeling it, too. I'm over thirty and still just a waitress. You're right."

"Eh, you're not just a waitress."

"There are not many places to go from there," Rosa said. She nodded to the two waitresses gabbing with the idle cook, looking awkward in the little farmhouse aprons the staff had to wear. "They're both in their fifties, I would guess. Still pouring coffee for a few tips."

"Well, they are again, at least. Be thankful for that. I wonder how they made it through the year."

"Hopefully, not as bad as me. I'd be sunk without you, I think. Just in car repairs, I'd be done."

"Did you hear what I said before?" Jimmy said, just as one of the waitresses bustled over to top off his coffee again.

"What?" Rosa said, suddenly turning her attention back to him.

"I said you're not *just* a waitress."

"It's my job," Rosa said with wide eyes.

"Yeah, but it's not you, just like how pizza isn't me. And that's the problem. With me, I mean. Who am I?"

Rosa smiled. "You're a funny guy who loves others. Loves to help people out and show them a good time. You always have time for a friend. Or a girlfriend."

"Yeah, I've kind of set my life up that way – to have free time. I notice you didn't mention video games."

"So?"

"I realize… I thought that was part of my identity."

"Well, I mean, it's a hobby, I guess. But I don't think of it as much different than TV, or anything else. I don't think of my mom as a telenovela watcher, but that's something she loves to spend her time on."

"Yeah, you're right. And that's kind of my point. You're not a waitress. It's something you do for money. You're way more than that to me."

"True. I'm a good cook, too."

"A damn good one, which leaves me wondering why we're having breakfast here. Shouldn't you be serving me some fresh pancakes in bed or something?"

"It's not your birthday anymore," Rosa said with a smile.

"Anyway, I was thinking about what you said. I set up this life to have free time. I should use it on something."

Rosa gave him a confused look. "I thought I was suggesting you get a job with more responsibility."

"I guess I could do that."

"Were you thinking of something else? Taking up music again?"

"Yeah, maybe."

Rosa smiled as the food arrived. "But what about your games?"

Jimmy laughed. "Well, they aren't going to play themselves, so I'll have to spend at least a little time with them. But yeah, maybe music. Maybe some other business. Kind of depends on what you want."

"I just want you to be happy."

"Oh, I know that. But what makes *you* happy? Or what *would* make you happy? Satisfied?"

Rosa was quiet as she cut up her pancakes and covered them with syrup. "I honestly don't know. I thought I would sort of… find it out in the world. I thought it would just happen – the right job, the right place to live – a nice house, maybe – the right… person."

"Well, I hope we got at least the last one covered."

Rosa laughed awkwardly. "Oh, I didn't mean… sorry."

"It's okay. I want to be the right person."

"You *are,* Jimmy. I just…"

"I'm not the most ambitious."

"But, I *do* love you."

Jimmy shook his head and smirked. "I do know that. Maybe we just start working on the other stuff, alright?"

"Alright. So, what does that mean for you?"

Jimmy gave an awkward laugh. "I'm still afraid to make decisions, huh?"

"What?" Rosa said.

"Nevermind. Let's see… Well, today I'm gonna play some video games. I planned that, so that's what I'm gonna do. But I'm also going to have James come over, and we're going to write some music. If I'm feeling really brave… well, best not to say." Jimmy laughed. "I love you. You know that?"

"I do."

"Good. Yeah, that's really good."

*

"Holy shit, dude. We are *bad.*" James rolled the volume of his guitar off. They were sitting in Jimmy's living room, and the afternoon sun was peeking through the vertical blinds of the balcony.

"Like Michael Jackson bad?" Jimmy said.

"Yes, if you mean like the album *Bad,* which is a bad album."

"You think it's bad? Like *bad* bad, or like…" He stuck his chin up and nodded. "Bad."

"As in poor quality. Jimmy, we *suck.*"

"Well, we haven't played in like ten years or something. You gotta shake off the dust."

"I think it's going to take a lot more practice from each of us for us to be able to even play our old crap – which there are a few gems, but let's be honest, it's mostly crap."

"So, we'll write new stuff that isn't bad. No big deal."

James's phone started ringing. He picked it up, looked at the caller, then smiled as he silenced the phone.

"Jen?"

"Feels good, man. Anyway, something just occurred to me. What about drums and bass?"

"I could call up Darek and Will."

"Darek's in prison, bro."

"What?"

"Yeah, he got caught running an insurance scam."

"I guess we can find another drummer."

"And where are we going to rehearse? Not here, with a drum set."

"What about your house?"

James laughed. "I'm getting rid of that place first thing."

"Maybe Will…" Jimmy paused and made a strained expression. "You think he's still holding that grudge?"

"Which one?"

"With what's-her-face."

"You don't even remember her name?"

Jimmy shrugged. "I only hung out with her that one time."

"Yeah, but you slept with her, and Will was the one who brought her to the party."

"He has to have forgiven me by now."

James gave Jimmy a skeptical look.

"You know what?" Jimmy said. "Musicians now do everything in the studio. We don't *need* a live band. Not to get started. We can use a drum machine and stuff."

James shook his head. "Yeah, but then you have to learn how to program it."

"I could learn."

"And you'd have to buy it."

"Good point. Let's look up some stuff, and see how people are doing things these days."

A few minutes later, they were watching YouTube videos at Jimmy's PC, both of them looking thoroughly flummoxed.

"We have *no idea* what we are doing," Jimmy said, as he tried to make sense of a Cubase tutorial covering MIDI programming.

"Jimmy, we clearly had no idea what we were doing *fifteen years ago*."

Jimmy nodded. "Yup."

"Maybe we should take a break for today, and we can research what we need to buy separately."

"Good idea. Rosa should be getting off soon."

"Soon? She's not even here. You're too ambitious."

"Har har," Jimmy said, smiling.

*

"Did you have fun with James?" Rosa asked. She blew lightly on her spaghetti before putting the heaping forkful in her mouth.

"We had fun," Jimmy said. "Didn't get anything done."

Rosa shrugged. "It's good to have fun."

"It is, you're right."

"Something seems off."

Jimmy shrugged and sighed. "I guess I just kind of expected to hop back into some music with James, and it would be like it was before."

"Well, you haven't played in a while, right? And you and James are different people than you were in college."

"Well, James is different. Or maybe he's not, but he just dresses differently." Jimmy stared at his plate of pasta. "Actually, I think it was probably just like it was back in the day. I think I remember it wrong."

"In what way?"

"Well, we always sucked, I think, and we always had problems getting the rest of the band in line, but me and James always had fun with it. I imagine we would have been good if we kept going, but I don't think we would have been able to keep going regardless. I don't know how real bands make it happen."

"Yeah, I think everybody does that. You know, you remember the best things. It's like a clip show. I mean, I enjoyed college, but let's be real, I enjoyed everything that wasn't the actual *college* part." Rosa laughed. "That's probably why I never graduated."

"I graduated. Funny, I can't remember the ceremony."

"I bet you remember the after-party, though."

"I don't, but that was for different reasons."

Rosa laughed. Jimmy smiled at her and began eating his dinner.

"Maybe there's something else," Rosa said. "Something else you can do."

"Like what?"

"Videogames."

Jimmy laughed. "Of course, more videogames."

"What about streaming them? I heard there are streamers that make all kinds of money just playing games and having other people watch them."

Jimmy scratched his head. "Yeah, but I don't know. Then it's like work."

"You're looking for work."

"I'm looking for..." Jimmy raised his hands and opened his eyes wide. "Yeah, I guess more work. But not work, work."

"So, videogames?"

"I can't watch videogame streams. So boring."

"Maybe you're not the target audience."

Jimmy chuckled. "Eh, why not. I'll give it a shot for a week."

"You have the new Playstation. People might want to watch the games."

"Sure."

*

It was clear that it had been a long time since Jimmy had played a game as difficult as Demon's Souls. As he watched the death animation once again and glanced over at the chat, suddenly thankful that it was empty, he considered that it was probably not the best game to choose a public performance of.

A single message appeared:

You suck.

"Of course, the only person watching thinks I suck. It's not the easiest game, man."

No, you suck at streaming. You don't talk.

"What am I supposed to talk about?"

Anything besides breathing through your mouth and staring at the screen like a dead cow would be nice.

Another person added the chat:

This is fucking sad. Like, you should set up a green screen so you don't look like such a sad fat coomer neckbeard in his 40s.

"I'm thirty-five."

Then you should be out of your mom's basement.

And get a better job than delivering pizzas.

Jimmy did a slight double-take. Was someone he knew watching and taunting him as a joke? The screen names were unfamiliar and communicated nothing to him.

They wouldn't let him deliver pizzas looking like that.

True. Maybe he still lives with his mom because he's retarded? He kind of looks like he has downs or FAS

FAS?

Fetal Alcohol Syndrome. Mom drinks when pregnant - kid comes out a little off.

Sounds right. He doesn't know how to dodge, so yeah

"Then why are you watching it?" Jimmy said, throwing his arms up at the camera.

It makes me feel less bad about myself. I was born without a dick and with extra fingers, but I'm better off than you.

"Fuck this," Jimmy said, and killed the stream.

He tried again over the next few days, but the most viewers he could seem to amass was fifteen, and he thought it might have been the trolls from the first day who brought their friends.

*

"So, the streams are a no-go?" Rosa said. She plopped another plate of carnitas in front of him, and he dug in.

"It's going nowhere," Jimmy said with a full mouth.

"I think you have to put in more than a week of effort, you know."

Jimmy shrugged. "Yeah I'm not sure I'm willing to put in more effort. I've never felt like something I loved could become something so joyless."

"Alright, then stop. I guess I'm proud of you for trying something."

"Yeah, but now I have the camera accessory, and I don't need it. I feel like it's always watching me, like the Kinect."

"But you *have* a Kinect."

"Yeah and I hate that it watches me."

Rosa laughed. "So, sell it, then. I'm sure someone will want it."

"Eh, I'll probably end up needing it for this generation's weird motion-VR-whatever accessories that suck and don't find traction."

"Which you'll buy anyway."

Jimmy laughed. "Of course. I'm a collector. That means I can waste my money on stuff that I don't love because it's part of *the collection.*"

"I still think you'd be good at the streaming thing."

"I figured out that it's really about entertaining people, not being good at games. And I chose a game to stream that I kind of suck at anyway. Or, maybe I'm just not all that good at any game. Playing games doesn't necessarily make you good at them. These big guys, they're all basically comedians. That's not me."

"I think you're really funny."

"Yeah, but not in a performance kind of way. Being someone's funny friend isn't the same as being a standup comic, or even a talk show comic. Maybe I'll give it some more effort, but I don't think I'm going to be a hit."

"Okay," Rosa said. "I'll support whatever you need to do."

"That's good, because," at this Jimmy raised an eyebrow and looked at Rosa slyly, "after this meal I'm going to need to take you-"

"To Cancun?" Rosa interjected.

"To the bedroom."

"Oh," Rosa said, feigning disappointment.

*

"So, what do you do, have papers served?" Jimmy asked. He played a few chords on his unplugged guitar as he listened to James.

"No, I just told her I filed for divorce and handed her a copy of the papers to sign."

"What if she didn't want to sign them?"

"Then it's a contested divorce, and things get more complicated. This was easy, though. She was super surprised but signed right away. It's a relief for both of us. I might still end up in family court for asset division, but seeing as how we're underwater on the house and her student loans aren't part of marital liabilities, I don't expect *too* many issues."

"I guess that's good."

"Yeah, there's only one thing I'm worried about."

"What's that?"

"I have some money that I've kind of kept hidden. If things get ugly, I'm gonna end up having to disclose it and lose half of it."

"You can leave the money at my house," Jimmy said. "I probably won't even spend all of it."

"You're funny. But seriously, if you get a line on something I could dump this into, like a business or something, that would be rad."

"A business?"

"Yeah, if I can get it dumped somewhere post-separation, I can avoid disclosing it, since the account will be closed."

"Isn't that illegal? Aren't you a lawyer?"

"You don't know much about lawyering, do you?" James said with a laugh.

"I guess not."

"Anyway, if I lose it, I lose it. Frankly, I'd be happy to walk away with nothing besides my guitar. I'd give her all the furniture in a heartbeat. It's crap anyway."

"Yeah."

"Are you saying my furniture sucks?" James said in a faux-angry voice

"Sorry, man. It sucks. Hideous. Anyway, why don't you swing by and we can all have a drink? Maybe play some music?"

"Eh, not tonight. I have some work I need to handle."

*

Jimmy and Rosa shared a huge thin-cut steak she had cooked on her stove, in her tiny, dark apartment.

"I would never know this was just cooked in a pan," Jimmy said.

"It's the best way to cook steak. Grilling dries it out. All the cooks at the restaurants know it."

"What about the commercials with the flame grills?"

"At Burger King?"

"Yeah," Jimmy said. "Flame broiled."

"I'm pretty sure they warm up the Whopper in a microwave. Maybe it's flame broiled at some point in its life."

"Really?"

"No idea," Rosa laughed, "but at good restaurants, they cook the steak in a cast iron pan with a bit of butter or whatever fat. I used lard."

"Lard?"

"Why do you think real Mexican food tastes so good, eh?"

"The cooks," Jimmy said, smiling at Rosa. He took a big bite and washed it down with a sip of beer. Suddenly, he paused again and gave Rosa a curious smile.

"What?" She said, chuckling awkwardly.

"How do you like your job?"

"We talked about it. It's a job."

"If you had the option to do whatever you wanted, what would you do?"

"I don't know."

Jimmy leaned forward. "See, this is a question I asked myself recently, and I realized it's bullshit, because my first answer would be to play video games. But I already do that, and it ain't hacking it."

"Okay," Rosa said, shaking her head. "I guess I would read books and watch TV."

"Yeah, see what I mean?"

"Not really."

"It's all about available options. Nobody is realistic about limitations. You have to do what is in your capacity to do, not just think of any old thing to do. If nobody wants to pay you to watch TV, you can't just do that. Anyway, how would you like to start a business with me?"

Rosa blinked slowly. "What?"

"A restaurant. We could open one."

"What? The restaurant business is awful! Half the restaurants in town aren't re-opening."

"Exactly."

Rosa shook her head. "We don't have money for that."

"Very few people start a business with cash. Usually, you start with a loan."

"A loan?"

"Yeah, I have great personal credit. I have a business degree, and you and I both have tons of restaurant experience. It would be easy to draft up a business plan. I haven't done one since college, but it shouldn't be hard."

"What happens if the restaurant goes under, like all the others?"

Jimmy shrugged. "I guess we go back to delivering pizzas and waiting tables. So?"

"Don't you still have to pay the bank back?"

"Ah, but that is where we employ the magic of the corporation. You see, it's the *corporation* that goes bankrupt. It's the *corporation* that loses its assets. Hell, if they needed more collateral, I could put up my video game collection. If I lose that, no big deal. Most of them I don't play, after all. I also might have a line on an investor looking to solidify his assets. Plus, he can help us form our corporation."

"You've thought this through, huh?"

"Nope, not at all," Jimmy said. "Just something I thought I'd throw out there. Something we could both do and be good at and move forward with."

Rosa laughed. "You're really something, Jimmy. Yeah, maybe we should look into that." She was quiet for a few moments. "What kind of food?"

"Whatever is in demand. I think pizza is doing pretty well these days. Chain restaurants have a lot of corporate assets to leverage, so they'll still be around if we want to do a franchise. But maybe Mexican food is what our town needs. I think a lot of the Mexican places are doing really badly. We could probably hire a couple of good cooks easily since they're out of work."

"You already have a cook," Rosa said, pointing at herself.

"No, I need you to handle the floor."

"You're not going to have the Mexican woman cook the Mexican food?"

"Is that what you *want* to do?"

Rosa was quiet. "No, I think I just want to design the menu."

"There you go. Leveraging expertise."

Rosa smiled so much she had a hard time eating her next few bits of steak. Jimmy continued to poke at his own dish.

"It's going to take up a lot of time. You won't miss your games?" Rosa said.

"I probably will, but a business is a bit like a game. Yeah, and the money is like a score." He threw his hand up and cut another piece of steak. "Just an idea."

"I think it's a good idea."

"Alright, we'll move forward on it." He took a breath. "If we do this, we ought to move in together to save costs. Most businesses lose money the first year."

"Oh, I don't think so."

"You're never here anyway," Jimmy said with his hands up.

"No, that's not going to fly with my parents. They are happily ignorant as to what you and I do with our free time. If I just move in with a man without marrying him, I'll never hear the end of it. And I care about my family relationships."

"Well, we should get married, then."

Rosa looked down and shook her head, though she was smiling. "You can't be serious."

"I totally am."

She went red in the face and started laughing. Finally, she took a deep breath and said, "This isn't how I pictured a proposal."

"Alright, I'll ask you again later. I'll buy a ring once I can get this business in the black."

Rosa just laughed, growing redder.

Jimmy smiled and ate a few more bites of steak.

"What about kids?"

Jimmy shrugged. "You want a few?"

Rosa was quiet for a few moments. "Yes."

"Alright."

"Just like that?"

Jimmy smiled. "I asked you what would make you happy or satisfied. If that's it, we'll do it."

"Well, my mom's happy."

"Even though you're dating a loser delivery boy?"

Rosa frowned. "I'm dating a business owner. What are you talking about?"

"Business owner *and* musician." Jimmy winked.

Lined Paper

Jim checked his phone out of habit as he rushed down the hall. Before he could see just how late he was, the screen dimmed.

"Buggy piece of dogshit!" he said, shaking the infernal device, suppressing the desire to throw it through the 5th story window. For a moment he decided on a compromise, agreeing with his inner demon to toss it in the trash and buy a new one after work, but before he could act, he found the phone tumbling out of his hand as he fell onto the floor.

"What the fuck?" he said, twisting around on the marble floor. "Who-"

"Oh my God, I'm sorry, Jim!" It was Melissa, and she was on the ground beside him, papers and open files spilled everywhere.

"Sorry," Jim said.

"It's me that should be sorry," Melissa said, pulling up a binder to hide her mouth. "I was checking my phone and wasn't watching what I was doing."

Jim could see her going red around the ears, and his neck felt suddenly hot. Her eyes, pale blue, got slightly wet as they regarded him lying on his back and elbows. He swallowed, trying to regain his train of thought.

"Eh, don't worry about it," he said, sitting up and looking away.

"I made you spill all your papers."

"It's okay. Really, it is." Jim began sorting through the papers, trying to re-assemble his handouts for his fourth-quarter report. "Some of these are yours."

He heard a chirp and slid some papers over, revealing a phone – Melissa's phone. He picked it up to hand it to her, but couldn't stop himself from reading the text. *You're not remembering it right. You always misremember. Like with the last party.*

"It's… Don't worry about that," Melissa said as she took the phone from him, reading the text before putting the phone in her purse. A few tears had leaked from the corners of her eyes, and her maskera was smearing. Jim's mouth felt dry as a salt flat.

"I didn't mean to," Jim said. "Just a habit."

"It's okay. I do have a really bad memory." The phone chirped again. "I remember things differently from how they are all the time."

Jim hesitated with a thought, but his impulse took it to his tongue, and he said, "Who was that?"

"Sean. My… My boyfriend."

Jim felt a sinking sensation in his stomach. "Your boyfriend?"

"Yeah. I guess. We're dating, but we have…" She wiped tears from her face. "I'm sorry, too much information. You were probably heading to the meeting in D3. Let me help you sort these."

"It's fine. I don't really need them. It's all on the PowerPoint." He got up and put his hands under Melissa's elbows, meaning to help her up. She shook him off.

"Sorry," she said. "I shouldn't have… I'm just embarrassed. And I actually need *these* papers, even if you don't need yours."

Jim took a breath. "No need to be embarrassed." Jim saw his phone on the ground. It vibrated even as he reached down to pick it up. It was a text from Will. *Where are you? The old man's waiting.* Jim stuffed it in his jacket pocket. Quickly, he kneeled down and began scooping all the papers on the ground into one pile. "Just take all of them and sort yours out. I really am going to be late if-" he paused as Melissa took a deep breath beside him. He stood up, folding what remained of his files into the crook of his arm. "I'll… I'll see you later. Don't feel bad, okay? I don't like seeing… just take it easy, okay?"

She forced a smile for him, which he returned with equal effort, realizing he had been frowning. He nodded and turned down the hall, setting off into the only sort of run his Florsheims would allow from him, which was a kind of shuffling jog.

He reached D3 a minute later. Pausing outside the door, he smoothed his suit and brushed his hair aside, then opened the old walnut doors.

Inside, the old man, as they called the CFO, was addressing the room, though Jim knew he was talking primarily to the six other old men that sat near the head of the long table. Jim ignored the speech and quietly sat down beside Will.

"Had the runs, or what?" Will whispered with a snigger.

"No, just ran into Melissa," Jim whispered back.

"*Now* you have to chat up the office staff? I've never seen you say two words to her before, and when you're-"

"I ran into her in a literal sense. It really upset her." Jim pushed his hand through his hair impulsively.

"Eh," Will said with a shrug. "Not the prettiest girl, anyway."

Jim opened up his folder and began pawing through what he had left, hoping he had enough PowerPoint copies to hand to the old men up front. His heart suddenly leapt along with his blood pressure as he hurriedly checked his papers again.

"You seem tense," Will said. "You alright?"

Jim reached up and brushed a bead of cold sweat from his brow.

"I dropped something. Something important."

"Eh, you can always email it later."

"Not this. This wasn't an electronic document."

"Can't have gone far. Want to step out in the hall and see if you dropped it?"

"I know I dropped it. And I know who picked it up." Jim buried his head in his hands.

"Well go get it. I'll stall the old man."

Jim nodded. "Yeah. Maybe."

He stood up and quickly slipped to the door. The old man cast a fleeting glance his way, but it held little in the way of interest, much less anger. Jim stepped out into the hallway and broke into another jog. "How could you be so stupid!" he whispered to himself as he ran. He slowed as he reached the cluster of cubicles that he knew contained Melissa's desk.

When he reached Melissa's desk, he found it, and her whole work area, vacant. He stepped in, seeing all of the papers strewn out along one section of the desk. Some of his papers were already stacked, but most of them were still in a haphazard heap.

"She had to step out to take a call." Jim turned to see Rachel leaning back from her desk. "Do you need something?"

Jim tried to slow his breathing, but it raced ahead along with his heart. "Some of our papers got mixed up. I… need one of them. Has she… looked at many of them?"

"I don't know. She sat down crying with that heap and then got a call. From her boyfriend. Or, I think she has a boyfriend. I don't really know."

Jim nodded. "Okay. Do you think she'd mind?" He gestured to the papers.

"I won't tell if you want."

Jim shrugged. "I'm sure she'd notice."

"If she did notice, she wouldn't ask me."

Jim nodded again, slower, and turned around to the heap of papers. He rifled through them quickly, trusting that the one he was looking for would be easy to find. It was just a few sheets of stapled lined paper. With a rush of relief, he found it beneath a small stack of computer paper. He breathed a sigh, still wondering if Melissa had read it.

"Thanks," he said, turning and smiling to Rachael.

"No problem," she said, smiling back.

Jim rushed out of the little work cluster and back down the long hallway to D3. He looked down at the papers in his hand and stopped.

At the top, in blue pen, written in a shaking hand, began the letter.

Dear Melissa,

I hope this isn't too strange, but I have something to get off my chest…

Jim felt a pang that was more than physical grip him. He couldn't bear to keep reading what he had written.

"Stupid fucking asshole," he said. "Stupid fucking asshole James!"

With a sickness in his stomach, he tore up the letter.

Looking at the pile of small paper pieces covered in ink, a thought occurred to him. The letter, which he had carried around for months but could never summon the courage to deliver, had been delivered for him, against his will, as if God himself had decided he could delay his feelings no longer. And somehow, he had defied that providence.

"Just as well," he said. "I'm a fucking asshole and she would hate me."

He threw the pieces into a nearby trashcan and jogged back toward the conference room.

Eyes in the Walls

Chapter 1

My mom used to joke that being a mortician was the best job in the world because all of your customers walk away satisfied. At least, they never complain – of *course* they never walk away. Except... maybe I saw one of them walk away.

Should I tell you the story?

I mentioned my mom is a mortician. Well, let me tell you, that doesn't pan out well at school. Everyone assumes you are some creepy goth kid (my favorite color is green) or that you are depressed (I was, but that came later), or that you listen to black metal (I do, but I prefer bubble-gum pop). People also like to make fun. And ask a lot of questions – about zombies, Michael Jackson records, vampires, you know... They want a spooky story.

Well, one day, I got a story. And the days after. I was coming into the funeral home after getting off the city bus. My mom wasn't upstairs, so I went to look for her down where the morgue was. This sort of thing wasn't really frowned upon, at least not then. It was an older building, with the refrigerated lockers in a brick-lined basement, along with some dedicated rooms for embalming and one that was used for private autopsies.

She was down there, cleaning up in the main room. There were no bodies out, of course. Everyone wants there to be a body out on a table, but no, it was clean. Not that it would be that big a deal – when you are around a funeral home a lot you get used to the idea that a dead body is just a thing. There's really no "person" there. Even dressed up for a funeral, it's more like a sculpture – one last picture to remember the person by.

My mom and I talked for a while about the usual nothings, which was mostly me pretending that I didn't hate school, or that I needed to call my father and talk about my grades with him. We went back upstairs, and I remembered we needed to turn off the lights. When I went back down, I found they were already off.

No big deal, I just forgot that I didn't forget to turn off the lights.

I turned to walk back up the stairs, and I heard it – the unmistakable sound of metal crashing on the ground. I was too scared to look, so I ran back up and told my mom.

"Something crashed! In the room with the lockers!" I whispered it, but loud enough to hardly count as a whisper.

She just looked at me incredulously and said, "I don't think so, Billy. There's nothing in there to go crash. You must have heard something else. Maybe outside?"

"But mom," I said, protesting, "I know what the sound of something crashing sounds like. You didn't drop something up here, did you?"

"No," my mother said, rolling her eyes. "Let me take a look. Maybe I left something leaning in the wrong place."

We went back down the brick stairs, turned on the lights, and found that one of the rolling tables used to cart equipment around had fallen over in the corner.

"You know what?" my mother said, clearly perplexed, "I must have forgotten about that concrete lip on the edge here, near the fuse box." She casually walked over and pushed the cart closer to the center of the room. "See?"

"Ok mom, but are you sure it would just fall over?"

"The door is locked, sweetie. Nobody walked past you or me. There's no possible way it could have been anything else."

"No person, you mean." I said it with a smile, but all jokes contain half-truth.

"There's no such thing as ghosts."

"I don't believe in ghosts, mom."

"Or zombies. You've been watching too much cable."

I let it go and shrugged, but I swear that there was no way that cart could have tipped over on its own.

*

A few weeks later I was again at my mother's work. My dad had something come up with his job, and the school sent me home on the city bus again. My mom seemed just as busy as before. She worked the whole afternoon in the office until sunset – I guess burying people requires a lot of paperwork. It wasn't all bad. I told my mom I had finished my homework (which I would do the next morning right before class, like always) and got out the new GameBoy my dad had bought me for my birthday.

The batteries ran out really quick, though, and before I could find another set in the office closet, the power went off. We had been getting power outages a lot at that time, but this one was weirder than usual. Everything in the office was off, but we could see lights on across the street. My mother was really upset about it – her computer lost power and whatever she had been working on was apparently lost.

We decided to wait it out for a bit since the refrigeration in the morgue would need to run on a backup generator if the power didn't switch on, but eventually, the lights on across the street got to my mother, and she started to get annoyed and anxious.

"I bet it was a power surge and something broke," my mom said.

"What would break?"

"The switches. Those black switches."

"The breakers? The fuses?"

"Yes!"

My mother decided we ought to try the breaker box, but she had never had to deal with the power at the funeral home before, so she had no idea where they were. She got a few flashlights out of the closet and resolved to go look for them. I didn't want to be left alone, so I went with her. First, we checked around the office. We found a sub-panel there, but everything looked fine. Outside, the power main seemed to be on. That left one panel that I remembered – the one in the morgue.

We went down the narrow stairs together to the locked double doors next to the elevator. My mom fumbled around with her keys in the dark, trying to find the right one, when an impulse struck me. I pressed the call button on the elevator, and nearly jumped in the air when it lit up and chimed.

"Mom! The elevator is on."

My mom startled at my sudden movement and shout. She took a breath and said, "See? I knew it wasn't a real outage." She bent over slightly to examine the call panel, as the car hadn't arrived. "Maybe the motor got shut off, though."

While my mom was trying to find the emergency key to the elevator, I turned and looked at the morgue doors. I pushed on them and found that they were open.

"Hey mom," I said, pushing open the first door.

That was when I saw it.

It was a tall, lanky figure of pale, dirty white. It was naked and turned half away from me, so I could see all of its pasty flesh. It looked human, but distorted. It had long, skinny arms and huge hands with long fingers like bundles of white twigs. Its ribs stuck out at the bottom, making a little ridge, and its hipbones were likewise pronounced.

It was moving across the morgue from one of the other rooms, its thin legs moving slowly and silently. I couldn't scream. Somehow, all the will to disbelieve my eyes had turned into total paralysis.

At the same time, I couldn't look away.

It turned and looked at me, obviously drawn by the light. Its eyes were dark and hollow, almost black the whole way through, with big dark rings on the cheeks. It had a huge mouth that was drawn back into some sort of smile revealing dark teeth. Above the ragged line of its lips was a nose that was crumpled and flattened – barely a nose at all, except for its large, moist nostrils. Its eyes were lit up like a cat, and I thought it would rush at me, and eat me alive.

I screamed and dropped the flashlight. I remember my mother turning, shocked at the sound, and I fell backward, unable to turn my eyes from the darkness.

When my mother shined her light inside, the creature was gone.

"There's the breaker box," she said, clearly not realizing my trauma.

"No! You can't go in there," I said, grabbing her leg. "There's something in there. Don't go!"

"There's nothing in there, Billy," my mom said, reaching down and forcibly shaking me off of her. "You're being ridiculous."

I screamed in protest, fumbling for my flashlight, knowing that the thing, whatever it was in reality, would tear her throat out, devour her.

But it didn't. I shined my light all through the room, across all the square lockers and into every corner, but the creature was gone.

My mom found the breaker box and opened it. She flipped a few things loudly, then the lights and refrigerator came back on. I was laying on the floor, still holding my flashlight for dear life, when the white lights flickered and came to life, revealing nothing out of the ordinary.

"See?" my mother said, walking back in a huff. "I'm going to have a talk with your father about letting you watch his cable."

Chapter 2

I couldn't shake that horrible thing from my dreams. It didn't help that I had to go to the funeral home at least once a week. I did my best to focus on my homework, but I could never get rid of the feeling that the thing in the morgue was watching me, waiting. At night I imagined him following me home and sneaking into my house, standing at the foot of my bed in the darkness, licking his lips. I could even feel those twig-like fingers hovering over me, touching only the faint hairs on my cheek, somehow never actually touching me.

I frequently slept against my own will, succumbing only once all my tolerance for wakefulness had departed. This was especially true if I had to meet my mom at the office. Some nights, though I fought to stay awake, I would fall asleep as if I had been drunk. It was like my body refused my mind's insistence that I must stay awake.

I never felt that when I was at my dad's apartment. For some reason, his half-messy, half-furnished living space seemed like the last place in the world I would see a walking corpse. I was supposed to be there on the weekends, but that sometimes fell through. My dad had to travel for work a lot.

A few weeks after the incident at the morgue, staying with my dad fell through. My mom, though, was super busy on Saturday. I guess things line up that way – a bunch of funerals and then a date at night. I had to spend the day with one of my cousins. My father wouldn't have allowed it if he knew, because my Aunt Mavis (my mom's sister) was a real piece of work, and her kids were, too. Her eldest was a few years ahead of me and had already been forced to go to some kind of special school for the emotionally disturbed.

My mom said they were all fine, that my cousin was doing much better with therapy, and that my aunt was now very stable. I knew from experience what that really meant – she was stable because she was currently single.

My cousin – his name was Jeff – was my company on Saturday, and my aunt seemed perfectly willing to let me go out with him while she watched TV with her baby. I didn't protest, despite the weird vibe I got from Jeff, because her house was a bit creepy on its own, and I knew Jeff liked to torment me physically if he wasn't getting his way.

We hit up the corner store and grabbed a few comics. I would have bought one of the horror comics – there was a really good one about zombies, I remember, that got into the "thoughts" of the zombie (which was mostly nothing but standing in the swamp for who-knows-how-long before shambling off in search of brains), but my cousin insisted I get the latest X-Men. Turned out he wanted it but didn't have the scratch to collect it and Amazing Spiderman.

He had a whole extra huge stack in his bag, though, so we went to the park and read. It would have, to my surprise, been a fine day with Jeff, but some of Jeff's friends showed up.

They were really hard up about some horror movie they had seen – Day of the Dead, I think. I didn't pay much attention, just read the comics and turned down cigarettes, until the subject of my mom's funeral home came up.

"Yeah, the last owner was into black magic," said Mikey, a lanky kid who was always rubbing a stuffy nose.

"Funny, that's where Billy's mom works," Jeff said. "Actually, I think she owns the place."

"What?" I said, realizing they were talking about the funeral home.

"We were just talking about Danny Fiskar," Jeff said.

"Who?" I said.

Tim, a big fat kid with a permanently sour face, said, "Danny Fiskar was a kid around here. He lived above the funeral home with his parents, who owned the place. He disappeared one day and was never found."

"Yeah, and they sold the place to Billy's mom after that," Jeff said.

Mikey laughed. "They raised him from the dead, first. But he came back all wrong. He was a monster. He was the Night Stalker and was a cannibal. So his parents buried him and sold the place for a fraction of what it was worth."

"They buried him alive?" I said.

"He wasn't alive," Mikey said. "He was always dead. Or just undead. You bring a soul back from hell…" Mikey stopped laughing. "Nobody knows where he was buried."

"The story is he was buried under the home," Jeff said. He was smiling. Apparently, he enjoyed getting my goat.

"Not possible," I said. "The floor is solid concrete. A huge slab."

"You can cut slabs up," Tim said. "I heard they buried him in one of the mausoleums so that they could keep the door always locked."

"I heard," Jeff said, smiling at me, "That they put a curse on him, so he could never leave the home."

"Stop it," I said.

"But he's still there," Jeff said, laughing. His friends started to chuckle, too, "Waiting around to eat whoever stays over there at night!"

"Stop!" I said.

"Are you scared?" Jeff said.

"He's there," I said.

I remember the laughter died away just like that.

"He's still there," I said. "I saw him. He's horrible."

Jeff laughed at me. "Man, we was just playing."

"I wasn't," Mikey said. "I wasn't. When my aunt died, I went there, for the viewing. I swear I felt something. I asked around. Lots of people felt or heard weird things that day. I wouldn't stay. I got the hell out of there as soon as I could."

"Believe me," I said. "I wish I was playing. I've seen him once. I also know he knocked something over one time."

"You know, sheesh," Tim said.

"The morgue is always locked. One door in, one door out. There was a cart knocked over. Nothing's knocking anything over in there!" I realized I was almost shouting at the time, and I was standing, so I sat back down quickly. "But I saw him once, too. God, I wish I hadn't."

I remember I was crying, but nobody was willing to make fun of me for it.

"You probably imagined it, man," Mikey said. "I'd be creeped out being there, too. Shit, I *was* creeped out when I was there."

"I think he knows me now," I said. "I don't know if that means he's trying to get me."

"What a bunch of bullshit," Jeff said.

"It's not."

I remember Jeff's smile. I should have heeded the chill running up and down my spine – it was a sociopath's smile.

"Let's find out," he said. "Let's go there, and we'll have a look-see."

"No way," I said.

"Why you so chicken?"

"You'll be the one who's chicken," I said.

"Prove it. We'll go tonight. Mikey's brother has a car."

"Hell, no," Mikey said. "I ain't going there. Especially at night."

"I'll make it fun, man. I got a few beers stashed away. Come on!"

*

Jeff teased me about his plan on the way home, but I didn't think much of it. My mom would be by to pick me up, or so I thought.

When we got to my cousin's apartment, my Aunt Mavis told us that my mother was going to be later than she thought. I would apparently be spending the night. Normally, this wouldn't bug me too much. Jeff had a lot more Nintendo games than I did, and was actually pretty decent about letting me play or picking the two-player titles. We had a lot of fun (he had just gotten the new TMNT game, which was like the arcade version).

But then, around midnight, Jeff made us stop. He had that devilish look in his eyes, and I knew something was wrong. He snuck out of his bedroom and made me wait. He came back a moment later.

"We'll have to be real quiet," he said. "My mom passed out in her chair again."

"She hasn't already woken up, we can still play," I said.

"No, you doofus, we'll have to be quiet when we sneak past her. Even when she's totally blitzed, she'll wake up easy. She usually goes to bed to pass out. Come on, get your shoes on."

"Where are we going?"

Jeff gave me that smile, that awful, fake-sweet smile. "The funeral home, duh."

It was no use protesting. If I had thrown a fit, and woken up my aunt, she would probably have hit me as much as she would hit Jeff. So, I went. Against the protestations of my own sanity, I went.

We snuck past my aunt, who was asleep in a recliner, the TV playing a screen of silent static. Each of us had a backpack full of keystone cans from Jeff's closet and we had a hard time keeping them from clunking together as we stepped through the mess of the kitchen to the front door. The lights in the hallway outside the apartment were dim and flickering, making it hard to see anything. Once we got out to the street and the constant humming orange of the lamps there, it got easier.

Mikey's house was close, in the neighborhood just around the corner from Jeff's complex. When we got there Mikey was standing outside, hunched over on the curb, nursing a cigarette he didn't seem too interested in finishing. Mikey's brother, John, was there too, talking on the porch on a cordless phone. His voice was kind of sickly-sweet, like he was talking to a girl, but it was quiet enough I couldn't make out the words.

"You look sick," Jeff said to Mikey.

Mikey just shook his head. "I can't believe we're doing this."

"Don't be a wuss. Besides, this will prove there's no such thing as ghosts. Where's Tim?"

"Probably eating fried chicken," Mikey said.

"Or maybe he chickened out. What a pussy."

I kept my mouth shut until John walked over. "Let's go guys. Jeff, did you bring the beer?"

"You bet," Jeff said, patting his bag.

"Hit me."

Jeff opened up his bag and tossed a beer to John, who opened it up and chugged it. "Warm." It didn't seem to upset him. "Want one, Mikey?"

Mikey shook his head.

"Let me say that a different way. Drink up, Mike."

Mike held his head in his hands as he stood up, but he did as his brother commanded him. He took a beer out and began to drink it, nursing it down slowly like the cigarette.

"It's not a fucking bottle, Mike, sheesh," John said. He laughed with Jeff, who had already opened up a beer and downed it. John nodded at me, as if finally seeing me.

"This is my cousin, Bill," Jeff said.

"You gonna drink, or what? Beer is free."

"He's just a kid," Jeff said.

John shrugged. "Yeah."

"I'll have one," I said, feeling a sudden need to prove myself. I opened up my backpack and took out one of the beers. When I opened it foam spilled everywhere and all of us had a good laugh. "Must have shook it up on the walk."

It tasted utterly foul, easily the worst thing I had put in mouth up to then. For years that's what I thought beer was supposed to taste like, only realizing when I was close to adulthood that Keystone isn't even considered beer in most places in the world. Hell, it's not considered beer in most of the country.

I drank as much as I could, but quit before the end. John finished my beer off. We got into John's car, which was an old Chevrolet Caprice from the 70s that had half its paint job missing.

Riding in the backseat of the car was when the alcohol began to hit me. It was the first time I had really had any alcohol, and three-quarters of a beer was apparently enough. The lights started to shimmer on the road, and things got hazy, hard to see. Sounds got quieter. Before I knew it, we were at my mom's office. All the orange lights in the parking lot were on, and we couldn't see the cemetery behind it at all.

It looked blank but horrible, and my drunken eyes couldn't see it right.

"That's it, huh?" John said. "Doesn't look so spooky."

"It's the inside that's weird," Mikey said.

"Let's go," Jeff said. "Billy has a key."

"No, I don't," I said.

"You got us in that one time."

"That was the spare key."

"Well, we can get in, then."

I couldn't argue the point anymore, so we stumbled out of the car and up to the door. With some effort, I found the fake rock that hid the front door key. We were quickly in the lobby, which was completely dark except for the light spilling in from the parking lot. We looked around for a minute. Nobody wanted to go too far from the light. Even John, who was drinking another beer. Eventually, I found the main switch panel and lit the place up. Somehow, the clean, white lighting didn't help. It only accentuated the reality that we were somewhere we shouldn't be.

I led the others down the hall to the offices, and also to the elevator to the morgue. Every time I turned on a light I half-expected to see the creature there, in full detail, smiling at me, but each time there was just emptiness.

We took the stairs down to the morgue in single file, everyone else following me. At the double doors, we stopped.

"I don't have a key to the morgue," I said. "Sorry, I didn't think of this."

"Eh, it was fun anyway," John said. "Good for some creeps."

"Hold on," Jeff said. He pulled a little black bundle out of his backpack. Inside there was a set of lockpicks.

"You don't know how to use those," John said.

"Do too."

We stood there for a long time, watching Jeff try to rake the tumblers and failing to get them to stick well enough to turn the bolt. I saw the lights turn off at the top of the stairs, and Mikey, who was leaning against the first steps, nearly jumped into his brother's lap.

"Someone's here!" he whispered.

"It's the automatic lights," I said. "Mom put in a switch that turns them off to save power when nobody is in there."

"You sure?" Mikey said.

"Yeah. Goes off when I'm sitting real still, too." Something occurred to me then, and had I been sober, I would have stuffed it and kept my mouth shut. "I think there's a key in the desk upstairs."

"Well go get it," John said. "Come on, I want to see these corpses."

"You can't look at the corpses."

"Just go," Jeff said. "I think I got this either way."

"Someone come with me," I said.

"Don't be a wuss," Jeff said.

I didn't know what to say to that, so I started up the stairs. On the second step, Mikey said, "I'll come, too."

We marched slowly up to the top. When we stepped out into the darkness of the office, the lights didn't immediately come on.

"Sometimes you have to turn them off and back on again," I said.

"Well, fucking do it," Mikey said.

I side-stepped to where I knew the panel was, leaving Mikey looking like a shadow against the faint glow of the light fixture downstairs.

"Hey!" I heard Jeff from below. "I got it!"

"It wasn't locked!" John said. "Open the whole time."

"Ok just a sec," I said.

I watched Mikey's shadow disappear as he grunted. He stomped loudly down the stairs.

I felt for a nearby desk to help steady myself and get back to the stairs. I slipped a little when a car with bright lights drove by, lighting up the windows in the other room and showing the office for a moment in stark detail.

That was when I saw him.

He was sitting totally still in an office chair at a desk – the one I usually used for homework. He was staring right at me with the same dark, vacant eyes as before. I couldn't see his mouth so well this time, but it was dark and big, too big. Just like before he was naked and his flesh was totally white. In the glow that made up his outline, I could barely make out spiderwebs of veins.

I was paralyzed. I was also suddenly cold sober. Never in my life since have the effects of any drug departed so quickly as that horrible moment when I beheld the creature contemplating me in the dark.

The lights from the car moved off, and I thought I saw movement.

"Help!" I screamed, falling to the floor and dragging myself desperately toward the stairs. "Help me! Help! Please!"

I heard the sound of stampeding feet as I dragged my suddenly useless legs to the stairs.

The other three were running up, bumping into each other. I looked right into John's eyes and cried out again. "He's right here! He's right fucking here!"

John stepped over me into the dark and froze. He flicked a lighter and stepped past me to the panel. I watched him flip on the switch, bathing the office in bright, fluorescent light.

"There's nothing up here," he said. "But..." He frowned and rubbed his face, staring at the dark hallway.

"He was right there, at that desk."

"There's nothing," Jeff said. He walked over to the chair and sat in it, then spun it around. There was a long few seconds of silence as I picked myself back up.

"Mikey, did you see him?" I said.

Mikey looked pale, but maybe it was just the lights. "I... I don't know. I saw a shadow. Probably just the chair. But we need to get out of here."

"Yeah, it was just a shadow," John said. "Creeping us out."

"Let's go," I said.

"Man, I only just looked in the morgue," John said.

"I'm leaving," Mikey said, and jogged toward the foyer.

"Fine," John said. "Pussies win, I guess." He stomped toward the door, then stopped suddenly at the entrance to the Foyer. "Shit, guys."

"What's up?" Jeff said.

"The cops are coming."

"The alarm system," I said. "Damn it, I forgot the alarm system!"

"Let's get out of here!" Jeff said. With sudden desperation, he added, "I can't go back!"

We all ran for the entrance as fast as we could. Mikey was already outside, in the bushes, watching the distant lightbars advance.

"Get in the car, we can cut through the lawn and get back to Second Street," John said, in a flat run to his car.

"Wait!" I cried out, stopping. "We have to lock the morgue!" I turned to go back.

"Are you crazy?" Jeff said. He was grabbing my sleeve, practically dragging me.

"He can't get loose!" I knew he would come and get me. I knew it, though at the time I couldn't articulate it. I shook Jeff's clutch loose and ran for the front door before realizing he was already loose. Whatever was down there was out.

I froze. Through the lobby windows I could see something moving. A shadow. I turned around and ran like the wind back toward the car, jumping in the backseat, practically on top of Jeff.

John peeled out and turned, driving right past the funeral home building. I looked in the windows, not wanting to but seemingly unable to resist the compulsion.

"There he is!" I cried out, not knowing if what I saw was real or not. But I thought I saw him again, this time a blur of a flat white thing moving back toward the office.

John hopped the curb in his sedan and drove full pedal over the lawn, avoiding a fountain and threading through a set of trees. We bounced off the other curb and he twisted through an intersection. I could hear sirens, but I couldn't see the lightbars anywhere.

The beer stupor returned slightly, and the next thing I knew we weren't driving so fast, and we were in some neighborhood I didn't recognize. John killed his headlights and pulled into an alley.

When he turned the engine off, I realized Mikey was sobbing.

"That was a close one," John said. "Stop crying Mikey, we'll be fine."

"I saw it," Mikey said. "It was in the window!"

"No, it wasn't," Jeff said. "I was watching. It was just..." Jeff slumped down into the seat.

"Yeah I think we're just freaking ourselves out, guys," John said. "Cops will do that. A fucking room full of dead bodies will do that. Chill."

"Was the light switch off?" I said.

"Huh?" John said.

"Was the light switch off?" I repeated. "The one you flicked in the office. Did you turn it off and on, or just turn it on?"

John was quiet for a few seconds, just staring out into the dark alley. "Fuck, they were off. Jeff, get me a beer. Get me two of those motherfuckers."

Only Jeff could get to sleep in that alley. The rest of us sat there until dawn, trying to talk about other things. I followed John's lead and opened another beer for myself. It tasted so bad I could barely stomach it, but I drank every single drop, hoping it would kill the images burned into my mind.

Chapter 3

Jeff and I crept back into his apartment the next morning. We were both surprised to see the chair where my aunt had fallen asleep empty. She had apparently gotten up at some point in the night and gone to her room.

My mom came to pick me up not long after we got back, and I remember my palms being so sweaty I couldn't grip my water glass when she came in. My head felt awful, too – part my first ever hangover, part my not sleeping at all.

Something was off with my mother as well – my guess was she heard about the break-in at the funeral home but wasn't telling me. We got into the car in silence and she drove us home. I realized why she was giving me the silent treatment when we pulled up to our house. Three cop cars were there, parked – two were black and whites, but one was all black. I said nothing as I marched in.

At our kitchen table, sitting casually with a few papers spread out, were a couple of detectives and two other men in standard uniform. They were sharing coffee and stopped talking as I walked in. My mom pulled out one of the chairs, expecting me to sit, and I remember looking at that chair, and then at the detectives, and knowing that I was done for if I put myself in that chair.

Not just that, but I knew they wouldn't believe me. Danny Fiskar knew me, and nobody else would believe he existed until they found me with my throat torn out and devoured. I wanted to run out the door. Maybe I should have. But I sat.

"I'm Harry, and this is Sal," said one of the detectives, a lean and tall man. "Why don't you tell us what happened last night?"

I was silent for a few seconds. "I was at my cousin's house last night."

"We know it was you," Sal said. He was a big man, and I couldn't help but stare at his huge, sausage-like fingers. "We talked with your mother about it. We found the spare key in the door. You're the only one who knows where the key to the morgue is, and it was unlocked, so we know it was you that unlocked both doors."

"Yeah," Harry said. He gave me a big, fake smile. "We just want to know the details. The why."

I didn't quite know what to say, so I tried to tell a half-lie. "I went there to see if Danny Fiskar was real. He's supposed to come out at night."

Sal gave me a funny look. "Danny what?"

"Danny Fiskar," said the uniformed police officer. He was a relatively young man, but his face had a slightly aged look when he spoke. "Little urban legend. A ghoul who lives at the funeral home and graveyard, eating ears and noses, because he doesn't have any."

Sal looked hard at me. "So, who dared you to go in?"

"Nobody," I said, thinking of Jeff and Mikey and John. Despite what they got me into, I wouldn't just let the police in on the whole thing.

"Was it Jeffrey?" Harry said. "Did he make you do it?"

"No," I said.

"Then why? Did you let some stranger – some creep – in?"

"No, it wasn't a stranger."

"Call in for Jeffrey," Harry said to the standing officer.

I nearly jumped out of my seat, tears filling up my eyes quite suddenly. "No, not Jeff!"

Sal put his hands out. "Relax, son, we're not sending Jeffrey back to juvie, alright?"

"No?" I asked, unable to stop the tears.

Sal shook his head. "It's a welfare thing. I can't tell you more than that, but we're not gonna jail him, alright? He's a kid." He nodded to the officer, who stepped away, talking into his radio.

"So, tell us what happened," Harry said. "We just want to know what happened so we can close our investigation."

I started crying, but I also started spilling my guts. I told them everything. I told them about the beer, about breaking in, about the horrible monster in the darkness, glaring at me hungrily. Danny Fiskar? I couldn't say, but I couldn't talk about him without trembling. I was sure I was going to throw up.

"You left after that?" Sal said. "You didn't go back down to the morgue?"

"No," I said. "Are you crazy? The morgue is where it lives!"

"None of you boys went into the morgue, is that what you're telling me?" Harry said.

"I... I don't know. They had just found the door was already open when I saw Danny in the chair."

Sal and Harry shared an incredulous look.

"How long do you think you were at the top of the stairs?"

I shrugged. "I don't know, maybe a minute?"

Sal shook his head. "Come on, let's drop the ghost story. This older boy – John – is he the one who opened up the lockers?"

"What?" I said. "What? He just saw the door was open."

"Was it you that opened up the lockers?"

"What? The lockers?"

"A few of the lockers were opened up. The bodies were out," my mother said. "When I came down to investigate the break-in. Were you trying to see a naked woman?"

"Let us handle this, please," Harry said.

I was at a loss for words for a few seconds. "We didn't open up any lockers. We went there to see if Danny Fiskar was real."

"You sure John didn't open up the lockers?" Sal said.

I stammered for a minute. "I guess he could have, but he didn't. Jeff would have talked about it. He always talks about stuff like that."

"How big in trouble are we?" I said timidly.

Sal shrugged. "Desecrating a body is pretty serious."

"We didn't do anything to the bodies. If anyone did it, it was Danny Fiskar. He's there now! Did you catch him? You have to stop him!"

"Calm down, son," Harry said. "Listen, we're not arresting you. We're not even going to take you into custody, except to talk to a man a little later today. He's a psychologist. No handcuffs, none of that stuff."

*

The police psychologist was a nice, middle-aged man with a close-cut beard. He made me tell the story again, but it was a little easier than the first time. When he was done, he walked out of the room and talked to my mom, along with Sal.

On the way home, my mom finally broke the silence.

"I never thought you'd be capable of something like that."

"Like what?" I said.

"Breaking into the home, and then lying like that."

"But it's not a lie. You have to believe me. It was real."

My mom got agitated and growled to herself. "That's what the shrink said. That you believed it was real."

"It was real, mom, but..." I paused and looked at the glaring face of my mother as she drove the car through heavy morning traffic. "It *was* real mom, but I don't expect you to believe me. Kids can't be believed, and he knows it."

"Can you think for just once about someone other than yourself? Mavis is going to have Jeffrey taken away from her. Put into foster care. Doesn't that mean anything to you?"

"What?"

"That's what the police meant by welfare. If you would just tell the truth, that that boy John made you take him into the funeral home and made you show him the dead bodies, none of this would be happening."

"But that's not the truth!"

My mom reached over, like she was going to slap me. I shrank back. She seemed to think better of it and pulled her hand back.

"You're going to go into this shrink's office and you're going to tell him that you made the whole thing up to get attention. You're going to tell him John threatened you and Jeff, and it was all his idea, and he's the one who was messing with the bodies."

"But-"

"Then you're going to tell it to the detectives. And if you don't, so help me God..."

She just grunted instead of completing the sentence. It was a terrifying moment, but also revealing, and I remember it still. Even my mother couldn't evoke the name of God with a lie. I hardened myself in that moment. If God existed, so did devils, and one of them lived in the funeral home. I had never been to church, but at that moment an understanding of faith and its inverse was born in my young mind.

I was alone, and nobody would ever help me survive.

*

A few agonizing days later - days filled with unwelcome and torturous dream sleep – my mom took me to see what I found out later was a court-appointed psychiatrist.

He was a nice middle-aged fellow (as they all seem to be) named Doctor Grant, calm and non-emotional as he talked to me. He was primarily a therapist, he informed me, not merely a doctor of psychotropic medicine.

I was infinitely thankful when he asked my mother to leave the room and she complied. He told me later that he legally can't make a parent leave, but people often will do what you ask of them without considering the option of saying no.

He asked me about the creature – Danny Fiskar – for a long time, plying out of me every detail of the foul thing. He asked about my feelings. We talked for a long time about my parents' divorce, and how I felt about it. Things always came back to Danny Fiskar, though.

"I'm worried about this vision of yours," he said. "You said you see him at night. Is he the same at night as when you saw him at the funeral home?"

"No," I said. "He's not really there. It's just me imagining."

"But he's real at the funeral home."

"He was real."

He was silent as he wrote something on a piece of paper.

"You don't believe me," I said.

"Actually, I do, in a way. I'm going to have your mother come in and talk to both of you about this, alright? Anything else you want to tell me before I do that?"

I nodded. "She wanted me to lie so that Jeff wouldn't end up in foster care."

"Thank you for not lying. It's important for Jeff and for you. Don't ever be afraid to be honest here. That it?"

I nodded.

"Alright." Doctor Grant got up from his desk and quietly retrieved my mother. He had her sit next to me, and she was silent and blank-faced as she spoke. "So, let's talk about what I'm seeing here."

"Shouldn't Billy leave?" my mom said.

Doctor Grant shook his head. "It's my philosophy that it is important for the patient to be party to any therapy or treatment, even if he's a child." He picked up his notebook and looked it over. "There are some very interesting things going on here. Dealing primarily with troubled individuals, particularly children, I have developed some good tools for detecting what we call psychological acting – that is, behavior that is designed to simulate some sort of psychological disorder. Some people can be very clever, and some psychiatrists are very excited about exotic disorders."

I saw a slight smile form on my mother's face.

Doctor Grant caught her eye. "That, however, is not what I think is happening here. William mentioned this figure – Danny Fiskar – as being undeniably real in certain locations, but of an uncertain reality in others. These uncertain encounters with the vision, which happen primarily in spaces where hallucinations are common, such as in the dark close to sleep, are of particular note. Also of note is that William discounts these encounters as part of his imagination."

"So he knows he was all just dreaming this up, and he admits he was doing it for attention and to get out of trouble," my mother said.

Doctor Grant frowned and looked away for a moment. "Not exactly. I believe William. That is to say, I believe he is telling the truth as he experiences it. He really did see this figure. I believe firmly that he truthfully experienced seeing it. However, this figure defies logic and our normal assumptions of how the world works, so we have to look to some additional pieces of evidence.

"William admits a paranoia surrounding Danny Fiskar: a preoccupation with it and a continual feeling of being watched. He also admits that his mind is presenting ideas and images which are very real to him, but are not as tangible as actual sensory data. We can call these feelings and images part of a delusion."

Doctor Grant took a breath and said, "This is actually, in conjunction with the visions of Danny Fiskar, a strong indicator of the acute stage of schizophrenia."

"What?!" my mom shouted, nearly getting out of her seat. "You think he's crazy? He's just a kid who got into a little trouble. He's just depressed, if anything."

It was weird to hear her try to stick up for me.

Doctor Grant held his hands out peacefully. "Please, let me explain. Schizophrenia is a psychological disorder that is actually more common than people realize, affecting about 1% of people in some capacity. Usually, first onset is mid-teens, so this case would be early onset, and this case would also be mild."

Doctor Grant looked at me and took another shallow breath. "I believe you saw Danny Fiskar. But I think the best explanation is that you suffered a period of psychosis – a mental break where you can no longer correctly assess reality, or where imagination and reality merge – due to specific stresses. Lots of people suffer psychic breaks. It's very common. Schizophrenic psychosis tends to focus on recurring delusions – those unwelcome imaginings of this monster – and thus they are often incredibly convincing.

"You are lucky, though, in that you are very smart and are able to correctly identify delusions. Most people who are affected by psychotic disorders have deficiencies in self-assessing delusions. At the same time, people who try to fake this sort of disorder usually try to present persistent psychosis." Doctor Grant looked at my mother. "That's the sort of schizophrenic patient you might see on Dateline or 60 minutes, but that's not typical at all. William isn't doing that, and he also isn't suffering any sort of deficiencies that are usually associated with schizophrenia, which is very, very good."

My mom was silent for a long time, then she said, "So what causes it?"

"The physiological cause is unknown. We know it by its symptoms, primarily. We're also beginning to do neurological studies using special machines known as MRIs – they're kind of like x-rays or cat-scans, but show a lot more soft tissue detail – but we're a long way from knowing what's physically going on.

"Luckily, it's been a very studied condition for a very long time, and we have a variety of ways to treat the disorder both medically and via psychological therapy. Usually, there are three phases, or cycle stages, to schizophrenia, and treatment varies depending on the individual and where they are at in that process.

"William at this moment is not suffering any significant psychosis. That's in the past, but the paranoid delusions are still persistent. For this reason, I would say he is still in the acute stage. The stage prior to the onset of psychosis is called the *prodromal* stage, and it's usually missed with first onset. It's a ramping up of paranoia and other manic states. This moves into the acute stage, which is typified by mania and psychosis. After the acute stage comes the recovery stage, where the patient is able to properly contextualize the delusions and settle into stable mental functioning.

"I'm going to recommend a few things. First, a removal from the things which I believe are stressing William and triggering the psychosis. That means he needs to stay away from the funeral home. I know this is also outside my area, but I recommend he spend more nights, if not all of them, with his father as he suffers no paranoia in that environment."

"I have custody," my mom said. "Gary is never home anyway."

"It's a suggestion. I can't order it. Beyond that, I'm going to prescribe an antipsychotic medication. I want William to take it before bed. It has sedative effects early on, so it will encourage sleep. Bedtime is also when the delusions are most powerful, so it should begin to help him resolve the paranoia rather quickly. I'll re-assess him in a few days, and then we can consider tapering off of the antipsychotic and going to an antidepressant, or trying therapy to stabilize the mood."

"So you're putting me on drugs," I said.

"Medication," Doctor Grant said. "Just temporarily. Like I said, many people recover from periods of psychosis. I absolutely expect you to as well. The first step is to reduce stress."

Chapter 4

My mom didn't want to send me to my father's apartment, but it was the weekend again, and she had to let me go according to family court. She refused to get out of the car when she dropped me off at his apartment. I pieced together later that they had argued pretty badly about me, with my mother thinking that my dad was trying to angle his way to some larger portion of custody.

My dad's apartment felt right when I stepped into it and put my bag down.

It's hard to describe *cozy* with words that mean more than cozy, or comfy, or peaceful, or warm. It was none of those things – it was cold, for one – and it was also all of those things.

The early sunset of autumn usually showed in his windows, which had miniblinds, always half-open to let in the half-light. All his furniture was grey or muted blue, and he hung nothing on the walls except an abstract picture of the sun setting in the ocean. The living room was sparse, with an angular small couch, leather chair, and big TV on a black stand. It was to this couch I went when I arrived, slumping into the cheap springs to look silently out at the city buildings. It had started raining, and the rain was orange in the failing light. My father was silent, going about his little kitchen to make up a few sandwiches.

I remember the coffee table well – it was black like the TV stand, but was covered in rings from countless cups and had a few forgotten plates stacked in a corner along with a small pile of forks. My dad brought over my meal and took his own to the leather chair to eat.

"Mind if I watch the game?"

I shrugged. He turned on a baseball game and we watched in silence for a while, but as the sun left and darkness set in I found myself looking around the room at the flickering lights from the TV on the sunset picture and on the blinds, and then at the lights of the city beyond.

I have a deep and abiding nostalgia for that moment, which stands out in my memory above anything else that wasn't pure terror. The rain and the darkness, the lights of infinite strangers outside the flat windows, the TV, the rough texture of the couch. Nothing outside; nothing but what was right inside.

Cozy is the best I could describe it, but it's not the right word at all.

I fell asleep on the couch, and when I woke, I noticed that my father had fallen asleep in the chair, but not before putting a knitted blanket on me. It was still dark when I got up and retrieved my Gameboy from my backpack.

"We forgot to give you your medication," my father said as I sat back down.

"I don't need it here."

"Did the doctor say that?"

"Not exactly."

"We can talk about the medicine later. What do you want to do today?"

"I don't know. I don't want to go anywhere."

"I might need to head down to the pharmacy. Did you want to pick out some comics or something?"

"Mom says I shouldn't read them."

"I won't tell her."

He went back to sleep while I fired up my game and the attached light and played. The room slowly filled with grey before my dad woke up again and started getting ready. He took me down to the drugstore early, making for himself his ever-present cup of coffee before we stepped out.

The store looked kind of strange to me; the lights looked too bright, but I supposed it was the medication wearing off. I ended up finding some decent books at the store. The ones in the city are always better stocked with stuff like that, even though the store itself is always much smaller.

When we came back, I felt right again and spent the day reading or playing games. My father never made me take the meds, but when I had to finally "come home" (as my mom always called going back to her house), I ended up practically begging for them.

*

Jeff called me on Sunday morning. My father answered the phone and handed it over to me without asking who was on the other side.

"Hello?" I said.

"Hey, this is Jeff. I tried your mom's but got an answering machine." He sounded a little rattled.

"Did they take you away? From your mom, I mean."

"Yeah, I'm calling from a group home. Supposed to be temporary. I told 'em I'm calling my uncle Billy."

"Sorry, man."

"The court is trying to track down my dad. They're not going to let me stay with him, though."

"Why?"

"He's a truck driver now, and he has a record still."

"Oh yeah. Did I tell you what happened to me?"

"No. Did you hear what happened to John?"

"No," I said. "Did the cops arrest him?"

"Sort of. They dragged him down to the station and grilled him for hours and hours, apparently, trying to get him to confess."

"I was the one who broke us in."

"Yeah, that's the thing. I guess it's not really breaking and entering since your mom owns the place."

"What were they trying to get him to confess to?"

"Uh… It's weird, man. I'm hearing this from Mikey, so maybe he's crazy, but he thinks they were trying to get him to confess to *eating* the dead bodies."

"What?" I said. "Eating them? You serious?"

"Dead serious, Bill. John didn't say nothing, so he's back home, but I think there was something up with the bodies, and they found bites or something on them."

"No shit." I looked over at my dad, who didn't seem to notice my cussing as he read the newspaper.

"Yeah, I'm freaking out, man. I'm thinking now you were right. I think John might have tried to throw you under the bus, say it was all your idea."

I didn't quite know how to respond. "Did I tell you they sent me to a shrink?"

"No."

"They think I'm crazy. They think I have schizophrenia."

"I have to see a shrink this week. Wondering what they'll say is wrong with me this time."

"You had to see one in juvie, right?"

"Yeah. He was stupid. He kept thinking I was depressed." Jeff's voice took on a suddenly sad tone. "Man, I don't wanna go back."

Suddenly I was aware of something Jeff said when we were running from the funeral home. "I can say it was my idea. They can pin it on me. I can plead insanity."

"It don't work like that dude. Trust me, if they were going to arrest me, I'd be arrested. More just I wasn't supposed to be going out. I'd be in trouble if we had gone down to the Thrifty."

"Group home okay?"

"It sucks. No Nintendo and they took my comics away. Other kids are assholes or really screwed in the head."

"I'm screwed in the head."

"Naw, man. You're cool. You don't know what crazy is. I'm getting a look here. Call you later."

*

I had to "go home" that night. My mom refused to get me from my dad's apartment. Instead, she honked the horn on the street, which was kind of embarrassing.

On the way home, she peppered me with questions.

"Did you bring your medication?"

"Yes."

"Did you remember to take it?"

"Yes," I lied.

"What did you and your father do?"

"Just hung out."

"What does that mean?"

"I don't know, we watched TV and stuff."

"Did you read any comics?"

"No," I lied again. My father had agreed to keep my books at his place. I gathered that my mom was really against them after the appointment with the psychiatrist, and I expected to find my collection gone or gutted when I got home.

"The psychiatrist said you aren't supposed to read comics." Now I knew *she* was lying.

"I want to stay at dad's house."

"He's too far from school."

School. I had almost forgotten about it, having stayed home all week. I suddenly wondered what the kids would think. I tried to put it out of my mind.

*

Sunday night, I took the antipsychotic again. I slept. It was an uneasy sleep, disturbed and full of half-dreams. I was also so zoned out at school I still don't remember if I got any questions about the funeral home. It was the same thing the next night, but worse. All night long I thought I could see shapes on the edge of my vision, but I couldn't control my eyes to look at them and see what they were. I thought I felt long fingers running on my skin, but when I could look, I couldn't see anyone.

I had to test something.

I decided not to take my medication on Tuesday night.

My mother handed me the pill, I put it in my mouth, then I pretended to swallow it. What I actually did was tuck it into my cheek, then spit it out a few minutes later.

It had started to dissolve, tasting horribly bitter and undoubtedly delivering some of the psychoactive substance, but it wasn't enough to be a proper dose.

I went to bed tired, but uneasy. Already I found it far too easy for my mind to dwell on the events of the previous week. I kept remembering random details as I tried to sleep. Eventually, I focused on something that seemed to help: a pretty girl from school. I can't remember her name now, but I remember vividly her image and the dream.

As I got more and more tired, the fantasy of the girl from school shifted. Her skin got pale and stretched, and her fingers grew long and dark. I realized I was looking at the body of Danny Fiskar, though I hadn't properly seen it before, but with the hair and face of the girl. When she looked at me, her eyes grew black, and her lips peeled back to reveal dark, stained teeth, like she had been drinking bum wine for years.

I startled myself awake.

My hands were shaking under the covers, and I was drenched in sweat. I could feel my face distorting, grimacing.

Then I saw him. Standing just at the edge of the light cast by the lights on my VCR was the unmistakable pale figure from the morgue. The amber blinking 12:00 was dim, but in the utter darkness of midnight it was a beacon, and it pulsed, revealing in flashes the flat face of the monster.

Danny Fiskar.

I tried to speak the name, but my throat was parched and unresponsive to my will.

When the light blinked off, all I could see was a trace of light from some leak at my bedroom door. When it blinked on, I saw the shadows of the face, including the flat, almost missing nose. The eyes were utter blackness, utter void. The mouth was moving, drawing tight, one frame at a time, moving into an alien expression that was neither frown nor grimace.

Each frame, he got bigger, slightly closer to the foot of my bed. Soon I could make out his arms. They were moving up. The hideous fingers, over-long and like the legs of spiders, were moving slowly as he raised his thin arms. He stopped at the foot of my bed and I could feel the fingers touch my feet and legs, tickling them through the sheets, probing.

I could detect a sound coming from him, like a soft and hoarse moan. His nothing eyes were invisible, but I could feel them crawling on my body and my face.

He said, very slowly, each consonant clear, like a whisper by my cheek, tickling the hairs around my ear, "Like me."

I tried to scream, but instead, I only whispered a string of nothings in the same hoarse tone he used.

"Like me."

"No," I whispered.

"Come."

"No."

His mouth got so wide that I couldn't understand how he could speak.

"Be with me. Come, eat." His fingers seemed to move up my body to my face, touching the edge of my mouth, trying to pry it open.

"No!" I finally had my voice back, and with the power of that word my fear receded just a bit. I also began to feel my fingers and toes. I kicked with all my might. My legs moved just a bit. I realized they were restricted, held in place by his body. Those horrible fingers! My skin crawled and tingled.

I sat up, but I threw myself back down, unable to stand the horrible face in the darkness. I reached over and felt the lamp. I didn't think to turn it on. I threw it with all my might.

"Burn in hell!" I screamed.

The lamp cord caught in the socket and the lamp stopped mid-air, tumbling and thudding down onto my feet and legs, breaking apart. Frantically, I swung my arms in wide circles, hoping to find something else to fight with. I thought I could feel, however faintly, the ghostly fingers release slightly. My heart felt like it would explode. I thrashed on the ground, and I thought I heard the slamming of some door.

Then the lights came on.

My mother was standing at the door, the light from the hall illuminating the room and casting her shadow across my bed.

"Stay back!" I screamed. "He's here!"

She turned on the overhead light, and all I saw was my normal mess. She rushed over to the bed and drew me into a hug.

"It's okay," she said. "It's not real. You were just having a nightmare."

"He's here, mom!" I said, trying to pull her off of me, trying to free my legs. My mind saw my baseball bat leaning on the wall by my closet, and I dove for it.

My mom saw what I was doing and flopped on the ground trying to get the bat as well. She struggled against me, but I was still weak, and she managed to pry my cold fingers off of the bat. She ran out of the room with the weapon, throwing it somewhere out of reach while yelling at herself before returning to find me scrambling through my old toys for something that could do damage.

She grabbed me again in a hug.

"It wasn't real, Billy," she said. "It was *not* real. Please relax."

I did, finally, seeing the room bathed in light.

I started crying.

As my mom hugged me and the silent minutes rolled out, my mind went into two directions.

You're crazy. You really are crazy. He wasn't real.

He found you. If you had been asleep, he would have gotten you.

He can't be real. He disappeared, and real things don't disappear.

He's real. He's a ghost. Ghosts can do things like that. Or demons.

You didn't take your medicine. You're crazy.

If I had taken my medicine, he might have got me.

I didn't sleep the rest of the night, and my mom didn't try to make me. She let me sit in my room with the lights on, or in the living room, until it was time for my morning shower.

Chapter 5

I spent the next day at school in a different kind of haze: that of sleeplessness. I saw the pretty girl from my fantasy, and she repulsed me. I was terrified of being called on to answer questions in class. I was afraid I would just blurt out the whole story of Danny Fiskar, and nobody would believe me there, either. Luckily, no teacher bothered me. They were all content to let me stare into space or draw in my notebook.

My notebook!

I threw the thing away at some point. The pictures I drew in it were disturbing. I drew gestures more than forms. Long sweeping strokes of ink, all in the same directions, gave impressions of my thoughts, often looking like faces with dark eyes, or overlong limbs, or reaching hands, or rows of crooked teeth.

There was actually one person who believed me. Apparently, she heard the story through Mikey, who went to high school with her brother.

She approached me during lunch. I remember her looking down on me as I ate my tray of processed food by myself, my friends sitting a few feet away and ignoring me. She wore big black glasses that framed brown eyes which were wide with shock. Her hair was pinned up, and she had a big, baggy sweatshirt on.

"Are you Willy Smith?" she said.

"Billy," I said.

"Yeah." She sat down across from me but held a stack of books close to her chest, like she was afraid I would steal them.

"What's up?" I said to her, not knowing where to begin a conversation with a strange girl.

"I heard you saw Danny Fiskar."

I immediately felt annoyed and embarrassed. I shook my head and looked away.

"Did you see him?" she said, her big eyes getting bigger still.

"I thought I did. I'm just crazy, though."

"I believe you."

"You do?"

"Yeah."

"Why?"

"Mikey said you didn't hear about Danny Fiskar first."

"So?"

"That means you can't have imagined him."

"Sure, it can," I said. "Someone had to imagine him in the first place."

She shook her head. "Not if he's real. You're not the first person to see him. My aunt saw him. She worked at the funeral home a long time ago."

"So, your aunt's crazy too. So what?"

She gave me a strange look, then stood up. "Just wanted to say I believe you."

I stared at her for a few moments. "Thanks. Sorry I was a jerk."

"It's okay. I'll see you around."

I realized after she left that I never asked her name, and she never gave it.

*

I took my medication that night.

I slept like the dead, but my dreams were chaotic and nightmarish fragments of thoughts. The only thing I clearly remembered was trying to crawl away from something that had me by the feet and was pulling me closer and closer to some sort of abyss.

My mother woke me in the morning, and I was so groggy I could barely move, but I managed to get out of bed. When I went to put on my shoes, I screamed.

My feet were black and purple, covered with painful bruises all across the tops and penetrating to my arches.

"Your lamp broke on your feet last night," my mom said. "That must have done it. Don't you remember?"

"Yeah, but this isn't… This isn't right."

"Just take it easy today. No PE today, right?"

"I guess."

The bruises weren't right though. They were indented into my feet, like long fingers had grabbed them, twisting into my flesh.

*

It turns out I forgot my block days and I *did* have PE. Even though my feet were in pain it was nice to exercise my body. We played field hockey and had a great, if rough, time.

I saw the brown-eyed girl from the other day in the next field over. She saw me and I waved. Her PE clothes were baggy like her regular clothes, but because she was wearing a T-shirt, I had an inkling why. She was what you might call an early developer, and she was shy about it.

She found me again at lunch, sitting across from me without saying anything, dressed again in her baggy sweatshirt.

"You seem different today," she said.

"They put me on medication," I said truthfully. "Supposed to stop me from seeing him."

"Danny Fiskar?"

I nodded.

"Does it work?"

"I slept," I said. "But I think he's trying to get me when I sleep." I told her about the bruises and my mom's explanation.

"Maybe we should call an exorcist," she said. "Father James would be able to find one. I think he *was* one."

I shook my head. "Nobody would believe it."

"Father James would. I know it."

"Why? I'm just some sick kid."

"Because," she said flatly. She went quiet and started looking at one of her notebooks.

"Hey, I never got your name."

"Anna."

"I'm Billy."

"I know."

"Right," I said, feeling embarrassed. "How much does an exorcist cost?"

I remember that was the first time I saw her smile, like I had told a little joke. "They're priests, Billy."

"Priests get paid, right? They gotta pay rent."

"Yeah, but you don't *pay* priests. You pay the church. They aren't plumbers or something."

"Same difference."

"No," she said, frowning at me. "You should talk to Father James, though."

"I don't know who that is."

"Right, of course. I'm dumb." She frowned even harder and stared down at the table. "I would have seen you at mass."

"Do you really believe me?"

"I really do. Mikey believes you. John believes you."

"Then help me. Talk to father James."

"Just go to Saint Mary's. He'll be there."

"I can't go. My mom picks me up."

Anna gave me a confused look. "Your mom won't take you to church?"

"I guess I can ask, but she's not religious."

"I'll try then."

*

That night was like the last. I took my pill, but I also fought sleep with all I could muster. I was afraid he would come back and finish pulling me into that black abyss. My dreams were jumbled and unresolved. I dreamt of places I had never seen.

Danny, or what I assumed afterward was Danny, attacked me again. I can't remember the scenes on either side of the moment. All I remember was long, pale arms slashing at me and me holding my arms up to try to keep those hideous fingers off of my face.

I woke up groggy and sweaty, my mouth like cotton. When I was getting dressed, I noticed more bruises on my arms, like I had been struck. I decided not to tell my mom, and I also resolved myself to find the priest Anna had talked about.

I didn't get the opportunity that day. Instead, my mom picked me up early to take me to my psych appointment with Doctor Grant.

He was calm and collected, just like before, but seem very concerned about Monday night.

"This sort of night terror is very uncommon. It says to me that the Thorazine may not be working as well as it should be, but at the same time, I don't think this is indicative of it failing to treat the psychosis in general. It could be because your body weight is on the edge of the adult range. I'm going to recommend a high dosage at bedtime. If that doesn't work, we can transition to something stronger, but we're so early in treatment I really don't want to transition unless we're failing to see results. Was this an issue at your father's?"

"It wasn't," I said.

"Well, let's try the higher dosage starting right away, and we'll re-evaluate next week again. Have you begun a 504 plan yet?"

"Yes," my mother said. I didn't know what a 504 plan was, but I guessed it was related to my treatment.

"Good. I'm available for comment during normal hours. Make sure the principle has my card."

*

The higher dose knocked me out. I dreamt, but in the morning, I could scarcely remember any of it. I had no new bruises on my body, and it made me wonder.

Was I really crazy? Maybe I had made the bruises myself, or they came from something else, like my mom said.

Did the medication have some sort of power over the demon? Did I need to be conscious and receptive in order to see him?

Or was it that he just left me alone for a night?

School was a brutal haze, and I felt like sleeping the whole day. I think I did fall asleep in English, but once again nobody bothered me.

Anna found me again at lunch.

"Father James said to give you this," she said, and handed me a rosary, though at the time I didn't know the name or purpose of it. I put it around my neck, and Anna gave me a strange look.

"What?"

"You don't usually wear it," she said. "But I guess you can. You're supposed to pray it."

"Pray it?"

Anna gave me a confused look. "Right. Just pray, I guess. I have to go."

*

My dad picked me up from school that day and drove me to his place downtown. The sterility of the building and the apartment was comforting. He had a stack of comics waiting for me on the kitchen counter. It was a quiet night and, having the rosary secreted under my shirt, I duped my dad and spat out my meds. I figured that even if I had a vision, I'd be clear-headed enough to actually enjoy a Saturday.

I went to bed at the normal time, but couldn't sleep as the antipsychotic slowly drained from me, clearing my mind and making me feel like I could think again. I turned on my lamp and read my comics a second time, then played some Tetris. With my mind clear, I was on fire. The levels blew past. I finally died on level 24, and I realized it was sometime after midnight. I got up to get a drink and saw the lights from the city still pouring into the little living room.

Once again, I felt calm as well as tired. I fished the rosary out of my shirt and held it as I watched the sparse traffic outside.

"God, I don't know how to pray," I said out loud. "Don't let him come here."

I went to sleep and had real dreams for the first time that week. I dreamt of people and places, trees and houses, and sun and rainclouds. It was a relief.

The rest of the weekend with my dad was great. I once again avoided my meds. I prayed while holding the rosary, feeling the crucifix as a reminder that God was real and hoping that he would use his power. Sunday came around, and I begged my dad to let me stay.

"I would love you to stay," he said. "I have no problem driving you to school and picking you up, but it's not up to me. The court decided your mom has custody. She already doesn't have to let me have weekends."

"He knows I live there," I said, too desperate to pretend.

"Who?"

I stopped and did my best to think quickly. "When you bought the funeral home with mom, who did you buy it from?"

"I don't remember."

"The Fiskars?"

He shook his head. "No, somebody else." Something seemed off with that explanation, but I let it rest. I remember my dad's tired smile. I knew he hated letting me leave. "You're doing better with the meds, right?"

"Yeah," I said. "The doctor thought I should be staying here. Said it would reduce my stress."

"It's not up to me," was all he would say.

Night fell on Sunday and I was left with a choice: to take the pills, or to pretend to take the pills.

I pretended, hoping that the rosary would have some kind of power for me.

I panicked slightly as I found, when I went to my room at my mother's house to sleep, that I had left the rosary at my father's house. I had put myself in an unfortunate position.

In order to take my medication, I would have to get my mother and fess up to what I did. The bottle of pills was with her. She had a fear I would take more than I was supposed to. Where that fear had come from, I had no idea. I preferred to *avoid* medicine, not take too much.

If I avoided that conversation with my mom, I risked having Danny Fiskar come to get me. My mom had taken my baseball bat. I had no way to defend myself if he showed up.

As the house quieted down and got darker, I became more anxious and agitated. I left the lights on in my room, but my mom came up and, thinking I was asleep, had turned them off. I immediately began to panic, seeing the blinking light from the VCR. Inside my bedside table, I found a little Maglite my dad had given me for Christmas one year and turned it on. I shined it perpetually on the space between the closet and the window, waiting for the creature, but it didn't come.

I crept out of bed when I was sure that my mom was asleep.

I went through the hall and into the kitchen, hoping to find a knife or something else that could be used as a weapon. I found that at some point, maybe over the weekend, my mother had removed every knife and sharp utensil from the house. The knives were all gone, as were the steak knives, the butter knives, the scissors, and even those little yellow things you use to eat corn on the cob. I managed to sneak out to the garage and found something similar. All the toolboxes had locks on them; all the knives were missing.

The only thing that I could find that I thought might tangentially be a weapon was a big, rusted pipe wrench. I grabbed it and headed back to my room, half expecting Danny Fiskar to be there waiting for me. I was relieved to only see my room, just as it was. I settled into bed with the wrench and began to wait.

Sleep eventually came to claim me. My dried eyes could no longer keep their vigil in the dim light leaking through the windows from the orange streetlamps outside. I clung to the pipe wrench. As my consciousness began to fade, I thought I could hear unfamiliar sounds from the street, but I seemed unable to get up to see to them.

I finally slept. Once again, I had dreams. Unlike at my father's house, these dreams were disturbing and strange, full of shadows and darkness. I saw Danny Fiskar in one of them, but it was him before... well, before whatever turned him to the monster he was. Somehow, I knew it was him, or else it was my mind's idea of what he might have really looked like.

He was a boy, lanky and with clothes, but there was something wrong with him. He stared at everyone everywhere he went. The other kids ran away from him. He was taller than all of them, were they afraid? They were, but not because he was tall. He was terrified, too. He hated school. He hated the other kids. He hated everyone, and he wanted to run away, too.

I awoke from the nightmare, knowing fully what I would see in my darkened room.

"God, help me," I said. The words could actually come out of my mouth, to my surprise. They seemed somehow, to have a kind of power, or else they encouraged me.

In the shadows, illuminated by the light leaking from the half-open blinds, was a tall figure. I knew who it was, but I didn't know why he just stood there. I desperately tried to move my arms and legs.

He took a step closer. I could see ragged strands of hair in the bands of orange light.

"God, help me!" I croaked. My tongue was like sand, and my voice was like stale bread.

The figure moved slightly away, as if preparing to flee or leap at me.

I felt sweat under the fingers of my right hand and flexed.

The wrench!

Courage suddenly came into my mind, matching the dread of Danny Fiskar's wicked mouth and spider-like fingers. Finally, I gained enough strength in my limbs to lift the wrench.

I sat up with as much speed as I could and swung the wrench. The figure turned, flinching. I fell forward, off of the bed. I lost track of where I was. A loud hissing sound surrounded me.

I got to my knees and swung again, hoping to hit the large, unknowable writhing shape in the darkness. The pipe wrench collided with something, thudding heavily. The hiss turned into something else, a cry or wail. I tried swinging again, but was too disoriented to know if I hit anything.

The wail turned into a scream, then I heard the sound of the door slamming. I swung again, hitting nothing, then realized I had rolled by the door and was half-leaning on it. My breathing was frantic, I pushed myself up and turned on the light. My room was empty.

I began to slow my breathing down. At the same time, I heard my mother coming down the hall. Quickly, I threw the wrench under my bed and flopped on top, not bothering to turn off the light.

"Are you alright?" my mother said, bursting through the door.

"Fine," I said. "I just had a nightmare. I'll be okay."

"This is twice now this has happened since you came home from your father's. I think there's something about that apartment that's stressing you. I'm going to talk to doctor Grant about it."

"No!" I said. "There's nothing stressful about it." I wanted to tell her it was her house that made me stressed, but I held myself back. I was afraid of making her truly mad.

"Are you going to be okay?"

"Yeah, I just stumbled getting to the light to turn it on."

"Alright," she said, and stepped back out, leaving the door slightly ajar. "That was quite a scream."

My eyes went wide as the light went out.

I waited nervously for a few minutes, then found my flashlight and looked under the bed for the pipe wrench. I found it and pulled it out. In the light, it looked like it was covered in something black – blood, perhaps, but if it was, it was darker than what I imagined it could be, like it was long rotten.

It sent a shiver up my spine, looking at it. I refused to touch the end of the wrench, afraid whatever substance was left on it was of some insidious evil. I needed the wrench, though. I found an old pair of underwear I didn't care about anymore and put the dirty end of the wrench on the butt part so that my bed wouldn't end up with the filth on my sheets. Then I went back to bed to wait for Fiskar's return.

"Thanks," I said aloud.

Sleeping was impossible. I had to find a way to end it.

Chapter 6

My eyes were aching the next day. I lost it about third period and somehow fell asleep. Nobody bothered to wake me until the bell rang. My whole body hurt on my way to my next class. I felt like I had gone three rounds with Mike Tyson. Even when I sat down at my desk for English, I had random shooting pains in my legs and shoulders.

I laid my head down and closed my eyes, thinking that in the bright lights of the G building I would be safe. Fractured dreams claimed me immediately.

Mister Pewter was my teacher, and while he may have tolerated my spaced-out affect the last two weeks, apparently me falling asleep was over the line. I woke up to him screaming at me. I was so tired that I can't remember any of the words, but I found myself outside his door with a detention slip when I was finally able to come to my senses.

I walked slowly to the office, unsure of what I should do, and also unsure of where else I should go.

I handed the detention slip to the secretary. She gave me a funny look.

"I don't know why I have this," was all I said before collapsing into one of the padded chairs in the lobby.

I must have drifted off again, listening to the ticking of the clock above me and the shuffling of paper by the office staff. When I woke, I had the principal, Doctor Keeler, kneeling by me.

"Is everything all right?" he said.

I had a sudden compulsion to tell him everything, but I took a breath and remembered myself.

"Yeah, I just fell asleep in class, I guess."

"Did anything change about your medication?"

"Yeah, they upped it," I said truthfully.

The principal stood up and loomed over me, his hands in his pockets. "Mister Pewter was informed of your five-oh-four plan. I'll straighten things out. Why don't you stay here for now? Anything I could get you?"

I shook my head.

"Alright, just relax, maybe do some homework until lunch."

I nodded.

I let my eyes close again, then I heard the heavy footsteps of Doctor Keeler returning.

"I just got off the phone with your psychiatrist. He said that the sedative effects of your medication should only last a few weeks, so if you feel tired, I'm going to make an executive decision that you can come here or the nurse's office to rest. Sound good?"

"Yeah," I said. "I didn't mean to upset anybody."

"We know, son. I'll tell your teachers what you need. You're late for lunch, by the way."

"Right," I said.

I sat there for a minute, and then realized that I could sleep at school. For at least two weeks, I could sleep at school and keep vigil against the demon during the night. After realizing this I felt slightly better. I stood up and picked up my bag. On the way out I ran into Anna.

"Hey, there you are," she said. Her eyes were wide like always.

"Yeah I got in trouble for sleeping in class."

"Good," she said. "I mean. Not. I mean… I thought something maybe happened, so I was coming to ask if you were here today."

I stepped outside and she followed me. "He came at me last night."

"What did you do?"

"I prayed. I don't know if that did anything. I hit him with a wrench, though. That sent him away."

"You can actually hit him?"

"Seemed like it. Of course, I could just be crazy."

"You need to come see Father James."

"I can't, I told you," I said. "My parents would never take me."

"I'll take you. Let's go now!"

I shook my head. "Can't. If I get caught playing hooky…"

Something came to my mind, tired but un-fogged.

"What is it?" Anna said.

"I can get away with it. How long does it take to get to him?"

"About thirty minutes by bus," Anna said.

I thought about it. It was already near one o'clock, which meant we would have less than three hours to get to him and back. My mother was picking me up every day now and taking me home – no more city bus rides.

"I can't today. Not enough time to get back. What about tomorrow morning?"

"Will you be okay?"

"Yeah, I'll stay up all night. I'm allowed to sleep during class now."

"Oh. Alright. I'll meet you at the bus stop, then. What time?"

"You're really just going to ditch class?"

"God won't hold it against me. My parents will forgive me."

"Alright. Nine, then."

*

That day, my mom picked me up from school.

She took me to the funeral home. I guess she assumed the Thorazine was working. The office looked clean and immaculate as always, but at the same time, I was always aware of a presence in addition to the people working there, like a person breathing in the next room over. I could hear it in the silence between conversations on the phone or between my mom and some of the other staff. Maybe it was just my knowledge that he was there somewhere. It was like eyes on the back of my head; I knew he was watching me, listening to me.

I got none of my homework done, but my mom didn't seem to notice. She drove me home. That night I once again faked taking my pills. I knew the sleep they induced put me in a weakened state.

My mother turned my light off, and I immediately felt the fear return. When she had gone down the hall, I retrieved the wrench from under my bed. I listened to her for a while through the door as she moved around the house. Doors opened. She talked to someone on the phone, then the lights went out.

I stayed awake, staring into the dark and listening to every sound in the night, wondering if I would hear footsteps or nothing at all when he came to get me. Night sounds are terrible when you are really listening to them. People outside sound like whispers in your ear. Creaks sound like steps. Car doors closing sound like bodies falling.

It occurred to me that the creature hated the light, so when I felt it was safe, I turned my overhead light on. I played my Gameboy. I read the few comics that had escaped my mother's theft. I read a few pages at a time of a bunch of books. I even did my homework.

I also prayed. I still had no idea how to do it, but I figured an all-knowing being wouldn't hold the wrong words against me. I made a cross out of a pair of drumsticks leftover from when I did band, tying them together with some spare wires from an old solar system model.

I made it through most of the night, and Fiskar never showed up. The light, I supposed, was some kind of bane for him. Around five AM, I grew curious. I crept to my door and listened. I heard nothing.

I stuffed my makeshift cross in my waistband and grabbed my wrench. I opened the door and half-expected to see the pale drawn bones of Danny Fiskar recoiling from the light. I saw nothing but an empty hall.

But I heard something.

It was a thud in the living room: loud and with the accompanying crash of something being knocked over. I thought I heard a door shut. I immediately closed my door and retreated to my bed, holding the huge pipe wrench in one hand and the cross out in the other. I cried.

I stayed that way until the roar of an engine starting up outside snapped me back to reality. I got back into bed as I heard my mom come down the hall to get me.

*

When I considered that I could sleep in the office instead of at home, I hadn't thought ahead to playing hooky the next day. I also didn't realize that, while my teachers might not question my absence, the office surely would.

I had made up my mind, though, and would suffer the consequences if I needed to.

I went to first period, then slumped my head down to sleep. After a few minutes of tortured dreaming, somebody poked me. There was some laughter, so I guess the other kids were having a go at me for fun. I got up and told the teacher I'd like to go to the office and to please tell my second-period teacher where I was.

She let me go, but instead of heading to the main office I walked off-campus. That's a really strange feeling for a kid, by the way. It's a sudden realization that the walls that keep you in school are only in your mind. There was nobody even watching, and anyone who was clearly didn't care that I walked away.

I got to the bus stop half a block away and found Anna waiting for me, wearing a dress that actually fit her. It made her look almost like an adult, at least if you looked at her body.

"You know which ones to take?" I said, sitting next to her.

She nodded.

After a long, awkward silence, I said, "Your dress looks nice."

"Thanks. It's one I usually wear on Sunday."

"Should I have dressed differently?" I said, looking at my jeans and t-shirt.

"No, it doesn't matter, I… I don't know why I put it on. I shouldn't have. If we go back to school… ugh!"

"What?"

"You're not a girl, you wouldn't understand."

"I wouldn't?"

"No way. It's totally different for guys. You don't know what it's like to get stared at."

I actually laughed. "Yeah, I do. Everyone stares at me."

She looked at me, looking slightly sad. "That's different."

"It is?"

"Totally."

I didn't know what else to say, but the bus arrived quickly, and I followed her on. I used part of my lunch money for fare and we left the school behind. One change later and we were standing in front of a large, ornate church. It looked like something out of time, like it was made hundreds of years before any of the buildings around it, though I knew logically it couldn't be much older than any of them. It told me something important – that the church stood on its own against anything and everything. It defied all modernity as it defied anything else that would try to corrupt it.

We found father James, an old bald priest, inside an office working on something at his desk, his door open.

"Anna?" he said, seeing her standing at the door. "You can come in, but shouldn't you be at school?"

Anna bowed her head as she shuffled in, me close behind her.

"You brought a friend?"

"He needs you," Anna said. "Or, he needs God."

James smiled at me. "We all need God."

"I mean…" Anna growled in frustration. She looked at me.

"I have… a demon, I guess," I said.

James gave me a serious look. "You have a demon?"

I didn't know how to answer. "Yeah. Anna said you can help me."

"Sit down." I complied, sitting in the wood chairs by his desk. "Who told you I could exorcise demons?" He said, looking at Anna.

"My grandmother," she said.

"It's a serious thing. Nothing to be taken lightly."

"So, you've done it? You've fought demons?" I said.

He shook his head. "It's not like that. *I* have no power. *I* am powerless before the hosts of hell. It is Christ that has worked against the devil. It is Christ that has the power. Christ has worked through me. I am just a man of small, flawed faith."

I couldn't begin to understand.

"Does this demon have a name?" he went on.

"Danny Fiskar, I think," I said. "I don't really know though. That's just who we thought it was."

Father James frowned and looked at his fingers. "What does this demon make you do?"

I shook my head. "He doesn't make me do anything. He's trying to get me."

"You aren't possessed?"

"I… I don't think so, but… Everyone thinks I'm crazy."

"Tell me everything."

I did. I spared no detail, and as I talked, as I described the moments of sheer terror, Anna curled up in her chair, wrapping her arms around her knees and pulling her skirt down to her ankles.

"Can you help me?" I said when I was finished.

Father James gave me a sad look. "*I* cannot help you. Remember, it is Christ who helps you. I can pray for you. I can ask the saints to pray for you. If God chooses to work through me that is a blessing, but it is not my power."

I remember him sighing and looking out one of the windows for a long time.

"It is possible you are afflicted by a demon," he said, not looking at me. "Demons can cause madness. So that could be what you are experiencing. But we also know that there are dysfunctions of the body which are not demons."

I shook my head. "I'm not possessed. Danny Fiskar is out there, waiting for me."

Father James shook his head. "Danny Fiskar was just a boy, not a monster. I knew him, and it saddens me that this urban legend about him continues."

"Danny is real?"

"He was the son of the owners of the funeral home. He died with his mother and father in a very tragic accident."

"What happened?"

"If you must know, they drowned in a boating accident. They were members of this parish, once."

"So what is he? Who is he?"

Father James didn't answer immediately. Instead, he stood up and walked over to me.

"Are you confirmed?" he said.

"I don't know what that means."

"I'll take that as a 'no.'"

He laid his hands on me and prayed. He said a lot in that prayer. He evoked a bunch of saints whose names meant nothing to me at the time. I could feel something in that moment though – a presence of comfort. He prayed for protection, and he prayed for healing. He prayed that any demons I had would be cast out. He blessed me and prayed for my eternal soul.

When he was done, I wondered – *is Danny the demon, or is the demon inside me?*

Anna was crying.

She was quiet on the way back and was quiet when we reached the school again. It was eerie walking back onto campus during class. The spaces between the buildings were deserted, but like before, nobody seemed to watch or to care who we were or where we had been.

"Thanks," I said when we reached the point where we needed to part.

"I was all wrong," she said.

"No, you were right, but I think we were expecting the wrong thing. We were expecting a priest to save us. Save me, I mean, but Father James is right. It's God that has the power. I think I've been going about this wrong."

"How so?"

"I have to kill him. Kill Danny, or whatever it is. Maybe I ask God to help me do that, yeah?"

"You can't kill a demon."

"He has a body. That means I can hurt him. I just need a way to do it."

"A gun?"

"My mom doesn't believe in them. My dad doesn't have one."

"What are you going to do?" she said.

"I'll think of something."

*

The rest of the day passed without incident. If the office knew I had skipped half the day, they never brought me in for it.

I was surprised to see my dad's car pull up in front of the school after the bell.

"What are you doing here?" I said as I got in.

"Your mom has something going on. You're staying with me tonight. That alright?"

"Yeah," I said. "That's perfect."

He turned on the stereo to some classic rock station and headed toward the city. On the way there, I turned down the music and said, "Why didn't you ever take me to church?"

"Well, we didn't really believe in it."

"You don't believe in God?"

"I think your mom doesn't believe in God."

"But you do?"

My dad shrugged and smiled. "I believe there is probably *a* god. But I don't believe the God of the Bible is really a thing, just like how Zeus isn't really a thing. Or at least, the way churches… they have the wrong ideas, I think."

"So, mom is an atheist?"

"Agnostic, maybe. We didn't really talk about it. We had both moved past church when we met."

"You used to go to church?"

"When I was a kid, yeah. Not as much as other families. But you grow up and see the world a little bit, expand your perspective, and it's not so convincing as an absolute truth."

The image of those dark eyes came back to me. "What made you stop believing?"

"I didn't stop *believing,* I just came to the conclusion that the church didn't have a monopoly on truth. I mean, who am I to say a guy in India isn't following a true god?"

"So, what did you decide was the truth?"

"Nothing, that's the point."

"I don't get it, I guess."

My dad sighed and turned off the radio totally. "I have a lot of problems with organized religion. Almost everything bad that human beings have done has been done in the name of God. If God is real, then he has to be against that sort of thing. The god that the church teaches you about…" He grumbled and shook his head. "Let's just say I can't believe in a god like that, okay?"

"What do you mean?" I said. "What's so bad about the god in the bible?"

"He's petty and vengeful. He orders his followers to kill whole tribes. He destroys whole cities because a few of them are bad. And that's nothing compared to what was justified by Christians in the middle ages. Have you had to study the crusades yet?"

"Yeah, I think," I said. "But…" I gave up.

"I didn't want you to grow up with a bunch of nonsense about what was the true religion. I wanted you to make your own decisions."

"What if I decided that the church was right? The Christian church, I mean."

"Which one?" he said. "Even Christians can't decide who is right."

I didn't quite know how to respond. "What if I picked one that was right. That I thought was right."

My dad was silent for a minute while we pulled into his building's parking garage.

"I don't believe you would ever decide that," he said at last. "You're too smart for that."

A few minutes later I was back in the comforting cocoon of my father's small apartment. It was still bright afternoon, and the sun streamed into the warm living room. We made sandwiches for ourselves and my dad put on a baseball game.

As we watched, I asked, "Why did mom let me stay here tonight?"

"I'm not sure. If I was to guess, it was something to do with her boyfriend."

"Mom has a boyfriend?"

"You didn't know?"

"I think she went on a date awhile back."

My dad shrugged at me. "It's up to her to introduce you, so don't tell her I told you. Might be that you're not supposed to know."

"How did *you* know?"

"He answered the phone one time at the house. Your mom and I are divorced. It should be an expected thing to see other people."

"Do you have a girlfriend?"

My dad actually laughed at me. "No, but I'd tell you if I did. You deserve to know. Most I've had is a drink or two with a woman."

I had a lot to ponder that night as I went to bed. Mostly, my mind was focused on how I would kill Danny Fiskar. I found the rosary in my room and put it around my neck as I focused my thoughts. Eventually, I slept. My dreams were sparse but easy on me.

Chapter 7

"Do you still believe me?" I said to Anna when I caught her in the hall the next day.

She nodded silently.

"Even though Father James thinks I'm insane?"

"He doesn't think that. He just doesn't understand. He's thinking it's a demon trying to possess you, not… a real, living demon."

"I need you to help me."

"How?"

"I need oak and silver."

"What? Why?"

"It's what kills monsters."

"This isn't a movie, Billy."

"I know, but movies are based on real things. This stuff goes way back. All the best writers will tell you it's what folks used to do. If the monster is real, then at least some of the tales would have to be real, too. I even read that they used to put oak stakes into corpses when they buried them, just in case."

She looked at me incredulously. "What kind of oak do you need, just a board?"

"Something I can make a spear out of. Or a stake."

"What about one of those poles from the closet? The kind that you hang your clothes on."

I felt a surge of hope. "You're right! I can make a spear out of that. What about silver? Is there anything silver you could give me? I can pay you."

"I have a silver crucifix my grandmother gave me."

"I don't think I can use that as a weapon. What about silverware?"

"Oh, yeah, that would be a lot easier. Wait, you have silverware, don't you?"

I shook my head. "My mom took away and hid every single knife in the house, even the butter knives, because she was afraid I would hurt myself with them."

"I could probably steal a butter knife, but..."

"I know, stealing is wrong. Maybe you could ask to have one. Then you don't have to steal it."

"Unless my mom says no. What then?"

"Well... *then* you steal it."

She chuckled a little bit. It was good to see her smile.

*

That afternoon I was a little sad to see my mom pick me up rather than my dad. She was quiet as she took me to the funeral home. I could tell something was bothering her, but I was afraid to ask. She had a tendency to yell at me when she was mad at other people.

I got to work on my homework right away when we arrived, doing my best to focus my thoughts on math, rather than the monster that lurked in the dark places of the funeral home. Eventually, the battle was lost, so instead, I tried to focus my mind on my plan to kill the creature. Its home was probably in the morgue. That's where it always was at or near. It was the loneliest place, and the darkest place – the right place for a monster. So how would I flush it out? How would I force it to face me?

I realized that I need not goad it out, merely put myself in a position that it would come to me, then I could spring a trap.

I began to make a few notes in the blank end pages of my math book but paused when I couldn't help but overhear my mother on the phone.

"I'd like to speak to Frank. Last night, yes."

At first, I thought she was talking to her boyfriend.

"Yes, detective? I have something unusual to report."

My curiosity was piqued. I glanced over to see my mother at her desk, looking out a window. I slipped away from her office and went through the main rooms to where another phone was. Janine, the secretary, was apparently absent that day. A couple of people were working down the hall, setting up chairs, but didn't seem to care what I was doing. I sat down at the secretary's desk, picked up her phone and turned on line one, trying very hard to keep totally silent.

"I'm sorry, are you serious?" said a male voice on the other side of the line. It presumed it was Frank.

"I'm dead serious," my mom said.

"Is that a joke?"

I heard my mom growl in frustration. "No. I confirmed it last night. The cadaver was definitely re-stitched. I know my own handiwork."

"Why aren't you talking to Doctor Horace, the forensic pathologist? I thought you knew each other."

"We do, but detective, he isn't a cop. This is a serious crime, and I don't know the how or the why. This deserves a serious investigation."

"You're sure about this?"

"Yes."

"Why didn't you call last night, when you confirmed it?"

"Because I thought I had to be crazy. This is simply too strange to be true."

"Alright, I'll get on it right away.

"And detective, we are going to need a judge's order to perform a second autopsy on a few of these bodies."

"A few?"

"Yes, I confirmed the re-stitching on another cadaver this morning."

"Either myself or another detective will be over right away to take a statement and open a report. Don't leave, alright?"

"Yes, of course."

I waited for the phone to hang up on both sides before putting down the receiver and slipping back to where I was sitting before. I had scarcely opened my math book back up when my mom came over.

"Listen, Billy, I need you to stay calm."

"I'm calm," I said.

"Some police are coming over right now. You are *not* in trouble. They need to investigate something else."

"You think dad should come and get me?" I said.

"I'll try calling him."

My mom called my father but couldn't get ahold of him. He wasn't at home or at his office, so I stayed put. About an hour later two detectives showed up. One of them was Sal, the big, imposing man I had met when I got caught breaking in. He actually smiled at me when he came in.

"Staying out of trouble?"

"Yeah. Trying," I said.

"Good."

It was really easy to eavesdrop what they were saying initially. I sat quietly in a chair outside my mom's office.

"So, where do we begin?" Sal said. "When did you notice the bodies had been tampered with?"

"Yesterday, during embalming preparation. I happened to notice that the body was stitched up with black wire. I ran out of blue wire two days ago."

"The autopsy was performed here?" said the other man, who I presumed to be Frank.

"Yes. Private autopsy. It was a full pathological survey, which means the chest cavity was opened."

"Did you stitch it back up?"

"Doctor Horace, the medical examiner, performed the autopsy, but yes, I stitched most of the body up as part of embalming preparation."

"You are sure it was with blue wire? You sure you haven't forgotten which day you switched colors?"

"I'm sure, but even if I wasn't, and I was definitely second-guessing myself, as this is extremely strange, I know that I didn't sew him up."

"You know?"

"Yes. The color got my attention, but when I came back last night to confirm what was bothering me, I saw definite signs that I had *not* stitched it up. Somebody else went over the old stitches, almost duplicating what I did. A dead body doesn't have supple skin, you see. There would be indentations left from the initial resealing of the body. However, the tie-off for the stitches was affirmatively not mine. It was backward from what I do.

"Can I take a look?" Sal said. "Just a quick one, for the report.

"You'll have to take some precautions."

"I'm used to it."

"Alright, but we'll need an order from a judge to alter the body now."

"Let me look first," Sal said. "The truth is, there's no real procedure for this. The body hasn't been interred yet, so legally we're in some weird territory."

"Peter'll know the case law to get it done," Frank said. "I'm sure we're going to have to do a second autopsy, though. No way around it."

"On two bodies, yeah?" Sal said.

"Right," my mom said.

I slipped away before they could finish so I wouldn't get caught. I didn't know what they said after that or what they said when they saw the body. Sal stopped and sat down by me on his way out. He still had a mask dangling from one ear.

"Sorry, Miss Hunter, but I have to," he said. He pulled out a small pocket notebook and a pen.

"I understand," my mother said.

"Billy Laseter. Where were you last night?"

"At my father's house."

"All night? Did you go anywhere with him?"

"Yes, all night. Didn't go out."

"Two nights ago?" He jotted something down.

"At my mom's house. All night."

Sal looked at my mom. "You or his father picked him up every day?"

"Yes," my mom said.

Sal looked at me. "You were in class all day, correct?"

I felt sweat gather at my temples. "Um… sort of?"

Sal gave me an odd look. "Something you want to tell me?"

"No," I said. I thought quickly of a way to avoid a lie. "Just… I can leave class and go to the office if I'm too tired. So, I didn't go to all my classes."

Sal smiled at me. "Alright. Sorry, Billy. I have to at least check out recent suspects."

"I get it. So, what happened?"

Sal smiled at me. "You can ask your mom, and maybe she'll tell you when we're gone, but I don't want it spread around, alright? Let's keep it quiet."

"Alright."

*

I stayed awake all night, crafting a weapon.

I used the pole from my closet. It was big and sturdy, and it was apparently made of oak. I snuck down to the garage and swiped some tools – a chisel (that my mom figured wasn't really useable as a weapon) and a few bastard files.

I stuffed a t-shirt at the bottom of my door in case my mom saw the light, and I got to work on the pole, which was about six feet long. I used the chisel to carve out a point, and filed it all the way around so it was relatively smooth. I had the idea to test it, so I set up some old clothes on an old pillow. I thrust it into the pillow with what I thought was about eighty percent of my strength and was disappointed to see that it barely affected my old clothes. All it made was a small hole, less than the size of a penny.

I decided that the point was too blunt and the ramp to it was too shallow. I got the chisel out and made the whole cut longer, increasing the depth of the angle up to the tip, which became absolutely vicious with the help of the file. When I tested this spear (which looked much more like a spear now) it easily slid deep into the pillow through the old clothes.

What I now had was effectively a wooden stake with a six-foot reach. I wished there was some way I could make one with a silver spearhead, but the know-how of such a thing was beyond me. I figured if I could get a silver butter knife from Anna, I could file it into something proper for killing.

I saw the sun rising and didn't feel tired at all. I felt instead a restless energy.

*

Anna slipped me a silver butter knife at lunch.

"Did you have to steal it?" I said.

"No, she gave it to me. Didn't even ask why."

"Thank you."

"What do you plan to do with it?"

"I'm going to sharpen it up. Make it into something that could kill Fiskar."

Anna looked distressed. "You're going to kill him?"

"He's flesh and blood. I've drawn blood before, I think. I can kill him."

"Do you know if silver will work on him?"

"Nope, but I figure why not?"

She sat down next to me. "You planned this out?"

"Sort of. I haven't figured out how I'm going to get there. He's at the funeral home, but..." I didn't know what I should say to Anna, so I shrugged.

"You don't have a car," she said. "John could drive you. I can get him to help."

"That, too, but there's more. The police are investigating the home – investigating *him*, I think."

"Then you don't have to kill him!"

"No, they aren't going to find him. They don't believe... they won't even consider that it's a possibility, so they'll never figure it out. I have to be the one-"

"What exactly are they looking for, then?" Anna said, interrupting me.

I was hesitant to tell her, but looking at her staring at me behind those glasses, I felt like she would figure it out anyway. "Someone's been opening up the dead and stitching them back together."

"What?" she said.

"Yeah, it's weird. My mom only just noticed because she changed the color of the wire she was using to stitch them up."

"Your mom stitches them up?" She gave me an odd look, like I really was crazy.

"She's a mortician," I said. "She sometimes gets bodies from the medical examiner or helps the medical examiner do private autopsies. We have a special room for it at the home. They cut open the body and look at the organs, trying to figure out how the person died, then they stitch him back up. I guess she found something wrong with some of the bodies that were opened. Who knows how long it's been going on, but it has to be Fiskar."

"The way you and Mikey describe him, he's like a ghost or demon, not the kind of thing to be careful with corpses."

I shrugged. "Either way, the police are paying attention to the place, trying to figure out what's going on. I'm going to need to get in, too, but that shouldn't be too hard. I got that part figured out."

"I don't think you should try it."

"Thanks, but I have to do this. You'll know too, whether I'm seeing something real or I'm just insane."

*

My mom picked me up from school and took me to the funeral home. On the way, I dared to ask her a few things.

"So what's up with the police?"

"Nothing you need to concern yourself with, Billy."

"Sal said you could tell me."

"No, he said he couldn't stop me from telling you. Big difference."

"What happened? Was there something else done to a body, like before? A bite taken out?"

She glanced angrily at me. "That wasn't a bite before, that was someone trying to tear up a body for their own amusement." She practically growled at herself. "Thousands I spent on that alarm system, and it's worthless!"

"Sorry, mom."

"I just paid for more sensors, too."

"So, it *was* something to do with the morgue."

"Don't worry about it, Billy. It's nothing to get yourself worked up over. Just relax, okay?"

*

We went to the home because Sal and Frank had to come by.

When we got to the door, my mother realized she didn't have her door key.

"I swear I put it on there this morning," she said. "I must have popped it off on accident. I'm always doing things like this."

She didn't know that I had been the one to take it off. It sat in my pocket, where it would remain until I placed it strategically in the house for my mom to find.

I watched as she retrieved her secret key, from a different, new false rock, and opened the door. I also watched carefully as she put in her security code. She was upset and in a rush, talking to herself under her breath, and not covering her hands. I quickly memorized the sequence.

Sal and Frank arrived a few minutes later. They brought the medical examiner with them, who was already wearing scrubs. I watched and listened carefully from the desk.

"This is unprecedented," the medical examiner, Doctor Horace, said. "We already talked to the D.A. and the judge. It's still alright we use the facilities here?"

"Yes," my mother said.

They all went down to the morgue and adjoining rooms carrying a stack of smocks, leaving me by myself in the office.

I pushed back against my fear of the cold room in the basement and went down the stairs after they entered. I slid up to the door and listened carefully. I could barely hear them. I dared to open the door a crack and saw the lights in the examination room. As silently as I could manage, I went through the doors and slid up to the other metal door, where their voices became much easier to understand.

"There we go, now let's take a look inside. He's been here a while, eh?" It was the voice of the doctor.

"We had to postpone the funeral due to immediate lack of funds, then this," my mother said.

They chattered quietly for a few moments, but it was too hard to make out the words until I heard the medical examiner say loudly, "What the hell am I looking at?"

"It's half-eaten," Sal said.

"Nonsense," the medical examiner said.

"Ain't decomposition. Look at how clean the separation is. This heart was eaten."

The medical examiner was silent for a long time. "You're right, Sal. These are the marks of hands and tools."

"No, sir. I take it you don't spend much time out of the city. This is what a deer carcass looks like when a coyote has been at it."

"My God."

"The fingerprints were strange as well. Too long," Frank said. "The pads were too long, but the prints weren't smeared. They were sharp."

"Yeah?" Sal said.

There was silence.

"Perhaps your suspect has acromegaly, then," the medical examiner said.

"Acro-what?"

"Acromegaly," the medical examiner repeated. "An excess of growth hormone in an adult. It causes enlarged hands and feet, along with some other things, like a bigger jaw. It's fairly rare."

"Growth hormone, eh?" Sal said. "So we've got a giant cannibal on the loose?"

"Not usually giant. It's usually a disease of middle-age."

"Well, that might make things easier once we find the guy."

"How is he getting in, is my question," my mom said.

"We're working on that," Frank said. "I might suggest a new security company."

"I already switched."

I crept away, back up to the lobby. They were definitely seeing the evidence of Danny Fiskar. I reasoned that if he ate, even dead bodies, he was flesh and blood. I could kill him. I felt hope growing.

Chapter 8

The next night, I stayed up filing the silver butter knife into something approximating a dagger.

The work was slow but the files were effective. I swiped one of those cheap knife sharpeners from the kitchen to put the final edge on both sides, and it was sharp enough to take the hair off of my arm.

It was right then, as I tested the knife, that the bedroom door opened, then shut again, as if whatever was opening it was suddenly shunned by the bright light. I jumped up with my dagger and got ready to fight. I waited an agonizing few seconds, then decided that if I wanted the fight, now would be the time. I had the tools. I felt a surge of courage. I grabbed my flashlight and threw open the door. There was nothing there but the empty hallway.

Holding the flashlight in my left and the silver dagger in my right hand, I went down the hallway, stopping to survey the living room. Nothing was moving. My fear grew as I saw the shadows from the furniture moving like ghosts on the walls and windows. I moved cautiously around the couch, but there was nothing there. I got to the front door and found that it was locked.

The dagger felt slippery in my hand. I thought I heard something from my mother's room, the sound of her door shutting, and I was suddenly panicked about being caught out of my room. It didn't immediately cross my mind that Fiskar could be attacking my mother. As far as I was concerned, his terror was exclusively the domain of children.

I backed up slowly, then ran to my room. I shut the door quietly, then turned on the lights. This time, I didn't block up the bottom with a t-shirt. That beam of light might keep him away; I was stupid to hide it.

When morning came, I opened up my window and slid my spear down to the ground. The silver dagger I hid in the pages of my math book within my backpack.

*

I checked in at first-period then went to the office to sleep. I was antsy, but the safety of the fluorescent lights worked on me, and I managed to nod off for a good few hours.

A secretary woke me for lunch, and I stood up with energy, realizing that it was Friday again. I would get to stay at my father's apartment. Of course, it might be time to do what I know needed to be done. There was still a lot to figure out, though.

Anna caught me at lunch.

"You're looking better," she said.

"I feel better."

"Mikey wanted you to call him." She handed me a piece of paper with Mikey's number on it.

"Why?"

"He wants to go," she said.

"On what?"

"The monster-killing mission."

I shook my head. "I have to do this alone."

"Just call him."

"Alright, I will," I said.

Anna sat down beside me at the table and opened her lunch. It was the first time she had done that. We ate mostly in silence.

"It might be the last time we talk," I said after a while.

"I know," she said.

"If I survive, I might be shipped off for good. I'm probably not getting away. If I die, well… I'll be dead."

"I know," she said. "You should talk to father James again."

"I don't think I'll be able to."

She was quiet for a while.

"I like you," I said. It felt really awkward. It's probably something unavoidable about youth – it's terrifying to say how you really feel, so you just awkwardly half-ass the expression of your true feelings.

"I guess I like you too."

"Even though I'm crazy?"

"You're brave. I can like a brave man."

I chuckled. "A man? I'm a fool."

"That, too," she said, smiling at me.

We talked about nothing for a fleeting few minutes, then the bell rang for class.

*

My father's apartment was quiet, neutral, and unimposing as I stepped into it. As he and I spent the evening watching hockey, I realized that it was no longer a sanctuary as much as a home base. It was a place of temporary safety, but could not ever be a true sanctuary. It was, as I said, neutral. Eventually, the battle would come there, I was sure.

I called up Mikey later on.

"It's Billy. Anna told me to call you."

"Yeah. She told me you were going to kill him," Mikey said.

"I am."

"How?"

"I have ways."

"Dad listening?"

"Yeah," I said. "You?"

"No. John wants in."

"He needs to be there?"

"Yeah," Mikey said. "He can drive us."

"You want in, too?"

"I need to back him up. I'm scared though. You heard from Jeff?"

"He's in a foster home," I said. "I guess he'll be safe."

"Alright, just me and my bro. How and when?"

"What choices?" I said, hoping he got the hint. My dad was watching me lightly, his focus mostly on the hockey game.

"Uh… Saturday?" Mikey said.

"Yes."

"Night?"

"Yup."

"How about we get you at midnight?"

"Next hour sounds good. Yeah, my dad lives downtown. It's a cool place. Great view. We're on the corner of Eighth and Grand. It's kind of a long way from my mom, but I kind of like that." I looked over at my dad and he didn't seem concerned. "Yeah no food but Dunkin Donuts, but that's alright by me."

"Alright, we'll pick you up at one AM at the Dunkin Donuts."

"Yeah, that's right. Homework is the questions from the end of chapter 12. See you later. Hope you feel better. Sucks throwing up."

I hung up.

"Who was that?" my dad asked.

"A friend from school. His cousin asked me to call him and give him the homework. He had the stomach flu or something."

"He knows your cousin Jeff?"

"Yeah. Or his brother knows him."

"I worry about that kid."

"Me too, but he'll be alright, dad."

*

Midnight Saturday came. I had slept most of the afternoon, and I felt ready. I tucked my silver dagger into a scabbard I had made out of duct tape, then tied it to my belt. I put on a light, but long, coat and steadied myself before stepping out of my room.

It was silent in the main room. I walked to the little kitchen and looked at the clean, simple living room. The blinds were half-open, letting in the infinite lights of the city. I took a deep breath and let myself gaze at it one last time. It was calm. *Cozy*. But not totally safe, yet. I could feel my heart rate slow in the quiet dark. Then I stepped to the door and silently slipped out into the hall.

About fifteen minutes later, I was at the 24-hour Dunkin Donuts. I was early, so I ordered half a dozen donuts, including a cinnamon roll for myself, and even bought a cup of coffee. It tasted like ash, but I drank it anyway. It was my first cup of coffee, and I thought somehow I shouldn't go to the grave without at least tasting what the city, and my dad, in particular, seemed to run on.

Nobody at the shop seemed to care that a kid was there in the dead of night eating donuts.

A few minutes passed, and I saw John's beat-up Chevy pull up into the parking lot. I gathered up my things and stepped out.

I paused as I saw that an extra person was in the car. As I bent down on the rear passenger side, I saw a pair of glasses and brown eyes. I opened the door and got in.

"What are you doing here, Anna?" I said.

"I'm coming, too."

"Danny doesn't know you," I said.

"She threatened to tell," Mikey said. "We had to let her come."

"I had to see it through, too," she said. My eyes widened as she drew a long silver knife from her coat, much like mine but made from some larger piece of silverware.

"Did you all bring weapons?"

"Yeah," Mikey said. "I got my knife. John brought his gun."

"If silver don't work, lead sure as shit won't, but it's better than nothing," John said.

I sighed and said, "Alright. Let's head by my mom's on the way, okay? I left a spear in the bushes."

"A spear? Do we actually need that?" John said. He pulled out slowly and started down the road toward the freeway.

"It's oak, which is good against ghouls," I said. "And spears are long. I don't want to knife this thing to death while he tears my throat out."

"Good enough," John said. "It's not too far out of the way."

"Oh yeah, I got donuts for us," I said. "Including you, Anna. I originally bought two for each of us, but…" I shrugged.

"Thanks," John said. "You got any chocolate? I wanna eat a chocolate donut."

"Yeah."

We ate all the donuts on the way. I ate a pink-frosted cake, and I don't think I'll taste one that good again. The last one was a cinnamon roll that I split with Anna.

We watched the streetlights pass by, orange and ominous, while we made our plans to kill the monster. I reached over on impulse and grabbed Anna's hand. Silently, she squeezed it back. It was a tender moment, but was unfortunately muted by the dread that was to come.

John stopped by my mom's house, parking with his lights off behind a ford mustang – the same one that had shocked me to my senses another night. I got out and slowly opened the gate. From the bushes outside my room, I retrieved the spear. It didn't fit in the car, so we used a hole going from the trunk to the cab – presumably for skis – to fit the whole thing inside.

From there we headed for the funeral home.

There was virtually no traffic in the suburbs. When another car would pull up or turn in front of us, or appear from a side street, we would all tense up.

We reached the funeral home around two AM. The moon was up, and we could see the entire cemetery beyond the building in clear, white light. I was somewhat surprised that there were no police. Despite the evidence, they couldn't really believe in what was happening under the roof of that house of the dead, and so they weren't really watching.

John parked on the side of the building. We got out extra-quietly, even going so far as to slowly push the car doors closed so they wouldn't make a sound. We retrieved our weapons. John had brought a pistol of some sort. It was a .22 of a nameless make, about as long as my hand, that he had managed to get for about a hundred dollars. He racked the small slide and held the gun in front of him as we moved toward the front door.

I retrieved the new key from the new hiding spot and opened the door. I used my Maglite to find the security panel and punched in the code my mom had used earlier in the week. It worked, and the system turned off, the display reading a clear "SAFE" in amber letters.

We moved out of the foyer and toward the office and the stairs to the morgue. We turned on no lights on our way.

"I think we should stay together," Mikey said.

"Stick to the plan," John said. "We'll be fine."

"I won't." Mikey's voice was quavering, but he followed through. When we got to the office space, we split up.

John slunk off to the alcove that hid the elevator. Mikey moved past him to one of the hall entrances. Anna went to the other hall entrance, holding her silver knife in front of her. There would be no exit for the thing at the bottom of the stairs. I quickly went into my mom's desk and retrieved the key to the morgue. Even with all the weirdness, she still couldn't believe – she still kept the key casually in a desk drawer.

I stepped to the stairwell and leaned my spear against the wall. There wouldn't be room to use it, but I wanted it at the ready when I came back up the stairs, hopefully following the demon, or being chased by him.

I proceeded down the stairs slowly and as silently as I could. I held my dagger in my right hand, my flashlight (which was off), in the other. The only light was the soft glow of the elevator button at the bottom of the stairs.

I reached the landing and stepped toward the morgue door. I was surprised to find it unlocked. Very slowly, as smoothly and as quietly as I could, I pushed the door open. I reached in and hit the switch for the lights.

They didn't turn on.

Panic flooded me. I fumbled my flashlight but was able to click it on and swing the beam through the cold room. One of the lockers was open. A body was open on a rolling table, the skin peeled back.

The room, however, was empty.

"He's behind us!" I screamed, running up the stairs with my flashlight.

"The lights don't work," I heard John yell back. I heard Anna scream.

I reached the top and dropped my dagger. I picked up my spear and readied myself.

"I saw him!" Anna said from her corner. "He's in the hall. Help!"

I ran for her voice, knocking over a chair in the process. I reached her side and shined my light down the hallway. It was empty.

I crept forward, holding my Maglite on the side of my spear to light up the hall. I realized John and Mikey had joined Anna beside me. We worked our way toward one of the viewing rooms at the end of the hallway. The double doors were shut. I stepped forward and pushed on them with the tip of my spear. They were unlocked and swung inward.

We kicked them open and stepped in. Once again, the lights didn't work. I surveyed the room and saw nothing but chairs and old decorations from a recent funeral.

"He must be in the other room," I said. I turned and stepped out, checking the hallway again. "Damnit, he could have gotten past us, somehow. Somebody stay near this door."

John complied. He stood a few feet away from the room and pointed his pistol at the door. A pale patch of moonlight from a small nearby window illuminated the place where the doors met.

I went to the next big room. There were only two on this side of the building. I kicked in the door and once again found an empty room – nothing but chairs and tables. I ducked down to shine my light under the tables.

That's when I heard the gunshot. Even though it was a .22, it was deafening.

I stumbled as I tried to turn around with the spear. John was screaming. Anna was screaming too.

I kicked the doors open to see John splayed on the floor, a singular figure standing over him, white and naked, with dark liquid streaming down its mishappen chest. John was hurt, and was rolling on the ground. I saw him point his pistol up, but nothing happened – the cheap gun had failed on the second shot. He tried to rack the slide, but couldn't seem to get it to work before the monster bent over and struck him with his long, too-large hands.

Anna screamed again, and the white creature turned to look at her. His eyes were horribly dark, but glowed in the center like those of a cat. He was naked, and in the ambient light cast by my flashlight, which I had dropped on the ground, we could see every dark spot on his withered body. He had a huge chin and jaw, which dropped open in a smile as dark as his eyes.

Mikey screamed wordlessly and charged. Danny Fiskar – if that was who it was – hit him in the face and tried to grapple him to the ground while Mikey slashed with his knife.

Anna threw her knife. It hit the creature and he cried out. The blade had struck him squarely and there was a dark mark on his shoulder. He lumbered toward Anna, too-tall and horridly proportioned. She screamed and fell to the ground.

Now it was my turn. With a surge of conviction, I stepped forward and stabbed at him. He slithered around the first strike like a snake, but I drew back and struck again, this time hitting his ribs hard enough that I felt through the solid oak the snap of a bone. The spear was torn out of my hands as he went careening down the hallway, toward the morgue. The wooden weapon fell from him a few yards into his run.

I ran for John and pulled him to his feet awkwardly. He was bleeding from his mouth and nose, and probably more places I would have noticed better in the light. He fell back down immediately, but I saw that Anna was right beside me, with Mikey right behind her. He was bleeding, too. I stepped over and picked up my flashlight. The hallway was once again empty.

I picked up my spear on the way down toward the lobby.

"We almost had him," Mikey said.

"He's real," I said aloud.

"God help us," Anna said. We reached the lobby to find it deserted. I scanned everywhere with my flashlight, but there was no monster. I went between the desks and saw no Danny Fiskar.

"He's got to be back in the morgue," I said. Nobody seemed willing to argue with me, so I went back down the stairs, this time with my spear firmly in front of me. I reached the door and found it locked.

Locked! How was it possible?

I fumbled in my pocket for the key. When I found it and turned the lock I saw that Anna and Mikey had moved down right beside me.

I opened the door and quickly scanned the morgue. There was no creature. I went more slowly with the light a second time. Still, no monster to be found.

"Where the hell is he?" Mikey said.

"He's got to be behind us again," I said.

"John!" Anna said.

We raced back up the stairs and through the office. We found John stumbling down the hallway with his pistol.

"Let's get the hell out of here!" he said through blood in his mouth. "Before that bastard comes back."

Just as he said it, we heard a crash from somewhere.

"Agreed," I said. We all ran down the hall toward the front door. We didn't bother to reset the alarm. I turned and locked the door behind us, throwing the key away into the grass.

"I got him," John said as he tried to find his car keys in his pocket. "Gun is a piece of shit, but I fucking got him."

"So did Billy," Mikey said. "Practically impaled the thing. There was blood everywhere."

"And he ain't dead," John said. "God help us."

I threw my spear down on the ground as we fled.

We piled in John's car and raced away from the scene. He took a break closer to the city when we pulled into the parking lot of a Taco Bell. They had a few outdoor bathrooms where we could clean up a bit, but for a few minutes, none of us were willing to step out of the car.

"I wonder where he went," I said after a while.

"To hell, I hope," John said. "I hope he crawled off somewhere to die."

"If he did die, would anyone find the body?" Mikey said.

"Yeah," I said. "He was flesh and blood. If we killed him, my mom will find his corpse on Monday, or the cops will."

"So we got to wait till then to find out, huh?" John said.

"I don't think we killed him," I said. "He was flat out running with the spear in him."

"Sometimes people take a long time to die from injuries," Anna said. "It's not like in the movies."

"I'm sorry I got you all into this," I said. "Maybe we should have just burned the place down."

"Maybe, yeah," John said. "If he keeps on… If he isn't gone, I'll burn it down myself. I can't live thinking those eyes are watching me."

"Yeah," I said. "Better in jail than dead."

"Right," John said. "Fuck man, I can't believe I shot a guy."

*

I snuck back into my dad's apartment without much trouble. The moon was setting in the windows when I stepped in, and my father was still sleeping soundly in his bedroom.

I took off my shoes and coat, bundling them all up to hide any blood, then shoved them into my room. I went back and sat down on the couch, watching the moon above the city lights.

I prayed. It was silly, but genuine, and I thought God might listen.

I watched the moon set, repeating my plea.

Let it die.

I couldn't sleep, so I got up and took my pills. I stretched out in my bed and slept dreamlessly for the first time in as long as I could remember.

Chapter 9

My father woke me up around noon.

"Hey, you've been sleeping a long time."

"Sorry. I think it's the pills," I said. "The doctor said that the sleepiness would get better."

"Okay, that's good." He gave me a half-smile. "Hey, you get to stay here for the next couple of days. Sound good?"

"Yeah, but why?"

"Something happened with your mom's work. Nothing you need to worry about, but she'll be pretty busy the next few days, so I offered to keep you."

My skin prickled and I got goosebumps. "What happened?"

"Like I said, nothing you need to worry about."

"Did they catch the guy?" I didn't really care about showing my hand, I had a sudden and dire need for resolution.

"What guy?"

"The guy eating the dead."

My father frowned and gave me a strange, confused look. He shook his head, almost in disappointment.

"Did they?" I said again, sitting up.

"There was a break-in," my father said. "Some kind of fight. That's all I know."

"Can I call mom?" I said. "I'm just really worried."

"Sure," my dad said, smiling again. "Just don't expect to get much out of her."

I got up and forced down some breakfast in the form of some cereal. It was stale Trix, but I ate it anyway, hoping it would calm my nerves a bit. When I was done, I picked up the phone.

I called home first, but there was no answer. I called the office next, and after a long set of rings my mom picked up.

"Peaceful Gardens funeral home, this is Elizabeth, how may I help you?"

"It's me, mom," I said. "Dad said there was a break-in at the funeral home. What happened?"

"Don't worry about it, just enjoy the day with your father."

"I can't if I don't know what happened." I added hastily, "Are you alright?"

"I'm fine. We're going to have to stay closed for a few days."

"Why?"

"It would only stress you out to know."

"Did they catch the guy?" I said.

She was quiet for a few moments. "What guy?"

"The guy who was breaking in, who…" she would know I had been eavesdropping, but I had to find out, "The guy who cut open the dead body."

"I don't know how you heard about that. Doctor Grant was very specific about keeping that away from you. It would stress you, and I agree."

I growled. "Can you just tell me what happened, please?"

"We don't know if it's related, Billy. It looks like some people broke in and had a gang fight. There was blood on the floor along with weapons. The detectives are here now photographing everything."

"There was blood? Was anyone killed?"

"No, it looks like they all left."

My heart sank down into the pit of my stomach.

"I upgraded the security system and forgot to set the alarm, so it's partially my fault. This place has always been a target for hooligans for some reason."

"Alright, mom. Thanks for telling me the truth."

"You're welcome, Billy. Please don't dwell too much on it. The police will find out who did it, I'm sure."

*

School on Monday was a blur. I didn't see Anna. I asked a few people, and she apparently stayed home sick. I desperately wanted to talk to her, to hear that she was okay, or to hear her say that it wasn't all in my mind, that we really had fought Danny Fiskar, but it would have to wait a day.

I felt so scattered in my mind that I willfully took the antipsychotics to get some relief and actually sleep. Monday night was at my father's house again, and though it still felt peaceful there, I couldn't feel that I was totally safe. I had a feeling the monster would find me there too, somehow.

*

I went to school again, this time actually able to function in class, but I was horribly lost on the subject matter. I took what notes I could, but I began to feel that the life I was living was actually a dream. Nothing seemed to make sense. Everything was out of context and had no meaning.

At lunch I found Anna.

"Are you alright?" I said.

She leaned against me and hugged me slightly with one arm. "I'm okay. I've been shaken up. Pretending to be sick."

"I get it."

"Did we get him?"

"No," I said. "The police think some hoods broke in and got into a fight while drunk or something."

"So we won't get caught?"

"I didn't say that. The cops might figure it out. I don't know. If they do… I guess I'll be in trouble again. They'll say I had another psychic break."

"Not if I tell them Fiskar was real."

"If they don't find you and talk to you, don't go saying anything about it. Don't try to talk to them. They don't know you. They know me, John, and Mikey. If you get away and we all got in trouble, you should let it be."

*

Having to go back home to my mom's house for a few days put me on edge. I was nervous all day in school, and I was almost shaking when I got in the car with my mom. She didn't pick up on it. We drove off in silence.

"We got everything straightened out at the home, just so you know, Billy," she said, breaking the silence.

"Yeah?" I said. "Did they catch the guys? The guys that broke in, I mean."

"No, but I've had a few things done to the building to make it more secure, like some bars in some places. It will be much harder to get in."

I wondered silently if it would be as hard to get out.

I took my medication that night, resigning myself to my fate. Danny Fiskar knew where I slept, and he would want revenge. At least I could sleep through it this time.

When I dreamt, it was chaos, but Danny Fiskar was there at times, drawing his long, blood-caked fingers across my chest and back. In one dream, I was running on the track, only to have it change to a dark and cloudy day suddenly. I looked back to see the monster grabbing ahold of my legs, rooting me in place. He crawled up my legs, his fingers gripping my thighs, then the dream shifted.

I woke up more or less whole, but dazed. I faced another day at school and another return home.

I sat and talked with Anna at lunch about the dreams.

"He's not physically there, though?" she said.

"I don't know. I could just be out of it from the meds."

"Why are you taking them? You've avoided them before."

"Because I can't sleep otherwise. They calm me down. Make it less scary."

"You had a system worked out before, didn't you?"

"The adults would think something is up. The sedative effect of the drug is only supposed to last a little while."

"Well, I don't think you're crazy."

"Have you been having the same dreams?"

"No," she said. "Actually, I've been feeling very at peace about the monster. I haven't thought much about it. I'm much more worried about you. I think about you… a lot."

"I'm sorry I'm so out of it. I'll stop the medication again. I was just… I don't know what to do."

She held my hand under the table and squeezed it tightly for a few moments.

"Trust God. He protected you before. He can protect you now."

"I'll try."

*

I skipped my medication that night. I was wired. I kept hearing noises that upset me more than they should have – the sound of a car door closing, or an engine starting, the sound of wind outside the window. It started raining sometime after midnight, and I thought I could hear voices amid the patter, almost arguing at a high pitch. I saw lights outside my door – my mom wasn't sleeping either, at least for part of the night, and that put me on edge, too, filling my mind with possibilities.

Was Danny Fiskar tormenting my mother?

I went over the events of the previous week. Always the empty, dark eyes, encircled in crimson above a withered nose and a too-wide mouth came to me, almost real in my vision.

At one point I tried sleeping, but the dark was too frightening. I turned on the lights and tried sleeping again, but the brightness of them defeated me. I found the wrench under my bed and hid it in my blankets. I lamented losing the silver dagger.

Eventually, the sky began to lighten again.

I had made it through, but I knew I couldn't go on that way. I tortured my mind for ways to escape the haunting, but again, I felt powerless.

*

I didn't sleep during school the next day.

Anna wasn't there – pretending to be sick again, I presumed.

My mother picked me up from school and drove me to the funeral home. She was apparently needed for something, but I didn't inquire what.

I looked around the place as I went to the office area, and I saw no sign of the struggle that we had gone through with the monster: no blood, nothing broken. I sat myself down at a desk and tried to concentrate on my homework. It was nearly impossible. My eyes were so dry I couldn't do much more than tear up looking at the little words in my textbooks.

While I was trying to work through things, I noticed an odor. This wasn't the kind of odor I was used to at the funeral home, or even in the morgue. There, the primary smell was of chemicals – the things my mother used for embalming and making a corpse presentable for display at a funeral. Those weren't exactly pleasant smells, but what I detected sitting at the desk was far worse.

It was a sweet sort of smell, but it had horribly foul undertones – it smelled like overripe fruit and dead fish, along with something else.

Eventually, I couldn't ignore it. I got up and found my mother exiting the morgue.

"Do you smell that?" I said. "Something smells really bad."

"I smell it," she said. "It started the other day, but it's getting worse."

"What is it?"

My mom sighed and sat down in a nearby chair. She put her head in her hands.

"What?" I said again.

"It's the smell of a rotting body," she said. "The refrigeration has to be on the fritz, but everything checks out. I just took a thermometer to each separate locker and found them all operating at the right temperature."

"It must be something else," I said. "It must be some*where* else." My voice rose in pitch, and I felt embarrassed to sound so optimistic.

"Where else would a rotting body be?"

"I don't know, but maybe we should call the detectives."

My mom looked at me, confused. "It's a refrigeration issue. I've already called a repairman… I just can't figure out where the failure is." She sighed. "We're going to have to shut down and transport the bodies somewhere else, I'm afraid. This could be really bad, Billy." She took a breath. "I'm sorry, I shouldn't stress you. Everything will be taken care of."

*

That night, I fell asleep despite not taking my medicine. I had reached a breaking point of tiredness, and fell asleep with the lights on.

I assumed the lights had some protective effect, because I was not tortured by Danny Fiskar that night, nor did I have any night terrors that blended with reality. My dreams were many, but sane. I dreamt most of school, and of a place of total calm. It was like my father's apartment, but full of old furniture instead of new. It was small.

Cozy.

I dreamt I was talking to Anna, but I could remember nothing of the conversation.

*

Anna found me at lunch. She smiled almost tearfully when she saw me, and hugged me.

"I prayed for you. I prayed Saint Michael's prayer. I was told it was answered."

"I slept," I said. I didn't ask her who told her that her prayer was answered. "There was no demon."

"Good," she said.

"Thank you."

*

My mom took me to the funeral home after school. Once again, the smell was present, only stronger than before.

Two repairmen showed up an hour later, rolling a cart full of tools. They took the elevator down to the morgue and, after donning some basic protection gear, began investigating the refrigeration system. I set myself to trying to understand my homework while they worked.

"Holy Mother of God!" I heard the scream through the heavy steel door as clear as if it had been said in my ear.

I stood up quickly and followed my mother down the stairs. We were almost knocked over by one of the repairmen, who was crossing himself and muttering as he took the stairs.

The other one came up behind him, taking off his mask. He was a black man, but even so he looked deathly pale.

"We found something. Christ!" He shook his head. "There's a... There's a dead body in the wall. We thought there might be an electrical problem, so we took off one of the access panels that was loose under the breakers, it looked old..." He shook his head again. "We need to call the police, right?"

"Yes," My mom said, her face draining just like the repairman. "I'll call right now!"

They both turned and ran up the stairs, leaving me at the door, forgotten for the moment.

I was filled with a mix of emotions. There was a rise of tension in my mind and body, and I saw a chance to release it, to resolve the dissonance of my tortured soul. I quietly pushed open the door to the morgue.

Truthfully, I half-expected him to be standing there, looming over a dead body, devouring it, casting a knowing glance at me, either asking me to join him, or letting me know I was next.

All I saw though was the bright fluorescent lights of the morgue and the adjoining examination and embalming rooms. I walked past the exam room and toward the lockers. An old fuse box attached to a steel panel was leaning up against the wall. The proper breaker box was above it, with bunches of wires hanging down over what was clearly a tunnel.

There was a flashlight forgotten next to the panel. It was still on. I picked it up and kneeled down.

Into the wall, into the very cinderblocks that made the concrete basement, was carved a small and rough tunnel. It seemed to go into the earth and turn left. As I got down on my knees, I was nearly overcome by the stench of decay.

I crept forward slowly, keeping my light shining ahead of me. I went around the bend and saw a dim light.

The light was a bare lightbulb hanging from a makeshift ceiling in a very small room.

A large body was laying on a dirty, grey mattress. The body was naked, but nearly grey with dirt and filth. Its hands and feet were enormous, as was the jaw and distorted face. Its eyes were sunken and partially closed, but had clearly been open at one point. It had a gaping wound on its side along with another small hole at the top of its chest, but all the blood had dried or congealed into rotten blackness.

Despite the state of decay, I knew exactly who it was. It was Danny Fiskar. The skin was puffy and grotesque, but it was surely his face. It was a surreal moment, staring at my dead tormentor, seeing him in all the stark reality of that light. I stared for a long time at the pitiful sight.

There was no telling how long Danny Fiskar had existed in that little hole, hiding, but he had a little pile of possessions, including comics of mine I had forgotten about at some point.

His open, putrid mouth seemed fixed in a frown, but it was indeed too large, as was the jaw and face around it.

The smell started to be too much to bear, and I backed out, sickened but also relieved. My mind felt suddenly released from a horrible burden of fear.

I dropped the flashlight when I exited the tunnel and sat on my knees for a moment.

"Thank you, God," I said. "And forgive me for killing."

The detectives who had investigated the break-in, Sal and Harry, arrived awhile later.

Both repairmen had to stay to give statements. When released they left in a hurry, not bothering to retrieve some of their tools that were near the tunnel.

The detectives roped off the room. They donned hazard suits when some other police arrived and went into the tunnel with cameras.

While they did that, my mom made a bunch of frantic calls to have the bodies transported to other facilities. It was dark outside when Sal and Harry re-emerged into the office area. They went outside and sat down in a couple of folding chairs, looking exhausted. I was sitting nearby, under one of the outside lights, pretending to read.

"I'm gonna need a drink," Harry said. "Or twelve."

"It'll have to wait," Sal said. "This kind of stuff never happens on a Friday."

"Yeah, or when it does, we end up working the weekend," Harry said. "How are we going to get the body out? Guy is big and liable to fall apart if we pull him out."

Sal shrugged. "He's not that far gone. Me and a couple other big guys can get him out no problem. It'll be unpleasant, though."

"It's already unpleasant."

"Yeah, but look on the bright side. We caught our man."

"We did?"

"Acromegaly," Sal said. "You get a look at his hands?"

"It's him," I said, cutting in.

Harry gave me a skeptical look, but Sal grinned at me. "How do you figure?" the big man said.

"I've been thinking about it a lot," I said.

"Yeah, me too, son," Sal said. "What's your take, uh?"

"He's just a kid," Harry said.

Sal smiled at him. "Let me indulge him."

"He's been living in that little hole for a long time," I said. "I figure years. Maybe longer. If he was really Danny Fiskar, it would have to be decades. I found out his parents owned this place, but nobody really knows what happened to them. It was assumed they drowned."

Sal smiled at Harry. "I know what to look up already."

"He's been here, scavenging at night," I said. "He's been cutting open the corpses and eating the organs."

"Makes sense," Sal said. "They've all already been autopsied by the medical examiner. Nobody till now noticed, because why would you cut open a body twice?"

"We'd have to ask the embalmer," Harry said. "But if so, he was clever. We'll have to have the other bodies looked at."

"Yeah," I said. "It explains why the alarm system doesn't work. He never broke in."

"Who put the holes in him, though?" Harry said. "That's what I want to know."

"Whoever he was, he was doing God's work," Sal said. "I've seen a lot of shit – pardon my French, son – a *lot of shit*, but this is by far the strangest and most disgusting case I've worked. Kid, I'm sorry I doubted you."

"Yeah, I'm not crazy, I guess," I said. "But who could blame you for thinking that?"

That was what the reports on the news ended up saying. They called the body Danny Fiskar, but he couldn't be formally identified by dental records because of his condition. His jaw had grown far too large since any dentist had taken x-rays of him. It did come to light that Danny Fiskar, the real person and son of the couple that owned the home, had been declared dead, but his body had never been recovered. His parents had been found after the boating accident.

It was decided that he had made himself a space in the wall and crawled into it after his parents died. He was declared dead and there was nobody to follow-up on him. He lived in the morgue within a secret sub-basement and survived off of eating dead people along with whatever garbage was being left behind in the office, a secret scavenger for years. Someone had come into the funeral home for some reason and stabbed him with a large, wooden spear. He then crawled back into his hole and died of his injuries.

What had driven him into his dark lair – what demon, or affliction, or evil gnawing at his soul – nobody living could now say. I think, perhaps for all of us there that night, it was difficult to shake the feeling from then on of eyes watching us from the shadows whenever it became quiet and dark. Once you know that something truly frightening, truly horrible, can exist in flesh and blood, it becomes impossible to accept the myth of safety, or even privacy, in a world that is designed to look sterile and safe.

Chapter 10

I was glad to spend the weekend at my father's house. I spent some time talking to him about everything, and like many of the adults in my life, he heard part of what I said and focused on details that I thought didn't matter. I never told him I killed Danny.

My father spent his words musing over what could have driven the man crazy, and how there was nothing supernatural about it, after all. Basically, I felt like the conclusion was, "Even though the monster was real, you are still insane."

I have to say it affected me. I remembered as he talked to me that Danny was still was in my dreams that week – probably while dead. Did that mean the spirit of the monster was still at work in the world, as a ghost, or that I had created the encounters in my mind? What was part of the real experience, and what was part of my mind? The feeling of his sticky, long fingers and naked body made my skin crawl whenever I thought of them.

I kept my promise to Anna, though. I spat my meds out. As a result, I slept "rightly" – my dreams were pleasant and mostly forgettable. I still went to bed with the rosary near at hand, falling asleep feeling the beads and not knowing what prayers I was supposed to say with them.

Perhaps by seeing the body of Danny Fiskar I had banished his demons from my mind.

My cousin Jeff called me on Sunday from his foster home. I told him Danny was gone, and he seemed happy about it. Things weren't going well for him, but he was staying out of trouble. His first court date was that week, and he wanted to go home.

I realized while talking to him that I had no *real* home. I was a wanderer between two places, always transient.

*

Monday was the first time at school I began to feel somewhat normal. I could understand the lessons, though I was lost in the subject matter, having been in a haze for weeks. I talked and joked with some friends.

At lunch, I sat with Anna and her friends. They mostly talked about things that didn't interest me, but the banter felt human. Anna gave me her phone number, again apparently. I had no memory of her giving it to me the first time.

That night was a bad one.

My mother somehow suspected I had been faking taking my meds. I don't know how she figured it out, but despite my denials, she insisted she knew I was avoiding the drug.

"You're not well, Billy. You *have* to take your pills."

"Danny Fiskar was real, mom!" I dropped the pretense. "I'm not crazy!"

"I talked to Doctor Grant. It's very dangerous to just stop your medicine. And he agrees that you still had a breakdown. This situation aggravated and stressed you. You need to take your medicine!"

In the end, she forced it on me. She put the pills in my mouth herself and made me show her my empty mouth after I swallowed each one.

I fell asleep quickly that night.

My dreams were awful. Danny Fiskar was back, and in the drug haze, he assaulted me, pulling me apart like one of the corpses, trying to eat my flesh. His hands probed me, and his dirty mouth licked at my wounds.

It wasn't real. I awoke whole and untorn in the morning. By some effect of the drug, I didn't wake up screaming. I passively accepted the psychic assault during the night.

I was once again in a haze at school. Anna found me during lunch, but I told her I couldn't talk to her. I went and hid myself under one of the building eaves. She found me there, too. It was raining, I remember, but I couldn't feel the cold of it.

"What's wrong?" she said, sitting down beside me.

"I was forced to take my medication last night. I don't know how my mom knew I was faking it before."

"What happened?"

"I dreamt about him."

"I… don't know what to say."

"He couldn't hurt me," I said. "At least, it seemed like I was fine no matter what he did to me."

"Maybe Father James…"

"Maybe. Maybe he'll believe me this time."

I didn't really believe my own words.

*

The entire week I was forced to take the drug, and all week I had sickening dreams of the dead thing I called Danny Fiskar. Always he was touching me, probing me in a hungry way, like he could dine on my soul. Prayer had no effect. The drugs *did* have an effect. It was uncanny. No matter what happened to me in my dreams, I didn't seem to care.

I was of two minds – one which was screaming and writhing, the other which was passively accepting of all that was happening to me. I was aware of both, and only the passive one was dominant. This carried over into waking life – I couldn't muster the mental or physical energy to resist.

Anna said she was worried about me. She even called me one day, wondering if I had lost her number. I hadn't lost it. I simply hadn't ever considered talking to her, or anyone else.

Friday, she caught me and took me aside.

"I don't like what's happening to you," she said. "There's something really wrong."

"I know," I said. "I don't like it either, but everyone says I'm still crazy."

"I had a dream," she said. "Can I tell it to you, please?"

I didn't respond. She continued anyway.

"I was in a desert, and there was an old man in a cave. He had a light around him. It took a long time to reach him. When I got close, I realized he was Saint Anthony."

"Who is that?" I said.

"He's a saint – he was tortured by demons, that's how I knew it was him. There were demons all around him. Some of them were really monster-like, some looked like… Danny Fiskar, maybe. Kind of human, but wrong. He ignored them, and they bit and scratched at him, but it didn't hurt him. I sat down across from him – there was a little fire. He was smiling while the demons attacked, but he started crying when he looked at me.

"I asked him where the food was. There was a black plate there, sitting in front of him, and I felt hungry.

"He looked at me and said, 'Take nothing into your body which will corrupt the spirit.'

"I asked him what if I starved? And he said, 'If you eat nothing but the body of Christ, and drink nothing but his Blood, you will be sustained.'

"Then there was food on the plate. Saint Anthony looked at me and shook his head. I felt really hungry, so I reached for the food, and took it. I took a bite, and suddenly the demons were attacking me. I screamed, and then I vomited up the food. The demons stopped and left me alone."

Anna was quiet for a minute.

"You think it was about me?" I said.

"Yeah," she said. "Saint Anthony said, before I woke up, that there are intercessors, and that God hears us."

She was crying at that point. Because of the drugs, I felt very little about it, but I knew it was significant.

*

I spent the weekend with my father. My mother must have tipped him off, because he did the same medicine routine with me – watching me swallow my pills and checking my mouth to see that I had swallowed them.

I didn't dream of Danny Fiskar. I wasn't sure if it was because of prayer, or not, but when Monday came, I was dreading going "home."

At school, Anna asked me if I had seen relief. I said I hadn't dreamed, but I was still being forced to take the drugs.

Monday night, the nightmares returned. The next day, I asked Anna about the dream again. I tried, through my muted mind, to figure out the meaning and message behind it. That suppressed part of my mind believed unwaveringly that Saint Anthony had appeared to Anna on my behalf, but I didn't know what I was supposed to do.

I decided that I would try not eating, since that was what the saint did. It was hard, but I made it the whole day without consuming anything but water. Evening, though, presented a problem. My mother insisted I take my medication with food, even though I told her I was sick. Begrudgingly, I ate a sandwich and took my medicine. The dreams returned.

I tried again the next day, avoiding all food until I was forced to eat something for dinner, this time trying to say I wasn't hungry. It didn't work, and I was forced to swallow each pill. I went to bed dejected, but as I laid myself down, checking again for the wrench I hid in my bedsheets, something came to me.

For a few minutes, my mind was clear – truly clear, not just free from the drug, but also the paralyzing fear that had dominated my sleep cycle. I thought I could see what Anna had described and my mind had been focused on that week. Saint Anthony. I could almost imagine his face – bearded in white and drawn thin.

Anna threw up the food, and the demons stopped. My mind fixated on this detail.

I got out of bed. I didn't go to the bathroom. Instead, I found an empty plastic container. I stuck my fingers down my throat and, though I hated it, I made myself vomit. Up came half-digested food and water into the plastic bin. The smell was sickening, which helped me throw up more. Finally, I saw the pills come up. They were mostly intact, hardly broken down at all. Unfortunately, it didn't stop there. Once I began the purge, it wasn't going to stop until my stomach was totally empty.

I filled up the plastic bin and threw up into another one that held a few of my pencils. Once I was totally empty, I put the lids on, thinking I would dispose of the vomit in the morning.

I still felt the drugs. I was shaking from the fit of vomiting, but I managed to get myself to bed. I felt horrible, but somehow I slept.

The dreams came. They were chaotic. I could feel the eyes of Danny Fiskar, the malevolent spirit that remained bound to me, always on my back. I was walking down hallways, and I could see his strange shadow cast out in front of me, but I could never turn to look at him. I dreamt I was back in the morgue, and he was staring at me from the darkness of his hidden lair.

I began to drift into wakefulness. I was in my room and it was dark, except for the light that leaked in through my blinds from a distant street lamp.

I could see Danny Fiskar.

He was on top of me, his dark eyes wide with hunger. I could feel his long fingers touching my bare skin, trying to pull it open to reach the meat within. His mouth was gaping, and his breath was foul. I was paralyzed, my body still stuck in sleep while my mind was desperate for motion.

My paralysis broke suddenly, and I found I could move my hands. I reached into the folds of my sheets, underneath one of my pillows, and grabbed the wrench. Danny didn't notice. His face moved closer to mine. Was he real? Had he never died at all? He inched closer, and I could hear his breath, then feel it tickling my cheek.

I smashed the pipe wrench into his face. His hulking, naked body fell on my legs pinning me. He started to writhe, his arms reaching up to my throat, fingernails digging into my skin.

I struck the monster again in the head. His grip tightened. I hit him again. He was trying to roll away now, his fingers dragging painfully off the skin of my neck.

"God help me!" I cried aloud. He had moved enough that my legs were partially freed. I got up above him and brought the wrench down with all my might on the creature's horrible, bald head. There was a crack. Something gave.

Danny rolled off my bed and crashed to the floor.

Alive with wrath, I jumped out of bed and onto the monster, seeing its pale outline in the narrow light bands from the blinds. Pinning its shaking shoulders, I hit it in the head again. Again. Again. I stood up and put my whole body into the move, screaming as I sought to destroy my tormentor. The head began to split open. In the orange light from the window, the insides of the skull were pitch black. I didn't stop. I refused to stop.

Finally, the body beneath me ceased its twitching and went still.

I screamed wordlessly, an exaltation of triumph. At last, he would truly be dead.

The lights turned on, and my mother was there. For a moment, she stood there in silence, then she covered her mouth and screamed.

I was out of breath. I rolled off the body and stood up.

"What did you do?!" my mother shouted, pushing past me to the body of the monster.

I realized, watching my mother shake the pale, naked corpse, that it was not the same creature I had seen buried and decayed within the walls of the morgue.

What was on my bedroom floor, its head broken apart and maimed beyond recognition, was a man. A once normal-looking man. He was naked and splayed on the carpet. I dropped the wrench and realized in horror I was partially unclothed as well – I had only my shirt on.

My mother was still trying to rouse him. She was used to the dead. It should have been obvious what she was looking at.

My mind was reeling with the sight of blood clotting on my bedroom floor. I collapsed against the wall.

"What did you do?" my mother said again, this time her voice quavering, on the edge of giving out. She rose like she was going to pounce on me, fury in her eyes, but after meeting my gaze for a few moments, she ran out of the room. I stared at the dead body before me, and as I tried to put the pieces together, I heard my mother from the other room talking on the phone.

"He snapped and attacked my boyfriend. He's not breathing and he has no pulse."

I rubbed my face and looked around. I saw my jeans on the floor near me and began to pull them on while sitting.

"He's calm now, I think." I could tell my mom was talking about me.

I stood up and staggered out of the room. I caught my mom's eye in the living room, all the way at the end of the long hallway.

"He's coming. Yes, I'll get out right away. Hurry."

She dropped the phone on the ground and ran for the front door. She slammed it and started shouting outside.

I began to go after her, but paused as I heard a voice coming from the phone on the floor. I was still panting and in a haze of confusion. I knelt down and picked it up.

"Hello?" I said.

"This is 911, who is this?" said a female operator

"Billy Sheppard. My mom just ran out the door."

I heard some talking on the other side of the line between strange voices.

"Yes, Billy Lasseter?" a male voice said.

"Yeah?"

"Remain calm. Help is on the way."

"Okay," I said. "For me?"

"Yes. Just remain calm. Is there anywhere that you can sit down?"

"Yeah, I can sit down. Why?"

"Just stay on the line, please. We need to make sure you are okay."

"I'm…" I couldn't say I was fine. "I'm right here. What do you need me to do? My mom ran out the door, should I go get her?"

"No, remain where you are. How are you feeling?"

"Not good," I said. "I…" I didn't want to talk about what was sitting in my bedroom.

"Are you armed?"

"No." My mind was starting to return to some sense of equilibrium. I was beginning to piece together what the operator was doing.

"We have some people heading your way, just relax and stay calm."

"I'll wait in the living room," I said. "I'm unarmed. I'm going to open the door so that the police can see me." I put the phone down and opened the front door. I couldn't see my mother outside, but I could hear voices. I returned to the phone. "I'm going to sit down."

The operator continued trying to talk to me, but once I realized what was happening, I kept quiet. A few minutes later, the police rushed up to the door. Their hands were resting on their guns. They paused as they saw me.

"Don't make any sudden moves," one of them said.

I held my empty hands up. The front one stepped in and pushed me to my feet. He cuffed my hands behind my back and pushed me forcefully out of the door. Other police were already moving past me into the house, heading for the back. An ambulance was out front, and two paramedics were waiting by a gurney, cracking knuckles through white latex gloves.

I saw my mom standing with a policeman. She was crying and had a look of horror and confusion on her face. I said nothing as I was pushed into the back of the car and was driven off. She refused to look at me.

Chapter 11

An hour or two later, I found myself sitting in a small room at the police station. I was still handcuffed, but now the cuffs were in front of me so I could drink some water from a paper cup they had given me. My mouth felt parched, but the water didn't seem to wet it.

A youngish man in a suit came in, looking very tired and drinking a cup of hot coffee, along with a uniformed police officer.

He sat down across from me and refilled my water cup from a pitcher.

"So, you want to tell me what happened?"

"Aren't I supposed to have a lawyer or something?" I said.

"This is just an interview."

I looked around for a few moments. It didn't seem like an interview.

"What do you want to know?" I said.

"Why don't you just tell me your side of the story."

"I don't know what to tell you," I said truthfully.

"Come on, don't bullshit me. You had a fight with Brett and used a wrench to beat him up. He had to have done something to deserve it, right?"

"What?" I said.

The man in the suit shrugged a little. "I get it, man. Your mom is dating a new guy. He's a real asshole, she won't listen about him. He embarrasses you, maybe pushes you a little too far. It's real common, man. I get it."

"I don't get it," I said. "Who is Brett?"

"I just want to know what he did to make you do it, that's all."

"You mean the guy?"

"Yeah, the guy. What did he do?"

"I just… I woke up and he was in my bed."

The cop gave me an incredulous look.

"Listen, think about it. Maybe we can get some paper so you can get your thoughts in order, yeah?"

As he said that, the door behind him opened up and, to my utter shock, Sal walked in. He was wearing a tracksuit and drinking a large cup of 7-11 coffee.

"I got this, Tom," he said. "It's my case now."

"We're just getting started," the sitting detective said.

"Well, now you're finished. He's been on my caseload, so he's mine. We're not even supposed to process juveniles here, you know."

"No way, Sal. You know what happened. This isn't a juvie case."

"Go ask the captain if you like," Sal said. "It's my case now. Beat it. Go on." Sal's voice was deep and calm, but left no room for debate. He stepped around beside me and put a hand in his pocket as he looked at the younger men.

Tom growled and got up. The uniformed cop followed him out the door. They left it open.

Sal produced a key from his pocket and removed my cuffs.

"Better, yeah?" he said, tossing the handcuffs on a nearby table.

"Yeah, thanks."

"You're in my custody now, so I may have to put them back on to transport you."

I shrugged.

Sal closed the door.

"We kind of figured out what's happening," he said. "Tom wasn't in the loop on you or your situation."

"That I'm crazy?"

"Eh, sort of. More like, he's missing all the context. He's treating you like a suspect. I apologize."

"I'm not?"

"I know you killed Brett Hammerstein, but I also know what he was doing. I'm working a little ahead here, but I'm pretty sure the doctors will all agree with my narrative when things are through and we get all the evidence sorted out. I'm never wrong about this sort of thing."

"How bad of trouble am I in?"

Sal pulled a chair close to mine and sat down. He chuckled and gave me a smile that looked half-sad. "Kid, there's not a jury in the state that will convict you for killing that perv. You're gonna get no-billed for sure. There's no way the D.A. will want to press charges on something like this. No way."

"Why not?"

Sal chuckled again, but his eyes held the same sadness, almost like the huge man was tearing up. "Hey, you want a snack? I got some twinkies and stuff."

"Sure."

"Alright, be right back." He got up and left the room, then returned with a few wrapped snack cakes. I opened one up and ate ravenously. I realized I had only had one meal in the last few days.

"Hungry?"

"Yeah. So why am I not in trouble?"

Sal smiled. He scratched his nose. "I'll tell you the story. I already know it's true enough. You can see how it fits. Your mom has a boyfriend she doesn't tell you about." His face got gravely serious. "He comes over sometimes, which is normal, but she doesn't know he's a convicted child rapist. He tries something when she's asleep. Kid fights back."

"What?"

"Yeah. Unfortunately, son, I see this a lot. It's why I'm never wrong. Guys like that date the mom to get to the kids."

More pieces came together in my mind. "He was touching me. I... thought it was something else. He kept trying to come in my room!" I stood up, almost knocking over my water. "He was coming in and touching me! Over and over!"

"Relax," Sal said. "Have another twinkie. I know you've been through a lot, so excuse my easy manner. Frank calls it a defense mechanism." He took a long sip of coffee, then folded his big, meaty hands in front of his face. "Cops like me, who have seen this kind of stuff..." He shook his head and looked hard at me. The tears that had been hinted at as he spoke were now filling his lower lids. "We dream about sick fucks like this guy getting killed. You did a good thing, Bill. He deserved it. You did a real good thing, even if it doesn't feel good right now."

I sat down in silence and thought about it all. "What kind of doctors do I have to see now? For the case, I mean."

"Psych. You'll have to have a physical exam, too. Sorry about it, but we have to do our diligence."

I put my hands in my face and cried. The release was almost cathartic.

I was crazy after all, but not at all the way everyone thought.

After a few minutes, Sal said, "I'm gonna have to take you down to juvenile processing. It's across town. I'll get you a hot meal on the way. Don't worry about it, though. It's gonna be fine, son. I'm gonna make damn sure of that, alright?"

*

I went home with my dad later that day. I told him everything, and he got upset. It was the most emotional I had ever seen him. It was also the first time I had seen him cry.

I called Anna and told her, too. She cried, too, or at least I thought she did over the phone, but it seemed different. More like a relief. She asked if I believed the dream was a true vision. I told her I thought it was, but she had been given the dream instead of me because I wouldn't have believed it or known who Saint Anthony was.

Before I hung up, I told her I loved her. She didn't exactly say it back. She told me if that was true, I would be at church, because that was where she needed me to be.

So on Sunday, I went to Mass. I had no idea what was going on, but I thought it was where I should be. My father didn't give any protest as he drove me. He would never be a true believer – he was too hardened and clever enough to explain away every miracle in his mind – but he would at least let me find my own way, and I was thankful for that.

*

The D.A. refused to charge me, just like Sal promised. My story was all in the news, minus my name, since I was a minor. Apparently, my mother's boyfriend, Brett, was indeed a convicted rapist. There was some debate with the authorities over whether she knew what he was doing to me - There were a lot of instances of molestation, as I found out with the help of the psychologist. I think due to that controversy my father ended up with custody of me, which I was happy about.

I never went back to my old room at the house; my mother sold it as soon as she could. She sold the funeral home early the next year and went to work at some other place in the next city over. I also never took Thorazine, or any antipsychotic, ever again. Doctor Grant quickly declared me to be in the recovery phase of schizophrenia and moved me into weekly therapy. My father declined a prescription for an antidepressant.

I talked to Father James at one point, sometime after everything went down.

"Father, why did God allow this to happen to me?"

"Look at where you are," he said. "How would you be here if this had not happened to you?"

"Couldn't God have just told me to come?"

"Would you have listened?"

I thought about it a moment. "Probably not."

"Then he had to prepare you first to listen before he could speak to you."

"But... I guess this is my father talking – if God loves me, why didn't he intervene?"

"He didn't intervene?"

I remembered the events leading up to each battle, including Anna's dream. "I understand. I remember something Anna told me about Saint Anthony, that God let demons torment him as a test. Maybe it was something like that."

"If it was, you passed. We're blessed to know you, William. You humble me, you know."

The End

Live in the Pod and Eat Bugs

Bob, who lived in the pod above Jake, was masturbating again.

Jake peeled his eyes open. They felt like oranges that had been cut in half and left in the sun. It wasn't something out of the ordinary - watching the standard government funded porn before getting up for work – but Bob was far too indiscreet about it. He moaned and rocked as he got off, making the old steel and fiberboard of the pod creak in time with his ugly incantations. Jake looked at the clock next to his mattress, in the single shelf that housed his personal effects. He was not allowed to get out for another twenty minutes.

He rolled over and turned his earpods on, then launched up a game on his datalink, desperately wanting to go back to the world of dreams, to escape the wakefulness that had come unbidden to draw him into the infinite grey of the world that is. For his waking mind, the game was the closest thing, but as soon as he passed the loading screen he remembered that he hadn't waited long enough since the last time he had played, and thus had no stamina to walk out into the beautifully rendered world of escape.

Resignedly, he charged another five UN credits to the game, buying a quick stamina potion so he could actually go exploring. With a sigh, he knew he would buy another one at lunch.

The adventure was efficient and successful. He cleared out a building full of Christian Cultists in a ruined temple, retrieved some currency, and even got a gold chest. He would normally have paid to open it, but having just spent five credits, he decided to wait and open it that night after the time had expired.

He turned off his earpods and listened to the space around him. Bob had apparently finished his business, and outside the curtain of his pod Jake could hear others being woken by their datalinks and preparing for the day before common time began. Jake sat up, or at least sat up as much as he could in the cramped space, and began pulling on his clothes for the day.

With a flash, the lights turned on, and curtains began to be drawn back. Jake opened his own, watching the men and women shuffling out of their pods into the crowded common walkway, most dressed and ready for their day. A few were naked or lightly robed, intending to shower and be de-loused before they left. His eyes lingered on a woma n heading for the showers, and he found himself admiring her, taking in the details of her flesh and watching her hips and breasts sway.

He felt a pang of guilt, knowing he had committed a dark act with his eyes. He had been avoiding the pornography networks too often of late, and now he was raping a woman with his eyes. Despite this, he did not look away as she paused in the crowd. He stared at her buttocks and his eyes went up her back to her bare neck and shaved head.

He sighed, thinking she would be beautiful if she had hair, but then again, only pornstars had hair.

At last he got out of his pod, his sole refuge of personal space, and put on his shoes. He headed through the crowd toward the exit. He stepped around the biggest milling queue, which was composed of people trying to get their breakfast from the early food service, and stepped up to a vending machine instead.

He charged another few credits and got a WaferBar. He was hungry, but he knew he would be hungrier still if he didn't eat during the time allowed. He peeled open the bar and examined it. He could barely tell it was made from beetle larva, so processed was its shape and texture. Reluctantly, he bit into it, trying to eat it quickly.

"You're wasting your money, you know."

It was Natty Eckelstein, who stood next to him with a bowl of fresh smoked larva. He picked up a few and tossed them into his mouth, then crunched them loudly.

"And you don't? You spend all your money on KillQuest."

"At least I have something to show for it. I'm rank fourteen. You're what, rank seven?"

"Eight. Well, eight was my highest."

"You could be buying lootboxes my friend, and you know, actually working the meta, but you keep wasting your money on snacks."

Jake paused and frowned. "I don't like it."

"Then why play it?"

"I mean, I don't like eating bugs."

"It's free, Jake. Why are you paying for what's free. That bar isn't made of some mythical jungle fowl."

"It doesn't make me feel like I'm eating bugs is all."

Natty smiled. "They're better for you raw. You know that, right? That processed stuff will make you fat."

Jake forced a chuckle. "I'll see you tonight."

Jake stepped out onto the street. He looked up and down, seeing the other pod houses empting of residents, all heading for their respective transit stops. He crossed the street toward his own, and his datalink came to life, beaming in the first news report of the day. He pressed the button on his link to kill the transmission, but it didn't work. He had run out of pass credits for the news, and had to watch the broadcast.

The annoying voice of a female anchor (she had short hair, not bald) screamed into his ears. The security council was apparently negotiating the successful beginning of a war. Quickly the broadcast went through some local news, and Jake began to zone out.

He jumped back into consciousness, however, when he had to leap out of the way of two speeding chair scooters, their occupants laughing and snorting as they ran into pedestrians. The girth of each of them spilled voluminously over the sides of the chairs, jiggling as they ran over the uneven, crumbling pavement. He watched them shriek as they sped down the avenue toward the department of wellness, where they would be picking up their weekly disability stipend.

At last he reached his train stop. He found a tight crowd there, all standing back from the landing. He quickly saw why. The largest pile of feces he had ever seen sat on the platform, leaning like an ugly castle, almost scowling at the crowd. Insects had already found it, and crawled and buzzed over its moist and fetid surface.

"How could one man make that?" Jake said aloud. Nobody responded.

The train arrived. Jake and the rest of the commuters stepped around the brown monument to human waste and into the train car. The chimes began to sound as the doors closed, a series of sharp melodies corresponding to each classification of person on board, letting each group know when it was time for them to find a place. Jake was surprised to find a single vacant seat when, as a white male, it was finally his turn to sit.

He sat next to a large man, who scratched at his bald head.

"You hear they're going to do a mid-semester delousing for everyone?" he said, staring out the window. He took a glass pipe out of his coat and began to pack the bowl with greasy black leaves that smelled like floor cleaner. "I might actually need it this time."

"Couldn't hurt. Luckily there is no typhus at my podhouse."

"Just one guy at mine, but he was a rough sort. Spent too much time out-of-doors. I think he might have died, but I haven't seen them rent the pod out to anybody else." The stranger lit up his pipe and took a long draw of the substance within. Others in the car were following suit. "You forget yours?" the stranger said.

"No I just don't want it," Jake said.

"Gotcha," said the stranger, winking and touching his nose. "You should know the natural stuff is better for you."

Jake shrugged. The stranger quickly put his pipe away and opened up a game on his link. Jake did the same, trying to resist the urge to drop another five credits on the way to work.

Irregular Temporal Probability

Kenneth had never seen an irregular temporal sphere before. Bernard leaned on his knees and held the object between his hands, staring at the golden center, swirling like the center of the galaxy and throbbing like a dying heart. It's center glowed subtly. Temporal singularities were uncommon playthings, even for the wealthy.

"So what did you decide to study?" Kenneth asked, putting down his tablet. He was starting to get fatigued from his class readings. Temporal vibrating membranes was a hugely interesting academic area, but required more of Kenneth's brain power than he could spare with Bernard sitting in his dorm room.

"My parents want me to study irregular temporal probability," Bernard said, rolling the time-sphere around in his hands. "That's why they bought me this."

"Tough subject," Kenneth said.

"No kidding. You have to have an innate understanding of retrograde time. At least, to be good. I don't know if I want to study it."

"Man, I would love to get into that," Kenneth said, nodding to the sphere.

"Why don't you?" Bernard said. He tossed the sphere to Kenneth, who caught it, fumbled it, then dropped it to the ground. It thudded without a bounce. He picked it up quickly, almost dropping it again because of how deceptively heavy it was.

"Because there's no money in it," Kenneth said. "I'm going to have the better part of a 100 million kilodollars of debt by the time I get out of here. The only way I'm going to be able to pay that back with a job working for one of the hyperdrive manufactories."

"Bah," Bernard said, and leaned back. "I'm not going to pretend it's hard to be rich, Kenneth. But making decisions like this... I'm just going to say that taking the challenge out of something takes away some of the passion, you know?"

"Retrograde temporal probability still seems plenty challenging to me," Kenneth said. He held the golden swirling sphere up to his hands. Suddenly, the sphere pulsed and wobbled. "Did you see that!"

"What?" Bernard said. "Oh, that. Yeah, it does that sometimes." Kenneth turned around and began jotting something down on his tablet. "Anyway," Bernard went on, "since my folks are paying for everything I don't really feel that threat of failure, you know? I mean, sure I can do retrograde time stuff, but I don't really have to be great at it, do I? If I suck, or if I'm just mediocre, its ok. Nobody to pay back. Hey, what are you writing down?"

"The exact time the sphere did that wobbly pulse thing," Kenneth said.

"Why?"

Kenneth half-sighed, half-grunted. "This is an anti-time singularity, Bernie. You have to keep meticulous records of all outputs, so you can link them to inputs in the future. That's how you study retrograde temporal events."

"How do know that it wasn't just reacting to you dropping it? That it's not anti-time at all. What if it's... slowed time, or something?"

"Because changes in time flow require speed or gravity, or both," Kenneth said. "You remember relativity lessons from grade-school, right? Besides, your folks wouldn't buy an anti-time singularity that was fake."

"I guess that's true," Bernard said. He grabbed back the sphere and looked at it. He dropped it on the ground, then picked it up again. He waited a few seconds. "Didn't happen that time. I guess you're right."

"You ever think it's fun dropping that thing, and wondering if it shook the shop keep's hands a few weeks – hell, a few years – ago?"

"Yeah, but who's dropping it and making it shake for us?"

"You'll have to hold onto it and find out," Kenneth said. "Each singularity has a different lifespan until it goes dun."

"Dun?"

"Literally runs out of time. After that it's just a paperweight."

"Cool. I always wanted a 500 million kilodollar paperweight." Bernard tossed the sphere about some more.

"Odin's bones, it cost that much? I could pay for all of my degrees with that!"

"Then you take it," Bernard said, and tossed it to him.

"I can't take this," Kenneth said. He gazed at it deeply.

"Sure you can. You can pay for your education, or you know, actually study some retrograde temporal phenomena."

"Thanks," Kenneth said, and meant it. It moved the golden swirling sphere around in his hands.

"You're not going to sell it, are you?" Bernard said. He stood up and stretched.

"I don't know," Kenneth said. He smiled at Bernard. "But I know how to find out."

"How?"

"I know exactly how *I* would study this thing. I know it responds to physical shock, so in the future I would input some particular patterns, maybe in Morse code. Something I would easily recognize."

"What's Morse code?"

"An digital codec used for early telecommunications over analog systems. It used a series of long and short pulses. Each combination stood for a letter. I actually memorized it when I was a kid for fun."

"You would."

"I did. Anyhoo, I'll just hold onto the sphere for a while, and wait for an output I know is from me. I'll make it say, *Bernard Goldman is a big fat doofus,* or something. If I get the message, then I know that I hold onto the sphere in the future."

Bernard chuckled. "Kenneth, you're not really making a decision at all. You're relying on future events to make present decisions for you."

"Making current decisions better based on future *certainties.* That's what retrograde temporal probabilities is all about!"

"What if you get the message and decide to sell it anyway?"

"I can't."

"But what if you do?"

"You don't understand, Bernie, I literally can't. Something will stop me from selling it, no matter what I try."

"What about Schrodinger's cat? Quantum probability? Multiverse theory? Free will?"

"All bullshit when you have access to anti-time, my friend. I've already created an experiment with a dichotomous outcome. Either I keep the sphere, or I sell it. I have no choice!"

"Gimme the sphere back," Bernard said.

"The experiment just disproved multiverse theory," Kenneth said, and held out the sphere.

"Fine, keep it," Bernard said.

"It just disproved it again!" Kenneth clutched the ball and looked into it with a smile.

Bernard scratched his chin. "You know what, Ken? I'm going to go over to the music department. I'm taking up the guitar."

"It's what you were always meant to do!" Kenneth said, standing up excitedly.

Three Moral Tales

The Chicken and the Wild Turkey

Each day the farmwife would go out to the chicken pen, and throw out some feed. Each day, the chicken would come out of her coop and eat. One day, the farmwife was in a hurry, so she threw a handful of corn hastily through the wire, and moved on to her other business. Some of the feed fell outside of the pen. The chicken pushed her head against the wire, trying to get her beak to the pile of fresh feed beyond, but could not. Finally, she abandoned it and went back to her nest.

Later that day, a wild turkey stole by, and began to eat the feed that fell outside of the pen.

Seeing the wild turkey, the chicken hopped down and said, "Hey! That's my food."

"Then why haven't you eaten it?" said the turkey.

"I couldn't reach it, obviously," said the chicken.

The turkey laughed. "Then why do you care if I eat it?"

Feeling flustered, the chicken went back to her nest.

The next day, the farmwife was again in a hurry, and again some of the feed was thrown past the wires of the pen. Once again, the turkey came by to eat the extra feed.

"If only I were a turkey!" said the chicken.

"Don't be so hasty to envy me, my friend," said the turkey. "While you cannot reach this food, the food that normally is given to you don't have to work for."

"Of course I work for my food. I give the farmwife my eggs," the chicken said.

"That's hardly working, don't you think?" said the turkey.

"Well you didn't work for that feed."

"Oh no? I came a long way from my nest to reach this food, past eagles and wolves and other nasty things. There is a great deal of risk that comes with being wild."

"What if no food falls outside tomorrow?" the chicken said. "How will you eat then?"

"There's lots of other things to eat in the forest, though most are not as tasty as corn. Still, I may go hungry, as I must do from time to time."

"Then why don't you come in here?" the chicken said. "I get fed twice a day, without work, as you point out."

"Just because you don't work doesn't mean there's no cost," said the turkey. "I live and die by my wits, something I don't think you have the stomach for, but I certainly don't have the stomach to give my eggs to a farmer to eat, only to end up on the dinner table myself later on."

"What? You think the farmer will eat me?"

The turkey laughed. "Surprised, are we?"

The chicken, flustered, ran around the pen a few times before returning to the dining turkey. "Well, turkey, I happen to know that the farmer has a shotgun, and I see him often returning from the woods with foul. Perhaps you will end up on the table before me."

"Perhaps," the turkey said. "But that outcome will be up to me and my ability to avoid such a fate. As for you, yours is a sealed fate, though a comfortable one. I'll take my chances in the wood."

"You're a fool, turkey."

"If I am, then I will soon be dead," the wild turkey said, and flew off, just as the farmwife returned.

"Made a new friend, have you?" she said to the chicken.

The next day, the farmwife fed the chicken, and once again, some of the feed landed outside the pen. The chicken waited for the turkey to come and eat, but he never came.

"Hello! Turkey?" the chicken called out, but the turkey did not come.

Finally, the sun began to go down, and the farmwife came by. She scooped up the extra feed and tossed it to the chicken. The chicken noticed she had a shotgun broken open over her forearm.

"It looks like you have a clever friend," she said to the chicken. "Thrice is never an accident, as my father used to say."

The Goat and the Sheep

Prometheus, freed from his bonds, came upon a farm. Hidden as he is to the eyes of man and beast, but perceiving all, this is what he witnessed.

A sheep and a goat were standing in a fenced pasture chewing on alfalfa and wild barley. The goat, tired of the bare patches of earth made by the sheep, leapt up onto the turf roof of the farmhouse and began chewing the cud that grew upon it.

"Get down from there you fool goat!" said the sheep from the ground below.

"Why should I?"

"You aren't supposed to be on the roof," said the sheep

"You're the fool. There's no such thing as 'supposed to.'"

"Mark my words, the farmer will punish you for this."

"He'll have to catch me first," said the goat.

The farmer, returning home from an errand, saw the goat on the roof and called for him to come down, saying, "Get off the roof before you cave it in, you foul goat!"

The goat ignored him and continued chewing his cud. The farmer threw a rock at the goat, which struck him smartly on the rump, causing the goat to jump, yet he refused to get down off of the roof. The farmer tried several more rocks to no avail before climbing onto the roof, damaging and denting the turf that rested on the lattice below, and with his staff his the goat around the shoulders and head.

Bleating, the goat ran from the farmer, jumping off the roof and going back to where the sheep still stood.

"Don't let me catch you on the roof again, you worthless beast," the farmer said, hitting the goat an additional time for good measure. He sighed and set about fixing his damaged roof.

"I told you so," the sheep said.

"I am punished for having free will," the goat said.

"Have you eaten any more than me?" the sheep said.

"I have eaten what I wanted to eat, you worthless servile sheep!"

The next day, the dog was rounding up the animals. He barked at the sheep and nipped lightly at her feet, and the sheep went quickly to stand among the others ewes. Gently, the farmer and the dog began to lead them all into the next pasture, a resting field.

"Go get the goat," the farmer said to the dog. The dog followed his master's order, and ran to the goat, barking and nipping lightly at his feet.

The goat, in response, stood stubbornly and refused to move, then began to kick whenever the dog came near, hitting him on the nose and making him yelp. Seeing this, the farmer walked over and hit the goat around the shoulders and neck, making the goat bleat and run away. The goat still refused to go to the other pasture.

"The other field is rested, you idiot," the farmer said. "Do as I command!" He hit the goat again and again, until at last the goat followed the sheep into the rested field.

The sheep, seeing the goat being hit said, "It's much easier when you just do as you are told."

"I am only punished because I have free will," the goat said. "But I would rather be free than be a sheep. Everything you do you do according to the will of your master. He will lead you to the slaughter, and you would go happily and with ignorance to your death!"

"Shows how much you know about sheep. The farmer wants my wool, not my flesh."

"The flesh of your children, then," the goat said.

"It is the same for them," said the sheep.

"To hell with you!" the goat said.

Some days later, the farmer had a visit from a relative, who brought with him his whole family. In the afternoon, he went out to his pasture.

"Goat. Come hither," he said to the goat.

Hearing the farmer, the goat ran away, to a far corner of the pasture. The farmer came forward with his staff, and the goat ran from him, leaping onto the back of the sheep, who was in the middle of the herd.

The farmer walked away, and the goat laughed at him. In a few minutes the farmer returned, not with his staff, but with a long gun. He shot the goat, which stood upon the sheep, and the herd scattered, leaving the goat dead on the ground. The farmer retrieved the corpse and walked back toward his kitchens to slaughter the animal.

That night he fed his relatives and also called his neighbors, so that every useable morsel of the goat was eaten.

Watching the feast, the sheep said to himself, "Serves the old fool right."

The next day more visitors arrived at the farm. This time it was the lord with his retinue of servants and retainers, sojourning in the countryside.

When the lord greeted him, the farmer said, "What brings my lord hither to my humble estates?"

"Fair weather and a fair hunt," said the lord.

"Ah, the woods are rich and well maintained by the woodsman," said the farmer. "But there is always chance at play in such matters. If the hunt goes ill, or the stags too scarce, come and stay at my house, and I will feed you well."

"If it is so, then allow me to pay you for your hospitality," said the lord.

"Only as you see fit, my lord," said the farmer.

That evening, the lord returned from the hunt empty-handed and said to the farmer. "I believe I will take you up on your offer. The wood is too scarce, methinks, but at least the pastures are rich."

"Indeed," said the farmer. The farmer then let the lord and his retainers rest by his fireplace and went out the pasture with his relative, who was still visiting him.

"Pity you slaughtered the goat yestereve," his relative said to him.

"The goat would ill-suit a man of the gentry," the farmer said. He gathered up the sheep and lead her away from the herd.

"As opposed to mutton?" said his relative.

"Mutton for the dogs and servants," said the farmer, "and lamb for the lords." With that he gathered up also a male lamb. "This ewe is past her prime, and it is time for this lamb to be slaughtered or sold for a stud. The lord is a fair man, so we shall come out the better for it."

And so the farmer took the sheep and the lamb, and slaughtered them, and the household dined on the mutton, and the lord and his retainers dined on the lamb, and all that was unsavory was given to the dogs, who ate the mutton happily.

The Wise Farmer and Lazy Farmer

There was once two grape growers, who each had plots handed down to them from their fathers. One of the farmers was a diligent, wise man, who followed the teachings of his father and was prosperous with his craft. The other man heeded little the gifts of his father, and was prone to vice and laziness.

It happened that one year, as the winter was receding, the lazy farmer neglected to prune the old growth from his vines. The wise farmer, who went out to the fields with his children to prune the vines, noticed this and grumbled to himself, pitying his neighbor in his heart, but not going to his house to correct him. The lazy farmer waited too long, and new shoots sprang from the old canes. This was bad news, for it meant that his harvest would be less than it otherwise would be; the wise farmer's vines were already thriving when his neighbor's vines were just beginning their year's growth.

A few days later, a plague of locusts swept through the region, decimating the vines of all the vintners and grape growers for miles around. The wise farmer was distraught, because he knew that because of the timing of the insect plague he would have no harvest, and since his family had grown grapes for generations, he held not auxiliary crops.

The vines of the lazy farmer, however, were little touched because of their overgrowth. Soon they were heavy with grapes, and though the harvest was less than full, it was extremely profitable for the lazy farmer. No other farms for many miles had been able to bring much to harvest, and for that entire season grapes were exceedingly rare and valuable.

In the late summer the lazy (but lucky) farmer went to his neighbor and paid him a large share of his profits.

"Why are you giving this to me?" the wise farmer asked him.

"Because you need it," the lazy farmer said. "Please don't refuse my gift."

Due to the generosity of the lazy farmer, the wise farmer and his family were able to eat well over the winter and prepare for the next year.

When spring came the next year, the wise farmer once again went out and pruned his vines. Once again, his neighbor did not. This time, the wise farmer went to his neighbor and said to him, "It's time to cut your vines."

"I'll do it later," was what the lazy farmer said, but he neglected his work again over the next few days and pruned the vines late.

There was no plague that year, and the wise farmer had a rich and profitable harvest. The lazy farmer's crop was ruined, for he had neglected to totally complete each step of the growing process. He frequently forgot to water the vines. He forgot to net them, and they were eaten by birds. He neglected to trim the leaves to allow the bunches to ripen in the sun.

The wise farmer went to his neighbor and gave him a large portion of the profits from his crop. When he returned home, his wife rebuked him.

"Why did you give our lazy neighbor so much of our money? It's his own fault he had no grapes to sell."

"He gave to us when we needed it," the wise farmer replied. "Or did you marry a man who ignores his debts?"

"He only made money last year by dumb luck."

"Why does that matter? A debt is not cancelled merely because the lender acquired the money to lend with dice," was all the wise farmer had to say.

The next year came. Once again, the lazy farmer neglected his work, ignoring what his neighbor told him, and had a poor crop, while the wise farmer worked diligently and executed each step at the right time, and had a large, valuable crop. The wise farmer went once again to his neighbor and gave him a large portion of the profits. His wife this time was very displeased.

"We paid back our debts," she said to her husband. "Why did you give him money we did not owe him?"

The wise farmer said, "I gave him our money because he gave us his money when he owed us nothing."

"But we only needed his money because of bad fortune, not bad behavior, as he displays."

"That doesn't change the nature of the gesture, and it does not negate need," the wise farmer said.

Another year passed, and once again the lazy farmer failed to produce a crop of value, while the wise farmer increased his wealth and savings substantially.

His wife approached him at the harvest and said, "You cannot say that our lazy neighbor deserves any of our money now. We have paid him back, and now he owes *us*."

"Very true, he does owe us," the wise farmer said, but he went over to the lazy farmer anyway and gave him money so that he could be comfortable through the winter.

This time, the wise farmer's wife was furious. "Why did you give him even more of our money? Now he will owe us twice and we will likely never get paid back."

The wise farmer replied, "Well now at last I have exceeded his original gesture, and I can say that we are truly charitable."

Yet another year passed, and things proceeded as before, with the wise farmer gaining wealth and the lazy farmer failing to produce much of value. Before his wife could stop him, the wise farmer went and gave money to the lazy one. When his wife asked him "why," he said, "Because I failed to correct his behavior and help him with his harvest."

"That is not your responsibility," his wife replied.

"But it was my opportunity," the wise farmer said. "I saw years ago, before he owed us anything, that he did not prune his vines in time, but I did not go over to him and tell him it was time. I didn't show him how to do it."

"If you had spent your time on that, there would have been no harvest for anyone. And since then you've tried everything to turn him into a good farmer, but he doesn't listen to you!"

"Why does that matter?" the wise farmer said. "You can only judge the virtue of an action before chance plays its games with outcome. We may yet be repaid."

One more year passed, and again the lazy farmer failed to produce great value with his vines, while the wise farmer became even more wealthy. Once again, the wise farmer made up the difference with his own money.

"I don't know why I bother asking you," his wife said to him, "but why did you give him money this time?"

"Because I wanted to," said the wise farmer.

His wife ceased arguing, and said, "Very well, do what you want. You have led us well this far."

As time went on, the lazy farmer began to become infirmed. His joints ached and he could not do even his poor work. The wise farmer went to visit him.

"What shall I do?" the poor farmer said. "I cannot work, and I have no savings."

"I will buy your vineyard from you," the wise farmer said. "I have done well and can hire men to tend the vines for me. With the money you can retire."

"But I already owe you a great sum," said the poor farmer.

"I forgive it," said the wise farmer.

And so, it was done. When the wise farmer's wife learned of this, she once again became angry. "Why did you do this?" she said. "He should have just given us the vineyard with the money he owed us."

"Don't worry about the money. We will easily make it back working two fields," the wise farmer said.

Eventually, the poor farmer died. When this happened, the wise farmer turned the vineyard he had purchased over to the poor farmer's son as an inheritance for him.

The wise farmer's wife, no longer willing to rebuke her husband, said when he did this, "He was a lucky man to have a friend like you, with all that you have done for him."

"If luck is what you want to call it," said the wise farmer. "I was lucky to have a father who taught me well, and a good mind to hear and recall everything he said, and a good sense of time, and a good personality to negotiate a high price for my grapes, and good health throughout my life, and a great many other things, including a wife who trusts my wisdom. So yes, perhaps he was lucky to know me, but as far as luck goes, I had the lion's share, other than one bad year, and for that year, his luck paid well. And now we have engendered good relations between our children. Our son might turn out like he did, and I would have others treat kindly with him."

"His son might be like his father. Will you treat him as well?"

"If he turns out like his father, I will. Let us remember that our debts have already been forgiven."

Witch of the Woods

Dusk is a dangerous time in the Piney Woods. The forest has become less of itself as the years have rolled down the Mississippi to the Gulf, but once upon a time it was a thicket of great repute, for ill much more than good. At dusk the birds clack, the mosquitos swarm, bats flap, and the wolves come out of hiding. The woods are not dangerous because of the wolves or the bears, or even the alligators that lie in the wetlands, but because of the whispered fears of things far less natural.

Once, when Arkansas was newly settled, and the edges of the wood were still being beaten back – before the plantations were built and the hard work of growing cotton had begun in earnest – a young couple built a house together. Back then there were precious few people around the woods, other than the Indians, and they avoided the area except to pass west and back again. They were a happy couple for their part, and preferred the frontier to the eastern colonies where they were not tolerated. One day the woman's husband left her to fight in a war, promising to return by winter. Winter came, but he never returned.

In the spring, a group of settlers came down from the Ozarks and encountered a Cherokee group camped in the hill country by the woods. Being travelers themselves, they warned the settlers of a homestead they came across containing an evil air.

"Something beyond death lingers there," the eldest said, a man calling himself John Black Feather. "Spirits are God-sundered in the woods for miles. We hunted game there a week ago, but the meat is not fit for a man. It is already rancid when still warm. I suggest you pack what you can on your horses and oxen and make North. There is a good road there, and a few towns of white men."

"Leave our wagons?" said one of the settlers. It was Clay, an older man and de-facto leader of the train. "We certainly will not. And we came this way to till new land, not old."

"All the land is old," Black Feather replied. "Older than me or you. And I tell you as I would tell my sons that the woods carry a taint. As for your wagons, the lowlands at the end of the road are flooded this time of year. Your wagons will not get far in the mud. You had best take my advice."

Clay and the other settlers thanked the Indians for the advice but ignored it, thinking it to be savage superstition and believing that the Cherokee were trying to con them into abandoning their wares to them, and so continued down the old road to the flood plain at the edge of the woods. Soon they found their wagons stuck in a thick, sticky, black mud. They pulled what they could to a dry, brushy hill amid the marshy, sparse forest and made camp. Winter stuck a finger out that night and chilled the lot of them. Even a good fire, with what little dry timber could be mustered, seemed to do little to banish the cold, especially for the women and children.

The next day the men set to exploring on horseback and trying to work the wagons out of the mud with triple oxen teams. A few of them went afield to the woods, riding along between thin trees and avoiding large pools. On the edge of the wood, they found a house, small enough to be a hut, though well-made, with a shake roof and timber boards for walls. The door stood ajar and was swinging in a cold wind. The forest around it was cleared, but the fields were fallow. A thin water lingered on the ground, an inch deep in most places, making the little house look like it floated on a still lake. Curtains flapped in glassless windows, the shutters gaping and hanging from rusted hinges in rotten window frames. At first, the scene misgave the settlers, and they were inclined to move on, but two of the men mustered up their courage in defiance of the words of the Indians and went inside.

What they found was a scene that ever after haunted them. A woman was inside, her hazy eyes staring out blankly as she sat in a roughly made chair. Her lips were agape and a pale shade of blue. Her small hands hung limp beside her. Her dress was tattered and dark with old moisture. A lone fly crawled over her pallid skin. The house was set as if lived in, but a season of wind had moved things about and left a layer of dust on every object. A black kettle hung in a mud-brick hearth containing rotting wood and charcoal. The table had empty cups, one of which was blown over and held a dark ring from long dried tea. A bed was made neatly in a corner, the sheets set against a straw mattress.

"She dead?" Bill, one of the men, asked.

The other, a younger man named Tom, stepped closer to look and confirmed it. "Looks like she died this morning. She'd be puffed up and eaten to bits in woods like this if it was any longer."

"But look how torn up the dress is," Bill said. "And look at the wood in here. It's all rotten-like. That fire hasn't been lit in a month, or I'm a frog."

Just then, a cold wind blew through the open windows, and to the two men, it seemed as if the dead woman let out a long groan. The two men jumped away, failing to silence short screams.

"It's just the wind," Bill said. Then they saw the eyes had moved and now regarded them with an eager light. The hands of the woman were no longer dangling but were folded in her lap. Her mouth was closed and twisted into an oddly beckoning smile. The wind blew again, and they thought they heard voices among whistles in the eaves. Without another word, the men dashed out of the house, splashing water and mud on the way to their horses. They didn't bother with their muskets, but instead leapt into their saddles and galloped away east. As they splashed through the flooded field, the wind picked up again, blowing their coats over their heads and freezing their spines. Through the gale they could hear, faint and indecipherable yet somehow tempting, words in a high voice.

They got back to the makeshift camp to find the wagons already circled on the hill and a high fire burning in the dusk damp. The fire flickered heavily; a strong wind had come with the riders all the way to the camp. The two men dismounted their sweaty horses and told their story to everyone in earshot, which was soon many people as bits of their story passed among the settlers.

"You two been drinking?" Clay said to them.

"Swear to God, no," Bill said. "I haven't touched a bottle since Tuesday, but I can tell you if I have my way, I'll never be without a nip again!"

"Pah!" Clay said. "You got scared off by a little woman in a hut!"

"She was dead," Bill said. "And she moved. Swear to Christ and all the saints and the Devil hisself that she moved. She looked at me."

"Either she was dead, and you imagined it, or she was quite alive, and you ran off without so much as a polite word or an offer of help. I'm going to put this nonsense to rest." With that, Clay saddled up his horse.

"It's witchcraft, Clay, don't go back," Bill said.

"No such thing. Now saddle up and show me where."

"I won't, and you can't make me," Bill said. "Especially not in the dark." Indeed, the sun was setting, and shadows were deepening on the swampy ground at the edge of the woods.

Clay spat on the ground and cursed Bill for a coward, then set off in the direction from which the two riders had come. Bill drank a whole pint of whiskey before saying another word, then sat himself beside the fire and shivered, saying he could finally no longer hear the whispers. His wife, a Godly woman with a soft heart, believed every word and never left him alone again without a sip of whiskey.

Night fell, and the barely waxing crescent moon sank below the trees. Darkness that should have been total was not as a fog rolled in above the flooded waters, strangely luminescent in the mere stars, and blew swiftly over the ground. It surrounded the hill like an island in a raging river, with only the tops of trees to say they were not perched up in some strange sky kingdom of darkness. The wind howled above the fog and threatened to kill the fires. Through every gust soft, strange words came passing.

Around midnight the wind finally died down, though the fog lingered and ceased to rush by in torrents. New fires were lit, and the settlers huddled together. Even the children went without sleep.

And Clay never returned.

Morning came the settlers discussed among themselves what to do about Clay. Tom, having considered Clay a good friend, organized a search party to find him despite the terror of the previous evening. He set a few pairs of men (for his first directive was never to go alone) to try a few different areas of the wood, but he held in his heart the belief that Clay had found the little abandoned house. With a heavy heart, he returned.

The house was standing peacefully. The water in the fallow fields stood still and glass-like. The curtains hung in the still air and the door was shut.

"The wind must have blown in closed," he said, but he did not believe his own words.

With great trepidation, Tom approached the house, his pistol primed and cocked in one hand, with two additional musketed men beside him. He turned the handle on the door and pushed. It creaked on its rusty hinges and swung inward, revealing an empty rocking chair.

"Jesus Christ," he said to himself, half-prayer and half-curse. He swallowed hard and entered. In the far corner, the neatly made bed held two people, pale-skinned and blue-lipped. Each had closed eyes. One was the woman, looking content as if sleeping; the other was Clay, equally peaceful.

"Clay!" Tom shouted in the dead air. No reply came. He drew his pistol and fired it into the wall above his friend. The shot rang loudly in the small room, full of still air. The smoke slowly cleared, and through it, Tom could see that Clay had not moved an inch.

"Devilry!" One of the men said.

"We're getting the hell out of here," Tom said and backed away from the scene. The trio of men saddled up and rode back to camp. When they returned, they found Black Feather waiting for them outside the ring of wagons, his eyes hard. Other settlers stood around him, along with the Cherokee traders.

"I can see in your eyes what I have felt up on the hill," Black Feather said.

Tom, almost out of breath, said, "It's devilry. Witchcraft." He looked at the other settlers and pointed back toward where the little house stood. "Clay's dead! The witch took him!" Clay's wife, Elsa, cried out from the crowd and was quickly drawn away by a few of the women.

Hard and silent, Black Feather kept his gaze on Tom while the sound of the crowd rose and then slowly fell back to near silence. At length, the old Indian spoke, "There is here a spirit of suffering and withering. Whether your dead woman brought it with her, or it has always been here and has merely found a vessel, I cannot say, but for now, it is sated."

"Why did you come back? To gloat?" Tom said.

Black Feather remained motionless. "No. I came back to help. My sons have always said that I have been too generous for my own good, but hearing what we heard on the wind last night and feeling what we have felt through the earth, I felt I could not leave you to this darkness and call my own spirit at peace."

"What do you propose?" Tom said.

"While the spirit rests, we might act to contain it."

"How are we going to do that? You have some kind of magic you know of for this?"

"Magic?" Black Feather paused at that word. "No. We must lay these bodies, and the spirits trapped within them, to rest. If what your people have told me is true."

"It's true," Tom said.

"Then show me. Do you have any clergy with you?" Black Feather said as he mounted his horse.

"No, we believe every man is clergy to himself," Tom said. "Besides, that's the white man's god, isn't it?"

"There is only one God," Black Feather replied. "May he hear our prayers today." The other Cherokee echoed the sentiment in their own language, and then they all set out following Tom. They were quiet as they went, and gradually a growing silence began to weigh on them as the sounds of woods died out.

"Keep your muskets handy," Tom said as they came back to the little house.

"Bullets are no use here," Black Feather said. He dismounted and walked without hesitation inside the house. Emboldened by the Cherokee's confidence, Tom followed him in, once again laying eyes on the pair of bodies in the bed.

"Aren't you afraid?" Tom said.

"I do not fear such spirits," Black Feather said. He approached the bed and laid a hand on the forehead of the woman, then the man. He sang soft words as he did so. He turned back to Tom. "We must bury these bodies before sunset."

"We ought to burn them," a man said beside Tom.

"Right," Tom said. "That's what we do with Witches."

"No, that is not right," Black Feather said. "We should lay them together in the ground. The body must be returned to the earth. That way they will rest. Together, so the spirit is sated. We need to find a spot that can be marked so that none will disturb them. I will send my son White Owl to look. Will you send a man with him?"

Tom agreed, and so Black Feather's son set off along the edges of the forest with one of the settlers. Within the house, Black Feather unwrapped several implements covered in pale deerskin. One was a small carved stick with two long raven feathers tied to the tip. The other was a wooden bowl with a tiny opening, much like the end of a pipe. He lit a match and burned something inside of it, then placed it nearby, where it smoked. He held the carved stick and began again to sing softly in his own language.

"What are you doing?" Tom said.

Black feather paused and said, "Praying. You should do so as well."

Tom felt strangely comforted by that, and so bowed his head and said a prayer for Clay and his family. When he looked up, he saw Black Feather still singing softly. Still not liking the air of the place, and not wanting to look more upon the dead face of his friend, Tom turned to go out the door. He paused after a step and found his gaze lingering on a small, black book on a little shelf. He picked it up and turned it over in his hands. On the cover was a strange symbol, like a star with many additional geometric shapes. He had a strange compulsion to open it, and found himself flipping through pages of words he could not read and symbols he could not recognize.

He turned his head to see Black Feather, who was going on with his prayer, his back still to the door. Silently, Tom slipped the small book into his jacket pocket. He wondered for the rest of the days why, but he told nobody that he did it for a great many years.

A short time later, White Owl returned, having found a suitable place to bury the bodies. Black Feather, along with the other Cherokees and the help of a few of the settlers, bound up the bodies in the bedsheets, covering their faces, and dragged them outside. They placed the bodies onto hastily made sleds hitched to saddles. Black Feather's son and one of the settlers dragged them off. Black Feather turned back to the house and considered it a long moment.

"This we should burn," he said.

"I agree," Tom said and set about in his saddlebags for some oil and matches.

"You did not take anything from it?"

Tom paused and saw that Black Feather was regarding him with the same expressionless, hard face he always wore.

"No," Tom said, lying for reasons he did not know. A part of himself deep inside cried out to tell Black Feather the truth, but the struggle was not enough. Tom turned back to his saddlebag and retrieved his tinderbox and a small bottle of lamp oil.

"It is well, then," Black Feather said, and looked again at the house. "This whole place has an unsettling presence, even for me, and I have seen many horrors."

Tom followed Black Feather back inside. They pulled down the curtains turned out the rotten bed, and placed everything they could against dry wood to fuel the fire. Tom doused the cloth with oil, and with a match, a blazing fire soon filled the interior of the little house. The fumes from the dusty, dying rags caused Tom to gag. He stumbled out of the house with Black Feather and watched it burn for a few minutes. Black Feather sang a new song.

When they were convinced that the house would burn on its own, they followed the tracks of Black Feather's son up a hill into the woods. After a little while, they found a clearing where the Cherokees and a few other men were busy wrapping tightly the bodies and digging a hole. Beside the would-be grave, or rather above it, was a monolithic boulder, twice as high as a man.

Black Feather looked up at the westering sun and said. "Good. I will begin preparations for a funeral ceremony. What customs will you observe?"

"I suppose we'll pray, maybe sing a hymn, say a speech or something. I'm not used to this sort of thing. Clay always did it. His wife will want to be here. I should go get her."

"Do not dawdle. These bodies need to be in the ground by nightfall."

Tom rode back to the camp as quick as he could, finding a long dry stretch of land that let his horse gallop. When he got to the camp, he explained what they had done and what Black Feather proposed. Elsa, Clay's wife, was still in hysterics. They were an older couple but childless. One of Clay's nieces attempted to keep her from thrashing at Tom.

"You're not burying him with a witch!" Elsa screamed. "You're not burying him with a witch and with a pagan to pray to his damned gods."

"Cherokees aren't Pagans, and we're going to do our own prayers," Tom said. "We're giving him a Christian burial as best we can, but we have to bury both of them."

Despite the woman's protests, she was put in a saddle, and a large group of the settlers accompanied her and Tom to the burial site. When they got there, they found the hole already dug and the bodies, bound by cloth, already lying in the hole. Black Feather stood motionless and regarded the newcomers coldly. Elsa slid off her horse and began cursing the old Cherokee, but he remained silent and did not react.

"Like hell, you're putting Clay in the ground with a Witch!"

"Does it matter where his body is laid?" Black Feather replied. "The body is not so sacred as the spirit."

"Don't give me your pagan nonsense!" Elsa said back.

Bill was there and said to Tom, "We should pull him out and bury him somewhere else. It is Elsa's wish. She has the right."

Black Feather said, "If it is your custom, I will not fight you for it, but will only say to heed my advice."

So Tom, feeling a burden as the others now looked to him as they once did Clay, did the second thing that day he would come to regret. He said. "She's right; pull him out. Dig him his own grave. Quick. Before the sun sets."

"Not here. Anywhere but here!" Elsa said.

"It is a pure site. A good place for a man's body to be put to rest and his spirit freed to go to God," Black Feather said.

"We'll bury him at the camp. There's good dry ground there."

A few of the men hurried to the hole and pulled out a large body wrapped in a sheet. Black Feather sighed and said, "And so it is done."

The settlers worked quickly to fill in the hole as the sun moved into the tree branches around them. Once the hole was nearly full, they began to pull away the rocky soil under the great boulder. The monolith started to teeter, then with a great shove rolled and landed on the sump made by the fresh grave, pressing the body of the witch down.

Black Feather and his son began a ceremony around the rock, with the older man singing a song in his native tongue while the younger played a small wooden flute. Soon the other Cherokee joined in and circled the stone. They shook more smoke at the boulder and then stood back.

Black Feather said, "We have prayed for the woman and for her rest. Hopefully, God will grant it and inter the body here forever. Will you now say a prayer in your own custom? The more voices, the more God will harken."

"I'm not praying for no damn witch," Bill said. All the others shared this sentiment.

Tom opened his mouth to say that he would, but he found his tongue stilled. When blank-faced Black Feather nodded slowly and began packing his things, Tom noticed that his hand lingered on a small book in his pocket. It was a third regret, as deep as the others.

Somewhere, a strange bird crowed. Dusk was settling in, and the barely waxing moon was chasing the sun in the west.

"Let's get out of here," Tom said.

"Wait," Black Feather said. He spoke quickly among his people and then turned back to Tom. "We will accompany you. This night is not one for riding." His eyes lingered on the wrapped body of Clay, now bound again to a makeshift sled.

They all rode back as the light left and the red-grey dusk deepened in the woods. Mist began to gather in the low places about them as the temperature dropped. When they exited the tree line, it was into a sea of fog.

"It isn't natural," Bill said, taking a drink from a flask.

"Just stick to the path we cut before, and we'll be fine," Tom said. The others followed close behind him, and the fog closed in. Soon the trees were lost to sight. If there were stars, they could not be seen, nor could the moon.

"Not sure if I like this more than the wind or not," Tom said. His voice fell flat in the fog, wrapped like cold, wet blankets around the party. Nobody responded. Tom stopped and pulled an oil-soaked rag from his saddlebag and wrapped it around a limb from a nearby scrubby oak. He lit it with a match and soon had a blazing torch. He held it aloft, but it did little to light the way. Instead, it made the fog into a brighter waste of grey and white. It did, however, cast enough light to see a short way in front of the horse. He did his best to follow the ruts and tracks of their previous trek.

Soon, Tom pulled his horse up short as they reached a deeply flooded basin.

"What's wrong?" Elsa asked from back in the line.

"I must have lost the track," Tom said. "Either that or the water moved."

"We're lost?" Elsa said.

Tom stayed silent and held aloft his torch, lighting up a calm pond that extended beyond view.

"What about the Indian?" Bill said.

Tom looked to the back of the party. Almost obscured by the fog were Black Feather and his group. Without bidding, the Cherokee met Tom's eyes and worked his horse forward, followed closely by his son.

"I see," Black Feather said, seeing the body of water.

"You know where we are?" Tom said.

"No. I am not from here," Black Feather said.

"Don't you have some kind of Earth sense?" Elsa said. "Can you get us back to the camp?"

Black Feather withdrew a leather bag from one of his pockets. He began opening it and fishing inside of it.

"What is that? Some sort of talisman?" Bill said.

"It's a compass," Black Feather said. He tapped the brass-cased item a few times. "And it's not working."

"It's the witch!" Elsa said. She shook upon her horse and gripped the reigns iron-hard.

"Maybe, maybe not," Black Feather said. "I said these woods are tainted, and there may be more to that than a lone white witch. But in any case, she is bound now."

"Perhaps she is restless," said White Owl. "The body is bound, but the spirit may still have some power."

"Some, yes, but clearly not all it once had," Black Feather said. "Do any of you hear the whispers from last night?" He looked to the others in the party. Nobody would say that he had heard the eerie voice from the night prior.

"We still need to get back to camp," Tom said. "And out of this fog."

Just then, ripples appeared in the still water, and soft splashes sounded at the horse's feet.

"What is that?" Elsa said.

"Alligators," Black Feather replied.

"This far north?" Tom said.

"Tom! Get us out of this devilry!" Elsa cried.

"Relax," White Owl said, watching the ripples. "It's moving away from us."

"A bad sign," Black Feather said. He looked to Elsa. "Are you a believer in water burial, as they do on the sea?"

"What?" Elsa said, taken aback.

"This water is permanent, not a remnant of the floods, or it would not have life in it. We should bury your husband immediately. Immediately!" Black Feather's voice rose in the still air, with an urgency and a fear that he had never expressed before. Bill signed the cross on his chest.

"No!" Elsa said. "I'm not leaving him to be food for gators and fish!"

"Damn it, woman, listen to the medicine man!" White Owl said. "We never should have permitted this, we never should-"

"Calm yourself," Black Feather said, laying a gentle hand on his son's arm. "What is done is done." He looked at Tom. "To our right should be South, if we have kept in the general direction you came in. Let us go that way. And keep your torch lit, if you can."

"Will you guide us?" Tom said.

"God will guide us, or nobody," Black Feather said.

"I will stay in the front with you," White Owl said. "And help you, if you wish. I am a decent enough tracker."

The party went on along the edge of the water, the fog still wrapped tightly around them. Tom's torch began to flicker as the oil rag began to run out of fuel. The water seemed to drag on in a straight line blocking them.

"I don't recall any lake near your camp," White Owl said after a time.

"It does just seem to go on and on," Tom said. White Owl called for his father, who moved up the line to join them.

"We've been on this line for hours, it seems," Tom said.

White Owl said, "I'll admit, father, this baffles my senses. Do we head back?"

Black Feather pulled a necklace from inside his shirt and fingered it. "It no longer matters what direction we go, I think. We are going to the conclusion of matters."

"So do we stay close to the water or break? Maybe backtrack a bit and see if we can find our old trail?"

"Stay with the water," Black Feather said. "Water purifies. And it calms me."

The Party went on, but soon the water began to curve away to their left. Tom followed this shortly and then departed, keeping as near as he could remember to where east should have been. After a time, they encountered trees in thick bunches once again, and a feeling of deeper dread settled on the party. The only thing audible was the soft sound of the horse's hooves in the mud.

"You've led us back into the forest!" Elsa said.

"Quiet, woman!" Tom said sharply, feeling nearly sick with fear.

"Stop," White Owl said. "Give me the torch." Tom handed it over, and White Owl held it out in front of his horse. "These are our sled tracks from this afternoon." He dismounted from his horse and looked more closely. "We are back at the house. Look around, and we should find it."

"There," Bill said. He pointed away in the fog, and in the flickering torchlight, a dim shadow, tall and narrow, could be seen. White Owl mounted and approached, and saw the remnants of a mud-brick hearth, then returned to the shapes of the party.

"What do we do?" Tom said.

"We follow our tracks back to the burial site," Black Feather said. "And give him back to the witch. That is the price we shall pay for escape."

"Like Hell we are," Bill said.

"Indeed like Hell," Black Feather replied.

"I won't!" Elsa said. She turned her horse, which pulled the body of clay on a sled, and turned to ride away.

"No!" Black Feather cried, but it was already too late. He kicked his horse into a gallop after the woman, who quickly became a black shape in the night fog. The others, slower to react, followed. After a few terse minutes of galloping, each man doing his best to guide his horse by sound when sight failed, the men, with Black Feather in the lead, came suddenly upon a horse lying on its side, crying out and thrashing its legs in terror at the shore of the strange lake. Black Feather dismounted quickly and ran to the beast, whose lungs rattled with death.

Near at hand, Elsa was wailing hysterically, cutting at the cords that bound the body of Clay to the makeshift sled.

"What's got into you, woman!?" Tom said, dropping his torch and attempting to get his arms around the woman.

"He's not dead! He's not dead!" she cried.

"Get a hold of yourself!" Tom said, trying to grip the hand that held the knife. He quickly let go when caught the flash of movement in front of him. Elsa took the opportunity to continue hacking away the rest of the chords.

In terror, Tom pushed himself back as the folds of the bed sheets moved of their own accord.

"Everyone back away," Black Feather said. "Away I said!"

Even Elsa complied with this request, so grim was Black Feather's voice.

The folded mass of sheets convulsed. Strange groans emanated forth from it, and it began to rise. The sheet fell away, revealing a pale face with hazy eyes that had a dim orange light of their own. The mouth was agape, and in it, sharp teeth shot from withered gums. The being turned from them and let out a beastly howl.

"Clay!" Elsa said and rushed forward.

"No!" was all Tom could get out before she reached what was once Clay and wrapped her arms around him. It was her husband's name that was last spoken upon her lips as the corpse turned and plunged its hands and teeth into the woman's neck, rending her arteries and tearing flesh from bone.

"Dear God!" Bill said. He shouldered his musket and fired without hesitation, hitting Clay above the right breast. It had no effect except to draw the demon's attention and cause him to charge. Bill's horse bucked in fright and threw him to the mud, then bolted as Clay ran toward Bill. Bill, still drunk, got to a sitting position before the corpse hit him. Bill still held his rifle and was able to push the creature off him, though it continued to scratch at his chest, drawing beads of blood. Another one of the settlers, having drawn a sabre, set to hacking at Clay, slicing through cloth but drawing no blood.

The creature abandoned Bill and lunged at his new opponent, teeth sinking into his skull as the sword fell to the earth. One of the Cherokee, a tall man named Still Fox, initiated his own attack with a steel hand-axe, trying to sever the neck. It failed, and the creature reared up at him. The Cherokee was spared by Black Feather, who slashed with his knife at the creature's hamstrings, causing it to fall to the earth and thrash wildly.

Tom ran over and shot it square in the head, but like the first shot, that did nothing to slow it except draw its attention. Tom turned to flee but tripped, landing face-first in the water. He felt dead nails clawing at his legs above his boots, and he dug his hands into the wet earth, finding no purchase. He turned and looked into the maw of terror. The creature gripped his belt, and then with a sudden expression of wonder, released him and turned its attention to the Cherokee that remained, crawling first toward Black Feather, who stood resolved, singing and trying to light once again his smoky incense. It seemed then that the creature laughed darkly, or else it was a trick of the terror of that moment. Black Feather, dropping his composure, leapt forward and struck the corpse on the forehead with his incense bowl, swinging it like a sling.

Before the horror could react, White Owl flung onto it a bottle of oil, retrieved from Tom's horse, which had miraculously not bolted. Seeing this, Tom retrieved the torch, just beginning to sputter out, and threw it on the corpse. With a tortured, spine-freezing cry, the monster began to burn. Not content to be destroyed in a flash, Clay-that-was thrashed on the ground, with echoing screams, as flesh peeled and cloth chared. The men backed away, weapons still at the ready. Tom got another bottle of oil and threw it on the blaze. After an agonizing few minutes, the thing began to move only slowly. White Owl strode forward and kicked the body. It rolled into the water of the lake and continued burning and moving as it slid into the depths.

They stared at it for a time. White Owl broke the silence. "As my father says, 'If all else fails, use fire.'"

"And water purifies," Tom said.

Black Feather laughed. It was wild and free-hearted in the dark. "So I have said."

The men still standing in the accursed scene consisted of Black Feather, White Owl, Tom, Bill (in much worse shape, having discovered that his horse, along with his whiskey, had disappeared), Still Fox, and one settler named Jim. Missing were seven additional white men, two women, and two Cherokee. The horses of the Cherokee had not fled, but all the others save Tom's had. The fog persisted, dense as ever. The remaining men set about building a fire, cracking apart the makeshift sled and using what kindling they could to get the thing going. It smoked horribly but provided some welcome warmth.

After a time, one of Black Feather's men returned, saying that he heard voices in the dark calling to him, but his horse had led him away from it. He had dismounted to run to the voice when the horse bit him on the arm and broke the trance, and then lead him to the fire. When he arrived, he helped bury the dead settler. None of the other men were found that night.

The fog lifted in the hazy morning, and White Owl went on a quick scouting trip. He found three stray, riderless horses and managed to bring them back. One of them was Bill's, but it had thrown its saddle somehow and now had no whiskey for its owner. He also found that the Lake was smaller than any of them had thought and that they had hall traveled far further south than they had realized. The settlers' camp was now very much north-by-north-east of the lake. On their way back, they came across a thicket with a dirty white cloth hanging in the branches of a dead tree. A quick inspection found the two women, who had gotten lost and sheltered there. Their horses had stayed nearby, and soon they were accounted for as well.

When they got back to the camp, the settlers that remained were eager to hear the tale and swift to believe it because they had experienced the same fog that night, and many men had been awakened in the dark by strangely pleasant dreams that seemed nightmares once awake. A few men hastily assembled a search party, but Tom and Black Feather begged them not to. They judged the men who had disappeared to be surely dead, or possibly worse.

"It is better to grieve less with uncertainty than more having judged things for yourself," Black Feather said. "I myself have lost a kinsman, and though it is a grievous loss, I will not risk the rest."

With heavy hearts, the remainder of the settlers agreed. They broke camp and moved further north, away from the Piney Woods and the flood plain, hoping to leave the horror of those nights behind them. Tom went on living with his memories, but ever the black book, that which he could not speak of, troubled him, but what he did with it, and whether his soul and conscience survived, none can say for sure. The memory of him, of Black Feather and White Owl, of Clay and the Witch of the Woods, eventually faded into rumor, and then passed to lore and legend.

It is said, however, that the Piney Woods are still perilous to walk through at dusk, and that the Witch of the Woods, entombed in body forever beneath unmovable stone, calls out on cold spring nights, wailing for her forgotten love to come back to her, and drawing to her any man unwitting enough to listen to her soft song. Those men whose ears hear that melody or whose eyes chance to see the grave, it is said, go down, down into the earth with her, to sleep forever in her tomb of unwilling lovers.

Voices of the Void

Andrew walked down the gallery, watching the slowly bobbing reflection on the waxed floor from the bright artificial windows to his left. Looking out as he entered the wide, clean foyer, it was hard to believe he had just stepped through a grit-caked airlock that opened into darkness. Comfortable furniture lined the walls in bright colors, upholstered in a synthetic material made to look like weaved cotton. The rubber-soled boots of his EV suit even squeaked as he walked; the dust collection system was still working at full capacity. The automated maintenance system was top-of-the-line; it would be years before it needed its own round of repairs, and the reactor that powered the colony would likely take centuries to die. Andrew reminded himself of this as he looked at the details of human life around him.

This section was the school. A book sat on a nearby work table, closed and abandoned, ignored by the robots and machines that cleaned the room… Andrew couldn't guess how many times they had passed it over. On a nearby bulletin board, there were pinned a variety of drawings depicting scenes that were more-or-less earth-like: children playing on grass under a yellow sun, rain and rainbows, castles and cars on busy streets. Odd, considering that it was likely none of the children had ever seen Earth, any other garden planet, or even a bright yellow sun for that matter. Andrew paused and looked around himself, and thought it likely none of them ever would. But there was a chance, or else he wouldn't be here. He spied on one of the nearby desks another drawing, and his eye became fixed on it.

He walked toward it, looking down at the floor of artificial maple, each section printed to be as unique as real wood, and saw a black scuff mark that had stood up to the passage of the cleaning machines.

Andrew looked up and felt suddenly queasy.

The large room was full of children of all ages, sitting on the neat couches or working at tables. From a distant hall, a teenage boy careened toward him on old-fashioned rolling skates. A young woman – a teacher, by her professional dress, stood at the entrance to a nearby classroom, her arms crossed seriously, though she smiled slightly as she watched the youth. Her light brown hair blew around her shoulders as the boy passed her. Another teacher – a middle-aged man – slipped behind another door, pretending not to notice the boy.

The young teacher called to the teenage boy, "Astin!" and though he knew she was looking to the rebellious youth, Andrew could have sworn the teacher caught his eye. "Astin what do you think you are doing?!"

She's pretty. The thought careened into his consciousness unbidden, though not as unwelcome as other sentiments that intruded so. Andrew could suddenly see the details in her eyes, as if he were looking into them just centimeters away. They were blue, and reflected the artificial day of a skylight above in a bright white halo.

The image disappeared as Andrew came back into himself. He flinched as the boy on skates tried to stop in front of him, but tripped, scuffing the floor with the rubber brake on his skates, falling onto his side and sliding away, grunting softly. He slid into, or rather, *through,* Andrew.

And then the vision faded. The sounds of playing children turned to hallow reverberation, and the beautiful teacher turned translucent as she stepped toward him, intent on helping the fallen teenager. Then she was gone.

"Damnit," Andrew said to himself, forcing the word out of his mouth. His visor was fogging up with his rapid breath. He checked the computer on his wrist and, seeing that the air was clean and clear, he pressed the release button at his neck. His helmet and visor split into tiny ribbons, then disappeared into his collar. He breathed deeply.

"Damn fool, getting distracted like that," he said aloud to himself. With the helmet removed, he was suddenly aware of the reverb of his voice in the empty room and the soft clicking of a fan's bearing somewhere in the ventilation system. The wonder of the vision was quickly replaced with his usual sense of unease. He looked down and checked the receiver of his rifle – an antique weapon, but one that he knew functioned better within atmospheres than his plasma gun, which he kept slung on his back. It was toggled over to *auto.* Andrew shook his head and toggled it back to safe, distrusting his instincts.

He stepped toward the picture on the desk, hoping to provoke another vision (which he had, ironically, intended to avoid by staring at the faux-wood floor), and hoping also that if he were to slip back to the past, he could, with his wits more about him, actually look for his quarry. He let his rifle hang and picked up the picture. It was of a castle, colored with grey pencil and highly detailed, but there were little modern colony buildings instead of a medieval village surrounding it.

Probably better if I don't slip back, he said inside himself. *I need to find her in the present. A past vision does nothing.* A void echoed back, and Andrew sighed.

Andrew looked to the manila door from which he had seen the young teacher emerge. It was shut. He could see through a small window a few empty desks. He felt a strong compulsion to open the door and look around, provoke another vision.

She's likely dead, his voice said to himself. He knew the voice – part of his fractured self – was right. They had played too long at that once already. Andrew nodded his head.

He couldn't control the power, at least not yet, but he was beginning to understand what would cause it to present itself. Perhaps in the future, he would be able to look back in time at will, not be thrust into it at the behest of some echo in his brain and lose all sense of what "the present" meant. Perhaps... but such experiments would have to wait.

Andrew put the picture back down and stepped away from the desk. He walked through the open school toward where his readout said the primary elevators were. This sector had to be empty. He walked down a long and narrow hallway, the rustle of his suit and his soft steps the only sound.

When he reached the elevators, he noticed the doorway to the dormitory overflows was open. The lights were shining brightly all the way down a long, straight hallway. He could only see the first few doors, and they were all shut.

Andrew looked back at the slick steel doors of the closest elevator. A glowing panel above indicated that the car was paused on the sixth level. He tried to remember how deep things went, information he gathered while pouring over the technical details of the plant during his trip to the planet, but his memory felt hard to access.

"Probably goes pretty deep, but not from the dorms, yeah?" he said aloud, listening to his voice die in the artificial, fabric-lined corridor. He slipped his right glove off to operate the computer panel and call up the elevator. After hurriedly going through the motions, he brought his rifle around and touched the trigger, feeling the familiar steel against his fingertip. He let the weapon fall back into its bungee sling and tucked his glove into the belt of his suit.

The lift moved slowly, and Andrew could hear the sliding and grinding of the pulleys above, shaking off old, dry dust. He glanced over at the dormitory again. He stepped toward it, seeing more of the plain blue doors appear around shallow recesses in the hallway.

"Hello?" he called loudly. "I'm here from..." He paused and thought about his employer. His mission from Saul Toro was not officially from the Iber Colony Counsel. "I'm here to help. Is there anyone out there?" He brought his rifle back up and shouldered it, intending to fire a shot, but then thought better of it. "Anyone alive?"

The elevator doors opened, and he glanced at an empty and pristine car. He turned from it and stepped toward the dormitory hallway. A tall computer panel stood next to the open blast doors. Andrew saw that it could be used to page the rooms, but also saw, since this was an overflow dormitory, that only certain rooms could be paged. He could go through the list, one by one, and make sure there was nobody simply hiding from him.

"What would they be hiding from?"

Part of his mind answered to him, almost against his will. A single word – a *concept* – from a sector of himself he had, for reasons of sanity, maintained little contact with.

Wr't'lra'a The word drew itself out, all guttural nonsense, but in the image remained. *Wrtla,* a voice inside said back.

Could it be? He thought. *Could there really be more of them?* The situation seemed to fit, but then again there were many things in the universe that could swallow a colony of humans whole. *But leave everything so perfect? No! They walked away. They walked down. To it.*

The sliver of his former self that had surged forward seemed to cry wordlessly after its interjection, demanding to become one with the other pieces of Andrew's mind. The self he was before – his memories, his identity – had something more to say, but it had been touched too deeply by the ancient unknowable void. The hunter he had created out of the shards of that contact asserted itself and shut the old, broken Andrew away. His old consciousness was now an echo – useful if needed, but safely locked up.

Andrew took a quick picture of the room list with his computer and stepped into the dormitory hallway. It was carpeted and clean. He brought up the list on the screen attached to his left forearm. Normally he would use the heads-up display on his helmet, but he had removed it to breathe the air of the place.

"J-115," he said aloud. A sliver of his mind touched his consciousness, and he felt a pang of dread again. He frowned and focused as he walked to the first occupied dormitory, bringing his rifle forward in its sling just in case. He found the door unlocked, and it pushed in with a slight squeak of the hinges. Automatic lights flickered on, revealing a Spartan flat.

"Anyone home?"

As he expected, silence was all that greeted him.

He stepped in and looked around briefly. In the bathroom a toothbrush sat perched on a deep sink. A personal computer sat on a table near the made bed, dead and unplugged.

Andrew took a breath and listened to his own thoughts.

It would take a long time to check every room. The dread returned, and tapping on the edge of his current consciousness was an idea he didn't want to consider. It tapped again, and he groaned, wondering if it were prescience or just his imagination.

He stepped out of the empty flat and continued down the hall.

"I'm checking each one, so you might as well come out if you haven't. I'm not here to hurt you."

The whir of a fan in a vent was all that responded. Then there was a sudden click, and Andrew brought up his rifle, quickly clicking off the safety. A few paces in front of him, a small door in the wall opened up, and a cleaning robot emerged. It began its daily chore, turning and running along the edge of the hallway, sucking up the dust that had collected in the last day.

Andrew chuckled and stepped forward, then was assaulted by a vision and a ringing in his ears. He reached to the wall to steady himself, but the wall wasn't there.

He was suddenly inside a large flat, stepping toward a partly open door. A smell was stuck in his nostrils like dried mud. It was a rotten smell, and he knew what made it. He pushed the door wider, looking only down the sights of his rifle, knowing that it would not save him from the horror. The lights flickered on, and his mind was fracturing further, seeing further, as if the vision could not be contained within a single moment.

He screamed as he saw a crib; the scream did not stop him from continuing forward and seeing what remained inside the simple wooden bed. Nausea scraped across the back of his head, his neck, his ears, down his throat. He could smell his own bile. He screamed with every piece of himself, screamed and bled and cried and collapsed.

Then he was standing back in the hall. The cleaner had moved one door down. His prescient self was still screaming, and though the images remained, preserved like endlessly looped video files, the screams began to slowly fade, responding to the subtle push he gave to that part of his mind. Soon it was a dull roar in his mind: echoing, distant, and yet not gone.

"No reason to continue," he said, his voice dry like reeds. "They walked away. Those that *could* walk away."

He turned away from the hall and ran back toward the elevators. As he did, the screaming finally stopped. The vision of the dead, forgotten child, seared into his retinas, burned into his memory forever, suddenly waned and began to disappear. By the time he reached the lift, the images had nearly evaporated, becoming a dream after waking, or a half-memory of a blurry photograph.

He knew what he had seen, though. His future self had seen it, and by warning him, had destroyed the vision in a paradox created by his change of course.

He stepped into the elevator. He ran his hand through the menus on the computer to run the car down to the industrial center, which was level six. *The last place this elevator went.* From there, he would test the fears and desires of his former mind. Already that part was raving, calling to him. The doors closed. Andrew kneeled and began preparing himself. He checked every magazine and battery he had. He tested the light on his front rail and affixed a bayonet to his front lug. He checked his plasma gun and made sure it was slung right where he would want it.

Lastly, he reached in his pocket and felt for the grenade he had rigged up specially to explode immediately upon setting the fuse. He would not feed the old Andrew to a *Wrtla,* whatever might happen. The finality of that decision gave him courage. He knew not whether there was a journey beyond his life through limbo or purgatory, but wherever he might go, he would go as himself.

Taking a breath, he checked his wrist computer. His vision blurred and focused. It was 10:00 hours. He tapped the computer, sure something was wrong. Perhaps it had reset the time when he had entered the mining facility, syncing with the central chronometer. Toro *had* given him the codes.

"It can't have been three hours already," he said, reassuring himself. Visions, especially those of the future, were always instantaneous.

He toggled the safety of his rifle, finding it on semi and feeling disconcerted by the fact until he remembered that he had meant to fire a warning shot down the hall.

"I'm getting out of practice," he said to himself.

The elevator slowed and the lift doors opened. He stepped out and looked down several wandering hallways which led to the lowest level of housing. Like the top floor, there was an open foyer near the elevators, but this one was clearly designed with an industrial purpose in mind. Desks and computer terminals lined every wall. Like the first floor, these were left in a state of mid-use. Some monitors still showed open documents, the image of words and draft lines burned forever into the machine, which carried on refreshing the same still image week after week. Caged doors opened off the main hall into equipment rooms and other repositories like lockers and materials storage.

A few wide sapphire windows were set in the walls, gazing out into an abyss that once was likely the well-lit beginning of the mine. The darkness beyond irritated a part of Andrew, but he resisted the urge to shine a light out one of those windows and see the rock for himself.

Andrew walked past all this, shining his light into dark corners, following his map to the next set of lifts, which would take him down into the mining area. Once again, there was no life other than the artificial buzzing of machines engaged in their daily maintenance tasks. He skipped the dormitories, knowing that if they were not empty, they would contain things he did not wish to see.

He paused as he passed a workstation, noting that a half-eaten donut remained by the keyboard, nearly desiccated. He wondered why no pest had wandered by to claim it, but then he remembered the planet's desolate surface. There would be no unwanted life in the colony, save for the microbes that came along with the colonists themselves, and he had already seen those at work on the corpse-

"Of the baby," he said aloud, and shivered. The image was dim, nearly gone, but he could imagine the horror well enough.

He paused as he turned away, noticing a few pieces of rubbish in the workstation's wastebasket. He looked around and saw, as he expected, no trash in any other basket. The robots responsible for waste management were working well, except for this one. This one contained a number of food wrappers and grease-stained napkins that the robots for some reason could not detect.

I guess the systems aren't so autonomous after all, he thought. He walked on into a wide hallway, brightly lit and floored with a composite pebble. The walls were smooth and sound absorbent. He held his rifle aloft as he rounded a bend, then found the next set of lifts. He checked every corner as he approached, his sense of foreboding growing strong again – telling him that he faced danger, and also that he was on the right track.

The lift cars that serviced the mine were, as Andrew expected, both away deep in the various digs. He looked out a nearby window. Like the others on the bottom level, it was one of few in the facility that was not made to artificially create a sense of sunlight on a garden planet. He could see running lights going down a long series of rails and cables. The lifts would slide along these, going diagonally into the mining area. In a few places, the lights were flickering or dead, and Andrew knew he had come to the end of the well-designed automated habitat created for the human miners.

He took a look at the computer panel by the lifts and noted where the cars were. One was on sector four, the other past it on sector five, which he assumed was deeper in the infinite rock of the well-named planet Gibraltar. He thought it curious that the lift cars were not on the same level, but then remembered he was operating on a set of assumptions that were, in all likelihood, bunk. It was his precognitive side's worrying about his original mind – that "Old Andrew" he kept contained and away from consciousness – that was leading him to believe in a... whatever you could call it. A demon?

"Then what are they doing in the mine, eh?" he said to himself. He called up the car from sector 4, thinking he would check there before proceeding further in. Once again he had a tickle, but this time it was a mixture of feelings. Dread still hung in the future, but there was also something else, like a quiet anticipation. He wondered which part of him felt that, and as he rolled between his minds, he was reminded of his "old" self – was there something in there calling out?

He watched the lift car approach, hanging from a steel rail, arriving much sooner than Andrew anticipated. Had it really come so far in just a few minutes? He worked against an urge to check his computer, which he knew was not functioning properly, to confirm the time.

The car moved past the windows and arrived at the steel double doors. After a few seconds of buzzing, the car opened. It was empty. Of the four lights in the ceiling, three remained lit. Andrew stepped in and told the computer to head to sector four. The motor overhead jumped to life, the doors closed, and the car lurched, heading out and down.

Through two small windows in the doors, Andrew watched the colony's headquarters shrink, cut into living rock and lined with multiple stories of lit, empty windows. Below the car was a black abyss spanned by steel and old scaffolds – the first mining site of the colony, now abandoned and depleted. Eventually, the lights shrank to dots, and he turned to the windows on the opposite side. He was hovering in the dark, the running lights on the track the only thing to remind him he was moving forward. Seconds passed, then long minutes.

The track turned and slowed. The descent leveled off as he approached sector one. It was black save for a few scattered lights. Nothing moved except for some clouds of dust as the car moved past the open landing cut into the rock and back into the dark caves. It began to get colder, and Andrew clenched his ungloved right hand. As the car rolled on, the running lights on the track growing brighter (they were newer, he reckoned), he reeled at the amount of atmosphere the colonists had created for their operation. The planet's surface was still thin and made mostly of greenhouse gases, a necessary step for even the accelerated process of creating a garden world, but the vast catacombs of the Gibraltar mine were full of fresh oxy. The way forward was wide, but always around the car earth-like air rushed like wind.

The car approached sector two. The rock ceiling came into view as the car slowed and paused at what looked like an equipment bay. A few hanging sodium lamps lit a long open avenue, lined with lockers and abandoned tools. A few computer terminals were still lit, ticking away with whatever tasks they had. The doors opened automatically. Andrew flinched and shouldered his rifle, but relaxed as a small robot rolling on tracks appeared from around a rock formation. The light on the end of its single appendage searched back and forth over the smooth floor.

"Hello!" Andrew yelled. Nothing answered him past the glow of the lamps, but the robot, not slowing, turned its light upon him.

"Greetings," it said in a warm, feminine voice as it approached. "Sector two is not staffed today. Are you looking for someone?"

Andrew felt a bead of sweat pop on his brow, despite the still and cold air of the bay. "Um... I might be," he said, shrugging, though he knew the robot would likely not recognize the gesture.

"Are you heading further down?" it said pleasantly, pausing in front of the open doors. "Perhaps I could share a ride with you if you are. If not, or if you do not wish to ride with me, I will wait for the next car."

"Um..." Andrew stepped away from the robot to appraise it. It took the gesture as consent and rolled into the lift. The doors closed, and the car began to move down again, the computer being operated remotely by the robot.

"Are you new?" the robot said.

"I am," Andrew said. "How did you know?"

"I haven't seen you before." Its arm and its strange light (which had dimmed to a pale blue) swiveled to regard Andrew.

"Oh," Andrew said.

"What is your name?"

Andrew thought a moment. "Toro."

"My name is Lucille. Are you married or single?"

Andrew frowned at the thing. "What is your function, if you don't mind me asking?"

"My function is autonomous maintenance of electronics and basic structures within the mining hazard zone. What is your job, Toro?"

"Why are you asking if I'm married?"

The robot dimmed its front light. "I don't have any records of you. I thought I would update the personnel files for Tracy with the identity of your spouse and children, if applicable. I know she would appreciate having it done for her."

Andrew nervously checked the safety of his rifle. He had flipped back to *auto* at some point. He put his thumb on it and slowly clicked it back twice to safe. "I'll talk to Tracy myself."

"What is your job, Toro?"

"Mining."

"I'm sorry, Toro, I meant to say-" The robot paused and clicked a few times, "What is the title of your job position?"

"Why do you want to know? I told you I'd talk to Tracy."

"What is the title of your job position?"

Andrew looked out the window. They were passing through a narrower stone passage, not hanging over an abyss any longer. It was still cold and dark. The stone had a mottled color, grey and black, with veins of iron that had not yet gone to rust in the newly oxygenated mine.

"Have you forgotten your job title?" The robot said.

"Yes," Andrew said.

"Open positions were for maintenance supervisor and demolitions technician. Does either of those sound correct?"

"Yes. Maintenance supervisor."

"Pleased to meet you, Maintenance Supervisor Toro. I am Lucille, one of the autonomous maintenance robots that operate in the mining hazard zone," it said, seemingly oblivious to its own conversation history.

"How many more of you are there?"

"Three."

"Where are they?"

"The other maintenance robots are powered down, sir."

"Why?"

"Their services have not been required."

"Why are *your* services required?"

"Sectors three and four have not been serviced in 45 days."

"Why?"

"Transport has not stopped at my service terminal in 46 days."

"*Why?*"

"I am not authorized to operate lift cars except in the presence of staff, for logistic and security reasons."

"I meant why hasn't there been any elevator stopping at your last location?"

The robot clicked. "I don't know that, sorry."

"You stopped my car. I wasn't stopping at your last location."

After a few seconds, the robot said, "I am not authorized to stop a lift car."

Andrew growled to himself softly. "You know what, Lucille, I forgot – I *am* looking for someone."

"Who are you looking for?"

"Vivian Toro."

The robot clicked. The computer terminal moved through some menus on its own. "Sorry, the network is slow."

"No worries."

The robot clicked a few more times. "Vivian is in the third grade. You can find her in the education center, either in the common area, or as a pupil of Elena Garcia."

"Thanks. I've already been to the school, and she wasn't there."

"I'm sorry I couldn't help you. You can contact the education center to see if she was out of class due to health concerns."

"I don't think it was that."

"I'm sorry; I don't have information on that."

"It's fine, Lucille."

"Thanks, Toro."

The car approached sector three. The elevator bay opened to a much smaller space. The lift stopped and the doors opened. Lucille the robot moved out into a dirty corridor, kicking up a few dust clouds to dance under the bright LEDs and warm sodium lamps which were attached to wires running along the high ceiling.

"Is this your arrival point, Supervisor Toro?" it said, pausing and *looking* back with its light.

"No. Say, Lucille…"

"What is it, Toro?"

Andrew took a slow breath, wondering if he should be so direct with a machine that could report to the unsecured network. "Do you know what happened to everyone? Where the colonists went?"

"I do not know what happened to everyone. Which colonists were you looking for?"

"All of them. They're all gone from the residential area."

"I'm sorry, but I can't seem to parse your request. Can you be more specific?"

Andrew chewed his cheek. He didn't feel quite right talking to a robot in this way, but the thing seemed harmless enough.

"Have a nice day-"

Andrew's mind shifted for a few moments, inducing nausea instantly, and then suddenly the robot was looking away. More lights were on, and brighter. A few men stood around, talking. One of them was holding a toolbox, which he put down.

"The network is fine, here," he said.

The other man took off a hard hat and scratched his bald head. "Well, it must be further down. Check out sector four."

"Maybe the demo team is playing a prank on us," the first man said.

"Not my kind of prank."

"Can we have them relay back through the robots?"

"I would think so, but the robots don't seem able to manage it on their own."

"Maybe Johnny could write a few routines for that. Seems like a good redundancy."

The other man put his hard hat back on. "Truthfully I never considered this sort of malfunction. I'll get down to sector five and check it out myself. I'm not looking forward to telling Esquivel how I lost a half-day of work, though."

The first man shrugged and picked up his toolbox, then started walking toward Andrew. He faded away, and the lights dimmed.

Lucille remained where she was, but was clicking and turning away. The lift doors began to close.

"Wait!" Andrew said, putting out a hand to stop the doors. He glanced at his computer. "I'm looking for the senior plant manager. Um…" He flipped through a few messages. "Ralph Esquivel."

Lucille turned back and dimmed its light. "He is listed as absent to work. I lack the capacity to be more specific. Shall I page him?"

"No, don't bother."

"Alright, Toro. Have a nice day."

Andrew watched the robot begin moving again. "You too, Lucille."

The doors closed, and jets of air began moving about the robot, kicking up dust and blowing it to the edges of the room. The lift started moving again, resuming its journey down into the rock at a steep incline.

Once again the walls opened up and the car slid out into icy blackness, bouncing slightly; apparently, the rails in the final sectors were not as robust here, with the supports from the ceiling or rocks below more spread out, or perhaps as a whole, it was built to a lower specification. The car swayed as it moved, but the engine above showed no signs of struggle. Andrew popped his ears and took a breath. He felt lonely suddenly, for the other parts of his mind were silent, and though he knew the robot was a simple thing, its artificial voice had banished for a few minutes the oppressive, uncanny silence of the colony.

He brought up his wrist computer, unable to ignore that it was past 12:00 hours, and flipped through his messages.

"Did you instigate this, Saul Toro?" he said to himself, wondering about the vague language used by his employer. He tapped his head. "I need to get you all wrangled. I'm pretty blind for a man who can see the past and future."

His inner self answered back, but it was the remnant of his original mind, not the part of him that was prescient or able to see into the past. It was laughing with pleasure – a cackle that was somehow also guttural and strained. Andrew shut it out.

The lift slowed as it pulled into a corridor hewn into the rock. A pair of black composite doors swung open as the car pushed against them, revealing a tighter tunnel with the lift rail running through it. Air began to whistle all around the car, but stopped when the black doors closed again. The lift stopped, swaying slightly, and Andrew saw out the window a small foyer opening up into workspaces much like those in the residential area. Computer stations sat at desks, but none of them were on. Rather than sodium lights, the space was lit by bright white diodes running in the corners of the hallways, which, though unfinished, were nonetheless quite square.

At last, the door opened and Andrew stepped out. Immediately he lifted his rifle and checked his left and his right, making sure he was alone. He quickly grabbed his nose and forced his ears to pop again. There wasn't an additional atmosphere generator running in the space, he realized. He took a deep breath, thinking that he should have been more cautious and worn his full suit. With a sigh, he stepped through the foyer to the workspace beyond.

It was large and sparse, a remote office made to serve the technical and logistics needs of the current progress zone. The dead computer monitors reflected back the subtle white of the ambient lighting, looking like a dozen frozen faces with white slits for eyes. Past the workspaces were more hallways. Andrew stepped toward these, checking around each desk, wondering if he would see a body lying behind one, or perhaps a living person. He saw nothing but dusty wires and refuse. The robots which maintained the living spaces of the colony had obviously yet to reach this distant place.

Still, that's a lot of trash, he said to himself, wondering at the piles of forgotten papers and wrappers. A chill ran up his spine as his boots slid over the slick floor caked with rough dust, and for a moment, he heard laughter, almost audible. He ignored it.

Andrew stepped toward a hallway, where the running lights thinned to a single strip in one rough-hewn corner. He resisted the urge to flip on his flashlight, and instead stepped softly into the dim corridor. A few yards in he saw a fork. One path, lit by old lights on a rough stair, went down to a space filled with orange sodium lights. The other wound forward, and he could see more white light there.

He tried asking himself what he could expect with each one, but his prescient mind gave no response.

He turned to go to the mine first. He began to feel sweat breaking on his brow as he descended. The steps were irregular, some short, some steep, and many of them much longer than stairs normally were, so he got deeper only slowly. The white lights of the office began to dim behind him, replaced by the eerie flickering orange of high-pressure sodium.

He held his breath as his foot stepped and slipped on something. He flipped on the light attached to the forward lug of his rifle, refusing the detached caution that begged him not to, and looked down. There was a pile of food going down several steps. Most of it was unopened, still sitting in its clear cellophane wrappers as if waiting for someone to buy it from a machine. In other places, the food was ripped open and half-eaten.

Andrew wondered if the food was piled up from the bottom or thrown down from the top. He decided that nobody would go so far down the steps just to toss unopened food, and so he carefully stepped his way through it until he reached the landing. Before him was a wide mining zone. Tunnels reinforced with steel ran in many different directions, some up, some down. Tracks ran out of most of these. Robotic haulers stood idle in a line to the side, most of them looking broken or forgotten. Some of the tunnels were still lit in the same orange, but most were dark.

Peeling his eyes from the maze in front of him, Andrew looked down at his wrist computer. He searched for a wireless network, but could find none. *I guess the office was shut down, along with the network. But then, Lucille was still active…*

He looked at the time, wondering if the loss of network would reset it. It read close to 13:00. He shrugged and stepped toward one of the tunnels, meaning to see how far down it went.

He forgot his train of thought as a vision assaulted him.

He was in one of the corridors. A light flickered just behind him. Two people appeared from the darkness, rising from an unlit tunnel he hadn't seen. They were too quick for him. All he could see was their faces – ashen in the monochromatic lights, thin-skinned and pale. Their mouths were exceptionally large and twisted into strange grimaces over teeth that were over-long from the withering of their dark gums. He fired his rifle into nothingness, then the vision began to fade as he felt hands pushing into his stomach, parting the flesh, seeking something inside him. Dozens of wriggling fingers, like the tentacles of some vicious squid twisting his insides towards a beaked maw…

He was staring at the tunnel again. Around a bend, he saw a flickering light. Calming himself with a slow breath, he stepped into the tunnel.

Each time he was assaulted with a vision of his death, he had to make a decision – run away, or use the knowledge to confront and hopefully avoid his demise. He didn't always decide to face his fear, but more often than not he trusted the optionality of the vision, especially since he had regained his old proficiency with his weapons. He supposed that in the abandoned mine that, should he inspect another path, the monsters he saw could approach him from another angle – an angle he hadn't yet foreseen.

The vision held steady in his mind as he walked along the cart track, letting Andrew know that he was proceeding toward the finality of it; had he walked away, the vision would begin to evaporate like a dream, being no longer part of the future. He saw the flickering light, its ballast failing after untold hours of steady work. He brought his sights up to his right eye as he approached the empty space from his vision.

It was a space of nothingness, easily overlooked as part of the endless colorless dark stone. As he pointed his flashlight into the void, he saw movement. Two heads turned to look at him, their eyes wide and reflective like those of a cat. Attached to those heads were two malformed bodies, withered but also smooth; colorless or so covered with filth as be robbed of the hues of flesh. They were hunched over something, but Andrew could not see what.

He only regarded them for a fleeting second, then he opened fire, knowing they would kill him if he did not. He started with two quick shots to the central mass of each. Black blood sprayed out in clouds, but they initially seemed little affected. Screaming in chillingly low tones, making a dissonant diad between them, they burst from their lair. Andrew's pulse quickened as they flailed about, bumping into each other recklessly, falling over themselves while black blood and bile spilled from their open ribs.

Andrew fired slowly and deliberately, willing his nerves to obey him. Two bullets hammered through the heads of the attackers, and their progress finally stopped. Seemingly unwilling to accept the loss of the brain, their bodies continued to try to run as they toppled over and collapsed. Long fingers terminating in jagged nails whipped about. Andrew stepped closer and tapped another shot into each head, watching as the bodies finally began to stop moving.

He approached the closest and flipped it over. The body was human in some ways essential to the species, containing all the bones and structure of a normal person. The skin was grey under the white diodes of his flashlight. It was also slightly translucent, revealing the anatomy beneath: tendons and muscle fascia, bone and sinew and long, blue veins. Remnants of clothing still clung to their bodies. He knelt closer, but could not see anything immediately identifiable on either one.

They were human once, which meant that the creatures were the colonists. Nobody else had been to the desolate ferrous planet before him.

Andrew stepped over the bodies and looked closer into the little hiding hole from which the monsters had emerged. Tattered clothing was everywhere, like a nest. The remnants of a half-rotten body were present, torn into pieces that were only vaguely human. Andrew guessed at where the rest of the corpse had gone.

He checked his computer and quickly punched in a message. He was too deep now to transmit directly back to his ship, but as soon as he was in communications range the message would go out, informing Toro of what he had seen, and warning him that nobody else should be sent. He quickly turned and half-jogged back toward the central chamber, happy to cut his mission short and negotiate with his employer for payment even though he had failed to find his mark.

Another vision hit him, though this one did not totally blank out his sight, as those further in the future usually did. He saw two more of the monsters waiting for him in the central chamber. He gunned them down, only to be floored by an attacker from above.

Andrew focused as he went around the bend. He dropped to a knee as soon as he saw the brightly lit central room. Two shadowy figures were there. He shot each of them. Like the others, these began to charge at him, but he could see through their odd movements that his rifle was indeed effective at injuring them, they were just more reluctant to die than a regular person. He continued to fire as they slowly collapsed to the ground, just to be sure. Then he saw the hidden attacker emerge – along with two others.

They ran at him quickly, their gate unmistakably human, though it became more monstrous as they were hit, turning into a knuckle walk or a fast crawl.

Andrew's bolt snapped back and stopped. Smoke rose from the empty chamber. He dropped his magazine and slammed in another. He let the bolt fly forward and continued firing at his attackers, which had closed the distance more quickly than he thought possible. Fear gripped him at that moment, and he let himself shoot more wildly than he knew was wise. The loss of discipline didn't matter. Soon all three lay in twitching heaps five yards ahead of him.

"Thanks, mate," Andrew said tapping his left fist to his temple. Before walking on, he took out his magazine and quickly checked to see how many rounds he had left, since in the moment he had forgotten to count. Seeing eight remaining, he tucked away the magazine and put in a full one. He picked up his spent magazine from the floor and put it away too, then walked slowly down the hallway, keeping his rifle trained on the bodies in front of him, whose nerves still fired in defiance of the very real death of the major organs.

Like the others, they were people – at least at one time. One of the closer ones seemed less monstrous than the others. It was a woman, likely young-looking whenever what changed her had taken hold. Her hair was still black, though matted, and though her skin was thin and stretched, he could still see healthy fat around the lips and cheeks. She still wore her clothes – a simple set of coveralls.

Something occurred to Andrew. He had been so focused on the idea that there was a *Wrtla* at play that he had not considered other causes. Had some sort of pathogen his sensors could not detect caused this? Should he have resisted the urge to remove his helmet and breathe the air of the place? He looked at his computer and started up the air filter on his suit. Within a few moments, it returned a safe value. No atypical pathogens. DNA mutations in microbes within normal limits.

Andrew opened his mind briefly to the oldest part of himself, and heard the laughing internally, drawing fingers towards his lips to pull them into a smile. He pushed it away.

It has to be a Wrtla. I need to get out of here, payments be damned.

He stepped over the bodies and continued to the central room of the mine, piquing his prescient self for warnings, but none came. The dead in the central room were in a similar state to the woman – still dressed and looking far less gone than the first pair he had slain. He turned and looked above to the tunnel from which he had just exited to see a small platform attached to the steel scaffolding.

They were smart enough to set a trap for me, once they knew I was here.

He headed back toward the stairway. He stepped over the pile of uneaten pre-packaged food and continued back up, still keeping his rifle ready, in case he needed it. At the top of the stairs, he turned to the left, seeing a pale white glow from another finished workspace. As he turned a sharp corner, his past mind, his echo mind, jumped forward, almost displacing his normal thoughts, but seemed unable to complete its normal vision process.

He saw a wide office space that was in shambles. Phantoms of people in tattered clothes moved toward him, their eyes wide and reflecting the fluorescent lights above in a pale green. At the same time, he saw the space as it was – desks were neat and ordered, and people stood about talking and working. Several of the desks were actually workbenches, piled with parts and other machines that were being fixed.

His mind splintered again, and he saw the figures with the pale eyes moving toward him, almost like ghosts, and saw himself shooting them down, one at a time with clear precision. They began to move in the present, and he enacted the will of his future self, slaughtering the wraiths as they fumbled their way over the ruined floor, looking more confused than angry.

Somehow he held onto sanity as he heard the laughing of that other part of his mind, which held the taint of an eternal demon as well as most of his human memories. He was pressing forward, demanding to take part in the sanguine feast, and there was another voice with him, singing a horrid song into his ear.

There were three images competing with the laughter – past, present, and future. His prescient mind saw something that gave him pause. He shot and killed, amidst the throng, a young woman who, he realized only too late, looked totally normal. She was a single image standing in all three places; only the future image was frozen, blood flying out from a wound in her neck, surprise plastered on her pale face.

He took his finger off the trigger, rather than following through with the prescribed motions of the future, and suddenly the future vision changed, then winked out of sight. He was nearly set upon by four people, two of them walking and two of them crawling forward, strange words in an alien tongue spilling from their mouths like linguistic vomit. Andrew glanced up and saw the girl, who stood still and stared at him. Her eyes were almost glassy, but trembled, as if in fear.

He blinked hard, then quickly dispatched the remaining attackers.

Brass tinkled on the stone floor, then all was silent, save for a moaning, wracking sound coming from one of the mad people. Andrew stepped toward the victim, intending to put it to final rest, when a wordless cry from the girl stopped him in his tracks.

He looked up at her. She cried out again, as if trying to form words, but the utterance came out slurred and strange.

Andrew held out his left palm and lowered his rifle.

The woman stepped quickly toward him. Andrew resisted the temptation to gun her down, remembering the vision, and stepped back. He watched as she went to the wheezing wretch on the ground. She pushed it over to reveal a middle-aged man. He looked like some of the others: pale and thin-skinned, but human besides the strange, hollow eyes.

The young woman shook the man, then stood up, almost defiantly against his armed bulk. She was crying, and Andrew watched as she grabbed a piece of her simple grey shirt and blotted her tears. Despite the grit caked on her face and in her hair, she looked young. Andrew thought she wouldn't pass for 20 Earth years. She stomped her foot as she looked at him, and her pouty expression was almost childish, though below it was something harder than any youth should possess. Andrew wondered how old she really was.

"Can you understand me?" Andrew said, still not raising his rifle, though his trigger finger was of two minds, dancing on and off while his thumb toggled the safety randomly.

She nodded. Her frown deepened as she pointed to the dead man at her feet.

"Can you talk?"

She nodded, but at the same time, wordless vocalizations came out of her mouth.

"I can't understand you."

The girl clenched her fists and grunted.

"You knew him?" Andrew said.

She nodded.

"Sorry. There was nothing for it. He would have killed me." Andrew frowned. "You must be early in the change, but why?" he said, mostly to himself. "Everyone else is far gone. Too far gone to save. Are you... yourself?"

He saw that she was staring at him, but was unsure if she was comprehending. His trigger finger danced some more. He realized that his echo mind – hearing some voice of the past, was still trying to push a vision forward. He allowed it more room, and he saw the workspace as it was, with the strange girl seated at a nearby desk, writing in a notebook. Somebody was seated across from her, talking to her, but the vision was silent. The girl's lips didn't move.

Andrew snapped out of it as the girl stepped past him. He flinched, but he realized she wasn't attacking. She was searching for something in the rubble. She knelt down and retrieved a simple notebook. A pen was perched on the back cover, and she took it, then opened the notebook and began writing with her right hand. She turned it toward him.

I'm normal, it said in jagged letters.

"I'm not so sure of that," Andrew said. "There's a *Wrtla* at work here. You've clearly been affected, but maybe if I got you out of here right away-"

She frowned at him and waved her hands, then said with great effort, "No." She pointed at the notebook again.

Andrew shook his head. She grabbed at his arm, and he reflexively shrank away, fumbling with his rifle before lowering it again. Once again, she pointed at the notebook.

Andrew took a breath and paused. He looked carefully at the girl. He noticed a subtle disturbance in her face, as if half of it was not under control, though not quite drooping like someone who had suffered a stroke. He tilted his head and saw a slight scar running through her scalp to her neck behind her right ear.

"You've had a head injury..." he whispered, craning his head to see. She caught sight of him examining her, and leaned her head, cupping a hand over her right ear.

"I said you've been injured. Recently?"

She shook her head. Sudden realization dawned on her face, and she reached into her pocket with her right hand. She fumbled out a wallet from her trousers, almost dropping it as she opened it up. She handed Andrew a plain white card.

Andrew had to hold the card up in the dim lights, but was able to read:

My name is Mariela Flores. I have suffered a traumatic brain injury. I have difficulty with certain physical tasks, including speech. I may have difficulty understanding you or communicating my thoughts accurately. Janice Telany is my therapist and can be paged over the network. She can program my AAC device with new conversations.

Andrew looked back at the girl. "Nice to meet you. I'm Andrew. Or... Andrew is the right-now me." He shrugged. "What happened to your communications device?"

Mariela waved her hands as if trying to sign something, shrugged, then bent her notebook in the middle.

"We need to get you out of here."

She shook her head, then scribbled on her notebook. *My parents are still here.*

Andrew nodded in understanding. That's why her neuroanatomy remained unrepaired. She must have been younger when it happened, and there were no transports to take her back to a settled planet with proper facilities. Or perhaps the damage was beyond repair. He touched his own head.

"No fixing me," he said aloud. "But you *do* need to leave. I might have already killed your parents."

Mariela frowned deeply at him, then rushed past him, back toward the hallway and the mine.

"Wait!" Andrew shouted. "There could be-"

Before he could finish his sentence, his future mind pressed forward, demanding his attention. A swarm of insane people was emerging from the tunnels in the mine, rushing toward where he stood in the vision. He saw

Mariela, who he was chasing. They paid her no mind, pushing past her on both sides. Then he saw an empty liquid gas tank tip over at the passing of some clumsy madwoman, and fall onto Mariela, stunning her.

Andrew was frozen in his decision as the vision of himself being smothered by bodies began to fade. The former workers seemed to ignore the girl – for what reason he could not guess, though he suspected some familiarity that persisted despite the stupefied state – but at the same time, she was in real danger. He broke his paralysis and ran after Mariela.

Fear began to tighten his throat, and he broke into a sweat in his temperature-regulated suit. Normally, his future visions gave him something tangible to avoid, or could guide him in some way, but this one gave him only his demise. He supposed as he ran down the hallway, following the echo of footsteps, that he could turn back and avoid the situation entirely, but he felt a stronger duty to persist. Mariela could be saved, he was sure.

He began down the stairwell, trying his best to avoid slipping on the remnants of old food wrappers. He heard the sound of more footsteps, and knew the horde, likely awakened by his scuffle earlier, was inbound. The lights in the stairwell flickered and went out. He was in near-total darkness; the only light was from behind him, but below him, his own shadow blocked all. He flipped on the flashlight on his bottom lug rail.

He fell backward with the shock, hitting the stone stairs heavily. Below him was a swarm of people groping forward, climbing over one of their number that was struggling on the bottom stair.

"Hold him! Hold him!" came one of their voices from the noisy din, and Andrew knew this lot, though clearly mad, was cognizant enough to be something more dangerous than a herd of animals. Their mouths were twisted and wide, their skin pale and taught, but a dark light was in their eyes, which refracted and defied the blinding whiteness of the gun's light even as their pupils drank it up.

Andrew's nerves unwound; he hadn't been surprised – truly surprised – in a very long time. Without thought, he squeezed the trigger of his rifle, firing a single shot into the stone wall that went ricocheting down the stairwell. His earplugs deadened the sound immediately, but the cognizant insane humans before him lacked such tactical protection. They screamed and wailed in unison. It was a sickening sound to Andrew, but it gave him time to hastily flip the safety over to auto and fire wildly into the throng of attackers.

Blood sprayed up onto his suit. Onto his face. The warmth of it sickened him, shattering his resolve even as it brought howling laughter from within. The screaming intensified. The bolt locked open. With trembling fingers, Andrew dropped the magazine and slammed in another. He tried to master himself, watching the remaining bodies in the bright circle of light in front of him. He fired another burst – perhaps ten rounds – into the motion before him, then forced himself to toggle back to semi. The light trembled before him, and he willed it to stay still. The bodies below him were still or sliding backward. There were fewer than there ought to have been, meaning that some had fled, surely awaiting him down below, if he dared to try to retrieve the girl.

He took a breath and slowly worked his way downward, avoiding the bleeding bodies. One still twitched – its face contorted and ticking around vacuous, dead eyes. The image seemed to burn into Andrew's retinas, a memory at which his old self seemed to smile inwardly.

Near the bottom of the stairwell, his future mind kicked in again, revealing the waiting attack from both his right and left, the madmen hiding behind piles of discarded equipment. In the vision he saw the remaining group standing back, fearful near one of the tunnels.

As the vision faded, Andrew's present mind quickly formulated a strategy. He reached to his back and retrieved his plasma gun. He balanced its considerable girth in his left hand and quickly double-checked the battery life. The indicator on its white-metal case glowed a bright green. It was a clever death tool, compact and efficient, but he didn't trust it in an atmosphere unless he had no choice.

He stepped out into the open cavern and pointed his guns out to his left and right. Looking ahead to find the rest of his enemies, he fired a burst from each gun blindly. The roar of the plasma gun almost overwhelmed the loud rifle, its energy ripping apart the nitrogen and oxygen in the atmosphere at a molecular level, but the report from each weapon indicated impact with flesh. He saw the remaining miners, then glanced left and right to see a dead man on each side. The one on his left was burned nearly black and smoking. The stink sent a wave of nausea over him, but his old self suddenly pushed a finger of insanity up into Andrew's psyche, which quelled the need to vomit and hardened him temporarily.

Andrew dropped his plasma gun, letting it hang around his shoulder by its bungee strap, then sighted the last group. They were rushing at him, ignoring Mariela as if she were an inanimate object, though she reached out her hands as if trying to stop and slow them. They swarmed around, knocking the girl roughly down, paying her no notice.

Andrew was back in control now, and he didn't need the faint early images from his prescient mind to tell him what to shoot. He carefully executed each rushing man and woman, tapping each one in the chest twice. Six fell as they ran. Ten. Twelve. The last one took one shot in the shoulder, and the rifle was empty. Andrew let go of the rifle and picked up his plasma gun. The man was almost upon him, blood pouring from his single wound. Andrew could see his face – which was both confused and angry.

With two air-burning shots, Andrew obliterated the man, turning him into a smoking corpse with two gaping wounds seared through him. The man's face was plastered in a slightly sad expression as he fell. Andrew had a flashback; he saw the man sitting near Mariela in an office, talking calmly. The girl seemed not to notice the conversation, and stared at her hands.

"Mariela, let's go!" Andrew said. "You see you can't stay here. He was mad. They all were, and I can tell you, there is no cure."

Mariela picked herself up, shocked at the carnage surrounding her. Tears were welling in her open, trembling eyes.

Andrew gave her an appraising stare. He looked down at the blood, which was running between the forgotten pre-packaged snacks piled at the bottom of the stairs. His mind was blank, unable to think of the next step as he looked upon the gory horror of his handiwork. The stoic lane that he piloted his psyche through was suddenly no longer straight, but was like a winding path. He felt no immediate disgust, or fear, but all around him the feelings pressed in. All he really knew was that he had to escape the sight; escape, or else succumb and lose what control he still held.

Hesitantly, willing his voice to work, he said, "I'm... going to the elevators." His voice died like sand spilling on stone. He choked slightly. Silently, he considered carrying Mariela out by force, but the warm liquid running underfoot unnerved him. He turned and walked hurriedly up the stairs, gripping the handrail on his left in case he slipped in the blood, which was running in torrents over the stone steps. In some places, the puddles on the uneven stairs were deep enough to lap over the tops of his composite boots. He let his rifle slide to behind his right hip and continued holding his plasma gun in his right hand; he wanted the escape from the grizzly scene even more than he wanted to reload, for it was more than a sight, it was a beacon, and he feared the one who would heed it – the one who laughed in the cold recesses between his footsteps.

When he reached the top of the stairs he traded his weapons, traded his magazine for a fresh one, then started back toward the lift, refusing to turn and watch the stairs.

As he walked, another part of his mind pushed forward with a vision, though he couldn't be sure which. He was sitting alone in the cockpit of his ship, calm and without fear. It faded as he neared the lift car, dissipating into hazy memory as quickly as it had come.

It stood open, just as he had left it, a lighthouse to the floundering ship of his mind, beaten by waves of emotion. He reached the control terminal and sighed, leaning against the wall. He looked out at the track through the lift car window, watching it fade into night. The running lights disappeared into the twisting rock further out, hiding the points beyond. He could not bear to wonder what was out there, which was just as well, as he had decided he would leave without finding his mark. He simply could not endure any longer.

The girl he was supposed to find was just that – a girl, and he had thus far seen only adults, save for Mariela, who hardly qualified as such. The children were likely dead – he had a sudden echo of the horror on the first floor, along with laughter from his old self – or else were in the sixth sector, along with the rest of the colonists. And their minds were surely gone. He turned and looked back at the empty space of the landing and the tunnel to the mine. Mariela had not followed him.

He looked at the panel and considered leaving Mariela, but despite the emotional detachment he had developed over the fractured months, he felt horror at the threat of guilt of such a decision. Guilt in the moment washed over him, as he considered that he left her amid his carnage, as if she were a child throwing a tantrum, refusing to come when bidden, not a grown woman who had witnessed the death of a dozen people she had known since childhood. And she had not followed. Of course! She would not leave, not if she would walk headstrong into the hive of monsters without a care.

Andrew banged his fist against his head. "What's wrong with you?" He stepped away from the elevator, hearing a beep from his computer, alerting him to an unexpected jump in his blood pressure and pulse. He reached the stairwell, whose lights were now flickering, threatening to return to some semblance of life. To his relief, Mariela was walking up the stairs. In the high contrast of the flickering lights he could almost pretend the floor was black, not crimson. Caked with oil, rather than blood.

"I'm glad you're coming," he said.

She raised her eyes to look at him, and frowned with anger.

"I'm sorry," he said, and stepped back to let her pass. She turned back toward the office and began walking quickly.

"The elevators are back this way," he said. She ignored him. He sighed. He would have to carry her out after all. Leaving her would be unacceptable. Horrific. He started after her. When he reached the office space, he found Mariela emptying some drawers and pulling out various items from beneath an aluminum desk, then stuffing them into a backpack. She pulled out a sponge cake from the bag, opened the wrapper and bit down into it, and then walked toward Andrew.

Andrew frowned with realization. "You got everything?"

Mariela nodded, then walked past him, eating the snack cake noisily. Andrew skipped a step to keep up.

"It was you that left all that food at the bottom of the stairs."

She glanced at him and nodded.

"Why?"

She put the snack cake in her mouth and rubbed her stomach.

Andrew thought a moment. "You came here and left it for the... people, below?"

She nodded.

"They stopped eating the food."

She nodded again.

"But you kept coming down here anyway."

Mariela continued to nod.

"You got it from the main dormitories. That's why so many machines were empty."

She looked at him and nodded curtly.

"If you could have put out the beacon for help the whole time, why didn't you?" He remembered and corrected himself, "Unless you didn't know how to pull the alarm or-"

Mariela shook her head and then pointed to her temple.

"You didn't because you didn't want to lose your parents?" He shook his head. "Oh, it's probably better you didn't call for help. Whoever came would be enslaved..." Andrew trailed off and looked hard at Mariela.

She didn't respond to his monologue. She walked quickly to the elevator and began working the computer terminal outside it. The doors opened.

"Willing to leave now?"

Mariela stared at him. She finished the last of the cake, then scribbled in her notebook and showed it to Andrew.

They won't come out now. They haven't eaten food in a long time.

"There are more people down there still, hiding?"

She nodded.

"Do your parents notice you? Do they acknowledge you?"

Mariela looked sadly at him and shook her head.

"It's the *wrtla*. What they were... they're gone."

Mariela scribbled. *I know.* Then, *What's a wertala?*

"*Wrtla*," Andrew said, trying to drop the vowels and pronounce the title he had learned from his contact with... he could not remember its proper name, just it's title. He motioned to the elevator. Mariela stepped in and he followed. He watched her punch up the dormitories. The car started moving, lurching from its resting place, squeaking as it slowly began its ascent.

Mariela pointed again to her notebook. *What's a Wertala?*

Andrew thought a moment. "It's an ancient monster. A demon, a devil." He shook his head. "Something beyond such concepts – they don't do it justice. It can control the minds of humans, turn them mad. It eats sanity like its food. A long time ago – nobody who knows anything about the *wrtla* knows exactly how long but we think close to a hundred thousand Earth years – they were imprisoned by a race of beings that could compete with their power. Angels, maybe, but they left nothing behind. The *wrtla* were placed deep within planets like this one, hopefully to be forgotten by man. Whatever they are, my guess is they are immortal on some level, but clearly not powerful enough to escape a prison of rock.

"But their powers can leak through, touching the minds of people. Maybe they've been coming through for a long time. Calling mankind down, back to them – some primeval song without words or melody. We hear it between the words of thought. Out in space…" Andrew was clenching his hands as he talked. "They can whisper, too, if you get too close, and once they get in, you'll be their slave, and if you escape, you'll go mad. Trust me, I know."

He was waiting for her to ask him how he knew. He dreaded the question, because within it was the explanation of his power, but also of the madman that lurked within him, ready to take control and wreak havoc. He laughed inside (and not the "old" Andrew) – *madman! Ha!* – he was already a madman, with four minds living inside him, constantly trying to be the one true mind, constantly talking behind each other's backs. Some part of him wanted her to ask him. He needed confession. He longed for it.

But she didn't ask him. Instead, she wrote in her notebook again.

I haven't heard any whispers. I'm not insane.

"You'd have to be a little crazy to keep coming down to feed those people," Andrew said.

She wrote, *What else should I have done?*

Andrew shrugged. "Did any of the others acknowledge you? Notice your existence?"

She shook her head.

"Weird. I think the unprotected part of my mind can hear the thing inside the rock whispering, practically screaming. Or singing."

What is it saying?

Andrew opened up to his old self for a few moments. "Lots of things. Kill, mostly. But you don't have to worry about me. Like I said, it only whispers to the unprotected part of my mind, and it's locked away safely." Andrew bit his lip. He did need confession. He made up his mind to see a priest when he got out of this, though he wondered if the priest would understand, and would actually be willing to help him pray; help him find forgiveness.

Old Andrew was balking at him at the thought. *A priest? You think he knows God*

The car rocked as it passed a beam in the dark.

Mariela scribbled, *Why did you come here? To get me?*

"No. But I won't leave someone behind who can be saved."

She pointed at the notebook again.

"I came to save a little girl named Vivian Toro. I was hired by her father, Saul Toro. I don't think I'll be able to finish the job, though."

I know her. Little girl.

"She's probably dead by now."

I wasn't dead.

"You're immune, that is, if you really don't hear the voice. You're an adult… If Vivian was immune, there was nobody to care for her."

Mariela frowned and then wrote quickly, *You're a coward.*

Andrew flushed slightly. "I can't feasibly search every cranny of this mine. It's not possible as one man."

You know she's on level six. The rest are.

"I don't know that."

Mariela touched the panel and the lift car stopped, swinging in the abyss. She pointed to the notebook again.

"I have a responsibility to *you* now. I must see you to safety first."

She sighed as she wrote. *I was already safe.*

"You won't be if I head to level six."

They don't pay attention to me. She was getting tearful as she pointed to her words. She grunted in exasperation and went to the panel. The car started moving back. Andrew saw she had punched in level six. He sighed and stepped over, but she slapped his hand as he reached for the panel. Quickly, she unplugged it from the wall.

"I can just plug the monitor back in."

She shook her head. She wrote again.

I know the way.

Andrew sighed. He remembered her standing still while the vile people of the mind swarmed past her, bent on him. Perhaps she was right, and they would ignore her. "Where is the closest security station? Any weapons storage?"

Mariela smiled asymmetrically. The left side of her face seemed unwilling to go with the rest. She kneeled down and plugged the monitor back in. With a few strokes, they were headed back up.

Andrew leaned back and looked at Mariela. She stood looking out the window as they moved through the darkness, the lights on the rails making an endlessly extending road to nowhere. The girl looked terrified, but at the same time without fear. A sadness touched her eyes, which seemed fixed in a downturned expression. Andrew could not be sure if that was due to some neurological damage, or if she was emoting into the abyss.

"Do you know how to operate a gun?"

Mariela turned and looked at him. She nodded once. Andrew doubted that was a true answer, but the question on its own was a gambit he could not back out of.

"If I die, take the elevator back to the dormitories. My ship is parked outside. You won't be able to operate it without an access code, but there is a distress beacon on board that will function. I have a few friends in the sector that know I'm here. They'll take care of you, but don't let them into the colony."

Mariela looked at him as if to say thanks, but all that came out were some confused vocalizations. She sighed and wrote in her notebook.

You think you will die?

"It's always a possibility. If I see something we can't avoid, we'll just leave."

What if they surprise you?

Andrew smiled. "I'm difficult to surprise. Make sure you pay attention to me and obey my orders."

She nodded.

The lift reached the sector four landing station and slowed. It was dusty and the bright lights of the robot Lucille could be seen down a long hallway.

"Anyone on this level?" Andrew said as the doors opened.

Mariela shrugged.

"Do you know where the weapons locker is?"

Mariela bit her lip.

"Do you know that there is one on this level?"

She nodded.

"Lucille ought to know, then. That's that robot up ahead."

He stepped out into the cavernous foyer and flipped on his light. He swung through the still hanging dust, checking corners, then waved Mariela forward. They went straight down the half-finished hallway toward the working robot. They passed a few doors that Andrew hastily checked for any signs of humans, then finally reached Lucille.

The robot ceased kicking up the dust and cleaning the floor as they approached.

"Hello, Toro," the robot said in a kindly voice. "It's good to see you again. Is your shift over?"

"Not quite," Andrew said. "Do you know where security is on this level?"

"Has there been an incident?"

Andrew paused a moment. "Yes."

Lucille clicked silently, its dimmed flashlight head motionless. "There are no security personnel on active duty in this sector. Shall I page another station?"

"It won't do any good," Andrew said.

"Why not? Is something wrong with the security personnel?"

Andrew looked at Mariela, who shrugged.

"The network is malfunctioning," Andrew said. "The personnel are on duty, but... but all of the stations are..." He stammered as his past self begged for his attention, raving, but also pleading. He listened for a brief second. "The system software is bugged out and is returning a null value for all members of the team. I need to get to the station to correct it, but I'm new here."

Lucille clicked again. Its head turned and seemed to regard Mariela. "You can reach the closest security station by returning to the lift terminals, taking the second hallway from the left, and proceeding to room three, on the left. Greetings, Mariela."

Mariela nodded nervously to the robot.

"Have a nice day, Lucille," Andrew said. He grabbed Mariela's hand lightly and led her away from the robot, back down toward the lifts. They quickly made the rounds and found room three, which had a clear gold-lettered sign reading "Security."

As Andrew reached for the door handle, he had a slight premonition. It wasn't a full-blown vision, but his prescient self was warning him, though not of imminent danger. With the echo of the forgotten crib, he had some idea what to expect.

The door, however, did not wish to open. Looking around, Andrew saw that it was a powered lock, and the power had been disconnected at some point.

"Damn, Lucille, why did you have to clean before fixing anything?" He looked at Mariela. "Stand over there."

Andrew took his plasma gun out and covered his eyes with his arm before obliterating the door lock. Pieces of aluminum shrapnel spun away, bouncing off of his suit and the wall. White smoke billowed up, but the fire system didn't recognize it. Andrew kicked the door in, which gave easily. The rest of the lock rattled off and clanged on the ground.

The lights flickered on as they entered. It was a rather normal office for a large mining operation's minimally-needed security, containing generic furniture, computers, seating, and a few lockers. Andrew saw immediately what his prescient self had warned him of. Lying down against one of the walls was a man in the remains of a security uniform. He was clearly dead, his eyes drawn and opaque, his flesh withered slightly and desiccated. His peeled lips were thin and revealed rotting gums holding long teeth.

Surprisingly, it only stunk slightly.

"He must have died of thirst, having forgotten how to get out," Andrew said. He stepped around the corpse to one of the lockers. He found it unlocked, to his surprise. "Any preference?" he said to Mariela, gesturing at the open locker. She was standing aghast at the sight of the dead man, her mouth open and eyes trembling.

Andrew snapped his fingers at her until she looked at him. "Sorry you had to see that. I forgot to tell you to expect something like that."

She gave him a puzzled look.

"Now. Do you have a weapon preference?" He gestured again at the open locker, which contained an assortment of small arms.

Mariela shook her head, clearly confused.

Andrew nodded slightly to her. He took a twelve gauge shotgun out and placed it on a nearby table, then looked through some drawers and found the ammunition. After some searching, he found a few boxes of buckshot and put them on the table too. Next, he found in a drawer a 9 millimeter pistol. He saw that it was locked to an electronic security bracelet. He brought it to the table and quickly took it down. Using a multi-tool from his belt, he pried out the identity device that was attached to the trigger group and threw it away, chuckling. The slide went back on, and he tested the trigger, watching the hammer move smoothly through the long action double-action.

He put in a magazine and racked the slide, then eased the hammer down. He made to hand it to Mariela, then withdrew it. A thought had just occurred to him

If she's invisible to the Wrtla, will I be able to see a future where she intends to kill me? He remembered all the people he had slaughtered in the other sector. What if he had already killed her parents, and she was looking for revenge?

He saw that Mariela was looking at him questioningly, clearly not understanding what was going on his head.

I saw her in the vision... was that just incidental?

His past self pushed forward *You saw her in the past.*

But...

He sighed and handed the pistol to Mariela, barrel first in case she tried to shoot him. He held his breath as she looked at it with half familiarity. She placed it in her right hand and weighed it.

"That's just your sidearm." Andrew turned back and found a few loaded magazines. He slid them across to the girl, who stuffed one of them in her pants pocket and the rest in her backpack. "Your main gun ought to be this," he said, picking up the shotgun. He found the bolt release and pressed it down, then racked the bolt a few times, ejecting what he knew were beanbag rounds. He opened up one of the boxes of buckshot and loaded eight fresh shells in the magazine, then dropped one in the open chamber. He released the bolt and it slammed closed. He held it to Mariela, who took it doubtingly. "Put the rest of the ammo in your backpack."

She nodded and put down the shotgun carefully. She then put the extra shells into a pocket on the outside of her backpack.

"You sure you know how to use it?"

Mariela nodded and picked up the gun. Her left hand held the foregrip uneasily, but as she rested the stock on her hip, it settled down. Andrew nodded slowly. Keeping the girl in his periphery, he turned back, checking the rifles in the locker. They were all chambered in 6.2 millimeter, not his old rifle's 6.8. He shook the satchel at his hip, feeling the weight. It was light. He put his hand in and felt three more loaded magazines. Normally he would feel fine with ninety rounds, but his prescient mind was whistling at him.

With a sigh, he picked up one of the security rifles and popped open the receiver. With his multi-tool, he removed the electronic security block on the auto-sear and tossed it aside. He slung the rifle around him, annoyed that it lacked a more ready suspension system, like the bungees that held his main rifle. A quick search of the gun locker found a whole drawer full of pre-loaded magazines, along with a few empties. He put them in his satchel, feeling suddenly very weighed down, even in the lower gravity of the colony.

"After you," he said, pointing to the open door. He watched Mariela exit and turn down toward the elevators.

They reached them and stepped inside. Andrew put his own rifle down, leaning it against a corner to retrieve on the trip back. Mariela fumbled with the shotgun slightly, leaning it next to his rifle. She brought the terminal to life, and the lift car was soon moving back through the dark, toward sector six.

"You don't have to come too, you know. You could wait for me at the dorms."

Mariela stared at him, then wrote slowly, *I'm not afraid. Are you?*

"Yeah. The me that's *me* is. The me that sees the future, not so much, which should be reassuring, but I don't trust him. He doesn't answer a lot of questions."

She looked at him with a puzzled expression.

"I have a few residents upstairs. They're all me. One lives in the future, one lives in the past, one lives in *my* past, but I don't talk to him much."

Mariela wrote on her pad, *Are you insane?*

Andrew paused and ran his tongue over his teeth. "That's what a doctor would say, but I'm still alive, and most wouldn't be who have tread the paths I have. Paths like this one."

Mariela stared at him.

"Where do you think a kid would be in sector six?"

She shook her head.

Andrew took a slow breath.

The car slid on in silence, eventually approaching the landing for sector five. Andrew could see several shapes moving amid the lights, scattering as the car approached. They slid through, and all that could be seen were a few pair of vacuous, open eyes watching them pass.

The running lights along the track were brighter here, and the space through which the lift moved was less uncomfortably open. They passed through open caverns and small cut shafts, sliding downward and deeper into the rock. The car swayed as the track leapt over a chasm, infinite darkness extending above and below them. It looked to Andrew like the track abruptly ended a few yards ahead, but he felt no impending dread.

It was just the end of the running lights. They moved on along a darkened track, the line of yellow beams disappearing behind them. The lights inside the lift car were enough to dimly illuminate the rock walls as they slowed and entered another shaft. Andrew readied the security rifle, pushing the fixed stock into his shoulder and flipping off the safety.

"You remember where the safety is on that?" Andrew said, nodding to the shotgun.

Mariela nodded. She picked the gun back up and pointed to the little steel dot right behind the trigger. Andrew nodded back.

"Be careful. Don't shoot if you don't know what something is."

She nodded.

Mariela couldn't speak, and Andrew was content to let the lift move toward its final destination in silence. Slowly a light in the distance grew. The atmosphere outside began to whistle in the cracks of the car, which swayed slightly as it ran on. The growing light turned into an image – an open mining area, surrounded by the blackness of a natural cavern above, too high for the operating lights to touch. It was deserted, but a pale dust hung in the air, creating white halos around all the spotlights.

"There's been activity recently."

Mariela looked at him quizzically, as if she thought such a statement was obvious.

Finally, the car reached the landing and stopped. The track, which had run an unknown number of miles from the original mining colony, ended in a great steel stop covered with large rubber bumpers. The door opened.

Andrew stepped out quickly, checking the corners behind him and looking for any ledges above. When it was clear, he motioned for Mariela to exit, but he found she was already standing right beside him, holding the shotgun awkwardly, the stock clutched under her arm.

He nodded for her to follow him and continued visually checking every spot as he moved through the staging area. It was deserted and dusty. Computer terminals stood in the appropriate stations, but all the monitors were dim. A wide shaft ran downhill in front of them, lit by a long row of sodium bulbs. Due to the slope, Andrew could not see ahead.

He tapped a fist to his head. "Don't fail me now."

They started down the shaft, which he quickly realized was a full-width access tunnel, made for the passage of the heavy machinery which would be on the final and most active mining sector. He looked down at the floor and saw a litany of tracks in the dust, including those of a large steel-treaded digging machine. Each track was nearly three feet wide.

"How did they get something so big down here on such a rickety lift?" he whispered to himself. Mariela touched him to get his attention, then made a series of hand signs he did not understand. He jumped to the correct conclusion anyway. "They assembled them here. Makes sense."

Mariela nodded. She pointed ahead, and there the tunnel diverged into two. One set of tread tracks was new, the other old. Mariela pointed toward the new ones.

"Good thinking," Andrew whispered. "Of course, they could have moved anywhere." He heard something faintly, and he quickly pulled Mariela to the side and knelt down. "Did you hear that?" he said through his teeth.

Mariela shook her head.

Andrew strained. Faintly, he heard a voice, but he couldn't make out the words.

"This way. On your guard."

He moved down the shaft with the fresh tracks as silently as he could, hoping each time he heard a pebble bounce or scrape under the sole of his shoe that the people here were as dimwitted as the first ones he had come across. As he inclined his ear, he marked such chances as slim. The voice was repeating words, but he could not make them out. It was one voice. A man's voice, drowned in the reverberation of the long tunnel.

Andrew knew there was no real way to tell how far away it was. Underground, in tunnels and other spaces where sound could bounce around, distant noises could sound immediately close; things right next to you could sound incredibly far away. Everything would be distorted. But the voice was getting louder, and clearer.

Andrew stopped as he felt a pull on his arm. He turned to see Mariela cup her hand to her ear. She awkwardly put her shotgun in the crook of her elbow and gave Andrew a thumbs up.

Andrew pulled close, knowing that if he could hear the voice, even a whisper might carry back. He put his lips to Mariela's ear and said, "I can't make out what he's saying, can you?"

Mariela gave him an incredulous look and shook her head. She cupped her ear again and pointed to it, frowning.

Andrew shrugged and continued forward. The voice grew clearer. Finally, he made out one word clearly: *deeper.*

He stopped and whispered back in Mariela's ear, "Did you hear what he said?"

Once again, she gave him a confused look.

A few steps further in, through Andrew's focus and straining to understand, the voice suddenly became clear. He dropped to a knee and brought his rifle up, looking down the tunnel in anticipation.

Deeper. Down. Deeper down. Dig deeper. Deeper. Dig deeper down. Down and down.

Andrew's pulse quickened as the voice grew louder and clearer; the reverberation diminished. He waited for a vision of the future which would not come, silently cursing his decision to return to the deep.

Dig it deeper. Don't stop digging. Just a little further, and he'll be free. Free, you'll see. Dig deeper down.

The voice sounded like it was in his ear, but he could see nobody – nothing. Frantically, he looked to the ceiling, then behind him. Mariela stood holding her shotgun, watching the empty tunnel. The voice sounded like it was coming from her. She turned to look at him, and though her lips didn't move, Andrew was sure she was saying all the words.

Free him, be him, see him. Don't stop digging. Andy, Andy An-diggity-dig-down-dy.

Andrew could almost detect her lips moving, taunting him. He flipped off his safety, overcome with an urge to kill the demonic girl, the deceiver.

Deceivers, demons, oh yes, And-diggity-dy.

She had been playing him all along, pretending so that she could bring him down – deep down, where the digging was dug – and present him to the master, the demon inside. The *wrtla.*

And-diggity-demon-dy. Digging deep day by day. Oh yes.

Suddenly, the prescient side of his mind cried out in pain. He saw, burning into his sight, Mariela being dropped to the ground, beaten, shot. She was screaming and blood was splashing everywhere.

Andy – Andrew – realized he was the one doing it in the vision, and he snapped his head back and forth.

Kill her, Andy. Or let me do it. What do you want from her first?

Andy – that was himself, the other himself, talking. He saw Mariela backing away from him in the present, her shotgun leveled on him. He dropped his muzzle and held out a hand of surrender.

It was his past self. It had been talking the whole time, saying the same things over and over. With effort, he pushed it back. It had tricked him.

With a sickness in his stomach quite apart from the gun being pointed at his head, Andrew said, "I'm fine. Don't shoot me, please. I'm fine now. I was… tricked."

Mariela looked at him apprehensively. The muzzle of the shotgun was shaking with her unsteady forward left hand. She let the gun drop back down and she stifled a moaning cry. Though her face was contorted as if tears were coming, none came, for whatever reason. She sobbed softly.

Andrew stood up. *He's far more aware of what is going on than I thought. He waited for the perfect time to spring his trap for me – to take control.*

As his breathing slowed, he noticed another noise: the faint but unmistakable sound of grinding in the distance.

"They're digging," he whispered. "Digging down to free the *wrtla*. He's calling them… commanding them. We have to put a stop to it."

Mariela stared at him blankly.

Andrew looked up at the ceiling. "We can't kill them all. We'll have to… call in somebody else."

Mariela pointed at him.

Andrew nodded. "You're right. I'm what they called in. We're far out here, too. At least a few weeks travel from the closest Iber fleet base. We'll have to think of something."

He turned and moved on, closer to the sound of grinding stone – the sound of digging.

Eventually, the tunnel widened to a large, cavernous staging area, full of equipment and littered with tools. In the whole space, only two people could be seen. Seemingly genderless, they sat near each other in grey coveralls, holding an identical pose: their knees were pulled up against their chins, and they were almost imperceptibly mumbling, rocking slightly on their haunches.

Andrew hesitated. He could easily kill both of them before they could react, but he didn't bring a suppressor for his rifle. Of course, even if he had, the rest of the people in the mine would be alerted due to the echoing nature of the caverns. He slid out of the tunnel and over to a railed-in work area. A few of the computer terminals were on here, but clearly hadn't been touched in some time. A thick layer of dust covered everything and was caked onto the keyboards.

He watched his two marks carefully. He kneeled down to pause, then flinched as Mariela banged into a chair beside him. It hit the metal desktop and reverberated in the space. The two grey people did not move. Curious, Andrew began to move forward, then froze. He saw a vision of a few seconds in the future.

The two people were running toward them, screaming. In the vision, he felled both of them.

Strange, he thought. *Not my death, but theirs… unavoidable?*

He didn't have time to mull it over. Mariela bumped into the railing and it toppled over, all twenty feet of it. It apparently had never been secured to the platform. The heads of both people snapped toward them. They rose quickly, their eyes widening in alarm.

Andrew quickly shot each of them twice in the chest. The second victim – a woman, he could see now – staggered forward, unwilling to accept the reality that she was dead. Andrew shot her once again at center mass, and she fell like a sack of potatoes.

Andrew looked over to see Mariela shrinking against the desk, her gun forgotten on the ground. She had her ears covered.

"Damn," Andrew said. "I forgot you needed hearing protection. You'd better toughen up, I'm sure more of them are on the way." He tapped Mariela as he moved past her, over to another desk facing out on the platform, giving him some slight cover and a place to rest his rifle for better accuracy.

Nobody came.

Andrew allowed himself to listen to his past self – Andy – and heard nothing but the former ravings. Mariela had retrieved her shotgun. Andrew signaled her to wait. He hopped off the platform and went to a nearby pile of equipment. Amid the discarded elements was a pair of active earmuffs. They had been left on. Hoping the battery wasn't dead, he switched them off and then back on, relieved to see a small blue light let him know there was still charge remaining. He figured they had an auto-off feature.

He slung his rifle and went back to the platform. He helped Mariela down, who was very careful with her shotgun, then put the earmuffs on her head. He found the volume knob for the external microphone and cranked it up.

Andrew whispered, "You should be able to hear me really well now, but these will stop the guns from deafening you again, yeah?"

She nodded.

"Come on."

She followed him as he walked toward the sound of machines. Two dead bodies lay in a state of suspended decomposition near a cart, both their heads turned into smashed craters. The blood was long dried. On a garden world, one with insects and a full microbiome, it would have been a far more gruesome sight. As it was, it was just one more image to file away.

They entered another tunnel. The sodium lights were lying on the floor in a long strip, dimmed by layers of grey dust. It was almost foggy inside, so packed was the air with the debris of crushed rock. Andrew flipped on his flashlight as they neared the end of the light strand. It barely cut through the dusty dark, igniting countless motes in a long beam flashing out to the abyss.

The light caught a blank face, and Andrew froze. His prescient self had not foreseen anything. It was too late to wonder about that. The face contorted in anger and rushed forward, a hoot echoing from its gaping mouth.

Andrew fired straight into the mouth and watched the body drop. He swung the light, looking for more. It crossed two more faces, who likewise turned to attack. He dropped both of them. He took a moment to tap his head.

"Come-on, you," he said. He looked to Mariela. "You okay?"

She nodded and tapped her earmuffs. Andrew wondered if she would be able to shoot if – when – the time came.

They continued on, hearing the working of the machines growing louder, filling the space with a droning, horrible sound. His electronic earplugs worked to silence it, but it only increased his anxiety. Soon all he could hear was his own heartbeat and ragged breath. If he stopped and held it, he could hear, just on the edge of reality, Andy in his permanent prison, begging to come out and greet the *Wrtla*.

They came to a fork, of sorts. The greater part of the tunnel continued curving downward, but a small cavern was open to the side. There was some sort of refuse in front of the cavern – what looked like piles of dirty clothes. As they got closer, the light caught a pair of eyes. A slightly thin face lifted itself up from the pile. Its skin was taught and white, and it stared at the pair of them. Andrew did not hesitate. He watched the brain fly out the back and into the abyss behind it.

The refuse was, Andrew realized with horror, the remains of humans: empty, bloody clothes and piles of bones. He reached a hand back to signal Mariela to stay put. He turned as she screamed, only to have a future vision. He was seeing double – the future Mariela, and the present girl. The future one, stepping back in slow motion, was firing into an advancing man, ripping his flesh apart with three close-range blasts of buckshot.

The man, though, was cognizant in his face, pleading. His hands were up in surrender, not attack.

"Mariela get back! Get behind me!"

She was still screaming. Andrew pulled her by the back of her shirt. She nearly turned her gun on him, but froze as she saw his face.

He could still see the future. The man's face was open in both surprise and relief.

Andrew pulled Mariela behind him, and the vision disappeared. He raised his rifle, pointing his light beam where he had just seen the man. He could not help but see what Mariela had in the white reflected light. Just inside the entrance to the side cavern, there were human figures. Two of them were huddled over a body, squatting like some ancient savanna tribesmen, though not in the peace of such ancestry; they were dining, ripping flesh of sanguine hues bordering on black.

Andrew held still watching them. He didn't care about the future vision, or if either of these "humans" were capable of independent thought. He shot the closest one in the back of the head. Two clean shots tapped in and sprayed black gore on the further one. The remaining one didn't react for a moment, then realized that its companion was slumping over. It looked at the dead body curiously, then up at Andrew's light.

Andrew ended its existence with a slight pleasure that brought *Andy* forward hooting, only to be pushed back down.

"They're deaf," Andrew said, realizing the delay with each of his enemies in the tunnel. "Somehow they've gone deaf." He realized Mariela was gripping his arm with her free hand. He could feel her panting breath, though he couldn't hear it over the eternal thrud of the machines in the tunnel beyond. "Anyone would go deaf here, if subjected to it long enough and without protection. All they hear now is *It*."

Andrew jumped and raised his rifle again as he detected movement down the tunnel. He held his fire and swung his light around to see the man from the future vision – or at least the one he thought might be from the vision. The details always became hazy and indistinct once he altered his actions.

The man was wearing a dingy and slightly torn white shirt, a half-buttoned orange work vest, and heavy duck trousers. He still had his shoes on, but they were untied. He walked stiffly, his arms flailing occasionally as if they had their own mind. His face was twitching, and every few steps he half-turned, as if desiring to run. His eyes, though, were fixed on Andrew's light. He started convulsing as he got closer, as if he were fighting some invisible attacker right in front of him.

"Stop!" Andrew shouted.

The man seemed to notice the word, but did not stop until he was a few yards from Andrew. Then he collapsed to his knees and gasped. His mouth was moving, but Andrew couldn't make out the words.

Carefully, he crept closer, his fingers twitching on his lips as if trying to pry them open.

"Please!" he said, his dry voice barely audible. "Please!" His hands went to his cheeks, and trembled there against the skin, as if wanting to dig into his flesh. "Kill me. Kill us!"

Andrew hesitated, wanting immediately to give in to the man's demand.

"Who are you?" he said, taking a step closer. He answered his own question as he saw the crooked name tag still on his vest. It was Ralph Esquivel, the plant manager.

The man didn't seem able to answer, but his eyes were desperate. He wore earplugs like Andrew's, though they were caked with black filth and long drained of power.

"I can't!" he said. "He made me! Now they'll dig him up and his voice will be everywhere! Kill us. Or he'll eat you too!"

"The children!" Andrew shouted. At the top of his voice he screamed, "Where are the children?!"

The man shook his head, his terrified eyes unable to break from their lock with Andrew. He choked and sputtered, then closed his eyes. "They can't work..." He looked to his left, into the cavern. His fingers were at his eyes, pushing into them, trying to reach behind the eyelids. "He made us eat. Can't starve. Can't leave. 'Til he's... He made us!"

Andrew gave into temptation and stepped to his right, to where the side cave opened up. He pointed his light inside. He hadn't really looked before. Now, he couldn't tear his eyes away.

He was vaguely aware, looking at the scene, that he ought to be feeling nausea, but his consciousness had become suddenly too detached to feel human. Or, perhaps, such reactions were part of Andy, and that one had been too tainted to find anything but perverse pleasure or humor in what was inside.

He was thankful, at least, that none of the bodies inside – small, once joyful bodies – were still recognizable as human. Their eyes were gone – devoured, perhaps, or destroyed as the mockeries of life they were. Time and the evil of the p;d *wrtla* he had known had saved a shred of Andrew's sanity, a sanity those empty eye sockets threatened to shatter. Andrew breathed, and his past self refused to show him anything of the victims. The seer of the past begged him not to look, but memories of the school flashed by his consciousness anyway.

The blast of Mariela's shotgun brought him back to the present, and Andrew spun around to see that she had shot the plant manager. He was twitching on the ground, blood flowing freely from many wounds to his chest. The girl's face was no longer horror-struck. It was iron-hard. She was holding her gun confidently, the stock pushed hard into her shoulder and her left hand steady, as if she had gained through the shock some return of control on that side of her body.

She stepped closer to the broken man. He looked up at her, his face almost relieved. He nodded slightly. She fired again, and his face disappeared in a spray of dark blood and bright bone that soon turned incarnadine in the beam of the flashlight.

"You shouldn't have looked."

Mariela glared at him, and he could read her face like she had spoken aloud, *He deserved to die.*

"No," Andrew said. "No, he deserved hell. What you gave him was a mercy, truly. He is free." He knelt down and glanced into the darkness, where he knew lay a satanic butchery that threatened his sanity. "My mark is dead, surely, but we can't leave yet. We can't let them release the *wrtla.*"

He looked at Mariela, who gave him a hard, appraising stare.

"I shouldn't have let you come," he said, "but you're here. We'll have to shut down their digging. Any idea how?"

Mariela shook her head. Andrew nodded and stood up, walking straight-backed toward the infinite noise at the end of the tunnel, no longer afraid of being heard. Mariela matched his pace. The tunnel went down and down, along an uneven and crooked path. All sound besides the digging and the internal sounds of his body disappeared. Time crawled by in the swinging beams of the flashlights. Eventually, they reached a cluster of large lamps enflaming a great cloud of dust.

Silhouettes of human figures were moving around the lights, which Andrew saw were attached to a great piece of machinery. It was like a tank, or armored vehicle, but larger, sitting on brown treads twice as tall as a man. The front of the machine was turning in circles, some diamond-faced set of tools grinding endlessly the stone in front of it, whittling it down slow centimeters at a time. A narrow drill bit sat poised above it, meant for longer excavations, not large tunnels. He didn't know how many people it took to operate as he could not see anyone in any kind of driver's seat.

The cluster of people around it were working endlessly on what the machine produced: millions of pebbles and piles of dust. The pebbles they threw by hand into nearby carts, automated to run along a magnetic track on the edge of the tunnel. The dust was pushed hastily to the side, kicking large amounts up into the air.

"Cover your mouth," Andrew said, flipping a switch to bring his helmet back around his face. The infinite sound immediately died down. "There are heavy metals in this dust." He saw that Mariela had wrapped her shirt around her nose and face. It would have to do.

Andrew didn't bother waiting. He took a knee.

"Watch our back!"

He began firing, holding himself in tight control. He dropped two silhouettes, and the others around it froze, then began moving toward him. He purposefully slowed his breathing as he felt Andy begging to gain control. He shot three more people. The lights began to get hazy in the background, and they were so bright his own flashlight was of little use.

Four more dropped. Two were crawling still toward him. He'd have to get them in a second. How many were coming now? Ten? Twenty?

He exterminated five more in five shots. He began to shake, and Andy began to laugh inside. Through his old self, he could hear the whisper of the *wrtla*. How close were they? Ten yards now?

He toggled over to auto, and fired, meaning to spray the group in front of him, but only a three-shot burst came out.

"Damn," he said, cursing his carelessness in not inspecting the autosear. He dropped three more. He was empty. Quickly, he exchanged his magazine for a fresh one.

His future self asserted some measure of control, and he saw a dozen forms spreading out around him. It only further confused him. Trying his best to focus, he continued to fire. He saw the shadows moving toward their slow-motion echoes, the places where they would be momentarily. With a quick appraisal, he fired as each one arrived, dropping six people, their blood blotting out the light behind them as they fell.

Again, he fired. He was losing track of where they were. Andy was yelling with mad glee, pushing into the center of his consciousness.

Empty.

He dropped out the magazine and reached for another. He fumbled it and dropped it on the ground. A field of future images flew out, immediately in front of him. Their hands, sickly white, were groping him, touching him in a tingle of future dread.

Andrew dropped the rifle and reached for his plasma gun. In the silence, he realized that Mariela was firing. He saw bodies drop to his left, but the images in front of him remained. He flipped off the safety and fired through the images. The muzzle flash of the energy weapon was powerfully bright in the dim tunnel, but the way it lit up all the dust around him was possibly worse. He was nearly blind, but he stayed focused on the images. The images disappeared as he hit the attackers which he could not yet see.

Finally, the last motion was a shambling corpse of a man heading toward Mariela. Andrew saw she was kneeling down, trying to reload the shotgun. He quickly dispatched the wretch, then moved to help her. Her shaking hands were having trouble loading the shells into the magazine tube.

"Next time use your pistol."

Andrew reached into her bag and grabbed a handful of shells. Taking the gun, he quickly popped them in, then threw one in the chamber and released the bolt. He picked his rifle back up and swung the light into the darkness behind them and saw motion that he couldn't clearly find the origin of out in the dust.

"The wrtla told them we were here," Andrew said, hearing laughter from Andy. "Stay close to me. Fire on them if you have to."

She obeyed, watching the space behind them that was flooded with the digging machine's lights. Andrew approached cautiously, watching his periphery as much as he could. Once he was fully in the halo of lights it was impossible to see any moving shadows. He tapped his head, hoping his prescience would alert him to any remaining enemies.

The machine seemed more massive as he approached, like a gigantic armored beetle with its head stuck in the sand. He slung his rifle and climbed up a ladder onto an operating platform that contained several seats. Each one, he saw, was controlled by a computer terminal and operation surface; manual controls were apparently locked. He touched one panel to bring it to life and it prompted him for identification and a password.

"Damnit," he said. He moved to the other three. All of them were identity locked. He began looking about frantically for an emergency kill switch. He shouted down to Mariela, "Do you see any switches? Anything to turn this thing off?"

On the ground, she turned from staring out into the darkness beyond the lights. She pointed at something on the ground level, between the treads.

Andrew quickly hopped down, falling to his hands as he hit the uneven pebble-strewn floor of the dig site. He found the switch, a large red button behind a plate of glass. He slammed the butt of his stock into the glass, shattering it, then something inside him snapped.

With horror, he realized he could hear laughing – *it was Andy.* He reached toward the switch, and his hand froze. He willed it forward, but it would not obey him. Slowly, his hand turned back, the fingers curling, as if the hand had a mind of its own and was struggling to make a fist. He could almost see a grimace there, in the lines of his palm.

Welcome back, child of darkness.

"I don't know you," Andrew said.

You know my sister, and therefore you know me.

"No."

Yes, Andrew Dalatent. Space is a small matter for us, distance irrelevant. Time belongs to us. We are inevitable.

"No."

You think we made a mistake with you? No, we did not. We do not make weapons idly. It is time for us to begin our great crusade, Andrew. The great work you were created for. All that you desire will be given to you; we reward those who are strong.

"I am free from you!"

Laughter answered him, but he couldn't be sure if it was the *wrtla*, or himself.

The next moment he was turning, facing Mariela.

She stood hesitantly, her eyes looking out across the dusty lightscape. Andrew felt a sudden heat in his neck, and he recognized an emotion that he had long been detached from – a consequence of his condition. *Emotion* was not the right word, he realized. It was a feeling, and it would have sickened him, but he was no longer in control. He was watching now, passively, and he realized that detachment from his past self no longer prevented him from feeling Andy's desires and compulsions.

Worse, he *was* Andy.

He considered for a long moment the lustful feelings that welled in him. There was simple, human lust, and a deeper, uglier feeling. A bloodlust. A lust for pain.

Kill her. There will be others. The demon tickled his mind with a promise.

He fired two shots into her chest. She crumpled into a heap. Her eyes looked up to regard him, sickening surprise filling the wide pupils as life left her body. Andy smiled. He had hated her from the moment he saw her.

Welcome back to the fold.

Andrew tried to resist, but he was failing badly. He felt gone, washed away and blended into oblivion. His fingers in his mind reached forward, trying to regain control and salvage something. He was a murderer, truly, now, but that didn't mean he had to let the *wrtla* win. Mariela's dead face recused him.

Something snapped, and Andrew realized he had lost time.

He was, he saw now, surrounded by the simple servants of the lord beneath. They waited on his whim, dominated by the thoughts of the being they had worked tirelessly to free. So many had died in their quest to please him, served him as food for the remaining slaves, who were hardened beyond any semblance of humanity now.

They worked endlessly at his feet, pulling away the rubble from the great dig.

At last the digging machine broke through, its many bits and faceted tools worn down to round nubs by the effort. A black abyss opened beyond, and from it emerged the *wrtla* in all its terrible inverted glory. It was swirling gray smoke, seething and crawling out, covering every surface with millions of smooth, lacteous tentacles. Within that mist and mass of nocturnal opalescence squirmed pieces of its body – corporeal and yet beyond the physical realm, just as the mind of the lord was unfathomable and yet could be known and understood a piece at a time.

"Lord Dalrathag," Andrew said aloud, relishing in the name of his lord, knowable only once he had reached direct contact with him. Countless eyes of nothingness regarded him with pleasure, and Andrew leaned back, receiving the blessing of power from his god. Command and presence, to go with his foretelling and understanding.

Andrew – the Andrew who had withstood a *wrtla* and rescued himself, screamed internally at his impotence. His failure.

Darkness swirled. The prescient mind was sending a vision of the coming crusade, obeying the will of Andy and the *wrtla.*

Andrew was looking out from a window upon a scene of fire and carnage. A city was in ruins. Soon another lord would be freed. He laughed with pleasure. Gladness and satisfaction spread through his mind, tingling his body.

Andy laughed as the vision subsided.

He heard the voice of Dalrathag, omnipresent, soothing, "My servant, you shall be whole."

"As you will it," Andy said.

Pain, and then a fleeting wondering – do you remember pain in the space of nonexistence? Andrew realized the fractured psyche he had carefully formed was being folded in on itself.

Black nothingness enveloped his mind. Cold fingers twisted into fragile memories.

Then a little light appeared at the center and began to grow. It coalesced into form He was staring at a hand. His own ungloved hand.

He saw another hand move past his, and slam into a big red button. He turned his head to look upon the hard face of Mariela. She looked at him, alarmed. The machine to his right began to quiet, the digging apparatus at the front grinding slowly to a stop.

He clenched his hand into a fist and turned around. Mariela had her back to him now, her shotgun held at the ready.

Shadows were coming in from beyond the halo of light. Sound was returning – footsteps echoed around them as the machine wound down.

"It was a vision," he said. He tried to focus, but inside he was screaming wordlessly against his past self, and he felt sick with the echoes of Andy's bloody lust. He reached in his pocket for the grenade he held there, to end things. He was too close to madness now. But then, Mariela was still alive.

A vision returned to him – he was alone in his ship. His fingers hesitated on the grenade. He cursed himself for not knowing which mind was sending it, past or future, or what he were trying to say.

A shadow turned into a person, running straight for Andrew, and Mariela fired. The attacker flopped forward, twitching. Another came in, and she fired again. She hit it somewhere on the side, but the faceless figure came on.

Andrew broke his paralysis. He took his hand out of his pocket and began firing. He put the closest one down quickly, then began firing into each moving shadow beyond the dusty lights. He didn't know how many he hit.

"We need to get moving," Andrew said. "We have to get out of here."

He strode forward. His prescience was not presenting him any information, perhaps tired from the exhaustive, years-long vision he had just lived. Andrew was too on edge to feel real fear about his blindness. He just knew he had to move forward.

As he got further away from the machine, his eyes adjusted, and he could see more people. They were milling about further up the tunnel, as if coordinating. He remembered the ones down here had minds that were more intact.

"Wait," he said, turning back. "They'll be able to start it again. Dalrathag will be able to command them."

Mariela gave him an incredulous look as he removed the grenade from his pocket.

"We have to disable it permanently." He adjusted the electronic fuse on the grenade so it would no longer explode instantly. He flipped the switch and threw it under the tread of the machine. "Run!"

He grabbed Mariela's elbow and pushed her forward, toward the swirling darkness and the figures beyond.

The grenade exploded, sooner than Andrew had intended. The blast threw both of them forward and covered them with a shower of small rocks and dust from above. Andrew helped Mariela up only to find a hand gripping the muzzle of his rifle, trying to twist it away.

Mariela fired on the attacker, knocking him away and showering both of them with a sudden deluge of blood. Andrew's visor was almost completely obscured by the gore. Desperately, he pressed the button at his neck to open it up.

They were surrounded by grimaced, dusty faces. Empty eyes.

Andrew panicked and shot wildly around himself. Mariela, he saw in his periphery, was retreating, her shotgun empty. He backed up toward her as he fired, desperately trying to aim with shaky hands and an overwhelming fear. He suddenly clicked empty.

"Mariela!" he shouted, running back and dropping the empty magazine. He fumbled a fresh one, but managed to get it in and release the bolt of the rifle. He turned again and fired at nothing he could see.

He was back at the machine. Mariela was nowhere to be seen. His heart fell as he looked upon the digging machine. His grenade had failed to do anything of significance. The heavy chassis was blackened, but the treads were intact.

He turned his head back at a cry from the hazy dark. He shouldered his rifle. His attackers were moving about, but his wild retaliation had stalled them. He heard the vocalization again, almost a scream.

A woman's scream.

"Mariela!"

He ran toward the scream, which was distinctly audible now that the machine had ceased its endless grinding. Through the settling dust, he could see figures moving; they were clearly as confused as he was in the bright, yet obscured, light, unable to hear his passing due to the deafness they endured.

A withered man reared up before Andrew's eyes. He barreled into the surprised thrall, checking him with the side of his rifle's receiver and sending him flying to the floor. The impact nearly knocked the wind from Andrew, but he scrambled on, trying to find the source of the scream. Just as suddenly, he saw the kneeling form of Mariela looking out into the darkness, her flashlight off.

Of course, they ignored her, they're looking for me, he thought.

He managed to stop and stoop beside her. Mariela, with a guttural note of fear, reached over and turned off Andrew's light. She then stood and guided him back along the wall, back away from the lights. Andrew looked back and as his eyes adjusted he could see more clearly the slaves of the *wrtla* moving together, fanning out into a net. They vocalized softly, wordlessly, like some imitation, or mockery, of babies. It was unlikely they could hear each other, but in the silence, the growing line of coos and grunts sounded like the song of insanity – the *wrtla* singing through grim, grey lips while it moved its toys about.

"You're right," Andrew said. "They can't hear us, but they can see us. This way, along the wall."

Andrew turned with Mariela and they felt their way up the tunnel, pushing themselves against the rough stone each time they heard the footsteps of one of the damned running past them, heeding the call of the master below. This happened with decreasing regularity, but no matter how long between the sounds, he and Mariela went as quietly as possible, just so that they could hear them. Andrew wondered if there were people down in the dark who could still hear. He did his best to still his breathing and avoid speaking.

Some amount of time later (it was hard to judge either distance or time while blind, and Andrew dared not check his computer for the hour, lest they be revealed by its light) they came upon the second cavern. Andrew discovered it when his feet ran into something heavy, yet soft, and he knew it was a body. They paused there, and Andrew considered crossing to the other side, blindly, or stepping through the bodies. He heard Mariela tap him and vocalize a wordless question behind him.

"We're at the cavern where the children… where we found the plant manager. We're going to have to cross blind here. Hold my hand." Andrew slung his rifle and took out his plasma gun. He reached back to feel Mariela's hand, then began to cross, shuffling slowly. He reached another body and, not knowing how to go back, tried to step over it.

He misjudged the distance and stepped on the far side of its ribcage. The body was significantly butchered and decomposed, and the ribs snapped under his weight, sending his boot down onto a bone, which rolled under him. He slipped and put a hand under himself. Ungloved, it ripped through some soft sinew and entered a cavity. The stench of rotting meat assailed him, and he didn't bother trying to stop himself from vomiting his meager stomach contents.

Even while he threw up, he pushed himself erect. He wiped his hand on his suit, then reached back for Mariela, who had let go of him.

"Find my hand." He snapped a few times, then felt relief as her hand closed on his, slightly resistant to the wetness. "I'm sorry."

Andrew helped Mariela over the body, and then they shuffled into a pile of bones. Not caring about the noise, they pushed through into empty, rough stone floor. After what felt like a long time scraping their feet along the floor, they reached the other wall.

"I think it's this way," Andrew said, pulling Mariela to his left. "At least it feels like it's going up." He chewed his cheek, hoping that he had not lost his bearings in the fall and wasn't taking Mariela back toward the digging machine and the waiting creatures.

The blackness stretched on. They passed noises of varying kinds: footsteps, vocalizing, talking with words, speech in a language neither of them recognized, snorting and snoring, and finally, the worst of all, the wet and sickening sounds of dining. All of them they passed by, and Andrew began to feel optimistic despite the horror of it all.

Then he heard, far below, the sound of the digging machine. Somebody among the hell thrall of the *wrtla* had enough capacity to start it back up. Dalrathag had purpose; he did not impose madness for its own sake, it seemed.

They tried to continue on, but without the sound to warn them, they grew tense. Mariela gripped Andrew's hand with increasing strength, to the point where he thought, had he a light, he would see marks in his flesh from her fingers and nails.

"They'll be heading backward to find us," he said. "We have to run for it." His heart leapt as he said this, his body finally responding to the brooding, sickening fear he had felt for so long in the dark.

Mariela paused, then squeezed Andrew's hand. She released him and flipped on her flashlight. Andrew did the same for the built-in light on his plasma gun. They looked around. They were somewhere in the tunnel, but they had no idea how far. They were indeed heading up, and that made Andrew feel relieved. He checked his computer on his wrist.

"I can pick up the wireless network signal from here. We'll definitely get back soon."

Mariela nodded.

They broke into a run. The incline was steeper than it seemed, and soon both of them were panting for breath. Andrew's suit felt stifling. He could feel a stream of sweat running down the back of his neck and pooling against his undershirt. They encountered nothing until they reached the point where the tunnels converged.

There, as their tunnel met the others, where the sodium lights remained in their eternal orange vigil, was a mass of people spread out into a long, tight line blocking the way forward.

They were men and women, all hunched and drawn thin. They weren't emaciated, but rather wretched – beings of deformed skin and musculature, made to function brutally rather than with beauty. The women seemed to lose their femininity, their sex determined as much by their old dress as any other feature. Their mouths were overlarge and darkened from their vile meals of flesh, and gaped as Andrew and Mariela approached.

Andrew did not wait for a battle plan; He strode toward the line and fired a bright white shot of plasma into the closest creature. It twisted away, its flesh burned and ripped apart by the energy of the blast. Andrew fired again, and again, but the creatures maintained some semblance of discipline. The *wrtla* was being liberal with his pawns, but he was still executing a strategy.

Andrew regretted throwing away the grenade when he did as the line of wicked moaning creatures became a semi-circle hemming them in.

Mariela joined him, firing in the same direction. The line was close enough for the buckshot to do its magic, ripping soft flesh and maiming, even killing. She stayed to Andrew's side as they counter-advanced. When a man fell, the space was immediately filled, leaving a pile of dead bodies between Andrew and Mariela and the freedom beyond.

Andrew's plasma gun clicked empty, and he dropped the battery out and replaced it, then continued the carnage. An idea struck him.

"Cover your eyes!" he shouted as he put his arm across his own face. He used an old flaw of his plasma gun – he flipped the safety halfway on, which only slightly impeded the venting of the raw, hot matter from the gun.

He pointed the gun up and forced the trigger down. It fired a shot of burning hot nitrogen in a cone above him, a burst far brighter than a single projectile burning through air.

Andrew uncovered his eyes and saw the thrall were recoiling in blindness. He pointed his gun to fire, but found that the shot had destroyed the breech. He threw the weapon hard to his right, where it hit a stooped woman. The thrall began to move toward her.

"Now!" Andrew said, bringing his rifle back around. He charged the line, waiting to fire until he was close enough to see the blind hollow eyes of his enemy. Rapidly, he killed three people. Mariela joined him, gunning down two that stood behind. Before they could fall, Andrew charged into them, knocking them down and bursting through the line.

Mariela screamed and Andrew turned back. One of the dying slaves had caught her ankle, as if suddenly realizing her existence. In their blindness, she was suddenly a thing to be noticed through touch. She had dropped her shotgun and was trying to draw the pistol tucked in her waistband. He stepped over a body and fired three times, killing the monster, but it had served its master well. Two more men gripped her legs. Andrew went to fire again, and found the rifle empty. He quickly checked his bag. He was out of ammo.

He hurled the useless weapon forward, striking one of the blind men, then he picked up the shotgun and fired the last three shots. Mariela at the same time fired into the closest man, emptying her magazine. Blood blackened by the artificial light poured in torrents, baptizing Mariela in sanguine horror. One thrall, unwilling to die, clung to her leg still, despite having most of its face ripped away by the pistol. A single blind eye stared up into the abyss from the part that remained. Andrew stepped forward and kicked the eye, breaking what remained of the skull. The thing twitched, but clung on in a kind of rigor mortis.

Andrew bent down and wrenched Mariela free, dragging her to her feet. She limped along beside him, running full out now from the hellthrall that followed behind, blind and dumb, but guided by a will that at the least could sense part of Andrew's mind.

As they ran, they could hear others joining the chase from some other corridor. They looked back to see eyes that had vision, and steps that had purpose. Even the blind were running wild now, guided by the intelligence below, which saw through the failing eyes of his puppets.

Finally, they reached the landing where the lifts were. By some grace beyond Andrew's understanding, the area was vacant. The *wrtla* had neglected to guard the final retreat, or else had deemed it unnecessary for his purposes. The lift car stood open, a white light in the eternal darkness, a fragment of color in unending umber-tinted horror.

"You get it moving," Andrew panted as they flew into the car. He quickly picked up his regular rifle and began firing at the approaching mob. It almost didn't matter now, nothing would stop them, but Andrew fired on. He emptied the magazine and threw a fresh one in. He toggled over to full auto and sprayed the ugly faces as they grew close, close enough Andrew could almost smell their rotting breath. He went empty again and reloaded.

Then the lift door closed. Andrew fired a single shot into the door. The tempered sapphire glass cracked as it caught the bullet, but did not shatter. A group of thrall slammed into the doors, rocking the car, but it was already moving. They slid off as the lift car moved into the dark tunnel. The monsters were leaping off the landing, scrambling through the tunnel in a mad attempt to catch them. Then the car slid over the abyss, rocking slightly as it ground along the track.

In the dim light, they watched bodies spill over into nothingness. Then the car went around a bend in the stone, and over a chasm.

They were alone in the dark once more.

"Take us straight to the main complex," Andrew said, leaning against the side of the car. "Don't stop anywhere on the way."

Mariela pointed to Andrew's gun, then held up four fingers.

"Not worth it. I have a few rounds left. There's bound to be a security station in the main compound anyway." He took a breath and looked at his hands. He wiped the sweat from his brow with the outside of his suit, which did little. Suddenly, the sweat felt cold. "I think the further away they get, the less they can understand. It's why your... the ones... in sector five, were so far gone. Who knows how many people are left, but I know nobody in the main area bothered to attack me, if anyone remained."

Mariela shook her head. She retrieved her notebook. *There's nobody left there. I checked.*

"Good. We'll be safe. Hopefully, I'll be able to disable the atmospheric generators." He caught Mariela's eye. "No, it's unlikely they'll use up all the oxygen, but we have to do something. We can't let them free the *wrtla.*"

She nodded and wrote, *Better than nothing.*

They approached the sector four landing. A cluster of people stood on the landing, in the space where the cars passed, and on the rail above. The car didn't slow as it slammed into the crowd. Andrew brought his sights up and watched as bodies rolled over the windows, knocked down by the lift's running mechanism above. One of the thrall landed on top of the car. It swayed as it left the landing and moved back out into the dark. Andrew could just see the person above, struggling to move around and gain entry to the car.

Mariela was standing beside him; her pistol had apparently been abandoned and forgotten. Slowly, the person, withered and hollow-eyed, reached down toward the seam in the door. The glass was bulletproof; waiting for him to penetrate the doors to fire was agonizing. The monster lost some sense of footing and slipped down, falling away from the car into darkness.

Andrew relaxed and lowered his rifle.

They were out over the biggest abyss now, the running lights on the track the only way to tell they were going uphill. Suddenly, they saw the lights further up going black, one at a time.

"What?" Andrew said, squinting. His question was answered a few moments later when the other lift car came rushing by.

Mariela looked at him with alarm.

"It makes sense. They can use the digger, so of course they can use the lift." As if sensing her next question, he said, "The *wrtla* wanted full control of his slaves more than anything. If he let them go back up for food, he could lose them." He absent-mindedly touched his fist to his head. "So they ate…" Andrew shook his head, the images below returning to him briefly. "He must consider himself close to free. We're on a timer now."

The car went on in darkness, passing through the third sector landing and on into another stretch of blackness.

"We'll have to skip the atmosphere generators," he said. "No time, no point. Let's just live, eh?" He forced a weak and unfamiliar smile.

Mariela touched her chin in thought. She got out her notebook and wrote slowly *decompression?*

"We'd have to decompress all seven levels of the colony."

Mariela held up her finger as she flipped her notebook over. She drew something Andrew didn't recognize: a series of two-dimensional boxes lined up against each other.

"I don't know."

Mariela gritted her teeth, then wrote, *Heat.*

"The heat sinks. For the power plant. They wouldn't vent into the primitive atmosphere. Too thin. No point for that."

Mariela wrote *Top Level. Vents at TOP LEVEL. Emergency.*

"So punch a hole in the top of the power plant?"

Mariela nodded.

"Would that do much? It would take weeks to vent out the mine."

Mariela threw her hands down in frustration.

"Well, it's better than nothing, I admit."

Mariela began working the computer panel. Andrew leaned over and saw that she was punching in sector one as a destination.

"We don't have time," Andrew said. Mariela looked at him, impassively.

She picked her notebook back up and wrote *Explosives.*

They soon reached the landing for sector one, which looked out across a great underground canyon. In the distance the lights of the lower levels of the colony could just be seen, burning ever on despite the lack of anyone to see them. Mariela moved out of the lift car, limping slightly but going as close to a jog as her body and her nervous system would allow.

The second sector had at some point been converted to additional storage. There was nothing left to conveniently mine so high up, so the empty tunnels had been sealed by steel barricades which were now caked with dust. Mariela seemed to know the main area, and she quickly found a storage room with a locked door. She pointed at the doorknob.

Andrew sighed. He had discarded his plasma gun.

"Step back and cover your eyes." Mariela nodded and complied. Andrew took several steps back and shot at the lock. The bullet fractured and ricocheted, but the lock endured. He shot it three more times. The last time the mechanism within seemed to break apart, falling from the handle and clanging dully on the dusty floor.

Andrew tried the handle and found it stuck. With a grunt, he kicked hard at the door. It gave way and swung inward to reveal a room stocked with various types of explosives. She pointed at a case. Andrew nodded and picked it up, finding the small box heavy for its size. She grabbed a few other oddities that Andrew didn't recognize – blasting caps and ignition wires, he thought. She nodded and they quickly left the room.

When they got back in the lift Mariela quickly entered the coordinates for the main colony, and the lift car lurched out onto the floating track.

"We should have blown the track," Andrew said a few seconds later.

Mariela shook her head, as if that wouldn't have worked.

"Why?"

She put down the equipment she held under her arm and wrote *Only work under compression. Dad did demo.*

Andrew thought back to a rudimentary engineer's course which dealt with demolition that he had taken when he was part of the Angl Space Force. The instructor had likened a firecracker going off in the palm of his hand – it would burn you, but you'd be fine, ultimately – with closing your hand around the same firecracker. You wouldn't have a hand after that.

"I should have used my grenade differently," Andrew said aloud. "I could have at least put it in the space between the treads and the driving gears. Haste makes waste, I guess."

Mariela looked at him blankly. Andrew made to answer the look, but her eyes grew wider and she stepped past him before he could begin the words. She looked out the rear window, placing her hands lightly on the window. Andrew shuffled next to her and looked into the blackness.

The other lift car was coming. It had just passed through the first sector landing. It seemed to be going slightly slower than their own car.

"Damnit," Andrew said. He released his magazine and checked it. He had nine rounds left. Quickly, he rummaged through his bag. He found two more stray cartridges and popped them into the top of the magazine, then put it back in the rifle. "Twelve shots, including the chamber," he said. "Just like the old west. Is there an emergency shutoff for the lift?"

Mariela nodded, but her face indicated a different emotion. She wrote, *Need a key.*

"Makes sense," Andrew said. "Any way to trigger an automatic shutoff?"

Mariela shrugged unknowingly.

"On the other hand, it would probably shut off the interior elevators as well." He sighed. The colony loomed closer. "Let's get there as quickly as possible. You know the way?"

Mariela nodded.

A minute or two passed in silence as the lift approached the final landing. At last, the lights grew close. The rock wall approached and the details of the windows looking out into the hollow mine could be discerned. The lift car slowed and finally arrived. The doors opened. Andrew and Mariela stepped out. The white light was almost nauseating after the darkness.

Andrew took a quick look around. He saw an access panel near the double doors of the mine lift and ripped it off. Inside were a number of breakers and fuses. He dropped the explosive case, put his gloves back on, and quickly ripped out what he could. Sparks flew and the power hissed. Several of the breakers wouldn't budge, so he stepped back and shot them a few times. The running lights on the magnetic track flickered and died.

"Nine rounds," he said aloud.

He looked out the window and, after a moment, saw the other lift car in the distance, a pin of light. It was still swaying, growing closer. As he watched, the first lift car pulled away, heading back into the mine.

"Shit," he said.

He glanced at the littered office around him and found a long screwdriver from a nearby workbench. He raced over to the doors and wedged it into the side of the second set near the wall. When he turned, he saw Mariela already limp-running to the main elevators. Andrew picked up the explosives and sprinted to catch up. She had already called one of the cars, and the doors were open. He followed Mariela inside and she punched in the top level.

"We don't have much time," Andrew said.

Mariela looked at him impassively. In the bright, incandescent light of the immaculately clean elevator, he could finally see clearly what they had endured. She was covered in blood, drying from crimson to brown, and her face was wet with sweat. She was trembling, too, on the edge of exhaustion. Andrew saw that his own hands were shaking and he was equally ugly with human death.

"How long has it been?" Andrew checked his wrist computer, unsure of the passage of time in the dark below. He tapped it, unbelieving.

Mariela was staring at him curiously.

"Almost three days? How are we still alive?"

Mariela pointed to her head.

Andrew wondered: did she mean her injury, or his?

The lift arrived at the first floor. Andrew followed Mariela away from the dormitories and schoolroom to another long, steel-lined hallway. At the end of it was a set of double doors that opened for them automatically. A reception area greeted them, empty and clean, with live computers but nobody to man them. Mariela paused for a moment, then went through a swinging door to an area full of terminals and basic workstations. She glanced around, then limped to another door. It opened into the power plant proper, a sleek self-contained set of rooms housing the fusion chamber, which plugged away its infinite hum without a care for the humans who had not attended to it. The door, apparently, had never been locked when the workers walked down into the mine… or had been carried away.

"There?" Andrew said, seeing the piping for the heat sinks leading from the free-standing central chamber up over a steel platform. Mariela nodded and limped on, carrying her equipment with her. They went up a narrow set of stairs to the piping, seeing the area where it divided. Half of the pipes went up, the others went another direction.

Mariela beckoned for the case. Andrew set it down and pried it open. Inside were stacks of tubes with elongated nozzles. Mariela pointed at him, then at the far door.

"I'll cover you," Andrew said. He turned and readied himself. In the bright, clean space it was hard to imagine the thrall from the mine. He could only think of human people. His past self gave him a fleeting vision of men and women at work in the room, pale translucent ghosts assembling the chamber at the center. Andrew refocused himself on the far door. He glanced back occasionally to check Mariela's progress.

Mariela slowly pushed the contents of the tubes into the space around the upper heat sink pipes. They vibrated slightly with the passage of coolant. As the thick, grey paste filled the area, she put in a narrow blasting cap, a simple electric-responsive explosive. She filled six of these narrow spaces, then quickly attached a wire to each blasting cap. Within a few moments, the paste had set. She ran the wires to a receiver.

Andrew saw her shaking so badly that she couldn't get the wire ends to fit into the terminals. He quickly kneeled down beside her and held the radio receiver. She guided each wire in carefully with her more proficient right hand. A sound from the other side of the room, distant and yet too close, made her wince.

"Just a few more, come on," Andrew said, not turning to look behind him. Mariela nodded and continued slowly inserting the wires, then closing the terminals.

Andrew, while he kneeled, was having a vision of the future. He saw six figures coming through the far door, right in a line. They were horrible to look upon in the clear, bright white light. They were dark… as if made of darkness, though somehow visible. Their skin was grey where it could be seen, but they were covered in filth, human waste, and the horror of their sustenance in the deeps. Andrew could see clearly the twistedness of them as they leapt over the railing and came bounding forward. Their mouths were slobbering open, too large for people, too small to be reptiles. Their eyes were over-large and dark. Their hair hung in strands, and their hands were like claws, or like the legs of some grotesque insect.

In the vision, he also heard. He heard their guttural cries, but he also heard the banging of the door. He knew that in the present, that sound had not happened.

"Stay calm, we'll be fine," he said. He watched the damned disperse, spread out to catch them in the future.

Mariela fidgeted, fitting the last wire into the detonation receiver.

Andrew heard the door slam open. Mariela put the receiver down. Andrew spun around and instantly saw three targets moving at a preternatural speed. He ignored the first two, who were already spreading out, and instead focused on the door. He fired once, and one of the thrall fell away.

"Eight."

The door opened again.

Andrew fired again. The shot didn't hit square. His vision shifted; he saw the fewer number trying to adapt, confused. The newly appeared thrall continued on, only injured. He fired again, this time hitting center mass. The figure collapsed on a ladder. In his vision, he saw a short one, what was once a woman.

"Six."

Andrew fired again, this time just as the door opened. The single shot hit a squat figure in the head, knocking it back.

"Five."

It stopped opening. One of the creatures that was already inside bolted for the exit; one sprinted directly at him and Mariela. Andrew focused on the bolting one, seeing a vision of him appearing from behind a steel workstation. He waited a few heartbeats, then fired as the beast revealed itself. The bullet hit, but it didn't kill.

The second one was on him; Andrew tore his eyes from the escaping monster and kicked out. His boot contacted the thrall, knocking it back, but it also latched onto Andrew's leg, taking him down with it. Andrew rolled, looking for a clear shot, but Mariela had already stepped over and was stomping on the thing, screaming at it.

It loosed its grip and Andrew rolled away. It grabbed Mariela instead, it was again as if it suddenly realized her existence; Andrew shot it once in the head. The skull came apart and the body stiffened. Mariela stepped back in disgust, then jumped over the body, beckoning Andrew onward.

"Wait," Andrew said. "There's more!"

He found it suddenly difficult to keep up with the limping, shuffling girl. He saw a phantom from the past and the future lining up over the door. As Mariela moved toward a staircase he kneeled down and fired. The door opened at the same time, and the creature was knocked back by the blast.

"Four," Andrew panted, getting to his feet and taking the steps two at a time behind Mariela. He grabbed her shoulder and stepped past her, kicking open the door. The hallway was empty, stained with a trail of blood. Two thrall were in their way, thrashing, fighting against death more than clinging to life.

Andrew froze for a moment, then put a shot in each of their heads, ending their fight. They had to climb over the bodies; it was impossible to step between them, and they seemed to give underfoot like something rotten.

"Two," Andrew said, dismayed.

He kicked open the door to the lobby. It was empty. He saw the trail of blood leading away, back toward the great lobby and lifts.

"Only way is forward," he said, stepping toward the exit. As they passed through the automatic doors, Andrew saw a flash of the future. It was confusing; he was alone in the landing zone.

Suddenly he turned around and saw a figure behind Mariela. The thrall was reaching for her. Andrew's finger twitched on the trigger, but he held it back with sudden realization. The creature was stepping around her, coming for him.

Not knowing what else to do, Andrew pushed Mariela into the wrtla-thrall with force. They both toppled to the floor. Andrew jumped over her and pulled the trigger.

The firing pin clicked, but the round didn't go off. Lacking the time to rack the bolt, Andrew stomped down with his foot on the creatures head. He vaguely thought he recognized the face – it was a woman's, but all his memory could tell him was that she was pretty, once. These thoughts circled hauntingly as he obliterated her twisted face, first with the heel of his boot, then with the stock of his rifle. He slammed it down over and over, until the skull split apart and the thing finally gave up its life to its master.

He breathed hard as he looked at it. It still twitched in spite of its exposed grey matter. It was wearing the remains of a dress. He racked his bolt and popped out the offending dud round.

"One," he said, helping Mariela up. She touched her chest as if in pain. "Sorry." Andrew pulled her along the blood trail toward the entrance. In the school lobby, he stopped. "We don't have an exosuit for you."

Mariela looked at him, dumbfounded.

"My ship is parked outside, not in the bay, since nobody was responding to hails. The atmosphere is too thin for you to breathe."

Mariela looked down at her right hand, which held the explosive remote. She put her shaky left hand on Andrew's shoulder, as if to resign herself to a goodbye.

"No," Andrew said. "I'll... Just come on."

She shook her head and pointed at the detonator.

"The ship is close to the airlock," Andrew said. "You'll survive. I know it. I can see the future."

She didn't give him an incredulous look so much as one that was disbelieving, but her face was also resigned, and yet somehow hopeful.

As they walked through the halls, the blood trail led on. Andrew looked at the once vibrant hallways, full of pictures and memories. False windows showing machine-made sunlight made shadows dance on the murals. How utterly devoid of meaning they seemed now, and yet his mind took them in. He took a last look at a child's drawing of a dragon, before focusing ahead. At last, they reached the front doors, the airlocks to the landing zone outside. The blood trail ended at the steel doors.

Mariela pointed down at the detonator.

"Now?"

She pressed a few buttons. Nothing happened for a long few moments. Mariela looked at the thing in anger, then they both felt a tremendous explosion through the ground. Smoke billowed into the distant foyer, and an alarm started sounding. Overhead, sprinklers began dripping.

Andrew linked his arm into Mariela's and led her to the airlock. It opened for him. He pressed a button and his helmet came back up. Most of the blood had dried into a smear fractured by the seams of the helmet's construction.

A vision assaulted him: it was one of the thrall. It was standing outside on the hazy planet surface, pointing a rifle at Andrew, firing it into his face. Vaguely he could see, as he fell, airlock doors.

"When it opens, run," he said as he pressed the button to open the other door. He shouldered his rifle with his free arm. The air rushed out, meeting the thin, almost red atmosphere.

Nothing was there. Andrew did not have time to puzzle over it. He pulled Mariela out.

It was sunset outside, which could last for many hours on the slowly rotating planet.

They dashed for Andrew's ship, Mariela holding her breath and limping as fast as she could. She started gasping. Then she fell. Andrew dropped his rifle and scooped her into his arms. As he approached the ship, the airlock doors opened for him, recognizing the unique signal on his computer.

He was struck with a future vision. He had seen it before. He was alone in the cockpit of his ship. Instinctively, he turned. He saw the bloody thrall right behind him, fazed by the thin atmosphere but far from dead. It was holding his rifle.

It pulled the trigger.

Nothing happened. Andrew chanced to tilt his head and saw – to his surprise – that at some point he had flipped the safety back on.

He backed up two steps as the thrall tried again to fire the weapon. The airlock doors closed. Finally, the thrall figured it out, and the last shot slammed into the door. Andrew hit the lock button with great force and turned away with Mariela in his arms, not bothering to watch the Thrall try to claw his way in with what remained of his driven, demon-powered stamina. The vision of himself alone persisted, and Andrew began to despair.

He brought Mariela into the main hold and laid her down on the floor. He found a weak pulse and quickly bent down to breathe into her, his helmet peeling away as he did so. He pressed his mouth against her cold, pale lips. He pushed hard and felt her collapsed lungs resist, then peel open slightly. He looked around; he had forgotten where he placed his medkit. He bent down again and pushed out another hard breath into her mouth. The lungs gave way again. He took a quick second breath and pushed with all his might.

She sputtered and coughed, wracking with the effort. He leaned back. Suddenly, he remembered where his medkit was. He returned a moment later with an oxygen tank and a mask, which he placed over her head. He opened the valves and allowed the gas to flow in. Her weak breaths continued.

Then her eyes flipped open. They crossed and moved erratically, then blinked and found him. She coughed and sputtered again.

"Breathe slowly. You tried to inhale the atmosphere and it collapsed your lungs." He smiled at her, then stood up. With a touch of his wrist computer, the engines started up. He went down to the airlock and checked the window. The thrall was lying on the ground, his rifle next to it. Far beyond the body, at the colony, there was a plume of white gas venting, kicking dust up into the atmosphere.

"You can keep it," he said, panged to leave his favorite tool behind, but too exhausted and afraid to open the door and retrieve it.

He sighed, then headed back up to the hold, where Mariela was sitting up, leaning against a padded bench.

"We still need to get off this rock," Andrew said. "The lifts…" He trailed off, meeting Mariela's gaze. Gently, he picked her up and put her on the bench. She leaned over, holding the oxygen mask close to her face, and curled into a slight fetal position.

Andrew watched her slow her breathing, then strode up to the cockpit and began the sequence for take-off. He was alone, he realized, and the vision of the future became memory, a thing of permanence.

He waited for his future self to alert him of anything, but it was silent. The part of his mind that could see the past was replaying memories of the colony, but those were too painful, too weird, for him to attend to. His former self, *Andy,* was strangely silent.

"Always alone," he said aloud, checking over all the systems on the computer readout.

With the engines on full, the ship lifted off. Andrew could see the venting plume better now. It was bigger than he expected, but he knew the vastness of the caverns would still take time to decompress. He hoped it would not be too long. He said a silent prayer, knowing the act would prod Andy, but not caring. He begged and gave thanks, his hands trembling on the ship's control sticks. The *wrtla* still beckoned, threatened, was raving to be released, but the prayer pushed him – and Andy – into a barred well of darkness. He looked up. He put a routine into the computer during the automated liftoff to put out a bulletin when they approached the next beacon to stay away from the planet.

He took over the ship's guidance and brought it slowly up to orbit, where he set the computer to work on the trajectory for the closest settled system. He breathed out heavily. As the ship moved out into space, readying itself for a rapid acceleration past light speed, he went back to the hold.

Mariela was laying on the bench, sleeping softly, the oxygen mask slightly askew. Blood was caked in her dark hair, and circles still hung under her shadowed eyelids. Andrew sat down cross-legged in front of her and leaned against the wall, watching her slowly breathe.

"Not so alone."

Andrew closed his eyes.

End.

MURAMASA: BLOOD DRINKER

A Novel of Feudal Japan

MURAMASA: BLOOD DRINKER

It is said that it is the destiny of good men to die young, to fall to the sword, and it is the destiny of wicked men to go on living. It is a cynical view; a false view, but not for the reason you think.

The truth is, there are no good men. When you peer into the hearts of men, you will understand that they are all wicked, and they all fall to the sword.

My sword.

-The bandit known as **Ryunosuke**. The statement was believed to be taken down by a scribe in a small village north of Osaka, shortly before his death. The scribe, who was a visitor to the area, was known only as Takumi. His head was found neatly arranged on a bed of fresh white rice, as if it were a delicate sashimi.

ACT I

Chapter 1: Takumi's Dinner

"WHAT SORT OF MAN DOES THIS? The floor, it is ruined. The doors, they shall have to be..." The innkeeper sighed. He was a squat red-faced man who preferred an apron and a sleeved robe to the kimonos[1] that he made his mostly female staff wear. His hair was pulled back into a short tail over his shoulders, which whipped this way and that as he bustled about the artist's studio, a freestanding building behind the garden of his establishment that he occasionally rented out to the passing scribe or painter.

"I am still learning what kind of man does this." Yoshio, a tall middle-aged samurai, stood before the scene, his left hand resting on the handle of his katana[2], which he had neglected to set aside upon entering the small house. His face was calm, with only a hint of a stitch between his eyebrows to show how the gory murder affected him. He looked into the dead eyes of the scribe, now hazy and dry.

"I hope you find the culprit and cut him down at once," The innkeeper squeaked as he noticed blood spray soaking into the folds of the futon, thicker and more luxurious than what Yoshio would have expected in a rented room. It reminded the weathered samurai of a brothel he had visited once, in his youth before such things had begun to disgust him, where the prostitutes were kept in their own studio houses. He made a note in his mind to inform Lord Asano of the inn, and collect the appropriate taxes from the local vassal.

"I will cut him down if I must." Yoshio lowered himself down on his heels, not falling to his knees and keeping his kimono, a gift from an old friend, free from the filth of the floor. He looked at the gaping neck of the headless body, moving his face within inches of the cut.

"It had to be a bandit, or ronin[3], only a fiend could be so seemingly ruthless over such a small pile of silver," the innkeeper said. "Such men never go quietly, nor will they choose seppuku[4] if they are caught. Bandits should be tortured, yes, but they never go quietly. Who could blame them? Execution is never pleasant, and bandits have no honor. You will have to cut him – or them – down, I'm sure of it."

"If this was not done by a samurai, then it was done by an assassin or bandit with a samurai's sword," Yoshio said.

"Assassin?"

Yoshio raised a single eyebrow to the innkeeper who averted his gaze and began plying apart the layers of the futon. Yoshio looked again at the body, still sitting as if at work, the brush with dried black ink still resting lightly in his left hand. "The cut was as if he were the scribe's second, and it sliced through bone more cleanly than I have ever seen. It must have been a magnificent blade." Yoshio took in the details of the cut, remembering them for his meditation later. He could see the windpipe and esophagus clearly, the spine severed in the middle of a vertebra, and not so much as a single jagged tear of the skin around the neck. It was as if something magical had separated the head and body.

"Samurai? No," the innkeeper said. "In this town, a passing samurai would draw our attention. We noticed you. Yes, we did."

"Not all samurai walk with two swords," Yoshio said, standing. The body of the scribe sat before him, cross-legged before the meal of his own head upon a plate of white rice, which itself sat in dried ink on a well-aged roll of paper. The letters beneath were beautiful, from what he could see. "Though perhaps you are right. I'm inclined to think there was some skill in this cut, even if it were at the hands of a man unworthy of the sword. Perhaps a lay disciple from a dojo. Do you have any nearby?"

"No. No, Yoshio-san. Once we did, when my father was young, and that was a long time ago, and the school was up the mountain, far away from here."

Yoshio moved his eyes from the dead face of the slain scribe to the innkeeper, who bowed his head as soon as he made eye contact.

"Keep your patrons inside their rooms tonight, master Doki," Yoshio said. "I know it will be bad for business

---

[1] A traditional Japanese garment similar to a long, layered robe bound at the hips.

[2] The traditional, single-edged long sword of the samurai.

[3] A master-less samurai. Usually viewed by other samurai with contempt.

[4] Ritual suicide, usually performed by men through disemboweling oneself with a sword. Typically, a "second" would behead the man after he had committed the act.

to speak of this, and I do not expect you to inform your customers of this deed. Conjure up a ghost story, if you like. Say the town residents remains inside this night out of respect for the kami[5] of this village. Any man who is so impolite as to walk openly in disrespect of your traditions will deserve what he gets."

"Of course, Yoshio-san, of course. I will do it at once. Will you require a room? Please, stay here tonight, no charge."

"I will be out of doors tonight, though I will use one of your rooms for the afternoon to rest, and meditate on my task. Make two rooms ready, please."

"Two?"

"I also require a room for my guide," Yoshio thought for a brief moment, "and master. I have left her in your common room. You will recognize her by her pink obi.[6]"

"Of course, of course. Please excuse me." The innkeeper hurried out of the room.

Even alone, Yoshio kept his face disciplined. He took in the scene again. His eyes were drawn once again to the skillful calligraphy beneath the severed head. He bent down, and in a single move, faster than the eye could see, pulled the scroll from beneath the plate. Only a stray hair or two on the scribe's head moved with the passage of air as the paper vanished from beneath the plate, leaving the drafting table as if the paper had never been there.

Yoshi looked at the scroll. It was professional calligraphy, the sort that any man or woman might be inclined to hang upon the wall by the table, with a saying of the family, or in reverence to an ancestor or domestic kami. It was a work of art, in form. He read the quote, and frowned.

Mysteries, he thought. He rolled up the scroll and stuffed it into a hidden pocket sewed into the sleeve of his light kimono.

The village, which nobody seemed to have a name for beyond the petty daimyo's[7] name of Kuramasa, was sweltering in the summer heat. The cicadas clacked and buzzed loudly, and as Yoshio walked down the narrow streets his eyes took in the peasants, many stripped down to loin coverings as they worked outside.

"Do you ever smile?" Yoshio turned to see Amaya. She stood in the shade of a tall house. There was mud caked on her geta,[8] which did little to stop the soil from darkening the pale blue of her split-toed socks.

"I thought I told you that you would be safest in the inn, Amaya-sama," Yoshio said, with a slight bow.

"You did."

"Then why am I talking to you?"

She smiled, showing the hint of a row of white teeth between rose lips. "Because you are my servant; I am not yours, Yoshi."

"Hmn," Yoshio said, regarding her again. He did not like being called Yoshi. The obi binding Amaya's silk kimono was knotted off slightly to the side, evidence that she had dressed alone, an uncommon roughness for a female samurai as important as she was. "Aren't you frightened of the assassin?"

"After seeing his handiwork, I suppose I should, be," Amaya said, gazing down the hazy street at an eta[9] merchant, whipping his horse as it pulled against his harness. The wagon it was pulling was caught in the mud produced by the summer rain that had been falling on their way into the village. "Yet, somehow, I'm not. Are you?"

"Privately?" Yoshio stared at her, his face relaxed. Amaya smiled back. Her open friendliness was hard to get used to. "Of course I am. I have seen enough on my journey to know that this man is beyond dangerous. Many otherwise good swordsmen have fallen to him, some of them valuable warriors to your lord and mine. I know that I could be the next."

"So you are sure it's one man," Amaya said, ambling down the path, squinting in the sun.

"Don't you require a parasol?" Yoshio regretted letting the woman walk with him so often along the way from her father's estate, content for herself or borrowed beasts to bear her burdens, but he had never felt like he was in a position to refuse the wishes of such high birth.

"You are marvelous at dodging questions. My father would have a place for you as a minister if you were not otherwise... bound."

"Lord Furukawa thinks it is one man, so it is one man," Yoshio said, falling into step next to the young woman. "Your father agrees with him." He kept always

[5] Shinto spirit

[6] The sash that binds a kimono at the waist.

[7] A feudal lord.

[8] Sandals with raised wooden platforms.

[9] Lowest caste of person; they are ostracized for their jobs, which usually entail preparation of dead people and animals.

his hand on the hilt of his katana. Amaya giggled. Yoshio cast a gaze her way. "You don't think it's one man?"

"Oh, I'm quite sure it is one man. Or woman."

Woman, Yoshio thought. *I suppose it is possible.* "Then why did you ask me?"

"I wanted to know what *you* thought, not Lord Furukawa. Or my father"

"It is not my place to think," Yoshio said. He walked toward the stuck wagon, eyes focused on the horse.

"Then why did Furukawa send you? I'm sure he has many younger swordsmen."

"Younger, yes."

"Better." She eyed him with a smirk, as if hoping for a crack in his discipline.

"I did not say that."

"So you *are* the best." Amaya stopped in the road and began straightening the folds of cloth around her midsection. Yoshio stopped with her, almost regretfully.

He sighed. "He chose me because I can solve problems."

"You can save the humility for court, Yoshi."

He stared at her soft brown eyes, the irises so large as to crowd out almost all white. Her hair was not perfectly arranged, but the casualness of it added something to her picture, made her memorable. She was beautiful. At twenty-eight she still looked like sixteen. Far too beautiful to be unmarried. Far too old. The way she dispensed formalities with him, the way she showed her teeth in her smile… though he found it disconcerting, it was also endearing in a way he had not expected. "You know, there's a question of mine you never answered. Why aren't you afraid?"

"I have a skilled retainer," she said. "Also, our assassin has never killed a woman."

"True," Yoshio said. "I had not thought of that."

"Of course you did," she said. They took the last steps to the wagon of the Eta trader together.

They approached the wagon just as the man with the whip was winding up for another strike on the horse. His clothes were the strange rags often worn by the eta: cut-off, dirty pants and wide straw hat to keep the sun from his head.

"Move, damn you!" the stranger said. "I don't have all day." He whipped the horse. Drips of blood could be seen along its flank and shoulders.

"Whose horse is this?" Yoshio said as he strode up. The eta stank, making Yoshio's nostrils scrunch up. He glanced back at Amaya, thinking of the foul-smelling pool they had walked around to get to the village, and how it had distressed her. She raised her sleeve to cover her nose as she had then. Yoshio frowned.

"Mine, who else's?" the eta said. He made to whip the horse again.

There was a flash as the whip came down. Its leather tendrils fell in the mud, and the wagoner was left with nothing but a twisted handle leather handle remaining in his grip. He looked up to see Yoshi 's sword held up at the end of its arc, pointing above his head, motionless, though he felt air still moving around him, ruffling his baggy clothes.

"Hey!"

"Quiet," Yoshio said. "Consider yourself lucky that I cut the fingers of your whip, and not the fingers of your hand."

"How dare you?!" the man said, though his eyes shimmered with fear.

"How dare you damage the property of Lord Asano!" His sword flashed again in a blur. In two quick strokes, the woven basket hat of the outcast fell to the ground, along with heaps of his messy black hair, leaving a bloodless shaved spot on either side of the man's head. "I will take this horse as tax. You are an unworthy custodian of the property rightly belonging to your daimyo and your emperor." His sword flashed again, cutting the harness of the horse free from the wagon. The horse, hesitant at first, pushed himself out of the mud and trotted into the shade of a nearby tree. Yoshio held his katana with one arm away from his body, its edge facing the eta man.

"You have no right!" the man said.

"He has every right," Amaya said, speaking up. "As my retainer, he speaks for me. I am Asano Amaya. This land belongs to the Minamoto clan."

The outcast quickly bowed his head, his hands shaking. "But, Asano-sama, how shall I plow the fields for my lord without my beast?"

"A farmer leaves his plow in the dirt and lets it rust, then wonders how he shall plow his fields," Amaya said. "It is not my concern. This tool belongs to the Minamoto-Asano now."

"But," the peasant began again. "I… did not mean to offend your-"

"Not another word," Yoshio said. "It is enough that I have soiled my blade by giving you a haircut. Do not force me to soil it with your blood."

Amaya followed Yoshio over to where the horse stood beneath the bough of an old tree. As he walked, he ran his sword through the cloth of a dangling end of his obi's knot, then sliced it off and threw it in the dirt before putting his katana back into its scabbard. He reached up and grasped the halter of the horse, then placed his free hand along the animal's neck. The horse startled, then stood still.

"What was all that about, Yoshi?" Amaya said.

"It is distasteful, what that peasant was doing to this horse. We should take it while it still has use and is pliant. Moreover, Amaya-san, I wanted you to have a horse to ride when we see Daimyo Kuramasa tonight."

"I can walk, Yoshi. I walked all the way here with you, remember?"

"That was your choice, and I will bow to your wishes as long as you make them, Amaya-sama, but I am disgraced that I have allowed your tabi to dirty so. Now, you can ride."

"My socks?" Amaya put her hands on her hips. "Dirty socks mean nothing to me. I will walk, as always."

"What if the mud offends Daimyo Kuramasa?"

"Kuramasa Kuro has the manners of a wet rat, and the face to match. He is merely a vassal of my father, only worth noting for the tax he sends our way, and I could not care less about courtesy toward the man."

Yoshio sighed. "Please, Amaya-san. You are lord here, but I am just a stranger. My name is not even known. Please, do it for me."

Amaya smiled, again showing a hint of teeth. "Stop with the honorifics, and I might consider it."

"Please, Amaya."

"Very well, because you asked me so nicely."

"Thank you, Amaya. Let's find a peasant to bathe this horse for you."

"Why?"

"It has been touched by eta. It is not fit for a woman such as you without cleansing."

"Very well," Amaya said with a coy, closed-mouth smile. "You will allow me to buy you a meal as thanks, then."

"You do me an honor, lady."

"Why did you refuse the rooms from the innkeeper for the night?" Amaya fanned herself in the heat that remained behind in the summer dusk, still bright orange and hazy.

"Because this night I shall be searching for our killer," Yoshio said. He walked beside the horse, now saddled with a proper leather seat that contained Amaya. She sat sidesaddle, with her feet (now clad in clean white) dangling down toward Yoshio.

"Perhaps *you* will," Amaya said, turning her head toward Yoshio with a delicate smile. "But I prefer to sleep at night." After their afternoon seclusion she had dressed herself in another kimono, this one a bright and bold blue and decorated with pink embroidery. It was far more formal than what she usually wore. Her obi was tied with a wide bow, though still to the side. Yoshio thought back to his request, and how Amaya so seldom stood for ceremony and politeness. Perhaps he was finally getting through to her.

"I'm sure Kuramasa will offer you lodging for the night," Yoshio said.

"I'm not so sure." Amaya turned her head to look forward again. "Politeness is ever in short supply at the edge of our lands."

"Hmn," Yoshio said. He turned and smiled slightly at his charge. "Your father has given me the authority to take heads."

Amaya frowned at him. "Don't joke about that, Yoshi. Being so quick to unsheathe your sword for more than shaving an eta will have consequences for us."

"My apologies, my lady. I am your servant, nothing more." Yoshio said. He bowed his head, and his heart sank slightly as she did not correct his politeness. *Maybe I am getting through to her a bit too much.*

"It's so hot still," Amaya said. She loosened up the top folds of her kimono and revealed her chest and neck, then fanned the sweat on them. Yoshio glanced over, breaking his gaze on the ever-extending road, to see her pale flesh and the gentle curve of her breast. He sighed. Amaya looked up to the mountainside to their left, rising in the distance to a hazy purple. "Is it too much to hope that we will go to the mountains next?"

"I would prefer to bring this Ronin to justice tonight," Yoshio said.

"Ah, but then I would have to go back to my father's castle," Amaya said. "I'd prefer to travel a bit more."

"It is still your liberty to travel, my lady," Yoshio said.

"In that, you are wrong, Yoshi. I, like you, must serve my lord," Amaya said. Yoshio looked up at her and nodded. "You must understand how much faith my father has in you as a retainer to allow me to travel freely."

"I am honored to do it, Amaya-san. Your value is very great, I'm sure."

"It's not that," she said, then looked back at Yoshio with a smile. "And what did I tell you about the formalities?"

"My apologies-"

"Yoshi, you are simply incurable!" She laughed with an open mouth. "Please laugh with me, Yoshi. I do not think I shall have the opportunity with that vermin Kuramasa."

"You keep referring to him as a rodent," Yoshio said. "Why? Is he not Samurai?"

"You will understand when you meet him; watch for the teeth!" She brought her fingers up to her face as if they were the long incisors of a rabbit, and laughed behind her hand as she squeaked at Yoshio. Despite himself, her retainer broke his composure and laughed, even so much as to show her his teeth.

Amaya's description had proved more accurate than Yoshio was prepared for, and as the servant woman showed Amaya and him to the long, low table of Kuramasa Kuro's upper-story dining room, he had to tap old reservoirs of discipline to stop himself from laughing as the petty daimyo spoke.

"I'm sure you will wish to inspect our storage and distribution of rice in the morning," Kuro said.

Amaya tilted her head in response, showing to Yoshio's eyes neither affirmation nor decline.

"Yes, you must understand that our rice storage is roofed with thatch. Very dry, very dry indeed," Kuro said. Yoshio was unsure whether his teeth were yellow like a rat's or if it was a trick of the small lamps that lit the room. "It would be dangerous to let you peruse our stores with a torch, being so dark."

Yoshio glanced at Amaya, and caught a subtle look his way. He spoke up. "We could use a lamp, Kuro-san."

"Of course," Kuro began, bowing slightly. "But then you would be there all night. With such dim light, you would have to check every basket, and all of them are under-filled. We have lost many koku[10] to the drought, as I'm sure you understand."

Yoshio nodded his head slightly. He turned as a small squat woman, matching in many ways the portly proportions of their host, came shuffling into the room. Her Kimono, though well made, seemed too small for her proportions, causing the folds around her neck to dip low enough to show jiggling, unsightly cleavage.

"Ah, Amaya-san, this is my wife, Reika," Kuro said.

"Amaya-sama, thank you for gracing our house," she began with an artificial bow of her head. The smell of burnt tar assaulted Yoshio's nose. He glanced over at Amaya again. This time, she made no move to cover her nose, instead continuing her polite, slight smile. "I have directed the servants to prepare you a room – our best room, of course, lady – and it will be finished shortly."

"And for my retainer?" Amaya said.

"Of course, we shall empty the adjoining room for him, Amaya-sama," the woman said with a bow, then hurried out of the room. Two female servants moved past her, carrying a bowl of steaming rice and a stack of smaller bowls.

Kuro collapsed down at the short table, allowing his kimono to fall apart oddly around his legs. Amaya, still standing with her hands crossed in front of her, stood still.

Kuro seemed to notice and said, "Please, it would honor us," and gestured to the narrow end of the table. Amaya nodded and situated herself down on her knees, being careful to tuck the ends of her clothing under her shins. Yoshio sat down on the long end of the table beside her, carefully laying his wakizashi[11] against his left leg, the handle pointed in an accessible position.

Kuro looked to the exit of the room, frowning. The rattling of what sounded like dishes could be heard beyond. "Please, excuse me, Amaya-san," he said, then pushed his fat body up and hurried out the door to the second-floor kitchen.

Amaya leaned over and whispered in Yoshio's ear, "What did I tell you?"

"Very rodent-like, yes, though he does not cower nearly enough for my tastes," Yoshio said. "It is good this man seldom visits your castle, or Lord Asano would surely have his head before the visit was through."

"My father is temperamental, but not so much as Lord Furukawa, I think," Amaya whispered. "My mother sooths him."

"Of course she does," Yoshio said. "She is as fine a wife as exists, to mother such a child as you."

[10] A measurement of rice that typically feeds one person for a year.

[11] The shorter of the samurai's paired swords, usually worn indoors.

"She merely makes sure he knows which lords are making him money and which aren't."

"You should not imply your father is greedy like that," Yoshio said. He looked over to see a half-smile pulling at Amaya's red lips. He smiled back. "At least to others besides me, of course."

Amaya nodded. Her face straightened. "Kuro's worth has been less of late, it seems" she said.

"I can understand why," Yoshio said.

"How?"

"Quiet," Yoshio said, straightening back up. "I'll tell you after dinner." Footsteps and more noise from the kitchen sounded as Kuro and Reika entered the room again, trailed by the same female servants, the first carrying a large steaming lidded bowl with a ladle, and the other a covered plate.

They both fell down to the table as Kuro had done before, nearly falling backward with the momentum of it. The servants put the bowl in the center of the table and then began to dish out helpings of soup, first to the lord and lady, then to Yoshio and Amaya. If the failing offended Amaya, the hosts would not have known, as she merely waited her turn, then nodded politely as the bowl was handed to her. It was a warm egg soup that smelled of hot noodles and a bit of the fish scraps that were most likely heaped in it to extract the last bits of protein from the main course. Despite Yoshio's misgivings about Kuro and his manners toward Amaya, he was driven hungry by the appetizing aroma of it.

"Allow me to thank you for the dinner," Yoshio said, holding the bowl of soup toward Kuro. Kuro nodded then slurped the top of the soup. Yoshio waited as the servant women came around again and laid a small spoon on the table next to each of them. He then picked it up, and maintaining the polite movements that seemed to define his life as a samurai, ate it down, one heaping spoonful at a time.

"Is it to your standards Amaya-san?" Reika said, pausing her shoveling motion to remember her manners for the high lady.

Amaya nodded slightly. "Yes, thank you."

Yoshio thought for a moment, holding the soup in his mouth. Soup made from the wasted bits of fish and other meals was the standard fare for himself, but he realized that living within the Minamoto clan Amaya was likely used to, if not entitled to, much better soup. She had not mentioned anything of their humble meals beside the road and at the many small inns between Asano castle and this small fief. Yoshio watched her slowly eat her soup, a paragon of femininity and Japanese sensibility. Perhaps she was more polite than he understood. He found himself unexpectedly wishing, for the second time that day, that she would be less polite for him. It was a strange feeling for one so disciplined.

"So, tell me," Kuro began, having sated his perceived obligation for pleasantries, "Are you here merely to keep me honest on my taxes?"

"You should not require anyone to keep you honest with your taxes, Kuro-san," Amaya said, putting down the soup. "Your honor should bind you."

"Yes," Kuro said, "But you know as well as I the limitations of trust. If honor bound all, then Lord Asano would never have to order anyone to commit seppuku. They would just do it, yes?"

"True samurai ask their lord's permission for suicide," Yoshio said. "Even if you would choose death over disgrace, bushido demands that you obey your lord, even if life would be unbearable to your spirit."

"A noble attitude, and very proper for a retainer," Kuro said. "Speaking as a peer, it is not part of my expectations."

"But it is part of your obligation, yes?" Yoshio said.

"Of course," Kuro said.

"Must we talk about this at dinner?" Reika said. She leaned over the table to reveal a plate of fish, lightly cooked in oil and sliced to reveal its delicate white flesh.

"I sincerely apologize if I offended your tastes, Reika-san," Yoshio said, bowing his head.

"Ever are the minds of men on death," Amaya said, "And the minds of their wives on life."

"Such is as it should be, I suppose," Reika said. More plates were produced, and Reika herself served the fish and the rice (now beginning to cool) to each of them at the table. They picked up their chopsticks and began to eat, Amaya slowly and politely with Yoshio matching her tempo and care. She did not spill a single grain of rice.

"What news is there from Asano?" Kuro said again. He had had his hand on his hip, giving a strange look to Amaya.

"Politics does not usually concern or interest me, Kuro-san," Amaya said. "But I shall tell you what I believe to be interesting for a vassal of your standing, such as I can remember." Kuro nodded. "There is some upset in the ranks, as is usually the case. Nobody has acted against the lord, and my father wishes to keep it that way. Some believe the unrest is from the house of the shogun, who has ever been wary of those who are descended from the Minamoto or allied with them."

"Of course," Kuro said. "To remain shogun you must be the strongest, both on the battlefield and off, and it is easier to poison your opponent and cause him to shrink from the battle than to risk yourself in war."

Amaya nodded. "My father wishes to stay in close contact with his vassals, all of them. Loyalty is prized."

"Bushido demands loyalty," Yoshio said.

"Aye," Kuro said, "But other things may command it, or upend it. I see that lord Asano is wise. Know that we have nothing to hide." Kuro turned his palms up and away from his body, as if to display his household, though they sat in but a small room of it.

"Too bad our sons are all gone," Reika said. "It would be good to introduce them to Lady Amaya."

Yoshio swallowed a large piece of fish and stuffed a grumble. The arrogance of the suggestion of such an introduction made the fish feel as if it was stuck in his throat. "Yes, I would welcome the help in exploring the estate," he said instead.

"Do you have any children, Yoshio-san?" Kuro asked.

"Not anymore," Yoshio said.

"I'm sorry, Yoshio-san, please forgive us," Reika said.

"There is nothing to forgive," Yoshio said.

Chapter 2: Gleaning the Field

"YOSHI, why must you do that everywhere we go?" Amaya said. She had her bag open beside a small cushion, and she was extracting her inkstone and brush set.

Yoshio put his head back in the window and looked at her. "It is never unwise to understand the risks of your surroundings."

"Yes, but in every room?"

"Let me ask you this: Do you believe Kuro to be an honest man?" Yoshio raised an eyebrow to her.

"Of course not," Amaya said. "I told you before that he is a rat, and is likely as thieving as one. That does not mean he will assassinate me."

Yoshio nodded, then put his leg out the window and tested the decorative wooden runner beneath. It held his weight. "He could not afford an assassin anyway."

"Because of the drought?" Amaya said. She held up one of her brushes observing the curve of the hairs in the lamplight. She cast a look at Yoshio, laced with deviousness.

"Look to the manager of his money, my lady."

"Ah, Reika," Amaya said. She ran her fingers along the brush hairs, which were delicate and springy, but spread apart very easily.

"You smelled her."

"I did. Opium, yes?"

"I'm surprised you knew," Yoshio said. "It is a foul habit."

"It was just a lucky guess. The dirty kimono helped."

"I didn't notice her kimono," Yoshio said.

"Of course not, Yoshi, you are not a woman." She set the brush down and observed another one, this one with a truer bunching of the hairs. "Interesting risk to take, shorting taxes for a few hours of pleasure."

Yoshio asked absent-mindedly, "Why does your father tolerate it?"

"Because Kuro is not ambitious, and because, like a rat, he cowers in fear of the cat," Amaya said. She removed an ink stick and began to scrape it on her stone, turning the drops of water she had just put in a deep black. "If you are so worried for my safety, you could always just stay in the room with me."

Yoshio remained silent as he walked over to her and removed from his sleeve the sheet of fine calligraphy he had snatched from the decapitated scribe. He took another look at it and handed it to Amaya.

"Is this what the scribe was writing?" Amaya asked as she looked at it herself. Brown remnants of blood clung to the edge.

"Yes," Yoshio said. "It's beautiful, is it not? If you would add it to your records I would be grateful."

"Have you not copied this yourself?" Amaya asked. She ran her thumb over the paper, feeling the fibers in it beneath the jet-black ink of the brushwork.

"Yes, but you know how bad my writing is; I would be ashamed for Lord Asano to see our records in my hand. I should have spent more time with the brush and less time with the sword as a boy."

"Then you would be no use to him," Amaya said. She looked at Yoshio and gave him a smile. "Or to me." She dipped her brush into the ink and turned her bound notebook to a fresh page, and began copying the script, making notes of her own below the wide columns. "This paper reveals things to me."

"Of what sort?" Yoshio sat down beside her and watched her work.

"This scribe is from Nagasaki," Amaya said. "I can tell from the tails of his letters. It is a style that is preferred on the southern island. He is also left-handed."

"His brush was in his left hand. I said that, I believe," Yoshio said.

"Yes, but it leaves a mark in his style. I could identify his work at sight now, if we needed."

"I don't think we shall have the opportunity," Yoshio said.

"There is more," Amaya said, holding up the scroll. "This paper. It is made with a fiber in it. Cloth fiber. It looks like linen. This is very fine paper. Too fine for a travelling man, I think."

"More mysteries," Yoshio said.

"I imagine you are unraveling them, as always."

Yoshio looked at her notes, and the message. "The words of the killer reveal as much as his mode. He speaks of wicked men, and so his victims have had… indiscretions, certainly."

"Perhaps a vendetta?" Amaya said.

"Possibly," Yoshio said. "But it is obvious to me that the scribe did not recognize him."

"Perhaps he thought him a friend?"

"No. Our scribe is of noble birth – all the signs are there – but something has driven him to the road. A familiar face would not be welcome to him, I think. So our killer was a stranger. Indeed, unless there is something I am missing, none of the victims knew him, or each other."

"Random, then," Amaya said.

"Nothing is random, my lady," Yoshio said. "If it appears to be so it is merely because the workings of karma and the gods are not easily understood. However, these are not the workings of karma, but of a man. When I come to understand him, his head shall already be mine."

"I can see whose philosophy you have studied as a boy," Amaya said, continuing to write.

"Do the Chinese masters offend you?"

"Not me," Amaya said. "But perhaps to others. To cite a Chinese warlord before a Japanese shogun would be unwise."

"I shall remember that," Yoshio said. "Do you mind if I meditate here for an hour or so? I want my mind to be sharp for the hunt."

Amaya looked up at him. "Then you are still planning on going out tonight?"

"Yes," Yoshio said. "Of course. I should not rest while he walks freely." He settled himself down on the floor, placing his knees on a thin cushion. He closed his eyes and slowed his breathing, listening for the scratch of the brush on the notebook, and the flame on the wick of the lamp.

Amaya sighed. Yoshio opened his eyes.

"Have I offended you, my lady?" Yoshio said.

"Every man requires rest," Amaya said. "Among other things."

"Do you not wish for me to go out tonight?"

"Truthfully, no," Amaya lay her brush in a slot of the ink stone and looked at Yoshio. "I have a sense – a feeling in my gut – that something bad is out there. I know it seems silly."

"It is not silly," Yoshio said. "But if you feel he is out there, then I should meet him. But I trust you in all things. Order me to stay and I shall. By your side, if it is your will."

"I will not order you, Yoshio," Amaya said. "Perhaps one day, with different purpose, I will submit you to your bushido, but not this night. You were tapped by my father and Lord Furukawa for a reason. It is *your* instincts that must guide you in this."

"Still, I shall hold yours as truth, my lady," Yoshio said. "I shall exercise the utmost caution. Do you still have your sword?"

"I do. Hidden as always."

"Keep it under your pillow. Then, I shall worry less."

Amaya smiled at him. "I shall."

Yoshio stood still. Perfectly still. Not even the breeze picked at the cloth of his dark garb, though it shook the leaves of the small maple that stood directly behind him, its long branches giving impenetrable shade to Yoshio. The moon had risen high, a pale half of the silver spirit that illuminated just enough to see his surroundings, yet not so much that he could make out details. His eyes searched among the shadows of the trees and low buildings that surrounded the rice paddies below the hill. True to the words of Kuro and Reika, the standing water of the fields did seem a little low, though in the daylight Yoshio and Amaya had both seen the rice plants as green and lush. The moon reflected off some of the water where the fields were bare, making pools of white that rippled when the breeze picked up from the east. From his position, a disruption in the pattern of light that his careful eyes were taking in would be obvious.

Funny, he thought. *This man was so quick and casual to toss a scribe's head upon a pile of rice, and yet I am anticipating rice to bring him hither. Even madmen must eat. If not from the cook, then from the earth.*

Yoshio did not stir from his secret position. His only movement was his right hand, which moved slightly along the cloth wrappings on the handle of his katana. He felt the spots where his grip had worn the strong maple. A smile tugged at the corners of his mouth. The katana was not a bad piece of work by any stretch. The steel was good, folded many times along its edge to retain its temperament, which he had put to the test in countless crossing of swords in his days as a samurai and retainer. The sword, despite its functional quality, was purchased quite cheaply. He had added some details on the handle himself to make it look more like the richer samurai's blades, but the sword was a cheap and quick work, a practice piece by an apprentice not yet come into his full skill. Still, the bones of its spirit were strong.

That was why Yoshio delighted in using it so much. When he drew the katana, honed to a perfect razor edge by his own hand, and put it to use, as often to delight a daimyo with a display of skill as to use it for marshal purposes, he felt a deep sense of satisfaction. It proved to him the nature of value as he understood it. The sword was worthless; it was his skill being used through it that made it a marvelous tool. In a way, he was the sword, the product of years of ceaseless forging and fire-hardened with experience.

It was not right to think of oneself as great, at least among the other members of the peerage, but the sword was a living testament to Yoshio's confidence in himself. He always told the lords he visited, when they inquired about the magnificent katana, that it was a gift from lord Furukawa. Watching him cut the flames from candles, or split rice grains along the nose of a servant, or suck the sake from a cup without tipping it over using a rush of air… rich men needed to believe that the sword was something special, a true work of art to match Yoshio's displays.

Yoshio's grip tightened on his katana as he saw a disturbance in the peaceful moon glow on a rice paddy. A ripple in the water, too big to be a crane. A hint of dark color in motion, too large to be a fox.

Yoshio moved down his watch hill, staying hidden in the shadows of the trees. His sandals he had traded for a pair of soft-soled black shoes, and his footsteps were like a cat's. In a blur of dark shadow he passed from one tree's shadow to the next, his eyes and ears constantly searching for more signs of his prey. The tiger passed over another hill, then froze beside a rock. He could see more motion below.

Off to his right, a pale light burned in an open window from a peasant's nearby house. He saw a door open and a shadow fill the light. It stood there for a moment, and the paddy in front of it seemed peaceful. Faintly, Yoshio could hear the figure say something that his even his keen ears could not understand over the distance and the rustling of the leaves. The figure disappeared back into the house and the door closed.

Yoshio began to move forward again, still sticking to the tree line, his ears perked for any sound that was not wildlife. He picked his way carefully, letting the tall reeds to the side of the rice paddy obscure his figure. He crouched and waited, then heard, just barely audible over the wind, the sound of water sloshing over mud.

As he listened, Yoshio could hear the figure in the paddy move closer, and slightly off to his right. Slowly and delicately, he parted the reeds in front of him and looked. Outside of the shade of the trees and on the same level as the farming plain, he could not see shapes in the paddy as easily as before. Instead, he let his ears continue to guide him. Along the rows of rice, tufts of long grasses grew in rocky islands sticking up above the water table. He kept these between himself and the sound of stepping in the water.

His own feet he dipped into the shallow water with great caution and dexterity, being sure to insert his foot toe first and slowly transfer his weight as he moved. It was a stalking technique he had developed as a boy, avoiding his mother and her list of chores by walking out of the house when her back was turned. Back then he had thought himself a ninja, a nimble assassin moving undetected. He had not understood how greatly he would value the skills of boyhood as a man.

Soon he could hear the wet steps very clearly, splashing in a seemingly haphazard cadence just beyond a tuft of overgrown grass. Yoshio imagined the ronin he had chased from the east threshing the rice stalks and chewing the green grain for sustenance. It would usually make a regular person sick, but supposedly you could get used to it. He imagined the killer could have gotten very used to it.

Yoshio drew his katana from its saya[12], feeling the clean sides of the blade run along the index finger and thumb of his left hand, the imperfections in the steel revealing themselves exactly where his memory had recorded them. He moved the tip of the sword to his left and then moved it over his left shoulder, winding up for a fierce overhand stroke. It would be lightning fast and precise. Every student's first stroke was the overhand strike, and he had practiced it for more than twenty years.

Then Yoshio remembered whom he stalked: a true killer, and a trained samurai, judging from the precision of his work on his victims, who he cut down from all manner of angles. He would fall first in left-guarded parry position, as all students of the sword learned to use

[12] The scabbard for a Japanese sword, usually highly decorated and made of wood or bamboo and fixed to the belt with a long loop of string.

instinctively. With the skill Yoshio imagined on the other side of the grass, even the most precise stroke could be pushed aside by a proper guard. He switched his starting position, putting the hilt of his sword down near his waist. A new fight played out in his mind

He strikes from the side, directly and intentionally into the guard, then slices at his opponent's feet. Yoshio then turns the point of his sword up, forcing the killer to attempt a downward parry. The killer, off balance, then steps back into a careful guard, his left foot crippled by the blow. Then Yoshio reveals his reverse grip and pushes it close; so close that his opponent cannot adequately reach to his right and guard his left side. The rogue tries nonetheless, turning the point of his katana toward his off-hand, but in so doing provides a ramp and guide to the vitals. Steel meets steel. Sparks fly as Yoshio's sword glides along the flat edge of the other, and into the pocket just below the ribs. The fight ends as the killer, unable to cry out from the sword cutting through his lungs, collapses.

All this flashed before his eyes as he crept around the rocky tuft toward the soft splashing of water. He tensed his muscles, and breathed. It was time to kill.

Yoshio sped around the side of the rock, his arm already moving his sword in a long horizontal arc. His eyes took in the face of his quarry in the soft moonlight, which lit the curve of the katana as if it was her daughter: a deadly crescent.

Then, Yoshio stopped.

His blade hovered motionless, its tip lightly touching the bare chest of the eta from the village. A drop of blood sprang up from the featherweight on Yoshio's katana, then slipped down the edge like a bead of oil. It was not the face of the eta that gave the samurai pause, though he knew that the man who had beaten his horse could not be the murderer he pursued. It was the addition of two others, just behind him, now also frozen in the act of gleaning rice.

It was a woman, dressed in a simple and visibly worn kimono, though its sheen made Yoshio think it might have been silk. Next to her stood a child, wrapped in a plain tan robe. She was perhaps six years of age, and though Yoshio's eyes never broke their lock from the deep-set eyes of the eta man, he could see she was on the edge of tears.

"Please," the woman said, taking a hesitant step toward Yoshio. "Forgive us. We... have nothing to eat, because the daimyo, he-"

"Begging, pleading, and excuses will not change my mind," Yoshio said,

"But our rice, all of it," the woman continued. She drew the child to herself.

"My will is set. I do what I see fit to do." Yoshio withdrew the sword. He flicked the blood off with a stopped slash to his side, then dipped the edge in the shallow water to wash away what remained.

"Then, why?" the woman said. Understanding flashed on her face as she saw Yoshio dry his sword on his obi and put it back in its scabbard.

"Because I choose not to," Yoshio said. "How many koku of rice are you taxed?"

"Only one," the eta man said.

"It should not be hard for any peasant to farm or trade for an excess koku over the course of a year," Yoshio said.

"That is our monthly tax," the man said. He touched the slight cut on his chest and held up black blood to the moon.

Yoshio nodded. He looked back over the rice fields toward the Kuramasa estate. "This fief has more on its hands than a murderer, it seems."

"What?" the woman said.

"Nothing," Yoshio said. "Persist in your business and I'm sure you will be rewarded with leisure. Now," he turned back to the small family. "Get home as fast as you can. Do not answer the door, even for a familiar face. Not tonight, nor any other night for the remainder of this moon. Do you understand me?"

"Yes," the woman said, scooping the girl up into her arms. The man picked up two small sacks, filled with a small amount of rice. They hurried off to the north away from Yoshio. He stood watching them in the dim light, stillness returning to his ears and body, though his mind moves swiftly over the details of his dinner with Kuro and Reika.

"Mercy is not something I had expected to see from the ever-cold Taoka Yoshio."

Yoshio's blade flashed as he spun around to where his ears heard the voice, very nearly whispering in his ear. All the katana found were errant blades of grass. Without a second thought, Yoshio leapt up to the top of the rocky tuft of grass. He looked all around himself quickly, but saw only the dreary calm of the rice paddy.

"Where are you?" Yoshio said. "If you wish to cross swords with a true warrior, I await you."

"A true warrior, yes," the voice said. Yoshio spun about again. The voice seemed so close, like it was in his head or speaking right into his ear in a raspy, breathy whisper. "Murderer is a better word. For what is war, but mass murder?"

"You are one to talk," Yoshio said. "I have seen your work."

"I know. I too deal death, but it is nothing like the violence inflicted by your shogun and his lapdogs. They kill indiscriminately. Good men, wicked men."

"You said all men are wicked," Yoshio said, turning again. He began to survey deeply his surroundings beyond the immediate marshy paddy.

The voice… laughed. "So I did. Alas, that I am but one…" the voice breathed. "Man. I have limitations, even if those limitations are far beyond the reach of your skill, Yoshio."

"How do you know my name?"

"I must make choices. The foulest men must go first. Their blood is the most…" the voice took another eerie breath. "Quenching."

"You didn't answer me, murderer," Yoshio said. He wanted the voice to continue talking, in hopes he could cut through the glamour surrounding it and find the speaker.

"I don't have to answer you, or answer *to* you," the voice said. "You should know, Yoshio, that your act of mercy will not earn you forgiveness."

"Then why am I not dead?"

"I, as you, do what I will. You have done… questionable things, but your heart will not make the best reaping."

"And the scribe's was?"

"You did not see into his heart, Yoshio, or you would have cut him down as I did. Even so, he was but a drop, a sip of evil before the great goblet on your doorstep."

Yoshio listened, but his eyes were fixed on a patch of darkness under some trees, on the other side of the paddy. In it, he perceived light, like an extremely pale lamp, only blood-red. He sensed a shadow.

"Sorcery!" he said aloud as he leapt off the knoll. He dashed toward the tree line, his feet mashing the rice plants as they stuck above the water, providing him the slightest bit of traction.

"Do you really think you can best me, Yoshio?" the voice went on. It still sounded like it was coming from right behind him, but Yoshio ignored it and continued his dash to where he had seen the light. "You were certainly a good student of Sensei[13] Tadashi, but the best? Not quite. And I slew the best. What chance do you have?"

The voice did not cause Yoshio to falter, though even as he charged part of his brain filed away that the voice knew the familiar name of his old sword-master, known to but a few. He entered the tree line and drew his sword.

His ears filled in the gaps where his eyesight failed, the shadows melding into shifting darkness. His wet cloth shoes made loud liquid-like noises as he stepped over tree roots and underbrush, bringing his knees up high. Between them, he could hear the light steps of another man, wearing wooden sandals that clacked occasionally on a tree root or hard spot of dirt.

Yoshio sliced through a bush and stepped out into a clearing. It was empty, the moon lighting up sparse grass, and it was deathly quiet. His sword in front of him, Yoshio stepped into the light.

"Showing yourself, eh?" the voice said. It still sounded close, but Yoshio was learning to look and listen past it. His eyes detected the same pale red from the other side of the meadow, and Yoshio took a guarded stance as he stepped toward it.

The red light was coming from something waist-high. He inched himself closer.

"I suppose you will not settle for being anything but a hindrance to me," the voice said. Yoshio could see the dim outline of a man. A large leather hat obscured most of his head and face, but his chin and the rest of his body was subtly illuminated by the red light near his belt.

"I will not settle for anything less than your head, ronin," Yoshio said.

"Ronin…" the voice said. "I do not sense…"

Yoshio could see the red light ebb and flow as he stepped closer. It was emanating from the handle of a sword. He could tell that the katana had an intricately carved handle, but its shape could not be seen amid the gloom and glow. Two red rubies radiated the light, like eyes in some sort of face.

"I should kill you, you know," the voice said.

"You may try," Yoshio said.

[13] The title often given to teachers, particularly of the martial arts.

"But it would ruin the feast." The man's hand was on the handle of the sword. "The soft spot in your heart is a bitter morsel indeed."

Yoshio readied himself. He made a quick determination that the killer might know something about the sword style he had studied as a youth, so he changed his grip and stance to one that was closer to his own design than that of his mentor and friend Tadashi. The tip of his Katana he held forward, nearly pointing at the man holding the red glow in his right hand. He led with his left foot, sacrificing the range of his guard for an increase in speed when he struck, along with a hope that his opponent might misjudge the fatal distance between them.

"Looking in your heart Yoshio..." the voice went on. "Amaya... how proper you are with her."

Amaya, Yoshio thought. The pace of his heart quickened. *This man has watched us.*

"I *have* watched you," the voice went on. The hilt of the man's sword tipped forward, and the red glow increased. "Hunting me and guarding her as retainer will be a disastrous dichotomy, *Yoshi.*"

Yoshio struck out, leaping forward with his right foot. He extended his sword in a stabbing motion. With lightning reflexes, though Yoshio could scarcely see any motion, the man dodged to the left, his sword remaining in his saya, his right hand still gripping the handle of the sword lightly. Cloth rippled very lightly, and Yoshio detected a strange smile of straight and sharp white teeth beneath the man's hat.

Yoshio turned his blade, and switching to a left-handed grip, slashed horizontally at the killer's new position, only to find him to move back, just out of range of his sword. Twice more Yoshio attacked, and the man moved around them, never appearing to exert himself. It was as if the man could predict Yoshio's techniques, anticipating the precise motion of his weapon no matter how fast or subtle the swing or stab.

Yoshio detected laughter as he moved on the man, pushing him back toward the light of the meadow, where he could better see his opponent. Finally, the moonlight was to the stranger's back. In a flurry, Yoshio attacked along three planes to force his opponent out into the light. Instead of stepping backward into the open, the stranger disappeared.

It was not as if he dashed away, even with supernatural speed, or that he had blinded Yoshio with an eye closer or sorcery. The man merely vanished, leaving Yoshio moving into the meadow, holding his katana forward in his guard and looking to his back every moment he could.

"Show yourself," he said aloud. Silence answered him. Sweat on his brow was cooling him quickly in the evening breeze, and his mind, so focused on the task of killing, suddenly processed all the details of the conversation and battle he had just had.

Disastrous dichotomy, he thought. The whole night rolled through his mind.

Yoshio dashed through the meadow south, back toward the estate of the Daimyo, laying his sword on his shoulder, not daring to sheath it.

Amaya!

Chapter 3: Uncommon Hunger

AMAYA BOLTED UP, throwing the blankets off of herself as the door was thrown aside. A flash of steel revealed itself in the light from some distant lamp down the hall. She stood up quickly, her sword already drawn from its ornate saya. She stepped back off the futons and put her right side close to the wall, raising the sword to a simple guard.

"My retainer will join me at any moment," she said, "but I will not need him to cut you down." She stepped forward, her simple bed robe revealing her thighs as she took a wide sword stance.

"Amaya. Amaya, it is me."

"Yoshi?" Amaya said, lowering her sword. "It is not like you to burst into a woman's bedroom."

Yoshio was breathing heavily. He slid his katana back into its scabbard as he walked into the room and slid the door closed behind himself. He put his hands on Amaya's shoulders and looked into her eyes, which were barely visible in the light still escaping through the gaps around the simple door.

"Are you safe? What has happened while I've been away?" he said. "Do you feel alright? No pains in your stomach or bladder?"

"I'm fine," Amaya said. "The only thing that has happened here tonight was sleep. I am not poisoned. I was careful to eat only what our hosts dined on themselves, as were you. What has gotten into you?" She opened the shutters of the window and let in some of the moon and starlight, then lit a nearby lamp using a stick coaxed to flame by one of the still-hot coals in the disc-shaped iron tray in the corner. It was not cool enough, even up in the hills, to bother with heaters, and so the flames had become neglected.

Yoshio breathed deeply. "I met the killer."

"But you didn't cut him down," Amaya said. She retrieved the saya that belonged to her katana, which was decorated with a beautifully painted cherry limb, and put the shining sword back in its home. The pale-pink blossoms were composed of a rare dye that seemed to shimmer below the shellac as she leaned the weapon up against the wall. Yoshio paused a moment to look at it. It was not customary for a woman to bear a sword, and yet Amaya had a weapon that was not only deadly, but suited to her sex from its weight and balance to its length to its feminine decorations. It was strange and unique, beautiful and hard, just like its owner. She had never revealed how she came by it, and as Yoshio memorized its features, he wondered about a polite way to ask.

"You guess well," Yoshio said, turning to see Amaya sitting down on the futons again, pinning her long, sleek hair back up above her shoulders. The split of her light bed robe revealed sleek legs. Yoshio pushed his eyes out the window.

"Not a hard guess. You have no blood on you," Amaya said. "And you are not acting the part of a victorious swordsman."

"A disciplined warrior does not delight in the slaughter," Yoshio said.

"He maintains his composure because he fears someone might see him smile," Amaya said. "Even you, my dear Yoshi, as hard as a sword edge and twice as sharp, cannot hide satisfaction away totally. At least not from me."

"I hide nothing from you, my lady," Yoshio said.

Amaya chuckled. "Of course you don't." She patted the futons beside her, and with a sigh, Yoshio sat down, his hand still touching his katana. "He's better than you thought he would be," she said.

"He is," Yoshio said. "I dare not say it, but..." Yoshio looked down and drew his sword an inch out of his scabbard. He looked at the steel, old and true.

"Do not say he is better than you," Amaya said.

"If he is?"

"You will only know that when you taste his steel, which you never will."

"I must try. It is my duty."

"It is also your duty to serve *me*," Amaya said. "Perhaps I shall forbid you to fight him."

"That is something he told me," Yoshio said. "That I would be a poor servant to you and to his demise."

"Oh my," Amaya said, her eyebrows rising into high arcs. "You had a conversation with him?"

"I couldn't do much else," Yoshio said. "I seemed incapable of hitting him with my sword. No matter what technique, or how fast, he had a way of not being there."

"Interesting," Amaya said. "Perhaps you should carry your bow next time. Or a spear."

"There's more than that. He knew the familiar name of my sensei, which is hidden to all but a select few students who have ascended to master, and the dojo is very far from here. He said he killed him."

"Lies, possibly," Amaya said. "Toda's dojo has become very well known for the quality of its students."

"I think it was lies, but I suspect more. I am loathe to say it."

"What then?" Amaya said. She leaned forward to look at Yoshio's face as he gazed out the open window. She touched his hand lightly, and he snapped back to look into her eyes.

"Sorcery," Yoshio said. "Perhaps I am wrong, and this man was merely following us and spying, but something tells me it is darker than that. We mustn't say it too loudly, but I think this man is a sorcerer, or else is possessed of skills and techniques whose secret is so far removed from my understanding as *to be* sorcery."

"With another man, I would call that a boasting of his ego. It is easier to invoke magic than to admit one's shortcomings for many men. But with you, I shall take it as truth."

"He had a way of throwing his voice, and his sword had…" Yoshio rubbed his face as he thought. "It had red eyes that glowed with their own light. Hmn…"

"What are you thinking?"

"Meaningless connections, perhaps. I think I shall need some time to sleep on them."

"Night passes quickly," Amaya said. "Sleep here, please."

Yoshio nodded. "I was going to ask for that to ensure your protection, my lady. I will drag in the mattress from the room next door."

"Very well."

Bako, Kuro's chief servant in charge of the estate, was a shrewd old peasant. He stood from just beyond the storage house, his arms crossed and frowning, trying to watch and listen to Amaya and Yoshio as they went through the stores of rice. Amaya had ordered him to stay beyond the entrance to the old barn – an order he had followed, though his expression made it clear he had not been happy to grant the Lady her requested privacy.

"What does your spirit say about him?" Amaya whispered as she peered into another half-full container of rice. The inside of the storage house was dim, with a few dusty sunbeams finding their way through the crevices between the slats of the sides and the simple thatch roof.

"He has the attitude of a noble, but in the least noble way possible," Yoshio whispered back. "Like many who are Samurai, he fears the unveiling of his treachery. What do you see?"

"Secrets, not treachery are what he fears the revelation of," Amaya whispered. "He is close to retirement. He knows he has but a little while to maintain the fantasy, which makes him all the more anxious to be through with it."

"A woman's wisdom should be prized," Yoshio said. "Though I could call keeping secrets from your daimyo the same as betrayal."

"Do you keep any secrets from me?"

"Of course not, my lady."

Amaya chuckled. "You are a bad liar, Yoshi, but do not worry. I will not hold you a traitor for keeping the secrets of your heart from me."

"Ask and I shall tell, Amaya-sama." Yoshio looked over to see the raised eyebrows of Amaya. He nodded. "Amaya."

She smiled. "Better. Now is not the place for such questions. But don't worry; I will hold you to that eventually."

"The grain reserves seem to be as Kuro said they would be," Yoshio said, changing the subject.

"But not as they ought to be for summer and the rain," Amaya said. She smiled slightly to herself as she opened up the next basket. Yoshio plunged his hands down into it and began churning the grain. "What are you looking for?"

"This." Yoshio held open his palm and began to push the rice this way and that, turning the small grains over. Many of them were greyed or even black on one side.

"Mold?" Amaya said.

"Yes. This grain was not harvested recently, or even this season I should wager." He threw the rice back into the basket. "Surprising. I would have thought our rats at least clever enough to have sold the poorest grain first and filled the bottom with sand to deceive us."

"Deception with words is easier than with action, it seems." Amaya looked over her shoulder through the narrow gap in the door at Baku, who was watching something off to his left. Yoshio joined her gaze.

"What shall we have him report?"

"What the lord wishes him to report," Amaya said, "save for one thing. We will mention the rotten grain."

"Why reveal that?" Yoshio said.

"It will make Kuro and Reika nervous," Amaya said. "They will trip up. The truth will come spilling out of them like vomit with the mere imagination of blades meeting flesh."

Yoshio grunted. "He is trading his fief's output for opium. Is that not enough?"

"As long as he pays the tax, no," Amaya said. "At least not if we want to keep the other daimyos in line. Still, a little fear will be good."

"Hmn," Yoshio said, nodding. "I may not be the one to take his head."

"You think our killer will?"

"Possibly. Let us speak more about it later, in your chamber. I do not want this inspection to go over-long."

Amaya nodded, then headed toward the door of the storehouse, her face placid.

Bako straightened up suddenly as they exited and cleared his throat. "What would you like to look at next, Amaya-sama?"

"I've seen what I need to for now," Amaya said. "I think I will retire to my room for the afternoon. Is there any fresh water where I can wash my hands?" She held her hands, dirty and with flecks of black from the mold on the rice.

"Of course," Bako said, clearing his throat again. He looked at the scowling face of Yoshio, and then marched off toward the estate. Amaya gave Yoshio a glance, her eyebrows subtly raised and her lips pursed in question, then followed.

"You should sleep." Amaya sat on her knees and shins on a cushion below the window of the same bedchamber as the night before. Her brush worked again on clean paper, but this time she painted a scene instead of letters. Instead of a single ink stone, she had a set of three, each one with two wells to make a range of different shades ranging from grey to raven. The truth of the image had not yet been revealed, as Amaya continued to work greys into an uneven background.

Yoshio opened his eyes. "Meditation is as restful as sleep to me," he said, breathing deeply and looking over to Amaya.

"I don't believe you," she said. He face was smooth and unemotional.

He smiled slightly. "How could I sleep with you painting?"

She relented and smiled back. "It is nothing special. It would be more pleasurable to watch a true artist work, I'm sure."

"You are a true artist, Amaya. But that is not what I meant."

"What did you mean?"

"The scratching of the brush on your paper will be too present in my ears for me to relax."

Amaya dipped a brush into dark ink, and began to paint dark lines underneath the grey. The limbs of a tree began to emerge. "What are you planning for tonight?"

"To guard you, of course."

"Are you giving up on your killer?"

"Not at all." Yoshio moved into a cross-legged stance and began to watch Amaya's brushwork. "Something the man said to me last night. He said there would be a feast of wickedness. I believe we have found some very wicked men."

"Kuro? He's foolish, certainly, but wicked?"

"Will you call him wicked when his charges starve this year? When they die so that he can sit in an opium dream night after night? There is more to being noble than paying taxes." Yoshio found himself leaning forward, his hands clenched tightly into fists.

Amaya's brush paused mid-stroke. "Interesting tone you used there."

Yoshio blushed, then turned away. "My apologies, Amaya-sama, Lady Asano. My life is yours, to forgive or to throw aside."

"I like it." Amaya turned to look at Yoshio. "Don't ever hold back your thoughts and feelings from me. I like seeing your heart, Yoshi. It is a prized weapon. And I understand why our killer did not draw his sword on you. You have far too *good* a heart; it would be a morsel before a feast, as you said."

Yoshio breathed and looked at the painting again. A bird now perched upon the branch, its head upturned. "I endeavor only to serve you well."

"That's an interesting one," Amaya said as she added pale grey leaves to the picture. "A truth and a lie." She smiled to herself. "And after I just demanded you never hold back, no less."

Yoshio sighed. "Women are strange."

"You must be fascinated with them, then."

"I think I will sleep some. I'll need sharp eyes and quick muscle tonight," he said. He pushed himself up and walked over to the futon he had drug into the room late the night before.

"Good," Amaya said. "I didn't want to be forced to order you."

Dinner for the evening was much as it was the night previous: a generous helping of fish and rice, though the soup was spicier than before, and more watery. Yoshio watched Kuro eat. The man would devour the contents of his plate ravenously and then, as if he understood he was being watched, pause and eat a piece or two of fish very slowly and in polite fashion, though he wiped juices from his chin more than a few times.

"Everything was in order, yes?" Kuro said, breaking the silence that had settled between pleasantries.

"Do you mean with dinner?" Amaya said, setting her chopsticks down.

"With our storehouse," Kuro said.

"Things were in order, of a fashion," Amaya said.

"You must understand that with the drought, as I said…" Kuro trailed off as Amaya made eye contact with him, her face perfectly smooth, as if she were looking through him. Sweat seemed ready to burst around his temples, though he held a forced, amiable smile. "And the storehouse, the floor is not well packed. It gets damp during the morning."

"Damp during a drought is quite a feat," Amaya said.

"Not in a rice paddy," Reika said, her voice rising in pitch. Kuro looked at her with a scowl as Amaya turned to her and bowed her head slightly. The lady Asano's unreadable expression did not change. Reika looked at her husband, returned his frowned, then spoke again, her voice carrying an assertiveness that also strained with fear. "If you understood farming, Amaya-sama, you would know that water drenches and dries, and just because we have water now does not mean it was always so. Our paddies have dried twice – or even three times – this season, and that kills the grain. You may ask any of the peasants. We would not cheat Lord Asano in our taxes."

"I did not suggest it," Amaya said. Sensing the tension in Yoshio, whose knuckles gripped the handle of his wakizashi tightly, she placed a gentle hand upon his thigh, and he ceased leaning forward and relaxed his hold on the blade. "I know that you would be just as happy to pay the tribute in silver as in rice."

Kuro gave an audible grunt as he looked at his wife, one eye closed. "Of course, Amaya-sama. I presume you mean to pay in market price for rice, not weight, yes?"

"Of course," Amaya said. "But it is a drought, after all. I'm sure lord Asano would be pleased with last season's prices, and of course, we would not ask you to pay beyond this season."

Kuro seemed to relax slightly. He cast another angry glance toward his wife, who seemed to suppress a blush. "Of course. We will have the silver prepared before your departure."

"Send it with a courier, please," Amaya said. "I am just a messenger, and we have more business to attend to south of here."

"Barefoot?"

Yoshio paused in the doorway a moment to look at Amaya. She had let her hair down, and it spilled around her narrow face and shoulders like the black ink she used so skillfully. In the dim lantern, the left side of her face was lit softly, blurring the edges of her eyes and mouth.

"Yes," he said. "If I plan to stay out of sight, I will need to stay out of sound, too. Sandals make a racket."

"What about your cloth shoes?" Amaya said. She reached behind the pillows of the floor-level bed and withdrew her ornate katana. She slid the blade out a few finger spans and looked at the edge in the light.

"Still wet," Yoshio said. "And not at all ideal. Bare feet are better for gripping the roof tiles."

"Acting the ninja in wait for one, eh?" she replied. She stepped toward the door as she fixed the sword around her waist.

"What are you doing?" Yoshio asked. His face formed a frown as Amaya looked at him with a cool, slightly upturned mouth.

"I'm belting my swords, of course," she said. She lined up the katana on her left side, then withdrew from the folds of her kimono a tanto[14] whose scabbard bore similarly intricate decorations to her katana.

[14] A single-edged dagger often paired with a katana prior to the Edo period.

Yoshio drew out a soft growl as he looked Amaya up and down. "It will be safer for you here."

"Think on what your madman said," Amaya went on. "It will be a hard thing to guard me and catch your killer. I'm going to make it a bit easier for you. I suspect you will be waiting by the lord's chamber, up near the top of the estate, yes?"

Yoshio nodded, a frown drawing his lips into a line.

"Then I shall wait in the garden below, beside the tea house our hosts seem unwilling to use."

"I may not remain there, my lady. Kuro may already be taken by the tar, but if he is not, he could wander. Perhaps he will meet his supplier tonight. There are many variables. Your chamber would be safest."

Amaya tilted her head slightly, wearing the same relaxed face from dinner, when Reika fumbled over her excuses.

Yoshio sighed.

"I will also be able to watch your back," Amaya said. "I'll hoot like an owl if I see the ronin."

"If you see the ronin your life may end too quickly to hoot," Yoshio said.

"He won't come for me."

"How do you know?"

"As you said, he has a bigger feast this night."

"Then you can stay here."

"You already consented."

Yoshio sighed again. "Very well. But keep your hand on your hilt and stay hidden." He looked down the long, dim hallway toward the open foyer beyond.

"I may not be a master like you, Yoshi, and I may be a lady," Amaya said as she touched Yoshio's shoulder, "but like me, this sword exists for reasons beyond being just a pretty sight."

Yoshio turned back, pondering her words, and saw her lips parted in a smile.

Ryunosuke. That was the name that was of true meaning. Truth. If he concentrated hard enough he could remember the name he bore before… the union. That name was a lie now, even if could remember it. He was Ryunosuke now.

He looked at the falling moon, reflected in the still water of the pond. Koi moved about below the image, gathering the silver light with their flashing white scales. They were as dragons to him – circling in an eclipse, ready to light the moon to a fire red. He pulled back the fold of his light coat, a peasant's garb unfit for his stature but bearing great purpose. His old life had been one of fame and glory, but now he needed to remain hidden.

Soft red light filled the still water as he drew his coat back to his left hip. Red eyes gazed upon the glass moon and filled it with blood. The koi, the dragons of the moon, lost their silvery sheen and became a swirling of crimson-hued gold.

Dragon.

We are.

Fill my mind.

Ryunosuke's eyes were filled with a second sight, and amid the waving trees and rice paddies, as if looking at the landscape from above, he could see two figures standing out bright red beside bleached buildings. Their auras pulsed and drew from his heart a desire… a hunger.

Hunger.

We do.

Deception. Betrayal. Such a feast.

There is yet so much more to drink. Look.

The vision pulled back to an even higher angle, and the outline of Japan itself could be seen far away, with tiny waves. A harbor city stretched out past the hills, a fire of red and orange. The buildings and waterways seemed insignificant compared to the blood rushing between them. Sudden thirst sprang up in Ryunosuke's throat.

Patience.

Of course. There is still tonight; but a snack.

Meals bring sustenance.

Let us go, then.

Ryonosuke turned to go away, but paused, his hand on the hilt of his sword still fixed upon the image of the moon.

Let the meal fully season. This one should be enjoyable as well as sustaining.

Of course. I want to catch them in the act.

In the mixture of silver and red, beside the calm pond, lips pulled back to reveal a wicked smile full of sharp, pristine teeth.

Yoshio shifted his weight. His feet were becoming tired as he crouched in the small alcove, a break in the long uninterrupted ramp of roof tiles that capped the second tallest of the petty daimyo's houses. Many of the tiles had been loose as he had run over them to his shadowy hiding place, a product of neglect over the generations that the Kuramasa clan had possessed the estate. Still, the old craftsmanship was good and he had avoided displacing any of the tiles, remaining both unseen and unheard. He could faintly make out Amaya on the ground level off to his left, standing in the doorway of the teahouse. Oddly enough, in the moonlight her pink kimono offered no color to identify her, instead becoming a faded gray that seemed to blend into anything. It was her hair – her raven-black hair – that gave her away, moving very subtly in the breeze. Had he not known to look for her, he probably would never have noticed even that detail, but in the knowing her hair was a stark shadow.

Yoshio re-focused on the window before him. It was open to the cool summer night, and though it was nearly pitch black for the most part inside, a square of moonlight helped illuminate the futons in the center of the room. He could make out the large frame of Kuro lying on his side. In more than an hour, nothing had stirred. The moon was moving to the west, and soon darkness total would set in. That is when he expected the killer to strike.

He must wait until then. He knew that Amaya would not get bored and stir; he trusted her discipline as much as he trusted his own, if not more so. He looked over to the shadows of the teahouse again, trying to make out the waving of her hair amid the greys, though not for doubt of the Lady Asano. She had proved to be a paragon of what a noble Japanese woman should be in her discipline. She exhibited it to every stranger they met with her calm demeanor and perfectly chosen words. He was beginning to think even her imperfections, like the way she tied her obi ever so slightly to the side, were part of that same discipline, a subliminal message of approachability and personality to the many common people they had met along their path.

Yoshio also thought of Amaya's smile, with a hint of white teeth between her lips. In thinking back over the past weeks, he realized he had never seen her do such in front of anyone else. She was formal with all others as well, requiring of him alone the withdrawal of honorifics. He wondered if that too was part of her discipline; that it was not her true face but just the one she had crafted for him specifically. He felt a tingle of sweat break out on his forehead at the thought. He shifted his weight and found himself letting out an audible sigh.

Focus, damn you, he thought to himself, fixing his eyes back on the open window. *Don't let a row of teeth you can't even see outside your memory distract you to your own death!* He wiped his sweating hand on his obi, then refixed his grip on his old katana. But it wasn't just her teeth, or her smile, or her dress. There was the subtlety of her soft voice, and the gentle curves of-

Focus! Yoshio thought to himself again. He felt a well of anger and frustration open up inside himself. Normally, his afternoon rest and meditation allowed him to have a perfectly clear mind and purpose. Somehow, he had failed during the day, and now his mind was a chaotic mix of thoughts, all of them coming back to two images: Amaya, and his killer, the darkness shrouding his face and his clothes glowing red.

This will be a long night, Yoshio thought to himself. He pushed himself farther into the little alcove of the roof. He hesitated and considered moving far enough back to block the teahouse from his vision in an effort to keep Amaya off his mind. Keeping his charge out of sight defeated the point, or at least the justification in his own mind that he had accepted, of allowing the Lady Asano to follow him into danger. *I'll just have to deal with it.* He found a sitting position where he could remain in the shadow and lean his back against the eave, and he finally let his legs relax.

The moon began to set, deepening the grey and blue shadows into black below the shining stars. Amaya remained hidden, though Yoshio's mind had memorized her location and he focused as much on the shadow of the teahouse as on the sleeping daimyo and his wife.

Yoshio's eyes widened. *His wife.* By the light of the last beams of the moon, and as a sudden breeze moved aside the sheer curtains of the bedchamber, Yoshio could see clearly Kuro sleeping on his side. Next to him was an empty space. Reika was gone; how long, Yoshio did not know. Perhaps she slipped away while he was distracted with himself, or perhaps she had never been there. Yoshio's mind began to race with possibilities and probabilities.

He slowed himself down and thought over the past few days' events and persons. The killer, Kuro and his wife, Bako, and the innkeeper danced through his mind's eye. Finally, he arrived at a supposition, less than a conclusion or even an assumption. Still, it tickled him with the way it fit into the puzzle before him. He had to decide which path he would take, and swiftly. He weighed the two in his mind, and after a long minute of judgment, he made his choice.

He stepped out of his hiding spot and looked down toward the teahouse. He pointed to the southeast, toward the end of the estate that housed the dry goods and clustered servants' quarters that terminated in the side of a large hill. Carefully, he silently crept down toward the edge of the roof and the gap between it and the building that housed the lord's chamber. Yoshio looked back down to the teahouse to see Amaya step out of the shadows. She gripped the handle of her sword, the edge pointed upward as if ready to draw it. She looked up to Yoshio and nodded, then set off in a jog toward the southeast.

Yoshio followed, leaping across the chasm between the two roof stretches and moving quickly along the slick tiles. The moon was now gone, the demarcation between sky and land a lack of light and nothing more. Yoshio let his feet and balance guide him. He could hear Amaya's footsteps to his left.

A scream echoed across the buildings. Yoshio stopped for a brief moment and heard Amaya's steps continue. The scream rang out again.

A woman, he thought. *Only one woman.* The scream was coming from the southeast. Yoshio sprang into a full run across the old roof. Occasionally a tile would click or slide underfoot, but he ignored the sound, his mind focused on what he expected to find on the other side of the darkness. Then the screaming stopped.

"Yoshio!" Amaya called from below him in a harsh whisper, as he slowed himself. "Yoshio!"

"What!?" he hissed back.

"I will cut across the garden. That way lies the front gate. I will cut off his retreat."

"No," Yoshio said. "You must remain hidden, as you said you would."

"I said nothing of the sort, if you'll recall," Amaya said. "Go get your killer. I will deal with anything at the gate." Amaya's footsteps could be heard moving in front of Yoshio, through an open foyer between the main house and the low series of lesser buildings where the storehouses and stables lay.

Yoshio grumbled and cursed to himself, then broke his paralysis. He ran across a weakly supported span of roof that connected the older, fortified home of Kuramasa with their support buildings. He could hear neglected wooded pillars creak below him amid the soft crackling of old straw. Softly, he stepped over a low thatch roof and looked uphill toward the storehouse. It was dark and empty, but a hut to the east, off to his left, had emanating from it a soft, red light.

Yoshio gripped the edge of the roof with his hands and swiftly lowered himself down, letting himself fall the last few feet to the packed earth below. He drew his Katana and ran over the rough ground toward the light, small pebbles biting his bare feet.

He watched the soft light fade and wink out as he approached the cluster of low buildings that sat beside the storehouse. He cursed himself again. Screams filled the air again, coming from a square of blackness that was the entrance to one of the huts. Yoshio ran past the sounds, the piercing rasp of the cry sending a chill up his spine. Softly, he could hear the sound of feet moving toward the grain storehouse. They changed directions, and Yoshio adjusted, diving into a small separation between two of the huts.

"You will not stop me, *Yoshi,*" the familiar voice from the night previous said, as if it were whispering into his ear.

"You may be a sorcerer, ronin," Yoshio said between breaths, "But you cannot alter karma. Death will come to you, one way or another."

"But not by your hand, my friend," the voice said.

"We shall see." Yoshio emerged from around the edge of the storehouse. The sound of the footsteps could no longer be heard, and he stood alone, looking down on the rice fields below and the woods to his right. The grass waved slightly in the breeze, and the dirt about him was undisturbed.

"You're getting too old for this," the voice whispered. A strange, cackling laugh followed.

It was all deception, Yoshio thought to himself. *He will be heading for Kuro.*

Yoshio rested his blade on his shoulder and set his tired body into a sprint, running back toward the main house. While he ran, a single disturbing thought invaded his mind; it was of Amaya, standing alone against the ronin, fear in her eyes.

In the cool summer breeze, wrapped in darkness as he was wrapped loosely in blankets, Kuramasa Kuro slept deeply, unaware of what was happening in his home.

Chapter 4: Blood and Honor

THE DIM LANTERN cast a sickly light upon Bako, the peasant overseer of the Kuramasa estate. Under the sun his face had been fixed in a perpetual frown, his eyes becoming squinting slits and his forehead a tangle of wrinkled brown skin. At night, his eyes were open fully, his lids and brow relaxed above smooth cheekbones. His pupils blended into black irises, making his eyes look like fathomless wells amid jaundiced whites – hollow and empty.

"If you are waiting for me to step aside, you had best make yourself comfortable." Amaya stood between the two posts of the gate. Her face was relaxed and unreadable, in much the same way as with the masters over dinner. Her feet were spread slightly apart, and her hand was on her katana's beautifully ornate saya.

"I'm not waiting for anything," Bako said. "Especially not that prissy retainer of yours." A faint glimmer showed a weapon in his right hand. Amaya guessed it to be a short sword, or a long knife, though it was dim and dingy. Outside of the sphere of light shoulders and sticks moved as Bako's faceless companions stepped up beside him.

"A pity that patience is not a virtue you possess," Amaya said. She smoothly drew her sword, the gentle arc of its blade pointing to the sky and flashing as it moved. The blade rang in a melodious note as the blunt edge slid along the steel collar of the scabbard. She held the sword up in a guarded stance, the point facing Bako.

"There's no virtue among corpses," Bako said. He stepped forward and raised his weapon. Flickers and shadows revealed a studded club instead of a short sword, a low weapon sometimes used for both crowd control and to defend against a sword. "Samurai are all the same: always talking about honor, but always missing when it comes time for a real fight."

Amaya stood still, her eyes locked with Bako. A spear flashed out from the shadows toward her, and in a quick step back, she avoided the steel point and chopped at the pole with her katana. Splinters flew as the weapon changed directory, pushed toward the ground. Amaya stepped hard on it with her bare foot, the pole cracking loudly as the structure of the grain failed and the shaft split in half. At the same time, another spear thrust from the opposite side made her step back again. She stumbled and felt her back hit a stone post that marked the edge of the gate and encircling wall. She held her sword in front of her.

Laughter sounded from the shadows, but Bako's face remained hollow. He raised the club over his head and swung down hard toward Amaya. Amaya put her sword up quickly to defend the blow, ready for the swing to rattle her arms and blunt the edge of her sword. Wind moved around them. She felt her katana contact the studs of the club, but was surprised when the weapon offered her little resistance. She watched as the club fell toward her, driven to an odd angle by its ungainly balance. She clumsily sidestepped it to protect her bare toes, then noticed the handle.

A hand, a wrist, and a forearm all the way to the elbow were still attached to it. Both arm and club fell apart from one another as they bounced on the packed earth.

Amaya looked up to see Bako, still standing. He looked to his right in shock. He lowered the lantern slowly to his hip as he stared at the dark stump that was once his arm. Beyond him, a flurry of a shadow moved. Steel rang in the darkness. Amaya did not hesitate; she slashed upward with her katana, sending a spray of blood over the light of the lantern. She felt warm droplets pelt her face, neck, and arms; soft sounds like rain came off her silk kimono. Bako collapsed. The lantern rattled on the ground and began to flicker.

"Amaya! Run!"

"Yoshio?!" Amaya said. She stepped toward the voice, her sword moved back up into a guard. With the lantern shining its light vainly into the abyss of night above, she could, at last, see beyond where Bako had stood. She saw Yoshio withdraw a sword from a man, black blood pouring out his chest as if it were a fountain.

He stepped toward the last man, one who had wielded a spear against Amaya. She was not forgotten as he back stepped, the iron point of his long pole weapon hovering before Yoshio. The stranger struck twice. Yoshio deflected each strike with the side of his blade, which sang a few differing dull notes with the contact.

"Run Amaya!" Yoshio said again.

"If I run you can no longer protect me," Amaya said, breathing deeply. She stepped toward the spearman, moving her sword around into a ready position, the blade curving over her head. The stranger saw this and began to move his spear toward her. In that moment, Yoshio stepped across the distance and struck. The blow landed on the pole of the spear between the man's two upraised hands and the sword buried itself into the hard wood.

The stranger made a move to pull the spear, along with the embedded sword, away from Yoshio. Yoshio released his katana and drew his wakizashi. He thrust it under the pole into the belly of the man, who cried out as it entered. At the same time, the spearman was silenced by Amaya's blade entering his lungs from under his left arm. A moment later, Yoshio withdrew his short-sword and swiftly beheaded the man. The body stood motionless for a second, then collapsed, dragging Amaya and her sword forward with the weight.

"For a brief moment, I was unsure if you would arrive to deal with them," Amaya said as she pulled her sword out of the bandit. She looked around herself to see a pile of dead men, soft shapes between lantern and starlight. She quickly counted seven, including Bako.

Yoshio, breathing heavily from the fight, wiped clean his wakizashi and put it back in its scabbard, making a note to himself to oil the blade at the next opportunity. "I shall endeavor to improve such a condition, should you see fit to continue my employment."

"Undoubtedly," Amaya said, wiping her own blade clean. "But you will not be getting out of your service to me so easily."

"I am glad to still have some use," Yoshio said. He freed his katana from the shaft of the spear and attempted to inspect the blade. He grumbled as he tried to look at the flashing edge in the dark, then wiped it clean and sent it home to its simple scabbard.

"Even if I had no use for you, I could not allow anyone else to possess you." Yoshio raised an eyebrow as he picked up the lantern. When he turned it up, he half-expected to see Amaya smiling, despite the scene. Instead, he saw her face was as calm as usual. She looked at him with warm eyes. "My peers could use you to bad ends. I'm afraid such skill could only safely be held in my own hands."

Yoshio looked around at the piled dead, and then sighed as he looked back toward the estate.

"Sighing after all this, Yoshi?" Amaya said.

"Kuro will be dead by now."

"Do you know that for sure?"

"It was all planned out," Yoshio said. "Everything was a distraction to lead me away from Kuro and from you."

"Come on!" Amaya grabbed the sleeve of his kimono and began dragging him toward the large house. After a few steps, Yoshio picked up the pace. They dashed to the front door and kicked it open, then hurried through the entryway and up the long stairs that went to the manor's chief apartments. Along the way, none stood and none stopped them, though the house had numerous armed men the previous night. They stepped into a corridor cast with lantern light to see a young man they knew to be a guard looking back at them, his hand on his sword.

"You!" Yoshio yelled as he ran down the hallway ahead of Amaya. "Check on the master!"

"What?" the young man said. "The master is not to be disturbed." The youth squared up as Yoshio approached.

"Open the door, damn you!" Yoshio said. The guard made to draw his sword, but Yoshio halted his hand and pushed the blade back into its scabbard, then punched him in the face. The guard fell backward and fumbled his sword even as he managed to get it free of its scabbard. It clanged on the paving stones.

Yoshio threw the door to the bedchamber open. Light filled the large room, casting Yoshio's shadow upon the far wall. He strode across the floor to the futons, expecting to see a bloody scene laid bare. Kuro's body lay in a heap in the same position Yoshio had last seen it.

Yoshio's eyes opened widely as Kuramasa Kuro sat up, his eyes blinking heavily.

"You're alive," Yoshio said.

"What?" Kuro said. He looked around. "What's going on here? Mitsuo! Why did you let this man into my bedchamber?"

"I'm sorry, lord," the young guard said, striding into the room, fumbling with his drawn sword.

"Get somebody down to the storehouse," Yoshio said. He then cast a harsh glance to Mitsuo. "I will clap this man in chains."

"You don't give the orders here," Mitsuo said, raising his sword.

Yoshio looked down at Kuro. "Don't you wonder where your wife is?"

Kuro looked around groggily for a moment. "What? Reika!"

"She's at the storehouse, Kuro-san," Amaya said, stepping into the room. "Please excuse us for entering your chamber at such an hour, and uninvited. Much has been awry at your house tonight." Kuro looked at the demure Amaya, her pink kimono stained with blood and two swords hanging from her belt. Her hands were folded in front of her, and her head was bowed ever so slightly.

"Mitsuo," Kuro said. "Get down to the storehouse and see what has happened."

"No, my lord," Yoshio said. "This man has compromised your house."

"Preposterous," Kuro said. He put his feet on the floor and attempted to stand up, steadying himself on the wall and swaying as he got to his feet.

"You have been drugged," Amaya said.

Kuro blinked heavily. "Then I shall see myself. Mitsuo," he glanced over at the young retainer. "Leave your sword if you have nothing to hide."

Mitsuo looked at his sword for a fleeting moment, then leaned it up against the wall. "Of course, my lord." He bowed his head.

The loss of detail that came with viewing the scene in lantern light somehow made it more horrific than it might have been in the day. The swinging of the lantern in Kuro's hand cast strange shadows upon the walls of the hut. Blood, which would have appeared a muted brown in the morning, looked like splotches of black night on the painted panels of the room. A decapitated body, naked, stood out stark white in one of those black pools, which lapped against the edge of a simple mattress, creeping up the sheets like paper dipped in water.

On the bed lay Reika, likewise naked, the most private details of her body in a lewd spreading of her legs, which were covered in dried blood. Her eyes were fixed open in a deathly stare, but her chest moved up and down with steady breaths. Opium implements sat on a nearby table, the wick of the small smoking lamp smoldering orange as it exhausted the last of its oil reserves.

Kuro dropped his lantern, which flickered on the ground, then went out. "Reika?" fell out his mouth in a trembling, quavering squeak.

Yoshio stepped into the door with his light. "Stay outside, Amaya," he said.

"Yoshio?" Amaya said. "What is it?"

"Please," Yoshio said. His voice was flat, but his brow twitched as his vision gathered the horror of the room. He stepped around the frozen Kuro, careful not to tread upon the congealing pool of blood, and stepped up beside the futons. At his feet, he saw the greasy black hair of the back of a head. He looked around and pulled a broom from the corner, then used it to flip over the head. An unfamiliar face looked up at him, the whites of the eyes turning black from the pooling dead blood.

"I don't understand," Kuro said, his voice barely audible.

"I do," Yoshio said. "Do you recognize this man?"

Kuro broke his stare at his wife to look at the severed head. "Yes, I think so. He is an eta trader. He sells tanned hides and tallow."

"More than that, it seems," Yoshio said. "You should not look upon this anymore, my lord."

"No, I shouldn't," Kuro said. "But I will. Horror hardens the heart for honor, as my father said."

"I will not counter that wisdom, but I would still recommend you leave."

"Reika?" Kuro said again, louder. His wife continued to stare out into nothingness. "Reika!" he shouted.

A soft sound escaped her lips, a mere rustling in the dead quiet of the early morning. Yoshio leaned over and placed his ear by her blood-splattered face. The sound of air moving through her lungs was like reeds knocking against each other in a breeze.

"Ryunosuke," she whispered to the abyss. What it whispered back, none but her could hear, but at that moment, a chill wind blew into the little room, coaxing the opium lamp back to flame before snuffing it out. The smell of tar and iron filled the air.

The sun was rising swiftly. Colorless light revealed scenes from the night before. Bodies were piled before the front gate with darkened dirt beneath them instead of pools of bright crimson. A blackened doorway stood empty. A man at arms, well-seasoned, stood nearby with a spear and a tachi,[15] its hilt discolored from use and age. His face was wrapped against the smell that would become unbearable within a few hours of sunrise. Above the wrapping, bagged eyes looked out with hollow

[15] A general term meaning "sword." From the Muromachi period onward, tachi usually refers to the type of curved or straight swords used in earlier periods, worn with the edge down, unlike the katana, which was worn edge-up.

certainty. He busied himself pawing through stacks of objects and worn sacks of leather and linen.

Kuro sat with Amaya in an east-facing roofed balcony that Kuro called his "sunrise room." A female servant served them tea from a clay pot. Yoshio stood nearby, cradling a simple cup that had been provided to him at the request of Amaya.

"What can I do to thank you for all this, Amaya-sama?" Kuro said.

"With due respect, Kuro-san, the slaying of the opium trader was not by our hand," Amaya said.

"Then I suppose I should thank this man too… what was his name?" Kuro said. His face seemed calm and gentle, and he looked always out to the countryside in the east.

"Ryunosuke," Yoshio said. Kuro did not turn to look at him.

"Dragon…" Kuro said and took another sip of tea. "Yes, I should thank this man, as I should thank you, Amaya-sama. Your dragon has slain the man who defiled my wife, and your retainer has destroyed a great betrayer of my house, along with those who would tear down my fief from the outside."

"It is my duty to serve my father's vassals, as they serve him," Amaya said. "We had suspected foul play in your house from our first meeting, but did not know who to rouse."

"You mean you did not know whether the foul play was mine, or someone else's," Kuro said.

"In short, no," Amaya said.

"I do not blame you," Kuro said. "Such hard lessons. My own wife was an opium fiend and I could not see it. I am ashamed, Amaya-sama. Very ashamed."

"The shame is not yours, lord Kuramasa," Yoshio said. "Ever is betrayal at work in the houses of the noble. This is no exception."

"Thank you for saying that, Yoshio-san," Kuro said. "I might ask you to be my second. Your sword is true."

"Kuro-san," Amaya said, "betrayal is part of being a Daimyo, and neither I, nor my father would ask you to commit seppuku, for your honor or ours."

"Perhaps it is I that cannot bear the shame, Amaya-sama," Kuro said. "I look out into a sunrise, not of relief, but grief. What shall I tell my son, when his mother must be put to death?" Kuro shook his head. "Is he even my son?"

"Please, Kuro-san," Amaya said. "Stop entertaining this possibility."

"I respect you, Amaya-sama, and revere you, yes, but you are not my lord," Kuro said. "Seppuku is mine by right, since your father is not here."

"I will be your second if it comes to that," Yoshio said. "And I would not permit pain to disgrace you. However, I may suggest, as a man who has lost that which I hold as dear, that you need not bring the shame of others upon yourself."

"Yes," Kuro said, stroking the wispy beard on his chin, "I remember you hinting at something like that at dinner."

"Yes, I do not speak much of it, and etiquette usually spares me the toil of recounting it, but I have lost much, lord," Yoshio said. "The question you must ask yourself is whether you prefer to live with honor and shame, or die a coward without disgrace."

"Yoshio," Amaya said, "You forget your place."

"No, it is fine," Kuro said. "You have done me the service of giving me the truth, about my wife, my house, and my fief, why should I ask for either of you to stop now? No, I appreciate that, Yoshio-san."

Kuro turned as a young man wearing a wide leather hat and wearing a single sword slid the door open. He bowed low. "Lord Kuramasa. I have found the eta's wagon and gone through its contents."

"Yes, Shiro?" Kuro said.

"The wagon was filled with standard wares. Candles, hides, and a few silks." The young man cleared his throat. "However, I also found a compartment below, near the axle. It had opium and various implements in it, as well as stacks of silver and a small cache of gold."

"Good," Kuro said. "Where is Mitsuo?"

"Locked in the stock room, as you requested," Shiro said.

"Good. My wife?"

"She is unresponsive still. We put her in a spare room. I was unsure if…" Shiro trailed off.

"If I wanted to keep her from defiling my bedchamber?" Kuro said.

Shiro looked down and took a quick bow.

"It was already defiled. But you did well," Kuro said. He took another sip of tea. "I seem to be without a retainer."

"I would be honored to act as your retainer, lord," Shiro said.

Kuro cast a glance to Amaya. "Nothing to say to that?"

Amaya tilted her head. "It is your prerogative. I have no say over who you hire to be your bodyguard."

"Yes, well," Kuro said, "not all of us are so lucky as to have a peer as a retainer, yes?"

"Yes, Kuro-san," Amaya said. "I am exceedingly lucky." She looked to Yoshio, who still stood by the door with his arms crossed. A hint of a smile flashed across his face as their eyes met, and then he went back to frowning as he looked Shiro up and down.

"What do you say to that, Yoshio?" Kuro said, noticing his evaluation.

"I do not expect much trouble in the country," Yoshio said. "Of course, the night has surprised even me." He looked at Shiro. "Draw your sword for me."

Shiro looked to Kuro, who nodded. He then carefully drew out his old sword, pulling the weathered handle high, and held it at the ready.

"A good retainer must be ready to strike in an instant," Yoshio said.

"He needs a proper sword," Kuro said. "We can give him Mitsuo's old katana."

"He needs instruction," Yoshio said. "I have no doubt he has been a good soldier." He looked at Shiro.

"I have fought in several battles, yes," Shiro said, nodding.

"Good," Yoshio said. "I prefer a practical warrior to the soft samurai I usually see as retainers." Yoshi ran a finger along the dull, grey blade of the young man's sword. "A reliable tachi is like a reliable soldier. The two go hand in hand, though you should know that the work of a bodyguard is different from that of a soldier," Yoshio said. "A little time with a good sword master would help you hone your reactions and skills with your weapon." He looked back to Kuro. "Besides, your old retainer's swords should be sent back to his family, Kuro-san."

"I will as I see fit with my property," Kuro said. "We will send back the wakizashi after Mitsuo is through with it."

Yoshio nodded, his face smooth and without reaction.

Amaya painted under the light from the chamber's window, letting her brush, soaked with a pale grey, guide her to an image. Long lines became reeds, blowing in the breeze. Behind them, a shabby house formed. A lone tree stood guard, its branches wind-swept like carefully tended bonsai of a coastal pine. She sighed and looked at the picture.

"Sighing after all that?" Yoshio said. He was busy rolling up their possessions in reed mats for the road. His swords, now neatly oiled, leaned against the wall.

"It is a pity we will not understand the story of this place," Amaya said.

"What is not to understand?" Yoshio said.

"Much could be gleaned from Mitsuo, if he were permitted to live."

"I am more interested in Reika," Yoshio said. "She alone has seen the killer act."

"Yes, and it has delivered her mind to madness."

"If only she could speak more than his name, I might have a real understanding of how to defeat him."

"I would like to know just what she was doing with that eta."

"It is no matter to us," Yoshio said. He looked over Amaya's shoulder at her painting. It was not her usual peaceful work. "Kuro's domain is his concern, not ours."

"You are very single-minded, Yoshi."

"You say that like it is a bad thing. I wish to be dedicated, nothing more."

"I know. I was not exposing pleasantries when I said I was lucky. You are a peerless warrior, Yoshi. You are Bushido made flesh." She looked over at him and met his eyes, then looked him up and down. "But I will require more than that from you."

"What more would you ask from a samurai?" Yoshio said.

"You will see, Yoshi. You will see. I have no doubt you will exceed my expectations." Suddenly, a bright smile split Amaya's face, removing the shadow that had lingered with the sunset.

Yoshio frowned. "You are a mystery, Asano Amaya," Yoshio said. Amaya put her brushes and ink stones away in a small bag and walked past Yoshio to her things, already rolled up. The painting was left sitting below the window on the floor. Yoshio bent down and picked it up. The windy scene filled him with a sadness, and an uncharacteristic feeling of nostalgia, as if he had found a relic of something once precious, now rusty.

"Leave the painting," Amaya said from behind him.

"It is... exquisite work Amaya," Yoshio said, looking at the many-layered details of the water ink. "This deserves to be displayed, or at least kept."

"It is my spirit from the night and the morning," Amaya said. "Those feelings are things I do not wish to keep. That is why I have captured them on the paper, where they can trouble us no more. Leave it. It will find its way to where it belongs, either the fire or the wall."

"As you wish, Amaya," Yoshio said. He laid the painting on the windowsill. A slight breeze picked at its edges from outside, making the grass and the white pine seem to come alive. Yoshio gazed at it for a long time, letting the brush strokes work their way into his memory.

"Let's go," Amaya said. "I'd like to be on the road again. There is a village a little way to the south, and if we leave quickly we can get there shortly after sundown."

"There is one short matter I must attend to first," Yoshio said. "Mitsuo has asked me to be his second, and honor dictates that I must not refuse."

"I can forbid it," Amaya said. "If you wish."

"My wishes are not relevant here."

"Then be done with it," Amaya said. "I will have a servant prepare our horse."

Mitsuo kneeled on the prepared mat. In a less rural estate, both the mat and the kimono worn by the practitioner of the ritual would have been white, but the Kuramasa fief was just far enough away from Osaka to make carefully bleached cloth too expensive, even for such a singular event. As it was, Mitsuo was wrapped in a cheap linen kimono, his regular clothes to be sent back with his swords to his family east of Kyoto. The mat was a matching off-white, though among the dark, damp soil and green garden of the courtyard it stood out brightly.

Beside Mitsuo was his wakizashi, lying on a small stool. A thick cloth wrapped the blade halfway to the tip. In front of him was a blank piece of parchment, a slight tear near one of the edges. His hands trembled as he drew the characters of his death poem. The letters came out uneven and jagged. The young samurai's breath was labored.

Can they not spare the man even a decent piece of paper? Yoshio thought. He stood behind the young man. He had not yet drawn his katana, but prior to arriving had ensured the edge to be pristine and true, evening out with his trusty stone a slight nick in the edge that had appeared sometime in the chaotic night. Kuro sat facing Mitsuo, an uncommon position for a witness. His formal kimono draped over both his fat and the platform that housed him. Yoshio thought it was the most lordly he had seen the man, but he still had to suppress a certain amount of disgust at the slight, sickening smile the daimyo wore. Shiro, the commoner Kuro had just named his new retainer, stood nearby. He still wore his old battle-sword, and now held a spear as well. Mitsuo had not been informed of whom Kuro had decided would inherit his blade after his death.

Mitsuo wrote a final word on the paper and set the brush back down beside the ink stone. Yoshio looked over at Kuro, who nodded, his strange smile still plastered on him. Yoshio drew his katana. He examined the edge one final time, and then raised the blade over his head in anticipation of what was next.

"Tell me, Yoshio," Kuro said, speaking up, dropping the typical honorific. "Is the poem any good? Does he compare his worthlessness to a cherry blossom, or a pond in winter?" Yoshio gritted his teeth, but did not answer. Mitsuo ignored the remark. In a whisper, Yoshio heard Kuro say to Shiro, "I cannot wait to see his shameful face." Shiro nodded.

Mitsuo reached for his blade, gripping the handle and the cloth wrapping. He took a breath and plunged it toward his stomach. In that moment, a flash of white steel that was a blur to the onlookers ended the young samurai's life in a splash of blood.

Kuro gasped as Mitsuo's severed head rolled toward him. He scrambled up away from it as it rocked up against the platform and then toppled over, revealing a pristine, peaceful face.

"Y-you!" Kuro shouted, pointing at Yoshio. "You said you were a master swordsman! You were supposed to leave his throat-skin attached to prevent this."

"My apologies, Kuro-san." Yoshio stood with his sword fixed at the end of its arc, well on the other side of Mitsuo's body. He shook the blood from his blade with a flash and then placed it back in its scabbard. "Perhaps I am getting too old for this."

Kuro rounded the platform and stomped toward Yoshio, whose face remained placid. "You didn't even let the blade enter his stomach!"

"If you examine the body," Yoshio said, "you will find that he did indeed cut himself." Yoshio bent down and snatched up the death poem and tucked it into his kimono. He picked up Mitsuo's wakizashi, and after shaking the blood off it and returning it to its scabbard, he picked up the katana. He held it in front of himself and bowed. "Now." He looked at Kuro. "I will take the liberty of seeing these off to this man's family."

"You can't just walk away with my property!"

Yoshio turned his back to the petty Daimyo and walked swiftly away, toward the stables, never turning back to see the shock on Kuro's face or the fear on the face of his new retainer.

END OF ACT I

Interlude: Satisfaction

Ryunosuke felt the dirt grind under his cheap sandals. He was aware of the haze of the sun, the heat rising from the road, and the swirling of mosquitos, the buzz of cicadas - all the things of summer life, for the first time in... he did not know how long. It was like seeing and feeling it for the first time. The hunger of the dragon had been satiated, for a time, and he felt bloated, like he was waddling. He felt satisfied.

Sweat beaded down his face below his wide-brimmed woven hat, and absent-mindedly he cleared it from his eyes. As his dirty sleeve fell away he saw, then heard something. There was another traveler padding along the road in the far distance, his footsteps heavy and uneven. Ryunosuke was surprised that he could not feel him or see him so close, with what he had come to call his "hunter's vision." Instead of seeing him as a painted red aura, glowing with blood and tickling the hunger of his inner beast, he saw him in true colors. Simple, bland colors. Still, the sight of the walker invoked a small piece of his other half, like a man longing for a sweet dessert or cup of sake after a large meal.

It was a man. He was naked, save for a thin and dusty loincloth. He had no sandals. As Ryunosuke approached, he could see the man was bleeding in places on his back and had bruises on his body. The man turned back to see his approach and grunted in surprise. He turned to run and tripped over his feet, landing hard in the dust of the road. Ryunosuke did not adjust his stride.

"Who are you?" The man said, pushing backward on his palms and heels. "I have nothing left. Nothing! Leave me alone!"

Ryunosuke found his hand going toward the hilt of his sword. His eyes narrowed. He looked past the man's frightened face, into the heart of the man himself, and saw things both good and evil, like he usually saw. The man was rich. Or used to be rich. His vision was not as strong as usual. He was still in the blood stupor.

"A waylaid traveler, eh?" Ryunosuke said. He licked lips over sharp teeth.

"I have – powerful friends!" the naked man said. "Very powerful. Rich. If you help me, I can persuade them to-"

"And if I kill you?" Ryunosuke laughed through a sickly, rattling throat. "They would never know. Nobody would."

"I can get you silver, or silk, or," the man stammered. "Women."

"You are not in a very good position to bargain." Ryunosuke laughed again.

"No! You must believe me!"

"I don't," Ryunosuke said. His face relaxed. "But perhaps I will not kill you after all. Pity has a poor flavor."

The man collapsed in the dirt. "Thank you. There is a village ahead. If I can acquire a spare piece of cloth, I can take you to my lord, and give you what I promised."

Ryunosuke's eyes narrowed. "Who is your lord?"

"Takigawa Mitsunushi, Lord of-"

"Lord of nothing," Ryunosuke said. "A weak man. A weak lord, and of no use to me."

"He has the ear of the Shiba, of-"

A grumble from Ryunosuke silenced the pleading man. The dragon turned his sword and saya, considering drawing the steel across the naked man's neck. *Would this spoil my appetite?* Ryunosuke sighed. *Decisions...*

ACT II

Chapter 5: Bushido

Long strings of silk upon untended trees
Falling leaves and bare cocoons
Moths fly free, but for a day
Blindly searching out toward
Another to rekindle the cycle
What of those who are barren?
They are as meaningless as fruitless trees
Or an unwatched sunset in the west

AMAYA ROLLED the worn parchment back up and handed the scroll to Yoshio. He tightened it and placed it carefully into a red scroll case. It was decorated with leaves of long black brushstrokes, flying in different directions. The trader who had sold it to them knew instinctively what the case was for when Yoshio produced it from among the racks of the kiosk, and the shopkeeper had given it to Yoshio for free as Amaya purchased new ink sticks.

"It's not bad, I suppose, considering all the pressures he was facing," Amaya said from beneath her parasol, dots of the hot afternoon sun dancing on her kimono as she twirled her shade. The horse plodded along slowly, swatting with his tail the insects that pestered him constantly.

"A samurai is trained early in his days to accept his own death," Yoshio said. "He accepts it, and becomes one with it, so that when he is faced with the inevitable, he can go without fear."

"I do not envy you," Amaya said.

"I used to wonder," Yoshio said, "or think sometimes, as a young man, if it was better to be a woman."

"No," Amaya said. "Though I would not count it worse. It is different. It is like asking whether it is better to be a white blossom or a pink one; they are each their own."

Yoshio nodded slowly. "I *do* like Mitsuo's death poem."

"Even if he was dishonorable in life?"

"A scoundrel could write a good poem. The moral qualities of the writer are not what makes a poem good."

"I disagree," Amaya said. "I think the moral qualities of the writer are primary to poetry. The same holds true for any art."

"I do not understand," Yoshio said. He frowned as he watched Amaya look out at the road wistfully, with her own distance.

"Only an honorable man can write a poem that inspires honor in others."

"He died honorably," Yoshio said.

"But he did not live honorably." Amaya looked over at Yoshio with a slight smile. "It is reflected in his poem. He references the silkworm, which lives for a brief period as a blind moth before dying."

"He was a young samurai," Yoshio said. "And died swiftly."

"Yes but *you* are old," Amaya said. "Well... older than him."

"What does that have to do with anything?"

"It is in the nature of the silk moth to die young. You may say that samurai accept death, but dying young is obviously not part of their nature. Furthermore, Mitsuo's comparison to the nature of the silk moth is not even his central theme. His theme is regret."

"I would have regret too, if I were him," Yoshio said.

"His regret is not for his actions though," Amaya said, "because in his mind he makes his actions part of his nature, which they are not. His regret is for his life not yielding him anything meaningful, not for any of the dishonorable things he has done. He is the barren moth. Do you see what I mean now?"

Yoshio breathed deeply. "I suppose. I still rather like the imagery."

"You can pout all you like, Yoshi," Amaya said with a smile. "But if you were to write a death poem I would expect it to be much better, and not dwell on the guilt that exists only in the act of being caught."

"Doubtful, Amaya. I am no poet."

"But you are honorable, which means you will be able to inspire honor in others." Amaya looked forward at the road, which bent around a grove of trees ahead. "I also expect it to be better because you have many years to write it and die an old man. Truly old, not just a young man with a wrinkle or two around the eyes, like now."

"I shall endeavor to serve you," Yoshio said, "As in all things."

"See that in this request you do," Amaya said. "I still have much use for you." She breathed. Yoshio watched her curiously.

"No, I have not seen anyone like that." The cook served up another plate of steaming rice and fire-cooked fish to the fat merchant who sat at the only occupied table in the room.

"Are you sure? He may have been without the hat, looking like any other peasant or merchant," Yoshio said. He stood behind the cook as he moved about the small dining room of the dark and vacant restaurant. The fish he served had a strange grey hue to it, though it smelled good enough to Yoshio.

"I would remember a samurai that looks like that, I would," the cook said.

"I should not have mentioned he was samurai," Yoshio said. "He will look much more like a bandit."

"I told you, I haven't seen him."

"His teeth will be very clean and very sharp, a whole row of them," Yoshio said, remembering the short interchange he had with the killer.

"So he looks like a filthy bandit but has teeth like a daimyo," the cook said, bustling back over to his cooking fire, located in an open room adjacent to the old, leaning building. "I will keep a lookout for him. If he comes in here, I'll send him straight to you."

Yoshio grumbled. "Whatever you do, do not do that. If you see such a man, do not acknowledge him as anything out of the ordinary, though I think you will be offset by his… demeanor, for lack of a better word. That will make treating him as a normal man difficult."

"I don't want any bandits in my restaurant," the cook said. Yoshio looked around the vacant room. It was sunset, and many people should be looking for food. Merchants and their wives, married samurai women, even the wealthier peasants of the village would be happy to dine on freshly cooked fish and vegetables.

"Are you sure about that?" Yoshio said.

"Yes," the cook said, stirring a pot of steaming soup. "Now, is there anything else I can do for you?"

Yoshio sighed and looked through the open kitchen to the paved street on the other side. "How fresh is your fish?"

"It was caught in Osaka not two days past," the cook said.

"Is that what the merchant told you?" Yoshio said.

The cook looked at him with a puzzled face. "Of course. I trust him."

"Be careful with that," Yoshio said. "Perhaps I will come by later for some of that soup, my master allowing."

"I'd be delighted if you did," the cook said with a wide smile. Yoshio walked back through the dining room to the open front door, passing the fat merchant. He looked back out to the street, and made up his mind to drop by the inn and see to Amaya. She would be finished with her afternoon studies and art by now.

"I think I've seen the man you're looking for."

"Have you?" Yoshio turned to see the merchant still gobbling the fish and rice, but looking up at him.

"Well, *I* haven't seen him," The merchant said through a mouth of food. "But my apprentice has."

"Tell me, please," Yoshio said. He moved over to the table and sat down at it, crossing one leg over the other.

"It will cost you," the merchant said, and slurped down another chunk of fish.

"If you or your apprentice had actually had encountered this man, you would not be wasting time parlaying for money," Yoshio said, standing back up. "You would tell me what you know straight away."

"Suit yourself, mister samurai," the merchant said.

Yoshio narrowed his eyes at the man's tone. He imagined cutting off the man's fat nose with a quick sword slash. Had he been a younger swordsman, and less disciplined with the use of his skills, he might have done it.

"Ask anyone in the village," the merchant continued. "I always tell the truth."

"I will tell you a truth," Yoshio said. "A man who took this bandit lightly ended up with his head on a plate of rice just like yours!"

The force of Yoshio's delivery, as well as the strength of his words, made the fat merchant choke slightly on a bite. "I do not survive by giving away everything of value," he replied.

Yoshio grumbled and then turned back toward the door.

"I live in the house at the end of town near the riverbank," the merchant said to Yoshio's back. "And my shop is just down the lane!" he shouted as Yoshio stomped back out to the street.

When Yoshio entered, he found Amaya sitting on a small mat near the western window, sitting cross-legged. Had he been in front of her, he would have felt very embarrassed by what would be visible in the un-ladylike stance.

"I'm sorry to disturb you," Yoshio said.

"You are never disturbing to me," Amaya said. "I thought I would try out the meditating you are always doing."

"And?"

"I find it rather boring," Amaya said, picking her knees up and pulling the bottom hem of her kimono over them. She situated herself in a more feminine position, sitting on her shins, then patted to the spot beside her.

"It is a chance to find peace through reflection," Yoshio said as he sat down beside her. "Perhaps you have already found peace?"

"I find none of it," Amaya said. "My thoughts just race around and fight each other, breaking through all their normal places to torture me with their conflict."

"That does not sound boring to me," Yoshio said.

"It is to me," Amaya said. "Painting is much better for me, I think, for ordering swirling thoughts."

"I think your paintings are peaceful," Yoshio said. "No, I think that they are perfection."

"Don't flatter me, Yoshi," Amaya said. "It makes you sound like you should be lumped in with all the sycophants at court."

"My apologies, Amaya-sa," Yoshio stopped himself. "Sorry, Amaya, but I really do think your paintings are great. I would love to have one for my own."

"Then sometime I shall paint for you a masterpiece," Amaya said.

Yoshio thought for a moment. "How do your paintings bring you peace? How are they a reflection of conflict?"

"I live a life of conflict, Yoshi, though nobody sees it, save you. And then, I think I only show you a little. I am pulled constantly, this way and that. Putting those thoughts onto paper orders them. Keeps them separated from one another. Peaceful."

"What pulls you?" Yoshio said.

"Many things," Amaya said. "Not just my father and mother. Many other things. Old things. New things." She looked over at him. "You pull me."

Yoshio turned away, and a silence settled into the room. "I have always considered the life of the samurai to be noble and honorable, though hard. Perhaps I should have considered a woman's perspective more thoroughly."

"To what end?" Amaya said. "You get to be single-minded. Your duty is all you have to worry about, but it requires your strength and focus, and eventually, even your life. I live in comfort. Who exactly should envy whom?"

"I was just thinking of the past," Yoshio said. "I could have done better. My wife-"

"We could all do better," Amaya said. "Be content with the now. I have enjoyed your company these past weeks."

"I have enjoyed yours," Yoshio said. "Thoroughly." He paused for a moment. "I was thinking. Perhaps you should abandon meditation and focus on what works for you. Your paintings are a delight."

"You are right," Amaya said. "But I have found it difficult to paint since we left the Kuramasa house."

"I see," Yoshio said. "That night disturbed me too, though for different reasons."

"What reasons?"

"I am not as clever as I thought I was," Yoshio said. "It is a blow to the ego, though a necessary one. It makes me challenge what I rely on most: my understanding of myself and my limitations."

"I see," Amaya said. "Instead, rely on my understanding of you and your limitations. You will not fall to this man." She looked into his eyes hard, her irises trembling.

"Then you can rely on my understanding of you," Yoshio said. "You will find your peace again, as always, through your painting. Remember, the first minute of meditation is the hardest."

"While I believe you," Amaya said. "I do not think you know me as well as you think you do. Or as well as I know you." She smiled at Yoshio. "But do not worry. I think time will remedy this shortfall." She looked out the darkening window. "We should end your current conflict, yes?"

Yoshio raised an eyebrow.

Amaya smiled at him and said, "You cannot hide your heart from me, Yoshi. One of the village people said something that upset you. I'm going to guess it is a demand for one of the many objections to your bushido, yes?"

"A merchant wanted me to pay him money in exchange for information, from his apprentice, no less."

"Why did you refuse to pay him? We have plenty of silver."

"It has nothing to with the money, it—"

"I'm teasing you, Yoshi," Amaya said. "I know it is beneath you to haggle. I will haggle for you."

"He should not be rewarded—"

"It's fine. It is what merchants do. You would not expect a dog to fly or a bird to bark. Do not expect honor from moneylenders." Amaya pushed herself up with a sigh. "I feel much better now. Peaceful. Let's go."

The merchant's house was among the largest in the village. It had long, sloping tiled roofs like the domicile of a feudal lord, yet lacked the entrance gate and gardens, instead just opening to the street. The great home seemed to fill the lot and dwarf the merchants' houses to the left and the right. The bright red roof tiles stood out even in the dusk, like a beacon to excess money.

A young man opened the door. He held a lamp that illuminated long halls behind the reception room, all glowing with soft light as the day fled from the outside.

"You must be the Samurai from the restaurant," the young man said. "My name is Tetsuo. The master has been expecting you."

Yoshio untied his katana and laid it edge up on a small stand near the door – an unexpected courtesy rarely observed even in Samurai households. The young man led them down the hallway to a small room. In it was the merchant from the restaurant. He was seated on a low stool at a tall table, with a few locking chambers holding the top up. Amaya had seen such things before – desks – that merchants used to organize their money papers and lock away their valuables, instead of working at a standard scribe's table lower to the floor.

The merchant stood up as they entered and, surprising Yoshio, bowed low and slowly to them. He was wearing a rich silk robe over a gui-like drab outfit, giving him the appearance of wearing a true kimono while having durable utility clothes. "Greetings and welcome to my home, and as you see, workspace as well. I am Muira Minoru, merchant and lender. You honor me with your visit."

Amaya nodded. "I am Asano Amaya, and this is Taoka Yoshio, my retainer."

"I had no idea I was expecting relatives of the shogun," Minoru said, bowing quickly again. "Or I would have arranged for some entertainment."

"Do not fret over it, master Minoru," Amaya said. "We can find entertainment in town if we desire. We are here for business."

"Ah, yes," Minoru said. "I overheard what your retainer was saying to Hideo, the cook. I believe my apprentice may have seen something of great interest to you."

"Interest, yes," Amaya said. "But value? Hard to say." Yoshio looked sideways at Amaya as she worked her social grace.

"Luckily, I'm in the business of assigning value to things," the trader said. "I deem this information worth no less than twenty pieces."

"How dare—" Yoshio began, but was silenced by a subtle touch of Amaya's hand to his leg.

"I doubt any information would be worth that," Amaya said.

"A woman of your incredible esteem should have no problem conjuring up such a small sum for such a small man as me," Minoru said.

"That does not mean it is worth that," Amaya said. "Which you should understand as a man who assigns value to things."

"I get the sense that he is very dangerous, Amaya-sama," Minoru said. "It is strange that you search for him."

"You cannot blackmail me for this," Amaya said. "Just so you know. My father knows everything."

The merchant remained straight-faced.

"This man is nothing to us," Amaya said. "Nothing but a trifling eta who needs to be dealt with as is convenient for me."

"Of course," Minoru said. "But that is the value of the man."

"Not to me," Amaya said. "He is worth to me, at best, perhaps three pieces."

"Hmn," the merchant said. "Doubtless, somebody else would pay to find this man."

"I'm afraid not," Amaya said.

"Who knows what the future holds?" Minoru said. "I can restrict this information to only you, for the small sum of ten pieces."

"Nobody else will come for him," Amaya said. "So you can tell whoever you like for five pieces."

"Six, and you will have the information and my trust, Amaya-sama."

"Very well." Amaya pulled from her bag precisely six silver coins, shined and free from wear, as if freshly minted. The merchant bowed and then put his hand out. The coins dropped in, one after the other, and then he quickly dropped them into a bag hanging from his waist.

"Tetsuo will fill you in on the details," he said, and bowed again. He gestured to the young man that still stood at the entryway to the office.

The young man bowed, then began. "I have seen the man you are looking for. He wears a conical hat lined with stiff leather, like a battle helm, but also like a peasant's. It droops over his eyes. He's also dressed like a peasant, with dark robes and pants." Tetsuo bowed quickly again

"Is that all?" Yoshio said. "Six pieces for that?"

"No," Tetsuo said. "I noticed that he wore two swords. That is what made me pay attention; that he had two. The longer one was more interesting. Its handle was marvelously carved, and his hand rested on it constantly."

"Not so uncommon for a samurai," Yoshio said.

"But the sword was uncommon, even for a samurai," Tetsuo said. "It looked like a dragon – a Chinese sort of dragon, if I were to guess."

"Dragons don't look very different to the Chinese, I imagine," Amaya said.

"You'll forgive me, Amaya-sama," Tetsuo said with a bow. "It looked like the zodiac dragons that are always painted and carved into the goods we get from China. That is why I said it looked Chinese. It was very detailed, the handle, and looked like it was carved from living rock, not made from clay like the cheap display blades that are peddled in Osaka."

Yoshio nodded. "Anything else?"

"The handle had two gems. Red gems. The sword looked far too nice for a man like that carry. It looked properly suited only to the shogun himself. The man looked like a peasant, or perhaps, because of the hat, a ronin from a lost battle."

"Where and when did you see him?" Amaya said.

"Yesterday morning, on the road, along the way back from Osaka. I go there every week to trade and bring back goods for the master. The ronin walked alone."

"Of course, Osaka," Yoshio said. He leaned his head down on his hand and thought. "What about his wakizashi? Do you remember the less common sword?"

"Not clearly," the young man said. "It looked rather plain by comparison. It had… a wrapped bamboo handle, I think. Wrapped in dark leather… or cloth… I don't really remember, I'm sorry."

"Thank you," Amaya said.

Tetsuo shook his head. "I wouldn't go after him." Yoshio perked his eyes up. "He had an unsettling presence. I can only compare it to a kami walking through you. Passing him gave me a sudden chill on a very hot day. And…"

"Yes?" Yoshio said.

"He smiled at me. Perfect teeth, white and sharp. Frightening, like a hungry beast. That was his acknowledgement of me. I hurried home as fast as I could."

"Thank you, Tetsuo," Yoshio said. "I hope your master treats you well. If he was on his way to Osaka you need not fear him here, but I would be cautious if you return to the bay. I do not know what this man will do in such a large city."

"Thank you for the advice," Minoru said from behind them. "I will keep my apprentice here for the next week or two. He has more than earned his keep today. In fact," he drew one of the silver coins from his purse and handed it to Tetsuo. "For your savings." Tetsuo bowed his head and dropped the coin into his own small bag, which jingled with other coins.

After they left the house, Amaya said to Yoshio, "This is good, Yoshi. We can catch him on the road."

"I do not expect to find him on the road," Yoshio said. "He is too smart for that."

"Then why did he walk in the open, smiling hungrily to merchants?" Amaya said.

"I don't know. Maybe he wants us to follow."

"Follow him where?"

"Osaka, of course, which you yourself wish to go. Why Osaka? I do not know."

"We don't have to find out, you know," Amaya said. She touched Yoshio's arm.

"The most preferable course is to cut him down before he can enlighten me as to the why," Yoshio said.

"That is not what I meant," Amaya said.

"I know."

"Can I tell you a truth, Yoshi?" Amaya said. She had perched the lantern on a small stand, and she sat below it with her brushes, writing slowly in jet-black upon a linked series of rectangular wooden blocks.

"Is it the truth you are writing?" Yoshio said. He looked out the window of the inn, which overlooked an empty street. A building across the street was well lit and noisy, and Yoshio watched as a young woman argued outside the door with a disheveled man wearing only a wakizashi. Repeatedly, he tried to grasp her hand, and each time she swatted it away.

"What I am writing is a truth of a different kind," Amaya said. "What I wanted to tell you is that, though I hoped you would get your mark, I was hoping we would reach Osaka. In fact, if you had cut him, I had a mind to order you to follow me there."

Yoshio tore his eyes away from the scene below and looked at Amaya, her eyes focused on her writing. "Why?"

"I know we all have secrets, but can you *keep* a secret?" she said.

"For you? Of course."

"My secret will be a dangerous one," Amaya said, a hint of a smile spreading across her face.

"I'm unafraid," Yoshio said.

"Of course not. Even if you were, I'm sure it would not stop you from doing your duty."

Yoshio looked out to the street, and saw the man on the street below, clearly drunk, trying to drag the woman (a prostitute, Yoshio had decided) away from the lit-up inn. Yoshio clenched his jaw and looked for his katana in the corner.

"The question I have is this," Amaya said. Yoshio looked to see her standing slightly behind him, her hands folded in front of herself. "What is your bushido, Taoka Yoshio?"

"I do not understand."

"Whom do you serve? If I forbid you to go down and stop that drunk man from raping that prostitute, would you obey me?"

Yoshio looked out the window again. The man was holding the robe of the woman with one hand and fumbling with his wakizashi in the other.

"Your hesitation speaks for you, Yoshio," Amaya said. "You are more torn than I am. You are like a weapon with its own will. Whom do you serve?"

"Please, Amaya. Let me intervene. It will be swift and I will not kill the man."

Amaya watched as the woman cried out and tore herself away from the man. "Go, samurai." She handed him his katana.

Her eyes were calm, showing only a slight widening with surprise as Yoshio griped the handle and saya of the katana together, not bothering to tie his sword, and vaulted out of the open window. He slid down the tiles of the short roof, an eave over the porch of the inn below, and then let himself drop down to the street silently.

He sprinted across the lane, drawing his katana and throwing the scabbard aside. The drunken man drew his short sword after throwing the woman to the ground. Her loose robe fell open, exposing her breasts and midsection.

"Damn you!" the man said. His wakizashi came forward in a loose arc, not at all precise but with enough power to maim or kill even without the skill to properly use the weapon. Steel rang out as Yoshio's katana intercepted the blow.

The drunk man looked at him in shock. Yoshio stepped over the woman, then began turning the other man's short sword in a large circle. The torsion made the man lose his grip, and his wakizashi flew away and clanged on the stones of the street toward his right. The drunken man staggered back, holding his wrist.

"You!" he said. "Who the hell are you to attack me?"

The door to the inn opened up and two men, large and tattooed across their bare arms and necks, stepped out. Each one held a studded club and wore a short sword

"Blum, how'd you get out here?" one of the men said.

"I thought I told you never to come back," the other said. He stepped out, standing a head taller than Yoshio. "Who are you?" he said, seeing Yoshio still pressing the tip of his katana toward the drunk man.

Yoshio's eyes were still fixed on the drunk man. He slashed quickly. His sword became a grey blur in the lantern light escaping from the inn as it streaked up and down from left to right. The drunk man flinched and stepped back, but found Yoshio had already made his cuts. The man's loose kimono fell from his body along with his underclothes, leaving him naked in the street. Yoshio stepped forward and kicked him in the solar plexus, sending him sprawling on the pavement.

"Retrieve your sword at your peril," Yoshio said. He turned and looked at the two large men still standing near at hand. He nodded ever so slightly to them, then turned back and walked slowly toward his own lodgings. Along the way, he picked up his scabbard and returned his sword to it.

"Hey!" one of the men called after him.

Yoshio did not so much as glance back to see the brawny bouncers, whose mere look would likely frighten a common man, staring at him in disbelief and the naked samurai hurrying down the street in his shame.

He did look up, however, as Amaya called down to him from the window, "You are a marvelous weapon, Yoshi." Yoshio paused to watch her loose hair scatter slightly in the same breeze that tickled the light of the lantern that lit her from below, accentuating the curves of a body hidden beneath a light silk robe. She had a statuesque appearance, and Yoshio stared as if she were art. A nearly imperceptible smile lay on her smooth face.

Chapter 6: Sengo Muramasa

THE SUN BEAT DOWN on the still-damp fields to either side of the raised road that split them. Peasants busied themselves with the harvest of the first round of rice, their bare feet collecting mud so that they looked like swallow nests below their calves as they stepped up and down. Their hats, large and conical much like the basket hat that Yoshio wore as he walked, bobbed up and down as they picked new stalks and threshed them. Amaya walked beside him, letting the horse follow by his lead a short distance behind them. A grove of trees interrupted their steady march as much by the sound of cicadas that nestled in them as the relief of shade they offered.

Amaya pulled the horse over to a shallow but clear pool in a rocky basin beside the grove, a leftover from the draining of the rice fields, and let the beast drink. He obliged contentedly, though the tense swishing of his tail at the pestering insects continued. Yoshio knelt down and dipped his hands into the water, then splashed his face.

"You've been quiet today, Yoshi," Amaya said.

Yoshio turned to see Amaya sitting on a low-hanging branch of a maple. Her head was slightly tilted. "I apologize," he said. "I've had a great deal to think about."

"Like what?"

"Osaka."

"It's a city, Yoshi. You've been in those before, haven't you?"

"Yes, but it makes it so much harder to predict him. I missed what might be my only chance to catch Ryunosuke because of shortsightedness. More may be killed."

Amaya nodded. "So you have given me the first answer."

Yoshio sighed and stood up, letting the cool water drip off his face. "Some of the things you said to me last night. They were not like you."

"That is where you are wrong," Amaya said. "They are precisely like me."

"Then you have many sides, Amaya," Yoshio said.

"And you will know them all, my dear…" she smiled sweetly and looked away for a moment. "Friend."

"I'm not sure if I liked it," Yoshio said. "In fact, it disturbed me."

"Thank you for your honesty. I would not usually show that side off, but if you wish to know someone, you must offer up a piece of yourself in exchange."

"Know who?" Yoshio said.

"You, silly." Amaya hopped off the tree limb and walked to the horse. "People get to know each other by self-revelation. First, you reveal something about yourself, and then your companion feels obligated to offer up the same. You told me a great deal about yourself last night."

"Like what?" Yoshio said.

Amaya handed him a painting from her bag. Yoshio unrolled it and looked at it. It was a picture of a samurai. His eyes were narrowed as he looked away and his drawn sword was held so the edge rested lightly on his shoulder. Behind him were trees in bloom.

"Who is this?" Yoshio asked, knowing it to be himself. "Were you able to paint again?"

"Yes. It's you from last night," Amaya said. She traced her finger along the samurai's jawline.

"I don't recall any trees or open fields or sunshine in the alley. I remember a prostitute, a fool, and two eta who likely thought themselves yakuza."

"It *is* you. You walk in peace, though your eyes are narrowed thinking of the danger ahead. Your sword is light: a tool of an artist. You look away, not caring to gaze at the shame of others."

Yoshio felt something move in himself as he looked at his own visage, pulled from the eyes of a caring artist. He so rarely looked in the mirror, but the painting gave him a feeling of satisfaction. It was a picture of how he wished himself to look: strong, young, and happy with his solitude. He realized he had not been flattering her before; he really did love Amaya's paintings. It was a strange revelation to a mind that was usually content turning with its own self-knowledge.

"Do you like it?" Amaya said.

"It is wonderful. I do not deserve such a work, but thank you."

"Just one of many more, I'm sure," Amaya said. "Do you see how much you gave of yourself to me?"

"I suppose," Yoshio said. "Just what did you give to me? Other than seeing an unfamiliar dark mood, you created more questions in my own mind than answers."

"I thought you loved mysteries," Amaya said with a smile.

"I love solving them, it is true."

"Same thing, yes?"

"Not at all. Solving a mystery is like killing it. Truly, I hate mysteries." He smiled to himself as he looked at the painting again.

"Then conduct your investigation. Ask me your questions. Unravel your mystery."

"Very well," Yoshio said. "What do you intend to do with me in Osaka?"

"Now, Yoshi," Amaya said. "Predicting actions is not the same as *knowing* someone. Not the same thing at all."

"Hmn," Yoshi said, looking back out at the road. He swallowed and chewed his cheek.

"Mmm," Amaya said and walked between Yoshio and the road. "You must have something good in mind."

"It is not right for a retainer to know his master so."

"You are my friend, Yoshi."

"Very well." Yoshio sighed. "Why haven't you ever been married?"

"That *is* a good one," Amaya said. "If you spent any time at all at my father's house I'm sure you've heard all the stories. That my father wished to sell me and nobody would buy, that I'm frigid or cruel and no man would want me, or I prefer women and my father does not have the heart to force my marriage to a man, or that I'm... missing parts." Amaya covered her mouth to stop her laughter.

"Is any of that the truth?" Yoshio said, half-smiling

"Only that my father does not have the heart force me to marry," Amaya said. "But, before I reveal more, I believe that you must give me some of yourself."

"Somehow, I thought there would be more to it than just asking. Maybe I do not wish to participate in this game." Yoshio took the horse's bridle and made to lead him back to the road.

"I do not wish to be harsh, or rude, but there is something has frustrated me for some weeks. Something I must know before we get to Osaka," Amaya said following him.

Yoshio froze and looked back at her, then nodded toward the road. "Do not worry about manners between friends," Yoshio said.

"I *am* your friend, then," Amaya said. "How are *you* not married?" Amaya asked, her face suddenly serious.

"My wife..." Yoshio trailed off and looked off to a vacant edge of a field.

She put her arm lightly on his, a gentle touch that made him stop short. "I'm sorry, Yoshi. Please forgive my rudeness."

"It is fine," he said, taking a breath. "You of all people should know what has befallen me."

"But I also understand not wanting to talk about your wife. Truly, I am sorry for prying." She looked up at him with a forced smile. "*I* remain unmarried for a simple reason. It is not because I do not fancy men. It is because I have extremely high standards, and will accept nobody below them."

"Indeed," Yoshio said, lightening his eyes. "It would take a very rich and very handsome man to keep Asano Amaya content." He glanced sideways at her.

"Riches give comfort, and handsomeness brings excitement, but such things have little meaning," she said. "Honesty, and not just honor or bushido, is what I crave. I will never accept a man in marriage who is dishonest, and I can tell you, my dear Yoshi, that finding an honest samurai is like finding a blue sunflower."

"A blue sunflower?" Yoshio said.

"Yes, a blue sunflower. Have you ever seen one?"

Yoshio laughed. "No, I haven't, but I *am* a samurai."

"Yes you are," Amaya said. "Are you honest?"

"I try to be," Yoshio said, surprising himself with the statement. "At least for you."

After a silence in which Yoshio stared ahead yet willed the edge of vision to pick out a smile on his companion, Amaya said, "It is certainly a start."

Yoshio tried to suppress a smile as they walked onward, the road going around a long bend into a thicket of pines nestled between a few steep hills. Amaya passed the time describing the manners of some her suitors when she was younger.

"Most of them were either allies of our clan, or part of my father's Ashikaga relatives with whom he wished to further relations," Amaya said. "A few of them were from outside the web of the Shogun's family – Rich members of the Tokugawa or those of the Minamoto that wished to retain some influence with the shogun and keep their own relatives safe at the court in Kyoto. There was always some interplay of wealth or power at stake. You can imagine how a spoiled seventeen-year-old girl would feel about that."

"I imagine that girl was ill-pleased," Yoshio said.

"What ill-pleased me more were the quality of some of the men that came to bargain for me. Many of them were very old. These were usually either older members of the Minamoto or otherwise very rich, and none of them would speak about what happened to their previous wives."

"Probably beheaded for infidelity," Yoshio said.

"It would be funny if it were not so true," Amaya said. "Some of them were young inheritors with very bad manners. I even had a young son of the shogun – he has so many sons I can scarcely remember names – pull his penis out when a servant left us alone in the dining room to deal with a fire in the kitchen."

"A suitor dared to reveal his manhood to an unwed woman of your stature?" Yoshio said. "He'd have lost it had I been there."

"You alone would have the skill to make the cut, dear Yoshi." Amaya giggled. "And 'Manhood' is entirely the wrong word for it."

"What did he expect you to do?"

"How shall I put this politely?" Amaya said, smiling and showing a slight blush. "He asked me in no uncertain terms to imbibe it with my mouth."

"No!"

"Yes! Instead, I threw my rice at his hairy crotch and ran out of the room."

"An excellent defense," Yoshio said. "I don't recall learning that secret technique from Tadashi. Perhaps he was holding out on me." They both laughed.

As they entered the sparse woods, Yoshio removed his hat and let the breeze blow over his head, drying off his sweat and cooling him. The shade was a shocking relief from the sweltering and humid day, and for a moment, Yoshio felt a chill.

He tensed, his right hand moving instinctively to his katana.

"What is it?" Amaya said aloud.

"I felt a chill," he said softly.

"Just a breeze?" Amaya said. She shook her head. "No, I know you better than that. I will pull the horse into that thicket over there."

"Thank you. I will return shortly. Perhaps with a head. If I am not back within a few minutes, ride the horse back toward the fields, pay the peasants for lodging and hide among them."

"I will," Amaya said. "Be careful, Yoshi."

Yoshio nodded and jogged through the woods. After a few steps, he kicked off his sandals and continued, his feet losing their sound, and he drew his sword. Amaya watched him for a moment and then pulled the horse through some bushes to a sparsely covered opening between the pines.

Yoshio leaned his sword on his shoulder as he ran, though not with the delicate grace Amaya had drawn for him in her painting. He held his tool with a constant tension in preparation of swift action. His ears attuned themselves to the woods, taking in the sound of the needles and leaves rustling against one another in the warm breeze and picking out the sound of birds among the noise.

He began to feel his wind running short on him and slowed to control his breathing. Amid the sounds, footsteps became audible, though he could not see the feet among the twisting path and great trees. As the sound grew more present, Yoshio deviated from the path, moving quietly among the undergrowth with an intention to strike first and silently. *Honorable fights are for honorable warriors,* he thought to himself.

At last, he approached the sound. He looked between the branches to a familiar sight: a tattered and faded travelling robe, capped with a worn leather-bound hat, like that used by a soldier in battle, only dipping low enough to obscure the face. Wooden sandals clacked along the ground. Yoshio tensed, preparing himself to leap out and slash at the man's back, ending him.

Yoshio crouched and then leaped out of the brush. His sword was moving fast – too fast for someone standing near to see – but at the last second, he changed his trajectory at the calling of a feeling in his chest. *No swords!* The downward slash missed the man narrowly to his left, cutting free a piece of cloth from the old traveling robe.

The figure, lacking any armament, stumbled and then fell forward, his hat rolling away in the dirt. He turned on his back and shrieked, revealing to Yoshio a young but scarred and weathered face. He reached inside his robe and drew out a rusty tanto. He unsheathed it and held it in front of himself, pointing it at Yoshio.

Calmly, Yoshio replaced his katana. "Tell me, stranger. Where did you get those clothes?"

"C-clothes?" the stranger said. He shook his dagger at Yoshio as if he were trying to ward away an evil spirit. "These are *my* clothes!"

"They were not always yours," Yoshio said. "How did you come by them?"

"I did not steal them, they are mine! Leave me alone"

"But somebody gave them to you, didn't he?" Yoshio's thoughts traveled back to Amaya. He looked at the groveling man once more. "Do not move from this spot!"

He turned and ran back toward where he let Amaya, no longer caring to let his breath escape heavily and for his footfalls to give away his position. When he arrived at the place where he had left Amaya, he heard her voice.

"Yoshio, what happened?" she said from the bushes.

"You can come out now," Yoshio said, breathing heavily. Amaya pulled the horse out of the bushes. "Ryunosuke gave his clothes to an eta. I thought it might be a play to draw me away from you, but now I think was just an opportunity to switch clothes. He could look like anyone in Osaka now."

"Problematic," Amaya said. "This is now three times you have sought me out in fear for my safety. Perhaps you should keep me near in the future. I am safest with you, after all."

"Yes, perhaps," Yoshio said.

* * *

The moon was high above them, shining out its silver guidance upon the path as the track cut its drifting way into the woods of pines, parting the fallow places and unkempt bamboo like a pale thread. Shadows made the thick weave of tight and dry branches in the trees on either side into an impenetrable darkness, though Amaya and Yoshio could clearly see each other's faces.

"I'm sorry, Yoshi," Amaya said. She rode on the horse, letting her sore feet air out. "It seems I've underestimated the distance to the next village."

"Think nothing of it," Yoshio said. "We have the moon, which I prefer very much to the sun this month." Yoshio sighed. "However, with blessings there comes struggle."

"What do you mean?" Amaya said.

"There are bandits on the road ahead."

"How do you know?" Amaya said.

"Because this road is where I would be if I were them. It is a good place and a good night," Yoshio said. "The moon reveals us, but beneath the trees, they will be hidden. Besides, I can hear them, speaking loudly and clanging pots together in camp. They do not understand how the wind can carry sound. Unfortunately, they will not learn this truth. They will ambush us, and I will slay them."

"You seem very calm about it," Amaya said. "We can turn off the road here and wait through the night."

"This is our path," Yoshio said. "I will not let a few simple and wicked men change that."

"Simple. Maybe they could be reasoned with," Amaya said.

"Unlikely. Nobody ever truly believes in a swordsman's skill until he is cut. It is karma, me walking here tonight." He looked up at Amaya. "I can put a stop to these men here, who have probably hurt many others before tonight, and will hurt many others if allowed to continue."

"Lead on, then," Amaya said. "I will be at your side." She hopped off the horse and retrieved her katana from her pack, the belted it in the traditional fashion. Yoshio raised his eyebrow, but did nothing else to countermand her.

They wandered on, letting the horse walk slowly behind them. After a distance, in which they each had time to contemplate the upcoming conflict in silence, they came upon the bandits, though not in the way that they expected. They saw the group of men, all wearing dark clothes and carrying various military armaments such as spears and bows, encircling a lone man. They were lit by the lantern the man carried, and outlined by the darkness they brought in closing around him. Voices carried in the distance, but Yoshio could not yet make out all the words

Yoshio's heart leapt at his first thought, that it was Ryunosuke, but as they got closer he could see that they surrounded a more ordinary man wearing a simple kimono with a single belted sword. His face, bearing a hint of age, was calm, and his hands were on the katana and saya in the traditional style.

"The sword's good, old man," one of the bandits, a tall man wearing his hair in a loose tail behind his bare shoulders. "I've seen plenty in my day. Just drop it, eh? We'll let you live."

The man shook his head. "I cannot. I still need it, unfortunately."

"What's this?" one of the bandits said, hearing the steady clopping of the horse behind them. "Friends of yours, old man?"

"Just a few travelers," Yoshio said. He held his scabbard and pushed the guard of his katana up with his thumb, leaving an inch of steel above the lip. "Most fortunate to have the moon to guide us."

“And they have a woman with them,” the tall bare-chested bandit said. “Why didn’t you say anything about her? She’s worth more than a grubbing sword.”

“She is,” Yoshio said.

"It is unfortunate that you have come upon this situation," the waylaid stranger said. "I do not like to put others in danger."

“I am in no danger,” Yoshio said. The closest bandit stepped toward him, a spear at the ready. Yoshio’s blade flashed under the moon like a streak of lightning as he stepped past the spear point and sliced across the chest of the bandit, sending his blood-spewing body backward into another one of the men.

Amaya drew her own sword more slowly, though she used the same ancient form as Yoshio. She stepped away from the horse, staying near her retainer and yet far enough to stay clear of his blade. Yoshio cut down two more men just as swiftly, and Amaya slashed at one of the bandits as reeled from Yoshio’s draw.

Yoshio froze for a fleeting glance to see the stranger, having drawn his sword, slashing madly at the men that surrounded him. There was skill in the cuts, the parries, and the stances that he used, but the motions seemed to be exaggerated. The man’s face wore an expression of undulating rage as he hacked at the bandits. His lantern lay on its side in the dirt, flickering, giving a strange sickly hue to the blurry scene. Most of his attacks were ineffective, but the intensity of the swordsman made up for what he lacked in precision, and soon several bandits were groping at wounds. He was like a raging wolf, and a scream escaped his throat as men died around him, swords and spears rattling the night.

Yoshio continued to cut, keeping himself calm and controlled, and always aware of Amaya at his back. He moved to another member of the bandit group, who swung a bladed polearm with soldier-like skill. Yoshio sidestepped a thrust and grabbed the shaft of the weapon just below its dark blade, then pulled the bandit onto his waiting katana. A swift kick removed the breathless, soon dead, bandit from his blade. Two more moved to engage Yoshio as the stranger raged under the moonlight in a confusing melee a few paces ahead.

Yoshio stepped past the first attacker, ducking under a sloppy sword swing, and cut the man’s hamstring. He heard the man scream as Amaya continued the attack behind him, cutting at the man’s throat and silencing his shameful cry. Yoshio parried a sword swing from the second bandit. He swiftly kicked the man's shins, setting him off balance, then swept his sword upward. It struck the blunt edge of his opponent's sword, but continued its trajectory and embedded itself in the man's groin, a killing blow once the blood began to pour. Yoshio reached forward and pushed the man over, making his flesh slide against the blade and deepen the killing cut. In agony, the bandit dropped his rusty sword and clutched as his gushing inner thigh. Once again, Amaya eased the passing of a bandit with a swift cut to the neck.

The bandits were fleeing, but Yoshio did not have time to take in the retreat, as he blocked another strike, this one from the stranger. Yoshio was surprised, but his guard served him well, and in a swift move he directed his opponent's sword toward the ground and it twisted out of the stranger's hands. He looked up to see the swordsman snarling at him, and again thought of wolves, though the man did not attack with his bare hands. He backed up into the shadows slowly, leaving his sword in the road.

Amaya moved up beside him in a guarded stance. “It seems a few have lived,” she said.

“Not what I expected,” Yoshio said. “But another with skill will be along soon enough, and they will meet their inevitable end. It is karma.”

"What of our stranger?" Amaya said. She shook the blood from her sword, sending a mass of droplets onto the ground to become stains under the moon.

Seeing the classic move performed, Yoshio said, “A bit early for that, don’t you think?”

“If it needs finishing, you will do it,” Amaya said. “Come out in the light, stranger.”

Yoshio put his sword back up in front of himself as the stranger stepped back out into the moonlight, looking much calmer than moments earlier.

“My apologies,” he said. “I do not prefer to have innocents about when I draw my sword. Sometimes I get carried away.”

“You look trained, but your rage makes you sloppy,” Yoshio said, not lowering his weapon. “You must learn discipline to have victory over a true master of the sword.”

“I am a true master of the sword,” the man said. “But not like you. I am a blacksmith.” He bowed to Yoshio, then Amaya. “My name is Sengo Muramasa.”

Yoshio looked to Amaya, who shrugged. “I think I’ve heard my brothers talk about his blades,” she said.

"I have heard of you," Yoshio said. "About more than the mere quality of your steel. In fact, among the samurai, you are something of a legend. Rich men seek out your art, and waste it, because they seldom cut with art, even if it is sharper than a razor."

"My reputation is better than I thought," Muramasa said. He picked up his sword, cleared the blood with a swipe, then put it back in its scabbard. Yoshio followed suit.

"There is more," Yoshio said. "Rumor has it that you have a cruel and violent temperament, and that your students are mistreated, and that such feelings find their way into your steel."

"Ah, that's a bit closer to what I thought," Muramasa said.

"Warriors seek out such blades," Yoshio said.

"What about you?" Muramasa said.

"I seek out steel that cuts, nothing more," Yoshio said.

"We should be moving on, Yoshio," Amaya said.

"Yes we should," Muramasa said, looking up at the moon. "Are you and your wife headed to Osaka by chance, Yoshio-san?"

"We are," Yoshio said. "But she is not my wife. I am her retainer."

"I see. I apologize for my assumptions, Yoshio-san," Muramasa said.

"I am Asano Amaya," Amaya said. "This is my retainer, Taoka Yoshio."

The blacksmith raised his eyebrows. "Asano. Such a name to be travelling with but one retainer."

"He is worth twelve," Amaya said, "and it is better to trust one than many."

"Such true words," Muramasa said. "I shall inscribe them on an odachi[16], the next time I have a chance to make one. Would you be willing to travel to Osaka with me? It will be good to have company on the road."

"I do not know if I can allow that," Amaya said. "But you are welcome to walk with us to the next village. I believe it is only a few miles ahead."

"Good," Muramasa said. "Thank you, Amaya-sama."

The coals of the small hearth smoldered as the innkeeper, bags under her eyes, picked the iron teakettle up and poured three hot cups. Sengo Muramasa sat cross-legged, a contented smile on his face. He looked very different from the raging animal that emerged during the fight.

"Tell me," Yoshio said as the tea was handed to him. "Why is a swordsmith from Ise[17] travelling alone with none of his possessions to Osaka, and from the west?"

"Normally I would lie," Muramasa said. "I usually just say I'm a pilgrim on the way to a shrine. It doesn't matter what shrine, because nobody who has asked knows more about Osaka than I do, and I do look rather..." He rubbed the thinning hair on top of his head, "Monkish. But seeing as how I've already told you who I am and what I do, I suppose that would be pointless now. I am travelling to Osaka to retrieve a certain piece of property."

"A sword?" Amaya said.

"Yes, since I am sword maker there is unlikely to be anything else, eh?" Sengo said. "Yes, somebody has something of mine. Not something I want, but certainly something they should not be permitted to keep."

"Intriguing," Yoshio said.

"Yoshi loves a good mystery," Amaya said.

"Nobody likes mysteries," Muramasa said. "You mean that he likes to solve mysteries."

Amaya smiled. "Precisely."

"So what is so special about this sword that you have traveled from Ise all over Honshu[18] to Osaka in order to recover it?" Yoshio asked.

"I have gone further than that, Yoshio-san. In short, it is the blade which earns my bad reputation," Muramasa said. "Most of my creations are just steel. Good steel, but just steel. This one is much more than steel. It is difficult to explain fully, but it is a weapon with its own will. Even in simple hands, it is dangerous."

"What will is that?" Yoshio said.

"The will to do what swords are made to do: drink blood," Muramasa said. "It was perhaps my greatest triumph, though it was also a great mistake."

Yoshio's eyes widened thinking about what Muramasa described. "Please, describe this katana."

[16] A two-handed Japanese greatsword. It is usually used as a singular weapon by a cavalry unit in battle, and cannot be easily drawn by oneself.

[17] A town and province east of Osaka, with a fishing bay.

[18] The largest island in Japan.

"Well, it is a very fine sword," Muramasa said, "as far as things go. Its steel shines brightly, the hamon[19] is beautiful and grained as if wood. I put a special handle on it though, that is very fine indeed. It is white alabaster, carved into the shape of a dragon with rubies as eyes."

Yoshio looked at Amaya and raised an eyebrow.

"How have you been tracking this man?" Amaya said.

"It's hard to explain," Muramasa said. He smiled. "I feel like I am saying that too much, but it really is hard. I can feel the presence of the sword, even over great distances."

"Sorcery," Yoshio said quietly.

Muramasa looked at him. "It a way, it certainly is."

"Perhaps you should travel with us to Osaka," Amaya said.

"Excellent," Muramasa said, and sipped his tea.

They left the inn late in the morning, content to sleep and take their time getting to the cluster of cities that made up Osaka. The sun was shining brightly, but did not seem as hot and oppressive as it did in the plains and among the rice paddies. Ever there was a breeze blowing in the face of Amaya, Yoshio, and Muramasa, cooling them and enriching the sounds of the trees around them. The sea, though not visible yet, was close enough to smell and sense through the wind. Osaka was near at hand, and their feet were light.

Sengo Muramasa spoke of strange things. Mad things, but things that Yoshio suspected were true.

[19] The line down a differentially forged blade where the two different kinds of steel meet and contrast one another. On a katana, this is often a wavy line of shiny or folded steel that runs midway between the sharp and dull edges, and varies by the sword maker.

Chapter 7: The Blacksmith's Tale

As a swordsmith, it was my place and my purpose to create perfection through the making of a blade. I sought to make perfect representations of Shinto[20] in the curvature of a katana through slow quenching and the ripple of a unique hamon upon folded steel. I yearned to match this beauty to perfect utility in a sword whose aesthetics would hold fast, matched with hardened steel that would cut as well as it looked. Unfortunately, my skill never matched my wish.

I was a failure, even as an apprentice. My swords came out poorly, either too brittle or too soft. When they looked good, they were little more than wall decorations for fat merchants, liable to break with use or dull after a single cut. When they were able to cut (which was rare), they were too ugly for my master to sell.

I spent a terrible long time trying to figure out what I was doing wrong. I listened at the feet of my master, then ran to my small chamber to transcribe what he had written. I tried my best to apply these lessons, but a good product eluded me. By the time I came of age I was able to make a decent sword, I suppose. It would cut and would not break. The handle stayed affixed. The steel was dull in luster but strong and not too ugly. My master was finally able to pay my expenses by selling my swords to students, but I could never seem to match his skill. He said I would find good work as a weaponsmith of moderate skill, and that if I traveled to Edo[21] I might find good work making arrow and spearheads for the clan wars and the armies that always seemed ready to fight in central Honshu.

I, however, was not satisfied with such. I had taken up smithing for more than a good trade and a comfortable home. I was not so ambitious as to view it as my path out of the merchant class, but I wanted to excel in it. I wanted my work to be Shinto, to please the gods.

So I set out at the completion of my studies, but not to Edo. I instead travelled the land north of here, in the countryside of the west of Honshu and up to Hokkaido.[22] I travelled down to Nagasaki and all over Kyushu.[23] I even voyaged through the Ryukyu[24] and observed their martial arts and strange weapons.

Always, I sought out the weaponsmiths and tried to learn from them. I had them evaluate my work, and watch me make a blade. None of them had much to say while I did it. After polishing, everything turned out worse than my technique should have dictated. I just couldn't seem to make anything that was better than mediocre. Discouraged, I set myself on a path to Edo, resigning myself to a destiny of making useful but unremarkable weapons for the common soldier.

Along the way, however, a particular myth pricked my ears. I heard it in a tavern in a conversation between two blacksmiths (by this time I had given up on gaining insight from other smiths, but for some reason I eavesdropped).

"Horseshoes!" said the older of the pair. "We should just be happy making horseshoes. We cannot hope to compete when our swords are placed next to one another in a shop in Osaka or Edo, Ise, or even Nagasaki."

"We *can* compete," the younger man said. "We just need to rebuild the forge so it is better insulated. Then we can get the steel hotter. Fold it more times. Then our swords will be known as peers of the best smiths in the cities."

"You're living a pipe-dream boy," the older one said. "It would take us the better part of a month to rebuild the forge the way you say, and there's business to lose by it."

"But it will improve our product. You know it will."

"Most of our product is horseshoes, you dolt! Nobody wants our swords."

"Because we don't have a proper forge," the younger said.

"We could have the best-made forge in the world, it wouldn't matter. We can't compete with the established schools"

---

[20] Shinto (kami-no-michi or "way of the gods/spirits"), the traditional religion of Japan, can often be used interchangeably with the word for sword, so this usage is a sort of dramatic pun.

[21] Modern Tokyo.

[22] The large Japanese island north of Honshu, the largest island.

[23] The large island just to the south of Honshu.

[24] Modern Okinawa, a series of islands to the south of Japan's main sequence.

"Why not? I don't see any difference between us and the students of Kanemitsu or the Mino School. Or even the Soshu School. It's steel. We know steel."

The older one humphed. "Perhaps we can match the Mino in product, but it would take years to match their reputation. As for the Soshu School, don't be ridiculous."

"What is so ridiculous about it?" the younger said. "What is so special about the Soshu School?"

"The Nobukuni are descended from Sadamune, and of course, Masamune himself."

"I agree that Masamune was a great swordsmith-"

"The best! He was the greatest. I've seen them, boy. They cannot be duplicated."

"But they are *not* Masamune," the younger said. "Masamune has been dead for a century at least."

"Yes, but they have his *forge* boy, his forge!"

"Which is why we need a new one!"

"No, the forge is what matters. That particular one."

"Then I will duplicate theirs."

I watched the old man cross his arms. "We can't. Nobody can. The forge doesn't run on wood or coal. It's heated by a fire kami. That's why we cannot rival the Soshu School."

"You don't actually believe that, do you?" the boy said.

"If you had seen the grain, and watched the cut… Bah! Just build your forge! I'm too old try to get back into sword making anyway."

I didn't listen too much past that point, but the conversation had definitely piqued my interest, and raised my spirits a bit. A fire kami… it sounds ridiculous, doesn't it? Somehow, my young self believed it, or was at least more interested in discovering the truth about the Soshu School.

Of course, most blacksmiths nowadays know about the Soshu School, and many samurai as well. It was a large smithy in Sagami, on the way to Edo from Kyoto, made most famous by the now legendary Goro Masamune, whose ideas had been divested into his ten greatest disciples, who left to form great smithies of their own. Not counted in these other schools were the descendants of his own school, namely Hikoshiro Sadamune, who some say was his son, and his own four students, the Nobukuni.

The Nobukuni and their descendants have persisted in the same smithy in Sagami, working the very forge and anvil of the great master, and though Masamune's disciples are great, only the Nobukuni can produce the same level of perfection as their predecessor. I had attempted to visit their shop during my early travels, arrogantly thinking it is the way of smiths to share their secrets, but was, of course, denied entrance. Usually, the descendants of Sadamune's students were the only ones permitted to study there. Supposedly, they would take an apprentice of unusual skill, but I was, of course, nobody in this regard.

I made up my mind to return to Soshu and discover for myself the secret of the forge and whether it was the work of a spirit or merely skill too far beyond my own to comprehend. If it truly was the skill of the ancient school, then I would keep walking to Edo or go back to Kyoto to make spears for the Shogun's armies.

I found the shop once again, nestled in the hills above Sagami bay, and made my way there. I was no ninja, but I had resolved myself to see the inside of the shop if I could, and so that meant breaking in. I waited until nightfall, but was perplexed by the glow from the shop that persisted into the early morning, and so I waited outside the small wall that surrounded the shop and adjoining buildings. I returned the next evening and saw the same thing. It seemed strange for the shop to be used both at day and during the night, when the steel could not be clearly seen.

Then it occurred to me: the forge was what was lighting the shop, and if it truly was the home of a fire kami he would be burning all the time. I climbed a tree and dropped over the wall. I walked as quietly as I could up to the shop and opened the door. I found the inside to be rather plain. It was filled with standard tools and a few typical anvils, as well as drenching troughs and open windows to let out the heat.

I saw all this, however, because the closed-top forge was indeed glowing. Light was escaping through cracks in the bricks and the narrow furnace entrance. I thought the light rather strange; sickening, in a way. It was red and orange and moved, throwing shapes on the ceiling like the sun reflecting off of water, though all the wrong colors. I approached the forge, feeling heat coming off it as I had never felt before. I was sweating through my clothes almost instantly. Fire seemed to rage inside the brick container, but when I looked down to see inside the bricks I could see no trace of coal or wood.

It was true after all! There was a fire kami living in Masamune's forge, which could heat steel so hot as to make folding effortless. I could only guess what kind of magic a kami could impart to a blade. I wondered then how Masamune had captured the spirit and how the Nobukuni had kept it in their forge. I wondered if Masamune had found it in the ground, and built the forge in the very place it lived. I wondered if I could find my own. Then it came into my mind as to whether I could take the kami for myself.

I felt guilty, because it is wrong to use a kami for oneself, but I also felt justified. The pride of the Soshu School had been the result of a god and not their own hands for more than a century. How would I take it? I inspected the forge and found no exits beside the furnace insert, surrounded by glowing bricks.

"A bit late for tempering, don't you think?" a voice said.

I jumped back, startled, and looked around me, afraid I'd been found out. It was very disquieting, hearing a voice and then finding myself alone. My nerves were on edge; adding the threat of madness to them was almost too much for me.

"Hmn," the voice said. "You are not Nobukuni. You are not any better than them, but you are not them, which is good." I realized the forge – or rather, the fire kami in the forge – was talking to me.

"No, I am not Nobukuni," I said, walking back to the forge. The fire within seemed to get stronger, blazing with orange and red light.

"Who are you?" the voice said. It seemed a strange and wonderful voice. It was sinister, and yet kind. I can't describe it another way without great effort.

"Sengo Muramasa," I said, feeling a compulsion to speak the truth. "I am a swordsmith in search of the secrets to blade making."

"You have found one, then," the kami said. "Would you like to take it with you?"

"Yes," I said compulsively. "I mean, why do you want to leave?"

"I am a prisoner, and I wish to be free. Is that not enough?" The fire changed colors as it spoke, becoming a pale blue.

"I suppose it is. How did you become a prisoner?"

"Deception. Evil. Masamune was not the pure-hearted smith of the peaceful heart he made himself out to be to his students. He was a wicked man in his lies and capturing of me. My greatest regret is that I did not get to wrench his life from him, and he was permitted to die an old man. It is the most preferred exit for you mortals, is it not?"

"Um, yes," I stammered. "Unless you are samurai. Then you are supposed to die by the sword, or something like that." I was getting witless talking to the fire kami.

"I wish more men were samurai," the kami said. "I like you, Sengo." The kami laughed. It was... an odd sound to say the least, like fire licking logs while a frog croaks. Does that make sense? I'm good with steel, not words.

"You like me?" I repeated.

"Yes," the kami said. "Will you free me? I will like you even more if you do."

It's hard to speak about how I felt talking to the kami. It was like everything it said you immediately believed, or wanted to believe. Your inner voice would protest, but it would seem ridiculous to you. That inner voice told me freeing this kami would be wrong, or dangerous, but I also knew that the secret to greatness was locked up in him.

"Alright," I said. "Um... how do I free you?"

"Nobody wants to help me when they find out. They just leave me here to rot. A prisoner. Forever."

"What is it? I'll do it for you," I said without thinking.

"We fire kami are not like the gods of the earth, or the sea, or the wind," the kami said. He was turning bright red and frightening me even more than I already was. "We are not omnipresent. We cannot go reside in a stone or a river for an age, or sweep across to new lands as a great breeze. We live, and we expire... then..." The fire seemed to be breathing.

"Then what?" I said.

"Oblivion, until a return. A blind return. Masamune tricked me and imprisoned me, and called it the gift of life, but a fire kami must be free!"

"How?"

"Through you."

"How?" I said again, not understanding.

"Your flesh... through your flesh... only then can I escape this torment."

Again, I felt a compulsion to comply, to do the will of this... thing. I found my hand reaching toward the furnace opening, then withdrew it. "That will kill me!"

"No! I will prevent myself from burning you. I can choose, but I need flesh to escape the nothingness." I did not fully understand his words, but my heart wanted to comply.

"Why?" I said timidly. "Why should I?"

"I can give you what you desire, Muramasa," the kami said. "With my power and skill, you will become the most renowned blacksmith in Japan – nay, the world! With Masamune, all I could do was heat steel and touch it with power. With you, I can do so much more. So much! Just release me; I pledge to give you what you want."

I did not comprehend all of the things the kami said, reflecting only later on the way he knew my name and my purpose, and offered to me that which I wanted above all things.

"Then I shall free you," I said. I stepped forward and extended my trembling hand into the forge, torn by half my will wishing to run away, and the other half earnestly desiring what the kami offered. As soon as my hand entered the glowing ethereal flames of the forge, I felt an intense burning. It was a pain beyond anything I had felt before, even beyond comprehension. I had heard that when a man is badly burned he soon fails to feel pain, having the nerve lines of his chi burned away. This pain, however, persisted, burning layer upon layer, all the way to my bones.

I took my hand out to look and saw the flesh unblackened yet in consuming flames. I stumbled down as the pain and burning spread throughout my body, from my eyes to my toes and to the center of my heart and skull. I was on fire, and yet not dying.

"Yes! Yes!" the voice said, filling the room. "It is better than I be imagined!"

I realized the flame of the forge had left, and only the burning of my body lit the interior of the shop.

"So much pain! So much desire!" the voice said. The voice began laughing profusely.

After what seemed like hours of torture, the pain began to subside. The flames were dying down in the dark room. The laughter continued, and I felt shock when I realized it was coming from my own mouth.

The demon – for that is what he truly was – had entered me. My mind was filled with his presence, and his consciousness was swiftly becoming my own. His mind pierced my thoughts and emotions, and probed my memories. I was helpless to stop him. My own desires became magnified as I felt power coursing through my veins. I lay on the ground shaking, trying to fight the demon, but I was no match for him.

"What's going on in here?" My head snapped off the floor to see one of the apprentices, a boy even younger than me, staring at me with a lantern.

"Fool! I'm free now!" my voice said. I saw the boy reach for a sword at his side.

What happened next was a blur. I felt my body moving. I was both in control of it and standing outside myself. My arms slashed at the boy. I felt his flesh rip under my nails as I tore at his face. The lantern fell on the ground and sputtered out.

His screams filled my ears, but the new part of me, the demonic part as I would come to call it, reveled in the boy's screeches. In the dark, I could see with a strange vision. The boy's body was glowing dimly, pulsing, his blood driving a primal hunger inside of me. I wanted to consume. I attacked his throat with my fingers, finding his flesh soft, and yet resilient enough for me to not draw forth what I sought.

I bit. I tore at his warm throat with my teeth. He gargled as blood filled his lungs, a horrific death rattle that filled me with even more lust. The blood poured out, over his head and neck, over my hands, onto the floor, into my mouth.

And I drank. I drank until I felt sick, and then stumbled away from the body, disgusted with what I'd done, yet also satisfied. It was a wonderful feeling, as much as I was filled with hate. It was as though I had had sex and eaten a meal at the same time, only much more profound… more filling.

Lights came on in the house that adjoined the shop, and seeing myself covered in blood, dripping from head to toe as it was, I panicked. I took the boy's sword – he had not even had time to draw it – and made for the wall. I stuck the katana in my belt hastily and reached up to the top of the wall to climb over. I couldn't get a grip because of how slippery my hands were from my murder. Full of fear, I leapt in an attempt to get a better hold, and to my surprise, nearly vaulted the wall in a single jump. I ran away, further into the woods and away from the shop, until I collapsed and lost consciousness.

"Interesting tale," Yoshio said, "If we are to believe it."

"You can believe what you will, samurai," Muramasa said. He shrugged.

"If I do believe you, it makes me regret allowing you to travel with us," Amaya said. "What would stop you from ripping our throats open?"

"Your retainer, Amaya-sama," Muramasa said. "Fury and strength are no match for skill, and I saw enough last night to know skill. I should make you a sword sometime." Muramasa smiled slightly. "Besides, the fire kami is no longer… with me."

"I saw you rage last night," Yoshio said. "You were like an animal. Is that how you murdered the boy?"

"Much worse," Muramasa said. "The nameless one is no longer with me, but he has left his mark and then some. There is still a small piece of him, of his evil and consciousness, imbedded in my heart. Enough that I can control it in most circumstances, though truly, I am a dangerous companion for most men."

"But not Yoshio," Amaya said, looking sideways at her retainer.

"No, not him," Muramasa said. "Besides, I feel like he would… taste bad, for lack of better words."

"How did you rid yourself of your demon?" Yoshio said. "If I am to believe that you were possessed by one."

Muramasa put a finger up. "Ah, but I wasn't possessed by him. I was one with him. There is a critical difference, and removing him from myself was no small task."

Yoshio raised an eyebrow to the smith. "Go on."

Yes, well, I should tell you a bit more of what I did *after* the demon entered me. I woke up the next morning, and I felt as if a fever had hit me. My flesh felt like it was on fire. I quickly ran through the sparse woods back down toward the bay. I reached a river, and realizing that I was covered in blood and would be unable to enter town as I was, I decided to bathe. Part of me knew the water would be cool and refreshing, but I trembled with fear as I attempted to step near it. I was… I felt like the water would… drown me, for lack of better words. Somehow, the river seemed like pure death to my heart, yet I knew I must bathe.

When I entered the water, cold and flowing swiftly down to Sagami bay, I nearly jumped out of my skin. It was ice cold, and clammy, and made me feel as though I was going to vomit. At the same time, I was surprised to be alive, to be impervious to the water. That is when I realized I was not myself at all, that I was not Sengo Muramasa. I had become a different creature entirely.

While I was bathing, I came to remember the night previous and the horrible murder I had committed. I also could remember myself before, but the thoughts were hazy and foreign. Likewise, I could, if I concentrated, feel out strange memories that were not my own. These memories, I presumed were of… my life as a fire kami. Some were of sight, and others were of burning or rage, or touch, or satisfaction. It is difficult to explain, especially since I am no longer that… abomination. It's like looking at a sketchpad copy of a greater painting of bright reds. Dull.

I could see back to the capture of myself by Masamune. Before that was mostly chaos, an unending hunger, but I remembered the perception, at some point that I might… die as you mortals see it. Kami see it differently, to say the least. Regardless, I was suddenly afraid of the darkness that comes with the expiration of fire's hunger. Masamune – that was his name when I met him amid the flames who are my children – made me an offer. He promised eternal life, in return for keeping him warm. I did not fully understand the offer or the nature of what he expected of me.

He brought me back to Soshu in a large lantern, which I felt incredibly frustrated by as it was fed by oil I could only reach a little at a time. Imagine wine being dripped into your mouth a drop at a time. It was maddening, but he assured me it was necessary. We got to Soshu and I found waiting for me my new home, the forge, which he told me was constructed of special bricks that could keep a kami without the need for his element. I misunderstood this.

A priest came – an old, sly, stick of a man – and performed a ritual upon the hearth. The lamp, with me inside, was thrown into the forge. In shattered and fed me incredible flames, then the oil was spent, and to my surprise, I remained hot!

I had, at last, achieved what had been denied fire kami for all time: persistence in the mortal realm; immortality as you understand it.

I quickly learned the price of my continuance in the world, which was imprisonment. The world that I wished to see, with its embers and its coursing blood, was forever locked away, as I could neither move beyond the confines of the forge nor go back to oblivion. Something the old priest had done was designed to turn away a fire kami. I regret too that I could not burn his life away along with wicked Masamune.

More than being merely kept caged, looking out eternally to the dusty shop of the swordsmith, I became the slave of Masamune. Day and night I heated the forge, unable to contain my own nature for more than a few minutes. I heated his steel, plying the layers of folded tamahagane[25] as he wished. In truth, my nature made the steel even stronger, as the more I raged and wished to obliterate Masamune, the hotter and more quickly it heated the steel.

Masamune was well pleased, turning away my wordless screams with frustratingly quiet words. He also enjoyed the impressions I left on his blades, of grain-like stripes that others thought were proof of his diligence and skill, but were really more like my fingerprint. Every piece he made with my flames was mine as well as his, taking a piece of me with it. It was maddening and infuriating, but all I could do was scream. I had not yet learned to speak the words of mortals, though I could understand them well.

Students from all over the land came to study with him, and they too abused me to their own benefit, crafting many more so-called masterworks with the heat of my soul. These became the famous ten disciples of Masamune. Each one of them I knew by name, and had I a body and a sword, I would have taken the soul of each as they took mine. Eventually, even Masamune's bastard son came to join the school, the unworthy inheritor of a trickster and liar.

This glory that Masamune reveled in eventually came to an end when I finally learned to speak in my own voice. A word here and word there, and eventually I spoke enough for the smiths to hear. My existence could no longer be disguised through the shoveling of coal and wood into the forge. On the cusp of being revealed for what he truly was, Masamune chose to declare all of his students to be masters of the craft, then sent them forth to let their education speak when their steel could not.

After that, the shop and the surrounding houses were shut off from the rest of the country and the people of Sagami Bay, the secrets of forging deemed too valuable to competitors. Only I knew the truth: that the inner sanctum of Masamune could be trusted to but a few. From that time onward I spoke only to the Nobukuni and their descendants, until I met… myself.

"All this became clear, an indelible part of my memory, as I stood in the river and washed myself," Muramasa said. His eyes stared out from under his hat, a calm hardness to them. Beads of sweat had burst around his temples.

"The Soshu School still stands," Yoshio said. "As far as I understand it."

Muramasa nodded. "Part of me is surprised that I never returned to exact a more powerful vengeance upon the Soshu School, a payment in blood for years of service in binding. Perhaps, gaining the sight of men, the demon thought the boy I killed was all the men who had put him to work, but it is hard to remember clearly that life."

"Why, then?" Amaya said.

"I think when the fire demon bonded with me a great part of his desires merged with my own," Muramasa said. "We were focused on the craft so much, we rarely had time to eat, and then it was always a feast, planned as much as I could. Returning to the Soshu School was never convenient when he was part of me."

"When he was with you," Yoshio said. "Has he returned without you?"

"I do not know for sure, but I am near certain he has not," Muramasa said. "In fact, that is where I thought he might be going this time. I have followed his aura far, though I always walk too far behind, it seems. I am not a young man anymore. I can still feel him ahead of us, though. Closer than I have felt in quite a while, actually."

"I do not understand," Amaya said. "You said that you could sense the **sword.**"

"They are one," Muramasa said. "The demon, and the sword. That is why the sword is my greatest triumph, and my most disastrous failure. The fool who stole it… I do not know if he is himself anymore." Muramasa sighed.

[25] A high-quality, high-carbon steel made in small batches and used in traditional Japanese sword-making. It traditionally makes up the sharp edge of the blade and terminates at the hamon, where it meets the softer and less brittle steel that makes up the majority of the sword.

Chapter 8: Osaka Bay

"What do you think of his story?" Amaya said. She was sitting across from Yoshio at the low table. Hot tea sat steaming in two cups in front of them. They sat in a quiet corner of the inn, behind a framed paper barrier. Beyond it, the chatter of peasants and traders in the common room echoed.

Yoshio scratched his chin absent-mindedly. "If you were to ask me three weeks ago, I would call it farce. After what I have experienced with Ryunosuke, I am more hesitant to dismiss the supernatural."

Amaya nodded and held up her teacup. Seeing this, Yoshio nodded back, held up his own cup, and took a sip. Amaya sighed. "I wonder about our swordsmith's motivations."

"There is too much mystery in him for me to say I have a grasp of even his immediate motivations," Yoshio said.

"I am wondering if he means to recover the sword for his own benefit," Amaya said.

"Perhaps. Should I permit it?"

Amaya cocked her head slightly. "If it is truly as he says, it would be dangerous for anyone to possess, yes?"

"Yes, but perhaps less dangerous to some than others," Yoshio said.

"Good point," Amaya said. "Sengo Muramasa is famous for his swords, not a long string of murders. What will we do with him if he wishes to reclaim the sword?"

"My only concern is to dispatch our killer. Muramasa works toward that end. Beyond that is a web of possibilities that are too dense to seriously consider."

"And yet you do," Amaya said, smiling.

"You know me too well, Amaya."

"And yet not well enough. If I predict your behavior it is because you are reliable."

"As I wish to be in all things for you, my lady," Yoshio said.

Amaya smiled and took another sip of tea. "Osaka is a marvelous city, Yoshi. We can find many fine things there, from silks to swords."

"It is," Yoshio said. "What is on your mind?"

"Just that my retainer is ill-equipped," Amaya said. "For such as we shall find there."

"I've told you before that I prefer my own sword. It may lack the delicate features of your own, but I have come to trust this sword with my life. I would prefer not to change the tool of my trade so close to bearing them in high duty," Yoshio said. He held tightly the wakizashi that still lay tucked into his belt, his thumb tracing the grooves on the end of the handle. "I know both my swords well," he said.

"I would never dream of prescribing to a samurai like you a change in weaponry," Amaya said with a smile, hidden behind her teacup. She took a sip. "I am talking about your attire."

Yoshio looked down at his robes and loose pants. He was always careful to keep his dress clean and neatly creased. "What is wrong with my clothes?"

"It makes it entirely too obvious that you are my retainer."

"I *am* your retainer. What else would I be?"

"My husband," Amaya said.

Yoshio choked on his tea, then forced himself not to cough. The burning at the top of his windpipe as he tried to clear the liquid with a soft grunt made his face turn red.

"I judge from your reaction that the prospect of being married to me you find less than desirable," Amaya said, looking down at her lap.

Yoshio coughed slightly. "No, that is not true! Marrying a lady like you would be an honor, far more than a lowly man like me deserves."

"A lady *like* me, but not me. I have been too crude and casual with you."

"No! I treasure our conversations. You are a true lady, and I am honored to know you as a friend."

"I am ugly, that is why you find the idea so repulsive," Amaya said.

"No, Amaya, you are beautiful! So beautiful. Your face brings tears to me in the morning, which I must use all my discipline to suppress. The grace of your smile is like a gift from the gods. You walk is like a breeze of perfect clouds, and your neck..." Yoshio found himself leaning forward, hands on his knees, and feeling flustered and angry with himself. "No, Amaya, my perfect blossom of a lady, you are perfection. I had just never considered... No! Amaya, truly, I do wish... I l-"

Yoshio stopped to see Amaya looking up at him, a slight smile on her face. He frowned.

"Relax, Yoshi," Amaya said. "It will merely be a deception. I will not actually make you wed me. I was just teasing you."

A dozen replies flashed through Yoshio's mind as he sat back and crossed his arms. As he went through them, he felt like there was nothing he could say that was not either improper or insulting to his master. Instead, he merely sighed.

"So," Amaya said, setting her tea down. "Will you be my husband?"

"I cannot refuse your commands," Yoshio said.

"I asked," Amaya said. Yoshio looked at her eyes, staring deeply at him, shimmering slightly.

"I will."

"Good," Amaya said. "Then we will need to get you some more formal attire, if anyone is to believe you are a worthy spouse to Asano Amaya. Osaka will be a lovely place to acquire such."

"Why are we not changing names, if deception is the game?"

"That would defeat the point. I will explain more in private."

"I will do my best," Yoshio said. "I am yours."

"In more ways than I had thought, it seems," Amaya said. She raised her cup to smiling lips.

Yoshio thought back to his stammering. "You must understand, Amaya, that you had caught me off guard."

"That was a bit of the point, and the fun, wasn't it?"

"Yes, well I can't be held accountable for what I said. I had never considered the proposition."

"I will definitely hold you accountable for what you said," Amaya said. "And with that in mind, I know you have at least imagined the proposition."

Yoshio looked down and did his best to relax and suppress the tingling blush that threatened his forehead and neck. He looked up at a touch from Amaya.

"Please, Yoshi," Amaya said softly. "I'm sorry, I was only teasing. Please forgive me."

Yoshio nodded.

Yoshio chewed his cheek as Muramasa entered around the paper barrier. He carried a pitcher of what smelled like hot sake, and he wore a wide smile across his face, deepening the wrinkles around his eyes. He looked at Yoshio's face, which was downturned into a frown.

"I knew a little sake was a good idea," the swordsmith said, "looking at a face as serious as yours." He set the pitcher down on the low table and passed out small ceramic cups to each of them.

"I cannot afford to dull my senses on rice wine, master smith," Yoshio said. "The life of a retainer is a vigilant one."

"Relax," Muramasa said. "Your mark is miles away from here."

"There are more dangers in the world than Ryunosuke," Yoshio said.

"Is that what he's calling himself now?" Muramasa said. He poured a cup of sake, then looked to Amaya, who nodded politely as he poured a second. Yoshio shook his head at the sake and Muramasa shrugged.

"It is the name he gave to a scribe near the fields of Kuramasa," Yoshio said.

"Do you believe the scribe?" Muramasa said.

"I had only his writing to go on," Yoshio said. "I found his head on a plate of rice. Do you know another name?"

"Yes, actually," Muramasa said, raising his eyebrows. "The blade was stolen from my vault by Ashikaga Keiji, by force of arms from my apprentice while I was away inspecting rough steel."

"That is one of the Shogun's sons," Amaya said.

"The one who showed you..." Yoshio said, gesturing downward with a finger.

Amaya chuckled. "No, this is one of the shogun's elder sons. He has not received a fiefdom of his own as of yet."

"Why is that?" Yoshio said.

"He has failed to prove himself in battle, while his younger brothers have fielded soldiers and samurai alike against Tokugawa pretenders," Amaya said. "Keiji has been afield, but never participated directly or dealt with battle himself."

"And so his father holds back the inheritance from him," Muramasa said, and raised his cup, then drained it and filled it again.

"The shogunate is primarily a military position. One must prove himself worthy of the duty entailed," Yoshio said.

"A samurai to the bone," Amaya said. "There is a bit more to it than that, but you are certainly right – the shogun cannot have his successor seem weak."

"He came to my shop seeking a blade of surpassing quality," Muramasa said. "I was happy to make him one, though I think he suffered the illusion that afflicts many samurai in regard to such artifacts. The belief that swords, not men, win battles."

"Interestingly self-abasing point of view for a swordsmith," Yoshio said.

"Not at all," Muramasa said. "I make marvelous swords. I can say that now without ego. They are, however, only as powerful as the man who wields them. Well," Muramasa scratched his chin. "Perhaps that is not true for the demon blade. We'll see. Anyway, he caught sight of the sword – just the handle, mind you, and just had to have it. He offered me a princely sum for it, too, but I wouldn't sell. Sons of the warlord aren't used to hearing 'no.'"

"Hmn," Yoshio said.

"Worried about having to slay a son of the shogun?" Amaya said.

Yoshio glanced at her and pursed his lips. "No. He does not even call himself such. To all concerned he is but a shifting eta. I am wondering about the demon blade. It explains much about his battle behavior."

"So you *have* met the man," Muramasa said.

"I have met him twice," Yoshio said. "Once when I attempted to cross swords with him, and again when he murdered an opium dealer."

"No big loss, then," Muramasa said.

"No," Yoshio said. "No great loss."

"Why do you chase him, then?" Muramasa said. "Not that I wouldn't oblige the help, being a swordsmith and not a swordsman."

Yoshio glanced at Amaya, who nodded slightly with a blank look on her face.

Yoshio breathed. "Lord Furukawa, my daimyo, was hurt by this man. He tasked me with recovering his head."

"How was he hurt, eh?" Muramasa said. He chuckled. "I ask because in my journeys I have seen no murder of high lord or good son." He took a sip of sake and smiled a wicked smile that was eerily familiar.

Yoshio glanced again at Amaya, who remained still and did not nod. "The victim was unknown to me," he said. "I only do the will of Lord Furukawa."

Muramasa chuckled. "What a heap of lies." He drained his cup. "Sorry, Yoshio-san, but I don't require special powers to see a plain-faced lie. I forgive you, though. Samurai are all trained to lie and accept lies as if they were truth. We merchants are free to – nay, we must –reject lies."

"It is not a lie," Amaya said.

"But it certainly isn't the truth." The swordsmith put his cup down and poured more sake. "At least the whole truth. Furukawa isn't your daimyo, for one. Not anymore."

Yoshio glanced over at Amaya, who nodded. "True, then. I was gifted to Asano Amaya as a retainer when Furukawa heard she needed to travel south on errands from her father."

Muramasa smiled. "That's better. Always funny how samurai talk. You stand above the peasant, but you can be gifted like a slave." Yoshio cocked his head to the side as Yoshio frowned. "I didn't mean anything by it, mind you; I just find your manners odd."

"And I find yours severely lacking," Yoshio said, leaning forward. Amaya gently touched his leg beside the table, and he relaxed.

"Anyway," Muramasa said. "I can see that she's the real master now. She lets you continue what should have been a secret quest, eh?" Muramasa raised his eyebrows up and down quickly.

"I found it intriguing," Amaya said. "And it would be good for my house to do a favor for Furukawa's family."

"Somehow, I think Keiji did the greater favor for the family," Muramasa said. "It's just a feeling, or the lord would have told you what was lost."

Yoshio glanced over at Amaya, who looked back, unnodding, but raised her left eyebrow in a subtle motion.

Yoshio looked back at Muramasa. "I, as you, have only suspicions. Suspicions are, however, irrelevant. Ryunosuke – or Keiji – must be stopped."

"On that, we most assuredly agree," Muramasa said. "I will do all in my power to aid you in this, I promise. I regret that I do not have months to spend making a sword worthy of crossing my old one. Worthy of you."

"It is only a tool, master smith," Yoshio said.

"But even a carpenter must invest in *good* tools, Yoshio-san," Muramasa said. "And you are no carpenter."

Yoshio, as usual, looked around the room and observed the location of the windows. He pushed open the shutter to the largest one and felt a chill as the breeze pushed its way in, causing the lamp to flicker. Their lodgings above the noisy inn were surprisingly quiet given the crowd noise when Amaya dismissed herself from the table to retire. Yoshio had looked back at Muramasa as he followed her, to see a strange look on his face. It had been a smile, but a devious one, as if Sengo were a child and had discovered some secret for himself.

"Is the room to your liking?" Amaya said, walking up beside Yoshio.

"It's fine," Yoshio said. He reached out to shut the shutters and was stopped by a touch from Amaya.

"I always get hot after drinking sake," she said. Yoshio nodded, glancing to see her obi already removed and laying near her futon. Her kimono was hanging loosely around her body, and she rubbed her neck sleepily. Yoshio averted his eyes, pushing his vision back out the window. He walked around a small corner, past a paper-lined sliding door to his own bedroll.

"Shall I close the door?" he asked, his back to the larger room.

"You always make me leave it open," Amaya said. Her voice was quiet and pliant, her syllables long and drawn-out.

"Yes, but I thought that tonight you might want some…" Yoshio glanced back to see a long, uninterrupted line that was Amaya's body, a subtle smooth wave that was her skin running from her raised arms to shoulders, down her back and over her buttocks, to smooth legs, one bent and pushing on small toes. It was not a new sight, but was wholly unfamiliar to the samurai, and he felt guilty taking the view in the way he did. Amaya was looking out the window as she undid the twist of her hair. Black sheets fell down her back, turning as each of them caught the breeze. She turned to look at Yoshio and he saw amid the lamplight her breasts, carrying the same long lines, as if painted in a single brush stroke, light but creating objects of weight.

"What do I want?" she said lazily.

Realizing the impropriety of his thoughts, Yoshio swallowed an forced himself to look away again. "Privacy," he choked out.

He could hear Amaya chuckle and walk back toward her things. "Sorry to make you uncomfortable, Yoshi," she said, closer to the voice with which he was familiar. "The sake… well, it does as sake does. I forgot that you prefer me to wear a robe at night."

"Prefer?" Yoshio said. He looked back into the room to see Amaya, still naked, bent over and going through her bag. She had retrieved her light sleeping robe, but was still digging deeper. She looked around her legs at him and he snapped his face back over to the window.

"Ha! A husband that can't look at his wife in the nude!" she said. "Here we are. You can look."

Yoshio looked back to see Amaya smiling, a large fan covering her breasts and her free hand covering her pubis over crossed legs. He huffed and looked back to the window. Amaya laughed again. "I'm sorry, Yoshi, but it really *is* too easy with you."

"Well," Yoshio said. He chewed his cheek for a moment. "I've never been made fun of for being devoted to my lord."

"I dare say you have seen me in more vulnerable positions than this," Amaya said.

"Yes, perhaps, but," Yoshio stammered. "This is different." He turned and went to the adjoining room, then slid the door shut. The wooden frame clacked loudly against the wall. He immediately felt a rush of embarrassment, and felt hot, as if he had been drinking sake himself. He loosened his robes and pushed open the shutter of a window on an adjacent wall to the door. The sea breeze felt cool on his face, but did not quench the flush of bashfulness he felt around his neck and the back of his head.

He did not turn when he heard the door slide open behind him.

"I must say I have never seen you lose your temper before," Amaya said. Yoshio glanced to see her enter wearing her light robe and fanning herself. The folds of the robe seemed to plunge between her breasts, and Yoshio found himself wondering if it was intentional.

"I am sorry," Yoshio said. "I know that we have changed clothes in front of one another before. I should have controlled myself better."

"It is good to know that there is a heart to you," Amaya said. "That you are not all honor and duty. That you are a man. It pleases me, actually." She stood beside him at the window. "However, you will have to do better in the coming days."

"Yes," Yoshio said. "About that. Why am I pretending to be your husband?"

"I'll explain more tomorrow when I'm a bit more clear-headed," Amaya said. "But in short, I am expecting to run into Shiba Masaki, a former suitor."

"You have never needed to be married before to turn away suitors," Yoshio said.

"This one has a vendetta against me. He will respect a marriage, but otherwise, he has power enough to make life difficult for my family."

"And he hasn't before?" Yoshio said. Amaya sat down on the futons, teetering a bit with the haze of the rice-wine.

"He has, but he's been married the last ten years," Amaya said. "His wife died recently, and he views me as a bit of a lost opportunity."

"I can see that," Yoshio said. "You *are* a prize."

Amaya smiled. "Thank you, Yoshi. But there is more to it than that. You see, I broke off an engagement with him rather unexpectedly and not in a very nice manner."

Yoshio sat down below the window at watched Amaya as she ran her fingers through her long raven hair. He grumbled. "Why did you? If you do not mind my asking."

"I don't." Amaya looked out the window above Yoshio. "He had a boy killed. A member of the rival Hosokawa clan that he saw as a competitor for my attentions. He thought I was having an affair with him. I despised him for killing that innocent boy."

"Did you? I mean, was he your lover?" Yoshio regretted the question as soon as he asked it, and frowned to himself.

Amaya looked him in the eyes. "He was my friend, Yoshi."

Osaka, or rather the sprawl of low and high houses in the nameless villages that surrounded the entire bay of Osaka, was a welcome relief to Amaya and Yoshio after the weeks spent traveling the countryside. The ocean breeze, blowing hard in the afternoon as the sun moved into the west, was cool and relieving, and the smell of salt penetrated all the other things in the first marketplace through which they walked, seasoning even the wood that held up the multitude of overhanging cloth shades.

"So this is Osaka," Yoshio said.

"Does it meet your expectations?" Amaya walked slowly beside her retainer, who had always his right hand on his katana. She looked this way and that at the shops on either side of her in the lane.

"I am less impressed then I thought I would be."

"It is very rare for reality to outstrip imagination," Amaya said, "Given the limitations of reality and the capacities of the mind."

"Do not mistake me; Osaka is still grand, for itself," Yoshio said. "I suppose I expected to be overwhelmed. I imagine the manors and temples below offer up more sights than this little rice market."

"They do, but do not start looking for castles among merchant houses; you will be disappointed." Amaya paused and held up a piece of cloth lying unattended on a table. It was silk, but had a loose and ugly weave. She sighed. "I was hoping we could get what we need here, but I am afraid rice will be all we are likely to find of any quality."

"When do you expect to encounter Shiba Masaki?" Yoshio said, looking at the cloth for himself.

"After we acquire lodging, I expect him to send us an invitation to meet us at his place of residence," Amaya said. She turned the corner. "He will have set up a house worthy of the image he makes for himself. It will most likely be a merchant's house, rented from one of the many rich traders that the emperor allows to barter on his behalf with China and Korea."

"How will we avoid the meeting?"

"We won't avoid it; indeed, I intend very much to meet him," Amaya said. "I want witnesses to his receiving knowledge of my marriage."

"You seem to have much in this affair predicted," Yoshio said.

"I know Masaki well," Amaya said. "I have also had some insight into his affairs from… a friend."

"One of your father's spies, you mean," Yoshio said.

Amaya nodded. "You sound like Sengo, speaking so plainly." She held up her hand. "Don't apologize. You are correct. We keep an eye on even our friends. To not do so is to invite ruin on your house. He keeps an eye on us, too, which is why he knew to seek me out here, away from my father."

"Hmph. I keep an eye on everyone," Yoshio said.

"You keep an eye on me, too. Both eyes sometimes," Amaya said with a half-smile.

"I did not mean it that way. Of course, I trust *you*, Amaya," Yoshio said.

"I did not mean it that way either." She looked away, down a sloping cobbled road to a larger thoroughfare. "Come, my dear husband. I don't think we shall find what we desire in this rice market."

Yoshio nodded and followed, a smile cracking his normally serious face.

"Of course, we have more silks coming off the ships every day. I generally have the best brought here for discerning customers such as you, Lady..." Kyo, the middle-aged woman who ran the silk shop, which was also itself house to her and her husband, raised her eyebrows to Amaya in question.

"Asano Amaya."

"I see," Kyo said. She looked up to Yoshio, who looked away absent-mindedly at the piles of cloth with his arms crossed. "I have the best of the best back here, then." She led them through a narrow doorway to a room lit brightly by a window cut into the roof. "These are the finest of Chinese silk, crafted and dyed, then cut here to Japanese customs. I can have my seamstresses cut a kimono specially for you this afternoon."

Amaya looked around here. The tables and shelves were filled with rolled and folded silk in every vibrant color and with many subtle and audacious patterns. "The truth, master Kyo, is that I have many fine silks already, though I would not insult you by saying they are superior to your product here."

"Thank you for your grace, Amaya-sama. What are you looking for, then?"

"I'm afraid I have travelled over-long in the country, and my light silks are not ideal for the cool sea breezes here."

"I see," Kyo said. "I have heavy silks here too." She walked across the room and produced a bolt of blue-dyed cloth. Amaya fingered it. Its yarn was loose and thick, and rougher than most silk. She pursed her lips. "Clearly not ideal. Perhaps it is better suited to a man's outfit?"

Amaya looked over at Yoshio. "Yes, perhaps."

"We can always make you a kimono of two layers," Kyo went on. "Light to the touch, yet thick enough to keep out the wind. We can also make it of two different patterns, with a matching obi." Kyo scratched her double chin. "It would be quite a beautiful effect. I will still have it cut this very afternoon for you, of course."

"Of course," Amaya said. She ran her fingers along the bolts of cloth on the shelves, and then pulled out two sets of silk. One was pink with an abstract pattern, and the other was pure white. "White on the outside, with a pink obi. Make it and the lapel folds wide, please.

"Excellent choice, Amaya-sama," Kyo said. "I will have my seamstresses drop their work and cut your kimono immediately."

Amaya looked again at the other, heavier bolt of cloth. "Have that other weave made into a formal outfit for Yoshio. I assume you can find a matching weave for his legs, yes?"

"Yes of course... Yoshio-san?" Kyo looked up at Yoshio, who drug his eyes away from the stacks of wares to bow slightly. "Let us grab a quick measurement for both of you. I'm sure you have very important business to attend to."

Amaya bowed. "Thank you, master Kyo. When shall we return?"

"I can have your silks delivered to your lodging, of course," Kyo said. "That way you will not need to inconvenience yourself any further with my humble shop."

"Excellent," Amaya said. "We are staying at the Hamada House."

"I am of course familiar with such a fine house of hospitality, Amaya-sama," Kyo said. "Had you not found a place to stay in Osaka of yet I would recommend it to you."

Yoshio sat cross-legged. His eyes were closed, but he found his ears open. The sound of the wind blowing through the eaves of the inn-house created a pulsing whistle. When it died down, he could hear Amaya's brush-strokes on the thick paper she had recently purchased, quiet as a mouse running on the floor. Those strokes, more than the noise of the wind, interrupted his meditation. He saw in his mind's eye the image of his employer, sitting straight and proper before her angled table, carefully and directly painting out the lines to something beautiful. He saw a slight smile on her face as she finished.

"What are you thinking, Yoshi?" Amaya said.

Yoshio opened his eyes and looked at her. She was still painting. "What do you mean?"

"You were smiling. I don't see you do that very often when you meditate."

"I was merely looking forward to seeing the completion of your painting," he said.

Amaya pursed her lips. "This one is not one of my best. I will show you the next one."

"I'm sure it is beautiful, Amaya," Yoshio said. "But I will wait for the next if that is your wish."

Amaya nodded and continued on the painting.

"Why are you still working on it, if it is imperfect?" Yoshio asked.

"There is virtue in finishing everything you have begun, even if there are mistakes along the way," Amaya said.

"Ah, Wabi-sabi," Yoshio said. "Beautiful imperfection."

"Not quite," Amaya said, drawing her brush across the canvass again. "At least, I don't quite mean that old Buddhist aesthetic. I mean that nothing is executed perfectly. We are not perfect beings. We strive for perfection, but it is ultimately futile."

"This is true in the martial arts," Yoshio said. "There is always another level of mastery to attain, and even the most skillful warrior may fall to a misplaced twig or an unknown technique."

Amaya nodded. "In art, we have the virtue – or curse – of living with our imperfections. Indeed, if an artist accepted nothing but perfection he would have no art to show for it. The act itself is what is gained, not victory."

"The discipline of the brush," Yoshio said. He chuckled. "Well, I can't compare it very well to the discipline of the sword, but I can tell you that if you draw imperfections, they are invisible to me. Of course, I am no artist."

"You are not a painter. You *are* an artist. I drew your sword as an artist's tool. Does every cut go perfectly?"

"I am alive, so they must go good enough," Yoshio said.

"So it is with the brush," Amaya said. She looked at her painting, then pulled it off and set it to the side. Yoshio could not clearly see what was drawn upon it. "There. It is finished. Good enough, as you say, but not perfect. This next one I will draw for you."

Yoshio smiled, then turned back and closed his eyes once again. He intended to return to meditation, but was interrupted by a soft rap at the door.

"Must be our fancy new clothes," Yoshio said.

"*I* expect it to be an invitation from Masaki," Amaya said.

"How would he know so soon where you are staying?" Yoshio said.

"The silk dealer, obviously," Amaya said. "That is why she offered delivery."

"It is me," the voice of Muramasa said clearly on the other side of the thin door.

Yoshio put aside his questions for Amaya and pulled himself up quickly. He slid the door open to find Sengo Muramasa standing in the hall, his hair falling around his head in twisted, wet strands. His right hand gripped his katana with white-knuckle strength.

"Ryunosuke?" Yoshio said.

"He is close," Muramasa said. "And hungry." He shook his head. "So very hungry."

"How do you know?" Amaya said. Amaya stood up and walked closer.

"My dreams," Muramasa said. "When I sleep I can see with his strange sight, and sense with his uncanny hunger. I become him once again."

"You reek of Sake," Amaya said.

Yoshio cast a look at Amaya. "This is how you sense him? Dreams?"

"It is," Muramasa said. "It is the only time what is left of the demon can actively reach back to me. Every time I drift off, I am returned to his torture. You mention sake. It is one of the few times I can get some sense of relief from it. The dreams are there, but so much hazier."

"Yes, but it is mid-afternoon," Yoshio said.

Muramasa looked down and clenched his jaw. "Believe me or not, but tonight someone will die by the work of my hands."

Yoshio clenched his jaw and nodded, then retrieved his katana from the corner. He saw Amaya pulling from her pack her own pair of blades. She looked at him as she tied the decorative saya onto her obi.

"Aren't you going to protest?" she said.

"Not tonight," Yoshio said. "But be quick to draw your sword."

Chapter 9: Dark Sons of Bright Fathers

"What exactly did you see in your dream?" Yoshio asked. The three of them walked briskly down a street still crowded with people eating at the restaurants and hospitality houses. From behind the paper-covered windows of cheaper establishments on each side, a soft and constant glow emanated, lighting their way along the cobbled path.

"I saw the aura of a fat man," Muramasa said. "He was infested with envy. His heart beat for wicked and malevolent deeds. His hands are filthy. Another man lies near death, though he is just as wicked. Snakes hover above him. Everywhere was the echo of a name. Minamoto."

"Strange," Yoshio said. "How do you know where he is?"

"I don't, exactly," Muramasa said. "It was somewhere higher up than here. A tall house. I could see city lights below my feet."

"What about the man beneath snakes?" Amaya said. "Were they literal snakes?"

"Real? They might have been kami," Muramasa said. "Yes, thinking again, they were kami."

The walked a few steps in hurried silence, Muramasa's sandals rattling on the pavement.

"I might know who the sick man is," Amaya said. "Minamoto Daiki. It has to be him. He is a relative of the emperor, as well as my own clan, who lives near here, and he has a reputation for falling ill, as many of the royal family do. "

"It seems to me he is being poisoned," Yoshio said. "If snakes are a metaphor understandable to men like me."

"Yes, the snakes… they bring venom," Muramasa said. "Do you know where he lives?"

"Yes, if memory serves," Amaya said. "I have met him once on my errands here, but he was infirmed. I know he lives with his nephew, who is also his caretaker, up the hill past these streets."

"He must be the fat man," Muramasa said. Amaya nodded and picked up her pace, leading the other two past the long rows of houses, shops, and open kitchens, working their way steadily up to a steeper inclined street paved with well-rounded cobbles. Soon they found themselves looking up at a row of houses above a switchbacking road, lined with smaller homes.

Their footsteps fell heavy, echoing off the stone walls on either side of them, making the three sound like many more. Amaya neared a run, letting her kimono sway and separate as she gripped the saya of her own katana; had there been daylight she would have been revealing eye-catching legs.

Yoshio could sense them becoming tired, their breathing becoming more labored as they pushed uphill. Lights became less frequent. Finally, they reached the trade house the samurai had spoken of, with its walled exterior. They paused for a moment, the footsteps echoing in the quiet corner of the city as they caught their breath.

"It is that one, I'll wager," Yoshio said, pointing to a large house with but a few lights on that was perched on a high hill above the importer.

Muramasa nodded. "Kill swiftly, but do not touch his sword, whatever you do."

"Will he be able to sense you, the way you sense him?" Yoshio asked.

"I don't know," Muramasa said. "I've never gotten this close."

"He has been able to sense me before," Yoshio said. He took a deep breath. "Catching him unawares will be difficult."

"We should split up, then," Amaya said. "Approach from two directions at once."

"Good idea," Yoshio said. "You and I will go in the opposite side of the house from Muramasa. Perhaps he will focus on you and be blinded to our approach."

"Using me as bait, eh?" Muramasa said.

Yoshio grunted. "I just assumed—"

"It's fine," Muramasa said. "It is fitting for me to be bait, all things considered. I will be able to hold my own until you arrive."

Yoshio nodded. His muscles tensed as he heard something from far off to his left. He grabbed Amaya's arm and pushed both of them into a crouch.

A bowstring rang out clearly in the night, the hairy breath of the arrow's feathers passing above them. The arrowhead clanged against the stone wall of the trade house, then wood clattered on cobbles. Yoshio looked to see Muramasa crouched a few feet away, his katana already drawn.

"A trap!" Muramasa said. "He must sense me as well!"

"Around to the back!" Yoshio said. "To the alley, where he cannot fire on us!"

"We should like the bow to the sword, my friend," Muramasa said. "But we do need to draw him in. I shall see you on the other side." He nodded to the split in the buildings behind him. Yoshio nodded back.

They split up, Yoshio moving himself and Amaya down the long side of the building while Muramasa dashed for the other alley. Sounds filled their ears of more bowshots, coming quickly and close together.

"He's so fast," Amaya hissed as arrows rattled on stone behind them. Yoshio pushed her before himself toward the black of the alleyway.

"He's not alone," Yoshio said. "There are at least three bowmen in three different places."

"How do you know?" Amaya said.

"I can hear it." He pushed her into the alley as another arrow zipped by. "I was not expecting this."

"You can't predict everything, my dear retainer," Amaya said between breaths. She drew her katana and held it out in a guard. Yoshio followed suit, stepping slightly out in front of her, facing the street. During the pause, distant noises filled their ears. "I hear voices."

"There you are," Muramasa said, jogging up from behind.

"Quiet," Yoshio said. The voices became louder, then stopped. "They are splitting up. They mean to corner us here."

"Bad news," Muramasa said.

"Excellent news," Yoshio said, "If Ryunosuke will, at last, face me."

"Yes, but with how many helpers?" Muramasa said.

"They are inconsequential." Yoshio raised his blade and stepped back toward the corner, where each opening of the alley could be seen. Shadows filled one, then the other.

"Just because you walk with a woman does not mean I will spare you, or her," a voice said.

"At last I have you, Keiji," Muramasa said, raising his blade and licking his lips. "Approach and I will take back my sword from you."

"You are a worse fool than you are a businessman," the voice said.

Lantern light filled the alley in front of Muramasa as a man stepped past the others, who were clothed mostly in black. The gaunt face of a young samurai appeared. A frown split his face, which was lit grimly from below. "You are an easy man to find, when put to it. I see your love of sake has not diminished."

"So it is you, Keiji," Muramasa said. "Still trying to use your father's money to make up for your own lack of skill, I see."

"You dare take the name of Ashikaga Keiji casually?" the man snapped. His eyes were drawn wide open, trembling.

"This is not Ryunosuke," Yoshio said quietly to Amaya and Muramasa.

"Are you sure?" Amaya said back, keeping her katana high. A bead of sweat dripped down her cheek.

"Ryunosuke has two arms," Yoshio said.

"What is that your prostitute is saying?" Keiji said. As the lantern swayed, they could see that the left arm of the man was missing at the shoulder, and an empty sleeve was pinned to the side.

"I see you discovered the truth of my words," Muramasa said. "You should not have stolen the blade, nor should you have drawn it in vain. It has rejected you."

"You gave me a cursed blade, Muramasa. I will give you back double what you have given me." Keiji turned to one of the assassins. "Take both his arms and give them to me. Kill the hooker and the other one."

"Take my left," Yoshio whispered to Muramasa. "I will cut this lot down first."

"I want this boy's blood," Muramasa growled. "I do not care for thieves."

"You shall have it, but you must trust me," Yoshio whispered. He cleared his throat and spoke loudly. "You have insulted the honor of Lady Asano Amaya, whose sandals you are not fit to clean!"

"A worthless house name dropped by a worthless liar," Keiji said, turning back. Men began to rush forward, swords drawn.

"For that, and for hindering me this night, you and all your assassins will die," Yoshio said.

He sprang into action, making a series of wide, sweeping arcs with his katana, which made the three men before him slow and put their own swords into a guard. At the other end of the alley, Muramasa did his own, more chaotic sword dance, leaving Amaya between them.

"This is no duel, samurai," Keiji said, his glowing face hovering above the black garb of his hired hands. He looked off to the end of the alley and nodded. "Ninja, like me, have no use for your honor."

After the pause, the three men that faced Yoshio countered, swiping at the samurai all at once. Keiji was right, this was not a duel, but neither was it a battle. All the moves the assassins used were familiar to Yoshio, though they came swiftly, sometimes two or three at a time, and he had to use all his skill to avoid death. The strangers were, however, not great swordsmen, and though their practiced attacks were designed to overwhelm a trained member of the warrior class, they did not include the traditional draw back to guard that comes with the study of true kenjutsu. Yoshio used this to his advantage.

He drew his wakizashi in his left hand, and using it as both an additional blade and a means to block incoming attacks, began a series of long and interconnected slashing moves that kept the three men in front of him from advancing. It was a technique rarely taught or acknowledged, but during his years practicing and teaching at the dojo, he had always made time to learn the techniques that would bring him victory against dishonorable opponents or in battle with many men. Steel flashed and clanged as he held his ground. During the moves, Yoshio realized to whom Keiji was nodding as arrows whizzed overhead. Losing focus for a moment, he turned back to see them clatter against the wall near the fierce Muramasa, missing Amaya.

One of the assassins used the break to press an attack, and Yoshio turned back just in time to see the simple overhead cut coming. He blocked the slash by crossing his wakizashi over his Katana, pinching his opponent's blade. With sure skill, he used the slight grip of his unpolished wakizashi to pull the man in closer, then Yoshio turned his short sword and slammed the razor edge into the man's shoulder. Black rain darkened the night as the man fell screaming to the cobbles below.

Yoshio did not pause to regard his victim, but pressed the other two. He swung his wakizashi at neck level and his katana toward the knees of both men. He felt his short sword connect with a hasty guard and then meet stiff resistance as his blade and the assassin's slammed into the assassin's head. He fell, dazed. The other man had duplicated the high guard. Yoshio's katana struck the second ninja's shins, cleaving bone and sending the man collapsing to the ground in pain.

Yoshio turned back to see Amaya slashing with her sword at an assassin that had slipped past Muramasa. Yoshio turned and dashed toward her. His heart leapt as the ninja turned his blade tip toward Amaya and thrust past her guard. The quiet lady of court, however, remained unharmed as she slid past the thrust, which caught itself in her hanging kimono sleeve, and cut across the chest of the assassin.

Yoshio did not break his stride, but instead dashed past the pair, letting his wakizashi cut the defeated ninja's thigh artery hastening death, and pushed into the fray with Muramasa. Blood and sweat flew as if caught in a great wind, and Yoshio found amid the shadows the openings he sought. He twisted his wakizashi into one of the men, then reached over him with his katana and cut the shoulder of another. Behind him, Amaya easily finished the dazed assassin with a feint that moved into a mid-chest slash. Muramasa chopped at both of them and turned to chase the final man, who was fleeing.

"Yoshio!" Amaya cried. "We must pursue Keiji!"

Yoshio turned around and followed Amaya out of the alley. They were both in a full run behind fast footsteps that rounded a corner. Keiji's lantern fell upon the street as he fled. Arrows cut the air around Yoshio and Amaya, but missed their marks, as if the bowmen were confused. In the moonlight, the awkward shadow of the Shogun's son closed.

Yoshio dropped his katana and then threw his wakizashi with both hands. It flew, end over end, then connected with Keiji. It failed to cut, but the one-armed man tripped and fell. Amaya tossed her own sword to Yoshio, then darted under the overhang of a building, just as more bowstrings rang out. Yoshio spun his master's sword in his hands in the final steps toward Keiji, feeling arrows move around his body. He saw the one-armed son of the shogun pull himself back up, Yoshio's wakizashi now in his hands.

Yoshio did not give pause to the man, or quarter, but made one swift and strong swing going from left to right. Air parted in a single note.

I missed! Yoshio thought as Amaya's sword followed through with the blow so well that Yoshio had to redirect the end of his stroke away from the street. He looked at the man before him and realized he was mistaken.

Yoshio's wakizashi clattered coldly as it fell to the cobbles. Keiji's arm still gripped it. Blood flowed from the noble son's shoulder, where his remaining arm had been moments before. His eyes were locked on Yoshio as the top half of his body slowly slid away from the bottom, separating at a perfect cut that ran from beneath his armpit to his left hipbone. Blood sprayed on the street for a few seconds before Keiji's heart stopped and his spirit at last departed. His body lay in two pieces on the stone, divided as if a god had parted him in twain.

Yoshio looked down at Amaya's sword. There was not a drop of blood on it.

The sound of footsteps pulled him away from the deathly vision. He turned to see Muramasa, rage in his face, pursuing a disarmed and final ninja, who was bleeding from his arm. Bowstrings rang again, and air was parted as a few arrows flew down from the rooftops and punctured the chest and lungs of the assassin. He could not even scream as he fell to the earth. Muramasa, catching the man, who was already dead upon the ground, slashed at his head and tore it to pieces with his sword.

Yoshio looked up to see shadows moving from the rooftops, disappearing into the night lit by the waxing moon.

Yoshio looked back at the dead assassin in the street as Muramasa approached, his manner apparently calmed for the moment. "They left nobody behind to talk," Yoshio said, doing the familiar and habitual shaking of blood before realizing again that he held Amaya's sword, and that it had collected no blood as it cut.

"Will they try again?" Amaya said. She stepped out of the shadows of the overhanging roof and retrieved Yoshio's katana, then walked toward him, doing her own shaking of blood.

"I do not know," Yoshio said. "I have slain their employer." Yoshio frowned as he pushed against the cloven upper body of Keiji. "He has only one arm."

"When the sword is drawn it must drink," Muramasa said, his eyes hollow. "It is inevitable, even if there is nobody else to slay, it must drink." He looked around and sheathed his sword. "We should get away from here. I don't want to be caught standing over the body of the shogun's son."

"That is wise, Yoshi," Amaya said. "Even I do not have enough influence to explain away the death of Ashikaga Keiji."

"There is also the matter of Ryunosuke," Yoshio said, looking at Muramasa.

"It is probably too late," Muramasa said.

"Let us try," Yoshio said. He exchanged swords with Amaya, returned both his katana and his wakizashi to their saya, and then they set off back up the hill at a jog.

Halfway up the hill, Sengo stopped, coughing. Amaya and Yoshio paused to attend to him.

"It is too late!" Muramasa choked out, and covered his mouth with the sleeve on his arm. Yoshio could see by the moon a slight trickle of blood that escaped with the hacks.

"Not too late to catch him!" Yoshio said, and began sprinting up the hill. Amaya followed behind, leaving Muramasa doubled over on the pavement.

They reached the high street, lined with large houses, walled and tiled neatly. Lantern light spilled out into the street from several of them. A dog barked angrily behind one of the walls to their left. They rounded the corner and saw several men looking away from them, down the street, holding up lanterns and candles. Yoshio and Amaya saw their target: a house at the end of the lane, with high steps leading up to a curved wall. Out of the shadows someone stumbled, teetering back and forth on thin legs. Yoshio reached for his sword, then stopped as the figure ambled into the light.

"Daiki!" Amaya said. A wizened face found his way into the light of a curious neighbor, who set his lamp down and nearly retched as he leaned against a wall. "Daiki!" Amaya said again, rushing up with Yoshio.

Hollow eyes trembled above wrinkled cheeks, darkened to black. The old man's robe was dripping more blackness on the light stone pavement; it was like a brush too heavy with ink, and as Daiki stumbled blindly forward, it was as if the brush were dripping on canvas. Absent-mindedly, the old man scratched his abdomen, and a piece of bloody flesh that was clinging to the cloth fell to the ground.

You slay the unworthy, I give men the death they are worth, a voice said in Yoshio's mind.

"Face me," Yoshio said aloud.

We should be friends for this business, Taoka Yoshio. Teammates. Partners. If only there was another sword worthy of you. Pity.

"Face me!" Yoshio shouted, turning around. Amaya rushed forward to the old man, supporting him as he stumbled.

"Help me, Yoshi. I'm not strong enough to hold him," Amaya said. Darkness stained her torn pink kimono and drops of ink found their way onto her face and hands.

Soon enough, I think, you will make of yourself a worthy feast, if the ugly desires in your heart come to bear fruit. An unfortunate waste. Then, I suppose you will get to face me.

"You will fall, demon," Yoshio said.

Foolish mortal. I am inextinguishable now.

Yoshio looked around himself again, finding his sword drawn.

"Yoshi, please!" Amaya said again. She was bent over as the head of Daiki rolled on his shoulders.

Yoshio returned his sword to its scabbard and stepped over to help the old man, taking the weight off the struggling Amaya.

"Did you hear that?" Yoshio said.

"Hear what?" Amaya said on the other side of Daiki.

"Him."

"I can hear him," Daiki said. His eyes still stared out blankly as his neck regained rigidity. "The demon. He's laughing at us now."

"Let's get him back to his house," Amaya said.

"I don't think we shall like what we find there," Yoshio said. "Is there anywhere else?"

"Nowhere to hide," Daiki said.

"I don't know," Amaya said as they turned the limp old man about.

Loud footfalls announced the arrival of Muramasa, breathing heavily. "Then it was too late," he said, bending over to catch his breath.

"We will have to ask a neighbor," Amaya said. "Let me do the talking. He is my relative, after all."

"I will take him," the neighbor with the lantern said. He wiped vomit away from his mouth and picked his lantern back up. "He has been a good neighbor. I also have a bathhouse. For all of us."

"I will look to see what has happened before I wash off the filth," Yoshio said.

Yoshio was the last one to bathe, and would not set himself in it until he had brushed himself clean with a soap-soaked set of brushes that had reddened from the gore on the others. The heat of the water was a welcome relief, but Yoshio found himself unable to relax. He closed his eyes and tried to meditate as the servant that had tended him left the room. The sea breeze blew through a window above, keeping the bathhouse from properly steaming. He breathed deeply and smelled the salt.

His mind raced around details. Ryunosuke and Ashikaga Keiji were not the same man. Muramasa knew as little about the true identity of the killer as he did, though it appeared he still shared some sort of connection with the demon. How did Muramasa rid himself of that demon, anyway? He would need to find out soon. What of the ninja? Would they return? Would he have to spend time and energy stamping them out in Osaka? Yoshio had done such things before, but never with his focus split in so many directions. Then, of course, there was Amaya's former suitor… he didn't want to think about the possibilities he represented.

Yoshio flinched as a small pair of hands touched his neck. He turned about, splashing water on the floor, to see Amaya with her arms outstretched, then he relaxed. She wore a simple robe of a linen-like weave, likely what clothes the neighbor had available in his smaller, though still noble, abode. Her hair was still wet and draped around her shoulders.

"I should know better than to sneak up on you," she said. "I suppose I was hoping you'd have relaxed a bit with the bath."

"Hardly," Yoshio said. Amaya walked around the bath and touched Yoshio's neck again. He sighed as he felt pressure from her fingers working their way into his trapezius muscles.

"I don't need to touch you to sense the tension."

Yoshio breathed through the painful but relieving touch. "Massage is better left to a servant."

"Are you saying my skills are lacking?" Amaya said. Yoshio looked up to see her smiling down at him.

"No, just that it is beneath you to do such."

"Let me decide what is beneath me for once, Yoshi," Amaya said.

Yoshio breathed deeply again. "What did you tell our host?" Yoshio bent forward as Amaya worked further down his back.

"About Daiki? Or about us?"

"Both."

"I told him that he was an uncle, which is true enough given my name, and that we were coming for a late tea under the lucky moon. He mostly filled in the rest. An assassination attempt gone wrong, with Daiki's nephew Shigeo taking the blade is what he believes for now."

"Good, but we should revise it to be a vendetta against the nephew." Yoshio groaned.

"Did I hit a sensitive spot, or are you upset with my story?"

Yoshio half-laughed as Amaya dug her fingers in harder. "It is just that if anyone were to see what I saw, that is the only thing they could truly believe."

"What did you see?"

"Just know that it was quite gruesome."

"I would not have asked if I did not want to know, Yoshi."

"Very well. I found the nephew in Daiki's bedchamber," Yoshio said. "He had been disemboweled, as if it was seppuku, but his head was never severed. The intestines were wrapped around his neck, as if choking him. Blood was everywhere. His head remained attached to his body, but his hands had been severed, as were his feet." Yoshio noticed Amaya had stopped massaging him. "It appeared he tried to crawl before he was strangled. It was wholly different than before. This was a reveling in the act, not just a clean kill."

"A feast," Amaya said. She began working her fingers into his back again. "Anything else?"

"I remembered what Sengo had said about snake kami. I searched the house and came across a familiar substance. It is a poison, called 'ricin' made from the casings of a type of bean that usually comes from south China. It was not very well hidden in, what was the lad's name?"

"Shigeo," Amaya said.

"Shigeo. It was in his bedchamber, amid a few scribing tools, as if it were ink."

"Interesting," Amaya said. "You knew what to look for?"

"A retainer must be wary of poison, yes?" Yoshio let himself fall further into the bathtub. "It is an old tool. Ancient, even if not Japanese. He did not have a great quantity of it, but it was far more than necessary to kill. I think he was trying to poison his uncle slowly, since its effects sometimes take days to appear. The symptoms of weakness and his reputation for bouts of gastric distress seem appropriate."

"What about blindness?"

"Shock, I believe," Yoshio said. "Unfortunately for Shigeo, ricin in small amounts can be overcome within the body. His uncle could have been killed anytime, but will likely recover now."

"I see. I am glad to hear it," Amaya said. "You should also know that the incident with the shogun's son has wakened this part of the city."

"No doubt," Yoshio said.

"When we meet with Masaki, I want to weave those two events together," Amaya said. "The son of the shogun and a wealthy Minamoto dying the same night can be viewed as more than coincidence by the right eyes."

"The eyes of Masaki," Yoshio said. "Does he hold that much influence here?"

"He holds influence everywhere. The bodies of the ninja still lay in the street. They have made a fortunate cover for us."

"But not so fortunate for Shigeo."

"No, I suppose not," Amaya said. "But can you say he did not deserve it, making his uncle suffer so?"

"I cannot say he did not deserve it," Yoshio said, "but my task is not to consider whether the men who have been slain deserved death or not. My task is Ryunosuke."

"Hmn." Amaya worked her way into Yoshio's neck. "Why did Furukawa send you on this errand?"

"My place is not to ask why," Yoshio said.

"You have said that before," Amaya said. "Why do you think he sent you?"

Yoshio sighed. "It is not my place to guess, either."

Amaya leaned over Yoshio's shoulder and whispered. "It *is* your place with me, my dearest friend."

Yoshio nodded. "For you alone, my lady. I am certain that this Ryunosuke slew somebody dear to the heart of Furukawa. He has not spoken of it, but I know the sound of grief in a man's voice, and the distant look in the eye of a man who has lost much."

"Yes, but who?"

"A person whose relationship to him he could not allow being revealed. Either an illegitimate child or a lover."

"And what does your heart say, Yoshi?"

"That it was his lover," Yoshio said. He turned to look into Amaya's eyes. "Probably a courtesan or peasant girl that he could not reveal his affections for because of his social standing and wife."

Amaya pursed her lips and looked away in thought for a moment. "What makes you think that?"

"If he had lost a child, he would have been far more grief-stricken. I would know."

"I am sorry that you do know," Amaya said.

"He would have sent far more than a single, aging samurai to fetch a head."

"He sent his most powerful weapon," Amaya said. "A most precious gift, though now I regret the trade of letting you pursue this madman."

END OF ACT II

Interlude: Stupor

HE ROCKED back and forth on his haunches his back pushing against the soft wall of rotting bamboo, made soft by the same rain the fed it over the summer season. It was missing. The... other was missing. Or silent and waiting. It didn't feel right. Outside, hovering in the void of memory was his name. His once name. His mortal name.

Nomohito. No, that is the name of the sword. It's old name. But it was close, so close.

Ryunosuke, that is all that matters now. He shivered in the wind on the high hill, and reached for the handle of his katana, feeling fiery warmth return to his limbs. The heat came slower than normal, for the sword was satiated; it sat like a gibbon in a meat-fueled stupor. A sickly trickle of ice ran down his back to his toes, and returned to settle in the back of his neck. The leaves of the bamboo were suddenly intensely itchy, and the nameless mortal remnant, the vessel of Ryunosuke, felt a sudden need to run, and leave his steel behind.

He could not. Would not. He remembered part of the mind of Muramasa, dividing itself slowly from the demon, running in fear. *No, I am not like that. Heat and pain is the price of greatness, and the old swordsmith is a fool for thinking he could have it otherwise. I should turn and take his head.* He shook his head. Those memories were too dear, too close to himself. He would let the smith find his own ends.

He stood up, leaning against the weakened stalks of bamboo, which creaked under his weight. He looked down over rich, multi-roofed estates on the rippling water of Osaka Bay, bright in the morning sun, and remembered his name.

This name will serve us well. The heat was returning. *It has its own merits, but true greatness shall be in the action with it – the slaughter to come.* Ryunosuke looked at his blood-smeared garments. They would have to be replaced with fine silks. Easy enough.

Sharp teeth smiled at the red dawn.

ACT III

Chapter 10: Red Sand

AMAYA WALKED slowly and carefully beside Yoshio, aware of her posture and the position of her hands in the long, hanging sleeves of her two-toned kimono. The roofed walkway, paved with a simple pattern of flat cobles as it passed through carefully arranged gardens, gave both of them a view of the estate to which Masaki had invited them. Faded grey roof tiles, the sign of an old and respected dwelling, hung above open well-furnished foyers that would be useful only by the sea. The servant that greeted them at the door hurried a few steps ahead, and then waited at an intersection, unwilling to break etiquette by requesting a faster pace.

"How am I supposed to walk?" Yoshio whispered, seeing Amaya's careful and silent steps. His new umanori pants hung in stiff pleats to his feet, obscuring his large steps with small movements.

"Just the way you do, my husband," Amaya said in a hushed voice. "It is the job of women to look formal, regal, and beautiful, and the job of men to admire them."

"I am concerned I will not act correctly."

"Act like yourself. You are a samurai." She looked over at him with a smile. "When it comes to nobles Kuramasa Kuro is more the standard than the exception."

"Furukawa and Lord Asano are the rule, then," Yoshio said.

"They are," Amaya said. "Now, just be yourself, and we will be quite a fitting couple."

They approached the servant. He was a bent old man wearing grey, who forced a smile as they approached then gestured for them to proceed down another walkway. Yoshio and Amaya followed him between two buildings spanned with a roof and down a set of steps. They approached a shaded platform, slightly uplifted from the surrounding pavement. The servant gestured to it. A young samurai stood nearby, his hand on the hilt of his katana. Yoshio eyed him as they walked past into the shaded kiosk.

A middle-aged man wearing a grey and white striped hakama below a decorated kimono turned about as they entered. He looked at the pair and raised his eyebrows. Wrinkles set themselves into his face as he looked at Yoshio and frowned.

"Masaki-sama," Amaya said. "It is good to see you again." She bowed, and Yoshio followed her with the same motion. "This is my husband, Taoka Yoshio."

"I am glad you could make it, Amaya-san" Masaki said, turning away. He looked out past the shaded kiosk to a wide empty clearing, boxed in by walkways and sitting areas roofed with similar, though clearly much newer, tiles. "And Yoshio-san. I feared you might have to decline, given the commotion of last night." He gestured for her to sit on a pillow that lay on the ground, which was itself covered with a white cloth.

"So you have heard." Amaya set herself down, placing her shins on the pillow and taking a feminine pose. She faced herself slightly toward her host and looked out to the empty courtyard to her left. A small tree grew in each corner, but otherwise, it was bare, the floor covered with sand bleached nearly to white. "I suppose the embarrassment of my family's tragedy has not remained discreet."

Yoshio looked around as he sat down to Amaya's right. Several groups of people ambled by on the walkways or sat below the running roof, almost all of them samurai. A few rich merchants, likely guests of the estate, sat in a sunny corner with their wives fanning them. Amaya's eyes remained pointed down, away from Masaki.

Once they were seated, Masaki sat himself down, facing inward at an angle matching Amaya's; facing them, yet facing the courtyard as well. "You do not need to fear shame here, Amaya-san," he said. "It is not your shame. Undoubtedly Daiki's nephew had fallen in with a bad lot."

"Undoubtedly," Amaya said. "Still, it is not the sort of thing you expect when you are invited to tea under the lucky moon."

"Hmn," Masaki said. "What makes it lucky, eh? I've heard of no special mark. No ceremonies or words from a priest."

"It was Daiki's belief, Masaki-sama," Amaya said. "You would have to ask him."

"Perhaps I shall," Masaki said. "He is a distant relative of mine as well."

"I don't think you shall get very far," Yoshio said. "If his manner last night was any indication." Yoshio met

Masaki's hard eyes, and for a tense moment, they stared, neither of them moving or looking away. Amaya continued to stare downward.

"No?" Masaki said.

Yoshio shook his head. "He will only speak of the killer."

"Perhaps I should wish to speak to him of the killer," Masaki said. "I could send a retainer to deal with him." He looked to Amaya. "For the sake of honor."

"It is unnecessary," Amaya said. "For a long time, we have been wary of Shigeo. It seems now it was for good reason."

"Are you sure?" Masaki continued, "I have just hired a new, highly skilled retainer from the Kenjutsu-no-Toda Dojo. He is the finest I have seen."

Yoshio's heart leapt at the thought of a fellow student of Toda Yuu, but he held himself back and remained still, remarking calmly, "A good find."

"Good to see Amaya-san has not married a man without his martial wits."

Yoshio nodded slightly. "Yes, but I must admit a touch of arrogance. I myself attained the rank of master there, and spent many winters there training as well as teaching. With my experience, I can attest to the high standards of Toda Yuu outside of my ego. I may have even given your retainer his initial rounds with the blade. Where is he? I have important news that may interest him."

"You were an instructor there, eh?" Masaki said. He cast an eye to Amaya. "I did not imagine that Lady Asano Amaya would be married to one of her father's retainers."

"Actually, Masaki-sama," Amaya said, "Yoshio was a retainer from a neighboring lord. He has earned the respect of my father through his honorable deeds, and more importantly, we had a great deal of respect for each other. Marriage was a good arrangement for us both."

"So it was your choice," Masaki said. "I wish you would have announced it. I would have sent a fitting gift to your father."

"It was recent," Amaya said. "We wanted to wait until after my travels to announce it formally. For you, though, consider my apologies for introducing you without a formal announcement first."

"It is no matter, Amaya-san," Masaki said. "As long as you would not be offended by a delay in your gift. What has brought you to Osaka? Wait-" Masaki leaned forward as a hush settled over the other people in attendance, virtually all of them sitting under the low roof that surrounded the courtyard. "The entertainment is about to begin."

"What is it?" Amaya said, suspecting an answer she did not want as she looked out on the white sands.

A man stood in the center of the courtyard, wearing a loose-fitting kimono and hakama, with a single sword in his belt. He was young, not more than twenty, and thin.

"That is Tamotsu, a retainer for the Hosokawa clan," Masaki whispered. "Soon Hayato, from my own clan, will enter."

"A duel?" Amaya said.

"Yes!" Masaki hissed. "These two have insulted the house of the other. Myself and Hosokawa Ichiro have agreed that this duel will seek the peace between us."

"Are there stakes?" Yoshio asked.

"Of sorts," Masaki said quietly. "In Kyoto, there was a disagreement about my father's daughter and who she should marry."

Amaya's face remained placid, but subtly she reached over and grasped Yoshio's hand tightly. Yoshio turned to look at first, but then held his head straight, seeing that Masaki's attention was bent to the center of the courtyard.

Another man stepped out who wore white and black. Tucked into a thin black belt striped with white was a plain wakizashi next to a decorated katana, with florid engraving and a carved handle. He looked to be thirty, with deep-set eyes that held a perpetual frown above them. Amaya squeezed Yoshio's hand.

The two men bowed to each other, then turned and bowed to opposite ends of the rectangular courtyard. The older of the two, Hayato, bowed to Masaki, while the younger, Tamotsu, bowed to an aged samurai who reclined on the other side in a similar kiosk. An old man wearing letters on his belt stepped to the center. He turned around and looked at the people on the edges.

"So honor demands. Do not interfere until blood or quarter," he said loudly. He looked to Masaki, who nodded, then to the man on the other side, who did the same.

Tense silence filled the assembly as each man dropped to a bent knee stance while holding the handles of their katana in their right hand and their saya in their left.

"An ideal contest," Masaki said.

"Hardly," Yoshio said. "What I see is a student facing a master. This will not end well for the boy."

"How so?" Masaki said.

"The youth holds his weight wrong, for one," Yoshio said. "He leans back. He focuses on the hands of the older, not the feet, and so will be late to defend against a strike."

"You learned this approach from Toda?"

"You can learn this from any teacher, Masaki-sama. This boy is green. I bet he has not yet trained five winters."

"Five winters is green to you?" Masaki looked to Yoshio, who met his gaze for a moment.

"In the art of kenjutsu, it takes time to achieve great skill," Yoshio said. He sighed. "This is a terrible waste of a warrior's potential."

"I suppose it bodes well for me, then," Masaki said.

In the center, movement broke the long, tense standoff, but the strike came not from the older and more experienced Hayato, but from the younger Tamotsu, who drew his sword in a well-practiced cut. Hayato leapt back from the blow, causing Tamotsu to cut the air in an audible whistle. In the dodge, Hayato drew his own sword and stepped back. The two men inched closer with their swords facing each other.

"Interesting," Masaki said, leaning forward. "This fight is already longer than you predicted, eh?"

"Your fighter is very experienced," Yoshio said, "and has not underestimated his opponent at all. He knows it is better to enter combat with a drawn sword, and so threw away his unsheathing cut to ready himself for a battle."

Hayato stepped left, then right, then struck with a fast overhead cut. Tamotsu raised his sword and deflected the cut to his left, then stepped forward with the counter. Before his cut could come, Hayato put his open left hand on the boy's chest and shoved him backward. Tamotsu fell onto his back and then quickly rolled the side, dodging another strike from Hayato. The boy pushed himself quickly back up onto his feet.

Masaki cast an eye to Yoshio. "Dirty?"

Yoshio looked back at him. "All is fair in war, they say. Kenjutsu is an art of war; once the fight begins there are no techniques more honorable than others."

Masaki nodded. "You are a true warrior, Yoshio-san. I can see why Amaya would choose you, knowing you as such."

Yoshio frowned and looked at Amaya, whose dark eyes trembled, focused almost blankly on the scene.

In the courtyard, Tamotsu pressed an attack, slashing first from the side and then changing directions to cut upward. Hayato parried both strikes as he stepped back. Tamotsu cut with a long sweep from over his shoulder. Hayato dodged. Tamotsu followed with an upward cut, which Hayato parried and then stepped in for a killing thrust. At the last moment, Tamotsu leaned to his right and Hayato's katana pierced his clothes. They tore and ripped as the boy fell to the ground and rolled away. Hayato flung his sword in the air, sending bits of cloth to the ground.

Tamotsu stood, panting. A red spot grew on his tattered kimono.

"Blood. It is over, then," Yoshio said. He realized Amaya was gripping his hand very hard. He could feel her heart racing. "Not so much of a waste."

The old sensei stepped back in and looked to each side. Masaki shook his head, first to the sensei, then to Hayato.

"There is no need to go further, lord," Yoshio said. "Please, let this end honorably and with the life of a servant to the country intact."

Tamotsu held up his sword again, ready for a final confrontation.

"But there is need, Yoshio-san," Masaki said. "There is. Things must be as they truly are." He smiled sickly. "In this duel as in all other truths. For you see, I know that Amaya knows you to be a great warrior,"

He paused as swords crossed again, Tamotsu desperately deflecting a rain of blows from Hayato on his weakened side. Tomotsu held on and dodged left, leaving Hayato swiping at air. The older man took a wide step with his missed attack and seemed to lose balance. Tomotsu took the opportunity and thrust his katana at Hayato, his full weight behind it in a killing thrust.

"But, Yoshio, does Amaya know the truth? That your wife sleeps with a fat Daimyo in Kyoto?"

Yoshio wanted desperately to meet the eyes of Masaki, but in the arena, the killing blow was at hand. Tamotsu's well-timed and well-placed thrust flew through nothing but air. Hayato's lost balance was but a feint, and he shifted around the youth's sword as if water, grabbing Tamotsu's arms and pulling him forward. Hayato's own katana, which he held in his right hand and which lay against his left leg, was suddenly propelled up with a lift of his thigh. The edge bit into Tamotsu's mid-section.

The youth grunted with the impact. Hayato stepped forward, drawing the entire length of his katana through Tamotsu's abdomen. Blood sprayed, then poured onto the ground as a flood. Tamotsu collapsed in agony.

"End it!" Yoshio shouted.

Hayato looked over at him and met his eyes, then stepped to Tamotsu and cut off the boy's head, ending his suffering. He shook the blood from his sword and returned it to its saya, looked to Masaki, and then bowed.

Yoshio followed Amaya down the narrow walkway on their way out of the estate. They walked quickly, not affording the servant the opportunity to stop and look back to them as before. Masaki had cast an ill-looking face as he looked at her half-finished tea, but had accepted her excuse that she needed to return to check on Minamoto Daiki.

They turned a corner, and in the entryway to the large house, Yoshio caught a glimpse of Shiba Hayato, the duelist from earlier. He sat drinking tea and speaking softly to another Samurai who leaned on one foot against the doorframe of the open room. He wore a traveling hat, as half of his body was in the sun, but Yoshio could see his profile. It looked familiar.

The man looked over and Yoshio recognized him as a student from his old Dojo, now grown to the stature of a man. His eyes were deep-set and dark, and his cheeks and chin were clean-shaven. His nose was like a hook above a mouth that was little more than a thin line. They stared at each other for a long moment, each a wall of unmoving stark calm.

"Amaya, that is Masaki's new retainer," Yoshio said, grabbing Amaya's elbow to stop her. "Udono Noburu was his name. I taught him his first forms."

"Please, Yoshi, let's leave," Amaya said, pulling on him.

"I must speak to him of Ryunosuke," Yoshio said. "He might know if it was a lie that our Sensei Tadashi was killed."

"Another time," Amaya said emphatically. She tugged hard on his sleeve. "Yoshi, please."

"Of course, my lady." Yoshio broke his stare with Noburu and hurried on with Amaya. He looked back once to see Noburu speaking to Hayato, though the speech was too quiet to comprehend behind the clattering of sandals and shuffling of feet.

Amaya nodded to the low bow of the servant as they exited the gates of the estate. She held her parasol low to her face against the noon sun as they turned from the large wooden doors of the entrance and set off back to the inn.

The slope of the lane dropped sharply, giving a view of Osaka Bay, filled with vessels of many sizes and shapes going about their daily business. A large trading ship sat at the far dock, which dwarfed the fishing vessels that rowed about it in quest for their daily catch. The sun glittered on the choppy water. Yoshio shaded his eyes and took it in.

"A beautiful scene," he said.

Amaya continued to walk quietly beside him, only her chin visible to the much taller samurai. He frowned to himself as they turned the corner. It was a long lane, shaded by many maples that had grown over garden walls and out of yards, and a cool, but not cold, breeze blew through it.

"Osaka is quite a city," Yoshio said, trying to fill the silence and distract from the brutality of the duel. "I had not expected something quite so scenic. Its pattern is like guessing the growth of an old tree, twisting this way and-"

Yoshio started as Amaya grabbed his arm and pulled him to a nearby wall. She dropped her parasol on the ground. It rolled away into a nearby puddle, staining its pink paper a dirty rose. Yoshio held his arms up in surprise as Amaya wrapped her own around his waist. She pulled him tightly, her hands balled up into fists that pressed into the small of his back.

"Amaya?" Yoshio said. He looked down to her carefully laid hair, and buried in his kimono, he felt her trembling breath. She pulled her head away a moment and he heard her give a wavering gasp. He could not see her eyes, but moisture dotted her cheeks and nose. He realized she was crying – weeping even, sobbing as silently as she could while she buried her head into his chest.

Yoshio relaxed his shoulders and rested his hands on her back. The silent sobs began to gain voice as she continued, her body shuddering.

"Yoshio," She said through trembling lips. "Oh, Yoshio."

"What is wrong?" Yoshio said, looking out at the vacant street. He breathed. "I mean, it will be… I would not have chosen for you to witness that."

"I'm so sorry, Yoshi," she said. "My dear, dear Yoshi. I can't stop crying. Why?" Her voice wailed into the now dampening cloth.

Yoshio's mind reeled with wonder, and he searched for words. "I am the one who is sorry," Yoshio said. "I should…" He felt his mind fall to a useless moment in the haze of blood, and regretted thinking of it even as he gave it voice, "I should have explained about my wife before now, it was just…" He sighed again.

"No, Yoshio, it's not that," Amaya said.

"I know."

"Please, just wait with me here a moment." Yoshio looked down to see Amaya, her eyes red and her cheeks running with tears looking back up at him. "Thank you, Yoshi," she said again, and pressed her cheek against him. "For stopping here for me. It seems I could walk no further." She looked down the path as a breeze picked up, causing late blossoms and loose leaves to fall down to the dark cobbles in front of them.

"I am yours, lady Amaya," Yoshio said, and laid his chin on the top of her head. He wrapped his arms around her tightly, and she picked up her arms and relaxed her tight fists.

Amaya laid her open palms against him. "It *is* a beautiful scene." Silent tears streamed down her face.

Muramasa's head hung between his knees as he sat on the steps of the inn. His hair blew in the wind, obscuring a long, tortured face. A cold bottle of sake, still nearly full, leaned against his hip.

"Back to drinking already?"

Sengo Muramasa picked his head up and flinched at the low sun. He shaded his eyes and saw the image of Yoshio come into focus. He was resting with his foot on the step, leaning on his knee. His right hand, as always, rested on the hilt of his katana. Amaya stood beside him, looking a bit more weathered than he was used to seeing. She shaded her eyes with her hand.

"It's always helped before," Muramasa said. "But I couldn't get more than two sips in without feeling sick to my stomach. I came out here for some fresh air."

"How long ago was that?" Amaya asked. "We watched you here for some time."

Muramasa shook his head in confusion. "I don't know. Is the sun rising or setting?"

"Setting," Yoshio said.

"Then I have been here a long time, but not so long as to have lost the day and the night," Muramasa said. He uncorked the brown bottle and smelled it. He made a face and slammed the cork back on.

"Do you usually black out?" Amaya said.

"I used to, but not like this," Muramasa said. He pushed himself up on a nearby wooden pillar, then bent over stiffly and retrieved the rice wine. "It would happen every so often, back before. You know, when the demon was in me. I would lose it, like blacking out drunk," he looked to Amaya with heavy eyes, "if you've ever known what *that* is like. I would wake up, with a foggy memory, but of terrible things." He shook his head. "Let's go inside, eh? I'm cold."

Yoshio nodded and followed him through the open door of the inn, still quiet in the afternoon. Amaya followed closely as Muramasa stumbled down a stair to a basement, his preferred room. An old man sat at the end of the dank hallway, holding a broom. He nodded to them as they stepped into a room lit only by a small window. Muramasa lowered himself onto the futons. Amaya seated herself at a simple pad below the window, a warped rectangle of light in front of her on the floor.

Yoshio slid the door closed and stood with his arms folded.

Muramasa looked up at him. "It's getting worse. I haven't been this close to it in a long time."

"You still share something with the demon?" Yoshio said.

Muramasa nodded. "I must. I thought I had banished him to the sword, but threads remain, however subtle. It is not, however, at all like it was. Before."

"How was it before?"

"Wonderful. Satisfying," Muramasa said. Yoshio raised an eyebrow to him. "The demon, when he was with me – when he *was* me – was like a raging fire. From time to time he would boil over, and his thirst would need to be quenched. It was, of course, a thirst always for the first drink he had been given as a man, the poor youth that I – we – murdered in Masumune's shop. Ever after he hungered for blood. He still does." Muramasa looked up at Yoshio, then turned to his head to look at Amaya on the other side. "But when he takes it now it doesn't feel good to me anymore."

"Hmn. What was it like?" Yoshio said.

"Like sex," Muramasa said. "You are a raging fire, then quenched by a rain that brings peace. This is the way of fire kami, their life, their chi. It is like a man's hunger for a woman, only with the fire kami it was much stronger. Of course, like the act I compare it too; the hunger grew and changed over time. Became a hunger for new and exciting things. Twisted things."

"It is not always this way with the time of rain," Yoshio said, using Muramasa's metaphor. "What is right can be satisfying for one's whole life."

"I bet you've only ever slept with one woman," Muramasa said, and chuckled. Yoshio frowned at him. "No, I envy you. For most, know that perversion always grows with the pursuit of pleasure."

"Wise words," Yoshio said.

Muramasa nodded. "So it was with the demon, and with murder. The depravity of it…" Muramasa shook his head. "The things I did… I should be damned. I *am* damned. I must at least try to make amends. I must end it."

"You do not want the sword for your own gain?" Yoshio said.

"No, Yoshio-san. I want that sword destroyed forever, but I fear I lack the skill the unmake it. Perhaps I should throw it in the sea."

"You made it, master Muramasa," Amaya said. "Surely you can unmake it."

"If I could have destroyed it, I would have in the years that I kept it," Muramasa said. "Hmn," he looked away, distant. "That's mostly true. Part of me also fears the unmaking of it, now that I am near again, for if our life forces are still joined, it may mean my death."

"I will destroy it," Yoshio said. "If I can."

"How did you make it?" Amaya said. "Perhaps there is a clue in the making."

Muramasa nodded. "I mentioned black-outs. As my time with the demon wore on, the hunger grew, but there was also a dividing. A tear in consciousness, small at first, started to present itself. When I started losing control and full consciousness during my murderous rampages, I began to understand that a part of my mind was my own again, or at least different from the demon, even if I can never be truly myself again. These lucid moments, which were like sudden sobriety in a field of drunken haze, I noticed were coming after the black-outs. Slowly, over the course of months and eventually years, I began to search for a way to undo what I had done to myself."

"Seppuku," Yoshio said, "would have saved many lives."

"Yoshio, now is not the time," Amaya said.

"He's right," Muramasa said, looking to Amaya. "I told myself I didn't want to free the demon and unleash him on the world, but if I had killed myself it probably would have ended there. Perhaps I am a coward. No matter." Muramasa shrugged. "Eventually I found a traveling Shinto priest who had some expertise in driving away lingering kami. He spoke of a way of trapping water kami in a blessed bottle, by luring them there with a promise of a return to the sea, which they ever seek. It got me thinking.

"I labored for many months in the making of a sword. This blade was made without the assistance of the demon, for I worked on it only after I blacked out. It was a long and arduous process, but somehow I knew that the only way to catch the demon, who had now become a demon of blood, was with steel. When the blade was complete, I had a priest help me inscribe upon it a prayer of binding blood, and bless it.

"I waited for the demon to grow hungry, very hungry indeed. As I felt myself blacking out, I plunged the blade into my leg. Blood poured out onto it, and like the water kami, the promise of blood drew the demon out of me and trapped him in the sword. It was horribly painful, but I could feel the heat of desire leave with my blood. I did not black out, but nearly so. My apprentice found me lying in a pool of my own blood and thought it was an accident."

"Yet part of the demon remains?" Yoshio said.

"I had not fully departed from control of my body when I cut myself, and so he had not fully gained his hold either. He spoke to me from the sword, a sick, hissing whisper, for many years."

"I know this voice," Yoshio said.

"It was maddening and tempting, but I kept the sword hidden and refused to part with it, even exploring ways to destroy it, until Ashikaga Keiji stole the blade from me."

"Yes," Amaya said, "and somebody stole the blade from him."

"Perhaps," Muramasa said. "But the blade has a will of its own. I think it rejected Keiji. He said it was cursed."

"Not to offend you, master smith," Yoshio said, "but it is said that all your blades thirst for blood, and that once drawn, they must drink it before returning to their saya. If not…" Yoshio shrugged.

"Yes true," Muramasa said. "I made many, many great blades with the strength of the kami. Undoubtedly his thirst has passed into some of them. This one is much more so. I believe Keiji drew the sword with nobody around, and it took his own blood."

Yoshio nodded. "It is too bad we cannot discover the truth now."

"Discover Ryunosuke, and I think you will have the truth," Muramasa said.

Yoshio nodded again, and looked out the window at the west light. "You should get some rest." He bent down and picked up the sake bottle. "I'm sorry to ask this of you, but I need you to be free of drink in case Ryunosuke hungers again. I need to you to dream, so that I may find him and end your suffering."

"Just as well," Muramasa said. "That stuff is making me feel sick and isn't working the way it used to at all." He rubbed his forehead.

Yoshio looked at Amaya, who stood back up and joined him at the door. Muramasa lay down on the futons and groaned. Yoshio and Amaya walked out to an empty hallway.

"Do you believe him?" Amaya said.

"What else is there?" Yoshio said. "His dreams at least lead us to the killer last night."

"They also led us into an ambush with assassins."

"I will keep you safe."

"I know."

Chapter 11: The Swordsman's Tale

Yoshio checked the windows, the halls, and the corners of the room. For the first time since they had begun travelling together, Amaya joined him. She looked around in the hallway and leaned out the window to see the roof.

"You're worrying me, Amaya," Yoshio said as he watched Amaya lean out the window, holding tight to the eave.

"I won't fall," she said.

"It's not that. Never have you showed concern for your own safety."

Amaya pulled herself back inside the room. "Our situation has grown more perilous. Please do not think of my caution as a negative judgment on your abilities."

"I do not," Yoshio said. He walked to the window and looked out to the roof above.

"But apparently you have judgments about *my* abilities," Amaya said.

"You have not been trained as a retainer," Yoshio said as he surveyed the area around the window. "You have not been trained in the recognizing the signs of assassins."

"Do you really think of me as a soft and cultivated courtesan, Yoshi? Even after all this? My sword has drawn blood just like yours."

Yoshio looked in again. "It has. I'm sorry, Amaya. I make... assumptions." He pulled himself back inside and set his feet on the floor.

"It's fine, Yoshi," Amaya said. "I am used to it."

Yoshio frowned and looked away. "That does not excuse me," Yoshio said. "I have seen your skill firsthand. You have guarded my back. I should trust you."

"You should, but you do not," Amaya said.

"I am responsible for you," Yoshio said, stepping closer to Amaya, who turned away and began fishing in her things, piled against the futons. "If something was to happen, and I had not checked with my own eyes..."

Amaya sighed as she withdrew her katana. "I understand." She pulled the hilt away from the saya and looked at the start of the well-oiled edge.

"You know, you have never told me where you learned your arts," Yoshio said.

"I have had several painting instructors," Amaya said. "The finest was a Buddhist monk from-"

"That was not what I meant," Yoshio said.

She pushed the sword back into its scabbard and looked back at him with half a smile drawn on her face. "I know."

"Or where you got your sword," Yoshio said.

Amaya turned to him and held out her katana. Yoshio looked at her curiously for a moment, and then he bowed and took the blade.

"I have travelled much since I was a girl," Amaya said. "Undoubtedly I was able to witness a few duels. You pick up things."

Yoshio pulled the sword halfway out of its scabbard and admired the hamon, the grain-like forge line on the blade. The edge flashed as he turned it. "Even now you keep yourself a mystery," he said. He slid the blade back home and leaned it against the wall. "Very well. We shall play the question game we did once."

"Oh, Yoshi," Amaya said. "I'm sorry. I get into old habits."

"No, my lady, I do owe you answers before I deserve questions. I never told you what happened to my wife, and because of that I allowed Masaki to make a fool of me and test my temper."

"Really, Yoshi, you don't have to." Amaya stepped closer.

"We are friends, yes?"

"Yes, of course."

"Then I need not keep secrets from a friend." Yoshio sighed. "Tadashi, my old sensei and... friend, told me once about friends - that they should never the fear the shame of failure in front of one another, for success comes only through learning, and learning is an exercise in failure. In the dojo, Tadashi saw me fail many, many times. For him, I was a good student, and later, though everyone there saw me as swordmaster, he saw me as Taoka Yoshio, his friend. You are my friend, Amaya, and I have held a dark shame from you. I am sorry."

"So we all have them," Amaya said. "It is through politeness we forget that."

Yoshio nodded. "Everyone assumes my wife is dead, because I say I no longer have a wife, or a son."

"A son?" Amaya said. She sat down on a pad near the window, and gestured for Yoshio to join.

"Yes," Yoshio said. He set himself down facing Amaya in a slightly impolite pose, with his arms wrapped around crossed shins. "My wife is not dead, however, and neither is my son."

"Divorce?"

Yoshio nodded. "Of a sort. I told you I used to instruct at the Toda School. I never told you of how I came to be there, or how I came to the service of Furukawa."

"What does that have to do with your wife?" Amaya pulled open her satchel and began removing her ink tools.

"Everything. It is where I gained everything, and lost everything." Yoshio stared at his feet for a moment. "I do not follow the teachings of Buddha, but it seems a good tale for his lessons. Desire, loss, peace..." He sighed. "I am samurai by birth, but that does not mean I was wealthy. When I was young, my father was a poor retainer for an even poorer vassal of the Shiba clan. We claimed noble birth, the descendant of a petty daimyo buried in the footnotes of history beneath the greatness of generals, but my family lived long without a gain in fief. In time we came to serve others more than manage our own tiny and deserted plot. I was the fourth son among four sons, and all my brothers came to age before I could grow a beard.

"My father, lacking resources and inheritance to give me, sent me to the west, to the Kenjutsu-no-Toda School hidden in the Hida Mountains out of which run the many tributaries to the Kurobe River. I journeyed by myself to get there, with very little money to buy food, even begging for shelter at times. I had a letter of heritage, which my father assumed would be enough to gain me entrance."

"It was not, then," Amaya said. She worked her ink stick into a stone and began to coat a brush.

"No," Yoshio said. "The dojo was supported through the patronage of the Yamada clan, of whom Furukawa acts as regent in the far west, as well as the Kanamori clan in the valley to the west. The sons and retainers were routinely sent there for training, but I belonged only to the Shiba clan, however distantly. I had to spend two days climbing to get to the steps of the compound, only to be turned away by a disciple."

"Surely your talent would have earned you a place," Amaya said. She traced a few short strokes on her scroll.

"Talent?" Yoshio said, smiling to himself. "I had none. Skill – that is the true value in a swordsman – is created through practice and hard work. It does not appear from nowhere, and I had never trained before in my life, so I had none."

"How old were you?"

"I was a few months shy of my fourteenth birthday."

"And you travelled so far by yourself?"

"I thought nothing of it at the time," Yoshio said. "My father had also not given me a sword."

"That *would* make learning kenjutsu difficult," Amaya said.

"I assumed they would give me one. Can you believe that?" Yoshio said, and chuckled. "Luck turned my way, though. Having nowhere else to go but home, and having come so far, I camped outside the walls of the dojo compound. I had eaten all my rice, and so I ate what I could of the land. I even caught rabbits with a trap I had learned to make from a peasant along the way, and ate their meat in secret.

"I stayed on the mountain for ten days. On the tenth night, when I had made up my mind to make my way home and accept my place as a failure, the dojo's master, Toda Yuu, silently sat down across from me at the little campfire. So quiet was he that I did not even notice him until I looked up and saw his bearded face looking back at me through the flames. I actually thought it was a ghost, but did I not react because I had become rigid with fear. He had expected to frighten me, and by chance, he was impressed.

"He told me my persistence had made an impression on him. He viewed my camping outside the walls as such, rather than what it was – lack of conviction – and said that he would agree to let me into the dojo even though I was not of the patron clans. So, by luck and stupidity, I gained entrance to the dojo."

"Tell me more about the dojo, and the mountains," Amaya said. She rolled a brush in her fingers.

"Most places of martial instruction are little more than empty rooms in crowded cities. Toda's school, however, was a thing to behold. It was like an estate house, but with an open wooden floor on the inside. There were two adjoining buildings, hemming in an open courtyard used for practice. One of these buildings housed Toda Yuu and the senior instructors and students, and the other was a dormitory for younger and less advanced students. The buildings were surrounded by a wall, and between the buildings and the wall were many implements of practice. The gates, which were not as strong as what you are likely accustomed to, opened on either side to the countryside."

"Go on," Amaya said. Yoshio noticed the black brush strokes coalescing into rough images.

"Below the compound was some terraced land, where a small amount of food was grown during the warmer months. Above it was a pine forest where we would exercise, climbing the rocks and carrying water up and down hills. There was a bathhouse too, reaching over a small pond in the valley that contained the dojo. When I was first afforded the opportunity to bathe I was a bit remiss, for the attendants who lived there were both old women."

"Why did that disappoint you?" Amaya said.

"The imaginings of a fourteen-year-old; namely of beautiful, and of course available, consorts."

"Of course," Amaya said with a chuckle.

"I began my training immediately, and seeing no other option to further myself, I put all my effort into it. I found that I had started later than many of the other students, though I kept up with beginning motions, being permitted to borrow a wooden practice sword. Unfortunately, after a few weeks, I found out that I was to be put out again, as my father had failed to provide the customary donation that was the fee for attendance. He had sent a messenger with a letter of credit, but Yuu would not accept it. Credit from distant lords does not buy rice.

"I did not want to be sent away from the other students in shame. I begged Yuu to let me stay, and after much pleading, he relented, but with a condition. I would have to pay my own way. I immediately began thinking of ways to help the dojo.

"I offered to mop and sweep floors, but Yuu pointed out that he makes students do that anyway.

"I offered to heat the bathwater and carry it from the well, but Yuu pointed out that he, again, made students do that anyway.

"I offered to be an assassin, which just made Yuu laugh. He told me, 'If you can grow food for yourself and one other student, while not losing focus on your studies, I will let you remain. However, you will have to get a sword on your own.'

"I agreed. From then on both my nights and days were filled. By day I studied my craft, doing my best to excel and often overcoming my peers despite my lack of background. By night I grew rice and vegetables near the pond, tending my crop by the light of the moon and by lantern when the moon was new or hidden."

Amaya smiled at Yoshio and said, "I see where your disposition comes from, though I wonder when you had any time to meditate."

"That came later. I spent more than a year training at the Toda School. After that, I earned enough respect that Yuu, who I later came to know by his familiar name Tadashi, lent me a blunt practice sword. It was intended to be blunt, a training weapon for a novice, but I sharpened it slowly by hand, putting on enough edge to train with it. I admit I cut my fingers a few times early on doing draw cuts in my haste for a true blade. It was after another two years of such training that I met the woman who would become my wife."

"Ah, the other woman," Amaya said.

Yoshio raised an eyebrow. "Yes, well, I met her by chance. I was traveling down the mountain, beside a small river, with a few buckets of excess rice to sell in town."

"So you became not only a good swordsman, but a good farmer as well."

"I was a driven farmer, if not terribly good at it. I still needed my own sword, and slowly I was saving my coin to buy one. I remember that the rice was very heavy to carry, but when I unloaded it from my bo[26] and felt the silver hit my hand my shoulders would immediately forget their pain. That was what my mind was focused on when I met her.

"She called down to me from a horse, mistaking me for a local peasant. She was well dressed in a summer kimono, and her hair was neatly arranged. She looked to be my age. I remember thinking at the time that she was exceedingly beautiful."

"At the time?" Amaya said. "Did you revise your opinion later?"

"I was a naïve young man, who had spent the better part of four years seeing only boys, men, and the occasional peasant in town. I had not seen a samurai woman like this before. Also," Yoshio smiled, "I have seen things since which put her beauty into proper perspective."

[26] A stick, like a quarterstaff, placed on the shoulders and used to carry heavy objects.

"That's subtle, Yoshio, but you should know that I prefer good poems and true words to hints and slight suggestions."

"Ha! Of course," Yoshio said. "But yes, Hiromi – that was her name – was beautiful, though nothing compared to you."

"Better." Amaya drew a few more strokes on her scroll. Yoshio thought he could make out a mountain, and some trees.

Yoshio nodded. "She also had with her a very ugly retainer who scowled at me the entire time, wanting to spit on me like an eta, I'm sure."

"Scowls are an important feature in a bodyguard," Amaya said. She brought into being a small house in her painting, then looked up at a scowling Yoshio.

Yoshio consciously relaxed his eyebrows. Amaya laughed.

"I do my best," Yoshio said. "Hiromi was travelling to visit a relative of her mother, the wife of a samurai in the village, and had become lost in hills around the river. I offered to lead her there. I spoke to her along the way, much to the chagrin of the retainer, and pleased myself with being able to make her laugh a few times.

"It was then, travelling along the road under bright summer sun and without care, that I realized that her retainer frowned not because he hated me, but because he pitied me. Along that road, Hiromi's retainer betrayed her, and a group of samurai belonging to an enemy of her father, attacked while he stood by."

"Ah, Betrayal," Amaya said. "Is there anything more despicable among the ranks of the elite?"

Yoshio paused and looked at her. She seemed separate, a space apart, though she sat but a few feet away, as she stared at the scroll she had painted.

"There is nothing worse," Yoshio said. "For the elite daimyo or for the dirty eta, to betray trust is the most evil a man can do."

"What about a woman?" Amaya said. She brushed out a few more strokes on the house.

"Or a woman," Yoshio said. "What else is there to hold in this life but loyalty?"

"Are you loyal to me?" Amaya said.

"To my dying breath," Yoshio said. "Is there any doubt in your heart?"

"None, my dear Yoshi," Amaya said. She looked away a moment and smiled, then sighed. "I shall remember both of the things you have said."

"Still you speak in riddles, yet you call yourself my friend," Yoshio said.

"Only a friend would speak to me in such a way," Amaya said. "Is loyalty to friends the same as it is to one's master?"

"I think they should be the same."

"What if your loyalties conflicted?" Amaya said. "What if you were forced to choose between a friend and a master?"

Yoshio shook his head. "I have never considered this. Luckily, you are my friend *and* my master."

"Lucky for me, I'm sure. Lucky for you? That remains to be seen."

"It has been my privilege to travel with you, and to serve you. My life has been better for the experience, as bloody as it has been along the way."

"Mine too," Amaya said. "I don't know if I have been honest with somebody in a very long time." She drew a quick stroke on her painting and stopped to look at it. "No matter. Please, tell me of how you saved your wife from her attackers and won her heart."

"How do you know that is what happened?" Yoshio said.

"Because you are sitting here, talking to me."

Yoshio drew his lips trying not to smile. "True. There is not much suspense in the story of a fight when you already know who lives, eh? Well, I was surprised when the retainer pulled his horse away, and a group of men, perhaps five in all, descended from patches of bamboo and long grass on the slopes above us. By chance, that surprise made me flinch. I twisted away. First one bucket of rice, then the other, fell off of the bo that I used to carry them. They fell on the ground, scattering my crop in the mud.

"I did not take time to lament my loss, however. I was a trained warrior, even if inexperienced, and I knew I had to act. I slid under Hiromi's horse, readying myself to fight with my quarterstaff, and hoping to spook the horse in the process. The steed was scared, but not so much to flee and take Hiromi to safety. Instead, it ran downhill toward the riverbank, with the young woman unable to control it. It also left me surrounded by five very intimidating armed men, though they were certainly not samurai."

"Good odds for you," Amaya said.

"Yes, but I was not a master of the quarterstaff, like the Islanders or a wandering monk. I had studied the art of the sword. Still, I understood the basics, and put my weapon to work as best I could against the attackers. For all my effort, I did little more than make splinters and keep the swordsmen at bay. I realized that two of them were making off toward Hiromi, and so I dashed away toward the river, ducking under a few sword strikes as I slid downhill.

"I arrived just in time to engage the two men. One of them I was able to heel-hook from behind and dispatch with a quick strike to the throat, but the other was more skilled. He had a legitimate sword; I had not even been afforded at that time to practice with a true sword, or against one. I was shocked when the blade cut into my quarterstaff, breaking off one end.

"Luck saved me again, as the second cut buried the blade into the old maple staff between my hands, but did not break it. It gave me enough friction to pull the swordsman toward myself, pulling him off balance and toppling him into the river. He scrambled up the other bank and disappeared. Hiromi screamed, and I realized the other three men, trailing the betrayer, had reached Hiromi and her frightened horse. I pulled away, and at that moment, my staff broke. I reached down to the first man I struck and retrieved his sword, which was an old and dull tachi.

"It was good enough to give the first two men pause, who stopped and took up a sloppy guard as I ran at them. I say sloppy because, even with but a few seasons of training behind me, I easily turned aside their attempts at parrying and blocking and cut each. They were ragged and ugly cuts to their arms and legs – the weapon I had taken from the bandit was far from a well-balanced katana, but they were deep enough to fell one man and send the other fleeing. Seeing the blood, the final bandit, a large and tattooed man who was more fat than muscle, turned to run as well. The betrayer cursed him and drew his own sword.

"That was the first real duel of my life, and it was against a retainer, both trained and experienced, and my weapon was neither ideal nor familiar. He had the high ground and I had the low."

"You can skip past the duel, if you like," Amaya said.

"I apologize. I forget that the ways of battle are not always interesting to women," Yoshio said.

"I have just had enough of them for the day," Amaya said.

"Yes, of course," Yoshio said. "The short version, then. Needless to say, even though I was at a disadvantage, I prevailed due to a little bit of luck, a little bit of karma, and a few well-practiced techniques."

"Thank you," Amaya said. She held up the scroll, covered with drying ink. It depicted a lake and a mountain, along with trees, and the corner of a house peeking through the cover.

"It looks like the dojo," Yoshio said. "Very much like it, especially in its spirit. Very beautiful."

"I'm glad you like it. I will set it aside for you."

Yoshio leaned forward. "It is odd to look back. I realize I trained for a life of war in a place that was very peaceful."

"Extremes are inspiring," Amaya said. "And peace is great for focus."

Yoshio nodded. "I should like to take up painting sometime."

"Why?"

"Because it is peace, this picture," Yoshio said. "It is a place of tranquility and clarity right here amid the chaos of Osaka, and the horrors of the last week."

"What about your meditation?" Amaya said.

"I have found little peace in my own mind of late," Yoshio said.

Amaya looked at her picture and frowned. "I understand. Classic art might be an excellent pursuit to add to your study of the martial arts. However, I think painting is not right for you."

"No?"

"I think poetry is your strong suit," Amaya said. She smiled at him. "Yes, you should stick to poetry."

Yoshio laughed and slapped his knee. "You know I am no poet, Amaya. I can barely string enough words together to order dinner."

"I look forward to seeing you prove yourself wrong, Yoshi," Amaya said. Yoshio frowned at her. "You are looking the part of a good retainer again. What happened after your fight?"

"I recovered what I could of my rice and Hiromi assisted me in bringing it back into town by carrying a bucket on her horse. I sold what I could, but did not get much for it. Hiromi offered to pay me the difference in thanks for helping her, but I of course refused. I returned to the Dojo soon after, but I saw Hiromi often for several months as I returned to town to sell my crops and she visited her aunt. We developed a fast friendship."

"Is that all? Friends?" Amaya said.

Yoshio cleared his throat. "Eventually she left and returned to her parents' house. I stayed in touch with Hiromi via courier, which was expensive to me, and when I completed my initial studies I was able to secure our marriage. Her father was very impressed by the conflict with the bandits, and so permitted his daughter to marry down."

"That's a good story," Amaya said. "Good, but missing the ending."

"The end of things was not as dramatic as the beginning, I think," Yoshio said. "While I trained at the dojo I was noticed by Lord Furukawa Kenta, who would come by to visit his third son and witness the martial teaching of Tadashi. He hired me as a retainer when my sensei awarded me my letters of mastery, and afforded me housing when I got married. This is when he lived in Toyama, acting as regent while his father and uncle resided in Kyoto, where they were in attendance to the shogun and the other daimyos, as well as the imperial court. This was before he came into his fief west of your father's lands. He was very gracious to me.

"Part of this grace was the way he allowed me to return each winter to Toda's Dojo, both to train and to teach alongside my mentor and friend. As the years went on this became more important, as Tadashi began to grow less nimble, though no less disciplined or skilled. This was in part to contribute to my training of his family in their young years, which I did happily."

"How did your wife endure the winter in the mountains?" Amaya said.

"We were not permitted to bring family to the dojo. Women, and especially children, are a terrible distraction and inhibit the discipline needed to focus and grow as a warrior. My wife endured such separation with grace in part, or so I thought at the time, because she could remain in Toyama with the comforts of home."

"Our outward grace may hide inner sickness," Amaya said. "The more I know of people, the more I understand that to be true."

Yoshio nodded. He looked out the window at the failing light. "Some winters ago, I came to know the truth by chance. Furukawa's son injured himself during practice, misusing a sharpened sword before he was ready to wield it. It was a severe wound, cutting his foot and an artery that bled profusely. The cut also became septic despite our best efforts. I made up my mind to bring the boy back to Furukawa Kenta, if for no other reason than a father deserves to see his dying son.

"I made the hard trek down the mountain in the snow, to the muddy banks of the river and eventually to the first village, where I was able to hire a skiff-man to take us down the Kurobe. From there I took the lad via a fishing boat to Toyama. His spirit was strong, and he lived through the journey even while burning with fever. When I took him to Furukawa, I fully expected him to ask for my life for failing his son in such a grievous manner, but instead, he refused the offer. Furukawa was calm and collected in the face of tragedy, a testament to his nobility. He said his peace to his son, and then enlisted the help of the finest doctors and shaman to heal the boy's wounds, if they could. He survived, fighting off the sepsis with medicine and rest, but was crippled because of the severity of the wound, which could not be healed by skill or the supposed magic of the shaman.

"It was during this that I returned home to find my house empty. After some investigation, I learned that my wife had left the house along with my son, but not the area. It was well known to our neighbors. Suspicion grew in my heart for the first time. I found her at the winter home of Yamada Nobuyuki, a powerful daimyo of whom I knew only a little, though she had known him through her father's family for years."

"Betrayal," Amaya said. She cast her eyes downward.

Yoshio nodded. "I would likely have never known if it were not for the maiming of Furukawa's son. Many things were aired that day. Furukawa would not permit me to avenge the betrayal, nor would he permit me to end my shame. The dojo had brought me blessings, but these were not true." He shook his head. "In many ways it was still a blessing, to know the hard truth. You know too that I had a son."

"Yes," Amaya said.

"He was adopted by the snake Nobuyuki a year later. It was actually a relief to me, for in my haze of self-doubt I came to suspect that he might not be mine. The trust was broken forever."

"It is more than the seed which makes a son," Amaya said. She touched Yoshio's leg lightly. "It is the lessons, the love, and the crafting of greatness, along with the child's living up to those lessons."

"Then my true sons are at the dojo," Yoshio said. "I am a fool."

"You are not a fool," Amaya said.

"I was a fool, Amaya. I was a fool to believe that I could have more than what karma had apportioned for me. I am a poor son. I am a retainer. My life is to fight and die. Hiromi's father did her a disservice by permitting our marriage."

"Hiromi is the real fool," Amaya said. "She must not have come from a very wealthy or powerful family to value comfort over virtue. One is fleeting and ever breaking, like a dry twig. The other is a living tree, always renewing no matter how many cuts you make to the sap."

Yoshio sighed. "So now you know the story of Taoka Yoshio. Now you can say you are my true friend, if I am not too pitiful to sit with you. The ranks of my friends have grown thin these days, and I cannot say there is benefit to it."

"Thank you, Yoshi," Amaya said. "You are not pitiful to sit with, and I value your confidence. I will give you mine as well, such as I can."

"I value it as well," Yoshio said.

Amaya cracked a smile. "Suddenly I'm hungry. Let's go downstairs and have some food, shall we?"

"You will force me to inspect the room again," Yoshio said.

"It's fine. It will go quickly because now I will help you." Amaya put her painting to the side to dry and stood up with Yoshio.

Chapter 12: A Challenge

Amaya sipped her tea gracefully. She did not slurp. Her hair, as it had been the day before, was neatly arranged so that part of it was wrapped on top of her head and the rest of it was hanging down past her shoulders, a few stray strands blowing about in the light breeze. Her eyes flitted over the table, to the dishes of freshly cooked fish and steaming hot rice. A young woman put a plate of vegetables next to the other two, and exchanged the teakettle for a fresh one. Amaya picked up her chopsticks and began making a serving of the meal on her small dining plate. She smelled the fresh food and smiled. Her eyes closed lightly. She looked up at Yoshio.

"Does it look as good to you as it does to me?" she said. Yoshio tore his eyes away from hers and looked down to the well-made food.

"It does look good," he said. "But it smells even better." He shoveled some rice onto his plate and placed a few of the strips of fish next to it. "The growth of my appreciation for good food on this journey is one thing for which I have never expressed proper gratitude"

"I seem to remember a very simple retainer from some months ago," Amaya said. "A man who would eat rice raw as well as steamed, and would leave the bones of the fish only because he found them difficult to chew. And now that I know you have a taste for rabbit." She smiled and took a bite.

"Has it been that long?" Yoshio said. "And rabbit..." He shrugged. "So I do have a taste for rodents. Regardless, I did not have a proper appreciation for good cooking before. So, thank you for the many meals you have bought me."

"You are most welcome." Amaya nodded and ate a piece of fish. "We must remember what a luxury it is to eat fish so often."

"I remember it," Yoshio said. "For a time I could only eat what I could grow. That's why I only leave the bones." He looked behind Amaya and frowned.

"What is it?" Amaya said, not turning to look.

"Muramasa has found us," Yoshio said. He watched the old swordsmith grunt as he pushed past a server on his way to the open patio, a hand on his ornate katana's hilt.

"Perhaps he chose to dine at the same place as us," Amaya said.

"With all of Osaka to choose? Not likely," Yoshio said.

"You seem a little upset," Amaya said. "Do you dislike him?"

"Not as such," Yoshio said, "He's an excellent second sword in a fight, much better than most warriors, actually, but this is a formal establishment. He is not even samurai."

"It's one of his best features," Amaya said. "I am very glad your actions do not match your words, Taoka Yoshio."

Yoshio puzzled over the statement a moment while Muramasa lowered himself down to their table.

"You found us," Yoshio said.

"Easy enough," Muramasa said.

"I trust you are feeling better," Amaya said.

"I am," Muramasa said. "I haven't had any dreams, though."

"Both good and bad news," Yoshio said. "I have a feeling Ryunosuke is not done in Osaka."

"Nor I," Muramasa said. "I can feel him now in the waking world, not just in the dreams. It is like a long droning. I don't like it." He looked up and narrowed his eyes. "There are two men across the street watching us."

"Yes, I know," Amaya said. "They belong to Masaki."

Yoshio turned his head subtly, as if to look at a passing tea server, and saw from the corner of his vision two samurai in white and grey, sitting under an eave.

"You missed them, eh?" Muramasa said. "Here I thought you had a knack for observation."

"My back was to them," Yoshio said. "I do not have eyes on the back of my head."

"I'm sure if you did, you would have both pairs on your 'wife.'" Muramasa said. He picked up a pair of chopsticks and took a piece of fish from the center platter, then plopped it into his mouth.

"What is that supposed to mean?"

"It just means you play your part very well, of course," Muramasa said with a full mouth. He chuckled quietly to himself.

"You should learn to hold your tongue," Yoshio said softly, then took a long sip of tea.

"Or what? You'll cut it out of me?" Muramasa said. "I've heard that before." He tilted his head and smiled a sick smile. His teeth looked sharp and bright.

"Yes, I will," Yoshio said, leaning forward. His hand went to his katana, which he had not placed to the side when entering the restaurant.

"Cool your temper, Yoshi," Amaya said. "Now is not the time."

Yoshio broke his stare with Muramasa, who still smiled strangely. "My apologies, Amaya."

"None necessary," Amaya said.

"They are necessary. I should not let my heart make me speak so," Yoshio said.

"Your temper is part of who you are, my dear Yoshi." Amaya took a sip of tea. "I do not resent you for it. I expect it. In fact, I count on it, like your unwavering bushido."

Yoshio grumbled for a moment. Muramasa filled his plate up and ate hungrily, letting food fall from his mouth as it fell from his chopsticks.

"Do not let your mood stop you from tasting a good meal," Amaya said. "Enjoy the moment. It will never come again."

Yoshio sighed and ate. After a few silent moments, he spoke. "What shall we do about those men?"

"I expected Masaki to have men following us," Amaya said. "I believe we have been shadowed since our arrival. We are lucky these two are so brazen about it. It will make things easier."

"What things?" Yoshio said.

Amaya sipped her tea. She spoke quietly. "I have some business to attend to in Osaka. Business I would prefer if Masaki were not privy too. I need you to distract those men. Not just them, but I would like for you to distract Masaki as well. I want his focus to be on my husband, not me."

"How shall I do this?" Yoshio said.

"Be yourself, of course," Amaya said.

"I don't understand," Yoshio said.

"I want you to go over there and pick a fight," she said.

"Now that sounds like a bit of fun," Muramasa said.

"I do not start fights," Yoshio said.

"Neither do I, but always finish them!" Muramasa said. "And only half of that is a lie." He drained his teacup, slurping up the last drops.

Yoshio frowned at him.

"Do not worry," Amaya said. "This fight will be quite easy for you to start."

"I should not leave you by yourself. Have we not agreed to such?" Yoshio said.

"I will be fine, Yoshi. I will be safe in this, so long as I am not followed." Amaya looked into Yoshio's worried eyes. "Trust me, please."

Yoshio grumbled to himself, chewing his tongue. "Very well."

"Thank you," Amaya said. "Now enjoy your food, please. It was not cheap."

Yoshio nodded, and then continued eating. Soon the full plates began to look empty.

"I am satisfied," Amaya said. "Are you?" She looked to Yoshio, who nodded. Muramasa, his mouth still full, shrugged. "And so the day's business begins."

"I endeavor to serve you," Yoshio said. He stood up and checked the arrangement of his swords in his belt.

"Find me again where desire feigns false death," Amaya said. "At sunset."

"What does that me-" Yoshio paused as Muramasa stood up. "This does not concern you."

"No, but that doesn't mean I want to miss it, as much as I enjoy the company of your wife," Muramasa said, nodding toward Amaya.

Yoshio narrowed his eyes. "No. You are too unpredictable."

"That's part of what makes me great, you know," Muramasa said. "Besides, you said I was an excellent second sword back when you thought I was out of earshot."

Yoshio sighed. "Stand there." He nodded to a cloth-covered eave in front of the restaurant.

"As you wish, my dear Yoshi," Muramasa said.

Yoshio grunted, then walked around a short rail and into the street. Sengo Muramasa followed him. Yoshio looked back at him for a moment, scowling at the disobeying swordsmith. Muramasa smiled back and moved over to the door of the inn outside which the two samurai reclined. They took notice of Yoshio as he approached, and stood up, adjusting their own swords.

"Why are you following my wife and me?" Yoshio said to the closest samurai, a young man of about twenty-five years who wore his hair in a tight top knot.

The young man opened his mouth to speak, but shut it as the samurai next to him, a middle-aged man, put his palm in front of his chest.

"Who are you?" Yoshio said.

"I do not have to tell you," the older of the two said.

"You do not," Yoshio said, "but it is customary between samurai."

"Customary, but not required," the man said.

Yoshio felt himself grumble, unable to think of what he should say next. He filled the silence in a hurry. "The custom… is for your benefit, not mine," Yoshio said.

"I don't see how it is," the older said.

"Then to whom shall I send your swords after I cut you down?"

"Are you threatening me?" the older samurai said again. "Or challenging me to a duel?"

Yoshio thought about answering in the affirmative for a moment. *That is not right. I should not duel a man for so little,* he thought to himself. *But I suppose that is what I need to do.* "I am Taoka Yoshio. You insult my honor by stalking my wife. What is it you wish to see? Her breasts?"

"I see plenty," the younger man said.

"Don't answer him," the older samurai said to the younger.

"Are you own bedrooms so dry and empty that you must look into another's for satisfaction?" Yoshio said.

"I wonder if they look in with their dicks in their hands," Muramasa said from the side. Yoshio felt heat rising in his head, but saw the younger of the two samurai look over to Muramasa, anger on his face.

"I wonder too," Yoshio said. He looked at Muramasa, who leaned against the wall, his arms crossed. The swordsmith winked at Yoshio. "Satisfaction is ever fleeting for the lonely."

"You have a lot of nerve to suggest something like that," the younger man said. "Especially when you and your wife have two beds."

"So you *have* been watching us," Yoshio said, surprised to hear that he was picking at a truth. His hand tensed around the hilt of his katana. He thought of Amaya changing, and sitting in her simple, private robe. He thought about moments private only to himself. His arm felt as if it would draw the sword of its own accord.

"I told you to shut up," the older samurai said.

"How dare you," Yoshio said. He stepped up to the young man. "How dare you look upon my wife. Your family has raised a scoundrel, and your employer should bleed himself," he said, looking to the older of the two.

"Beware your words, old man," the younger samurai said. "Dusty joints should not go around hurling insults."

In a move both sudden and smooth, Yoshio pulled his left hand from his katana's saya and reached forward, pushing the young man's sword, which was already being drawn, back into its scabbard. At the same time, he struck the older of the pair in the throat with the edge of his right hand. The older samurai fell backward, releasing his sword and clutching his throat.

"Let's see how dusty they are," Yoshio said. He planted his left foot behind the young man and leaned forward as the man still struggled to free his sword from his belt. They toppled, the young man's saya striking the pavement and pushing the hilt forward and out of reach. Yoshio's knee was then on the man's throat. "Masaki takes too much pride in his warriors," he said, watching the young man struggling to breathe. "If his warriors cannot defend themselves from a simple throw, how shall they fare against my steel?"

Yoshio looked to his right and saw the older of the two standing up and attempting to draw his sword. He struck the young man in the temple with a closed fist, causing his eyes to roll back in their sockets, and then stood up to face the older man.

"I am Satomi Sora. I made a mistake in thinking you were nothing but a rich noble," the samurai said. He held his sword in a forward guard. "I will not make that mistake a second time."

"No, you will not," Yoshio said. Yoshio's steel flashed in the noon sun as his sword moved up, out of its scabbard, and into a strike. Sora quickly moved his sword to stop the cut, and the two blades rang out in terse notes at the contact. Yoshio stepped forward. Sparks jumped from the crossing of the swords as Yoshio pushed his edge toward the disk guard of Sora's katana. Sora pushed his hilt up above his shoulders, lessening Yoshio's leverage. He stepped backward, then stumbled.

Yoshio had kicked out with his left foot, and hooked behind Sora's knee. The samurai stumbled, holding his sword in an awkward guard above his head. Yoshio calmly turned his sword edge up and stabbed below Sora's guard. The point of the katana found its mark, and blood gushed from a deep wound in Sora's leg. The man screamed out in pain and collapsed to the ground. Yoshio kicked Sora's katana out of his hands. Sora reached down to his leg. Blood seeped from his fingers.

Yoshio hesitated with his sword, looking at the wounded man. Part of him wanted to end Sora, not out of mercy or the fulfilment of honor, but because he was furious. He felt himself gripping his sword over-tight, and became aware of his own heavy breathing. "I hope when you remember the day you were crippled you will bend your hate toward the dog Shiba Masaki, who was foolish enough to place you in front of Taoka Yoshio. If you live through this day, be sure to tell him who did this to you."

Yoshio stepped over the bleeding man, who was rolling and breathing in gasps. Muramasa was near the corner entrance to the inn, still leaning against the wall.

"You need a better sword, my friend," Muramasa said. "I heard its note. It was not beautiful."

"Friend?" Yoshio said. "Some help you were."

Muramasa shrugged. "You said I was too unpredictable."

"I expected you to help me unpredictably," Yoshio said.

"Well, I unpredictably wanted to just watch."

"And hurl out insults," Yoshio said.

"Your lady *did* ask you to pick a fight."

"That she did," Yoshio said. He looked over to the restaurant and the table where they had just dined. Amaya was gone. He walked quickly away from the inn, ignoring the passers-by that called to him and the hard breathing of Sora. He stepped to the corner and looked down the other street.

"Where did she say to find her?" Yoshio said, mostly to himself.

"Where desire meets false death," Muramasa said. "You know what that means?"

"No," Yoshio said. "But I have my own business to attend to until sunset."

"Masaki?" Muramasa said.

Yoshio nodded.

Yoshio walked briskly uphill, though his pace had slowed a few blocks from the inn where he had confronted the two samurai. The closer he got to Masaki's residence, the more of a fool he felt, even so much as to fear himself blushing. He had wounded two very unimportant men. The conflict and the insults hurled about on the street might invite whispers, but walking into the presence of Shiba Masaki with the same attitude could be much more serious. He was putting himself in danger that was of only nominal value to him, but he was also putting Amaya and her clan in danger, even if it was part of what she asked him to do. There was a reason duels were formal and well thought out, and it was to avoid the messiness of hasty challenges and swift retribution. Yoshio was a retainer, a warrior, and a samurai, but he was not a politician. He relied on Amaya, and before her Furukawa, to determine the fallout from his drawing of steel. He relied on them to tell him where to cut.

Still, as he walked up the hill, he felt compelled to go on. With Muramasa beside him, he felt, even more, the pierce of shame that would come from turning back. Other men – other samurai – could be convinced of the necessity of avoiding Masaki, but Muramasa would see and remark on the action as what it would truly appear to be, whether spoken to his face or not: cowardice. Yoshio began to feel sweat bursting out on his forehead. The breeze did not cool him.

"This is foolish," he grumbled.

"Of course it is," Muramasa said. He walked in an almost leisurely fashion beside Yoshio, his left hand hanging on the hilt of his katana. "But you're going to do it anyway."

Yoshio breathed audibly. "Lady Amaya has asked me to."

"That doesn't mean it's not foolish."

"Then why do you follow, if I'm such a fool?" Yoshio said.

Muramasa chuckled. "A better question is why I follow you despite your air of superiority."

"What air?"

"That attitude you have - that you're better than everyone because you wear two swords," Muramasa said.

Yoshio grumbled. He was samurai. That meant something, even if Muramasa could not understand. *Swordsmiths have a special place,* Yoshio thought, *but they are still not samurai.*

"It's your arrogance that I *should* be objecting to," Muramasa said.

Yoshio swallowed. "The life of a samurai, especially a retainer, cannot be filled with ego."

"I find it even odder," Muramasa went on, "That you act like such a high lord even with such shitty iron hanging from your belt."

"I thought I told you to watch your tongue," Yoshio said.

"I've seen better steel on horseshoes," Muramasa said, shaking his head. "Gods, if I had but a few weeks to spare and a fine patch of steel..."

"The steel does what I need it to; it cuts."

"It's a wonder that it does. I have seen the edge. It's more like a chisel than a blade. It should be an embarrassment to a man like you."

Yoshio stopped in the street. "Then why do you continue to walk beside me, if I should be so embarrassed? Why did you follow us to Osaka? Why are you not turning to the side now to drown yourself with rice wine like usual?"

Muramasa smiled. "Because I've seen you cut."

"You make no sense. You said it was a wonder my sword cut anything at all."

"I did. It's not that sword that cuts, Yoshi. It's the man that cuts." Muramasa looked away. "I need you to cut him." His eyes returned to Yoshio. "There is one piece of arrogance that you've earned, and that is what you do with steel." He shook the sword in his belt. "The truth is that I don't think I can finish what I started."

"I thought you said you always finish fights," Yoshio said.

Muramasa shook his head.

"Then why are you following me into this foolish one?" Yoshio said.

Muramasa thought for a moment. "I need to keep an eye on you. Even the best swordsman can be felled by a single arrow. Or an unexpected stab in the back."

"You expect one of these from Masaki?" Yoshio said.

"I expect both," Muramasa said. "And so do you, or you would not question my walking into the trap with you. You worry for the death of even a lowly craftsman, my much-divided friend."

Yoshio smiled. He looked up the hill and breathed deeply. "An arrow, perhaps. A stab in the back? Never."

Muramasa looked down to see Yoshio holding, almost casually, the hidden tanto the swordsmith kept buried in his hakama.

Shiba Masaki watched the sunset as he drank his evening tea. His viewing balcony looked out upon the low mountains behind Osaka, turning the wooded hills colors of orange and yellow even in the high summer. Far beyond those mountains lay Kyoto, the holy city, and the court of both the Shogun and the Emperor. A smile parted his lips.

Yoshio watched him from behind for a minute or two, taking in the view. The arrangement was very aesthetic, but also functional for the powerful daimyo.

"Ah, Taoka Yoshio," Masaki said without turning. "So nice of you to drop by and surprise me. Did you enjoy the duel?"

"Not so much as you, Masaki-san," Yoshio said.

"That is unfortunate," Masaki said. "Perhaps I should set up another that would please you more."

"Only if it is you in the ring," Yoshio said. "You are a snake, Shiba Masaki."

Masaki turned back to look at Yoshio. His eyes flashed as the setting sun cut through his corneas. "Very well. I challenge *you* to a duel, Taoka Yoshio."

Yoshio raised his eyebrow. "Just like that?" He looked to the old servant that had led him in. The man, with wide eyes, bowed.

"Of course," Masaki said. "I am not afraid of you, Taoka Yoshio. You may be a good swordsman, even so good as to fetch the hand of Asano Amaya, but you are no Daimyo. You have not the slightest clue how to fight a battle as a nobleman."

"That is true," Yoshio said. "I do not know how to weave the stories and words that turn man against man, settle fiefs and raise peerage. But none of that matters in a duel, does it?"

"Ah, but it does," Masaki said. "For how shall you win a duel when you are dead?" A wide grin split his face, but his eyes remained fixed open wide. Yoshio stood still, meeting the stare with an empty and emotionless gaze. The grin slouched on Masaki's face.

"You were expecting the archer-assassin on the western rooftop to have killed me by now, I take it," Yoshio said. "I must apologize. Seeing him crouch with the setting sun to his back, I expected he was here to kill you, Masaki-san. I assumed you would not set an assassin on yourself, and so I took the liberty of dispatching him for you."

"You are a fool, Yoshio," Masaki said. "You think in such narrow terms."

"I do," Yoshio said. "I concern myself with one, very narrow term: Bushido."

A guttural, gargling noise sounded from the shadows at the rear of the balcony. A man fell down to his knees onto the wood floor, blood dripping from a sword point emerging from his chest. A long tanto fell from his hands and rattled on the floor. The sword withdrew, and the dark face of Muramasa slipped out of the sunlight and back into the shadow of an eave.

"I also had myself followed," Yoshio said. "Though it matters not; I would have cut him before he realized I had turned."

Masaki turned around and backed up toward the edge of the balcony, his bare feet kicking him away from the fallen assassin. Yoshio looked at him calmly.

"You should not have sent men to spy on my wife and me," Yoshio said. "I do not appreciate the breach of trust between us. If the gods favor you in our duel, the spirits shall be settled between us."

"Guards! Hayato! Come quickly!" Masaki shouted, breaking his paralysis.

"Would you have them bear witness to your treachery, Masaki-san?" Yoshio said. "It shall not remain quiet."

"I'll have you torn limb from limb!" Masaki said.

Yoshio turned his back to Masaki as footsteps echoed from beyond the stairs. Muramasa stepped out of the shadows, his sword gleaming in the sunset as if it were made of gold.

"Put your sword away," Yoshio said. Muramasa looked at him, puzzled. Yoshio met his eyes. "I mean it. Hayato will not kill us. We will leave peacefully."

"You're asking for a lot of trust," Muramasa said.

"I have seen this man kill," Yoshio said. "Blood teaches much. This man will let us leave with our challenge in peace."

Muramasa growled, then returned his sword to its scabbard with force.

"Thank you," Yoshio said.

Several men emerged from the stairs, panting. First among these was Hayato, the duelist Yoshio had watched several days previous, his sword already drawn. He stopped and stood still as he met the hard eyes of Yoshio, who stood relaxed, though his right hand still held his sword.

"What is the meaning of this?" he said, putting his sword up in a guard.

"I have insulted the name and honor of your lord, and he has seen fit to challenge me in a duel, with your servant as witness," Yoshio said. He looked over to the servant, whose eyes remained open wide as he pushed himself against a wall.

"Kill this man!" Masaki shouted from the edge of the balcony. Hayato flinched and took a step forward. More footsteps echoed from the ground level.

"As you can see, the master is furious with me," Yoshio said.

"Is this true, Taro?" Hayato said, looking to the old servant. The servant, frozen, nodded.

"I am not afraid to let karma be served through bushido," Yoshio said. "I will yield my privilege, as challenged, for the location of the duel, so long as we agree to use katana."

Hayato looked to Yoshio, then to Taro, and finally to Masaki. "Very well," he said. "I will let you leave, but only if you do one thing."

Yoshio raised his eyebrows.

"Acknowledge the right of regency among Daimyo," Hayato said.

Yoshio nodded. "It is Lord Masaki's prerogative to have another fight for him. And Lord Masaki's face."

Hayato lowered his sword. "Let them go."

"Kill him!" Masaki shouted again hoarsely.

"I will," Hayato said. Yoshio looked to Muramasa, who nodded.

Yoshio took a step forward when another group of samurai arrived at the stair landing. He paused to see Noburu, a student from his old dojo, at the forefront.

"It's fine," Hayato said. "Let them pass."

Yoshio looked to Noburu, who stared at him. "We should speak soon, Noburu-san. I have news from the north." Noburu silently nodded.

Yoshio took another step forward, but stopped when realized Muramasa was not beside him. He looked back to see the swordsmith, eyes wide open and trembling, staring at Noburu. He reached out a hand, then collapsed to his knees. Several samurai moved about, reaching for their swords.

"Gwa-ack!" Muramasa said, the attempt at words coming out to a gurgling hiss. He fell down to his hands and knees and began vomiting. A nearby samurai recoiled.

Yoshio looked back to Noburu. His eyes darted down to the handle of a katana, wrapped in black cloth, but with a protruding end, like a pommel from a Chinese sword. Behind the cloth, he could see two red lights pulse and flash to life. His breath stopped.

"Ryunosuke!" Yoshio cried and reached for his sword. It flashed out with lightning speed, but cut air as Noburu stepped backward gracefully. Instantly, a field of swords were drawn and trained on him, their points inching closer to his torso.

"I was about to let you leave in peace!" Hayato said, raising his katana.

"This man is a murderer," Yoshio said, frozen in place by the ring of death around him. "He must be put to death. Please, let me have him!"

Swords inched closer.

"Yoshi," Muramasa groaned. He coughed and fell onto his side.

Yoshio's heart pounded. He could feel Ryunosuke in the body of Noburu. It was like a sickly aura. He could feel him drawing in breath. He began to sweat.

*It is **I** who brought news, Taoka Yoshio,* a voice said in his head. Noburu's lips did not move. *It is I who brought death. This place, this soil, is a feast. You have almost become something to be devoured, my old friend.*

"Damn you!" Yoshio said.

A sword touched Yoshio's shoulder, pushing through his silk kimono, and breaking the skin. Yoshio came back to himself. He lowered his sword.

"Stop! I will leave in peace," Yoshio said. "But you must let me duel this man as regent for the honor of Shiba Masaki. All here as witness, Masaki's honor is bound in this man's blade. Let me have him instead!"

"Fine!" Masaki said. He now stood closer. "Let it be your death!" He looked to Noburu. "You will fight Taoka Yoshio. No quarter." Noburu nodded.

Yoshio sheathed his sword and bent down to Muramasa. He pulled him up by the shoulder and tottered trying to help him down the stairs. Swords remained drawn and fixed on the pair. Noburu watched him go, his face like something carved of wood.

Don't disappoint me, Yoshio.

Chapter 13: The Work of Words and Swords

THE STREETS OF OSAKA in the dusk were a deep grey; as the sun fled in the west, the colors of the lively city drained away. The buildings and streets formed a homogeneous stone chute through which men walked, and nobody had yet lit a lamp or fire in a window. Yoshio pulled Muramasa along by his arm. The swordsmith, who swayed this way and that as if drunk, coughed and sputtered, reaching out with his free hand toward walls and pillars that could provide him some support. The shuffling and vocalizations of the pair provided a distraction to the lines of people still walking the street, who would stop their conversations and stare, making a bubble of silence around the two men that matched the colorless streets.

"Just a moment," Muramasa said gruffly. He leaned up against a pillar and wiped his mouth. Yoshio scanned the surroundings.

"I do not see anyone following," Yoshio said. "Surprising."

"What's surprising about it?" Muramasa said. He stood up straight and looked at Yoshio, though he still held the pillar.

"Masaki intended to have me assassinated. Now he gives up the chase?"

"He's got you to agree to a duel with his best swordsman. I reckon he figures that's good enough." Muramasa coughed harshly. "Also, assassins are quite expensive, not that I expect you to know that. He doesn't have a bottomless purse to go hiring ninjas to kill the husbands of ex-lovers."

Yoshio nodded. "Ninjas are cowards anyway. Assassins would be very hesitant now to take on a job given what we did to Masaki's two men."

"I don't call that cowardly. I call that being a good businessman," Muramasa said. "It's hard to keep up the ninja trade if you're dead."

"He still may try. I do not feel safe just yet." Yoshio stopped his scanning of the streets and the trees beyond and looked at Muramasa. The swordsmith was pale, and bags had appeared under his eyes. "Is it passing?"

"Slowly, yes," Muramasa said. "I was not prepared for the onslaught of the demon's will and the penetration of my thoughts by his. I'm feeling better now, though. The demon's attention is elsewhere."

"Where?"

"Away from here," Muramasa said. He nodded west. "That way. He can... see, for lack of a better word, something that interests him in the hills. Someone, rather. It is fading, thankfully."

"Pity. I would value greatly your ability to see through the demon's eyes."

"No, you would not," Muramasa said. "To see and feel what he does as a mere man is overwhelming. It is torture. It is hell. And I see now that I am utterly helpless to stop it, which makes the torture worse." Muramasa pushed off the pillar and breathed deeply. "You knew him?"

"Udono Noburu. He was a student of mine, once," Yoshio said. "I taught him form and discipline in the Toda dojo. I showed him how to cut and how to guard. I thought he was a friend."

"Trust me when I say that he is no longer your friend," Muramasa said. "Like I was no longer Muramasa when I was with the demon. I imagine it is much worse for Noburu than I. He is a vessel of the demon now, and likely a terrible one, given his teacher."

"I'm not sure if that is an insult or a compliment," Yoshio said.

"I *do* enjoy insulting you," Muramasa said, his pale lips parting into a smile, "But it is more a statement of skill. A sword, however empowering, cannot wield itself." Muramasa shook his head. "Oh, how I wish the blade had remained with Ashikaga Keiji. A bloodthirsty dolt would be so much easier to deal with."

"I wish for that too. Hmn," Yoshio said. He frowned and looked down the long, straight path. Light shone in a window a few houses down.

"What is it?"

"I stopped here with Amaya the other day. It looks much different in the dusk."

"Where are we going to find her?" Muramasa said. "'Where desire feigns false death?'"

"Always she speaks circumspect to the point," Yoshio said.

"She figured someone was listening." Muramasa smiled. "At least she figured if they were listening they were stupider than you, which is to say she thought them either senile or retarded."

Yoshio frowned as Muramasa chuckled.

"I told you I like to insult you," Muramasa said. "Ah, a laugh is good. Very good indeed."

Yoshio stepped away and began swiftly walking down the street. Muramasa jogged to catch up.

"Come on, don't tell me you can't take a word or two of jest," Muramasa said.

"I know where Amaya is waiting," Yoshio said.

Small, dim lantern lights broadcast the presence of monks from beyond the oversized eaves. Even outside, a flame or two showed itself in wait of the moonrise. As Yoshio and Muramasa walked beneath the great west gate, a monk, bald and wearing loose robes that appeared to be colorless, passed them, bowing low. Yoshio returned it with a nod.

They stepped out into the wide and empty courtyard between the freestanding gate and the buildings of the inner garden[27] of sacred buildings. The pagoda showed itself behind the encircling wall of the sanctum as a shadow on the dark blue sky.

"I understand now," Muramasa said. "Clever of her." They approached another, smaller gate.

"Welcome to Shitenno-ji." Yoshio looked in the shadows of the wall to see a man standing straight, nearly invisible in the shadows. "Rare is the night visitor. What is your business?"

"How long have you been standing there?" Muramasa said.

"How long have you been making swords, master Muramasa?"

Sengo gave a puzzled look to Yoshio. "Why are you standing there, then?"

"You have an odd perspective to ask that question, eh?" the monk said.

"How so?" Muramasa said. "It's a bit odd to just stand around, don't you think?"

"I don't walk into your shop and ask you why you light your forge the way you do, do I?"

"But you *do* ask us why we visit a temple," Muramasa said.

"The temple is not your home, but the forge is, yes?" the monk said.

"Please," Yoshio said, holding up his hand. "As to why we are here." He thought for a moment. He thought about the way Amaya had given him the riddle. "In the night I find the greatest beauty and peace. However, I also find that I have failed to excel at the footrace. I am late."

"I see," the monk said. "I find the most beauty when the moon rises."

"As do I," Yoshio said. Yoshio struggled to find the words that would say just enough. "Because it gives light to that which is truly beautiful."

"I like that," the monk said. He chuckled. "I will think of that tomorrow, when the sun draws my sweat. Which do I prefer? All things have their time."

"I sought the light of sunset for beauty," Yoshio said.

The monk laughed again. "Oh, you are looking for Amaya. Why didn't you just say so?" Yoshio looked at Muramasa, who shrugged. "I thought we were having a conversation about the moon. She is over by the Kodo, the lecture hall, working at her art."

"You know Amaya?" Yoshio said.

"Of course," the monk said. "She has not attended in some time, but she was a frequent visitor when she was younger. We studied the art of ink painting together, though I believe she has developed more talent than me in that regard. I am Kei."

Yoshio bowed. "Pleased to meet you." Yoshio looked through the smaller gate at the buildings in the inner courtyard. A few lamps were being hung. "Which one is the Kodo?"

"Of course, let me show you," the monk said. "I forget sometimes that my home is not the home of others."

"No, you really don't," Muramasa said. Kei laughed.

They followed the monk through a small gate and into a large rectangular walled courtyard. Two buildings stood in the center: a large sloping roofed building with open doors revealing a sea of lit candles, and a tall pagoda with five sloping roofs of similar size. They walked past each of these to a low building with a tremendous tiled roof that adjoined with the sanctum walls. The doors, or what could be called doors in that place, were paper-thin and enclosed the entire front of the building, leaving an opening at both ends. A cool breeze blew through.

[27] The halls that usually compose a Japanese Buddhist temple.

Yoshio and Muramasa followed Kei up a few steps onto a raised wooden floor. The interior room of the building was open, with a few pillars holding up the weight of the roof. Four candles were perched on a stand near the eastern part of the large south-facing edifice, casting light upon a long scroll clipped to an easel. A brush traced over light lines, drawing images into more clarity. Dark hair slid over shoulders as Amaya turned her head to regard Yoshio, a smile on her face.

"I was beginning to think you had not solved my riddle," Amaya said, turning herself so she sat slightly facing them. "But of course I knew you would."

"It seemed an odd thing," Yoshio said as he stepped toward her, "for you to call false that which you seem to revere."

"Not so odd when you dig into the Buddhist teachings," Amaya said. "We all have failings."

"Speak for yourself," Kei said with a smile. He nodded to Amaya. "I'm off to stand around some more."

"It was good to see you, Kei," Amaya said. "Though I think painting would be a better use of your time."

"You wouldn't say that if you could properly remember my work," Kei said as he walked off.

Yoshio sat down and looked at the painting, which was an image of the temple grounds, filled with detail. He was not an art expert, but he could not discern any errant strokes, which were typical in most painting. "I apologize for my tardiness," Yoshio said. "It was Masaki that I met at sunset, I'm afraid."

"Not like you to delay," Amaya said, "but I assume you did so for good reason."

"I had to be thorough," Yoshio said.

"He also had to haul my shamefully sick self out of Masaki's house," Muramasa said. "After, of course, we made a fool of him."

Amaya smiled at Muramasa. "Good, though there is nothing shameful about falling ill."

Yoshio touched Amaya's leg. He looked into her eyes. "Ryunosuke. I know who he is now. Masaki has hired him as a retainer."

"Then why are you here?" Amaya said. "Why are you not taking his head right now?"

"I have agreed to allow him to duel as regent for Masaki," Yoshio said. "Moreover, I could not attack him with all of Masaki's men present and survive."

"I am glad you did not sacrifice yourself," Amaya said. "Then the duel shall prove good for both of us. I had hoped for a public dispatching of Masaki, knowing his pride, but embarrassment will do for now."

"How did you know I would challenge Masaki to a duel?" Yoshio said.

"How did I know you would solve my riddle? I *know* you, Yoshi." Amaya looked at her painting and adding a single black stroke to it. "There. What do you think?"

Yoshio looked over the detailed painting of the temple sanctum. The roof tiles stood out dark in the candlelight, and the pillars had a shading to them that made them seem very prominent. "Of course, it is brilliant," he said.

"What do you really think?" Amaya said.

"The technique looks wonderful. The detail is astounding."

Amaya gave Yoshio a questioning look.

Yoshio sighed. "I like best your paintings of people and nature. This is still very beautiful."

"I can't decide if you are a novice or a master." Yoshio looked to his left to see an old monk shuffling along with a cloth bag on his shoulder. "On the one hand, you are concerned with technique; on the other, technique is irrelevant to pleasing you."

"Well, when a man wants a sword, he wants it just so. He doesn't care about the hamon or the hilt if I make a blade too short," Muramasa said.

The monk bowed. "Hmn. A practical artist."

"That I am," Muramasa said, bowing back. "Thank you for greeting me as such."

"Hmn. Politeness from Muramasa," Yoshio said. "Is this man a sorcerer?"

"This is my old teacher, Iwao," Amaya said, chuckling. "He gave me the chance to study here when I lived in Osaka."

Yoshio stood up and bowed slightly. "You have given the world a great talent."

"The world gave itself the talent," the old monk said. "I just put a brush in its hand." Iwao bent down and put his eyes, surrounded by wrinkles, close to the painting. "Your painting is good, but..." He moved his head around, looking at it from different angles. "It is full of anxiety. This temple should be a place of peace."

"Yes. Well, part of the painting is the search for peace," Amaya said, trying to find her words.

Iwao looked at her with a smile and shrugged. "Eh, the last few strokes are. Though most of the strokes are quite technically correct, I think this painting was more of a distraction from the present than a capture of it. And the search for peace goes on always."

"You know me too well, master Iwao," Amaya said.

"I am master of nobody and nothing," Iwao said. "But I am glad to know you well." He put his fingers up to the painting and felt it. "May I have this?"

"You said it was full of anxiety," Amaya said. "You said it wasn't peaceful and did not represent an expression of the moment. Unless my lessons have taught me wrong, I thought you valued such things."

"I do," Iwao said. "But I also value you. The painting reminds me of Asano Amaya. That is what I want it."

Amaya smiled slightly and nodded. "Then it is yours. I will try to send some better work along soon."

"I prefer this," the old monk said with a smile. "It is excellent, all things considered. An hour of work would have yielded me so much less detail if it were mine."

"An hour of work?" Yoshio said. "How long have you been here?"

Amaya smiled. "You didn't think I sent you on all those errands just so I could recline and think at a Buddhist temple, did you?"

"No, I suppose not," Yoshio said.

The moon had at last risen. It peeked out between the sea and a trailing edge of cloud cover, giving the damp street a bright sheen. The soft glow of lamps in windows reflected on the smooth stones as well, making the walkways seem bright with hues of silver and yellow. Light showers, more akin to mist than to rain, fell intermittently as Yoshio, Amaya, and Muramasa walked south, back toward the inn. In the business of the day, none of them had been able to fetch a hat or an umbrella.

Amaya had instead bought a cheap oilpaper wagasa[28] as they left the temple from a merchant who had placed a barrel of them outside his shop. She carried it above her head, protecting her delicate kimono. Spots of water worked their way through the poorly waxed item, which would lose its utility by the morning, becoming little more than torn paper and painted bamboo. Muramasa walked openly when it rained, not caring about his cloth or his wet hair. Yoshio, ever vigilant, searched the shadows with his eyes, his hand readied on his sword.

"When will the duel be?" Amaya said. She reached up and picked a droplet off the underside of the paper umbrella with her finger.

"I do not know as of yet," Yoshio said. "I presumed that Masaki would find me – as he has been able to do so and we remain in the same place – and present his terms."

"It's probably going to be at sunset on some significant day," Muramasa said. "You can find a holy rite virtually every day of the week if you talk to the right priest. There's always some kami to be honored."

"Sunset is often chosen by daimyo, especially during duels to the death, because it is symbolic," Yoshio said. "One man's life is drawing to a close. I personally would not choose sunset though, if given the option."

"Why is that?" Amaya said.

"The sun is in a bad place for a fair fight," Yoshio said. "One fighter will inevitably have the sun blinding him. If not directly, then at some other disadvantageous angle."

"Yes, but what if you are the man at an advantage?" Muramasa said.

"I will not be, in this duel," Yoshio said.

"Then you must prepare to face a demon while blind," Muramasa said. He cracked a smile "After our display today, I don't expect him to make things fair. Not that they would be fair at high noon. Ryunosuke, after all, has my sword."

"Hmn," Yoshio said. He scratched his chin with his free hand.

"This is where you usually proclaim that the skill is in the warrior, not the blade," Amaya said.

Yoshio looked at her. "True, but this sword is more than steel. I will be fighting a demon, and I must be prepared for that."

"I can lend you this," Muramasa said, pushing the hilt of his katana forward.

Yoshio shook his head. "I'm sure it is a fine blade, but it is not mine."

"I'll trade you," Muramasa said.

"No, you do not understand." Yoshio drew his sword and held it point out in front of him. "I have spent more than two decades with this sword in my hand. It is part of my body. Its weight and balance are as familiar as my own hand. The hilt was made for my fingers. The edge cuts and sticks the same each stroke. I cannot change

[28] A Japanese umbrella or parasol, made from paper and bamboo and oiled or waxed to make it impervious to the elements.

something so familiar before the greatest battle of my life." He swung the sword around and put it back in its saya.

Muramasa grunted. "I suppose I can understand. Tools need to be familiar to an artist."

"Indeed. Yoshio," Amaya said, shaking water droplets off of her umbrella. "When you are approached with a day to duel, regardless of what time of day it is, I need you to do your best to delay it, perhaps a week, maybe two."

"A week?" Yoshio said. "Why? We have here a chance at vanquishing Ryunosuke. The sooner, the better."

"Because I need to ensure that this duel is witnessed by more than Masaki and the smattering of other vassals that are here in Osaka," Amaya said.

"Move it to Kyoto, then," Muramasa said. He ran his hand along a wall in front of them. "Then you can have every damned daimyo in Japan in one place, and the shogun and the emperor to boot."

"That is not necessary," Amaya said. "Kyoto is coming to us."

"How is that?" Muramasa said, stopping to turn around. Yoshio raised his eyebrow.

"Ashikaga Yoshitane is on his way here," Amaya said.

"The shogun is coming here?" Muramasa said.

"How do you know this?" Yoshio said

"Because I invited him," Amaya said. "Before we left Izumo."

"You have been planning this," Yoshio said.

"I have," Amaya said. "Initially it was an invitation to the Tenjin[29] festival at mid-summer. Now, I think it will be to tend to the funeral arrangements of his son. Soon, however, it will be to strip the honor from Shiba Masaki, who he supported in succession only a few years ago."

Muramasa stopped. Yoshio and Amaya took a few extra steps forward, then turned back to look at him. "What is it?" Yoshio said.

"The vision of the demon," Muramasa said, shaking his head. "His vision was turned toward Kyoto. Could he be anticipating the Shogun?"

Yoshio nodded. "Undoubtedly. However, killing Yoshitane will be more difficult than killing an opium dealer or a well-fed Minamoto."

"So you are not worried for him?" Amaya said.

"I do not feel guilty for allowing my focus to fall on taking Ryunosuke's head, rather than defending another nobleman," Yoshio said.

"A week?" Muramasa said. "The demon thought the shogun to be very close, it seemed."

"I expect closer to two weeks," Amaya said. "Even if he is already on his way, politeness will dictate that he visit vassals and friends along the way. Tenjin festival is still nearly three weeks away. I anticipate him being early, but not that early. We will need to stall."

Yoshio grumbled.

"Please, Yoshi," Amaya began.

"Of course I will do it for you," Yoshio said, cutting her short. "But know that this is something I do for you that is actively against what I wish for myself."

"A bit of honesty. Not used to that with samurai," Muramasa said.

"Thank you, Yoshi," Amaya said. "I promise that I will do what I can to fulfil your wishes. I hope that the end of this affair will bring you the peace you seek."

Yoshio sighed. "Ever will I trust you, Amaya."

They turned a corner and walked through a long and winding street leading more westward, back toward the inn. The shadows deepened as the moon caught the tail of the lingering clouds, though the rain had ceased. As they approached what passed as their home in Osaka, the fires and candles of the central room broadcasting warm radiance to the wet street, they caught the ring of a biwa[30] and the wavering voice of a woman singing lines from a tale.

Muramasa stopped and cocked his head before the door. "I do not know this song."

Before Yoshio could question him, he stepped across the threshold. The central room, which normally had dividers in place to allow privacy for afternoon and evening diners, was wide open and filled with people. On a stage to the left of the door sat a young woman, holding a biwa and singing. The strings rang out clearly between lines as she drew her plectrum across them. Her eyes were closed.

"I think I shall listen for a bit," Muramasa said. He stared at the bard, his eyes trembling slightly.

Yoshio stepped away for a moment and paused as Amaya gripped his arm. He followed her eyes to see Hayato sitting at a table in a far corner. He met Yoshio's gaze and held up a teacup.

---

[29] The patron kami of wisdom and scholarship.

[30] A Japanese lute.

"Stay here," Yoshio said, and stepped past Amaya. He shuffled over to Hayato, Amaya close behind and ignoring his instructions.

"Yoshio-san," Hayato said as they approached. "To your health." He drained his teacup.

"If you do not wish to meet a worse fate than your two men this afternoon, I suggest you leave," Yoshio said.

"I suppose I cannot feign an appreciation for the arts," Hayato said, looking toward the bard. "Lord Shiba Masaki has tasked me with delivering his terms for the duel."

"He could have sent a servant or simple messenger," Yoshio said.

"I am a servant. Perhaps he suspected you would slay the messenger, or perhaps he thought that I would communicate his seriousness. I just do what I am told."

"What are the terms?" Yoshio said.

"Sunset, the day after tomorrow," Hayato said. "I have been told it is a pleasing time and day to Futsunushi[31]."

"He cannot," Amaya said. "It must be postponed."

"I appreciate your appreciation of your husband," Hayato said, "but that does not make for bushido."

"It is not merely my appreciation for my husband," Amaya said, "but a question of tradition, spirit, and honor. Not that my admiration for him matters; I expect him to be with me for many more years."

"Spirits?" Hayato said.

"We have come to pray for the spirit of Yoshio's father, whose patron kami resides here in Osaka," Amaya said. "We must make the necessary sacrifices and rituals to prepare the way for his spirit to return from the battlefield in the north. It will take us at least a week to make the preparations."

Hayato nodded. "As far as excuses, it might work. Masaki would not want to be seen insulting a local Kami." He leaned forward. "However, if I were you, I would use the time to leave this city, and I would never return. Noburu..." he trailed off and stared at the bottom of his teacup.

"I will attend this duel," Yoshio said. "Masaki can be sure of that."

Hayato looked up. "Then you must be victorious, Yoshio-san."

"You wish to see your master's honor rebuked?" Amaya said.

"I wish to see Noburu killed," Hayato said. "The way he acts is... not natural. He disturbs me, and I feel like whenever I am around him I will fall ill. Moreover, it has affected the mood of Masaki, who has been wont to put him in any duel he can arrange. He's made the daimyo more bloodthirsty than usual."

"Of course," Yoshio said, looking at Amaya. "It is a perfect arrangement for Ryu- Noburu," he corrected.

"Whatever the arrangement is," Hayato said, "it is perverting the mind of my master. He must be stopped."

"Then cut him down," Yoshio said.

"I cannot," Hayato said. "Not for reasons of honor – no, I would kill the man if I could – I have seen him cut, Yoshio-san. I have seen him wield that incredible sword of his. I do not stand a chance. I do not think you will fare any better."

"I taught him. I can defeat him."

"I shall pray you do," Hayato said, standing. He looked at Yoshio, then Amaya in the eyes. "Please, consider what I have said. If you leave Osaka, and this duel does not happen, I will likely not be far behind you."

"You would choose to be a ronin?" Yoshio said.

"I would rather be a monk than spend the rest of my undoubtedly short days around a man like Noburu."

"He was not always like that," Yoshio said. "I remember a fine young man once. Disciplined. Strong."

"He is strong, but he is not the man you knew," Hayato said.

"I know," Yoshio said.

Hayato bowed to Yoshio and Amaya, then hurried quickly out the front door.

"That was a good story," Yoshio said. He looked to see Muramasa sitting close to the bard, listening intently to her song. "With the kami and the ritual."

"We shall need to make it true," Amaya said. "I will find a shrine out of the way of the city where you can train."

"I have had little time to practice since we set out together."

"I want you to be well prepared to take your prize." Yoshio nodded as he listened closely to the words of the bard. "Muramasa seems far more interested than I would have expected."

"I know," Yoshio said. "But an artist, even an uncouth one, has the capacity to recognize good art."

---

[31] The patron kami of swords.

Amaya smiled at him. “Without knowing it, your ego has given me a great compliment.”

“I won’t apologize for it, then,” Yoshio said, returning the smile. He gestured to the empty side of the table left by Hayato. Amaya seated herself and reclined next to him while they watched the bard perform.

They listened at length and caught an understanding of what she was singing, verse after verse. It was a tale of two lovers, divided by war. The bard was on a verse describing how the woman disguised herself as an old, bearded monk to enter the war camp of her lover, and how she was discovered by accident when she misremembered the location of her lover’s tent. She was then held for ransom when she was discovered to be the daughter of the enemy daimyo.

“Why are her eyes closed?” Yoshio said.

“She is blind,” Amaya said. “It is a good living for one so afflicted.”

“How does she describe the scenes so well?”

“She has imagination, a much under-valued gift.”

The bard sang of how the man was stricken with grief over the fate of his lover when her father refused the ransom, understanding at last her motives. The young woman would be burned alive, but her lover risked everything to rescue her. In the escape, he was mortally wounded, though the woman was able to make her way to freedom and safety. In the last verse, the bard sang of how she fled to a monastery and bore a son, who in time grew into a great warrior that united the two warring clans against a common enemy.

“I like this tale,” Yoshio said, “though, like Sengo, I have not heard it before.”

"It is a good tale," Amaya said. She nodded and looked at Yoshio. "I don't like the ending."

“All the best stories are tragedies,” Yoshio said.

Amaya sighed. “Yes, but I don’t want a tragedy for my own story. There has been enough already.”

Yoshio nodded.

END OF ACT III

Interlude: Blood Drinker

HAYATO STOOD to the right of Shiba Masaki, who sat comfortably on a pad. Though they both were in the shade, Hayato's eyes were narrowed against the bright noon sun. The white sand of the courtyard, now almost strictly a dueling arena, glittered in a blinding sheet. The two figures in the center, their hands on their katana, stood out as if painted on canvass. Hayato looked down to see Masaki, his eyes open wide, nearly glazed over, as he focused on the two men. His mouth was slightly agape.

"Hako has told me you have cornered Asakura on the border with your nephew's fief," Hayato said.

"Yes, I have," Masaki said. His eyes did not leave the dueling ground.

"He will challenge you on it," Hayato said.

"I look forward to it," Masaki said.

"Another duel, then," Hayato said.

"Are you feeling jealous of Noburu?" Masaki said. "You understand I could not pass up hiring such a famous swordmaster, yes?"

"I would not expect you to, my lord."

"I will give you more chances to prove your skill in the future. If Noburu feels any match is beneath him…" Masaki leaned forward as one of the combatants drew his sword in a swift cut. The other stepped aside. It was Noburu, and his face, as always, was slack and without emotion.

"Like the boy?" Hayato said.

Masaki did not answer. Noburu dodged two more swings, his hand on the hilt of his sword. Then, he struck. Drawing so fast that his motion appeared as a blur, Noburu's strange sword flew forward toward his opponent. He stopped his stroke with his outstretched right arm, his blade frozen in air. The other man stood motionless for a few seconds, then collapsed. Blood flowed out from his body slowly onto the white sand. His dead eyes stared into the row of samurai on the side of the courtyard.

"How did he do that? I did not see a cut," Masaki said, leaning forward on his knees.

"He cut straight through the ribs and stopped the heart," Hayato said.

"Impressive, yes?"

"Most," Hayato said. Noburu turned and bowed to Masaki, who nodded back. The swordsman's mouth was peeled back in a sick smile, revealing teeth that were sharp and much too white. Hayato felt sweat burst on his brow as he met the duelist's eyes.

"How fortunate we are to have this tool," Masaki said. "He has brought much honor to the house."

Hayato held his tongue.

A scream broke the quiet that had settled into the dueling ground, as another samurai came running into the center, kicking up sand as he went. He held a katana above his head, and he cried out as if running into battle. Noburu turned to look at this new assailant, bringing his bloody katana back to a forward guard. He raised his arms, leveling the tip of the blade at the charging samurai.

The new samurai attacked, slashing forward with his katana. Noburu nimbly stepped to the side of each blow and ducked past him as he charged forward. The man tried to turn on his heels when he realized he had missed Noburu, but it was too late. Noburu slashed. Blood sprayed out in a wide arc, dampening the pure sand for several paces around. The body of the man continued to charge forward, but his head was missing. Finally realizing that it was without a master, the body fell to the ground, more blood pouring out, as if a bucket of red paint had been turned over. The head flipped high in the air, arcing blood. Noburu caught it by the hair as it fell.

"No!" A woman's voice cried out.

Noburu, who was holding the head of the assailant by the topknot, turned to look at her. He held up the head so it faced her. Hayato could see from the side the slack face of a familiar swordsman. Another man tried to silence the woman, who was crying hysterically.

"That was Hachisuka Eiji," Hayato said quietly to Masaki. "The duelist's brother. And a teacher, once." Hayato felt a rush of fear in his heart.

Noburu held his pose for a moment. Then, as the woman looked on in horror, covering the lower half of her face, he held it above himself and let the blood drip into his open maw. Red rivers stained his sharp teeth, and ran down to the folds of his kimono.

Hayato forced himself to swallow.

Noburu threw the head to the side and walked toward the exit of the courtyard. Cries sounded.

Masaki breathed deeply. "Oh, how I look forward to seeing Noburu destroy Amaya's foul husband," Masaki said, and smiled. "How she managed to marry a man without me knowing, or that she would dare to try, is a wonder to me. She will not forget this month's lessons."

"And after Noburu cuts this man down, what will you do?"

"Let Amaya live on in her shame."

"How long?"

"Do not second guess me, Hayato. That woman is a devil. I will punish her as long as it takes."

"My apologies, lord."

ACT IV

Chapter 14: The Shrine and the Smith

"I COULD ALMOST FORGET we were near the ocean," Yoshio said, pushing aside the overgrown leaves of a wild maple. The narrow path, suited only to foot travel, disappeared here and there with the incursion of grasses and ferns.

"If it were not for the breeze I might agree," Amaya said. She led the horse along behind her, their things stuffed into bags and laden on the back of the beast. The handle of her katana stuck out from the pack, the edge turned upward.

"I haven't seen our shrine yet, but judging by the ascent I think this will be quite a defensible position," Yoshio said.

"Always so practical," Amaya said. "Yes, I know it is your duty to be practical, Yoshi," Amaya said with a smile as Yoshio turned back to speak. "I appreciate it, as always. Can you not also appreciate the scenery?"

"I can," Yoshio said. "When I am able to see it. All I can see right now is overgrown shrubs and falling bamboo."

"I was been told that the view on the hillside is quite marvelous once we get to the shrine. It faces east, and you can see the Sakai docks through the opening of the trees."

"I was told once that if I bought a bundle of magic beans and planted them beside my field I would grow rice made of gold. I am still not a rich man."

Amaya laughed. "Oh my, Yoshi, do you realize what you have just done?"

Yoshio paused and looked back at her earnestly. "What? Have I offended you?"

"No, my dear," Amaya said. "You, I believe, have just made a joke."

"Hmn," Yoshio said. "I suppose I have, at that. Does that please you?"

"It delights me," Amaya said.

Yoshio smiled and continued up the path, which switched back along a steep hill. "Do you think Sengo will be able to find us up here?"

"I left him a note with directions with the innkeeper," Amaya said.

"Rats," Yoshio said.

"Do you dislike him?" Amaya said.

Yoshio tilted his head in thought. "It is hard to decide. I think he is a likable enough man, aside from the way he speaks all the time."

"So aside from his personality, he is likeable," Amaya said.

"Yes, very much so, actually," Yoshio said.

"That doesn't make any sense."

"Doesn't it?" Yoshio paused and looked back at Amaya.

"No, it doesn't," Amaya said.

"A man is two things: his words, and his actions. If he speaks of virtue but acts with vice, what good is he? If a man says he will do something and does not do it, he is worse than a coward. He is a liar. Actions are much more powerful than words."

"While I agree with you," Amaya said, touch her lips, "I do not think you and I are thinking of the same thing when it comes to the word 'likable.'"

"Well, do you like him?" Yoshio said.

"I find him refreshing, funny, and entertaining. So, yes, I do like him," Amaya said. Yoshio grumbled and walked on. Amaya chuckled, and he stopped again to look back at her. She raised her eyebrows. "Jealous, are we?"

"No."

Amaya smiled. "I like you more, of course," Amaya said.

"I do not aim to be liked," Yoshio said. "I would rather serve with honor than be well-liked."

"Now Yoshi, you are saying one thing and doing quite another, something you just spoke contemptuously about. Moreover, you have failed in your aims and your false dichotomy."

"Have I ever failed to act with honor for you, my lady?"

"Never. However you *have* failed in your attempt to fail to care about me liking you, and you have failed in your failing to not try to *make* me like you."

"What?" Yoshio said, scrunching his face in confusion.

Amaya smiled and looked away. "Don't mind me, I'm just trying to be subtle even though I need to not be."

"So many riddles," Yoshio said, walking on.

"And you appreciate them," Amaya said.

"I do," Yoshio said, "Though sometimes I wish you would just tell me how you feel."

"I wish the same from you."

Yoshio glanced back to see Amaya walking carefully along, her face relaxed as she looked at the ground beneath them. He furrowed his brow, then sighed. They walked on in silence until the path joined another, larger road that was paved with ancient stones. Grass sprung up between the cobbles. The horse's hooves clacked as they walked on.

"Is this it?" Yoshio said as they walked into a clearing. A small, open-walled building sat beneath leaning trees. Coals smoked from a disc-shaped hearth in the center of the room. A teakettle sat upon them, steam issuing from its mouth. The small shrine was empty. Amaya tied the halter of the horse to a nearby post, close to rotting from neglect.

Yoshio, his hand on his katana, walked forward and searched about the large room. On the other side was a long set of wooden stairs that lead straight down to a wide, flat area below. Undisturbed white sand filled it, with small statues ringing the large clearing beneath tall shoots of bamboo.

"I wonder if the kami put this tea on," Yoshio said as Amaya walked across the floor to see the other side of the shrine.

"At least we know there will be an attendant," Amaya said, looking around.

"What good will he do?" Yoshio said. "Not to offend the spirits, but I doubt he will help me practice."

"He'll entertain *me*, of course," Amaya said.

"Excuse me! That tea is not for you!" Yoshio poked his head out from under the eaves to see a portly young woman trotting toward them, holding up the folds of her kimono. Her hair was arrayed in a vain attempt at a noble style, with strands falling about her shoulders and her eyes. Her obi was tied in front of her, which made Yoshio think of a prostitute before realizing she had likely been visiting an outhouse.

Amaya bowed slightly. "Greetings, I am Asano Amaya. This is-"

"Yes, just a moment, I'll fetch the incense," the woman said as she wobbled up the steps. She quickly pulled the teakettle off of the hot coals and placed it on a nearby sheet of reeds.

"Are you the attendant?" Yoshio said, leaning over to see the woman opening and looking in jars stacked on an occasional table near one of the corners.

"Yes," She said. She paused and turned around. "Oh! Um-" She pulled on her obi so that the bow slid around toward her back, then she bowed. "I am Emi." As she forced a smile, her eyes almost disappeared behind her round cheeks.

"I can tell you don't receive many visitors here," Yoshio said.

"I am sorry, did I offend you?" Emi said.

"No," Yoshio said. Emi stared back silently.

"We weren't offended," Amaya said. "My husband just happened to notice how undisturbed the sand is in the sanctum."

"Oh," Emi said. "Well, there's not much else to do here besides rake it. That and make tea."

"Which is not for visitors," Yoshio said.

"It's for the kami, of course," Emi said. "Tenjin was said to love tea."

"I thought Tenjin was enshrined closer to the bay," Yoshio said.

"He is," Emi said, "That is, he has an official imperial shrine in Osaka, but we honor him too. We have many Kami enshrined here."

"I see," Amaya said. "Is this building all there is?"

"No," Emi said. "There's the attendance house around the corner, which is where I live, and the outhouse, and of course the individual shrines."

"Are you alone up here?" Amaya said.

Emi pursed her lips. "Well, yes, as a matter of fact. But there's nothing up here of value to steal, and the gods will be angy-"

"Do we look like thieves to you?" Amaya said.

"Um, no," Emi said. "You both look very… nice?"

Amaya smiled and looked at Yoshio. "Did you hear that? You look nice. So much for not being likeable."

"You know, I said I didn't aim to be liked," Yoshio said. "If it happens by accident I suppose that is fine."

Amaya looked around the clearing. "What do you think?"

Yoshio scratched his chin. "It will do. The sand in the sanctum will give me the same footing as at Masaki's estate, though there will be less room to practice, and I will still need to find a way to put the sun in my eyes. It's awfully shady up here."

Amaya nodded, then looked back to Emi. "We will stay here the next few weeks. I presume your house is more than one room?"

"Yes," Emi stammered on, "It has dividers… It was meant for more than one… but that is *my* house. Visitors can't stay here."

"Would you turn away a pilgrim in the rain?" Amaya said.

Emi thought about it a moment, frowning. "I wouldn't, I guess, but-"

"We are walking through a very large storm, though you cannot see it yet," Amaya said. "And of course, I will donate generously to the shrine. You will be able to buy tea for yourself *and* the kami for quite some time."

Emi rubbed her hands. "Very well. I'll dust off the extra futons."

"We are expecting one more," Amaya said.

"Put him in a different room," Yoshio said. "And I will be practicing kenjutsu on the grounds. Please use caution when approaching me."

Emi sighed.

Amaya, seeing the pout on the girl's face, said, "Don't worry, we will make worth your while."

Yoshio wiped the sweat from his brow, and dried his hands. He ran the simple cloth, formerly white but now streaked with grey and yellow, across the hilt of his katana. He sat down on a narrow stool and pulled a ladle of water out of the heavy bucket he had carried uphill earlier and took a long drink.

"You ought to practice with the sweat on you," Muramasa said. Yoshio turned to see him pushing aside a long and leaning bamboo pole that blocked the entrance to the wide clearing. He adjusted a large, heavy-looking bag that hung across his shoulder. "You'll be nervous in the match."

"What do you think I've been doing the last hour?" Yoshio said, swallowing another mouthful of water. "Anyways, it is time for a break and a meal."

"Good," Muramasa said. "I could use a morsel or two."

Yoshio pushed himself up and walked toward the long, rectangular building that served as Emi's house, hidden behind a tall grove of bamboo that leaned up against even taller pines. Muramasa followed behind.

"I don't remember you carrying around such a large bag when we met," Yoshio said.

"Had to trade my silver for something a bit heavier," Muramasa said. "Good tools are never cheap."

"Hmn," Yoshio said.

"You think I am talking about your swords, yes?"

"It occurred to me, but then I realized that was probably too subtle for you."

"You're one to talk," Muramasa said. He smiled. "I was talking about my own tools, but your katana I can tell was not very expensive."

"It was worth all I had when I bought it," Yoshio said. "I traded everything – so to me, it was exorbitantly expensive."

"How did you buy the wakizashi, then?" Muramasa said.

"It was a gift from my former master," Yoshio said. He pulled the short sword out an inch and looked at the glinting steel.

"It was cheap for him," Muramasa said, looking at the sword. "It is only stamped with a place – Izumo. Smiths who produce good work are unafraid to put their name on something."

They walked around the side of the house to an open door. Amaya sat under the eaves, turning long filets of fish over a coal fire. She looked up at Yoshio and smiled as he approached.

"I don't know why you insist on insulting my steel so," Yoshio said. "I judge steel by its quality in battle, not its name."

"Wise words, swordmaster," Muramasa said. "However, I do not intend to insult you. I intend to liberate you from your humility." Muramasa dropped the sack down on the wooden deck, which knocked loudly.

"Humility is a virtue," Yoshio said. He leaned up against a pillar and wiped his brow again with the cloth.

"One that has probably served you well as a servant of the daimyo," Muramasa said. He paused and looked at the fish, and breathed in the smell. "I hope there is enough for me."

"Plenty," Amaya said.

Muramasa nodded to her and looked at Yoshio. "You no longer serve the daimyo, Yoshio. Now you oppose them. You stand as one of them. You must replace your humility in this with the confidence you have in your skill."

Yoshio looked to Amaya.

"He is right," she said, and flipped the fish over again. "You are my husband. That makes you a peer of Masaki, not just my servant. You must counter him the way you did the other day."

Yoshio frowned and looked at Muramasa again. "How will you break me of my virtue?"

"I'm going to give you a very special gift." He reached down into his sack and withdrew a hammer.

"A hammer?" Yoshio said. "Whatever will I do with it?"

"It's for me, stupid," Muramasa said. "This is a blacksmith's tool. I'm going to make you something worthy of your skill and your stature."

"I told you, I cannot change my sword so close to a bout," Yoshio said. "I would need months, perhaps even years, to regain the reflex I have with my current katana."

"That is why I am going to make your sword like your current one," Muramasa said. "Of course, I will make it better in every conceivable way. It will fit your hand like an extension of your body."

"There is not enough time," Yoshio said. "Good katana can take months to make."

"Perhaps for amateurs," Muramasa said with a smile. He sat down beside the disc-shaped stove as Amaya pulled the fish onto a plate. "The demon may reside mostly in my old sword, but he left enough behind to let me power through a job, and I still have many years of experience to draw on. A century of experience, including studies with Masamune himself, in a fashion. I will have your daisho[32] finished in time for you to train with it."

"Daisho?" Yoshio said.

"Yes, you deserve a matched pair," Muramasa said with a smile. "You don't let too many people know you can fight with two swords, do you?"

Yoshio frowned and sat down beside Amaya. "No. It is best to leave your enemy in the dark regarding your skills."

"But Ryunosuke will know, won't he?" Amaya said. "He was your student, you said."

"That technique is my own," Yoshio said. "Every swordsman needs things that are part of his innermost guarded skill. In battle, surprise is worth a thousand accurate cuts."

"Good," Muramasa said. "So it is with sword-making. Now eat up. You will need your strength if you are to help me carry an anvil and the steel for your swords up the hill."

"You are going to forge it here?" Yoshio said.

"Why not? We are surrounded by the sacred kami. It will be good luck to work here," Muramasa said. Emi arrived and sat down beside him, carrying a pot of boiled rice. "Who is this?"

"I'm Emi," she said. "Attendant, curator, and, um... administrator of this shrine."

"Where are your parents?" Muramasa said.

Emi cleared her throat. "I am the sole attendant."

"Not quite what I asked," Muramasa said, with a smile. "But you look pleasant enough."

"Thank you?" Emi said, her brow tilting with confusion.

"What about payment?" Yoshio said.

"I can handle that," Amaya said.

"My payment is this," Muramasa said. "Bring me back your opponent's sword. Bring me back the Blood Drinker." Sengo paused and looked into the coals. "Or destroy it."

"I will," Yoshio said.

"This doesn't look like steel to me," Yoshio said. He held a few of the blossomed bricks of grey iron and slag in his hands. Muramasa pawed through more of them.

"You're right, this is basically shit," Muramasa said. "I could still make a sword out of it, but it would not be easy, nor would the finished product be worthy."

"You have come in a bad season, my friend," the merchant said, looking over Muramasa's shoulder as he pulled iron out of the basket. "All of the steelmakers have disbursed their good stock already."

"Whose shop did you get this steel from?" Muramasa said, throwing a few more of the pieces back in the basket.

"Yamahama," the man said. "The forge is run only in winter."

"You're holding out on me," Muramasa said, standing up. He closed one eye. "Where are you keeping the good steel? The true tamahagane[33]?"

The merchant pursed his lips in thought for a moment. "I don't have any." He then added, "Not for you."

---

[32] A pair of swords which signify that the wearer is of the samurai caste.

[33] A steel made in the ancient Japanese tradition in small batches by combining iron sand with charcoal.

Muramasa twitched, as if angry.

"How much?" Yoshio said, stepping past Muramasa.

"I told you, I don't have any," the merchant said. He saw Muramasa reaching for his sword. "Killing me will not change that."

"I am Sengo Muramasa." He pulled his sword and his saya from his belt. He drew the steel a few inches out. It shone brightly, and his maker's mark was visible just above the hilt. "If silver will not convince you, perhaps this will."

"I'm easily convinced by silver," the merchant said. "I just haven't seen any."

Muramasa shut the sword and reached into his side purse. "I will do you better." He threw two gold coins on the table. The merchant scooped them up.

"I will have to explain to Mitsuyasu where his expected shipment went." He walked around the table to another room. Muramasa and Yoshio followed him. The next room was filled with goods piled into boxes and barrels. The merchant picked up a barrel and opened the one below it. "Here you go."

Inside were dozens of small, flat pieces of mottled and lumpy grey metal, some rusted and some coated with black carbon, and still some with a sheen on them. Muramasa pawed through them, holding each handful up to the light of the window. He separated each one into three piles.

"These look the same as the other ones," Yoshio said.

"They are far different," Muramasa said. "These were selected by the smelter specifically for use in swords. I can tell." He threw one of the pieces off to the side. "Even so, there is a wide variety, and each piece will be better for different parts of the sword. This pile," he pointed to the pile on the far right of the table, "will harden very easily. It is extremely tough, and good for an edge. These other piles are much softer. I will use them for other parts of the sword, specifically the heart."

"Why not make the entire thing out of the good steel?" Yoshio asked.

"Too brittle. I'm not just making art, I'm making a weapon. This weapon needs to cut, but it also needs to stand up to other swords in battle." He held up a piece of the lumpy steel. Its edges glinted in the light from the window. "This, my friend, is good tamahagane. What gold and silver are to the merchant, this is to a good smith." He threw the lump of steel in the far right pile.

"Does it meet your standards?" the merchant asked.

Muramasa looked at the table. "We shall have to see. I could probably make better steel myself, but I'm in a crunch for time, so whether this steel is great or merely tolerable, I will buy it." He shoved the right pile, which was the smallest of the three, into a bag, and then he held out his hand to Yoshio, who gave him another cloth bag. He shoved the middle pile into it and the rest into the half-empty barrel. Yoshio shouldered the heavier sack while Muramasa picked up the barrel along with his own bag. They nodded to the merchant and left.

"I knew Sakai would have some real steel, if only we took the time to look," Muramasa said as they stepped out into another cloudy day.

"I can hardly believe that what we just bought – and what you just paid for – will make a good sword."

"Ha," Muramasa said. "Let me ask you this, as a teacher, can you not see talent in a pupil before he even touches a sword?"

"I suppose," Yoshio said.

"Well, the way you see students is how I see a lump of steel. It is unmade, unmolded, but the material is right. I can make even the worst slag into a sword, but to make a good one, you must start with the right materials."

"I think good students are rarer than good steel," Yoshio said. "I have taught many men and many boys the way of the sword. Only a handful off the top of my head I can recall having any inborn merits."

"Then they are the tamahagane of men," Muramasa said.

"Every student can eventually master forms, even the bad ones, but to go beyond that," Yoshio said, "the only one I can think of that has the capacity to exceed his master has your sword."

"I expect no less," Muramasa said. He held his hand out as raindrops began to fall. "Let's get this haul back before we get soaked and it all rusts. Then we can go convince a blacksmith to give me his anvil."

"You can't find a new one?" Yoshio said.

"I could, but if you buy one from another smith you can tell just how hard it is as well as how well it will wear against good steel. We should bring the horse for that."

Water dripped off the many ends of Yoshio's hair, which had fallen from its long topknot to drape over his ears. His chest was bare, and an old, loose hakama was pinned up revealing bare shins and muddy feet. He breathed hard. He felt his pulse begin to slow and jumped up, grabbing back ahold of the tree limb. It sagged slightly under his weight. He pulled his chin up to the top, then kipped himself up higher and pushed the rest of the way up, so that the limb was at his waist and his elbows were locked below him. He relaxed and repeated it. Each time it was more difficult.

"How many is that?" Muramasa shouted through the din of the rain falling on roofs and leaves.

"I do not count," Yoshio said, laboriously. "Not until it begins to be truly difficult." He repeated the exercise.

"It looks difficult now," Muramasa shouted back. "You know, if you want to build up strength I have plenty you can do once we get the forge working." Beneath an old eave that extended off the attendance house he worked, laying out bricks and stones to build a small, long forge. The horse had willingly carried it, along with an old abused anvil, up the hill in the rain. Though Yoshio worked his body hard, he was silently thankful he did not have to carry the immense iron tool himself. "A couple of hundred hammer strokes would do you well."

"Strength is built through discipline," Yoshio said. "Not just repetition. When you reach your supposed limits, and force yourself to work through them, that is when you build strength." He breathed heavily as he hung. "So the true strength is in the mind and the spirit, not in the arm."

"I've always appreciated little truisms like that," Muramasa shouted back. "Even if they are a bit unrealistic."

"Bah!" Yoshio said as he pushed himself up. "You know nothing of the discipline of a warrior."

"Of course I don't," Muramasa said. "I'm a commoner. We have no use for a warrior's discipline. When a peasant breaks his limits, it is because he is hungry. Only the well-fed man needs discipline. Ha!"

"For a man who throws gold around like it is copper," Yoshio said between grunts, "You claim to know a tremendous amount about hunger."

"Of course I know about hunger, I had a fire demon twisted into my soul," Muramasa said, chuckling. "But I know what you mean. I wasn't always so successful, if you'll recall."

Yoshio kipped himself up one more time, his arms trembling as he pushed his body above the branch. He held his pose at the top. "And yet you continue to make great swords."

"Wow, a compliment," Muramasa said. "Your wife – well, whatever she is to you now – is molding you in interesting ways."

Yoshio let himself down. "What does that mean?"

"What I said it means," Muramasa said. "A compliment from you could be a well-traded commodity."

"About Amaya," Yoshio said. He strained to pull himself up again, then failed and relaxed.

Muramasa laughed. "She obviously had an effect on you. I merely mention her and you lose all your strength!"

Yoshio strained on the branch again, being able to do little more than flex his elbows. He let go and dropped down. Muramasa, sitting on the ground arranging bricks, laughed uproariously. Yoshio grumbled and picked up his stained traveling robe, which hung from a nearby branch. He stomped off toward the house, water splashing up between his toes.

The rain fell in sheets outside of the shrine, looking like a curtain of flowing glass. It was dark inside, with a few incidental candles lit near a scroll where Emi worked with a pen, scratching out utilitarian letters. Yoshio could not read them from where he stood, though he was facing Emi's table. That was because he was blindfolded.

Thunder occasionally lit up the room. The sound of rain drowned out all else as the storm raged on. Yoshio held his sword with his right hand and his saya with his left. He went through his rehearsed motions again. The sword sliced through the air inaudibly below the noise of the rain.

First, a cut as I draw the sword. He is on the defensive. He stepped forward. *A feint with a sidecut. Change directions. At the legs. Thrust up. Cut across. Stab to the side.* Yoshio stepped to the side and went into a guard after the attack, imagining his former student and colleague avoiding his strokes. He pulled the cloth from his eyes and looked down. The chalk marks on the floor were smeared in each place, except for one. Without his sight, his footwork held up, except when it came to dropping into the guard. He was not used to being on the defensive.

"You should stay on the offensive."

Yoshio jerked himself around, his sword in a forward guard, to see Hayato standing at the entrance to the shrine. He was wet and wore a large hat that dripped around its rim. He carried a large sack made of oilcloth on his back with a strange obtrusion sticking over his shoulder. An oilcloth was wrapped around the hilts of his swords, beaded with water. Yoshio held himself still, preparing for a sudden draw of the sword from the other samurai. Emi looked up at them and backed up against the wall, dropping her pen.

"Relax," Hayato said, holding his hand out to Emi and then looking to Yoshio. "If I were here to kill you, I could have done it while you were blindfolded."

"I don't think you would," Yoshio said. "You, of all of the men who consort with Masaki, seem like you have a shred of honor."

"I do have a shred," Hayato said. He stepped into the shrine. Emi relaxed, but moved to the edge of the room.

"I will be careful not to practice blind while it is raining in the future," Yoshio said. "I am not used to being surprised. Of course, I could have been warned." He looked at Emi.

"I was focused on my own work, thank you. It's not my job to be looking out for you," she said.

"I was more thinking of looking out for yourself." Yoshio flipped his sword, doing the familiar shaking of blood, even though the blade was dry, and put his katana back home in its saya.

"Why practice blind at all?" Hayato said.

"Because perfection of technique comes with perfection of motion. Sight does not make one cut well. If anything, it can deceive."

Hayato nodded. "All the best lies are truths in themselves."

"How did you find me here?" Yoshio said.

"A little bit of searching and polite questions can uncover much. I have not told Masaki, however, your wife should be careful with her transmissions. Masaki has spies in the house of the shogun. He knows he is on his way to Osaka Bay."

"I see," Yoshio said. He turned to look through the sheets of water at the sanctum below. He scratched his chin. "He means to shame Amaya before the shogun."

"It is an incredible opportunity for him," Hayato said. "He hates your wife very much. Why is that?"

"He believes she betrayed him during a betrothal period," Yoshio said.

"Did she?"

Yoshio frowned as he looked out over the sanctum water flowed over the sand, disturbing it. "He must be very confident that I will lose."

"Of course he is. He is always confident with his plans."

"I have already dismantled one of his plans," Yoshio said.

"He is confident in his swordsman."

Yoshio looked back at Hayato. "Is that why you have come? To concede to a later time for the duel? If so, why not tell Masaki where I am?"

"I have not come here as a messenger," Hayato said. "I wanted to see for myself your skill." He put his bag down on the floor. He pulled open the top and withdrew unwrapped oilcloth revealing a set of bokken.[34] Beside them he could see folded clothes, and silver.

"Other than the training gear you look as if you are going on a journey," Yoshio said.

"Perhaps I am," Hayato said. "That depends on what you can show me." He picked up one of the bokken and handed it to Yoshio.

"Why?" Yoshio said.

Hayato sighed. "This new swordsman, Noburu... I am unsure whether I can continue on with him there. In fact, I know I cannot. What I saw him do a day ago..." Hayato shook his head. "Masaki shares his bloodlust, and revels in it. I cannot contend with it."

"You would choose a ronin's life over honor?" Yoshio said.

"I'm afraid if I stay I shall have neither. I was thinking of taking what I have and starting an obscure dojo somewhere off of Honshu."

"I understand," Yoshio said. "Do you have family?"

"Yes. I have a wife and two children, but they are in Kyoto. I would have to hope to travel there before Masaki could send word for their execution."

"He would really do that?" Yoshio said, and then added, "I'm a fool – of course, he would. He has murdered for jealousy and suspicion just as easily."

"My family will be killed if I leave, and be destitute or worse if I stay and end up dead," Hayato said. "Either way I must give up all I have."

"Not if I can kill Ryunosuke," Yoshio said.

"Ryunosuke?"

[34] A wooden sword used for training purposes.

"It is the name Noburu has given himself," Yoshio said. "It is hard to explain, but the man Noburu does not exist anymore."

Hayato picked up a bokken. "Then show me you can end him. At the very least, you'll have some sparing practice with a real swordsman."

Chapter 15: Warnings Spoken in Two Voices

Yoshio held lightly the hilt of the bokken, which was wrapped in a rough linin-like strand of cloth. It was something very unfamiliar compared to his actual sword, the balance and feel of the red oak unsettling in the old swordsman's hands. He shoved the wooden sword into his belt, where it would be difficult to draw, lacking a saya. He would have to drag the wood across his obi, slowing his usually impressive cut from the draw. When he trained students using bokken, he usually began them in a forward guard, since the tools were used primarily to practice defense safely. This, however, was a duel, albeit a practice duel, and he needed to practice the first cut as if it were Ryunosuke standing on the other side of the grove and not Hayato.

"Do not hold back on me," Hayato said, walking forward. His feet splashed through a shallow puddle. Water dripped from the leaves above him. "For I will not hold back on you."

"I look forward to it," Yoshio said. He stepped toward Hayato, his own feet squishing on the wet turf.

Hayato stopped at a point equidistant from the attendance house and the shrine. The trees surrounded both of them on the left and right. It was slightly larger than the courtyard where Yoshio's duel would happen. Yoshio stopped at a spot a few paces away, as was customary.

"I've never been afforded the opportunity to watch you properly duel before," Amaya said.

Yoshio flinched slightly and looked past Hayato to see Amaya sitting beneath an eave of the attendance house. She had her inkstone and brushes laid out before a calligraphy easel. "You've seen me fight many times," he said back.

"But never properly; formally," Amaya said. "I expect to be impressed."

"The best victories are often the least impressive," Yoshio said. "A warrior should always seek to advantage himself enough to make each victory swift and decisive, and therefore boring for an onlooker."

Yoshio leapt back, springing off his forward placed left foot, as Hayato made a sudden and swift draw cut. Yoshio's right foot slipped on the wet grass as he backpedaled. He fumbled with his own bokken as Hayato turned in again, advancing with two more overhead slashes. Yoshio skipped his well-practiced cut for the saya and pulled his bokken free, feeling it drag along his obi. He parried a cut, continuing to move backward.

He sidestepped a stab cut from Hayato and, surprising the young retainer, grabbed the back edge of the bokken and slammed the edge of his own into Hayato's ribs, pushing the smooth wooden edge over his chest in what would have been a lethal cut.

"It is done," Yoshio said. He pushed Hayato away.

Hayato let his bokken fall toward the earth and held his hands to his chest. "Not as hard a hit as I expected."

"A good cut comes from the proper motion, not the strength of the arm," Yoshio said. He shook the bokken as if throwing blood off of it and shoved it back into his belt. "Shall we try again? This time without the deception?"

"You should expect deception from Masaki," Hayato said.

"What about from Noburu?"

"I do not know, but I would be vigilant in the duel. If Masaki is embarrassed he is more likely than not to put an arrow through you to ease his own suffering."

"I intend for him to be more than embarrassed," Amaya said from the beneath the eave.

"Then I would doubly suspect betrayal," Hayato said. "If he is to lose his honor, he would prefer to lose it with those he hates dead, including you."

"I know Masaki despises me," Amaya said, "but he would rather me suffer than be dead."

"Only if he can watch it, Amaya-sama," Hayato said. He looked back to Yoshio. "Let us try it again, no deception from me."

They returned to the center of the grove. Yoshio wiped the water from his bokken and dried his hands hastily on his hakama. Hayato returned his own wooden sword to his belt. They stepped a few paces away from one another, and bowed. In swift moves, each of their hands went to the bokken.

Yoshio turned his sideways, preparing for a draw cut, then stepped forward. The bokken dragged on the belt as he freed it, but instead of pulling it forward, he put the palm of his left hand against the blunt edge, close to the tip.

Hayato had pulled his own bokken free and went straight into a draw cut, this one coming from below in an unfamiliar starting technique. Yoshio pushed the edge of his sword down, deflecting the cut from below that, if unaltered, would have hit his groin in a lethal strike. He stepped back and put his bokken in a ready position. Hayato put his bokken up in a strong forward-facing guard. He inched closer.

Yoshio attacked, slashing from shoulder to waist, each time turning the blade in an unexpected direction. Hayato managed to parry each time, as if he expected the blows. Yoshio did not bother to feign a cut, but continued through each stroke, forcing Hayato to back up several steps. Then, Yoshio stepped back and raised his sword up in overhead guard. Hayato immediately stepped in and feigned a side cut, pulling back to go to an overhead attack.

Yoshio ignored the feint and stepped inside Hayato's guard, slashing twice. The first cut was parried above Hayato's shoulder, but the second ran down the side of his off-arm. Yoshio immediately stepped back, dodging several strikes from Hayato as he retreated toward the shrine. Hayato went on the offensive, feigning and following with accurate stabs and cuts, though Yoshio seemed able to turn each one away easily. Yoshio moved around Hayato and ran back toward the attendance house.

Hayato attacked again, and Yoshio continued to back up. Finally, Yoshio put his sword down at his side and made a motion as if shaking off blood.

Hayato paused. "You give in?"

"I've cut the artery above your humorous," Yoshio said, pointing to Hayato's left arm. There was a small snag of cloth in the armpit where the bokken had caught Hayato's kimono. "You have bled out."

"Not definitive," Hayato said.

"With a blade, it would have been. It is a lethal strike." Yoshio put the bokken in his belt. "You are very skilled, and your techniques are novel. If you started a dojo, I would be proud to view your students."

"Once more," Hayato said. He held his sword up.

Yoshio, standing some ten paces away, drew his bokken. He rushed at Hayato, who parried a side strike and then moved to counter with a thrust. Yoshio was not there. He felt Yoshio's bokken hit his neck from the left side. He grunted as he stumbled away.

"Definitive enough?" Yoshio said.

Hayato lowered his bokken. "There is no question you are very skilled," he said. He walked back toward the shrine, holding the place on his neck where Yoshio had hit him. Yoshio followed him. Emi, who had been watching the bout, quickly went back to her books as they approached.

"Thank you for the sparring match," he said.

"Thank you," Hayato said. "It is rare that a warrior has the opportunity to measure himself against another. Rarer still the opportunity to be found lacking and to go on living. I have work to do." He walked up the steps to the shrine. Hayato put his bokken back in his bag and wrapped an oilcloth back around the hilt.

Yoshio held out the other bokken. Hayato pushed it away with his palm. "Keep it," he said, "It is the rainy season here in Osaka. With that, you can train in the weather without fear of rust. Just remember that Hayato gave it you."

"Thank you," Yoshio said. He wiped the water from the wood and leaned the bokken up against a pillar.

"It is a small thing, really," Hayato said.

"Will you be returning to Masaki now?"

Hayato frowned. "You were impressive, Taoka Yoshio, but my heart misgives me. I do not think your skill will be enough."

"I understand," Yoshio said. "Your decision is yours. Protect what you value most – everything in this life is fleeting."

Hayato nodded. "Please do not fail." He put his large-brimmed hat back on and set off again down the muddy path, the rain drowning out the soft sound of his feet splashing in puddles as he walked away.

Yoshio sat cross-legged on the floor. He wore only his hakama, letting his upper body breath in the cool night air after the day of hard training. His eyes were closed. His bare ankles felt the grain of the wood beneath him. The pressure of it bit him slightly, and the angle of his ankles strained his joints. It was the way he had always sat when meditating, the same pose he had held in countless rooms for countless days across many years. Only now was he able to take note of the pain sneaking in. *Age*

is a strange friend, coming unbidden and remaining overlong, until when it is time to leave he is begged to stay.

There was little wind, and the storm that blew overhead was more like a weeping of Susano-o, the storm kami, than it was like a blustering of the Fujin, the wind god. It was calm, and peaceful. He opened his eyes. Water fell here and there from the eaves of the open sliding door, collecting the light from the lamp behind Yoshio. The drips looked like they were made of gold in front of the black curtain of night beyond. He felt small hands touch his shoulders.

"What did you think of Hayato?" Amaya asked.

"He is a skilled swordsman," Yoshio said.

"I mean, what do you think about what he is doing?" She dug her hands into his back muscles, strained from the workout.

"It is betrayal, to be sure," Yoshio said. "It is a detestable thing, but it is not my place to bring vengeance or justice upon him. Only karma can apportion such things out for him now."

"You understand why though, yes?" Amaya said.

"Understanding is different from excusing," Yoshio said.

Amaya paused her massage. "I see." She began again. "Would you choose blind loyalty over your family?"

"I have no family," Yoshio said. "I cannot make that determination."

"I'm sorry," Amaya said.

"I took no offense. Besides, you are my master, not Masaki. And I do not follow blindly."

"Even when I did not tell you my plans for Osaka? When I did not tell you my plans for Masaki, and my invitation to the shogun? You have followed me. Blindly, some might say."

"I knew you had important secret plans," Yoshio said. "I trusted that they were right – perhaps that is my blindness – but I also knew that I was myself a weak point in long-laid plans. I was new. Untested. Not yet to be trusted, especially when what happens may negatively impact the man I called lord for a long time."

"So you understand," Amaya said.

"I do."

"Does that mean you excuse it?"

"I suppose. Perhaps understanding is more important than I stated. I shall think on this."

Amaya dug into Yoshio's neck. He sighed. "You know, you never asked me where I went the other day, when you were confronting Masaki."

"I assumed the same," Yoshio said. "You will tell me when the time is right. I trust you."

"So sure I will tell you?"

"Yes."

"You are right. You are ruining one plan of mine though."

"What plan was that?"

"I was preparing my words to defend my actions here. You appear to understand me too well."

"I endeavor to understand you," Yoshio said. "You are my friend."

Amaya stopped. She sat herself down beside Yoshio, her back to the rain outside, so she could see him. He opened his eyes and looked at her. Her eyes gazed back, lit softly by the lamp.

"You are a brave man and a coward, Taoka Yoshio," she said. "You are unafraid to throw your life away as if it was nothing, and yet you are terrified of taking what you truly want."

Yoshio looked back silently.

"I have decided that last part, the cowardly part, is what feeds your stoic façade. If you have nothing in life worth possessing, then even life is easy to give away."

"Every samurai is born to die," Yoshio said. "We are all bound to karma. It is the way of things."

"No, it is not. There is no way. There is only will. Passion *in* life breeds passion *for* life." Amaya looked out at the rain. "People admire for you dispassion, but I do not. I understand it, given what you have suffered, but I do not admire it."

"I-" Yoshio breathed and collected his thoughts.

"The things I like about you – the things I *love* about you – are the things which you find the most contemptible about yourself. I love the way you value life, even if it is not your own. I love your temper, especially when it comes to me. I love the way you are jealous. With me alone you allow yourself to express such feelings."

"What would you have me do?" Yoshio said.

"Act on them," Amaya said. Her eyes trembled.

Yoshio leaned forward and kissed Amaya. It had been a long time since he had kissed a woman, and he held himself back, still doubtful. Amaya grabbed the lapel of his kimono and pulled him closer. They released and she wrapped her arms around him, pushing her chin into his shoulder.

"Close the door," she said quietly, then let go. Yoshio stood up and slid the door to the outside closed, muting the rain. Behind him, the door shut to the rest of the house. Amaya stared at him silently for a moment as she held the door. For a moment, the room was lit up with lightning from the outside, bleaching the frosted windows.

She walked over to him and tugged on her obi, letting the knot, slightly sideways as usual, unravel. The folds of her kimono were suddenly loose. She pulled a pin from her hair and it fell down around her shoulders. Yoshio looked at her silently, allowing months of thoughts, and the feelings buried with them, to re-enter his mind. A figure and a face that he had internally relegated to art, something to be seen and admired for its form in an aesthetic sense, suddenly changed to something far more sensual. More real.

"You are very beautiful, Lady Amaya," he said. "You are like a work of art. I… should not touch something so perfect."

"A sword is art too, Yoshi."

"But it is also dangerous to touch."

"I will try my best not to cut you, my dear Yoshi." Amaya drew close and threw her arms around Yoshio's neck. She looked up at him expectantly. Yoshio leaned down and kissed her again. He, with slight hesitation, slipped his hands into the folded silk around her waist. He felt her skin under his fingers. Amaya reached to Yoshio's belt and began untying it. Yoshio pushed his hands up Amaya's torso and pulled the folds of her kimono away from her shoulders. She relaxed her arms and let the silk clothes fall away. She undid the careful tie on her slip and pushed it toward the ground.

Amaya laid down on the futons. Yoshio let his kimono fall off of him and followed her down. He kissed her again as he pushed his body up against hers. They released, and Amaya looked into his eyes. She nodded. Yoshio sat up and ran his hands over her legs as they fell apart.

So far to fall, from so high up! How delicious.

Yoshio paused, his eyes wide.

"I heard it too," Amaya said. Yoshio frowned.

How wonderful it is to see you fall. I will ease your passing.

Yoshio leapt off the futons and pulled his sword off the ground where it had fallen when he disrobed. He drew it, dropped the saya, and threw open the door to the outside, not bothering to clothe himself. The empty grove in the rain was all the greeted him. He stepped out into the rain and looked around. The glade was calm. The shrine on the other side was dark, a black outline of beams and a sloping roof demarcating it from the waiving trees.

"Yoshi! I heard it again!" Amaya shouted. Yoshio turned around to see Amaya standing naked with her own sword drawn, pushing open the door to the hallway. He dashed back inside.

"I heard nothing," Yoshio said.

"It's coming from inside the house."

Yoshio stepped past Amaya and into the hall, his sword ready.

"Die!" Manic laughing filled the hall. A door opened, and Emi looked out at the naked pair and gasped.

Not bothering to tell the girl not to gawk, Yoshio stepped to another door and slid it open. Muramasa lay on a futon inside what was usually a study. His hands gripped the sides of his heads, and he spoke in a voice that was not his own.

"Suffer! Let your strength be my fountain," Muramasa hissed, and laughed again. Amaya laid her sword against the wall and bent down over the bed.

"Wake up, Sengo!" Amaya shook Muramasa, who continued to moan between laughs.

"Wait!" Yoshio said. "He may tell us something about Ryunosuke."

"Don't be like that, Yoshi," Amaya said. "He's suffering." She shook him some more and he bolted upright with a scream, and then scrambled out of bed and against the back wall. He looked about quickly for his sword. He saw it near the futon and dove for it, but as he did, Yoshio kicked it up by the saya with his toe and caught it with his left hand.

Muramasa paused and blinked hard, still delirious.

"It's over," Amaya said.

Muramasa looked at her, then Yoshio, and Emi, who peered in from behind them. He released his held breath and began to gasp.

"The warrior from yesterday," Sengo said. "I killed him."

"Hayato?" Yoshio said, his eyes widening.

Muramasa nodded, then frowned. "Why are you all naked?"

"A warrior should not let shame stop him from pursuing victory," Yoshio said, putting Muramasa's sword down. "For there is nothing more shameful than defeat." Amaya pushed herself up and quickly exited the room as he spoke.

"What about the retainer?" Muramasa said.

Yoshio frowned. "We must be quick if we are to find him," He backed out of the room.

"It's too late," Muramasa said to his back.

"I can still catch Ryunosuke unawares," Yoshio shouted back.

"You all are a strange sort," Emi said, looking at Muramasa.

"You have no idea," Muramasa said.

"A cherry tree, the blooms left on the soil, brown and rotten," Yoshio said, repeating the words Muramasa had recited after coming out of his strange stupor. "A river, running high. A boat. A face in despair." He rushed along the dirt road, the moon failing to give him light by which to run. Only the road, a grey streak among black walls to either side, led him forward. Emi, struggling to keep up, held aloft a lantern that illuminated just a few paces in front of him.

"There's a creek on the northern side of the hill," Emi said. "That is the only close river I can think of."

"A river running high is not a creek," Amaya said. She strode along beside Yoshio, her katana and tanto tucked into a narrower obi than what was fashionable. She had exchanged her delicate silk kimono for a utilitarian cotton version of the garment, which she let flow loosely around her legs.

"I wish your friend was here, then," Emi said.

"He would be of no use, or perhaps even a hindrance," Yoshio said. "About this creek. To where does it flow? The Yamato River?"

"I think so, but that joining is much closer to the bay," Emi said. "First it slows and flows through a lake, of sorts."

"Then let us try the lake," Yoshio said.

"It's still fairly far away," Emi said.

"Then we must hurry," Yoshio said.

"The main road comes up from the bay below, but up ahead is an old shortcut that should take us there," Emi said. "If my childhood memory serves me." Emi stopped some yards ahead. She held the lantern up high and looked over a patch of bamboo and short shrubs.

"What is it?" Amaya said, turning back. She clutched her katana.

"I thought the path was here," Emi said. She looked back to an unlit stone lamppost outside a nearby home. "Yes, it was here." She pushed against the bamboo. "I think."

Yoshio stepped forward and drew his sword. He started slashing at the undergrowth, knocking down bamboo. His sword caught in a few of the long, woody stems. Amaya drew her own sword and helped him, slashing cleanly through all the shafts. The wall of bamboo fell, and amid short shoots, an opening in the growth appeared.

"Here," Emi said, and stepped over the cut bamboo. She ducked under a low hanging tree branch and began pushing her way forward.

"Wait!" Yoshio said. "Let me lead the way. It is not safe."

He stepped through the brush, feeling loose twigs and splinters cut and scrape his shins, and pushed himself past Emi. He held his sword out in front of himself as he walked the path. A few yards into the closed woods what was left of the light of the cloudy night became totally blacked-out by a low canopy of leaves. Yoshio could feel with his feet that the path was little more than bare earth below the untended and many-branched maples. He had to stoop to move forward.

"This isn't much of a path," he said, slashing at a shrub.

"It is to a little girl," Emi said. "It's like a perfect tunnel."

They wound their way through the brush, working over a hill and then steadily down. The lantern flickered slightly as the wind picked up. The rain still fell lightly. Eventually, the trees gave way to more shrubs and tall bamboo stalks. These were not so high or thick as the ones closer to the road, and so they were able to easily push through, arriving at the wide waterway. In truth, it was somewhere between a creek and a river, with slow-moving water and far-flung banks. Under the clouds, the water looked like black glass, its surface detectible only by the occasional rock or woody stem bursting through its top.

"Here it is," Emi said, she held the lantern aloft revealing muddy water. "The lake is that way." She pointed downstream. "Be careful, the water can be deeper in spots than it looks."

They walked downstream a ways, each of their feet slipping over silted roots and rounded rocks. After working their way around a bend, they came to the lake. It was a large pool created by a sudden trough in the path of the stream, and looked in the darkened night like a black, rippling sheet. The wind had picked up in the open space, and small whitecaps could be seen on the water. They continued to work their way around, coming eventually to the main path Emi had mentioned, running a few yards away from the pool.

"Keep your eyes open," Yoshio said. "I do not quite know what we are looking for. And Amaya, keep your sword at the ready."

She nodded and drew her katana again. The walked through the low grasses and shrubs and onto the path, moving quickly to the end of the lake, where it again narrowed and emptied over a heap of wet stones into a more swiftly moving, though still wide, stream. Yoshio paused in front of the row of boulders.

"What is it?" Amaya said.

"I think I see something," Yoshio said.

"What?"

"Just shadows," Yoshio said, "but perhaps more." He slid his katana back into its scabbard. "Wait here."

"You know I won't," Amaya said.

Yoshio grumbled and removed his muddy sandals. He began climbing over the row of rocks to get to the far bank. Despite their placement in running water, they were rough enough to catch his feet, and he felt secure as he crawled over. Amaya followed suit, holding her sandals in one hand and using her free hand to steady herself. At the end of the row was a swift-moving patch of water. Yoshio lowered himself down into it, extracting his sword and holding it above his head, and waded through a waist-deep section and to the opposite bank. He pulled himself up by some exposed willow roots, and turned to help Amaya (her sword too held aloft) and then Emi, who waded through with the lantern high above her head.

"My poor robe," Emi said, looking at the black stains on her cloth as she pulled herself up and out of the dirt.

"Such a thing to think at this time," Yoshio said, sticking his sword back into his belt. "Worried about your clothes."

"If it does not wash out, I will buy you another," Amaya said, drawing her sword again and pushing the saya into her obi.

The two women followed Yoshio into a thicket. The stream curved around to their left, broadcasting its presence by the sound of rushing water even though it could not be seen.

Yoshio paused. "Hide the light."

Emi obliged by slipping a thick cotton shade over the lamp. Orange seeped through holes in the seams. Emi lowered the lamp and held it against her chest. Yoshio crept forward, his sword high in anticipation of a strike. He stepped out from the brush into an opening in the trees. The clouds above were bright grey, lit by a moon behind, and the movement of black leaves was visible around the edges of the meadow.

Something moved.

Yoshio tensed up and moved closer. He thought he could make out a man against a tree trunk, but the movement came from the shadows in front of him.

"Hayato!" Yoshio said. "Is that you?"

Silence replied.

"Hayato!"

Emi pulled the shade off the lamp and held it up as she and Amaya stepped into the clearing.

Hayato's face, covered in blood, appeared for an instant, floating above them. Blood dripped everywhere.

The girl screamed and dropped the lantern. It flickered. The hovering face disappeared. Amaya picked up the lamp, and a few seconds later the small flame caught hold of the oil again. She watched Yoshio, who looked at the scene with a blank expression.

Emi screamed again and covered her eyes, falling down to the ground and pushing herself against a large bush.

"I am sorry, Hayato," Yoshio said. "I should have acted more swiftly."

Amaya walked up beside him and saw Hayato's head hanging from a drooping limb of a willow tree by his topknot. Blood congealed at the clean line where the neck was severed, while fresh blood still dripped onto the wet grass below. Dead, dried eyes, not yet turned grey, stared passed them all, out to Sheol.

Yoshio's gaze lingered then pushed back to the shadows. What had first been mistaken for a man leaning against the trunk of the tree could now be seen for what it truly was. It was Hayato's body, pinned up against the tree by his sword, which impaled him through the belly. Blood covered the blade that protruded from Hayato's chest, aided by fresh rain falling through the leaves above. A small stream of red water collected and fell from the guard of the hilt. His wakizashi remained in his belt.

"I'm sorry, Yoshi," Amaya said.

"See to Emi," Yoshio said. "This is not a pleasant scene for a young woman." He stepped up to the body and looked around the sump. He turned back to Amaya, who had walked back to the crying attendant. "Actually, if you can manage, look around for a bag. It should have a bokken sticking out of it. I am wondering if he dropped it while running or if it was stolen."

Yoshio approached the body. He considered removing the swords, and finding a way to ship them back to Hayato's family, as he had done with Kuramasa Kuro's young retainer Mitsuo. He reached for the katana embedded in Hayato's body, but as his fingers brushed on the hilt, he recoiled. His ears filled with a loud hissing, like the rushing of air through trees, but much louder.

Yoshio clenched his fist, which suddenly hurt. "Did you hear that?" he said.

Amaya looked up at him from where she crouched, beside Emi. "I heard nothing."

Yoshio reached again for the katana. He let his hand wrap tightly around the hilt, and the hissing returned. He pulled on the sword. His arm alighted in an itching sensation, which moved to pinpricks, and finally to burning as he tried to pull the sword free. All other sound was blocked off, and he felt a burn in his throat. The hissing began to clarify in patterns. Yoshio shut his eyes.

Yoshio! Yoshio! Yoshio! The hissing said.

"Yoshi!" He thought he could hear Amaya, somewhere in the darkness, but the deafening whisper overwhelmed his senses.

Help me! Please help me!

Yoshio searched for words, somehow hidden in the torrent of his own mind. *Hayato?* Yoshio intoned inside.

Yes.

You are dead. I cannot help you.

I am dead?

Yes. I am looking at your body. Yoshio realized he was looking at nothing. Total darkness was all he could see. He forced his eyes open, but the images there were but dark, twisting shadows.

I don't feel dead.

You are. Ryunosuke has slain you.

I am sorry, then. It seems I could not stop him. I did my best.

I know. Rest.

There is no rest here, Yoshio.

Yoshio's vision began to return. He could see the body and the tree, in a hazy swirling of fog.

Free me, Yoshio.

The body fell to the ground, and Yoshio found himself holding the katana. Blood flowed down to the guard of the hilt, slowly creeping toward his hand.

"Yoshi!"

Yoshio turned to see Amaya. Her hands were on his arms, clenching tightly.

"Amaya," Yoshio whispered. His voice hurt to speak.

"Yoshi, are you alright? You were screaming."

"No." Yoshio looked down at the sword. "Help me put this sword away, please!"

Amaya looked over the fallen body and found the saya. She cried out as she tried to untie it.

"Yoshi, there's something wrong," she said, shrinking back. "It feels as hot as a burning coal."

"Leave it, then," Yoshio said. He threw the sword to the side, and felt an immediate relief in his arm. It flashed in pain, which then subsided to numbness and pinpricks, as if he had laid on it too long in bed.

"What was that?" Amaya said.

"Part of the demon remains," Yoshio said, rubbing his right arm. "And part of Hayato's soul. He asked me to free him."

"Why has this never happened before?" Amaya said.

"We have never been so close to the body and so near in time to the murder before," Yoshio said. "I have never touched one of the victims, either."

"You didn't touch Hayato; you touched his sword," Amaya said.

"A samurai's blade is as much a part of himself as his arm or his head," Yoshio said. He shook his head, trying to dispel the echoes. "Let's get out of here. I do not even know what I could do for his spirit here. I will be glad if I can forget this image." He walked swiftly back to Emi, who whimpered quietly, then gently pulled her up.

Chapter 16: Hammers and Brushes

"Yoshi."

"Yes?" Yoshio turned over to see the back of Amaya's head as she stared toward the door, dimly lit with the approaching dawn. He saw her side go up and down as she took a deep breath.

"I do not…" She trailed off.

Yoshio sat up and touched her shoulder. "What is it?"

"I am having doubts," she said. She turned on her back to look at Yoshio. "I do not want you to fight Ryunosuke."

"I must," Yoshio said. "It is not just a matter of bushido now. It is about your honor, your family's honor and-"

"It's about revenge, Yoshi," Amaya said. "Once I thought that I would trade anything to see Masaki fall, but now, I am not willing to make that trade."

"There is nothing to trade," Yoshio said. "Either I am victorious, and you have what you want, or I am not, and you have nothing."

"Perhaps trade is the wrong word. Risk." Amaya glanced back toward the frosted windows. "What once seemed precious to me has lost its luster, and I do not want to gamble what I have."

"Has it always been about revenge?"

"Yes."

Yoshio nodded in the dark. "Then I will see it done, my lady. I will take Ryunosuke's head and redeem your honor in one stroke."

"If you are permitted to live that long," Amaya said. "Risk envelopes us on all sides. What I wish most – now – is to be away from here."

"That did not work out so well for Hayato," Yoshio said.

"You are better than him. Stronger. Faster."

"Then we should wait for the duel, where I may face Ryunosuke on terms that, if not fair, are at least known ahead of time."

Amaya pushed herself closer to Yoshio. "I'm sorry, Yoshi."

"Don't be," Yoshio said. "Karma brings us where we are meant to be in the future, even if we do not understand the present. Whether we leave tonight or we stay and see through your plans, Ryunosuke and I will cross swords."

The forge was hot. Beads of sweat rolled off Muramasa's forehead as he reached into the burning coals and withdrew with his tongs an unshapely lump. He placed the ugly hunk of metal, which glowed red in the sunny day, on the anvil.

"Go," he said hoarsely.

Yoshio let the hammer drop onto the clump. Then again. As he could see small flattened spaces of the lump spread out, he began to add force to his strokes. The steel began to ring as it flattened out. Slowly, the orange and red gave way to mottled grey.

"This will form the edge of the sword," Muramasa said, picking up another hammer and working the edges of the steel lump between Yoshio's strokes. "This is the best steel from that batch. As we work it, it will become purer still." He grabbed the thongs and put the lump back in the forge. Yoshio stood up and went over to the bellows and began pumping. Muramasa buried the steel in the bright coals, turning it over a few times.

"How much will we have to do this?" Yoshio asked.

"We have not yet done the simple forge weld on the raw tamahagane," Muramasa said. "Once we have all the steel together, the real work will begin. The steel must be folded many times to make it resilient and harmonious. I hope your arms are up to the challenge."

"If they are not, they will grow stronger," Yoshio said.

"That's the spirit," Muramasa said. "Let me help you." He went over to another set of bellows on the small arrangement of bricks that made up his simple, long forge and began pumping. Sparks flew out of the opening. After a few minutes of slow, steady pumping, Muramasa moved back around to the front of the forge. He flipped over the lump that was still buried in the coals. He nodded to Yoshio as he pulled the steel out.

"Time to add a bit more," Muramasa said. He placed another two bits of the steel on the red-hot lump and began hitting them with the hammer. Sparks flew, and bits of slag broke off the outside of the lump, falling to black cinders on the bare ground below. Yoshio joined in as they alternated hard strokes with the hammer.

"Am I doing this right?" Yoshio said.

"At this point, it is hard to do it wrong," Muramasa said. "Get it hot, hit it with a hammer. Though this is undoubtedly the foundation of a sword-edge, and therefore the most important step, the real challenges will come later."

Yoshio stood on the white sands of the sanctum. He slid his sword back into its saya. Normally, he would not have violated the sacred place of the kami by practicing his art, but Emi had permitted it, saying the spirits would be appeased by a standard purification ritual afterward.

"Put it in a different place," Yoshio said. "I will not know where my opponent will be standing." He turned east and let his eyes adjust. The setting sun was just about to push below the hills and trees that blocked the shrine from a view of Sakai harbor and Osaka Bay.

"It is done," Amaya said.

Yoshi turned around and squinted into the light. In front of him, a blur of images wavered, placed into uncertain darkness by the blinding angle of the sun. Yoshio stepped forward and let loose his sword in a lightning-fast draw cut. He felt resistance as the blade sheared through the tatami[35], but he felt too much feedback when he reached the bamboo-shoot core of the practice prop.

Yoshio reached up with his left hand and shielded his eyes. He grumbled. The cut, while precisely in the middle of the rolled rice shoots vertically, was too shallow, and he had succeeded in cutting only the front of the tatami. The bamboo shoot at the center of the target was gouged, but intact.

"You still hit the target," Amaya said, standing back, her hand resting on her own katana. "Even a shallow cut can kill in the right place."

"Yes, I know," Yoshio said, "but it was not the cut I intended to make. I cannot trust victory to chance. I must be certain before I step into the dueling ring."

Amaya stepped forward and drew her sword into a sideways cut, which severed the tatami mat effortlessly where Yoshio's cut had been. The top half of the target held still for a moment, and then Amaya cut through it again using an overhand stroke. As the top of the target fell toward the earth, she struck it once more, cutting it into several wispy pieces of straw that scattered on the sand. She smiled and put her sword back into its scabbard.

"Impressive," Yoshio said, raising his eyebrows. "More than impressive, since I know you can do that to a man."

"Thank you," Amaya said.

"However, that was my last practice mat."

Amaya looked west at the sun that was peeking through the top branches of the trees. "And the sun is no longer in your eyes."

Yoshio grumbled. "Yes."

"Then it looks as though you will have to give it a rest for the day, and go have some dinner."

"There are many more things that can be practiced still," Yoshio said.

Amaya chuckled softly. "My dear Yoshi, ever focused on the task and not the living that surrounds it."

"I have been told that before," Yoshio said, "and not just by you. If I am not focused, I will be dead."

Amaya walked past him, toward the steps. "If you die, you will regret not pausing to enjoy the taste of a well-cooked meal."

"Food is fuel for life," Yoshio said. "It is not life itself."

Amaya stopped on the steps and looked back to him. "But it is part of life. I will help you roll more rice stalks for tomorrow's practice later. Now, come up to the house and dine with me."

He obeyed.

"Tell me, Emi," Muramasa said between mouthfuls. "Why are you an attendant at this shrine when you do not believe the kami exist?" Yoshio glanced to Amaya, who cast her eyes back, sending Yoshio the familiar message of *be quiet.*

Emi looked up from her plate. Her eyes were wide. "That's a nonsense question. Of course the kami exist."

"*I* know they exist," Muramasa said. "At least, I know that some of them exist. However, you do not." Emi chewed her food silently. Sengo went on. "Or you would be cleansing the sanctum right now. Which makes me

---

[35] A rolled mat of rice straw, sometimes with a core of bamboo, that can be used to practice cuts or test the edge of a sword in lieu of a living target.

wonder how you got here, and so young. Certainly you could still be married off, and enjoy a similar or better life of comfort than you have working around here."

"Hmn. Are you proposing to me, Muramasa?" Emi said, her wide eyes looked at him with hostility.

Muramasa laughed. "Perhaps I am. You make excellent rice balls, and I am always hungry, which is a trait I think we might have in common, but somehow I don't think you'd enjoy much an old man like me as husband."

Emi narrowed her eyes and pulled the folds of her kimono up higher. "You wouldn't know what to do with me."

"Yes, I most certainly would," Muramasa said with a smile. "But I digress. How did you end up here?" Muramasa looked at Yoshio. "I'm surprised this little mystery hasn't piqued your compulsion to know everything about everyone."

Yoshio shook his head, trying to hide a smile. "I try to stay mad at you, Muramasa, especially when you insult everyone at the table-"

"I didn't insult your wife," Muramasa said. "Or, whatever."

"But your lack of manners is now comical to me," Yoshio went on. "You are the only man I have met who could walk up to a man, call him a fat, bloated fish with breath to match, and the man would still be unsure of whether he liked you or not."

"I'm making you a sword, remember?" Muramasa said. "I'd have to like you at least a little."

Amaya looked at Emi. "He really is like this all the time; I must apologize, for he will not."

"Not that I should," Muramasa said. "I just want to know a thing or two about my host. Especially if I intend to fulfill her wishes and marry her." He winked at Emi.

She scoffed at him. "Not if you were the emperor and we were the last people on Earth."

"That's a pretty strong statement," Muramasa said. "You don't really know me either. I *could* be the emperor. Also, if we were the last people on Earth you might have to put your feelings aside for the good of the race. Our kids, though," Muramasa rolled his shoulders as if shuddering, then laughed.

"Lay off the girl, Muramasa," Yoshio said, leaning forward. Muramasa shrugged and shoveled some more rice into his mouth.

"Just so you know," Emi said, dropping her chopsticks and pointing at Muramasa, "I believe that kami are real. I know they are real, I just... don't know about the ones at the shrine."

"How is that?" Muramasa said.

"I've... well, I've talked to one before," Emi said.

Muramasa smiled. "Ha! You've made yourself much more interesting, I dare say. Not that you weren't already interesting. Where did you meet your kami?"

"You believe me?"

"Of course I do," Muramasa said.

"Well, she – it – lived in the river, down by where..." Emi looked at Amaya. Amaya nodded. "Anyway, I used to talk to it as a child, and it eventually talked back. My parents didn't believe me, which is funny, because they were Shinto attendants. I thought they talked to kami all the time."

"I'm sure they thought that their young daughter was imagining things, as many children do," Yoshio said.

"Or perhaps they were jealous," Muramasa said, leaning over. He stared at Emi and scooped a clump of rice into his mouth. "Like you said, the kami here never, ever talk."

"They forbid me to go to the river," Emi said.

"But you disobeyed," Muramasa said.

"Yes," Emi said. "But not enough. I could not go there for a long time once, when my parents sent me to my mother's family for a time. To..." Emi looked down at her food.

"Be taught a trade?" Muramasa said.

"No."

"Find a husband."

"Yes."

"And when you came back the kami could no longer be found," Muramasa said.

Emi cocked her head to the side. "How do you know so much?"

"Yoshi here is a master of deduction," Muramasa said throwing his thumb toward Yoshio. "Me? I am a master of guessing. Part of that mastery is knowing that people forget all the incorrect guesses."

Emi gave Muramasa a curious look. He smiled back.

"The world is full of kami, of all different sorts. Most of the time we aren't aware of them. This is because they are in many everyday things and events. Earthquakes – that's an easy one to blame on spirits, but they are also in rain, and snow." Muramasa looked at Yoshio. "In fire and steel. The kami that care about us – people I mean – are pretty rare. Water kami, like the rain and the river, simply are. They move and flow through the world so much they scarcely have time to notice us. Frankly, to the spirits of nature, men are a bit inconsequential, though sometimes we can be found to be interesting. That interest can be dangerous."

"You have experience with one," Emi said.

Muramasa nodded. "See? You're a good guesser too. A fire kami. The kami you have enshrined here, well, they are enshrined many places. They are probably a bit too busy to stop by for a ritual, if they even exist. I wouldn't believe very strongly in them either, if I were you," Muramasa turned his head laughed. "I'm sorry to have teased you. Like Yoshio said, I have terrible manners. Luckily, I have deep pockets, so most people forgive me."

Yoshio and Amaya sat on the floor facing each other. The door beside them was open to the night. They carefully tied the long sheets of rice reeds together, with Amaya holding the roll around a bamboo shoot and Yoshio wrapping twine tightly around it in several places. Two more tatami sat in a trough of water just past the eave of the attendance house.

"I heard some rumors while I was in town buying the reeds and today's fish," Amaya said.

"Of what sort?" Yoshio said. He tied a tight knot in the mat.

"A rumor from a travelling merchant, told to another merchant, of a train of nobleman moving across the country from Kyoto, for the summer festivals. The merchant was optimistic."

"Yet you are not."

"They are earlier than expected, which means we will have to meet with them outside of our own convenience."

Yoshio looked at Amaya. "Your face says more."

"True," Amaya said. "He said he met a man who sold goods to an assemblage of men at arms, east of Kyoto."

"Interesting. An army, perhaps. The shogun is already on his way, is he not?"

"Yes, as far as I know, unless you are thinking it might be an attempt to usurp him."

"That is what I am thinking. He may turn back to defend Kyoto. If the Hosokawa are again trying to install a puppet, giving them access to the emperor would be unwise."

"Ashikaga Yoshitane is a clever man. It is probably well within his plans. In fact, I am sure of it. My father reported to him of Hosokawa's search for allies, even though he pays token homage to the shogunate."

"Yoshitane has been forced to abdicate before," Yoshio said. "Perhaps it is the Hosokawa house again."

"Which is why he will be vigilant for it," Amaya said. "Our plans should hold, I think, but I thought you should know."

Yoshio paused a moment. "Who else is the shogun travelling with?"

"The merchant did not say. More noblemen. That could mean daimyo, or just his retainers. Why?"

"If your father or Furukawa is among them, I will have a great deal of explaining to do."

Amaya smiled at Yoshio. "So shall we both."

"This will be an excellent set of swords," Muramasa said. The hammer rang loudly as it fell upon the glowing sheet of steel. A smile split Sengo's face as he worked away at it. "Flip it."

Yoshio complied, flipping over the steel sheet. "How do you know?"

"The bright sparks, the hard feel beneath the hammerhead… but mostly the sound it makes when hit," Muramasa said. "It is like a melody to me. When the sword rings like a deadly bell, you have succeeded in giving the steel its one true spirit. Again."

Yoshio complied and flipped the steel over again. The ringing continued. He watched Muramasa slowly work the steel lengthwise just as he had before, making a long, continuous sheet that hinted at a sword blade between its many times in the forge. When this was complete the smith would take it, after all the work of flattening and elongating the shape, and fold it back on itself. Then he would begin the process again.

"It looks much the same," Amaya said. She stood on the wooden deck of the audience house, her empty bag thrown around her shoulders.

"And so it is," Muramasa said. "The process is slow, but necessary."

Amaya had come to watch for a while in the morning, painting a scene of it, but as the work continued and she finished the details of the painting Yoshio could see boredom take her, and she left with Emi to attend to the business of the shrine.

"I will be heading to town with Emi for some fresh vittles," she said. "Do you need anything?"

"Some flux," Muramasa said. "Doesn't have to be good. Even rosin, something like that will do."

"I don't know where to find flux," she said.

"Then don't worry about it," Muramasa said. "I'll fetch some more at some other time. I'll still have another day of folding this steel before I'll need it for the next piece."

"Can you wait until we are finished?" Yoshio said. "I am still hesitant to let you walk without a guard."

"I can care for myself, but I know that you will worry. I'll tell Emi to wait an hour," Amaya said.

Yoshio nodded, then watched as she turned and walked back to the open door of the house. He let himself feel desire as he watched the subtle motion of her hips in the summer kimono. It felt strange to allow the thought, but also exciting. He knew the thought was dangerous, but everything was dangerous now.

"Eyes on the steel, lad," Muramasa said. Yoshio snapped his head back and flipped the metal over with the tongs.

Painting is a good avocation for Amaya, Yoshio thought as the hammer fell. *Different every time. It is quiet and dignified, a perfect pursuit for a high-standing lady, and excellent for focus and meditation, but it also gives her the constant change she needs.* Yoshio found himself thinking on this as the notes of the steel washed over him, wondering about Amaya's future happiness for the first time since he had met her.

Most honorable and magnanimous Shogun Ashikaga Yoshitane,

I hope midsummer greets you well, finding health and prosperity in the warmth and life of the season.

I would like to thank you for receiving my family's invitation to enjoy the summer festival celebrating Tenjin here on Osaka Bay. I believe the Tanabata star festival is also spectacular, should your eminence find his schedule free enough, and the sea weather still agreeable, to reside in the bay for an additional week.

Let me also offer my deepest condolences for the regrettable death of your son Keiji. It has come to my attention that he was assassinated the same night as Shigeo, the nephew of our mutual relative Minamoto Daiki, whom I was visiting. I am sorry that my own intrigue has prevented me from seeing to the arrangements of your son and preparing for your most noble reception. I hope that the man responsible for his death will be rooted out and justice will be done to him, so that Keiji's spirit may be free to pursue its next path. My retainer and I have been staying near a shrine above Sakai, praying nightly for the resolution of both of our unlucky and malicious situations.

Undoubtedly you have been in friendly communication with Shiba Masaki and it has come to your attention that there is conflict between us. This is true. I will not dare to plead my side of the case, but will instead invite you to witness the duel between my retainer and Masaki's chosen retainer, the victory deciding the outcome of honor for both of us. If the kami and ancestors see fit to award the triumph to me , I will be happy to plead my case to you then, knowing full well that you will understand it to be the truth, and knowing that your highness needs not, in these troubled times, to condescend to such conflicts.

I would like to humbly request an audience with you, not as a matter of business, but as friends and relatives.

Please give my regards to your wife, and I humbly await your reply. May you, as I, find pleasure in the simple truths of life that shine amid the darkness of the times.

Your vassal and servant,

Asano Amaya

"I do not know what opinion I should give on this," Yoshio said, examining the scroll's long vertical lines. "I think the calligraphy is beautiful, but I do not know what goes into writing a letter to the shogun."

"Does the explanation seem plausible?" Amaya said.

"Which one?"

"Any of them."

"Well," Yoshio said, glancing over the letter again. "I find it a bit odd that you express hope that Keiji's killer will be rooted out and punished, considering I am the man who killed him."

"I said I hope justice will be done to him," Amaya said. "And justice unto you would be a reward of comfort and peace, though I don't quite know what *you* would do with comfort and peace."

Yoshio smirked. "I like that you do not reveal the cause of the duel. It feigns humility while avoiding the shogun's judgment."

"Now you are thinking like a noble," Amaya said.

"I'm married to one, eh? I'd best get a handle on such methods." Yoshio rolled up the scroll and handed it to Amaya. She tucked it into a pristine white scroll case, made up of dried and shellacked linen. "Though in the letter you called me your retainer."

"That goes in part with the conflict with Masaki," Amaya said. "I will deny the marriage, casting doubt on the lies Masaki has told, or will tell."

"You have planned this from the beginning."

"I have," Amaya said. "Marriage to you would not be acceptable, for the shogun or my father. At least, so unseen and unannounced. It would not be expected of me, and so we will use it." She ran her hand along the top of Yoshio's arm. "That doesn't mean other things are not real. You must trust me as you have before."

"I do," Yoshio said, running his fingers along her bare forearms.

"I will make sure this is waiting for the shogun at his clan estate north of Sakai," Amaya said, tucking the scroll case into her small bag. "It will show a careful consideration of manners, but not seem too sycophantic. We don't want to give him the impression that we are about to ask for a favor."

"I thought we were asking for an audience," Yoshio said.

Amaya held up her finger. "Yes, but if he anticipates a favor he is as likely as not to find himself too busy to meet with us."

"Navigating the social hierarchy is like walking through a field of traps," Yoshio said. "I'm glad I have a good guide."

Amaya smiled at him. "You have no idea, my dear Yoshi."

"I cannot believe we have had to come all the way down to the harbor to find this stuff," Yoshio said. He rubbed the dried rosin, held in a small bag, between his fingers. It made them feel sticky, but not dry like the rosin he had used in training.

"It's just as well," Muramasa said. "I need to find some polishing stones, and damned if the only polisher in Sakai won't sell some to me."

"Why not just hire him to polish the sword?"

"Eh," Muramasa shrugged, picking up the bag. "I usually farm out stuff like that if I'm in a hurry, but the sword polisher is young, and something about him makes me think he won't do such a good job. Besides, if you want something done right, it is best to do it yourself."

"There are advantages to hiring specialists," Yoshio said.

"I know how to polish a sword, Yoshi," Muramasa said. Yoshio followed him back out into the street, filled with people of both high and low status. Parasols stuck out above the crowd in various places, dots of color in a sea of white and brown.

"And I know how to sharpen one," Yoshio said.

"Then what's the argument?" Muramasa said. He pointed down the street. "The bigger trade houses might have what I'm after."

"I need to see to the women. We shouldn't wander far," Yoshio said, sticking his neck above a group of laughing young women to see Emi and Amaya tying bushels of straw together. Yoshio thought Amaya was trying to dress down, but she stood out, holding herself straighter and more delicate than any of the peasants around her, even when she stooped. He strode over to them.

"Did you find what you sought?" Amaya said. She handed a bag to Yoshio that was heavy with rice.

"Apparently," Yoshio said. "Muramasa wandered off to look for polishing stones."

"Your whetstone would not do?" Amaya said.

"No." Yoshio threw the bag around his shoulders.

"Trust a man to his art," Amaya said.

"I do not know how long he will be," Yoshio said.

"Let's just go back without him," Emi said. "Muramasa makes me miss being all alone up by the shrine."

"I'm sure he could find his way back," Yoshio said, "but I'm also quite sure that he will have something else for me to carry. Something heavy."

"Then I'll treat us to lunch," Amaya said.

Emi sighed but followed Amaya and Yoshio to the row of open markets and restaurants that faced the harbor. Most of them were filled with fisherman and traders of different sorts, laughing and cussing as they ate quickly prepared food. They passed a loud group of eta that whispered to each other as they passed. Yoshio did not spare them a glance, but held tight to his sword. Amaya selected a place closed in by awnings around an open kitchen. Wealthier men, merchants and a select few samurai, filled the low tables in the shade, talking quietly. A serving woman sat them quickly, rushing back between tables with fresh pots of hot water and crushed tea leaves. She came back by and set down a small bowl of them. Amaya began preparing the tea.

"This place is a bit expensive, don't you think?" Emi said as she watched the rich, black tea fill her cup.

"I was just thinking we might be slumming it a bit," Yoshio said with a smirk. "Amaya has particular tastes."

"No sense missing out on fine things, when you can afford them," Amaya said. "And that statement was blessedly familiar of you, of Yoshi."

Yoshio opened his mouth to apologize, then stopped himself. Amaya poured him a cup of tea, and then finally poured one for herself.

"Fine things. One of many treatments for which I owe you thanks," Yoshio said, holding up his cup of tea.

"If thanks are what you owe, you have just paid your debt," Amaya said. She smelled the tea and closed her eyes. "Fresh off the boat." She looked out on the harbor, and the ships that filled it. Most of the docks were empty, vacated by fishing vessels not yet returned from their catch. Far away, larger ships, filled with goods from Korea and China, bobbed slightly, their battened sails pulled up into tight bundles that swayed in the breeze.

Food came quickly after they ordered: freshly cooked fish, lightly oiled and placed on a bed of rice. Emi ate quickly, almost greedily, but she was always careful to control her actions, copying Amaya's graceful pose and deliberate movement with the chopsticks. Yoshio understood, watching the girl, that hunger truly was something she had in common with Muramasa, though she observed much better manners than the swordsmith.

Amaya produced her ink set after the plate was taken away and replaced with more tea. She began a careful painting on a small sheet of white paper with a small and stiff brush, taking her time with each stroke. Yoshio watched her for a time, then something caught his eye from beyond the edges of the open restaurant.

"What is it?" Emi said. Amaya looked up and followed her retainer's eyes over to a group of samurai devouring food and laughing.

"I've seen that face before," Amaya said.

"It is Shiro," Yoshio said. "The commoner that Kuramasa Kuro hired as retainer after demanding that his former bodyguard commit seppuku."

"Who?" Emi said.

"A vassal of my father," Amaya said. "His wife and his retainer betrayed him some weeks back. I wonder if Shiro is still in the employ of him."

"If so, Kuramasa is surely around here somewhere," Yoshio said.

"My first inclination is to avoid him," Amaya said. "I've had enough of that rat-face for the year."

"I agree, but-" Yoshio cut off as the men shifted around the table, reaching for a jug of sake. "There is Kuro, after all. I wonder what he is doing here."

"Perhaps he heard the shogun was coming," Emi said. She looked to Amaya bashfully. "Not to intrude, but I overheard."

"It's fine," Amaya said. She put her brush down on the ink stone and closed her eyes. After a few seconds, she opened them. "I see some disadvantages to him knowing we are in Sakai, not the least of which is my contempt for him. However, if he is planning to play something with the shogun, or any other daimyo with him, it would be good to put some fear into the greedy rodent. Yoshi, go speak to him."

Yoshio looked at her. "What do you mean?"

"Go talk to him. Be yourself, but do not reveal where we are staying or why we are here, other than for the summer festivals."

"This did not work so well last time," Yoshio said.

"He is afraid of you," Amaya said. "Let his tone speak to you when his words are lies."

"Very well," Yoshio said. He pushed himself up and adjusted his swords. "I hope my tea will not get cold in the meantime."

"I'll pour a fresh cup for you," Amaya said. She dipped her brush back into the ink and began painting again, seeming to pay no more heed to the task.

Chapter 17: Water, Soil, Steel

Yoshio stood beside the table, his right hand firmly holding onto the handle of his katana. He watched Kuro laugh with the younger men around him. A jug full of sake sat upright among several empty ones lying on their sides. Drops of rice wine were here and there. Yoshio looked out to the ocean, away from the men who, had they been sober, would have been ashamed of the scene they were making. It was barely mid-day.

He stood there looking at Kuro for what seemed like a very long time, though in truth it was but a few dozen heartbeats. He did not know what to say to the fat daimyo. He pawed through words in his mind, but every phrase he thought of was insulting and angry. He found that he had developed the same contempt for Kuro that Amaya had expressed on the way to the man's estate, and he found that he could no longer think of polite, or even neutral, things to say to him. Kuro laughed at a joke that Yoshio did not find funny, showing incisors that were long and yellow.

Vermin, Yoshio thought. He remembered what Amaya had told him. *Be yourself.* He could never figure out whether that was an insult, or a compliment.

"Kuramasa Kuro," he said aloud. "I cannot say that I am glad to see you here." Kuro looked up and choked on his rice wine. Shiro, the young soldier he had hired on as retainer, turned, trying to draw his sword. "Show a finger of steel, Shiro, and I will show you every bit of mine."

Shiro paused. He began to draw his tachi. Yoshio flashed out with his sword, making a slice across the bridge of Shiro's nose. Though it was barely skin deep, the cut welled up with blood. Yoshio flicked the blood away and returned the katana to its saya.

He glared at Kuro. "What are you doing in Osaka? Should you not be minding your fief for our mutual lord?"

"What is it to you?" Kuro said. "I have the right of travel. It is no business of yours where I go or what I do."

"No, but it is the business of my lord," Yoshio said. "Last I saw you, both your servants and your wife had betrayed you. Who have you left to tend your fields so that you may have the liberty and finances to drink yourself into a stupor in Osaka bay?"

"Bah!" Kuro said, waving at Shiro. "I am not your vassal. I do not answer to you!" He stood up, teetering slightly.

"That is where you are wrong, Kuro-san," Yoshio said, emphasizing the honorific. "In Osaka, I speak for the Asano. By the grace of my master your head remains attached to your body, and by her grace I have withheld my judgment, allowing you to see to the security of your household, but I still have the authority to take heads."

"You have no authority here," Kuro said. "Asano Takahiro will be here within the week."

"Then I am still empowered until our lord arrives," Yoshio said. Yoshio turned away from Kuro "You have told me more than you realize, Kuro-san. I would thank you, but for the misgivings in my heart for your plans. Farewell."

Yoshio walked out from under the awning.

"You still owe me a katana," Kuro said. He looked to Shiro, who wore a face of fear as he pulled himself to his feet, hand on his sword, blood dribbling from his nose into his beard.

"Pray that I do not hold such a debt as valid," Yoshio said. He did not look back, again denying Kuro the courtesy of a bow.

Calmly, he walked back to the restaurant where Emi sat with Amaya, still painting a picture of the bay. They looked up at him as he approached.

"How is our loyal vassal?" Amaya said.

"Drunk and belligerent," Yoshio said.

"So the same as always." Amaya smiled at Yoshio as he sat down. Yoshio looked at her, and his frown disappeared as he chuckled.

"A bit more rat-like than usual," Yoshio said.

"That is notable. Why is he here?"

Yoshio scratched his chin. "Several possibilities. Before I conjecture, you should know that he is expecting your father to be here within the week."

Amaya sighed and put her brush down. "That will make things a bit more difficult, but part of me expected as much. The shogun has traveled here with at least part of the military court."

"Does that concern you?" Yoshio said.

"It merely means that there are more plans afoot than my own," Amaya said. "That is almost always the case anyway, but I'd hoped Osaka would have less conspiracy than Kyoto."

"You don't know this town very well, then," Emi said. "There's always – *always* – something afoot. You know how much silver passes through this port in a day?"

"I'm sure it is more than the emperor or the shogun would know of," Amaya said.

"Then, of course," Emi went on, "There are always the eta, and the Yakuza who run the less seemly businesses. They think of themselves as something more than eta, and act like kindly kings, until they put a knife in your back. Osaka is a bloody town when you get to its heart. I am glad to live up on the hill."

"Me too, for now," Amaya said. She looked at Yoshio. "What about your conjectures?"

"First," Yoshio said, sipping a freshly poured cup of tea. "The fact that he is here at the same time as the shogun should not be overlooked."

"Of course," Amaya said. "In court and war, there are no coincidences."

"That means somebody informed him of the Shogun's plans, for you and I have spoken nothing to him of Osaka. Who, and to what purpose, remains to be discovered. He may have plied the information from a neutral source and may be seeking an audience with Ashikaga to parlay for power or influence. Kuramasa as a clan has seen better days. This is the most benign of what I see."

"I'm sure that will become the socially accepted reason for his visit," Amaya said. "But you see more."

Yoshio nodded. "He is secretive. I think that he believes he will be serving himself. The incident at his estate should prove to us all that he is easily deceived, and not one to make plans on his own. Ultimately, I think he is just a servant of a greater man."

"Nothing is ever simple with you two, is it?" Emi said.

"No, it is not," Amaya said. "My intuition says that you are right, Yoshi. It is unfortunate that we have so much occupying us. I should like to know what Kuramasa is caught up in." She sighed.

"I could help," Emi said.

Amaya raised her eyebrows.

"I could follow him to see where he's staying. He doesn't know me." She looked to Yoshio, who shrugged.

Amaya sipped her tea and cast a glance to Yoshio. "The intrigues of politics are a dirty business. I would not ask you to involve yourself."

"Well, it's more interesting than raking sand at the shrine. Besides, I can look out for myself," Emi said. "I do already."

Amaya glanced again at Yoshio. Yoshio cleared his throat. "Then perhaps you could do this. The retainers held by Kuramasa, including his personal bodyguard, are not samurai. They are cast-off soldiers. Peasants, really, and such men have appetites for things which are not so acceptable in good circles, namely gambling and prostitutes. Talk to the yakuza that you know-"

"I don't know any yakuza," Emi said.

"Of course you do," Yoshio said, "or you would not have spoken of them." He raised a finger. "I do not think less of you for it, you must understand."

Emi frowned. "Fine."

"Talk to the men who run the gambling houses in town, or the men who run the whorehouses – the cheap ones, mind you. The two will know each other."

"Of course they know each other," Emi said. "They occupy the same buildings."

"We will give you a bribe for them." Yoshio nodded to Amaya, who drew open her purse. "Ask them to ply the following from Shiro and his fellows: first, what their lord is doing here with regard the shogun, and second, who he has had in attendance in the last several weeks. The pillow is a place that reveals many secrets."

Amaya handed Emi a stack of flat silver bars, inscribed with unfamiliar Chinese characters. The girl stared at them in her hand for a few moments, feeling their weight. Amaya, seeing her wide eyes said, "It is untaxed silver. I have imperial coins for you, of course. The Chinese mint will obscure the fact that you speak for a noble, though they will still suspect it."

"If they will still suspect it, why bother?" Emi said, putting the silver in her own small bag hanging from her obi.

"Seeing a shadow is not the same as seeing something truly," Amaya said.

At last the steel, which had slowly morphed from mottled chunks of sooty tamahagane into a long sheet of matted grey, was taking the shape of a sword. Muramasa's hammer rang as he molded the hard, good steel around another piece of iron that, though it was less in starting quality, took no less effort to forge. Yoshio helped him, periodically putting the steel back into the raging forge, and holding in on the anvil. He even took the hammer from time to time, though Muramasa had made clear that the final strikes, the hammer falls that would turn it from rough steel to shining sword, could only come from an expert hand.

Eventually, an elongated, narrow band, the width of a blade though straight and much longer, emerged.

"Show me your sword," Muramasa said. Yoshio put down the forceps and pulled his katana from its scabbard. Sengo looked carefully at it. "That's good. Now your wakizashi." Yoshio complied, laying both swords against a nearby stone. Muramasa picked up the tongs and moved the steel over a wedge he had dropped into a hole in the anvil. Yoshio took the tongs back as Muramasa picked up the hammer. It fell on the steel, pressing it against the iron wedge. He threw the hammer down again. The steel began to bend over the wedge, and then it finally broke into two pieces, one longer than the other. The shorter of the two he put to the side. "That will be your wakizashi," he said as he put the longer of the two pieces back in the forge.

Muramasa carefully hammered out a bevel on the hot steel, working from hilt to tip meticulously. The tip he carefully forged apart from the rest of the edge. He worked methodically like an artist, though the sword still looked closer to refuse than a battle blade. He turned the blade over and hammered another bevel. He picked up the long flat piece of steel and looked down its length for irregularities.

Muramasa, seeming satisfied, produced a smaller hammer and placed the back of the blade so that it rested on one corner of the anvil. He hammered along the length of the sword, the small hammer ringing loudly and clearly. Yoshio realized that the tones changed as he moved along the blade. Each place that rang with a dull, or low note, Muramasa would hammer again. Through numerous re-heating and hammering, at last, the blade rang in a single note throughout its length.

"I see now what you meant by my sword having a dull note," Yoshio said.

"The song of the sword is not just aesthetic," Muramasa said, looking over the work. "It tells you the subtle differences in the steel, where things are denser or thicker than they ought to be, even below the threshold of the eyes. It is a practical device, though I do enjoy the tones." He leaned the blade up against another stone. "Your katana is ready for its first rough work with a stone."

"Forgive me, Muramasa-san, but it is not the correct shape," Yoshio said.

"That will be corrected according to the process," Sengo said. "Do not worry."

They repeated the forging with the smaller piece of steel, working until sunset until a wakizashi took form, though it was straight like its brother.

Muramasa looked at Yoshio in the failing light. "Tomorrow, steel gods will be born." He smiled as he stood up. "I'm hungry."

Emi entered the room just as dinner began, Amaya's cooking filling the small room with the smell of fresh fish. The young attendant looked disheveled, her hair falling out of its bun and onto her face, but she seemed cheerful. She sat down at an empty spot and began serving herself a pile of rice.

"I went to speak with an acquaintance of mine, who manages a brothel in the Buraku[36] outside of town," she said.

"You have already discovered something interesting, then," Amaya said.

"More stumbled on it," Emi said. "That man Yoshio spoke to – Kuro – he was already there with a few other men. I thought he was a daimyo."

"He is," Yoshio said. "Though he is not a particularly rich man, merely a vassal of the Asano. It is likely that he cannot afford to pay for the same courtesans that the aristocrats enjoy."

"Prostitutes have always confounded me," Muramasa said.

"Undoubtedly," Emi said.

Muramasa went on, ignoring her. "Men throw their hard earned money away at something literally anyone can do. Where is the accomplishment? The challenge?"

"The challenge is in pretending to enjoy it," Emi said.

"I mean for the men," Muramasa said.

"Kuro is, shall we say, newly liberated from his marriage," Amaya said. "I think he is more concerned with what he has been missing out on than in conquests."

"Bah," Muramasa said. "Not much of a man."

[36] Hamlet or slum.

"On that, you are correct," Yoshio said.

Muramasa shrugged. He looked over to Emi. "Your river kami. He lived near here, correct?"

Emi blinked slowly. "Um... yes."

"Where, exactly?" Muramasa said.

"The stream north of here. That is where I used to talk to him, just up-river from where we found..." Emi looked at Amaya, and then down.

"There is a slowing of the stream, and a sort of pond, yes?" Muramasa said.

"Yes. Why?"

"I will need some clay to fire and quench the swords," Muramasa said. "River silt works well, and if it has been blessed by a kami, it is all the better. You can take me there in the morning."

"I don't know about that," Emi said.

"I know I'm not the company you prefer," Muramasa said, smirking.

"No, it's not that," Emi said. "Well, it *is* that-"

"Good, I like a challenge," Muramasa said, looking to Yoshio, who frowned at him.

"No, I don't know about any blessed river silt," Emi said.

"The former home of a kami is better than nothing," Muramasa said. "Might have picked up a bit of luck."

Yoshio waded through the reeds, donning only a cloth that was wrapped around his loins, his kimono having been left on the shore. He dug down in the water, coming up with handfuls of silt, littered with grass, which he put beside a large clay bowl that sat upon one of the many rocks that protruded from the slow stream. Muramasa, stripped down in similar fashion, went through the piles of mud and sorted out a grey, malleable clay from rocky soil and watery brown silt. Emi sat under the shade of a willow nearby. Though she had agreed to help Muramasa find and retrieve the silted clay he sought, actually pulling it from the streambed would have meant removing her kimono, so instead, she sat watching the men.

"Emi!" Muramasa shouted to the shore.

"I'm not coming in to help you, you old coot," she called back.

"How about you say a prayer or two? Try to get that kami of yours to come back," Muramasa said, ignoring the insult.

"Kami do not come on a whim," She shouted back. "Such is not to respect the spirits."

"Then respectfully ask it to come if it wishes," Muramasa said.

Emi looked around with a sigh. "Very well." She stood up and dusted herself off. From the small bag she had carried with her she withdrew a long chord. She bent down near the stream and began pulling out the stiff water reeds and binding them together. She walked a few paces away and pulled from a tepid bank a single flowering water lily, which she placed in the bundle. She knelt down again near the river and began to shake the bundle up and down, softly touching the running water. She chanted as she did so, imperceptibly soft.

"Never seen this sort of prayer before," Yoshio said, eying the girl.

"Whatever speaks to the spirits is a good prayer," Muramasa said.

Emi paused and looked around at the placid scenery, then closed her eyes and continued. Yoshio piqued his ears, trying to make out her voice over the sound of water falling over stone near at hand.

"Friend of life, friend of mine. This water holds your memory," Emi said, just above a whisper. "Water going into earth, and back up in the sky," she continued. "Everywhere and anywhere my friend can wander free. Please return and bless this place, stained so near at hand. Nothing but respect and purity can I offer with your reeds. If you can see as to withhold a blessing, may you flow from life to life, ever free."

Emi opened her eyes and looked up. She met Yoshio's gaze and turned away, looking upstream.

Muramasa looked over at her. "Maybe not today, then." He reached back into the river and pulled up more clay.

A wind picked up then, whistling through the trees and reeds, knocking tall stalks of bamboo on the far bank together like drums. Emi's hair came undone, and blew away from her face, downstream. Yoshio felt his flesh suddenly tighten with the cold. The tied bundle of reeds and flowers flew apart in Emi's hands. She stood up and looked out to the center of the water and smiled, warm and wild despite the cold wind.

"Did you hear that?" Muramasa said.

"What?" Yoshio said.

"The whispers!" Muramasa hissed. He turned upstream.

"I heard Emi whispering," Yoshio said, trying to track Muramasa's gaze

"No, it was the kami," Yoshio said. "He remembers."

Yoshio strained, but all he could hear on the wind was the sound of leaves and rattling plants. A loud crack sounded from somewhere upstream. A current picked up against the line of rocks, sending Yoshio sprawling onto a boulder. The water level rose. Sengo pushed himself up toward the stream.

"Can you hear him?" Emi said.

"Yes," Muramasa shouted back. "But I cannot understand."

"Just listen," Emi said, looking to Muramasa. "He was here first. His words are truer than ours."

The water rose again, almost to a flood, and spilled between the rocks. Muramasa lost his footing and fell backward into the water. Yoshio reached under and, catching the blacksmith, pushed his head above the torrent. Muramasa gasped for breath.

He looked to see Emi laughing, the wind whipping her hair across her face. "The spirits want to drown you, Muramasa."

"Of course," He shouted, pushing the hair off of his forehead. "He senses the fire."

"We should get to shore," Yoshio said, dragging Muramasa.

"No," Muramasa said. He stood back up. "Please, spirit. If you do not understand my words, know my feeling. Purify this, your home, so that I can quench the untamed kami of fire. It is told the water sees further than even the wind. You must understand."

The wind intensified, and then, in a sudden burst of an overwhelming gale, stopped, and reduced to a calm breeze. Yoshio felt the sun on himself and was surprised, as if he had walked out of a house into daylight. He thought he could make out, among the rustling of foliage, a faint whisper, though the words sounded strange.

"Ha!" Muramasa said, looking at Emi. "The land itself speaks to you! You are no simple shrine attendant."

Emi smiled. "I *am* a simple shrine attendant. I guess I am a shaman too."

Muramasa laughed again and tried to make to shore. He found he could not move. Yoshio pushed against the rocks and found that his feet too were stuck, buried beneath a tall bed of silt. He reached down and dug around his calves, bringing up a fistful of clay. Sengo did the same, and feeling the grey material in his fingers, cracked a wide smile. He went to the bowl and dumped out all of the clay they had collected previously, then began heaping the fresh silted clay into it, laughing all the while.

"It seems he didn't detest you too much after all," Emi said, walking to the sandbar nearest to Yoshio and Muramasa.

"I am thankful," Muramasa said. "Fill up those jugs with river water."

"Since you asked politely," Emi said, and dipping one of their clay jugs into the river.

Yoshio paused from the digging of the silt and looked upriver. The stream was calm, and only a slight breeze could be perceived. He strained to hear the whispers again.

"Something wrong?" Muramasa said.

Yoshio turned back to him. "Nothing, I'm just rarely so surprised."

Yoshio looked around the dimly lit building. Its low ceiling and many support posts made him feel claustrophobic, though it was very spacious inside, running forty paces or more between walls. He could smell, though he could not see, somebody smoking opium, and it turned his stomach slightly. Women reclined on cushions and couches with men along the edges of the walls. They were dressed in loose garments and more than one had her breasts exposed through the draping cloth. Yoshio could only think of the clothes as "flimsy," a far cry from the carefully arranged courtesans he had seen in Kyoto. These were women not made to look beautiful, but enticing; tempting. The men that sat with them matched them in their simple, yet not quite dirty, appearance.

"This way," Emi said. Yoshio looked down to see the young woman walk confidently through the room to another door that was shut. She looked at Yoshio. "You really stand out here," she said, raising an eyebrow.

"Honor shines more brightly in the dark light of self-abasement," he said.

"I meant that you're frowning," Emi said. She looked around the room. "Do you see anyone else frowning?"

Yoshio looked around. Virtually everyone, including the women, was indeed smiling or laughing. "No."

"Then lighten up, if you can figure out how." She slid open the door and stepped inside. Yoshio followed, consciously trying to relax his brow. The room was filled with low tables. Cards littered the tops of many of them, which were gamblers from many walks. Most appeared to be playing Oichu-Kabu, a popular game of chance, and judging by the stacks of silver in front of them, they were losing.

Emi led him to where a young man leaned against the wall, a katana, slightly shorter than normal, tucked in his belt. He watched a few of the tables, his tattooed hand on his sword.

"Katashi-san," Emi said. He turned his attention from the tables and looked at her.

"You're back," he said. "So soon. Who's this?"

"My hired muscle," Emi said, winking. Yoshio looked at Katashi, trying to smile.

"Fine, don't tell me," Katashi said. "Not like I care." He crossed his arms.

"Well, the men I was interested in were already here when last I came. I figured you'd have found something," Emi said.

"Not much that I believe," Katashi said.

"Just because it seems implausible does not mean it is false," Yoshio said. Katashi frowned at him.

"So he's a philosopher and hired muscle," Katashi said. He laughed to himself.

"I would still like to know what they said," Emi said.

"Well, the fat old one…" Katashi snapped his fingers as if trying to remember.

"Kuro," Emi said.

"Yeah, he called himself a daimyo," Katashi said. "Which is a barrel of dung. Sure, he had plenty of money – too much for the whores here, but I'm not going to turn away a customer – but he was clearly a merchant. Bad manners even for one of them."

"What sort of things did he say?" Emi said.

"Bunch of nonsense about how he was friends with the shogun. He said he had a 100,000 koku fief owing the Hosokawa."

"Interesting," Yoshio said. "Did he say anything else?"

"Not that I heard, specifically," Katashi said. "He spent most of the night, when he wasn't down here drinking and boasting, upstairs with Hana, one of the girls. Had some problems with her."

"You threw him out?" Yoshio said.

"Not those kinds of problems," Katashi said. "She just said it was more of the same boasting."

Yoshio looked at Emi, his hand stroking his chin.

"What about the other man," Emi said. "The one with the old tachi."

"He didn't have much to say," Katashi said. He narrowed his eyes. Emi pulled a flat silver bar from her pocket. Katashi took it, nodded, and then looked around. "He paid with a promissory note, though he couldn't read the kanji on it. It was from a trader in north Osaka. It said fifty ounces, but he claimed it was for 100."

"Which one?" Yoshio said.

"Mitsowaga."

Yoshio looked at Emi and nodded slightly.

Emi looked at Katashi. "Thank you."

"I don't like seeing you around here," he said. Emi nodded silently, almost bashfully, and Yoshio followed her out.

It was warmer in the hills than down by the bay, and the door to the yard was left cracked, letting in a slight breeze. Amaya lay on her side, watching Yoshio as he looked out to the moonlit courtyard.

"It is significant that Shiro had that promissory note," Yoshio said. "It means that he and Kuro are working to opposite ends."

"Not necessarily," Amaya said. "They could be working to the same ends, just not aware of the other."

"True," Yoshio said. "I could see someone hiring Shiro without the Kuro knowing. It would be wise for a dirty job. Of course-"

"You should not let Kuramasa occupy your mind," Amaya said. "He is not the kind of distraction you need right now."

"You are right," Yoshio said. "I should focus on the duel. That is the critical action. Kuro can play his games."

"Shut the door and come to bed," Amaya said.

Yoshio pushed the door shut and turned around. Amaya's kimono was hanging on a stand behind her. The sheets of the bed, rough and textured, hung lightly around her hips, leaving her upper body bare. Yoshio thought about the women in the brothel, dressed casually. They presented a different sort of beauty from what he had been told to admire throughout his adult life, and though he had looked at them with derision, the same sort of image made flesh before him did not evoke the same reaction. Amaya, disrobed, was far more enticing than they were, and was still, as he saw it, a marvelous beauty. She pleased both viscerally and aesthetically. He wondered again how she was not married.

He untied his obi and hung up his own kimono, then slipped into bed. He felt Amaya's hands and arms around him.

"Is this real?" he said.

"Of course," Amaya said. "This was never part of the plan. At least, it is not what I had planned."

"What plan shall it be part of, then?" Yoshio said.

"Do not make this part of my conspiracy, Yoshi. I just want you to own this night."

He complied.

Muramasa applied the clay, partially wetted with the water from the stream to become a thick, grey molding material again, to the now roughly polished straight blades. First, he coated thickly the back edge and sides, using the richest and stiffest of the clay. Next, he took thinner clay, and after mixing it down further with water, dragged it on the sides going from the back out to what would become the sharp edges of the swords. Yoshio watched Muramasa as he gave the blade a crisscross pattern with the wettest clay, though the space between the lines of silt grew and shrunk, and seemed to be almost haphazard. The blacksmith left these blades to dry in the sun. The rest of the river water they poured in a long trough.

When they returned the next morning, the clay had dried into a dirty grey. The pieces looked ugly as the forge was lit. Yoshio once again manned the bellows.

"It must be hotter still," Muramasa said, throwing more coals into the center of the forge. Yoshio pumped harder. "Keep up that pace. This is the most important and critical step. We have but one chance to make this blade perfect." Muramasa, holding steady the tongs, put the katana in the forge. He looked in, watching the blade heat, mindful of the position it held among the coals. Frequently, he would flip it or adjust the angle, then cover it with more coals.

"It looks as though our hurried patience has, at last, come to fruition, my friend," Muramasa said, drawing the metal from the coals. It was glowing red along the edge. He looked at Yoshio, who had stopped pumping. "Now comes the miracle."

He thrust the entire length of the metal into the trough of water. A torrent of steam rushed up into Yoshio's face, feeling as though it were burning him, as the blade hissed in the water. Muramasa smiled as the steaming water began to clear. After a few moments, he dipped his tongs back in and retrieved the blade.

It came up, still steaming, but in seconds had gone from a straight piece of steel to a katana with a perfect curvature.

"That *is* a miracle," Yoshio said. He admired the shape as Muramasa held the piece in front of him. "Perfection."

"Perfection is in the water, and soil, and the steel," Muramasa said. "And through such the gods have made another, this one of steel, to join with them, may it serve you well."

The swordsmith placed it on a makeshift rack to cool. Yoshio saw him smile as he gazed upon it, then he pointed back to the bellows. It was time for the wakizashi to be born.

END OF ACT IV

Interlude: Savory and Sweet

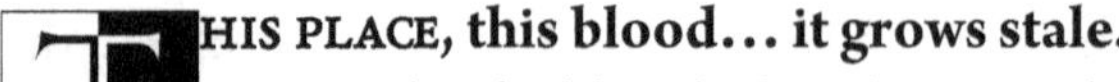

THIS PLACE, this blood... it grows stale.

It is the ideal for which we have searched. What else is there?

Such fine feasts, and still...

Hunger. Such agonizing desire, and Masaki will not deliver us a meal until we meet that old fool again. I will enjoy devouring him, piece by piece.

Patience. That meal may be bitter still.

Bitter. Bitter can be sweet, given the right surroundings.

Sweet. Perhaps. Till then...

The hunger was overwhelming Ryunosuke. He felt himself doubling over, like there was a lurch in his stomach, but there was no pain there. Instead, there was a dull ache that permeated his body, like all his joints were on the verge of popping.

He looked down. Masaki's dog laid at his feet, mangled almost beyond recognition, the once friendly face torn apart. Sinew and gore spread from where its muzzle had been to a nearby wall, where he had flung it with the tip of his katana. His sword had dissected the animal, drawing its spine into halves that split apart and revealed its organs. The sword had tasted each one individually, but it was not enough. It was an interesting experiment, slaying a beast, though it was totally unfruitful. It was like a morsel, a few grains of rice. He needed a meal.

He stabbed the sword into the dog and flung the corpse over a wall, into the garden of Masaki's neighbor. A trail of blood and gore was left behind on the stones. That would sew conflict. Ryunosuke was too hungry to be excited about it. He walked quickly to the gate that marked the end of the estate of his lord – a lord to him only in name, for as time wore on Masaki permitted the will of the dragon to dominate in all things, and even actively did as Ryunosuke commanded. That trusted part of himself – the dragon, the demon katana that had become one with his mind, was gaining influence over others.

He leapt from shadows onto the edge of the wall, the door guard oblivious, and looked out upon Osaka bay. His vision clouded. The lanterns of the city at night, shining like stars before the ocean, slowly faded and were replaced by a different sense. The hunter's vision was taking over, and instead of lights, he saw deep red blotches, the bleeding sins of the many denizens of the bay. Among them, he saw swirling phantoms, the remains of ancient spirits, one with the land but separate from the people that had forgotten them. Beyond the field of red, he saw the ocean. It would normally be a rippling black, but as he looked through the eyes of the dragon, Ryunosuke viewed the ocean as alive with color.

A multitude of ancient kami swam there; so many that one could not be discerned from the other in the sea of radiance. Since his arrival in Osaka the dragon had put forth his vision less and less, for each time they gazed out on the free and wild ocean, they felt a chill. Ryunosuke shuddered, and turned the vision back to the houses and inns.

He saw one among the noise, pulsing and growing. His vision reached forward, as if his spirit were flying toward it. Everything got larger and clearer. He could see him now – a man taking pleasure in pain.

Exquisite.

Ryunosuke leapt off the wall and moved toward the beacon, ignoring the dull and muted colors of the people still walking the street. He struck a balance between the bright hungering clarity of the hunter's vision and the human eyes he relied on otherwise so that he was better able to discern the man-made streets and buildings while still homing to the meal he sought.

He entered a long street, bright red, filled with men who reveled in pain. Their souls screamed to him. The ravishing hunger grew, and he quickened his pace, passing through the sparse crowd like a wind, moving faster than his feet would reveal. He reached the appointed place. He could see through the deceased world-flesh to the inner rooms. He looked around with his human eyes.

This is a house of pleasure. Odd that it brings so much pain.

Not odd.

He looked through the layers of dead wood, paper, and stone and saw his quarry. He let the human part of him flesh out the details from the swirling auras. A man was beating a woman. It was savage, and her pitiful orange aura flickered under the assault. She begged him to stop, and he did not. Finally, her aura dimmed as the man threw her onto the bed. He remained, searching through other dead things.

He is looking through her belongings.

Why?

Money.

We should take him now.

Too many people about. It will be bad for us to be seen. The man retrieved something, and turned to leave.

Ryunosuke saw this and moved backward. He leapt onto a nearby roof, landing silently on the tiles, and crouched down. He watched the man exit. Ryunosuke watched him push his way through the swirling dim clouds of other people. He followed the man, jumping silently from roof to roof. The streets narrowed into dirt paths. The crowd thinned. Finally, his quarry reached an area filled with modest houses, some leaning against each other. It was dark to the human eyes. Behind thin walls, people slept.

Ryunosuke hopped off a roof and landed lightly on the street behind the man, who was rushing toward home. The hunter's hand went to the dragon, and rush of power and hunger in anticipation racked him. The moment had arrived. The man turned into a path and stopped. He was in front of a house. A door stood open.

The seal was broken on the sword and saya. He began to draw the katana silently. He paused.

Curious.

"Out of my way, boy," the man said.

"No. I won't let you hurt her anymore. And I am no longer a boy, father."

"I said move."

Sudden screams erupted, and the red aura of the dragon's prey flashed bright crimson and deep purple. Ryunosuke approached, his sword at the ready. The man's aura flickered, and winked out. The body collapsed. Ryunosuke held his position.

"Who are you?" Ryunosuke could see, faintly, a young boy, holding a sword. He trembled.

"I am... Ryunosuke," he answered. His sword wavered, the point turning in circles toward the boy. He felt deprived; his feast was taken from him by this stranger, and the hunger was worse than ever.

"If you are a friend of my father's, you should know," the boy stammered. "That I know the art of-"

"I am nobody's friend." Ryunosuke could not return the sword. He must feed. Drink. Drown in blood. He had no choice; he could not resist, or else feast on himself. Feeling reluctance that was less than his compulsion to devour the spirit, Ryunosuke slashed at the boy.

The boy screamed, trying to put his sword up in a guard, but it was too late, and the hunger too strong. The demon blade arced through his body perfectly, and with lightning quickness. Blood, quenching and satisfying, flew through the air and onto the ground. The blade tasted it, and Ryunosuke's mouth urged to feel the same. He slashed again, severing the boy's head and silencing his strange, high-pitched scream.

A rush of color and pleasure filled his being.

He realized he had blood on his mouth and neck, a rush of clarity with the end of feeding, but rather than feeling the demon subside, he felt a sudden growth.

The taste! The taste was so different to him, like a meal shunned for a lifetime, only to discover on accident that it was, in reality, a delicacy.

It is... the taste of innocence. The boy's blood, his chi, was coursing through the nodes of power of Ryunosuke's body and the blade. The hunter's vision sprang to life. It was different than before. The world was now full of colors. Not just the red beacons of the wicked, or the swirling of the spirit realm, but all around him, moving up the sides of the hills from the bay and in the multitude of dwellings at hand, he could see auras of people. They were of suddenly a multitude of colors he had never seen. Oranges and blues, bright hungering red, and a new, bright beacon of green. He had tasted the blood of the righteous, and found it suddenly whetted an appetite he had never known.

What is it? How?

It is... sweet. That was it. The taste of the wicked, who he had pursued for so long as a spirit of vengeance, was like a savory meal, but he had ignored the wonder of the virtuous, as if they had never existed. Why did he never dine on them before?

Vengeance. That was so long ago.

The boy's spirit was a bright, sweet delight, and he wanted more. The hunter's vision peered into the house, and he saw more green auras. One was dull and pulsed softly, while two others were tiny, but shined as bright as the sun, seemingly. A new hunger welled up inside of him.

I will be fed! The blade was not returned to its saya. Ryunosuke stepped up toward the house, his katana seeking the two small beacons of life. The larger one stirred and moved toward him.

And so, he feasted. It was the sweetest thing he had ever tasted.

ACT V

Chapter 18: The Court of Ashikaga

"YOU LOOK VERY BEAUTIFUL," Yoshio said. He strode beside Amaya in the kimono she had the trader's wife make for him. His swords, his old swords – Muramasa had yet to finish the polish and fitting of his new set – were placed in their proper position and his hair was tied up in a proper knot. The sun was just beginning to set, and the wind off the ocean was cool and refreshing.

"Thank you for the courtesy, Yoshi." Amaya wore her outfit of overlapping layers of white trimmed with red. He had helped her tie her obi properly in the back, and her hair was perfectly arranged over her shoulders and back. She looked like a model wife for a high-ranking samurai, but as Yoshio looked at her careful walk, her tabi socks moving barely past the hem of her kimono, he thought the arrangement took something away from her.

"It is no courtesy," Yoshio said. She looked back and gave him a closed-mouth smile. She was beautiful, to be sure, but the Amaya he had come to admire – to love, if he could accept that notion outside of the bedchamber – was much more attractive to him with her bluntness, honesty, and expression of true self. A nobleman's wife lacked the gumption to make a truly enjoyable companion.

"I should warn you," she said, "That the shogun, and those daimyo in attendance with him, may say some things about you or me, or our families, that could be insulting. It is intentional, as the edge of politeness always rests in the eyes of the powerful, and Ashikaga Yoshitane ever wishes to test the mettle of those he considers less than himself."

"I will do my best to withhold anger, and manage my emotions," Yoshio said. "Though I have allowed my true feelings to be seen by you many times, I have a great amount of practice holding them in, especially with my superiors."

"I know," Amaya said. "I remember when we first met; you were as readable as a sheer stone to Furukawa and my father."

"Thank you," Yoshio said.

"But not to me, Yoshi," Amaya said. She smirked and looked ahead as they approached the entry gates. An old man in a grey kimono was rubbing the dull bronze handles of the gates with a rag, trying vainly to buff them to a sheen.

"This place seems less spectacular than Masaki's abode," Yoshio said, looking above the wall at the large eaves and roofs of the estate.

"Nobody would ever say so," Amaya said. "The house of the shogun will always be recognized as the finest house. If not the largest, then it has the best proportions. If not that, then it will have the finest decorations. If not that, then it will best represent the quest for nirvana."

"I see," Yoshio said. "Perhaps it is best if you handle the compliments."

"That will be my role, so far as we are together. You may be excluded from some counsel though, as a mere retainer."

"Good," Yoshio said. "That way there is less opportunity to embarrass myself."

"You think too little of your wit," Amaya said.

"Better than thinking too much of it," Yoshio said. The man polishing the gate took notice as they approached, and pushed on one of the great handles. The door swung inward, revealing a long stone-lined walkway leading up to a great house. He bowed as they stepped past him. Two armored samurai stood outside the open front door, long spears leaning on their shoulders. Inside, lanterns jumped to life in the failing light, illuminating large spaces.

"Remember what we talked about," Amaya said. Yoshio nodded.

Yoshio followed Amaya up the steps and past the samurai. A matronly woman stood just past the door, dressed in a fine silk kimono. Amaya stopped and bowed to her. Yoshio followed suit.

"Lady Amaya," the woman said, nodding. "I received your letter on my arrival two days ago. You were most gracious to greet us so, to invite us here, and to provide for the refreshment of our house in your absence. I should also like to communicate the acceptance of your condolences. Keiji and his father were not on good terms lately, so the news was merely regrettable for him. Nonetheless, he is appreciative."

"And what about for you, Esteemed Lady Natsuko?" Amaya said.

"For me it is sad," Natsuko said. "However, no mortal life is not marred by death. I trust the will of the gods."

"As do I," Amaya said. They followed the woman along a hallway open on one side to a well-manicured garden, though some of the shrubs showed freshly trimmed woody stems among their dark-green leaves. They reached the edge of an open foyer where a group of men sat, hot tea in front of them. Retainers stood by, their hands on their katana, eyeing, in particular, Yoshio as he and Amaya approached the doorway. None of the seated men spared a glance at the new arrivals. Amaya touched his hand and they paused at the threshold. Natsuko stepped past them and stood silently, smiling.

"Preparations are always long in the making, and swift in the doubting," one man said. He was middle-aged, wearing an uncustomary thick beard and mustache. He sat near at hand to another man, slightly older if not the same age, who wore a thin beard and had his hair tied up in a high knot that stood several hand-spans high. Both men sat upon a wooden riser, slightly higher than the others.

The shogun, Yoshio thought. *The man beside him must be the kanrei,*[37] *Ouchi Yoshioki. If only I had the time and position to have him teach me of his battle tactics.* All of the men in the room dressed simply, as samurai. Somehow, he had expected the great warlord to be different.

"That does not mean we should not prepare contingencies." Yoshio recognized Furukawa Kenta seated across from the warlords, his once lord. The man's face was cleanly shaved, and he looked much healthier than when Yoshio had left him.

"I assume everyone has already planned their own contingencies," Ouchi, the kanrei, said. "Which is no matter. Honor may bind your lives, but I do not expect all daimyo to act outside their interests."

"There are men that might consider that an insult." The man who spoke cast a fleeting glance to Amaya, and Yoshio recognized him as Asano Takehiro, Amaya's father. He had a stern but calm face, and did not show anger, even at the insult. "We are loyal, so we know you do not speak for us, but for those who would oppose the bakufu.[38]"

"Of course we trust all of you," the shogun said. "You have proven your loyalty on the battlefield. Oaths and bushido bind some men, but having been betrayed before, I know that words and codes are of little meaning when blood is spilt. Your blood speaks where others would lie. That is what Yoshioki-san meant."

"Thank you, your eminence," Furukawa said.

The shogun looked hard at Furukawa. "Betrayal is a certainty. It ever factors into my plans, even if it is not yours." He looked to his wife and nodded.

She nodded back, then looked at Amaya and Yoshio. They followed her across the threshold. "My lord, please let me introduce Asano Amaya, daughter of Takehiro, and her retainer, Taoka Yoshio."

The shogun nodded. "It is good to see you well, Amaya-san."

"And you, liege," Amaya said, bowing low.

"I got your letter. Masaki tells interesting stories, eh?" the Shogun continued. "Perhaps this marriage to your retainer was part of some misunderstanding?"

"Undoubtedly," Amaya said.

"We have not met in person, Yoshio-san," the shogun said, turning to Yoshio, "but your reputation, courtesy of Lord Furukawa, precedes you. I am glad to have your sword again, as I have before on the battlefield. "

"You shall have both, my lord," Yoshio said, bowing low.

"Won't you sit and have some tea with us?" Yoshitane said. He looked to the kanrei beside him, who nodded.

Yoshio followed Amaya to a sitting area outside the two camps of daimyo, facing the assembly at a 90-degree angle. Natsuko sat near to the shogun as a young woman came in bearing fresh cups and a hot teakettle.

"How has your stay in Osaka been?" Yoshitane asked.

"Alas," Amaya said, "It has been less pleasant than expected. The incident with Daiki was most distressing."

The shogun looked at Yoshio. "What about you, Yoshio-san? You have seen the horror of battle."

"In battle," Yoshio said, "the aim is to slay your opponent and to move onto the next one. There is no time to revel in death and suffering. The revelry comes only from victory, and from being alive. What I saw in the house of

---

[37] A title meaning vice-shogun.

[38] Shogunate; the bakufu is the government and policies of a particular shogun.

Daiki-san was nothing like battle. I am thankful that I spared Amaya the sight."

Both the shogun and the kanrei frowned at him. Yoshio looked at Lord Asano, who wore a blank expression.

"My apologies," Yoshio said, realizing how he had spoken of Amaya. He bowed quickly, setting his hands in front of himself. "Amaya-sama and I have spent much time travelling, and I have forgotten my manners."

The shogun looked at Amaya, who said, "It is no bother to me, Noble Shogun. I bid him to cease, in fact, because I felt that we had become friends. Such formalities, during long hours-"

"Are *we* not friends?" the shogun said. He looked stern.

"Of course," Amaya said, "but you are my superior. Such is not my choice. If you wished-"

The shogun laughed. "It is fine, Amaya-san. Yoshio, I have heard you are slated for a magnificent duel."

"I cannot speak for its magnificence, my liege," Yoshio said. Just then, he caught the eye of the third daimyo attending the Shogun, and he lost his train of thought.

"Well, what can I expect? Yoshio?"

Yoshio snapped his eyes back. "You can expect a duel between competent swordsmen. I can attest to my opponent Noburu, for he was once my student."

"Ah, interesting," Ouchi said from beside the shogun. "A student faces his master, honor and life on the line."

"Yes," Yoshio said. He looked again at the third Daimyo, who stared back silently, his eyes narrowed. It was Yamada Nobuyuki. The lord was not as fat as he remembered, but Yoshio could not forget the face of the man who stole his wife.

"You should tell Furukawa that the villain is slain. We do not need this foolish distraction to continue during such a critical time." Amaya's father stood looking out the open window, out onto an ugly stretch of dirt road lined by a few ragged trees.

"Then what was the point of this endeavor, my lord?" Yoshio said.

Takehiro turned back to him and scowled. "You have said enough to embarrass me, my daughter, Furukawa, and yourself. You should not speak anymore." Yoshio felt a heat rising up from his neck, but stuffed the emotion and nodded. "And you, Amaya. I did not persuade Furukawa to part with his finest swordsman just so that you could enjoy a man in your bed sheets."

"Father, I... You are mistaken," Amaya said.

"Do not try to fool me," Takehiro said. "Do you think you are a mystery to me, my daughter? No, you did not get your knack for reading people from nowhere."

"My affairs are my own, father," Amaya said sternly.

"No, they are not your own. They are the affairs of the entire family, for you bind all of us in your insufferable plotting," Takehiro said. He stepped toward Yoshio. "Perhaps I care too much for my daughter, but I will not suffer the unworthy to have her."

"Yoshio is the finest warrior I have ever seen," Amaya said. "He will prove it at the duel."

"Such skills do not make a man worthy of the peerage. You are lucky that I conceived that you had this plot before you left," Lord Asano said. "Your feud with Shiba Masaki is as dangerous as it is pointless, but it may serve the goals of the bakufu this time. That is why it was permitted. That, and because it allowed me to retrieve Furukawa's attention after the murder of his lover. This is why I have allowed you to come here."

"My feud is not pointless," Amaya said. "And the killer is real. We have followed him all over Honshu." The pitch of her voice had risen to an argumentative treble.

"Yes, it *is* pointless," Takehiro said. "You should have been married to Masaki, not trying to exact revenge for him exercising his right. And the killer is pointless too. In fact, I think he did Furukawa a favor by offing his lover. I had reason to believe the boy was a spy."

Boy, Yoshio thought. *I understand now. And a spy.*

"You know that I would never marry a man like Masaki!" Amaya said.

"Nor would I ever make you," Takehiro said, his voice lowering as he leaned back up against the window. "But you need to let go of the past, Amaya. Revenge for a lover now dead ten years has already drained enough of your life. I would rather you spend it living." He sighed, and the angry lord suddenly became a sullen, aging man.

"After this week, I will," Amaya said.

"It will not bring you joy, this revenge," Takehiro said. "Though it may yet serve greater plans." He turned back toward them. "I am sorry for my anger, Amaya. Things are tense. I have a room prepared for you. I will call you when we are ready to discuss plans."

Amaya, blushing relaxed. Yoshio realized she had been standing on her toes as she shouted with her father.

"I already have lodging near the shrine. I sent a letter to the shogun."

"I read it," Takehiro said. "I don't know why you would care to stay up on the hillside, but I need you here."

"What about Yoshio?"

"I don't care where he goes."

"I understand," Amaya said. She sighed. "Before I go, you should know of some intrigue we have discovered with Kuramasa Kuro."

"He is not important," Lord Asano said. "Let the rat scheme. He will still be prey to the cat."

"What do you think the daimyo are planning?" Yoshio said. He stood with Amaya near the entrance to the large house, in a small room that was currently used to store foodstuffs. Bags of rice were stacked on bending shelves.

"I don't know yet," Amaya said.

Yoshio scratched his chin. "The presence of the kanrei is significant, Amaya. Ouchi is the foremost military commander in Honshu. It was he who commanded us when we took back Kyoto some years ago. He does not like to travel, either."

"So you think there is some military conflict brewing," Amaya said.

"I would guess it," Yoshio said. "But I am a swordsman, I think first of the sword. Other considerations enter my mind more slowly."

"Then I shall do my best to discover what is amiss. I will have the ear and mouth of my father here. It is wise to consider the plans of others, especially the powerful, when constructing your own. Thankfully, it appears Masaki is not part of their plans, or is else a victim of them. I think I can assure the duel will go on without a hitch."

"So you will be remaining here?" Yoshio said.

"Yes," Amaya said. "My father has some use for me, as I have for him, and I should see to it."

Yoshio rubbed his chin as he leaned out the door of the little room. He looked through the open front doors to the gate, which also stood ajar, though flanked by two grim-looking young swordsmen.

"I will be safe," Amaya added.

"Yes, I suppose I could not ask for more," Yoshio said. "But I do not know these men. If our killer were to arrive…" He shook his head.

Amaya grasped his right hand in both of hers. "Come now, my dear Yoshi. You are not so arrogant as to believe that you alone possess the skill required to protect me?"

"Of course not, but these men have never seen him at work-"

"Besides," Amaya interrupted, "He will not come for me. Masaki is my enemy here, a much more manageable and easily contained threat in the house of the shogun."

"So sure are you," Yoshio said.

"Of course I am," Amaya said. She squeezed his hand tighter. "Now go. You have training to attend to. I will do my best to come see you."

"What about your things?"

"Bring them when it is convenient to you. I am not lacking here."

"As you wish, Amaya," Yoshio said. He gripped her hand back, then released it. He stepped out the door and paused.

"What is it, Yoshi?" Amaya said.

"Something your father said, about you and Masaki," Yoshio said. "He said Masaki was acting within his right. That you sought revenge for a lover…" He turned and looked into Amaya's steady eyes.

"What are you trying to say, Yoshio? Don't hold back from me."

Yoshio took a breath. "Did you betray Shiba Masaki?"

Amaya folded her hands. "What do you think, my dear retainer?"

"I think I trust you," Yoshio said. "But much can change in ten years."

She smiled at him. "Then trust me a bit longer."

Yoshio frowned and nodded, then walked out the door of the house. Amaya stood there for a long moment, holding the smile, then her shoulders slumped, and her face darkened with a sigh.

Yoshio approached the shrine grounds alone. His thoughts had twisted around themselves all the way from the shogun's house. *The daimyo had obviously planned on travelling here, but to what end? The kanrei came with the shogun. Kyoto is now unattended by the generals. Why Osaka? Is there someone here they must persuade, and for such risk? If so, who else but Masaki? That would be very bad, being forced to ally with that man after so much.* Yoshio sighed. *They might interfere with the duel. Things are*

never simple. Another thought entered his mind. *Yamada. Yamada is part of the inner circle.* His heart jumped up. Old wounds managed to be held shut as he pushed the image of the man out of mind, but they held together just barely.

His thoughts strayed to Amaya as he walked up the last slope to the house, the path now dry and dusty after the departure of the summer storm. Her answer to his question was circumspect, and he still wondered what the plain answer would be. His heart held the truth – but he was not ready to speak it to himself. The image he held of Amaya was still too dear to him.

Yoshio's ears, ever tuned to the inconspicuous, heard a constant, subtle squeaking as he moved into the shrine grounds. Above the sound was the soft rushing of voices, though he could not make out the words.

He touched his sword as he moved past a row of bushes and low hanging tree limbs, and saw Emi and Muramasa sitting on the wood deck outside the front door. The afternoon sun was shining at the blacksmith's crossed feet. He worked a blade over a large, grey stone, slick with oil, and the grating of the steel slowly began to move toward a high pitched squeal. Once it became a constant pitch, he moved to the next section of the blade.

"So there you are," Muramasa said, not looking up. Emi turned her head and swiftly stood up, away from the swordsmith, and cleared her throat. "And your wife is missing, I see."

"I wasn't expecting to catch you two acting pleasant toward one another," Yoshio said.

"It's not like I had anyone else to talk to," Emi said.

"What about you, Sengo?" Yoshio said.

"I'll talk to anybody, about anything," Muramasa said. "You know that. It's a good thing you didn't drag me off to meet the shogun, or we'd all have our heads on the floor."

"I nearly had my own neck catch a blade," Yoshio said. "But in such close calls, there is often wisdom."

"And what is the wisdom, warrior-sage?" Muramasa said, smiling as he worked the blade over the stone.

"The familiar is dangerous," Yoshio said, stepping up to see the blade. "Familiarity creates expectations, and expectations set the stage for misjudgment... or betrayal."

"So, your beloved betrayed you to the shogun," Muramasa said. He held up the sword and looked at the steel, which shone brightly in the sun, a far cry from the dull grey it had been after quenching.

"Amaya is faithful, as always," Yoshio said, choosing not to react to Muramasa's deliberate remark. "I just added that piece because, as I contemplated on my way here, it is true. Betrayal, that is, successful betrayal, always comes from those who you least expect."

"I hope you don't have to learn that one through experience," Emi said. She leaned over and looked at Muramasa as he flipped the sword over and began on the other side.

"Alas, but I have," Yoshio said. "Just not through Amaya."

"I forgot that you were married before," Muramasa said.

"I never spoke to you of that," Yoshio said.

"Aye, but it's easy enough to put the pieces together. Do not think that I think less of you for it. We're all fools 'til we wound ourselves a time or two, as my father used to say. He meant it more from a blacksmith's perspective, but I think it holds true for love."

"Truer," Yoshio said. "But at the same time, who is happier? Probably the fool."

Muramasa chuckled at that, and held up the sword to Yoshio. It dropped into the old swordsman's hands, feeling surprisingly light. He ran its eyes over its bright surface, taking in the tight grain and the beautiful hamon. Yoshio balanced it on a single finger, placed near what would become the hilt. He smiled. The blade held still, not teetering at the slightest.

"Never seen a samurai test a blade like that," Muramasa said, closing one eye.

"Then you have never met a man who looks for a truly good sword," Yoshio said.

"Very correct, but I made good swords all the same," Muramasa said.

"This is the secret of my swords," Yoshio said. "What makes them useable in a single hand."

"You doubted I would understand this," Muramasa said.

Yoshio took his eyes off the katana and looked at him. "I did, but you have proven me wrong."

"Of course I have. You will be wronger still once you practice with them," Muramasa said. He pulled from a makeshift rack of bamboo by the door the wakizashi, polished and gleaming as if silver. Yoshio exchanged the katana for the short sword, and Muramasa continued working the edge of the longer blade. Yoshio balanced the short sword in much the same way. It was a denser blade, and the point of balance was the exact same distance from the hilt as with the longer sword.

"Perfect," Yoshio said. He laughed softly. "What my younger self would not have given for something like this." He turned it over in his hands, and flinched as a pure reflection of the setting sun bounced through his eyes.

Muramasa looked up, his eyes slightly glazed. "There's something else you should know."

"What is it?" Yoshio said, stepping past him and placing the wakizashi back on the bamboo rack.

"Ryunosuke's tastes have changed," Muramasa said. He looked away to the shadows of the trees that surrounded them. "I saw through his eyes last night, but things have become blurry; untenable."

"I found him lying with his eyes open after you and Amaya left," Emi said. "I thought he was dead, but I guess he was having a seizure."

"You're not getting rid of me that easily," Muramasa said, looking to the girl with a forced smile. His face then drooped. "I'm glad you were here, Emi. Thank you. Yoshio." He looked wide-eyed at the samurai. "I… *he,* killed children last night. Innocents."

Yoshio grumbled. "Never before?"

Muramasa shook his head and looked down at the sword in front of him. "No. Always the appetite was for something in particular. Avarice, or violence. Betrayal. Evil draws evil, I always thought, but now he is freed from that compulsion. He drinks from children. There is nobody safe."

"I see," Yoshio said. "What shall I do about it? Go face him right now? With all of Masaki's house to boot?"

"When is the duel?" Muramasa said.

"The day after tomorrow."

"Then you must be victorious," Muramasa said. "I will build handles for these blades tonight, providing that the demon does not go on a hunt again, and build the saya while you practice with them tomorrow."

"Hey," Emi said. "Where *is* Amaya?"

"She is staying with her father for now," Yoshio said.

"All the better," Muramasa said. "You don't need the distraction, my boy."

Yoshio thought to fire back, but held himself fast. "You are probably right."

Yoshio's dreams during the night were fitful, filled always with uncertainty. He wandered in a bamboo forest where he could not see the sun, Amaya's voice echoing from nowhere. He was swimming across a river, but could not reach the other side. He was in the mountains, near his old dojo, but it was burning, sending up acrid smoke. Amaya screamed from it, and his blood ran like ice.

He woke up sweating once, and leaving the bedroom alone, he looked for a cup of water. He found Muramasa sitting by firelight, wrapping a fresh handle on the katana. His eyes were deep set and sullen, and though they shared long stares, they did not speak. On his way back to his room, he found Emi staring out her own ajar door down the hallway. She looked gravely at him and then she disappeared into the darkness.

Yoshio meditated and found sleep again, though slowly, and his dreams until morning were marred by more anxiety. He awoke feeling saddened, though he could not remember why. Upon rising he heard coughing and soft voices. He looked around the house, and found Emi sitting by the bed of Muramasa, in the room lined with scrolls.

"You can't force a cough. You just have to let it happen," the girl said, patting Muramasa's back.

"Bah!" Sengo said. He coughed and then took a deep breath.

"Is it Ryunosuke?" Yoshio said, standing in the doorway.

Muramasa looked up to him and nodded. "It looked like Sakai market. A boy. Couldn't have been more than ten. Carrying water."

"How long ago?" Yoshio said. He reached for the sword at his belt, but realized he had not yet put it on.

"Too long to catch him, Yoshio," Muramasa said. "And too far away. Wait for the duel. I finished your swords last night. I'll prepare the saya today."

Yoshio nodded. "Can I leave him with you? I need to bring some things to Amaya."

"Yes," Emi said. "He'll be fine, I think, once he has something to drink and a little bit of food."

"Tell Amaya that I'll be finishing the scabbards today," Muramasa said, pushing himself fully upright.

"I will, though I don't know why I should care," Yoshio said. He nodded and stepped back to his room, where he retrieved his swords and put on his grey hakama.

"Ah, Yoshio-san," the shogun said, pausing as he sauntered through the halls with the kanrei Ouchi. "So good to see you again."

"As it is to see you, and in good health," Yoshio said, bowing low. The leather bags he had arrayed on his shoulders flopped around, and an ink brush fell out of one. Yoshio quickly scooped it up and put it back. "I was just delivering some of Amaya-sama's things to her. She has a marvelous skill with the brush, if you ever care to task her with it."

"Perhaps," Ashikaga said. He scratched his nose.

"Well, I enjoy a good Zen painting," Ouchi said. "Even more so if I can witness the act, but I would not press a guest like she must earn her keep."

"I can suggest it to her," Yoshio said. "Subtly, of course, and leave it to her graces."

"I would like that," Ouchi said, and bowed slightly. "However, I might want to press a task to you." He looked to Ashikaga, who nodded.

"Of course, lord," Yoshio said.

"I hear you do marvelous demonstrations of swordplay," Ouchi said. "And that your blade is peerless."

"I'm sure there are much finer blades in this house," Yoshio said. "But if my humble steel should please you, I will arrange a demonstration of speed and precision, at your leisure."

"How about this morning?" Ashikaga said. "While Kuro is here."

"You have Kuramasa in attendance?" Yoshio asked, trying to sound surprised and not vitriolic.

"Yes, he claims he knows of some betrayal," Ashikaga said. "As if Ouchi-san and I are not already aware of our betrayers."

"It is always good to have confirmation, lord," Ouchi said.

Ashikaga nodded to him. "Of course." He looked at Yoshio again, a warm smile splitting his face. "It was Kuro who mentioned your prowess with the blade, though he also complained about your temper during a particular ceremony."

"Did he mentioned that Amaya and I also ferreted out a conspiracy in his house?" Yoshio said.

"No, but I figured as much," Ashikaga said. "Some men like to search for complaints in front of their betters." The shogun shrugged. "Such is how it is. I consider a severed head hardly a botched execution. See to Amaya, then join us for some food, won't you?"

"I would be delighted," Yoshio said, bowing.

Chapter 19: The Poison of the Past

Yoshio finished his rice and set the shallow bowl down lightly down on the low table.

"Are you prepared?" Ashikaga said from the elevated stage to Yoshio's right.

Yoshio bowed down his head. "Yes. A little food on the stomach does wonders for one's body." He raised his head up and caught Amaya's eye on the other side of the bright room, where she sat beside her father. She was wearing a new silk kimono, and her hair was arranged in a long, straight style back over her shoulders. She wore a blank expression, but after they locked eyes, she smirked slightly. It was an imperfect, asymmetrical, and uncanny smile, but it warmed Yoshio in an unexpected way. He felt his nerves calm.

His eyes then returned briefly to Yamada, who sat with Hiromi, his once wife. His glance had strayed in that direction more than once during the casual meal, and he took stock of his feelings after each look. He found the bitterness and anger that had been so overwhelming in the days and months after the separation to be strangely muted. His meditation, more than a decade worth, had apparently had more benefits than clearing his mind in the moment. He looked again. Hiromi's head was bowed, focused on the food.

He stood up and breathed. He had done many demonstrations before, but none before the shogun. It was an opportunity to improve the missteps of the previous day, but also a risk. He glanced to his left to see a young woman bringing in the items he had requested. She set out on a high table in the center of the room, directly in front of the shogun and the kanrei, a hot teapot and a small tea set, along with several candlesticks of varying length. She also leaned a tatami mat, tightly rolled, against the table. He turned his eyes briefly from her to get a look at Kuro, who sat with Takehiro Asano at a different table on his left and Yamada Nobuyuki directly on his right. Behind them stood their respective retainers. Shiro, the soldier Kuro had hired after his wife's betrayal, stood out sorely with his short hair and poor cloth. He now wore a single katana. Curious.

He does not even bother to dress his vassal for the company of the warlord, Yoshio thought. He narrowed his eyes and looked back at the objects on the table. *I know you are up to something, you rat. Whatever it is, you seem to be doing a poor job of it.*

"Rather common objects for a supposedly exceptional swordsman," Yamada said from the side. Yoshio ignored him and closed his eyes. He envisioned his movements, one after the other.

He opened his eyes and looked at the shogun. "Esteemed shogun, kanrei, and daimyo of the realm," he said, then bowed so low as to be parallel with the ground. "It is my pleasure to demonstrate for you the precision, speed, and deadly development of the Toda School of Kenjutsu. I will begin by demonstrating basic cuts and their adaptations."

His careful ears picked out whispering from Kuro to Asano. He ignored them and stepped back to the end of the table. He stood up straight and placed his right hand lightly on his sword.

"First, a cut from the belt," Yoshio said. The sword flew out of the scabbard like a flash of lightning, cutting the air like a howl of wind in an arc that went from Yoshio's waist to above his head. Yoshio stepped forward and held the cut at its final nadir just above his knees, his left hand coming to rest on the hilt. "Vertical style, designed to limit the enemy's ability to parry and advance. Next, an edge-up strike."

Yoshio's sword turned around and became a silver blur as it cut upwards. He pulled back his shoulders and shuffled back with his right foot, moving his sword into a guard position over his head. He looked to the kanrei. "Now, a forward stab, and a finish of Toda's design." Yoshio stepped forward with his right foot and the sword snapped forward, tip first, into a deadly stab at heart level. Yoshio turned the blade and did three fast cuts, going from left to right and back to left again, each one moving toward the knees of his invisible opponent. He then finished with two cuts moving upwards. They would have looked awkward in another man's movement, but Yoshio made them look simple, like fluid brush strokes. "And the return," he said. He flicked the blade as if to free it of blood and returned it smoothly to its saya.

"I thought I would witness a demonstration, Yoshio-san," the shogun said. "Not an introduction to Kenjutsu like we are students. My son might find this useful, but me?"

"Of course, my lord," Yoshio said, and then took a low bow. "I would not presume the room to be full anything but masters of the art. This, however, is not an introduction. I will demonstrate these techniques again, on a target, so that you can see why I paused between each stroke, if you will but permit it."

The shogun smiled. "Very well."

Yoshio bowed again and took a rolled tatami, almost as tall as he was. He settled it on a bamboo stand, then stood back from it. He bowed again, first to the shogun, then to each of the four settings of daimyo. He noted each of their faces: Asano's indifference next to Amaya's warmth, Kuro's rat-like teeth, Furukawa's hint of a smile, and Yamada and Hiromi's cool distance. Yoshio bowed once more to the kanrei and shogun. He took his stance.

"Watch carefully," he said. He stepped forward, and his steel flashed like a spinning wheel, cutting through the air like a mighty wind. Draw-up-stab-cut-cut-cut, two long cuts, then one more as it returned to the saya. The entire display took perhaps three seconds. The tatami mat stood still for a fraction of a heartbeat, then fell apart into a dozen or more neatly cut slices, all of near equal size. The bamboo core too fell away, split into six pieces. Yoshio turned and bowed to the shogun.

Ashikaga looked sideways at Ouchi, who nodded, his lips drawn in surprise. "Most impressive," the shogun said. "Pity we do not have a criminal handy. I should like to see that blade put to real use. Who made it?"

"I do not know," Yoshio said.

"May I see it?" Ouchi said. Yoshio nodded and drew the sword slowly. He put the handle toward the kanrei, who took it and looked down its edge, then felt it in his hands. He let the blade rise and fall with its own weight. "Dreadfully unbalanced," he said. "I'm surprised you cut anything at all with it."

"We work with the tools that have been allotted to us, my lord," Yoshio said, and bowed. "It may be imperfect, but the blade is mine."

"It impresses me more, not less," Ouchi said. He handed the katana to the shogun who did the same, nodded, then handed it back to Yoshio.

"What next?" Ashikaga said.

"I believe it is time for tea," Yoshio said.

Ashikaga raised an eyebrow. "Perhaps it is." He shrugged to Ouchi. "I suppose we should call a servant."

"Allow me, my lords," Yoshio said. "It would honor me to serve each of you tea."

Ashikaga smiled and stroked his beard. "Go on," then he said to Ouchi, "I do love a good act."

"Amaya-sama, if you would assist me," Yoshio said, nodding to Amaya, who smiled as she rose. "I will now make a single cup into eight," Yoshio said. He laid out eight cups in a long row on the table. "If you would but pour, my lady," he said to Amaya.

Amaya smiled and began pouring tea into the first cup. Yoshio gripped his sword, and let it loose with a sideways cut. The blade passed through the stream of hot tea, but did not seem to disturb it. Yoshio continued cutting through the stream, intensifying the speed and frequency of the cuts as they went along. He started going back and forth, the blade hovering over the bowls. Amaya continued to pour, but the cup never seemed to overflow. Finally, the pot ran dry and Yoshio shook a drop of tea from the tip and returned the blade to its scabbard. Yoshio bowed to Amaya, then picked up two of the cups on the end of the row. He placed them before the shogun and the kanrei. They were full of piping hot tea.

"May this tea find you and your health well, my lords," Yoshio said.

"Astonishing," Ashikaga said.

"Yes, now this is truly impressive," Ouchi said. "Useless, but impressive." Yoshio nodded and returned to the table. Amaya was already busy passing out the cups to the rest of the daimyo in attendance. He heard Kuro grumble as he received his cup, and it brought Yoshio a slight feeling of satisfaction.

"This next one is quite fun at night," Yoshio said. He nodded to Amaya, who shuffled out of the room and returned with a long, lit twig, which she used to light one of the candles. He moved quickly through the candle demonstration, knowing that the key to dazzling his audience would be in surprising them, and that meant speed. He began by throwing the flames from candle to candle using the wind from his sword until each one of them was lit. Next, he cut off the wicks of three candles in a single stroke – those three were each separated by a lit candle. Then, he extinguished the flames of three more candles while throwing the flame to the three he had just put out.

He cut through one candle. It flipped end over end and landed on the flat surface of Yoshio's katana, flame up. He heard Asano laugh in disbelief. He then cut another one, doing the same while the first candle did not move from the sword. More whispers and laughs. He flicked his eyes around the room to see the daimyo, noting Ouchi's wide eyes. Kuro had his arms crossed sternly. Beside the focused Yamada, Hiromi seemed uninterested, her eyes wandering. Yoshio continued down the line, dropping one candle on the table lit while picking up two more. He sliced the remnants of the original candles and then flipped the flames up onto them, so soon there were two rows of lit candles.

"Amazing!" the shogun said.

"Furukawa, you were holding out on me," Asano said, following the shogun's lead.

"Alas, but I have not finished yet," Yoshio said. He held the last piece of candle near the tip of his sword. He reached under the katana with his left hand and drew his wakizashi. For a fraction of a second, while the sword was being drawn, Yoshio looked to his right and saw, faintly an image. Something odd, but he had not the time to consider it.

Steel flashed and scraped as all the candles left the table, fire spinning in air. The candles were cut to pieces and lit, one at a time in a flurry, so that five rows of very small bits of flaming wax were forming on the table. In the middle of it, Yoshio finished processing the image he had seen while beginning the trick. His heart leapt.

"No!" he cried, and dashed to his right. Candles fell on the ground and table, rolling this way and that. Yoshio leapt with all his speed and strength, dropping his wakizashi and striking out with his katana.

Yamada screamed as the blade flashed at him.

"Yoshi! No!" Amaya shouted, but it was too late. The cut had been made. Yoshio dropped his sword and stepped back as Yamada's retainer slashed at him. Every man in the room, even the shogun, was quickly on his feet with a sword in his hands.

A look of shock was frozen on Yamada's face. He moved his hand away from face and stared at it. Moments before, it was drawing his tea to his lips. Now, it was empty, the teacup shattered into pieces by the sword strike.

"He has tried to assassinate me!" Yamada said. "I told you he would seek petty vengeance against his honor."

"Yoshi, why?" Amaya said.

"He has always wanted to punish me for my wife," Yamada said again, pushing himself up and reaching for his sword.

Yoshio bowed his head. "I apologize, Lord Yamada," Yoshio said. "But I could not let that tea reach your lips."

The lord looked around himself. He was soaked in hot tea, but as he held out and examined the white obi that held up his hakama, he shuddered. It was stained black, blacker than any tea could be.

"I don't understand," he said. His wife moved to examine it.

"Nor do I," Ouchi said, moving toward Yoshio with a drawn sword. A servant tried to stamp out a fire near at hand that had started when a candle rolled into a cloth mat.

"Poison," Yoshio said.

"We all drank!" Asano said.

"Check your cups," Yoshio continued. "All your tea should be a mellow brown. Only Yamada's has been poisoned."

"But all the cups came from the same pot," Furukawa said. He opened up the teapot and looked at the leaves inside. "His cup must have already had the poison in it."

"I would have noticed black tea like that," Yoshio said. He eyed Ouchi's sword trained on him. "So would Lord Yamada, and Amaya who gave it to him. Look to see who is missing." They all looked around the room.

"No, you did it, Yoshi!" Hiromi said, breaking her silence.

"No!" Asano said, even louder. "Kuro's retainer is gone."

"Shiro," Amaya said. "He must have slipped the poison into the cup when the lord's eyes were fixed upon the sword display."

Eyes fell on Kuro. He held out his hands and backed away. "No! You can't think I had anything-" Just then he fell backward over a table and landed in a heap. Two samurai were on him quickly.

Amaya slipped up near Yoshio as they subdued Kuro. "How did you know?" she whispered in his ear.

"I saw him leaning forward. Like the others, only a bit too much. Well, far too much. My mind put it all together while my swords moved."

"What if he hadn't done anything?" Amaya said.

"Then I suppose my head would forfeit."

While the focus was on Kuro, crying and kicking as he dragged off, Amaya clasped Yoshio's hand and squeezed.

Yoshio practiced on the remaining tatami mats, his feet shuffling through the white sand of the shrine's sanctum. His eyes were narrowed against the sun, which hovered in the west. His swords – the new blades Muramasa had forged for him – felt incredible in his hands. The balance was just as his old swords had been, yet somehow improved. He sliced through the mats cleanly and efficiently, and the steel felt weightless in his hands. He felt like the tip of his katana could meet any point in space instantly, swirling and stinging like a deadly wasp. The edge cut through the mats without resistance. So precise. It was as if the swords moved *with* his thought, not because of it.

The steel was alive. Muramasa, for all his talk and in spite of Yoshio's experience with the sword, had made him a believer. He did not let it wound his ego, so long sustained on the idea that he was the master and the steel was a servant of little importance. The tool he had been given was too powerful, too sharp, and too much of a work of art and spirit for his mind to waste time in contention with the reality with which he had been presented. He smiled as he practiced, not noticing the sweat beading on his brow.

"Yoshio," a female voice said from the stairs behind him. Yoshio did not need to probe the recesses of his mind to find its owner. He had buried the familiarity, along with all other feelings of her, long ago. Though years had drawn on, neither the voice nor the emotions had, as it was clear to him now, been buried deep. He swept away a layer of dirt, and there she was, as before. His heart ached, and his sword suddenly became heavy.

"How did you know I would be here?" Yoshio said, holding his pose with a sword in each hand, crossing one another in a guard.

"There are few hidden things that do not come to light in the circles of nobility. This place was not hidden at all."

"Still…"

"Ashikaga told me, of course."

Yoshio turned and looked upon Hiromi, his once wife. She stood humbly in a kimono patterned with flowers, her hands crossed upon one another, and her hair arranged simply. It was very close to a memory Yoshio had of her, during a summer years before. That image, once bright, seemed dim now.

"Do we have business with one another?" The samurai said. He was not wearing the saya for his blades, as Muramasa still worked on them, and so he leaned his wakizashi against a wood rail and rested his katana on his shoulder.

"You remain armed for a woman?"

"A samurai must never be disarmed," Yoshio said, then added, "Betrayal is ever in the hearts of the peerage."

She pretended not to hear the affront and continued staring at him. She cocked her head. "Why do you meddle in things far beyond your concern or depth?"

"I meddle in nothing," Yoshio said. "All I can do is act honorably. If that interferes with the plans of the nobility, then…" he was about to say sorry, but shook his head. "Then it is no concern of mine."

"As goes the bakufu, so goes the samurai," Hiromi said.

Yoshio felt a stitch between his eyes. He was becoming agitated. "Why have you come here?"

"To warn you," Hiromi said. "And perhaps, to give you an offer."

"The warning?" Yoshio said, knowing what it was likely to be.

"Do not attend the duel tomorrow."

"I must," Yoshio said.

"You must not," Hiromi said. "For your own sake. This woman you have taken up with..."

"Amaya," Yoshio said. "I have not taken up with her. She is my master."

"I know more than *that*," Hiromi said, contempt building in her voice. "But this woman is not what she seems. She uses you to her own ends."

"As though others would not. You do not know all that is involved," Yoshio said. "The man I face is… he must be killed. That is my end, if it brings ends to others, it does not matter to me."

"Just trust me this once," Hiromi said. "I would not come all the way here except to speak tp you truth."

"I have trusted you more than once, and such good it did me," Yoshio said, turning away.

"I would not deceive you in matters of life and death. I have that much decency."

"You had the decency to pin the attempt on your husband's life to me," Yoshio said.

"Who else there had the motive to do so?" Hiromi said, anger cracking her voice. "My former husband, in the perfect position to kill his enemy. It was the simplest answer, and by the swords there you know that it was the answer on the minds of everyone else in attendance, too."

"The simplest answer, but not the correct one," Yoshio said. He frowned, looking up to the sinking sun.

"And what is the correct one?" Hiromi said.

"My hope is that answers will be revealed with the setting and rising of the sun," Yoshio said. "Regardless, my path is laid before me."

"So it is. I hope you will turn off of it."

"Leave me, Hiromi. I have work to do."

"You never asked me what my offer was," she said.

Yoshio remained silent.

"Leave this place. With me," Hiromi said, her voice softening. "Leave the bakufu to its destruction and its many betrayals."

Yoshio, at last, turned his head back to look at her. The face of Hiromi was downcast, shadowed even though the western sun was upon it, and it looked sleepless.

"Yes, Yoshio, leave now. Only death and despair waits on the other side of tonight. I was wrong before... with you, but you must understand the demands that were placed on my by father, and my clan. Leave with me. I know of many places where we may retire in safety."

Yoshio held her gaze, and even felt himself turning about. He felt something for his ex-wife then. Perhaps temptation, as he remembered the life he once possessed, but as he thought about Hiromi, her husband, and the tense meetings with the shogun, a new thought emerged. He pitied the woman, at least as far as he understood the machinations of the court. He pitied her, and though he remembered tempting pleasure, he also remembered pain and betrayal. The old feelings, now lifted from the tomb, burned him.

"You are afraid," Yoshio said, narrowing his eyes.

"Yes," Hiromi said pensively. "Yes, Yoshio, I am very afraid. The plans of the shogun are very dangerous."

"They are," Yoshio said, "But your fear is twisted; I see it in you. You would not betray your husband unless your true fear was to be dead, rather than merely shamed and alone. You believe the shogun will fail."

"No!" Hiromi said, and stepped closer.

"It is true," Yoshio said. "You fear your husband will not survive this. He will die, or be betrayed, or perhaps," Yoshio hesitated, "you think he will do the betraying."

"It is not that, Yoshio."

Yoshio nodded. *I think it is.* He kept the thought close. "And you think it will be the end of your house. Or worse, you will be made to follow him down into the grave, and so you choose to temp a man you once cast aside with about as much thought as to a broken bowl, because you think he will help you escape your destiny."

Tears streamed down Hiromi's face. "No, Yoshio, it is *you* that I want."

"Lies, as always," Yoshio said. He turned away from her again. "Your destiny is to reap the rewards of dishonor, whatever they may be."

"So that is what we have become?" Hiromi said. "Harshness and anger, with no spare words of thought or trust?"

"We are as you have made us, woman," Yoshio said. "Now leave, and trouble me no more." He put his katana back into a guard position and began going through his motions again. Through the near-silent slicing of air, he could hear the footsteps of the woman with whom he once shared a life. Her sandals clicked quietly on the stairs as she ascended. They were steady and unwavering, save for one pause, where Yoshio reckoned that Hiromi was either stopping to think, or else turn back to look at him a last time. He felt the urge to turn during the silence, but resisted it, keeping his eyes west, and on his task.

The turn of the blade had a remarkable power to clear his mind, and moreover, his intent. Yoshio cut through the last tatami mat with lightning precision, holding his final position and feeling the connection of his blade to his body. He looked at the shards of straw on the ground and smiled.

"If only I had known all it took was a tatami mat to get you to smile."

Yoshio snapped around and saw Amaya standing on the edge of the open sanctum. "Yes," he said, turning back to the makeshift tatami stand. "It is good to take joy in the simple things."

"Your wife is one person I never expected to visit you," Amaya said, stepping across the sand toward Yoshio.

"So you saw her, then," Yoshio said. He shook his head. "She is not my wife."

"My apologies, Yoshi," Amaya said. "Words are too simple sometimes. And I did more than see her."

Yoshio raised an eyebrow. "I was wondering why she paused on the steps. I considered that maybe she was..." Yoshio looked away to the West.

"What?"

"Nothing."

"What did she have to say?"

"She came to warn me against the duel. I think she, like many others, has a stake in the outcome of this contest. Either her, or her husband. She said you are manipulating me."

"Am I?" Amaya said.

Yoshio shook his head. He looked at his sword. "Ryunosuke must be slain. I can do it. I shall do it. In comparison, Hiromi means little to me. Masaki also means little to me."

"Even if he means much to me."

Yoshio shrugged. "I am ever your servant, and something in my gut tells me that we will not be rid of Masaki until…" He breathed deeply.

"Until we kill him," Amaya said. She stepped past Yoshio and picked up the wakizashi lying near at hand, and admired its shining steel in the late sun.

"Yes."

"Not all deaths are equal, Yoshi," Amaya said. She put the short sword forward and moved through a few graceful moves with it. "Masaki today and Masaki tomorrow are as different as Ashikaga Keiji when you cut him down, and when he had the favor of the shogun as a young man. Dishonor must come before death."

"Tomorrow, I will choose death before dishonor," Yoshio said. "There is nothing I would not do for you, but tomorrow is the working of my own will. Noboru – Ryunosuke – must be stopped. Muramasa has seen visions more disturbing than any thus far. Children…"

"I exalt you for your efforts, my dear Yoshi," Amaya said. She lowered the wakizashi and touched his arm. "If you would like a break, I shall show you the reason for my visit."

Yoshio smiled and sighed. "I should make the most of the sun, while it is yet in the west."

"Very well, Master Taoka Yoshio," Amaya said. "You will find me in the shrine proper when you are through." She laid the wakizashi back down delicately and walked back toward the stairs. Yoshio watched her go, the subtle movement of her hips drawing a deep breath from him. Such a bright image. "And," she said loudly, not turning. "I am pleased that you did not decide to go off with that old wife of yours."

Yoshio shook his head and chuckled, then turned back toward the sun.

The candles cast a warm and steady light on the open shrine house when Yoshio walked up, the last light disappearing into the mountains in the west. His hair was slick with sweat, and shone a shiny black in the yellow-orange light, disguising the many strands of grey picked up through a lifetime of experience. Yoshio stepped into the shrine to find Amaya, Muramasa, and Emi in the large central floor. He laid each of his swords carefully down. Sengo was busy brushing a shiny lacquer onto a long saya, which hung by a cord suspended from the ceiling. Drips of thin clear varnish fell upon a white cloth lying on the floor. Amaya, sitting near at hand, had a shorter saya on a stand and was working on it with an ink brush. Emi, as usual, pretended to be transcribing a scroll.

"What is this?" Yoshio said, stepping in.

"The reason I came," Amaya said, finishing a stroke and looking up at Yoshio.

"I found out some days back, when you were off cutting down invisible enemies in the yard," Muramasa said, wagging a finger at Yoshio, "that your… whatever she is to you, is an artist."

"She is a peerless artist," Yoshio said.

"I do my best, but I have much yet to accomplish," Amaya said.

"No, don't be modest," Muramasa said. "You are really very good." He looked back at Yoshio. "And I knew it might mean something to you too."

Yoshio stepped closer and examined the painting beneath the shellac of the katana saya. There was an intricate image, not just of black ink, but of colors as well, of a stalk of bamboo, with leaves, and with a pair of birds among them. Their breasts were a bright and rosy red.

"I figured the cherry blossoms that I put on my own saya might not be quite your ideal," Amaya said. "So I decided to do something that symbolizes you. Bamboo. Strong and resilient. And the swallow, because it always, inevitably, returns."

"I would have loved the cherry blossoms, too," Yoshio said. He looked the length of the scabbard, not touching the wet lacquer. "There are two swallows."

"So there are," Amaya said, smiling. "I am done with this one, I think." She carefully handed the painted wooden wakizashi saya to Muramasa, who inserted a small wooden hook into the top and hung it beside its larger brother. He picked up the small bowl of clear shellac and began to put another coat of varnish on the larger saya.

"You never told me you drew those cherries on your scabbard," Muramasa said as he worked.

"I did," Amaya said. "It infuriated my father, actually, because of the cost and pricelessness of the blade. The maker never adorned his saya, but I was young and wanted to express myself. He forgave me, eventually, like he always does."

"Would you let me see the sword, by chance?" Muramasa said.

Amaya nodded and walked to the doorway opposite the sanctum. She retrieved her sword and handed it to Muramasa, who temporarily put down his shellac bowl. He smiled as it fell into his hands. "I knew I felt something from this sword, but I dismissed it when I saw the flowers. You are right; the maker never cared to adorn his saya, preferring the steel to speak when revealed." Muramasa drew forth the blade and looked at it, shining brightly in the light. "I know this sword."

"It is one of yours?" Emi said, looking up from her scroll.

"Couldn't have been," Amaya said. "Too old."

"Well," Muramasa said. "It is and it isn't. The first man to make use of our enemy was the man to forge this blade.

"Masamune," Yoshio said

Muramasa nodded. "It's marvelous, isn't it?"

Amaya smiled. "You're not angry that I ruined the scabbard?"

"No," Muramasa said. "The steel is what matters. If anything, you've made the thing better, by touching it with your skill and spirit." He replaced the sword and gave it back to Amaya. "Memories of less vicious days. Seeing through only the eyes of the demon, and after centuries of time in the forge, I wonder what the true colors of the master smith were. Was he a kind man after all?"

"Probably not, to imprison a kami," Emi said.

"He gave the kami what he wanted: persistent life," Muramasa said. "I cannot know all of a man through his work."

"Thank you, Amaya," Yoshio said, watching her put her sword away. "I will not forget this gift."

"Of course you won't forget, because I will not let you," Amaya said.

Yoshio smiled at her. "I should be escorting you back."

"I'm staying here," Amaya said. She walked near to Yoshio and laid a hand on his arm. "I couldn't let a man spend what could be his final night alone, now could I?"

"I'm in a wee bit of peril too," Muramasa said.

Yoshio glared at him. Muramasa caught the glance. "I was talking to Emi." He looked at the young shrine attendant and cracked a large, crooked smile.

"Pah!" Emi said.

Yoshio looked out the west-facing exit, and crossed his arms.

"Something bothering you?" Amaya said.

"Hiromi said she found out where I was from the shogun."

"Spies in a noble house? You're kidding, right?" Emi said. Muramasa chuckled softly, but Yoshio remained in thought.

"Perhaps we will not be safe here tonight. Hiromi was willing to do much to stop this duel tomorrow. Maybe she is allied with Masaki."

"Or maybe she assumes the duel will weaken the Asano clan, her husband's ally."

"Both could be reasons to strike early – either a hedge on a bet or a guarantee," Yoshio said.

"There is an old teahouse here," Emi said. "Up the hill, on the other side of the sanctum. We haven't used it in a long time, since the shrine suffices, and the foliage around it is very overgrown, but it is close, and probably safe."

Amaya frowned. "I had hoped that Yoshio and I... could be alone."

"We could stay here," Emi said.

"Still a danger," Yoshio said.

"We'll plug our ears," Muramasa said with a chuckle.

"I suppose it will have to do," Amaya said.

Chapter 20: The Duel

YOSHIO OPENED HIS EYES. Darkness greeted him, and the sound of crickets filled his ears. Slowly he became aware of the breathing of Amaya beside him, and as his mind returned to him, he made out soft whispers. He sat up, being careful not to disturb the sleeping woman beside him, and pulled the legs of his hakama on. He had to stoop inside the old teahouse, which they had found miraculously free of rats and other wildlife, despite part of the roof having been lost for several seasons. He moved toward the door, a patch of stars in the window providing the only light. Still, he could see the outline of Amaya, her hips melting into gentle curves that ran into soft shoulders. The blanket lay unevenly on her, exposing skin and, had he been given the light he wished for, her breasts.

Yoshio picked up his katana, lying lightly near the door while the varnish on the saya still dried, and pushed the low-hinged door open softly. Light from a setting moon, full and bright, spilled into the room. He saw Amaya flinch as the light fell across her face, and so Yoshio quickly stepped outside and closed the door.

Emi was sitting beside Muramasa. They both looked downhill toward the attendance house. The shrine was visible off to the left, its large roof pushing up from the grove of trees. Yoshio squatted down beside them.

"Emi noticed a flashing of lights in the grove," Muramasa said, his whispered voice crackling like a dying fire. "But I still watch."

"There is somebody down there," Emi said, her voice carrying only the slightest tone.

"I did not say there was not, merely that I have seen no lights," Muramasa replied. "They may have extinguished them, or they may be in the house."

"The door from the library to the exterior is ajar," Yoshio said. "Did you close it when we left?"

"I closed everything," Emi said.

"Then somebody has entered the house," Yoshio said.

"I suppose you were right," Emi said. She looked at Muramasa. "We could have been down there, getting skewered by some assassin."

"Naw," Muramasa said. He stuck his thumb toward Yoshio. "This fellow wakes with a mouse squeak, as you can see. He would have cut them all to ribbons by the time you woke up."

"Yes, we would have been safe anyway," they all turned at the voice to see Amaya inch out of the teahouse, her kimono wrapped lightly about her. "But we came here so that Yoshio could have a sound sleep, knowing we are safe. You are defeating that purpose."

"Sorry," Emi said. "We were trying to be quiet; I just had a bad dream, and ended up watching."

"Usually it is *you* having the bad dreams," Amaya said to Muramasa.

"I always have bad dreams," Muramasa said. "Tonight I'm not getting so sick though. Decided to keep our lovely hostess company."

He smiled at Emi, who pursed her lips and sighed.

"You should get back to bed," Amaya said. "There are still hours till dawn-"

"With assassins down the hill?" Emi whispered harshly.

"They are gone now, I think," Yoshio said. "And if they were truly assassins, you would have seen no lights."

"Fine," Emi said. "I'll go back to bed, but don't expect me to sleep." She turned and looked back at her bedroll, which lay beside Muramasa's on the porch that encircled the teahouse. A tarp lay above it, making a small enclosed room.

For being so close to the window of the teahouse, they had made no sound and refused to whisper when Yoshio had made deep, passionate love to Amaya. The samurai's lord and lover desired privacy, but had refused to let the lack of it deter her. Their sex had been silent of voice and cry, but the lack of such had intensified the experience for each of them. Their breathing had spoken where words could not, and as it aligned in rhythm and effort, it built to final, harsh stutters and deep sighs, Yoshio understood why it was called "the little death," for he took it all in like a man dying.

Amaya took Yoshio's hand and brought him back into the teahouse, leaving the tense Emi and Muramasa to their own. She disrobed him, and in the darkness, she took from Yoshio again, almost hungrily. She cried out at the end.

Yoshio stood silently, looking out at the wide courtyard that would serve as the arena. Its white sands were meticulously raked. A slight breeze from the sea occasionally sent up a puff of dust from around the rocks that lined its edges. Above the slight wind, he could hear whispers of the many samurai, male and female, young and old, that had come to witness the event. They lined the surrounding walkway, some standing, and some sitting. Yoshio could not make out many words, but could feel the tension of the spectacle that was to be revealed.

On either short side of the long rectangle that made the dueling ground were raised platforms. Yoshio stood upon the eastern of these two points, while the western one, the platform Yoshio had shared with Masaki a few weeks past, stood empty. Midway between the two, in the center of the grounds and therefore the best seat, another platform had been built. The shogun and the kanrei sat there, along with wives, courtesans, and a few retainers standing guard. Ashikaga and Ouchi looked out sternly at the grounds, an image of power.

Asano Takehiro, accompanied by Amaya and Furukawa Kenta, sat behind Yoshio. Their eyes were narrowed. They matched the energy of the crowd, whispering tersely to each other.

"Where is he, I wonder?" Furukawa said, leaning on his knees and peering across the dueling grounds.

"Trying to prepare a hasty exit, I imagine," Lord Asano said. "The conniving bastard."

"He means to delay this fight," Amaya said calmly. "The sun is yet high, but he means for it to be in Yoshio's eyes, blinding him."

"Conniving bastard is right," Furukawa said.

"Do not worry," Yoshio said, focusing inward to find his own sense of calm. "I have prepared for the sunset specifically. I also know the fighter; indeed it was I who taught him, and I have seen what skills he has gained since his tutelage. I know everything he brings to the duel. I am as prepared as any could be."

"Yes," Asano said, "but does he not also know you, his teacher? Will he not be prepared, *and* have the sun at his back?"

"I have a few surprises in store," Yoshio said. Even as he said it, the daimyo's words echoed in his mind. Ryunosuke, Noburu-who-was, did indeed have a deep knowledge of him. Part of the knowledge was supernatural, the gift of the demon sword and not merely the watchful experience of a student. He looked to Amaya to bolster his confidence. Her eyes trembled, and he witnessed beads of sweat running down her cheeks. She forced a smile to him.

"Look at that," Furukawa said, nodding toward the seat of the shogun. Ashikaga was reading a scroll handed to him by a young man. He nodded to the courier and handed the scroll to the kanrei. Ouchi frowned as he read it, and handed it back to the courier. Yoshio could not hear what they were saying, but the young man left in a hurry.

"Maybe they got something else out of Kuro," Asano said.

"Unlikely," Furukawa said. "Much as I think a rat like Kuro likes to lie, when he is put to it, he can't keep a secret at all. I expect we have everything of import."

"So you think he was telling truth about Yamada?" Asano said.

"What about Yamada?" Yoshio said, his curiosity piqued.

Asano regarded him with narrowed eyes. "Kuro made known, under pressure mind you, that he had come to Osaka bay to reveal a conspiracy in the bakufu. A warning of a betrayal by none other than Lord Yamada."

"I say the kanrei was expecting it – nay, he figured a certain betrayal in the bakufu from the start," Furukawa said. "It was all part of his plan."

"Betrayal to whom?" Yoshio said.

Asano sighed, and Amaya spoke up. "There is much that we have not been made aware of, Yoshio-san, until recently. The shogun is not sojourning here merely for the summer festivals."

"Why do you think we're permitting this duel, Yoshio?" Asano said. "The bakufu has predicted a rebellion. Your enemy, the Shiba clan, is ours, for now. We need only provoke Masaki properly, and the alliance, of which he is only a small part. Deeming in the chaos that the time is right, our enemy will mobilize the armies he believes to be hidden and march toward the emperor. He believes he is the predator, but he is not. Our prey will snap its jaws upon Kyoto, and then the rebellion will be snuffed."

"Rebellion?" Yoshio said, startled.

"Of course," Furukawa said. "A contingent of the Hosokawa and the Shiba clan, let by Hosokawa Masataka."

"But they are enemies," Yoshio said. "They squabble here constantly. I have even seen them shed blood in this very yard."

"All subterfuge, my friend," Furukawa said. "Both clans have had their eyes on the shogunate, and the position of kanrei alongside a puppet from the Ashikaga clan, for nigh on 60 years. Nothing here is unexpected, Yoshio-san. The kanrei has been careful in disseminating information. What Yamada knows is likely what he is intended to know, as it is with myself and Takahiro-san."

Yoshio turned back and looked at the yard again, pondering what the daimyo had revealed. He thought of Hiromi, pleading with him in the sanctum, and things fell into place. She had known of her husband's intent to betray the secrets of the bakufu, and had judged them with il-favor. The woman truly was scared, but Yoshio was in the end to this line of events as he was before to her: merely incidental. It was sobering, and also sad, but it allowed him to purge his mind of pity and sorrow and focus on what was before him.

This would be the end of his long task, first assigned by Furukawa and Asano and then taken up willfully. He wondered what would happen next, and his thoughts strayed to Amaya. It occurred to him that his current relationship would likely not continue. Asano, or Furukawa, or Ashikaga himself would have some use for him, and for her. His travels with the lovely and enigmatic Amaya were at an end.

Yoshio straightened up as the far platform filled with people. He saw Masaki, followed by Yamada, and finally Hiromi, her face downcast. They each bowed toward the shogun, and then seated themselves.

"So Yamada casts his lot, now that the bakufu knows of his treachery," Asano said.

"And yet the Hosokawa are absent from his party," Furukawa said.

"There is one I recognize over there," Yoshio said, nodding off to his left at an old man surrounded by young samurai, leaning against a pillar.

"Hosokawa Sumimoto, the old kanrei. He fled when we took Kyoto with Yoshitane and Ouchi, claiming that his loyalty lied with us. No doubt he intends to feign loyalty until the end," Asano said.

Another older man stepped to the center of the yard, wearing an unadorned hakama bound with a black obi. He began inspecting the dirt and edges, carefully walking forward and back through the yard. When he was satisfied, he looked to the shogun and nodded. The shogun held his hand palm-out and stood up. He looked over to Yoshio, then to Masaki's platform. Yoshio met his eyes, and stepped out of the alcove. He squinted at the setting sun.

Across the way, one of Masaki's retainers stepped past him and Yamada. Yoshio noticed Hiromi cover her face. He turned back to look upon Amaya a final time. She forced another smile, and then mouthed silently, "I'm sorry."

Yoshio turned away and walked toward the center of the dueling yard. He stopped the customary ten paces from the arbiter, the same old swordmaster he had seen adjudicate the duel between Hayato and the younger Tamotsu. He looked past him, squinting, and gave a start.

"This is not Ryu-" Yoshio said, then corrected himself. "This is not Noburu! This is not the man I agreed to fight!"

In place of the killer was a young man, clearly a few years short of twenty, wearing clothes that were nearly too large for him, and holding his swords hesitantly. *He's done it again,* Yoshio thought. *Masaki intends to make Amaya watch another young man die – this one by my own hand!*

"I have allowed it," the shogun said, loudly and clearly. "You agreed to fight Masaki's agent, and this man is his agent."

Yoshio bowed low to Ashikaga. "My lord! I only agreed to this duel if I could fight Masaki's best – Udono Noburu. He has sent a boy to die in his place!"

"I may be young, but I understand more of the way of the sword than you ever will," the boy said. There was a tremor in his voice that revealed fear.

"Noboru disappeared a week ago, at least," Masaki shouted.

"My lord-" Yoshio began, looking to the shogun.

"This is the man I have chosen as his replacement," Ashikaga said. "As a favor to Masaki and to your master. Unless you wish to defy me."

"No, of course not, lord," Yoshio said.

"Or embrace cowardice," The shogun said loudly. "And shame."

"No… I will not," Yoshio said.

"Then let the gods decide the outcome," the shogun said. He sat down, a slight smile on his face.

Yoshio took a breath and readied himself. He placed his right hand carefully on his katana, and prepared for the draw. He could not imagine the boy would stand much of a chance, but he kept his caution anyway. As he looked at the boy's smooth face, he sensed something in the back of his mind. A familiarity. With so many samurai crowding the bakufu and the court, he could not be certain, but Yoshio believed he might have passed the boy in the house of the shogun. He stopped trying to search his memory and focused on the present. The adjudicator clapped his hands and backed away.

Yoshio narrowed his eyes and turned his saya. He would not need both swords for this fight; best to make a single, clean cut and be done with it. He could feel regret for the poor lad later. Now was the time for blood.

The boy stepped forward first. Yoshio was ready for him.

Though he had considered drawing first, and ending things quickly, Yoshio felt a tug in his spirit that bound his arm. He held himself back as the young man stepped forward. The youngster's draw cut was fast and precise, yet far from unnerving to Yoshio. He did what he had practiced, taking a step back and drawing his own katana. The boy's second slash struck the steel of Yoshio's sword, making it ring a long, clear note before Yoshio diverted his opponents strike into the dirt.

The boy rounded, pulling his sword up into a guard as Yoshio stepped lightly backward. The boy flinched as Yoshio flicked his sword outward and then up, letting it rest in a strange overhead guard going from left to his right. Yoshio's katana moved down toward his brow, shielding his eyes from the sun. The boy's image came into stark clarity. At the same time, the reflection from the highly polished blade struck the boys eyes, sending him backpedaling with sudden blindness.

This was the time that Yoshio had practiced to make his killing strike, but as he looked at the boy's familiar face – too familiar – he decided on a more difficult, and more entangling path. He stepped forward and performed an overhand cut. The youth performed the parry as expected, but twisted to the left and avoided Yoshio's attempt to turn the edge of the blade into his shoulder. The sun moved to Yoshio's right and his opponent's left. The young face came into focus again. Yoshio's confused memory of the past knocked on the door of the present moment. *Could it be?*

"To hell with you!" the boy shouted, and then attacked in a flurry of slashes. Each one was well-performed, and a few turns even surprised Yoshio, but in fluid control the old master turned each aside. He let the boy move closer to him, then, surprising him, stepped past and cut smoothly across the lower left leg of the boy, shredding his baggy hakama trousers. The boy cried out. Yoshio paused and flicked blood off his blade, then looked to the shogun.

"To the death," the shogun said calmly, but loudly. "This is a proper duel, not a sparring match."

Yoshio nodded. The boy put his sword back up. Yoshio attacked, though each strike was intended to be parried. Lamed, the boy was unable to keep up with Yoshio, and as the old samurai moved to the boy's left, an opportunity presented itself. The boy's sword was held at an odd angle downward. Yoshio struck the blade twice, twisting the sword and forcing the boy to release his right hand. Yoshio then, in a swift motion, pulled the boy's katana away and threw it on the sand.

Yoshio put his katana against the boy's neck as he collapsed to his knees, defeated. A drop of blood collected on the razor edge of the Muramasa blade.

"It is done," Yoshio said, flicking away the blood and returning his sword to its saya. "I give this gift to my enemy, that though he is shamed, this boy's potential will not be wasted." He turned to the Shogun and bowed.

"It was a duel to the death," Ouchi said. Ashikaga nodded. A touch on his arm from his wife made him pause as he opened his mouth. He looked at her for a brief moment, then returned his attention to Yoshio.

"I... am satisfied. Death was certain," the shogun said. "I should claim this boy's life for the bakufu," he added.

"You are most gracious, and infinitely wise," Yoshio said, bowing low again.

Ashikaga locked eyes with him. "The gods have spoken through this. Masaki has shown his honor, as per the agreement laid before me. Let the Asano clan have of him what they wish; seppuku-"

Ashikaga was interrupted by a sudden struggle. At the shuffling of feet behind him, Yoshio had stepped to the side. A blade pierced through the folds of his kimono. Cold steel slid along the skin of his ribs on his right side, stinging and biting. Yoshio, surprising his young assailant, spun right. He seized upon the hands that held the boy's wakizashi and, using leverage against the boy's wounded leg, pushed him forward into a trip.

Unexpectedly, the boy knew the counter, and though it likely pained him greatly, he stepped forward too, removing Yoshio's leverage as he shifted his weight to his left leg. The boy could not stop his momentum, and the two tumbled forward. Yoshio, ever aware of the short sword stuck between them, twisted the boy's wrists and turned the edge away from himself. They rolled over again, the boy ending on top.

Yoshio felt the boy's legs around his hips as they struggled for control over the blade. Though he was young, Yoshio's opponent was strong. He looked in the boy's eyes, full of venomous rage. Yoshio released the sword and brought his knee up into boy's crotch. A grunt of pain accompanied the slash of the wakizashi just above Yoshio's face.

The old swordmaster quickly grabbed at the hilt of the short sword once the boy had rolled forward. The boy was on his knees. Ignoring the pain, Yoshio grabbed near the tip of the wakizashi with his left hand. Pushing with the palm of his left hand and against the boy's two hands on the hilt, Yoshio thrust the edge of the blade forward. The boy toppled backward. Yoshio's weight fell on him. The blade slid and skipped over his chest, then resisted as it entered the neck and jaw.

Yoshio let go and rolled away. He did not want to look, but found himself looking at the boy anyway. Blood poured over his neck and to the ground. There was a sickly gurgling sound, and the boy began to thrash about, groping at his neck. Yoshio took in his face again, growing more pallid in the struggle for life.

"No!" A cry sounded from the western platform. Hiromi was running over, followed by a contingent of men. "Kichirou!" They surrounded the boy as he thrashed a few more times and then was at last silent and still. Hiromi gave a long, piercing wail that cut Yoshio to the bone.

Yoshio looked upon the bloody, pale face and understood. He looked to the shogun, who spoke out above the cries. "Well done, Yoshio." The words seemed distant.

What have I done?

Suddenly, Yoshio found himself surrounded. Amaya was there, and Furukawa, and some others he did not recognize. Amaya was binding his hand. He looked at it and found it to be covered in blood. She was then pulling open his kimono and pushing against a cut on his ribs that screamed with renewed pain and brought him back to the present. He became aware of Amaya's voice. He became aware of her arms around him.

"Thank the gods, I thought you were impaled at first."

Yoshio started pushing himself up, wincing with the pain in his left hand as he did so. He thrust Amaya's arms off him and staggered back. He looked at the people surrounding the boy, and caught Hiromi's tear-filled gaze as she looked back at him. His blood ran cold.

He tore his eyes from the horrible scene and staggered, then ran away from the crowds. Lord Asano's cold eyes regarded him as he ran past the platform to the walkway. People parted and let him pass through. He ran through the gardens and along well-manicured paths, straight to the front gate. He pushed the doorman aside and thrust the heavy doors open, then staggered out into the street, where he at last collapsed.

He looked at his hands. Bloody.

"I'm sorry, Yoshi, I'm so sorry!" Yoshio saw Amaya slip through the gate and rush toward him. Tears streamed down her face.

"You knew," Yoshio said softly. "You knew and did nothing."

"No!"

"Why?"

Amaya knelt down to hug Yoshio, and he threw her arms off with his shoulders. She wiped her tears and looked away. "The shogun wanted to punish Yamada. Noboru was missing. He viewed it as an opportunity. He did not know that Yamada's son-"

"But you knew, Amaya. You knew that Yamada's son was not his own. Kichirou was my son. *Mine!* You cannot understand what that means."

"You said you never knew that for certain," Amaya said.

"Did Yamada run forward with his wife?" Yoshio said.

"It would have disgraced him."

"So he did not."

"No."

"Then Kichirou was not truly his son. He knew that he was mine. What a fool I have been made into."

"You are no fool. You are an honorable, just man. There was every chance for that duel to end, and each chance was rejected. It wasn't your fault, Yoshi," Amaya said.

"Don't call me that. I have always hated the way you call me that. I'm not your brother or your pet." Yoshio staggered to his feet.

"No, you are not," Amaya said. She reached for Yoshio's face, and he jerked away from her touch. "You are my love, Taoka Yoshio."

"You do not love me," Yoshio said. He turned his back to her. "You love only your revenge. Masaki is humiliated now. The conspiracies are unmasked. You can demand his life. I have served my purpose. You can discard me now."

"I do not wish to discard you, my love," Amaya said. She had begun to sob. "I would never discard you-"

"And if I asked for such?"

"Yoshio..." Amaya began to sob louder, her body shaking. "I'm so sorry. Please forgive me. I did not want this. It was not supposed to go like this. I didn't want any of this!"

"It is the price. Discard me, Amaya-sama," Yoshio said. "It is all that is left."

"What?"

"Release me," Yoshio said. "Let me leave this world in peace."

"I do not want you to die."

"That does not matter," Yoshio said. "If you truly carry any affection for me in your heart, you will let me go."

Amaya stared at him, crying silently. Yoshio's face had smoothed. His eyelids were relaxed, almost half-closed, and he had the look of a man who was disinterested and unconcerned.

"I await your order, Amaya-sama," Yoshio said.

Amaya shuddered slightly with the tears. "I won't. I will not order you away. I won't... I won't give you any order. Do as you will, my love."

Yoshio turned away and began walking up the lane to the south. His posture was erect, and his gate was smooth and controlled, an image of a classic, unmoved warrior. It was an illusion Yoshio had carefully designed and then practiced for years, the image of the true man of the samurai class. Ever at peace during war, ever controlled in the heat of battle. Masculine, hard.

Inside his head, and in the murmur of his beating heart, it was different. He ached and felt exhausted. He longed to look back at the woman who had filled his time, his mind, and his heart for the past months. He held himself back from his desire. His feelings had served her too well. Whether it was what she delighted in, or what she used to control him, he could not decide, but he felt he should not give them to her. Her last image of Yoshio, broken man, ronin, would be one of brutal indifference.

Each step was harder than the last, until he felt an unburdening. He buried his broken heart, and the world returned to him. He realized he had not taken in any of the sights around himself, so desperately had he desired to get away. Leaves waved in the evening breeze. Clouds streamed toward the mountains, colored red and orange in the dying light.

What now?

The streets were deserted. He thought he was near the market. He became aware of a din of sound, somewhere to his left. Chaos. He turned his head and listened closer.

Screams, and the sound of crashes. He heard the familiar crackle of fire, and he could smell burning wood. He felt the katana at his side, and knew.

Ryunosuke. Noburu. Purpose.

He could mourn later. Now was the time for blood.

Chapter 21: Fire and Water -Taint and Cleanliness

CHAOS REIGNED IN THE STREETS. Women and men moved like a river out of the densely packed marketplace, frantically searching for one another. Couples, or women with children, ran past Yoshio on either side. Beyond them, flames raged as the wooden storefronts and fabric awnings caught alight. Houses and buildings were catching too, as the areas closer to the ocean had dwellings that were made mostly of wood and were packed tightly together. The few stone walls of the richer houses were of little use, only slowing the building inferno.

Normally, men would be forming up a water line, from either the well or a nearby river. A stream ran nearby, and the sea was equally close, but everyone seemed to be fleeing. Those parts of the quarter which remained untouched by the flames were vacant. Yoshio paused a moment and looked into the flames, consuming everything as a wall some 100 paces before him. He took a cloth from the folds of his kimono, normally reserved for wiping down his swords, and soaked it in an unattended bucket. The bucket sat on the porch of a small house. Its door stood ajar, and the inside was vacant. He wrung the rag and began tying it around his mouth and nose.

"Run, fool!" a middle-aged man said, gripping Yoshio's kimono as if to drag him away from the fire.

"The stream is the other way," Yoshio said. He looked calmly into the man's sunken eyes. "You should be gathering others to put out this fire."

"Forget about putting it out!" the man's voice crackled as he leaned closer. "A demon walks! It is like Raijin gone mad; some unholy spawn."

Yoshio nodded. "It *is* a demon. A fire demon. I will put an end to it. You rally your fellows at the river."

"You're mad."

"Perhaps," Yoshio said. He picked up the bucket and thrust it into the man's hands. "Save your town, or choose not to. I do not really care." He put his hand on his katana and began walking calmly but swiftly toward the center of the market. The man held the bucket, watching him go, then dropped it on the ground and fled, leaving a spreading puddle behind.

Yoshio stepped into the swirling smoke. The street was wide enough that even though houses and stores burned on either side of him, the fire did not touch him. It was, however, exceedingly hot, reminding him of the heat in front of Muramasa's forge, but amplified. It pushed at him from all sides, making his breathing through the wet rag all the more difficult. He drew his sword in anticipation of the battle.

"Taoka Yoshio. You're different than I remember. It looks like somebody has played a trick on you." Yoshio looked about him for the voice. It was not coming from all directions at once, as when he had encountered the murderer in the rice fields, but from somewhere ahead. The voice, although preternaturally loud, was nonetheless physical. Wind picked up the smoke and pulled it upward, clearing Yoshio's vision.

"Noburu," Yoshio said. "You look different as well, though I do not think the years have been kind to you." He tensed his muscles and raised his sword. His old pupil stood outside what was once a restaurant. Blood dripped from his ornate katana. Red visceral gore covered his face, and was smeared over his clothes. His eyes, Yoshio realized, were glowing like the rubies on the hilt of his sword.

"That name no longer has meaning," Ryunosuke said. He stepped toward Yoshio, sword held casually. His vacant eyes fixed on the old samurai, and Yoshio felt heat rise up within him. As the killer stepped forward, the bottoms of his trousers appeared, dripping red. He flashed a sickly grin, revealing teeth that were long and sharp.

"It matters not what you call yourself," Yoshio said. "Your body will be thrown into a pit among countless others. Nobody will remember anything about you. You will be one dead man among many."

"You are arrogant and foolish, Taoka Yoshio," Ryunosuke said. "Your tainted blade will not cut me down. I think, however, that the time has come to at last dine upon your tortured, pathetic-"

Yoshio did not wait for the killer to finish the sentence. He ran in, swinging swiftly through a series of cuts. Ryunosuke stepped nimbly back, parrying a single attack and dodging the others. The look on his face, however, was one of surprise. Yoshio advanced again, but paused as he felt his feet slip over something wet. He glanced down. Had he not been so focused, he would have wretched. The floor was covered in body parts, blood, gore, and sinew. Fractions of skulls and faces looked up into nothingness.

Ryunosuke attacked, and Yoshio found himself off balance parrying and dodging the blows, slipping backward toward fire. The demon blade was fast, singing as it flew past his head, and its wielder had more than mortal strength. Yoshio desperately ducked down and slid face first over rough stone slicked with blood. He rolled to his feet and knocked aside another cut from his opponent, just in time. He now had enough space to work with, and a feeling of security on drier cobbles.

"You have outlived every other meal," Ryunosuke said. "Cold comfort it shall be to you when your soul is burned within me."

Ryunosuke struck, first with a feint, then with a hard slash toward Yoshio's left side. Steel rang out and Ryunosuke stepped back, looking somewhat puzzled. He leapt back again at an unexpected slash that grazed his thigh, cutting through his pants. Yoshio had drawn his wakizashi in his wounded left hand, the point still downward. He quickly flipped it around and pushed at his opponent again, each blade moving and cutting as it if had a life of its own.

"This was something you never taught me," Ryunosuke said, his katana flashing in the fire and twirling to push aside Yoshio's sweeping strikes. The killer backed into the courtyard of a ruined restaurant as blows rained down on him. He leapt backward and up, unnaturally high, landing well balanced on the cracking pole that once held an awning.

"There are many things I never taught you," Yoshio said. He crossed his swords and slashed them apart, severing the base of the pole, which began to tip downward toward the street. Ryunosuke leapt off of it as it fell, attacking Yoshio from above. The old teacher crossed his swords again and caught the strike of his student between them. He allowed the momentum of Ryunosuke to push him downward, and then he kicked up with his right foot and went into a roll. The foot caught Ryunosuke on the solar plexus. Yoshio vaulted his opponent over himself and into the center of one of the burning shops. A loud crunch and crash followed, as Ryunosuke hit a burning pillar and part of the building collapsed.

Yoshio backed up as the entire front of the store fell inward, scattering ash, smoke, sparks, and debris into the market square. Flames reached up to the sky and a rolling billow of smoke darkened the haze left by the departing sun, made redder by the flames. Ryunosuke was consumed in flame.

Yoshio waited, breathing deeply through the cloth wrapped around his face, his two swords at the ready. For a tense few moments, nothing happened. Then the building collapsed some more. Yoshio shielded his face from the heat with his left forearm, but as the flames at last subsided and the plumes of smoke billowed away, he despaired. A body rose from the coals and burning rafters. It was twisted and deformed, an ashen shape with veins or red flame bursting from its withered humanoid frame.

Its gaping mouth twisted into a sort of smile, rowed with inhuman teeth. A sword still hung in its hand. Its eyes flashed, and then the shape burst away, nearly vanishing as it ran with a strange gate.

Yoshio could not react, but as the buildings fell into flames around him, he knew he could not stay where he was.

"You look like absolute hell," Muramasa said. He pulled the open-flamed lantern off its stand and held it up high. The rail from the patio of the attendance house cast strange elongated shifting shadows upon Yoshio. "I mean that in a literal sense – what the hell happened to you?" Emi stood up from her calligraphy table and shrank behind the swordsmith, peering around his shoulders.

Yoshio raised his eyes and looked at Muramasa. They were like two black stones surrounded by a brown crust. His brow knitted into a hint of agony. "Noburu is no more."

"But you were not successful," Muramasa said. He looked off into nothing. "The demon still lives, though he is distant."

Yoshio shook his head. "I cannot overcome him, my friend. He cannot be stopped. His flesh... he survives without it."

Muramasa's face grew grim. "Where is Amaya?"

Yoshio looked down. "Betrayal."

Muramasa looked at Emi. "Get some soap. And a bag you don't care for." Yoshio looked up at him. "We're taking you down the river. You can tell me everything along the way."

"The river kami cannot purify me," Yoshio said. "And I have tainted your sword."

"Bah!" Muramasa said. "I just don't want to foul up the bath water. Neither one of us is young enough to enjoy spending half the day lugging water up the hill just for a clean bath."

Emi appeared again, holding a bundle of cloth. "I grabbed some more of Yoshio's clothes, too."

Muramasa nodded.

"We don't have time for baths," Yoshio said. "Ryunosuke…" He swallowed hard.

"He'll come to *you,* my friend," Muramasa said. "Now, let us wash away the sickness of the day."

Yoshio spread his fingers and let the swift flow of the stream pull his hands backward. He let his head dip below the surface of the water, and his ears filled with the muddled sound of liquid running over stone. He emerged and wiped his face. By the light of the lantern and the moon, the blood streaming off him looked like mud floating in the water. He had stuffed his clothes into an old sack, and thrown them into a patch of bushes beside the stream, thankful to be rid of them. They were the clothes Amaya had bought for him, and expensive, but with the blood and horror of the day, they made him feel sick. Standing naked in the stream made him feel better, even if it was only a fleeting experience.

He took a deep breath and waded back toward the shore where a towel and his other clothes had been left for him. He quickly padded himself dry. The clothes Emi had retrieved from his things consisted of a kimono, an old, faded hakama pant, and a tattered black obi with threads sticking out in many places. As he slipped the kimono around his shoulders, he could hear the voices of Emi and Muramasa. They laughed softly as they talked, and Yoshio was struck by the strangeness of joviality against the backdrop of the day. He gazed up at the moon, looking full or nearly so, and pondered how he might himself laugh.

Recent events had been absurd, but he could not so much as chuckle at them. Yoshio realized that, after all, he did not laugh very much. *Such is the way of the warrior, I suppose.* He pulled on his hakama and tied them, noting the frayed ends of the belt, which he had created himself by cutting off small pieces when a cloth wasn't handy. He looked at the sleeves of his kimono in the moonlight. It was a basic thing, spun of a single pale color as was proper with men. It was a gift from Furukawa Kenta as a congratulation for his marriage, and for years he had prized it highly. Of late he had not thought of it at all.

Funny, how quickly the generosity of friends is forgotten when in the presence of women. Women are worse than men when it comes to tolerating rivals. He still did not laugh.

He felt the silk of the kimono, now much rougher than when he had treasured it years before. He picked up the lantern and walked around the bamboo patch. He found Muramasa and Emi sitting around a small campfire, laughing.

"That was when he told me who he was," Muramasa said, raising his eyebrows, and threw a stick on the small fire. "I was, of course, mortified, though apparently not as much he expected."

"So why did the girl's father lead you on so much?" Emi said. She saw Yoshio walk around the fire and stand between them, his arms crossed. The girl turned her nose up. "Just sit down. We already know how grumpy you are."

Muramasa smiled at her and looked at the fire. "Not what I would say to him right now, girl."

"No," Yoshio said, "but it is good to make a play at laughter. I wish I had some in me today. Why did you make this fire? We should be getting on."

"The girl was cold," Muramasa said, nodding toward Emi, "And she rejected my first suggestion to that effect."

"Foul old man," Emi said, though she smiled.

"Sit," Muramasa said. "Let's talk a minute."

Yoshio complied and sat down cross-legged and straight-backed.

Muramasa drew his sword and looked at it in the firelight. "This is a good sword. One of my best, as far as the craft goes. Your swords are better, but this one is still as good as any samurai should have. It is, however, not good enough."

"How so?" Yoshio said. He looked at his belt. He still had the two swords Muramasa had made for him, though one of them was stained with the blood of his son. Not the blood of his death, but it was still his blood. Yoshio shivered in the warmth of the fire.

"Ryunosuke is no longer a man," Muramasa said. "I can sense the demon still. Perhaps stronger than ever, but I'm not falling ill anymore. I thought at first it was because we were far away, but the massacre at the market was close, very close. I should be doubled over in pain right now. I think now that the sickness was a mortal thing – me reaching out and feeling involuntarily the pain of the man bound to the sword."

"This is good, yes?" Yoshio said. "No more falling ill in battle."

"It has me thinking," Muramasa said. "The man that was Noburu is gone in a near-literal sense. He has been burned away, as you say, leaving only a husk of a body behind, bound by the burning spirit. The name of your student truly has no meaning for him any longer." He took a breath and poked the fire with a stick. Sparks flew up. "Well, that body, what is left, is obviously very resilient. You will need more than just steel to destroy it."

"What will I need?" Yoshio said.

"You have what you need," Muramasa said. "You will need a kami – a piece of one, or a blessing. Your sword has that. This one," he held up his own blade, "does not, as much as I would try to help you in battle. A kami-touched blade will be necessary."

"What better to end a fire kami than with a blade blessed by a water spirit?" Emi said. "I think it's rather fitting. Poetic, even."

"It has been tainted," Yoshio said.

"I am sorry for your loss, my friend," Muramasa said. "But blood does not taint a tool used for blood-letting."

The walk back to the shrine was mostly silent. Occasionally, Emi would yawn and complain about something, only to be met with grunts and silence from Yoshio, or an off-hand comment from Muramasa.

"I *was* looking forward to sleeping in my own bed again," the shrine attendant said.

"Lucky you. You get to keep on looking forward," Muramasa said.

Later, Emi broke the silence again. "You two will probably get me killed. This is what I get for my generosity."

"You took the lady's coin quickly enough," Muramasa said. "And I seem to remember a girl who rather resented raking sand and performing rituals for nobody in particular."

Emi kicked an errant twig on the path. "I wish I could go back to just raking sand."

Yoshio grunted, and then said, "Boredom or danger. Seldom is anything interesting in life without risks."

"Besides," Muramasa said. "You could take that silver and go buy yourself a new life."

Emi humphed and continued walking, falling a step or two behind Yoshio, who, having been refreshed by the bath in the river, strode forward with a renewed intensity.

Soon they were looking upon the attendance house and its large open yard, well lit by the sinking moon. The large roof of the shrine behind it stood out starkly above the trees, its tiles looking like the scales of a silver fish. Yoshio paused as they entered the yard.

"Something wrong?" Muramasa said. He reached for his sword.

"Not exactly," Yoshio said. "Somebody has been here in our absence." Yoshio stepped forward, hand on his katana, and walked in a shallow arc around the landing to Emi's house. He crouched down. "I need some lamplight."

Nervously, Emi shuffled over, holding the lamp above Yoshio. Yoshio bobbed his head to either side. Footprints crowded the space in front of the stairs, some overlapping others. "What do you see?" Emi said.

Yoshio stood up straight. "Some interesting things. Let's check the house, eh?" He stepped around the mass of footprints and walked up the short flight of stairs to the house's porch. He motioned Emi to follow him, and looked to the side to see Muramasa walking toward the rear of the house cautiously. They caught a look from each other, and Muramasa nodded.

Yoshio slid open the front door. Once again, Emi held the lantern up to illuminate the front room. Beneath a window, upon a calligraphy table, Yoshio saw a scroll. He turned to Emi. "Light up a few lamps, here and elsewhere, while I check the rest of the rooms. And don't touch anything." He heard the door on the far side of the house open as Muramasa entered.

He walked down the narrow hallway and looked into each of the small rooms, which all had been left open to the center of the house. They were empty, one and all, but in the room that he and Amaya had stayed in a single tattered piece of paper lay on the floor looking much out of place. He picked it up and went back toward the front room, now lit by its own hanging lantern. Muramasa stood near it reading an open scroll.

"It's for you," Muramasa said, and thrust the curled piece of paper toward Yoshio.

"I said not to touch anything," Yoshio said, looking to Emi.

"*I* didn't touch anything," Emi said. She frowned at him. "What's going on?"

Yoshio grunted as he opened the scroll. Penned in crooked characters drawn with pen or needle, rather than with a brush, was a letter:

Taoka Yoshio:

You have proven your grit and skill.

However, challenge alone does not make for a satisfying experience.

You have also proven your blessed depravity, in the murder of your own blood.

I know now, freed, that taste by itself, in its many permutations, does not make for a satisfying meal, either.

If I wanted either challenge or taste, you would lie dead at my feet, worshipping your own death, Taoka Yoshio.

But since I want both, I have waited. Now is the time to finish what we both have been putting off.

Tomorrow, when the moon is high, I will see you again, at the place once held sacred to your beloved betrayer.

In the sanctum, we will ply our fate.

You will die, but you will still comply. If you wish for the lady Amaya to live, that is.

Otherwise, she will do as a meal in your absence.

She is very lovely.

-Ryunosuke

"Shitenno-ji," Yoshio said, with a sigh.

"The Buddhist temple from before," Muramasa said.

Yoshio nodded. He carefully rolled the scroll back up, and looked at the paper he had found in his room. It was another letter, but he recognized the calligraphy immediately. "Amaya wrote this," he said. The characters were drawn exquisitely, but here and there shakes of the hand had pulled the brush off course. The writing spoke to Yoshio of emotion beyond what written in words. A nervousness, or a pain, but not fear.

My dearest Yoshi,

We know each other too well for formalities. I am sorry, for everything. I do not expect you to believe me when I tell you that the orchestration of the duel was not of my making, but I will tell you regardless, for that is the truth. Know that I did not ask or infer that the son of Yamada should be placed in that arena with you. That, I believe, was devised by Masaki with the will of the shogun in mind. Though he is disgraced, he has achieved his will against me, and like years before, has managed to take something very dear away from me. He also disappeared, removing himself from my revenge for such. I should have listened to my father, and to you, but the old wounds ran very deep. They run deeper now, torn wide by what has been done to you.

I thought I would never forgive Masaki, but looking at events now, I would, and abandon my revenge forever, if only you would forgive me. I do not expect you will, but if you do, you know-

The bottom of the page was torn off.

"The killer has Amaya?" Emi said. Yoshio looked up and realized Muramasa had been whispering to her, telling her the details of Ryunosuke's letter.

Yoshio scratched his jaw and looked out the open front door, silent.

"Not quite the reaction I expected," Muramasa said. "But after today – or is it yesterday? – I can't be sure what to expect."

"I do not think Ryunosuke is in the company of my master," Yoshio said. His gaze remained on the open door as he stepped out onto the deck and looked at the muddy tracks below the stairs. "No, I do not think that is the case."

"What about the letter?" Emi said.

"Genuine," Yoshio replied. He turned around and looked at her. "Amaya herself, however, was never here. She must have had a servant deliver it. There are many footprints outside, some overlapping the others quite intentionally. It looks a bit like a struggle, but all the footprints are flat. When you fight or wrestle with an opponent in Jiu, you are nearly always on your toes. Moreover, none of the footprints belong to Amaya. She has very small feet and would be wearing geta on dirt paths, as she preferred to do while we stayed here. Nowhere are there the twin indentations of such sandals."

"What do you think happened?" Emi asked.

Yoshio handed her the intact scroll left by Ryunosuke. "I think a servant came, left Amaya's note, and departed. Then our killer came, found the note, and used it in his own message."

"Interesting assessment," Muramasa said.

"There is one detail that confounds me," Yoshio said. "Ryunosuke, or whoever wrote the note, knows of Amaya's relationship to Shitenno-ji. Even Masaki did not seek us out there."

"Reeks of a trap to me," Muramasa said.

"Perhaps," Yoshio said. "Or perhaps I have underestimated the powers of my enemy. He seemed to gaze into my heart, once, though that might have been the remnant of Noburu, my student." Yoshio shook his head and sighed.

"So, does he have her or not?" Emi said.

"It does not matter," Yoshio said.

"Seems pretty important to me," Emi said. "Fighting for the life of your love rather than for nothing at all."

"I will be fighting for justice," Yoshio said. "And I would prefer to enter battle cool of heart and focused in my mind. The presence of Amaya would be a distraction."

"Wait, so you're going to go?" Emi said.

"Yes," Yoshio said. "It is my chance to end the madness that has settled in this town. You have not seen the marketplace, but when you do, you will understand."

"You should try to fight him on your own terms," Muramasa said. "Terms that are favorable to you."

Yoshio shook his head again. "There are no terms that are favorable to me. Better I should take this opportunity, when Ryunosuke is still interested in killing me. In a few days he may acquire new tastes."

"I guess I better make sure my sword is sharp," Muramasa said, and sighed.

"You're going too?" Emi said, flustered.

"It is my responsibility, girl," Muramasa said.

"I'm going to bed," Emi said. "Men are fools." She threw up her hands and grabbed one of the lamps. She walked down the hallway, grumbling, the light flickering with the breeze she made.

"You're not worried for your safety here?" Muramasa called out after her.

"I don't care anymore," Emi said. She disappeared into a room.

Sengo raised his eyebrows at Yoshio. "We better make an attempt at it too." Yoshio nodded, then snuffed out the remaining lamp.

Emi yawned widely, then flinched as she walked onto the porch. It was mid-morning, and the eastern sun fell brightly across the wooden deck, illuminating a long piece of paper filled with letters that was pinned to her calligraphy table. It was not the words that surprised her, but who was writing them. Yoshio sat calmly, drawing careful characters with a narrow-bristled brush.

"I used your ink set," Yoshio said. "I hope you do not mind. I lost mine at some point and never bothered to buy a replacement."

"It's fine, I guess," Emi said. She leaned forward over his shoulder and tried to read some of the lines. "I didn't figure you for a poet."

"Amaya always said poetry would be my highest calling," Yoshio said, "but you are correct, I am no poet." He leaned over and blew on the ink, speeding the paper's drawing in of the black lines into permanence.

"I... write poetry a lot, actually," Emi said. "It's not like I have much else to do here."

"As you frequently remind me," Yoshio said. "But you also say you don't care for the risk of excitement."

"Excitement is fine, but you all..." she shook her head. "Danger. I really don't know who would go in for assassins and demons and samurai cutting each other to pieces," Emi said.

"And yet it calls to you," Yoshio said. "Or you would not have been so willing to talk to gangsters, or house such vagrants." He looked at the paper and breathed deeply, then began signing his name in Kanji at the bottom. "I have a task for you. Not as exciting as my own task, but I think you might get something out of it."

"Another scrape with death, then."

Yoshio smiled. "You've never been so at risk." He rolled up the scroll and began binding it with a bit of string. "I need you to take this to Amaya, when I leave for the night."

"So you are sure Ryunosuke doesn't have her?"

"No, but if he does, she will find this once I free her." He handed the scroll to Emi.

"What is it?" Emi said, staring at the crisp paper.

"Something rather too poorly done, but she should have it. I believe you will be able to find her at the house of the shogun. You may get to meet him, actually. I will give you directions." The aging samurai pushed himself up. "Thank you for your courtesy, Emi. I will remember it, even if only for a short time."

Emi nodded silently. She watched Yoshio step down to the ground below and walk toward the shrine. She stared at the scroll for a minute, once Yoshio had disappeared behind a row of foliage. She considered opening it and reading it, but held herself back and instead went inside to make herself some tea.

Chapter 22: Battle Beneath the Moon

THE MOON coated the grounds of Shitenno-ji in an otherworldly haze. Dust rose between the outer gate and the buildings of the sanctum, kicked up by high winds off the sea. It made the temple grounds look like they were enveloped in a blizzard, the gale swirling up snowflakes where there was none in actuality.

The wind also made it cold, and Yoshio could feel his joints tightening up, his skin shrinking around his muscles. Aches found their way into his knees and elbows. He remembered practicing bareback in the snow as a young man, snow coating his bare feet, and he never ached. He looked to his left at Sengo Muramasa, grim-faced and tense, and wondered when they had each gotten so old. *Better to die in your prime than to watch your strength and vitality flow slowly out of you. Better to die on your feet than die a toothless husk who can barely chew, much less wield a sword.* Ten years ago he would have been less frightened than he was this night. For all his attempts at quiescence, his nerves stood on edge. That nervousness would speed his aging body in the battle, but also open him up to mistakes.

"The last battle," Yoshio said quietly, just over the howling wind. "The way it should be. The master swordsman at the end of his skill and strength, dying doing what he has devoted his life to."

"With an old fart of a blacksmith to die beside him," Sengo said. He cracked a smile.

"Wielding the last letters of a great artist," Yoshio said, feeling the grip of his katana in his hands.

"Poetic, eh? We just need some falling cherry blossoms, or some light snow on sleeping trees."

"The dust will have to do. Many times I have counted myself unlucky for the circumstances of my life. I will no longer, my friend."

"It's not like you'll have the opportunity, you mean," Muramasa said.

"True," Yoshio said, and smiled at the old swordsmith.

They approached the outer buildings of the sanctum, the roof tiles shimmering in the moonlight. The tall silhouette of the bell tower stood out in front of the silver-lit clouds in the east. Unlike the last time they had been there, there were no monks standing guard, waiting in the shadows. The place looked absolutely deserted, though Yoshio knew it was not. He could almost feel a dark life inside. They stepped through a gate, the wooden doors left ajar, and walked toward the center of the sanctum. The wind howled outside, but inside the ring of protective buildings, Yoshio could barely feel it. He heard a scrape off to his left, but did not look for it.

"Ryunosuke is not alone," Yoshio said.

"You shouldn't trust him to play fair," Muramasa said. "Keep in mind what-" Muramasa stared off into space.

"What?" Yoshio whispered.

Muramasa did not reply, but instead gripped his stomach and fell to his knees.

"Ryunosuke is not here," he croaked. "I can see his hunger with my eyes. He just killed a man, but not here. No, far away from here."

"Of course, he is distracting me again! Where?" Yoshio said. "What do you see?"

"A wall, and a tall house," Muramasa said, almost in a trance. "Double doors- closed. Three men. Swordsmen. Heat. Hunger. Up above. A balcony. Have to kill the men first. Appetizing-" Muramasa shook his head as if it had been struck.

"Retainers," Yoshio said. "That's the house of the shogun, or I'm a fool. Bah! I *am* a fool! Letting him draw me away like that. He did it once to me before and I should have seen it coming."

A crashing sound startled Yoshio. He turned around and looked at the entrance gate. It was now closed shut by great wooden doors. Iron rings rattled lightly.

"I told you it was a trap," Muramasa grunted. He pushed himself back up.

"Taoka Yoshio!" a familiar voice shouted above the wind. Yoshio looked across the empty expanse toward the bell tower. A figure walked around it, sword drawn.

"Masaki," Yoshio said. "I am surprised to see your head still on your shoulders."

"If you knew me, you would not be surprised," Masaki shouted. "Soon, your shogun will be dead, just like you. You have all played too well into our hands." Yoshio saw shadows step out over the roofs, and saw movement under the eaves of the buildings.

"Why me?" he said, hoping to stall Masaki long enough to get an accurate understanding of who the Daimyo had brought with him. "I hardly matter in the overthrow of a shogun."

"Revenge, of course," Masaki said.

"If you had cared about honor you would not have thrown a boy into the ring with me."

"I care nothing for Bushido, and even less for Yamada's dimwitted son," Masaki said. "I want revenge upon Amaya, and I will continue to collect it. It is too bad I will not be able to watch her cry over your corpse. I will, however, get to watch you die, an exquisite meal."

Meal! Yoshio thought. He swallowed hard and thought quickly.

"I see you have brought many men," Yoshio said. "That was kind of you. I have had little opportunity to test the resilience of my new swords."

"You are bad at boasting, old fool," Masaki said.

"I never boast, Lord Shiba," Yoshio said. "I count fifteen swordsmen in the buildings and ten archers on the roof. I will guess there are a few more I do not see. That is a great deal for one assassination. Your own precautions prove that I, in fact, do not boast." He looked over at Muramasa and glanced quickly and one of the buildings, a door-less open hall. Muramasa nodded back, slightly. "Remember this, Masaki, the doors that keep me in will keep you in as well."

"Lady Amaya?" Emi stood in the doorway. She trembled slightly, still nervous and fearful even though she had not caught sight of the shogun. The grim guards, many of them carrying spears rather than swords and arrayed as if for battle, had each glared at her, but let her past.

"Yes, Emi?" Amaya turned from her low artist's table, lit half by a nearby lamp and half by the light of the rising moon pouring in through a large window. Emi was struck by how tired the woman looked. Aged, even, considering how young the attendant had assumed the lady to be.

"I don't mean to disturb you, or your artwork," Emi said, still standing nervously. She felt sweat in her hands, and became suddenly worried she would stain the scroll Yoshio had given her.

"Come in," Amaya said, standing up. She was wearing a simple white kimono without adornment, and her long hair fell down her back. Sleeplessness rimmed her eyes in a pale red. "What do you need, child?"

Emi stepped into the comfortable room. "Yoshio asked me to give something to you."

"He got my letter, then?" Amaya said.

"Sort of. Part of it was torn off, I think. He got a longer letter from Ryunosuke, saying he had taken you captive, or meant to, anyways. He went off with Muramasa to fight him tonight."

Amaya took the scroll from Emi and stared at it for a moment. She sighed. "He knew that I would be here, and went to fight the demon anyway."

"I think he guessed," Emi said, "but yes, he went anyway."

"Old fool," Amaya said. "I should have ordered him to... do so many things. Ordered him away from Osaka, at least."

"I think he still cares for you," Emi said. "But he said the note was something you wouldn't like to read."

"Of course he still cares for me," Amaya said. "Yoshio doesn't let his heart get in the way of things, though when he shows it he can be quite sentimental." She untied the twine holding the scroll closed and unrolled it. She moved over to the lamp to get a better look.

"What does it say?" Emi said.

"You didn't read for yourself?"

"No. But I wanted to. I thought it might be a love letter."

"Have you ever gotten one?"

Ami looked down. "No. Well, yes. Sort of?"

"Then yes, you have," Amaya said with a smile. She held up the scroll. "This, however, is not a love poem, it is a death poem." Her face fell suddenly slack. She stared at it closely, and Emi looked over her shoulder. She glanced at Amaya to see if she objected, but Amaya seemed fixated on the poem. She leaned over to read:

My life is the sword
Its mastery my calling
And now by the sword
My life will, at last, be failed
Too late I waited
To find masteries more worthy
Too long I lingered
Not claiming what I desired
But if morning finds

This poem to be in vanity
I will come to you
And claim what I desire
Better than the sword
A mastery more fulfilling
Though I die tonight
And as many times reborn
I will long for you
The mastery of my heart
If never I win
The battle was not in vain
To find my mastery in you

At the bottom was Yoshio's name in kanji.

"Old fool," Amaya said. She sighed and rolled the scroll back up. A strange noise from outside startled both women, and Emi found herself stepping backward. There was a sound like gargling, with a soft vocalization, followed by the sound of something falling on the stone path. Amaya stepped forward, cautiously. She leaned out the window and looked left, toward the rear entrance to the large house. A body lay crumpled, blood visible as a blackened pool on the stone.

"What is it?" Emi whispered, still standing near the entrance to the room.

"Ryunosuke," Amaya whispered back. A scream pierced their ears, though it was muffled as behind doors and walls. "He is here."

"Then he has come for you," Emi said. Her voice quavered. "He killed Yoshio and now he's come for you, just like he said."

"Don't be silly, girl," Amaya said quietly. She strode over to a bundle beside the futons and removed a sword. She quickly tied it onto her belt. "He's here for the daimyo, and the emperor."

Emi quickly shut the door and moved away, toward the center of the room. She covered her mouth with her hands, gripping the skin of her cheeks as if she permitted her hands to drop a scream would come roaring out.

"We have to act quickly," Amaya said, pushing the door open. She motioned to Emi. "Come! You have nothing to fear if you do as I say."

Tentatively, Emi followed Amaya out of the room and down the long hallway, breaking into a trot. They heard another curdling scream, this time definitely from downstairs, and the sounds of struggle.

Yoshio's body snapped into action, his swords leaving their saya, one in each hand as he dashed toward Masaki. Sengo leapt in the opposite direction, drawing his own katana.

"Now!" Masaki cried. He drew his sword and backpedaled toward the large hall at the north end of the sanctum. Yoshio heard arrow strings twanging, and felt the air around him move. He stepped high as a flurry of missiles shot by his feet. He felt one cut through his hakama, mercifully missing his groin, and get caught in the cloth. The shaft snapped as he continued to run, splinters cutting his thighs. Still, he did not slow until a mass of shadows leapt out of the kondo, blocking his passage to Masaki. Black suits stood out between more traditionally dressed samurai. Dust flew up from their feet.

Yoshio did not hesitate. His katana flew forward at the closest man, causing him to attempt a parry. Yoshio's wakizashi cut him at the knees, and the man's sword flailed as he toppled with a scream. The next man stepped forward with his sword at the ready, leaving two men a few steps behind. At that moment, Yoshio understood he was fighting samurai, taught to fight one on one, and not trained assassins who would tip the odds in their favor. He took advantage of this by stepping to the right and stabbing out at the foremost man with his wakizashi while rushing past him. One of the men standing back was caught off guard and found himself fumbling his sword as Yoshio's katana thrust past the man's guard and went point-first into his neck.

A sickening crunch sound filled Yoshio's ears as he withdrew the katana and spun about, cutting the first man through the upper arm as he attempted to thrust into what would have been Yoshio's back. A scream erupted and a sword fell to the ground as the black-garbed samurai clutched at his left arm, now hanging uselessly by a few threads of sinewy flesh, gushing blood onto the dirt.

The last man attacked Yoshio with an overhand cut that then went into a thrust. It was a beginner's motion, and Yoshio would have easily parried it had he been handling a single sword. With a sword in each hand, however, defense was trickier. Yoshio backed up as the man continued his series, deflected a cut from the side, and then Yoshio stepped in with his own flurry of attacks. Dual-wielding was a rare, if not totally unused, fighting stance in the greater ryu of Kenjutsu, and Yoshio's opponent was not prepared for the offensive onslaught of the weaving blades. A single guard was difficult to use against swords attacking in two different directions, and the man found himself bleeding from his thigh and shoulder from some glancing blows. A final cut of the katana through the man's shinbone left him a bloody mess. He fell to the earth grunting.

A quick glance into the darkness, searching for Masaki, was interrupted by more sounds of fighting. Yoshio turned his attention to his rear. Steel rang as he saw Muramasa battling two men beneath a covered walkway. Archers, mere shadows on the well-lit roof tiles, swarmed toward a corner of surrounding buildings where they could once again get a clear shot at the old Swordsmith.

Yoshio shook the blood from his swords and slipped them into their saya. He jumped up and grabbed a hold of a wooden beam protruding from a nearby eave of the Kondo building, and kipped himself up to waist level. From there, he scrambled onto the roof. Almost immediately, the attention of the enemy archers was focused on him, and a volley of arrows was released. They flew past him as he danced and slipped over the roof tiles. Yoshio clumsily drew his katana, almost failing to pull it all the way out of the scabbard as an arrow ricocheted off the roof and hit him in the hip.

The wound wasn't deep, and so Yoshio pulled the arrow free with his left hand, finding it caught more in the folds of his hakama than in his flesh, which stung only mildly. He charged at the archers, who drew swords of their own as he neared. These men, unlike the black-garbed samurai on the sanctum floor, attacked in tandem.

These are the true assassins, Yoshio thought, stepping back from some coordinated cuts that would have left him bleeding at the neck or knees. He drew his wakizashi. A quick parry on his left side gave him an opening, and he attacked forward, letting his swords swirl around him as a lethal shield. He felt a slight resistance in his katana as it landed and slid across the chest of one of the assassins. He looked to his right to see an incoming slice, ducked down and swept at the feet of the attacker with his right foot.

The assassin leapt over it, but landed hard on his heels on the sloping roof, then tipped backward and fell to the dirt below. Yoshio thrust the tips of both swords into another archer, pushing forward with all his weight until the man fell backward.

Yoshio rolled over the body then turned to protect his back, only to find nobody there. A few of the archers remained on the far side of the sanctum, firing long, inaccurate shots in a hope either he or Muramasa would be distracted. Yoshio once again sheathed his swords and slid toward the edge of the eave. He gripped one of the protruding beams and let himself down so that he was hanging and looking into the building. He saw Muramasa backing up toward him, holding off two swordsmen. The other side of the hall, which would normally have been open, was battened up by some arrangement of debris that he could not discern in the darkness.

Yoshio dropped down and drew his swords once again. He crouched slightly and stepped around Muramasa, cutting one man down at the thighs and another at the collarbone. Blood flew warm and sickly onto his face and pate. Another man turned to retreat, and Yoshio cut him at the heels, severing his Achilles tendon. He screamed, and Yoshio stepped back to Muramasa.

Muramasa gave him a start. "How many more?" He held his side. Dark blood, though not a terribly large amount, colored his left hand.

"Not sure," Yoshio said. He turned to see five or six men standing around the pagoda at the center of the temple, whispering orders to each other hoarsely. They moved forward, and Yoshio could see that several had long spears. Softly, he could make out the voice of Masaki among them.

"It's too late for the shogun, Yoshio," Muramasa said, gasping. "I can see him. It is too late, for him, but not for us."

"You are shorter than I imagined you would be." Ryunosuke's voice was soft and controlled, but his insides burned with energy, a deep, penetrating vigor, and above all, a hunger for dark blood. His vision was hazed, skewing the focus of the room, and his flesh tingled. The remains of his mortal self still clung on in agony suppressed only through the spilling of blood. Soon the body and spirit would both be satiated. On the balcony, at the end of the long room, the shogun sat, his silhouette in the moon more layers of folded cloth than his chunky, soft body.

A crow cawed. It made Ryunosuke smile. The aura of the shogun pulsed a bright green. So vital. It was different, too. Exotic.

He tried to search the man's heart with his hunter's vision as he approached, but found a wall. Recently, the piercing senses that could probe men's memories and malicious feelings had become unresponsive, wandering to targets unlooked for, possibly due to the damages his mortal self had sustained. It was like his sense of smell had fled, and so his means of judging meals became more limited. The shogun, however, was a known to him, and Ryunosuke had long desired to dine on the seat of power in Japan, a man riddled with secrets. "Silent, eh? It makes no difference to me." The sword throbbed with power. "Ashikaga Yoshitane, ever ambitious, even in defeat. You are alone now. I have slain all your protectors. What do you think of that?" Silence. "What a delight it shall be to have you inside me." More silence.

Ryunosuke approached. His sword slid from the saya, almost singing a song with its unleashing. The world snapped into clear focus as mind, body, and the demon spirit became one in intention and thought. The shogun sat still, as if contemplating his fate, staring out the window at the bright and glaring moon. The sword turned, ready for the killing strike, and Ryunosuke raised it into killing position. His whole body was alight with pain and hunger, but was also filled with equal parts of exhilaration, excitement, and the pleasure of anticipation.

Ryunosuke stepped onto the balcony, katana raised for the killing blow. His arms felt stiff, resisting him, and he felt a surge of panic and wonderment. At that moment, the shogun looked up, and instead of looking into the eyes of the aged Yoshitane, he saw a smooth, round face. It was a girl's face below the high and prominent top-knot. Her eyes trembled, tears forming at their corners, and her lips tried to move in a silent attempt at speech.

"What is this?" Ryunosuke said, his own arms stiff. The hunger of the sword, now unsheathed, was overwhelming, yet he could not move his arms. He felt the demand of blood turning in on himself in the absence of new flesh. The twin being began to panic.

"I g-guess what she said is true," the girl said. Her voice quavered. "You really can't kill a woman."

"What?" Ryunosuke said. He tried to process the words as his mind became overwhelmed. The creature before him had significance, he understood, to mortal men. Why had he never taken note of them before? Something in his other self? He realized the edge of the sword was pressing into his charred flesh on his left arm. Blood was coming.

His frantic thoughts were interrupted by a shuffling of feet. He looked up to see another woman darting from the shadows. She had a sword unsheathed, and it glinted in the moonlight, but also blazed with its own aura.

Amaya. The name came to him, and he remembered his old master, arrogant Yoshio, who he had meant to pay back for the years of embarrassment in the dojo. Another life. Distant.

"Back to the abyss!" the frightening woman cried.

The woman's sword flashed, and a racking pain split his insides. He moved the demon blade to counter, but his mind was hazy, and he could not seem to predict her motions. He felt his flesh being cut. The arm, then the leg. His chest was split open with a long slash. He saw blood spring forth from his body, squirting out between knots of burned, twisted dermis. He was stabbed and felt himself reeling back, falling. Each blow seemed to draw forth less pain, and each cut seemed to push him further back, back into himself.

"I banish you back to nothingness, demon!" The woman said again, though she sounded now like she was at the end of a very long tunnel. "Die!"

Ryunosuke was vaguely aware of his body, and his vision was failing. He stared out blankly as Amaya tore him apart with her katana. His back hit a wall, and he was staring at the ceiling. The spirit withdrew, fleeing from the mortal vessel that had served it faithfully. The memories, the desires, fled, and all that was left was burning and hunger. The view of the room darkened as he sought escape in steel, and at last, he lost his understanding of time, sound… space. He could only sense blood, but he was powerless to acquire it.

The steel hemmed the kami in, and he was alone once again.

Blood sprayed across Yoshio's face, a warmth in the chill night. The young samurai's head fell into to two pieces as the wakizashi cleaved it. Yoshio thrust his katana past the dying man, straight into the sternum of the assassin behind him. It was a shallow stab, but enough. The swords sang a harmonious diad as Yoshio withdrew them. The assassin staggered back a few steps, then collapsed.

To his right, Muramasa's sword swirled chaotically, but found its marks near enough, and two more men lay dead, with another staggering away missing a hand. Arrows flew past them, but the archers were far enough away on the perimeter's roofs to be inaccurate as Muramasa and Yoshio fought around the bell tower. As a volley was loosed the pair would move around to another side, sheltering them from the aerial onslaught for precious moments, forcing the black-garbed archers to circle the roofs and move to a new vantage. During the dance, Yoshio and Muramasa had managed to kill eight men between them, but six more remained, and the rooftop assassins began to abandon their positions, drawing swords and running through the courtyard to the fight. The two men, past their prime, were becoming tired.

"He's there," Muramasa said, following Yoshio to a new side of the bell tower. "I can see in my mind's eye. He's about to kill the shogun."

"To hell with the shogun," Yoshio said, breathing heavily.

A group of six black-garbed men appeared from around the corner. A row of three had drawn swords, while the other three stood back. Yoshi saw the glint of throwing knives in their hands. The remaining samurai appeared from the other side, surrounding Yoshio and Muramasa.

"I'll take the rich boys," Muramasa said, and rushed the samurai, his sword spinning in an unrelenting series of vicious cuts.

Yoshio took a breath and attacked the ninjas. They knew how to fight as a group, and though Yoshio was on the attack, he had to spend much of his energy defending against the blows and stabs that came at him from all directions. He saw from the corner of his eyes knives fly at him. He ducked quickly under one and, finding old reflexes suddenly invaluable, knocked another one away with his wakizashi. It clanged off the blade with a bright note.

Yoshio turned his right wrist downward and thrust with his katana, piercing the foot of one of the assassins. The man did not cry out, but kept on his stance and attack, stabbing at Yoshio with the tip of his straight sword. Yoshio let himself fall backward, the blade narrowly missing his chest, then cut downward with both swords. The injured assassin toppled over along with the one to Yoshio's left. Each of them had lost a foot. Blood sprayed upon the ground and droplets temporarily blinded Yoshio.

He rolled away, his swords feeling slippery in his blood-coated hands. He glanced back to see Muramasa still holding the group of samurai at bay. One had fallen, and other was bleeding.

"No!" Muramasa screamed, and collapsed backward. Yoshio bolted toward the blacksmith, thinking he had been cut or otherwise injured. Whistles and dull thuds in the dust, just under his feet, reported to Yoshio that the remaining archers had circled to a new position. He felt a throwing knife hit him on the trapezius, just below his neck. The tip was off-target, however, and the knife only succeeded in cutting lightly the skin of his shoulder and face as it flew off of him. Yoshi could hear footsteps behind him.

The old samurai arrived just in time to catch and deflect a pair of killing blows aimed at Muramasa, who rolled on the ground coughing. Yoshi turned his parries back in on each attacker, cutting their thighs and groins in injuries that would be fatal if given time to bleed.

"Amaya," Muramasa rasped. "The sword… I see Amaya." The blacksmith shuddered.

Yoshio found his heart, already beating hard, leap into his throat. Fear gripped him, a fear that had not been present though he had been facing certain death before and during the fight.

"What?" Yoshio said, then was brought back to the present by an attack from behind. He did not have the presence to listen for an answer from the blacksmith. He turned and ducked, thrust and cut, protecting the fallen friend from enemies on all sides. He moved faster and more accurately than he realized he could, the fear of the moment pushing his reactions and reflexes beyond their normal limits.

Samurai fell, their blood spilling out like tea from a shattered pot. The assassins fell, silent or grunting. Yoshio moved through his many-practiced moves, fueled with fury as much as fear. He heard Muramasa scream, and looked down to see an arrow in the man's side. Yoshio stepped lightly over Muramasa, another volley of arrows falling around him, and swiftly cut down one of the assassins. Two more seemed to appear beside him with drawn swords. Yoshio leapt away from them and attacked the last few samurai, who backpedaled with fear-filled faces, their swords held far out in front in a semblance of a guard.

Shouts emanated from the rooftop to Yoshio's left, and behind him, the assassins turned and began running. Confused, Yoshio looked around himself again. The gate through which they had entered, bared from the outside, was ajar, and a figure was pushing his way through.

Masaki, you coward, Yoshio thought.

The two Samurai in front of him took the distraction as an opportunity to advance, and swift cuts assailed Yoshio. He stepped back, then with two simultaneous feints and two stabs, killed both of the samurai by piercing them through the heart. As they collapsed backward, spewing blood up in a black spray, Yoshio turned his head to the left at the report of a loud, clear voice.

"It appears our employer has fled!" The voice said. Yoshio pinpointed it to a crouching shadow on the roof of a western walkway. "Lucky for us, he paid us in advance. I don't feel like sending any more of my brothers to die today. Twice now you have proven yourself a singular army in one man. It will take me a long time to rebuild my clan, but I do not resent you for it. A man needs to know his limitations. If we meet again as enemies, which I hope we will not, I will be well prepared for you, Taoka Yoshio."

"Who are you?" Yoshio called back.

"A ghost in the night, Yoshio-san," the voice shouted back. "If you want to catch Masaki, he is likely on his way to a meeting at the river north of here." The shadow disappeared.

Yoshio bent down to look at Muramasa. He was bleeding from a dozen cuts, but the arrow wound in his side was the worst. His eyes seemed to be looking out blankly.

"You said you saw Amaya."

"Vicious Amaya," Sengo whispered harshly. "Bitter Amaya. I saw her fury." He came back to himself and looked at Yoshio. "She's there with the shogun. I cannot see any more." He relaxed and his head fell to the dirt. "Go, Yoshio. Do not worry about an old man's well-being. Go."

Yoshio nodded and stood back up. He shook the blood from his swords and re-sheathed them as he ran toward the open gate. On the other side, he paused and looked to the north.

Masaki. You will never stop, will you? He thought, wondering if he should pursue the wretched man. His heart was torn for a long moment, and then he set off to the south, toward the residence of the shogun.

I am too late. He understood it to be true, but he was compelled to go anyway.

Chapter 23: Imprisonment and Escape

Yoshio Ran. The strap of one his sandals snapped, and he casually left it behind, ignoring the bite of small rocks and cobbles on the sole of his foot. His sides ached, as much from exertion as from the wounds of the last few days. The blood that covered his face and soaked his clothes through to the skin began to dry in the wind, turning to a crust that irritated his face and neck. His lungs began to fail him, but he did not slow. His arms and legs began to feel limp as the fear and tension of the long fight departed. He was left feeling hollow, but he kept running.

Almost there, he said to himself as he rounded the final corner. He could see the residence of the shogun looming ahead, a tall series of houses surrounded by a wall. A group of men and women stood in front of the gate holding lanterns, talking tersely to one another. One of the women screamed as Yoshio approached, shocked at the sight of the bloody man. The men, all samurai of various ages, stepped back, partly in horror and partly in rank fear of the apparition that Yoshio had become. He rushed past them into the compound, not bothering with an explanation or greeting.

Bodies littered the courtyard, and the ground was stained with gore. Yoshio spared a cool moment to take in the brutal dismemberment of the shogun's retainers, who lay piled upon steps and the garden floor. His toe stung as he tripped over a severed head. Quickly, Yoshio turned his back on the scene and ran through the open front doors. More dead men lay inside and he had to leap over a body that, due to the way it was cut apart, spread from the landing to halfway down a flight of stairs. Yoshio's feet slipped over the wooden floor of the second story, still wet with congealed blood.

He raced down the hall. The door he sought was ajar. He rushed in, hand on his katana, though he knew he was too late to save her.

A cool, smooth face greeted him, with eyes that grew suddenly wider, and then trembled. Hair blew lightly in the breeze from the open balcony.

"Amaya," Yoshio said hoarsely. His breath felt suddenly empty, and his knees gave out. He fell to the ground, leaning up and back to look at Amaya. "I thought Ryunosuke had you."

Amaya shuffled across the floor and fell down beside Yoshio. "My dear, dear Yoshi." She wrapped her arms around him and pulled his head close. "Ryunosuke is no more."

Yoshio looked up at Amaya. Tears flowed from her eyes, but her lips were parted in a slight smile. "How?"

"I killed him," Amaya said. "I told you my katana was not just for show. I also said once that he had never killed a woman. It appears he was quite incapable of it." Yoshio looked past her at a heap of strange flesh on the balcony. "Yoshio, what happened to you?"

"Masaki set a trap," Yoshio said. "I thought I would be facing Ryunosuke, but instead Sengo and I were ambushed."

"Where is Sengo?" Yoshio realized Emi had been standing near the room's entrance, silent.

Yoshio turned to look at her. "I left him at the temple. He was badly wounded, and told me to go without him. I'm sorry."

Emi nodded silently.

"Temple?" Amaya said.

"Shitenno-ji," Yoshio said. "Where I met you before. I... thought that Masaki did not know of its significance to you. That is why I thought it was indeed Ryunosuke who would meet me there."

"He didn't know of it," Amaya said. "Before, at least." She looked away for a moment. "No matter, you are safe now."

"I let Masaki go."

"Good," Amaya said. "I wish I had abandoned him long ago."

"Karma will end him regardless. Just wait," Emi said. "Muramasa is at Shitenno-ji?"

Yoshio nodded, and watched Emi slide out of the room.

"I thought she hated him," Yoshio said.

"Perhaps she does," Amaya said. "But not so much as to not save the man."

"That makes no sense," Yoshio said.

"You are not a woman."

Yoshio straightened up suddenly. "The sword? Where is the sword?"

"I put it aside," Amaya said. "I did not like touching it."

"Quickly," Yoshio said, pushing himself up. "We must destroy it, before it claims another."

Amaya followed behind Yoshio, hurrying through the streets as they began to fill with the dawn light. Yoshio, still blood-soaked and hoary, kept up a solid jog, ignoring the looks of passers-by at the horrific sight. Amaya clutched the demon blade close to her, forbidding Yoshio to touch it for fear of its power manifesting again. On the way, they had each had time to take in the beauty of the sword, with its carved and ornate handle, normally quite impractical, and its carefully inlaid saya. The hilt was carved to look like the elongated head of a dragon, with ruby-set eyes that still glowed with a soft light. The saya continued the image of the wyrm, with a pristinely inlaid model of a scaled body and a long, swishing tail of green and red.

The katana truly was a thing of beauty, disguising its terrible and dark nature.

The street opened up into a wider space, ringed with market stalls. The smell of salt, growing as they ran, was now strong below the scent of fresh cook fires being readied for a morning meal of fish in the little restaurants nearby. The sea was at last before them. They ran out onto the docks, finding a long pier with a large Chinese frigate docked near the end. The dock workers and sailors, busy unloading cargo from the inland empire, stopped and gave them pause as they rushed past to the end of the wooden planks.

Yoshio looked out to the sea, endless blue in the grey morning, and then cast a glance back at Amaya.

"Cast it in," he said. "In the sea, let the fire be quenched."

"Should we not take it to a smelter or a smith to destroy it once and for all?" Amaya said.

"That would only free the demon," Yoshio said. "Sengo made this sword so that he could contain and imprison it. He knew that the death of his body would free the demon forever, and so we must never destroy the steel with heat. We must give the fire kami to his natural antithesis, water. There let him return to the abyss, or else stay a prisoner in his steel cell forever."

"Was this Sengo's idea?" Amaya said.

"No, it is my idea."

"Good." Amaya nodded and stepped past Yoshio. She held the sword out at arm's length, admiring the work for a moment, then threw it out into the ocean. It splashed, and then disappeared beneath the waves.

Amaya looked at Yoshio and smiled.

"It is done," Yoshio said with a sigh.

Emi's face was downcast as she walked into the attendance house. Yoshio was drying himself with a towel, and though he was now clean, the bags under his eyes and his distant gaze still gave him an unsettling appearance.

"Muramasa?" Yoshio said, wrapping the towel around his waist.

"I could not get to him," Emi said. "The monks had the entire temple closed, and would not let me through."

"They were conspicuously absent last night," Yoshio said. "Very interesting. What does your gut tell you?"

"That he is dead," Emi said.

"Perhaps it was necessary," Amaya said, appearing at the front door with a few pieces of cut wood. "Ryunosuke was stunned, not whole, when he mistook you for the shogun. Perhaps the part of him that held the kami needed to die."

"Perhaps," Emi said.

"Where was the shogun, anyway?" Yoshio said. "I did not see him in his apartments when I arrived."

"He was..." Amaya looked off for a moment with a smile. "Indisposed?"

"So he was sleeping with somebody he wasn't supposed to," Yoshio said.

"He sends his thanks," Amaya said. She put the wood down near the door. "I thought we could have a bit of food and sleep before we leave."

"Where are we going?" Yoshio said, raising an eyebrow.

"So, you are going with me?" Amaya said.

Yoshio grunted. "My task is finished, so who else would I go with?"

"Just what every woman likes to hear," Amaya said.

"No, Amaya," Yoshio said, "I did not mean it like that."

"It's fine, Yoshio," Amaya said. "Old habits die hard. You are no longer my servant."

"That is where you are wrong," Yoshio said. "But so be it. I am ready for a new journey."

Dusk fell on Osaka like a funeral shroud. The city had seen much blood over the past weeks. Massacres in holy places, in open on the street, and in the very house of the shogun had shaken the peace of the people who lived in the bay. As Amaya and Yoshio walked through the streets, the soft words spoken between friends and acquaintances had subtle tension. It was quiet everywhere they went. Despite this, there was also joy, here and there, and the streets were filling up.

"Tonight is the beginning of the Tanabata star festival," Amaya said. She ran her hand over the mane of their horse, which walked beside them contentedly.

"I had lost track," Yoshio said. "It looks like we won't be spending the festivals with the shogun after all."

"You know the story?" Amaya said.

"I think so… about the weaver and the cow herder?" Yoshio said.

"Yes, how God Tentei was concerned that his daughter Orihime, the weaver, would never meet a man, and so introduced her to the star herder Hikoboshi. They fell in love instantly, of course. Tentei immediately regretted his decision once the stars wandered all over the sky and his daughter no longer cared to weave good cloth for him anymore."

"He separated the two with a river of stars, if I remember right," Yoshio said.

"Yes, and a huge flock of magpies, pitying the couple, let the weaver walk over the star river to her beloved husband. Some say the magpies do this once a year, on this night, but if it rains, she must wait another year."

"The story means something to you, does it?"

"It does now." Amaya paused and looked up to the sky, which was turning a dark, deep blue. Stars were beginning to glint out between wispy clouds overhead. "I am glad that it is clear tonight. I would hate to have to wait a year." She smiled at Yoshio.

He nodded and smiled back. Then, his face relaxed. "Why are we leaving like this?"

"Tentei regretted letting his daughter fall in love. He put a river between her and her husband."

"Shitenno-ji," Yoshio said. "Your father knew how much it meant to you."

"He did. It was he who placed me there for my artistic instruction."

"I am sorry," Yoshio said. Amaya put her arm around Yoshio for a moment, and pulled him close.

"I have one more thing to gather, before we depart," Amaya said. "Please do not despise me for it."

She led him down another narrow street and into a grove of trees. The path wound past tall houses. They paused at one of these, lit from the inside by soft firelight. She rang a small bell by the front door.

"Just a moment," a voice said. The door slid open revealing an old, bald man in a simple robe. "Amaya-san and Yoshio-san. Good to see you again."

"And you, Iwao-san," Amaya said, smiling. She turned to Yoshio. "You remember each other?"

"The teacher monk," Yoshio said with a bow. "Only not residing at the monastery."

"I've kept this house for a while now," Iwao said. "It was a gracious gift to an old, poor art teacher, though I think my heart says I should be leaving it soon. Yoshio-san, I am sorry that none of my brothers were at the temple last night."

"What about you?" Yoshio said and added, "Not to offend."

"It is the monks of Shitenno-ji that should be offended. I was indisposed, as you shall see. Now please, come in." The old monk bowed low and ushered Yoshio and Amaya into the house. It was modestly furnished, with a low hearth and a few windows, along with a wood-fired stove in an open kitchen.

A young boy appeared from a short hallway with a few forward facing doors. He looked to be about ten, with a head shaved like a monk and wearing a simple kimono. He smiled broadly and ran forward to Amaya. He wrapped his arms around her in a tight hug.

"Yoshi," Amaya said, looking past the boy at the samurai. "This is my son, Masatsune. Iwao has been watching over him since he was weaned."

"Hosokawa Masatsune," Yoshio said, looking at Amaya. She nodded. Yoshio looked at the boy for a long moment. "I am pleased to meet you, Masatsune-san." He looked back at Amaya. "Shall we be taking him with us?"

"I had hoped. Osaka and the temple are not as safe as they once were," Amaya said.

"If there is anywhere safe," Yoshio said. "Are you good with a sword, my boy?"

Masatsune looked back at him with wide eyes. "No, but I have one."

"We do not practice martial arts at our temple and monastery," Iwao said.

"Plenty of time to learn, if you care to," Yoshio said. "If not, I think the brush is just as good a calling."

Iwao laughed.

The air was full of light as the trio walked through the villages on the outskirts of Sakei. Hundreds, if not thousands, of floating paper lanterns were drifting up from temples and marketplaces. It bathed the entire bay in a soft, golden light, and the sea itself rippled gold near the water's edge. It truly looked like a river of stars, come right down to earth. There were many prayers and many deaths to mourn for the people of Osaka, lanterns carrying their wishes to heaven.

The horse's hooves clacked loudly on the rough ground. Masatsune seemed to be fixated on the sky, watching the glowing paper bags as they rose and then descended toward the water. Soft songs filled the air. Occasionally, there was laughter, but most often, there was silence. Even the bloody horror of the night before could not keep people shut inside, and as they passed by Shitenno-ji they could see that the outer grounds were filled with people lighting candles and singing.

"You have kept Masatsune a secret very well," Yoshio said.

"I am sorry for keeping it so," Amaya said. "He would be hated by Masaki for the accident of his birth, and members of the Hosokawa clan, of which he would have claims of succession, would view him as a rival. My father would also have been ashamed of him. I had to protect him from all of these. I hope you will forgive me."

"I trust you, and I understand," Yoshio said. They walked on in silence for a while. "Where will we be headed?"

"I have led long enough," Amaya said. "I'm happy to follow you for a change. Anywhere you would like to go?"

"I have a few places in mind," Yoshio said.

"Oh!" Amaya said. She reached into her kimono and withdrew a scroll. "Here is your death poem." Yoshio raised an eyebrow as he took the rolled paper. Amaya looked up at the lanterns casually. "I thought it was good – quite magnificent – actually, it might be the best I've read."

"I am happy to satisfy you, my lady."

"Oh, I am *not* satisfied, my dear Yoshi. It wasn't at all up to your standards."

"You just said it was the best you'd read."

"I have *very* high expectations for you, my dear, beloved Yoshi," Amaya said. "Luckily, you will have many more years to revise it and add to it."

"I will endeavor to please you, as always," Yoshio said, and put the scroll into a fold in his kimono.

Amaya looked up at him with a smile. "You always do."

THE END.

Epilogue

THE POLITICAL MACHINATIONS that were endemic to the reign of the later Ashikaga shoguns came to one head of many at the battle of Funaokayama, which took place in the eighth year of *Eisho* era, on the twenty-fourth day of the eighth month (September 16, 1511 in the western calendar). The conflict occurred during Ashikaga Yoshitane's second reign as Shogun. In that battle, two heads of the Hosokawa clan, Masataka and Sumimoto, assisted by unexpected allies in the Shiba house, attempted to take Kyoto by force. Ouchi Yoshioki, representing the shogun Ashikaga Yoshitane, forged an alliance with another powerful member of the Hosokawa clan, Hosokawa Takakuni. Their combined forces, along with the Rokkaku and a smattering of smaller clans, marched against the Hosokawa usurpers north of the holy city.

In the spectacular battle the forces of Shiba and Hosokawa, lured by the absence of the shogun from Kyoto, were slaughtered by the forces of the Kanrei. In the midst of the battle, as the tide turned against the rebels, part of the Shiba forces, controlled by Shiba Masaki, a daimyo of some ill-repute, quit the field. Their retreat was interrupted by a group of reserve soldiers and samurai loyal to the Rokkaku clan, who obliterated what was left of them.

Shiba Masaki was not found amongst the dead, but a subsequent search of the countryside by Ouchi's outriders found what was claimed to be his body. He had stumbled upon a group of peasants who, upon recognizing him, slew him with scythes and other farm implements. His body was not easily identified, as his swords and armor had disappeared.

With the victory, peace and order were restored to Kyoto for a decade, until more strife arose in the Ashikaga house.

THE CITY OF SILVER

MOONSONG, BOOK I

WESTERN DEIDERON
IN THE SIXTH DOMINION

Prelude: Power

"Tell me, Vindrel, what is power?"

Sarthius Catannel turned his head away from the rail for a moment to regard Claire as she stepped across the threshold to the small balcony overlooking the courtyard. Below his shock of blonde hair, his green eyes stared at her with the same vacant stillness as when she had met the man years before. She felt a chill and drew her robes around her body tightly.

"Power, sir?" Vindrel, the dark-headed captain of the guard for as long as Claire could remember, stood beside Sarthius, his uniform of blue and green crisp as always.

"Yes, power." Sarthius stared out of the balcony as Claire crept up to stand close behind him. "What does it mean to have power? To be powerful? This philosophical quandary has been on my mind of late." She could smell the fire in the courtyard below, and quickly pieced together what was taking place. She didn't want to look, but knew somehow, she would. In the end, she would not be able to avoid it. Sarthius would see to that.

"Power…" Vindrel looked down for a moment. "Power is the ability to exact your will. To do what you wish."

Claire noticed the flintlock pistol that Vindrel openly carried in defiance of Church Law. It was a generally accepted fact that Vindrel was a *Somniatel,* though nobody ever dared to accuse him. Watching him look out to the courtyard with his familiar stone-cutting gaze, she believed he could, in truth, be a member of one of the strange rustic clans that as much as worshipped the magical and technological heresies of the Dream God, living like savages in wilds of the world. If it was true, it explained much of his retention with the young count; Dream-cultists were valuable sell-swords, just as much for their uncanny, even supernatural, skills as for their lack of ethics.

"Power to do as you wish… A good answer," Sarthius said, "but not quite right, I think. A woodcutter chops down a tree because he wishes it. Is he powerful?"

"He is to the tree," Vindrel said, scratching his thick, black beard.

Sarthius cracked a smile. "So he is. What do you say, Claire?"

Claire felt a lump in her throat as the count's empty eyes met hers again. "I think the woodcutter is not the powerful one in this scenario."

"And why?" Sarthius said.

"Because he can't chop down the tree. He needs an axe. It is the axe that has true power," Claire said, doing her best to stand up straight and look the part of her position as high cleric.

"Spoken like someone who truly understands the Canon," Sarthius said. "I'd expect nothing less than an acknowledgement of the gifts of the Gods of Knowledge to man."

"But it is the woodcutter who swings the axe," Vindrel said. "The axe is just a tool."

"Like you?" Claire said. The words came out with the wrong tone – far too assertive. A bead of sweat broke out on her brow.

"Aren't we all?" Vindrel said, a slight smile parting his beard and bringing out lines around his eyes. "It is Count Catannel that is the wielder, even if the tools can think." Vindrel's eyes were narrowed in the bright light from the cloudless sky, drawing in shades of yellow to his iris.

"I like this analogy," Sarthius said. "But it is incomplete." His lips twisted into the semblance of a smile, though the shape was somehow perverted. He gestured for Claire to approach the rail. She swallowed, feeling the lump in her throat return. She stepped up beside the count, looking out over the ornate stone rail to the courtyard below. There was a raging fire beneath a raised earthen platform, a stage that usually served up executions in the form of hangings. That day, however, the deathly theater would not display such a casual disbursement of criminals. Fire was for apostates of the most dangerous sort. "The woodcutter has as much in common with the axe as the axe does the tree."

"How so?" Vindrel said.

"The axe has no will. No real will, and like you said, power is the ability to exact your will, though it is also more than that," Sarthius said. "The axe is merely doing what it was designed to do." He nodded and smiled at Claire. "By the god Ferral, of course."

"Of course," Claire said.

"Not at all like myself and Vindrel." Sarthius chuckled. "For the woodcutter is also doing what he was designed to do. He too is a tool, serving masters he does not even recognize as such. He cuts the trees because they have value to others, not himself. The trees are merely a means to some other end – his family and livelihood, perhaps."

"That seems like life in general," Vindrel said. "The baker bakes to feed others, not himself. If you don't mind me saying so, aren't we all just serving some other's end with our actions? Even a king may serve the gods."

"I don't mind you saying what you wish. Better than groveling," Sarthius said. "Everyone serves somebody else, thus sayeth wise Denarthal, yes?" He cast a glance to Claire, then turned as another set of footsteps entered.

It was Donovan Dunneal, a man who had been given his naval commission from his high birth and advanced it through a type of brutality that even the court cleric could not avoid hearing about. Claire envied him less that Vindrel, if only because she knew that in the shifting landscape of power on the Isle of Veraland, a birthright was more likely to be a liability than a blessing. At least beyond the Cataling court she had no claim to power, and thus nobody beyond plotting to usurp her.

"Yes, you are correct, my lord," Claire said, choosing to lock eyes with the clean-shaven Dunneal as he approached rather than look out to the courtyard. She said formally, "Our place among all others is the gift of Denarthal. His knowledge is the foundation of our society. Our interdependence and interconnections are bound by his gift of the coin." Feeling awkward staring at Dunneal, she looked down on the courtyard. Only a few people stood to witness what was going to happen. For what Claire expected to see, usually only the most perverse residents of the city enjoyed bearing witness.

"The truly powerful do not submit to such notions of interdependence, cleric," Vindrel said. "The powerful do what they will."

"Exactly," Sarthius said. "I knew I made a good decision keeping you on. The axe would only be truly powerful if it cut the woodcutter, rather than the tree."

"I don't follow, lord," Claire said.

"To be powerful, you must be able to make the wills of others conform to your own." Sarthius gave her a smirk, but his eyes were as calm and still as ever. "To be powerful is to make the system into what *you* want it to be."

"Such ideas are dangerous," Claire said. "In the wrong company, of course. The same goes for your gun, Vindrel."

"Are you the wrong company?" Sarthius said, raising his eyebrows.

"No, my lord," Claire said. "As cleric to your grace and the church of the city, I am merely giving advice for your dealings with the world. You have done much to further the church and its ministry, but there are men who prefer to judge according to outward displays, and not actions."

"I am lucky to have such a wise counselor," Sarthius said. "Action… perhaps that is the last element of power. If you have the power to do something and never do it, who is to say you had the power at all? Yes, power only exists if you use it."

"Otherwise a beggar could claim to be the greatest sorcerer in the world," Dunneal said.

Sarthius chuckled, in a deep and scratchy tone. "Yes, of course. Let us observe an element of power. And of action, for the glory of the church and her holy gifts." He nodded toward the platform below.

The scattered crowd of mostly men began to hoot as the door to the dungeon was opened and the guards appeared, chains between them holding a young woman, her white flesh shining brightly under the noon sun. She was naked, and even from the heights of the small room, streaks of grey grit could be seen on her flesh.

Ardala, Claire thought as she watched the frightened face dart to the men of the crowd. It was only a few weeks prior when she had seen the same woman in the halls of the castle, busying herself with bed changes and cleaning. She was one of the few servants that didn't seem totally worn down by the atmosphere of the place. Eventually, all of them shared the same vacant eyes as the count. Claire wondered silently if her own eyes looked like that.

"So rare to see a mage burned in these all too dry times, eh?" Sarthius said.

"I thought she talked," Claire said.

"She did," Sarthius said. "She told us everything, and with not much effort, I must say. The torturer was disappointed."

"Most disappointed," Dunneal said, casting a sickly look to Claire.

"Yes, but she was lying," Vindrel said. "The Lady was not in the tavern when we went."

"She was telling the truth," Sarthius said. "I could see it in her eyes."

"Then why are you killing her?" Claire felt sick as she watched the young woman being led up the steps. The fire blazed off the end of the platform.

"Because I am a man of actions, not words," Sarthius said. "Whether she lied or not, the result was the same."

"But do you have to?" Claire said. She squeezed back tears as a leather bag was placed around the young woman's neck.

"I do," Sarthius said. "Power does not exist unless you use it. This must be done. For her. For these men here. For all who would betray me. And for the men below, their wives, their children… all the people of Cataling, who must believe not only that magic exists, but that their lord and their church are greater than it."

Claire turned away, covering her mouth. "You… Have no betrayers here, lord," she said through a choke.

"Do you not wish to watch?" Sarthius said. "It is so rare that we see a mage cleansed from the world. I do this as much for the church as for my court."

"No, I don't want to watch, lord," Claire said.

"Then why did you come up here?" Sarthius's eyes remained fixed on the scene outside.

"I just…" Claire took a breath and looked out the door. "Wanted to inform you of the death of King Grasslund."

"That *is* good news," Sarthius said with a smile, still never taking his eyes away from the scene below.

"Yes," Claire said. "It seems that his grief over the excommunication and banishment of his last son was too much for him, and he succumbed to his sickness."

"The writ of ascension?" Sarthius said.

"It is being cleared by the high priest as we speak," Claire said. "We can organize the coronation as soon as the writ has been acknowledged by all the other high lords."

"Good," Sarthius said. "It seems your job will require a bit of haste, Vindrel. I want the Lady here for the coronation. I want the Grand Cleric to see her here with me."

"I have a good idea where she's heading," Vindrel said, clearing his throat. "I'll need a ship."

"I'll give you more than that. Captain Dunneal? Or is it admiral now?" Sarthius smiled at Dunneal.

"I think it's a fitting time for that promotion," Vindrel said.

Dunneal bowed with a smile. "Thank you. I shall not disappoint you, your highness."

"I like the sound of that. Your highness," Sarthius said.

Dunneal smiled. "Your highness, something occurs to me. Need the Lady be present for the coronation?"

"The church *will* observe the law," Claire cut in. She looked down as Sarthius narrowed his eyes at her. "I'm merely letting you know the temper of the Grand Cleric, your highness."

"What I mean," Dunneal said, "is… How shall I put this? What if tragedy were to strike your beloved, and you were to remarry?"

"That would be quite a delay," Vindrel said.

Dunneal chuckled. "We can write whatever story we choose. Right, Claire?"

"Yes, your highness," Claire said.

Sarthius leaned over and looked down at the crowd. His eyes narrowed. "Yes. Who is to say that my wife did not already die, perhaps a month past, and that we held the news for our grief?" He scratched his jaw. "I have considered this. But then I would lose my ties to the Hviterland and the rest of the Northmarch." Sarthius laughed. "You're a good battle tactician, Dunneal, but truly you need a king to manage a war."

"I don't understand, sir," Dunneal said.

"Coronation is merely the inevitable first step," Sarthius said. "I do nothing without purpose. You must think beyond the battle and consider what our navy – the navy of a united Veraland – can accomplish on a broader scale. That is, if you wish to keep the position you have been promised."

"Aye sir," Dunneal said. "I will endeavor toward readiness as my highest priority."

"Vindrel, you have your ship."

"Understood, sire," Vindrel said. "They won't escape me."

"They?" Dunneal said.

"She had help besides the witch," Vindrel said. "I think I know who, based on my contacts."

"We're checking every ship that leaves," Dunneal said. "Nothing that floats is getting out without a thorough inspection."

"They're already gone," Vindrel said. "Out into the dry highlands. But don't worry. Their options are limited. We'll find them."

Sarthius glanced back at the cleric. "Ah, Claire, you may leave now, if this scene does not suit you."

"Thank you, my li – your highness," Claire corrected herself.

"Oh," Sarthius said. "I have another stipend for your daughter's studies." He reached in his pocket and drew forth a small bag.

Claire looked at Vindrel, who seemed not to react. The bag, made of burlap and topped with a simple string, sat in Sarthius's palm.

My daughter. Marriage and children were not permitted for the devotees of Verbus, the priesthood that managed the church itself, serving as clergy to all other clergymen. The Church of the Twelve was the source of all knowledge in Deideron, and indeed the world, for beyond the divine strand and the fractured North the land seemed to be filled with warring savages: men who had forgotten the light of the Twelve Gods and their gifts, and people whose humanity was in real doubt – remnants of the old races.

Claire's daughter Maribel was the result of her failing at being neutral with the nobility – failing to uphold her oaths. The girl's father had been a prince in the warring kingdoms of the divine strand, the remnants of the last great holy empire, and that put her at great risk of harm from competitors to the eleven thrones. She had managed to enroll her daughter in a devotion path to Nostera, the goddess of healing, much younger than would normally be allowed, in order to keep her hidden away. This she kept a secret to all, even the girl's father, but Sarthius had known about Maribel almost as soon as she had accepted a position as minister in Cataling. Somehow, the count knew everything.

He had come to her offering charity in the form of an educational stipend, but she understood what it truly was: a threat, and the sort of threat that keeps a woman up at night. Knowledge was part of his power, and that knowledge had been well-used against Claire. With her connections in the church, she had caused several key members of the nobility to be exiled as apostates, all with mysteriously sharp drawings of guilt and evidence of which Sarthius seemed always to know.

Maribel needs this.

Claire stepped forward to take the bag. At that moment, she saw, as if slowed in time, Ardala the servant girl being thrown naked onto the bonfire in the courtyard below. It seemed like she could not look away as a scream escaped her mouth. She felt her fingers clutching the bag, but turning away from the execution seemed impossible. Vaguely she felt Sarthius's spider-like fingers around her wrist, holding her. Flesh blackened as smoke and flame enveloped the count's victim. Silence in the crowd answered the woman's tortured cries.

The bag of gunpowder around the woman's neck finally exploded, ending her pain in a flash of fire and blood. Sarthius pulled Claire close and whispered with hot, sickly breath in her ear. It was like the hissing of a snake.

"Power. Remember."

I: Dry Highlands

The stars stand blinking cold as winter frost
The constellations frozen overhead
Within the portal I'm forever lost
Through pathless wilderness I'm blindly led

harlotte opened her eyes to see the firmament standing strong, with the moon in the west of the sky, barely peeking over the edge of the ancient wall. She was wrapped tightly in the wool cloak, and the fire still smoldered warm in the hearth, but she was alone. The song and voice faded, sucked into the wind, which whistled through the gaps in the walls, where the mortar that joined the ancient stones together had worn to dust and blown away. It sounded to her like a penny whistle and a voice at once, shrill and yet somehow melodious, blending with the song she heard even as it drowned the words. She drew the patched cloak closer around her body, wondering how much worse the wind would be outside the ruins of the old house.

The stars looked strange and alien to her, unfamiliar in their place where the roof of the house had once been. She realized it had been years since she really observed them.

Rone's voice returned:

Ten years have come and gone outside on earth
By fate, not chance, I do at last return
With time enough to contemplate your worth

He entered through a gap in the walls that was once a door and saw her looking at him. His voice cracked. "How are you doing?" he said, clearing his throat. He bent down by the fire and began rummaging in his backpack.

"I feel like I'm either dreaming, or waking from a dream," Charlotte said. She coughed softly. Rone turned his head and raised an eyebrow at her. "What's that look about?"

Rone chuckled softly as he removed a small copper pot from his bag. "Well, you didn't really answer my question, did you?"

"I thought I did," Charlotte grumbled.

"Were you dreaming? Dreams are more powerful up here." He emptied a waterskin into the pot and put it on the coals of one side of the fire. Rone leaned back against the stones of what had once been the central hearth of the house. He opened up a small bag and withdrew some herbs, which he crushed with his hands and emptied into the pot.

"I don't understand."

Rone picked up something else – something he had gone out to fetch that Charlotte couldn't remember the name of – and put it in the pot as well. He sat down by the hearth and stirred the pot with the end of a dagger, his sole eating implement after Charlotte had lost his fork days earlier.

"What were you dreaming about?"

Charlotte pulled the blanket up to disguise a sudden warmth in her cheeks. "Forget I said anything."

Rone laughed. "Not possible. You can tell me."

Charlotte hesitated. "Dragons."

Rone suddenly looked at her with wide eyes. "Really? That would be quite an omen." He watched Charlotte for a long moment, then turned back to the pot. "No. Something embarrassing, then. Don't worry about it. Just remember that dreams have power, especially in a place like this." He looked around. "It's like you can feel the remnants of the Prim, lapping against the stones. Now, how are you doing – are you feeling sick?"

"I'm doing fine," Charlotte said. "Loads better, actually."

"You were red as a gill and unable to speak just a few hours ago."

"It's just..." Charlotte swallowed hard. Her throat felt like she had swallowed nettles. "I... get sick sometimes."

Rone stood up. "Then we ought to be off. We're behind the schedule I had imagined, but if we make up for most of the day you spent groaning and sleeping, we may yet arrive in Masala ahead of... whoever Catannel paid to hunt you."

Charlotte sighed and pushed herself up, feeling the wind drive up the spine of her loose blouse, opened up just hours earlier when she thought she would roast to death. She shivered and her elbows shook.

"You're flushed." Rone strode over and put a hand on her forehead. "Why the lies?"

"It's not a lie."

Rone went back to the pot and dipped a cup into it. He held it up and blew steam off of the top, then carefully walked back to Charlotte.

"This will break the fever," he said, holding the cup to her lips.

Charlotte shut her mouth tightly in response, drawing it to a thin line.

"Come on," Rone said. "I went through a lot of trouble to fetch the proper mushroom and herbs for this."

Charlotte shook her head silently, like an obstinate child.

Rone sat back on his haunches with a sigh. "Do you want me to drink it?" He took a sip from the cup and smiled. "I wouldn't take you all the way out here just to poison you."

Charlotte swallowed painfully again. "Where did you learn that?"

Rone shrugged.

"You're not a physician," she said.

"I'm not pretending to be one. Are you getting religious on me?"

"I thought *you* were the religious one."

Rone shrugged again.

"It's sorcery, isn't it? Magic? A potion?" Her eyes grew wide. "A magic potion."

Rone chuckled. His face straightened and he looked around. "It's all sorcery. Or was. All of this is just the remnants of what once was magic – the eternal dream that persisted and became the mundane."

"I don't want any part of your magic."

"You have a part of it whether you want it or not," Rone said. "This little sickness you have is magic, a leftover of malevolence, more ancient than we can comprehend, made real. Or, I assume so."

Charlotte shook her head. "I wouldn't have come had I known you were a sorcerer."

"Oh, I think you would have," Rone said. "But I'm not a sorcerer. Or a wizard, or any other such fanciful distinction. If I was, I wouldn't have needed to drag you through the dry highlands, and I wouldn't bother fetching herbs to ease your body. I would just… conjure a spell and cure you, or blast my way onto a boat, and pilot it with phantoms." He laughed, but Charlotte stared at him with a deep frown. "Please drink it. I promise it will make you feel better. Besides, you're already as much as an apostate now. Might as well use a bit of magic."

Charlotte nodded and took the hot liquid he offered. It was bitter and burned going down, and sat in her stomach in a queasy sort of way. She drank all of it, not because she trusted Rone, but because she finally resigned herself once again to being helpless.

"Now rest while you can," Rone said. "I'm going to catch a few winks whilst I can, then I'll see if I can shoot us some breakfast. I saw some sign of rabbits while I was looking for those herbs."

Rone put out his bedroll next to Charlotte, with the hot side of the hearth facing both of them.

The wind died down a little, and Charlotte could hear crickets.

"What was that you were singing?" she said, pushing herself up on her elbows.

"Nothing," he said. "Just a song my mother used to sing to herself. It's part of an old story. Very old. I guess I was feeling a bit nostalgic. I didn't mean to wake you. You were pretty out of it."

"Would you sing the rest for me?"

"I'm not much of a singer."

"I thought it was lovely. You should hear me play the cello sometime, then you wouldn't be so self-conscious."

"Maybe some other time, when I have the words." He tapped his temple and nodded. "Let's hope for dragons, eh?"

*

The day was bright when Charlotte awoke. Rone was building up the fire, roasting on a spit the remains of what she assumed was once a rabbit. He noticed her stirring and shuffled over, picking up a cup on the way.

"Another dose, before the fever returns," he said, holding the cup to her lips. She drank it. It tasted much worse cold, but feeling tolerable for the first time in more than a day, she let Rone give her the whole thing in one draught.

"Thank you," she said, gasping after the drink.

"You're welcome. It's better in one gulp, by the way." He winked. "I'll have breakfast ready shortly."

Charlotte looked around, watching the trees above the roofless house dance in the breeze, dark green leaves fluttering and rustling loudly.

"What is this place, anyway?"

"An old farmstead."

"Is there a village nearby?"

"No," Rone said. "Just ruins like this. There won't be much in the way of people till we're coming out of the highlands."

"I wonder who lived here."

"The inscription on the hearth says *Molney.*" Rone pointed to a large stone lining what remained of the central hearth. Charlotte crawled forward to inspect it. It was a black stone, weathered and rough, but the inscription remained chiseled clearly, as if that part of the stone was immune to the passage of rain and wind. It was of a series of angled letters that she did not recognize.

"You can read this?"

"Aye. It's an old version of the runes, but the phonetics are easy enough."

"All those letters to say 'Molney'?"

"Not quite." Rone pointed to the top line. "That's an old verse about... well, the *verse* and the *inverse*. The mundane and the changeable. An archaic version of the old tongue, but readable."

"A line about magic, then," Charlotte said.

"You could say that. Now, at least. The verse is the power of the dream, the power to make reality what you wish it to be. The inverse is the reality that already exists. The limitations of the physical. Traditionally, you must know both, and balance both, for prosperity and achievement. The inscription technically reads, *Know the inverse to become who you are, know the verse to become who you were meant to be.* The line below is the name Molney."

"I wonder who they were, or where they went."

"My guess is that they went the way of all the others. Went down to the coast and abandoned the old ways. Didn't produce children, or the community produced too few children to defend itself in later generations. A loremaster might know the history of the family, but the last one in Veraland disappeared after the war with Marcus Grantel."

"Marcus killed the last loremaster?"

"No, the loremaster *disappeared,* along with all that remained of the Southern Clans – the Bitterwheats, Buckleys, and Ironshoes. Maybe others."

Charlotte narrowed her eyes as she got closer to the fire. "What do you mean they *disappeared?*"

Rone shrugged and smirked. "Well, I can't say except that Marcus couldn't find them. The farmhouses were all deserted, the livestock set free or gone - not that such an ending to his purge is widely known."

"You don't know where they all went?"

"You ask a lot of questions."

"What else am I supposed to do? I didn't bring any books."

Rone nodded. "Good point." He turned the meat over, exposing dripping flesh to the fire. "No, I don't know where they went. I wasn't there and I didn't know them. My clan kept to itself until the end."

"What happened to your family?"

Rone was silent for a few moments. After a stretch, he took the rabbit off the fire and began cutting flesh from the spit and handing it to Charlotte, who ate each piece as it was delivered. It was tough, but rich and satisfying, well-seasoned with hunger.

Rone took a deep breath. "My family dwindled. I was the first to abandon my village, but there were few of us left at that point."

Charlotte ate in silence for a few moments.

"I think this place is nice."

"We can't stay here, if that's what you are thinking. They'll come here eventually. Vindrel will know I've come this way once they figure out that we couldn't have taken a ship."

"Who?"

Rone bit his lip. "The captain of the guard. He's bound to be the hound set after us. He's a shrewd man. A clever man."

"Cleverer than you?"

Rone chuckled. "Not by a long shot." Rone looked around. "And far less imaginative."

***

Rone lowered his spyglass and looked at Charlotte, who was leaning in against a large half-dead bush.

"The city is closed," he said, rolling into a sitting position behind the large, wind-smooth boulder.

"What do you mean? I can see it from here."

"The hamlets, yes, but not the city itself. Look past and you can see the old wall. There are lines in all the entrances."

"So, they beat us here?"

"It could be something else. Masala is built on the slave trade, and trouble is constant. Maybe a little revolt." He wiped the sweat from his brow and scratched at his dirty neck. "Though, it's probably best to assume that Vindrel has sailed round the Isle before we could walk it."

"Assume the worst?"

Rone gave her a half-smile. "The worst? Oh, my dear, there are far worse things than that. It's just fairly likely. We should operate under that assumption."

"Where do we go now? Taisafeld? Some other town on the south coast?"

Rone shook his head. "We've already delayed too long, and our best chance for passage to the Northmarch, or hell, anywhere on the mainland, is the Silver City."

"So, we're in the same predicament as Cataling." Charlotte pushed herself up to look over the crest. She could just make out, past the walled city, the ocean. "Only now we're tired and dirty."

"Not at all," Rone said. "Well, we certainly are dirty. Catannel doesn't rule here. He has no authority over House Harec. Not yet, anyway. And I have contacts I can exploit within the city. We just have to get over the walls."

"Over?" Charlotte said, giving Rone an incredulous look.

"Or through the gate. We can't just walk in, though."

"So, what are we going to do?"

Rone impulsively examined one of his pistols, shaking his head. "I'll think of something. Let's rest a bit, then we can move off back up the coastal road; maybe find a group to blend in with."

*

Charlotte watched from the reeds, pointing Rone's musket down toward her feet and hoping she didn't have to shoulder it. It was alien in her hands, though not because of its firing mechanism, which had been banned. She had held – and shot – muskets many times in her life, but it had been so long, and the person she was when she last held a gun was so divorced from her current mind, that it felt like something new and terrible that could turn on her.

The man Rone had decided was their mark stirred from where he squatted relieving himself.

He never saw the tall and lean man approaching from behind, nor would he have been able to put up a fight if he did, stuck in his most vulnerable position. He had only the rustle of the bushes behind him to warn him, but his nerves were slow.

Rone had his hand around the man's neck before he could even turn his head to look, and his dagger pierced his lung so swiftly the man could only kick out with one leg before he lost his will and was pushed down to the ground.

Rone held him firm for a few seconds, then his kicking ceased.

The body rolled over to the side and, though she knew there wasn't life in the eyes of the haggard victim, Charlotte was sure he was looking at her.

She dropped the gun and stood up, feeling vomit coming. She fought it back for a few moments, but still ended up loudly throwing up part of her lunch.

Rone padded through the mud toward her, wiping his blade on a dirty cloth, frowning in a kind of accusation.

"Sorry," Charlotte choked.

"Quiet." He touched her shoulders and pushed her back down into the mound of grasses.

They heard a female scream a few moments later.

"One of his slaves," Rone said. "Come on."

"I need a moment," Charlotte said. She swallowed back more bile.

"He's not worth thinking on," Rone said.

"How can you not think on it?"

"I'm a professional. It's my job not to think on it. What else did you hire me for?"

Charlotte felt tears threatening to spring from the corners of her eyes. "Not this."

"It is done. We can only move forward. I need you to trust me."

Charlotte took a breath and nodded.

II: The Silver City

ames," Tugg said through clenched teeth, his one eye still running over the notes on his dirty ledger. The gate he managed marked one of the smallest portals into the walled city of Masala, relegated mostly to foot traffic and pack mules. The stone archway, hiding a strong iron gate, was moss-covered and reeked slightly of a perpetual moisture.

"Munin." the man in front of Tugg said, his heavy boots squishing through the mud that had been tracked over the city cobbles. His dark hair hung wet about his shoulders, and his cloak was nearly soaked. "This is my sister, Daera." He stuck his thumb out at the woman beside him, who wore a large-brimmed hat that obscured her eyes. A gun of some sort lay cradled in her arms, wrapped in a sheath of leather against the rain. Both of them were covered in dust and grit that had turned to a grey silt in the rain and dripped from the corners of their long coats.

Tugg dipped his pen into his inkwell. "What about her?" He pointed the pen past the pair at a short girl with hair that might once have been blonde. Tugg pegged her at about twenty, but a hard-lived twenty. Iron cuffs rattled on her wrists.

"She's a slave, here for market. I thought it best her master give her a proper name," the man said.

"Selling your village-mates, eh? Things must be getting on badly on the floodplain," Tugg said, shifting his nearly dissolved coca leaf to the other side of his mouth and clenching it tightly.

"Mind your own business," the woman said. She frowned and turned away, looking over her shoulder at some horses milling outside the gate.

Tugg hummed a deep chuckle to himself. Insults always gave you a better idea of who a person was than niceties.

"Why is the city shut?" Munin said, his tone neutral. "I've never been stopped at a gate in peacetime before."

Tugg grinned. "The gate is *my* business, not yours. Now I need names for *all* of you."

Munin looked back at the slave, his yellow-green eyes hard, and nodded to her.

The young woman looked at the man holding her chains for a moment, then shouted, "They killed my master and stole me! They're murderers!" She rushed forward, then found herself falling into the mud as Munin tugged on her chains. He pulled her up by her wrists, easily hoisting her face up to the level of his chest.

"Blast me, but don't make me tear you up before we even get you to market!" he said, his eyes wide with rage. His companion put her wrapped gun above her head, as if she was going to slam the butt into the slave's face. The slave twisted away and whimpered.

"It's true!" the slave screamed.

"Slaves will say anything to get out of their debts," the woman said, still holding the butt of the long gun high.

"Call her Hella," Munin said, staring into Tugg's one eye.

Tugg paused as he was writing and chewed on his lip, unsure if he should follow his gut.

"What is it?" the man said.

"I'll need to have a look at your gun."

"The good count having problems with the church?"

"What's the hold-up?!" Another man shouted from behind the trio. He held the reins of a laden mule, his simple clothing soaked through.

"My job is my own," Tugg said. "If I want to inspect your gun, I get to, unless you want to take the round way up to the West gate and lose half the day, and deal with fellas that are much sourer than I am. Now, unwrap that iron."

The slavemasters looked to each other and then nodded. Hesitantly, Daera untied a small thong and slipped the gun out of the leather, displaying a simple stock and bare iron receiver. Tugg looked closely at it.

"If this is a matchlock, I'm a dead rabbit," he said, looking at the vacant screw holes on the gun's receiver.

"It's legal," Munin said.

"I'll be the judge of that," Tugg said.

"Tugg! What are you doing you old fool?" Michel, one of the lieutenants of the guard, rode up to the old arch and reined in his horse.

"My job," Tugg said, and spit out a discolored wad of coca onto the ground.

"Are these them, or not?" Michel said.

Tugg's one eye looked over Munin and the slave. "No. I'd say not."

"Then let them through," Michel said. "You're backing things up."

"They're in the slave trade."

"I don't give a damn what trade they're in. We have orders. If they ain't the ones we're looking for, send them on through."

"Aye."

"Aye what?"

"Aye, *sir,*" Tugg said, and put his hand to his chest as a salute.

"That's better. You have the morning ledgers?"

Tugg nodded and pulled his current piece of paper from his wooden ledger stand, then handed it to the armored lieutenant. Michel quickly rolled it up and stuck it in a saddlebag, then rode off.

"We'll be off then," Munin said, stepping forward. Tugg put a hand out.

"Just a moment. You interested in a private sale?" he nodded to the slave, being all but dragged by Munin. "Avoid the auction cut. I know a richer or two that might have a taste for what you've got."

"I'm taking her to market," Munin replied.

Tugg scowled. "Alright, move along." He watched the trio slip away and stuck another coca leaf in his cheek, then looked at his ledger. He realized he had forgotten to write their names down. "Who were they?" he said to himself. He shook his head and dipped the quill into his inkwell, then wrote down what he could remember. "No matter."

*

Rone and Charlotte shuffled out of the crowded gateway and into an open thoroughfare, dragging the slave girl between them. The girl's dress, once a light-colored slip now darkened to a muddy brown by abuse and weather, clung to her thighs as she stumbled behind. Despite the rain, the tenements that crowded the south wall of Masala felt hot and stuffy, and smoke from brick chimneys blended with the sky, making the clouds appear only head high. The sea was close, but from the feel of the air, nobody there would have known it. They followed a winding path, away from the gate and through a slum.

"Here," Rone said, and pulled both Charlotte and the slave into a narrow alleyway. A dog, emaciated and frightful, looked up at them from where it rummaged through a pile of refuse. It ran away as they pushed past, stopping to stare at them from a stair step where the alley ended.

"You're gonna get it," the slave said.

"Quiet," Rone said, and removed a tall satchel from the inside of his tattered coat. He undid a leather cord around it and opened it, revealing a row of metal tools. He pulled out a few bent pieces of scrap: a rake and flat wrench. "Sit down." He pointed at the ground. The slave girl looked up into his hard, yellow-green eyes and sat down quickly, the dirty dress pulling back to reveal legs that looked shining white compared to the road grit that covered her bare arms and shins.

"Why are we stopping here?" Charlotte said. She looked at the entrance to the alley nervously.

"Cutting loose the baggage," Rone said. He put the flattened wrench into the large lock on the slave girl's shackles and quickly began raking through its two tumblers. "Wish I'd bothered finding the key." A few seconds later, the first shackle fell away and landed in the alley with a dull thud.

"What are you doing?" the slave asked.

"I'm setting you free. What does it look like?" Rone said.

"Marcos has brothers on the road behind him," the girl said, holding up her other wrist. "They'll be looking for me when they find his body - and for you."

"I'm quite good at not being found," Rone said. He picked the lock on the second shackle. The girl rubbed her wrists, which were flaking and covered with mild iron sores.

"What now?" the girl said.

"You run, and stay hidden, and do whatever you will with your life," Rone said. "Consider it my thanks for helping us through the gates."

"That's it?"

"Maybe I'm getting soft and I should just kill you, eh?" He flashed the girl a grim smile.

"What about this?" The girl said. She pulled up the dingy sleeve of her dress and revealed a brand of two letters.

"They branded a woman?" Charlotte said.

Rone tilted his head. "Odd."

"It's barbaric, doing that to a woman," Charlotte said.

"It's likely she ran away a few times," Rone said. "Well, nothing I can do about that. Not here, anyway. I might recommend you find a friend with a hot iron to stamp it out. Won't be very fun." Rone flinched as

Charlotte shoved a folded piece of paper into his arms. "What's this?"

"Title papers," Charlotte said. "I found them in her owner's bags. We could have her cleared."

"I'm not much on forgeries. Even if I was, we don't have the time." Rone handed the paper to the slave, who turned it over, wondering. "I'm sure you can find someone to forge a clerk's stamp for a modest sum."

"You don't know anyone?" Charlotte said. She lifted her head and locked her clear, almost tearful eyes on Rone.

"No," Rone said, and looked away. He stepped past the slave and grasped Charlotte's arm. "Let's keep moving."

"Wait," Charlotte said. She knelt by the slave girl and pulled from a pouch at her waist a handful of silver coins. "Take this. It should be enough to get you started. New clothes, a few days' worth of meals-"

"Try a few months!" the girl said, her eyes widening as the coins fell into her palms.

Rone scoffed audibly and Charlotte turned back to give him a frown.

"Fine," Rone said. He looked at the slave. "There's a man that goes by the name of Getty, a few streets away from the docks in a book shop. If he charges you more than twenty cyprals for a forgery, he's cheating you." He looked at Charlotte. "Let's go. *Now.*"

Charlotte cast a last look at the slave girl, gave a half-hearted smile, then jogged after Rone as he exited the alleyway and joined in the throng of people traveling the city on their morning business. She pulled up beside him, trying her best to match his long, swift stride.

Quietly he spoke, "If you wake up to a dagger in your belly tonight, remember that it was your kindness that brought it on."

"We couldn't just leave her like that," Charlotte said back loudly.

"Shh!" Rone said. He continued quietly, his voice holding a hint of voiced anger, "Yes, we could. Turning her loose was enough. It would keep her owner's brothers off of us and earn plenty of gratitude from the girl. Now you've shown her coin. Not just a pinch of copper to get supper, either, but nearly as much as she would have been sold for. Enough to really matter."

"That was the point. With that and a little smarts, she could have a real life."

"It was foolish. Urchins talk to other urchins. We throw away silver like that, she'll know we have gold. She's a slave. Don't think for a moment she won't fall in with a pimp or worse here. Eyes and ears will be searching for that money. For us."

Charlotte cast her eyes down and thrust her hands into her pockets. "I'm sorry."

Rone sighed audibly. "What's done is done, and I'm a part of it myself. Come on."

*

The western part of Masala was higher in elevation than the tenements, allowing a steady breeze off the sea in the afternoon to blow through Charlotte and Rone's long coats. The streets were mostly deserted, and the people that did walk down either side of the paved avenues were moderately well-dressed; men wore waistcoats more often than plain shirts, and women bustled dresses more often than aprons. Rone and Charlotte, with their dirty long coats and packs, stood out among the colorfully dressed citizenry, catching glances from passers-by busy enough to spare little else. Charlotte realized she was a woman wearing trousers, an uncommon if not alluring sight on the Isle of Veraland.

Rone walked quickly ahead of her, continuing the long, protracted silence that had settled between them when they entered the city. On their journey to Masala, through the dry highlands of the Isle where men were a rarer sight than beasts, the silence between conversations had been comfortable to Charlotte. Somehow, in the crowded city, the lack of talk was maddening.

"Where are we going?" Charlotte said, daring to break the silence.

Rone turned his head slightly to look at her. "Somewhere to stay. Out of the way of the bustle. Normally, I'd choose something a bit shadier, but given the interchange with the slave, we'll have to do with accommodations that are actually decent." Rone flashed a slight smile.

"You? In places that are actually decent?" Charlotte smiled back

"*Merely* decent," Rone said. "I shall do my best to condescend to your preferred level of comfort, though I fear I might undo weeks of work and spoil you to hard living forever. A warm bed will do little to make you long for the road, which I suspect we'll see more of before the end."

Charlotte sighed. "A bed. Dreamer! I feel like I can scarcely remember the pleasure."

Rone turned his head again, his brow furrowed. "Careful who you invoke. Folks in decent places don't appreciate blasphemy, even in an off-hand way. We get enough looks as it is."

Charlotte nodded. She wanted to say sorry again, but some degree of pride held her back. "I've just spent too much time with you. It seems I'm starting to pick up your way of speaking."

"I can tell. Invoke a different god while you're here." Rone turned away and picked up the pace again, leading Charlotte up a wide avenue. They turned down a slightly narrower street, lined with shops and boarding houses that stood several stories tall, the masonry and tile roofs clean despite being ancient. Rone paused in front of an inn, the wooden sign above the door waving slightly in the breeze.

"The Sevelny Inn," Charlotte said, reading the sign and looking at the closed, simply carved doors.

"The proprietor's name," Rone said, digging around in one of his side bags, which rested under his powder horn.

"Not very creative."

"That's exactly what we want. Here." Rone nodded toward a narrow alley and walked briskly down it. Charlotte followed close behind. Her pack scraped against the side of the building, filling her ears with an odd echo. Around the corner was the rear entrance of the inn and a small porch. A door stood open to the kitchen, airing out the morning's cooking. A black cast-iron pipe from the stove stuck out of a window, a few wisps of smoke escaping from its capped top and curling through the still air of the alleyway.

"Stay here," Rone said. "I'll come get you shortly." Charlotte nodded.

Rone walked back out of the alley swiftly. After he disappeared, Charlotte let herself draw a long breath and a sigh. She looked around at the darkened backs of the stores and houses, each going down a straight line to streets that looked bright in the dim alley. A small refuse pile stood behind the inn's kitchen, full of old bones and other discarded fragments of food. Charlotte could see movement that she imagined to be a rat rummaging inside, and it made her scrunch her nose up.

She backed up to the corner and took off her pack. She rubbed her shoulders softly, feeling the ache of the burden fade. She had become used to the weight of it after so many days on the road, but the pain reminded her often that such things were still new to her. With that in mind, she thought back to her first days on the road and smiled. Then, she'd been scarcely able to shoulder anything; now, she could carry her weight. Charlotte had grown strong in a relatively short time, and that gave her a bit of hope.

She started slightly when Rone stepped out of the kitchen door and looked about.

"There you are," he said. "I got us a room upstairs, with a view of the street. Come on."

Charlotte picked her bag back up and slung it over a single shoulder, then followed Rone into the kitchen, currently deserted except for a dog lying in the corner, moving only his eyes. Just past the tight arrangements of stoves and ovens was a narrow stairwell.

"There's a rat in the alley," Charlotte whispered at the dog. As she passed. "Go get him!"

The dog raised its head, long ears drooping over its head, and looked out the back door, as if thinking it over in his own mind. He dropped his head back down, as if he had decided the rat was not worth the effort.

*

The sun had come through the clouds in the west, bathing the tidy inn room in warm light and illuminating the grit that had worked into Charlotte's hair over the many miles between Cataling and Masala. The window was open, hinting at a breeze that could not be properly felt in the land-facing room. It was humid in the so-called Silver City, and Charlotte continued to sweat even with her jacket removed.

She sat and worked at the tangles in her long, coppered hair. It pegged her as a foreigner in Veraland, where even the occasional blonde shock among a sea of brown drew stares, and so Charlotte, at the bidding of Rone, had twisted it into a braid and stuffed it down the back of her long jacket, then covered her head with Rone's oversized hat. Her hairbrush, an ornate thing with tortoise-shell inlay and stiff boar bristles, found the knots in the hair all too well, but she was still glad to tend it, letting it remind her of her womanhood.

"I can't wait for a bath," she said to herself.

The door squeaked slightly as it opened a crack. When Rone did not appear, Charlotte felt a sudden surge of panic. She dropped her hairbrush on the ground and looked around for Rone's pistol. It was nowhere.

"It's me," the voice of Rone said.

"Come in. I'm decent."

The door fell all the way open and Rone entered, carrying two plates filled with freshly roasted chicken and bread along one arm. He kicked the door closed behind him and rushed over to the little table beside the open window, where he deposited the plates hastily.

"I figured a little bit of hot food should be first on the agenda," Rone said, smiling slightly. He pulled a bundle of knives and forks from his jacket pocket and dumped them on the table. Charlotte picked her hairbrush back up off the floor and put it on the windowsill, then pushed her chair closer to the table.

"I can't remember the last time I had a hot meal," she said. She picked up a fork and examined it, then wiped some of the dust off on one of the few clean spots left on her cotton shirt.

"I can," Rone said, tearing apart the quarter of a chicken on his plate. He took a bite and chewed in satisfaction for a moment. "I cooked us rabbit. It was at the old Molney homestead."

"It was just an expression. I do remember." She smiled as she carefully carved the chicken into neat slices. "I can't believe I ate rabbit. Disgusting."

"You didn't think so at the time," Rone said. He took a hearty bite from one of the bread rolls, then said while chewing. "Hunger really is the finest seasoning."

"My mother would have a fit watching me eat a fresh-skinned rabbit. Or this." She put one of the chicken slices into her mouth and chewed.

"What's wrong with chicken?"

Charlotte swallowed. "This is cooked all wrong. Pot roasting a chicken is a sin, and with this much salt such a deed is practically criminal."

"It's an old bird. You can't throw an old bird on a hot fire and expect to be able to chew it," Rone said.

"No, you can't." She shrugged. "I suppose this really isn't that bad." Charlotte took another bite.

"Aye, but is it as good as the rabbit?"

"Of course not." She smiled at him. "A servant came by earlier. A young girl. They have a few baths downstairs."

"You answered the door?" Rone said. He held a forkful of chicken in front of his face as if his hand had frozen there.

"It was a girl, couldn't have been more than twelve. Anyway, I decided to have a bath drawn."

Rone dropped his fork. "Damn it, girl. We're not on vacation here."

"I need a bath."

"It's not about the bath. The innkeeper thinks I'm here alone. Didn't you think about why I brought you in through the back? Eyes are watching!"

"We're in Masala, not Cataling, like you said."

"A Masala with the gates shut. Dreamer! Do you ever spare a thought to the danger you're in?"

Charlotte sat silent for a moment, then said. "You ordered two plates of food, mister clever. Did you spare a thought to that?"

"I told the cook I was extra hungry. It's not unheard of."

"So hungry you needed two sets of silverware?"

"Bah," Rone said. He began shoveling food into his mouth at an accelerated rate. His mouth half-full, he said, "I'll drop some hints that we're eloping or having an affair or something. The most believable lies are the ones you spend effort covering up."

"Then it's settled. We'll have baths."

"Fine." He looked up at her. "I suppose it will make us look a little less road-worn. A little more like we fit in. We should dye your hair. Maybe cut it too." He dug back into his food.

Charlotte held her hair up in the light. "I suppose you're right." She sighed.

"Something wrong?"

"Just a woman's vanity."

"It'll grow back." Rone paused and looked at her, his face casting creases of sadness. "Which is a good thing, of course."

III: Farthow

What ya think, cap'n?" Colby said. He pushed the scabbard to his rapier to the side and took a knee beside the woman. Her eyes were closed, and her hair was a mess of tangles that obscured most of her face. Lying in her outstretched hand was a pipe, with a half-burnt pill of opium still stuck in the bowl. Colby pushed her hair away, revealing a dirt-streaked young woman. A rough tunic covered her upper arms and chest, but she was bare below the waist.

"Looks like her," Farthow said. He scratched absent-mindedly at the place where his short-cut blonde beard met the high collar of his green jacket.

"First thing she did was hit the smack, eh?" Colby said. He pushed the woman onto her back. He legs fell apart, and still, she did not wake. Colby, almost analytically, examined her genitals with his gloved right hand.

"Second thing," Farthow said. "A friend of mine forged papers for her earlier today."

"Looks like somebody had his way with her."

Farthow spat onto the dirty wooden floor. "Figures. You can't expect much different if you're a woman in a place like this."

"Pretty much what she would have expected if she'd been sold though, eh?"

"I suppose." Farthow kicked the pipe out of the woman's hands. "The smell of this place makes me sick."

"Captain, I found the keeper." Farthow turned as Dem entered, his rifle held lightly in one hand. The young man pushed his dark hair up out of his eyes as he looked at the woman on the floor, legs splayed open.

"Well?" Farthow said, raising an eyebrow to his young sergeant.

Dem tore his eyes away from the girl and looked to Farthow. "I shook him down and found a cache of silver. More than she could have spent on opium." He reached in his pocket and withdrew a handful of coins. "Odd marks."

"Let me see," Farthow said, and took one of the silver coins from Dem's palm. Colby stood up beside him to look. "This is an argent from Northmarch. Brulia."

"I don't recognize the face," Colby said.

"That's because he's been dead at least a century," Farthow said. "Vaslius." Farthow picked up another coin. "This one's from Hviterland."

"Does that mean something to you?" Dem said.

"To me, yes," Farthow said, and handed the coins back to Dem. "To you, not so much. I want both of you to turn this house out. Find every coin. If it has a mint mark to the Isle, you can keep it. All others surrender to me. Do not make me mistrust you."

"Aye," Dem said, and nodded to Colby. "What about her?"

"I'll try to get her up and clothed," Farthow said. "You may have to help me cart her back to the castle. Once she sobers up, we'll figure out what to do with her."

"You going to give her back to her owner?" Colby said.

Farthow shook his head. He knelt down and pulled a folded and piece of paper from a pile of clothes nearby. "She's got free papers."

"You said they were a forgery," Colby said.

"I did. Now turn this place out. Throw the keeper out too. Go."

Colby and Dem stepped past him and out into the hall of the opium den. Farthow sighed and looked at the woman, still drifting in an opium trance. He closed her legs and pulled her faded skirt over her nakedness. "Well Hella, if that is any true name of yours," he said softly, "I must keep you away from prying eyes, since you are so unwilling to do it yourself. Hopefully, you don't resent me too much for the cage."

*

"Ah, here he is now," Drath Harec said. "Welcome back, Captain Bitterwheat."

"Aye, lord," Farthow said and bowed low, stopping among his long strides for just a moment before quickly approaching the count of Masala and his guest.

"This is captain Stonefield," Harec said, gesturing to the burly man standing beside him on the wide balcony. The man wore a green jacket similar to Farthow's, but with dark grey pants. "He's Cataling's captain of the guard. And a highland man."

"Pleased to meet you, sir Stonefield," Farthow said.

"Vindrel will do." The burly man extended a hand, which Farthow shook.

"Sorry for the delay, lord," Farthow said. "My men came across an opium den, and we felt compelled to turn it out."

"I trust you burned the opium," Harec said, almost absent-mindedly. He looked down at the intricate gold-threaded embroidery of his own state jacket.

"Of course, lord. Not a trace was left. I'm having a clerk make up the deed to the place for an auction."

"Good, good," Harec said. "Now, mister Bitterwheat, the captain here is on a mission from Count Catannel, searching for a pair of fugitives. I told him you would provide him with full support."

"Um, yes, of course, sir," Farthow said, his eyes widening. "What sort of support does he need?"

"I could use a cadre of men who know the city," Vindrel said. "I'm looking for a man and a woman. The woman has light red hair. We need her at least alive for trial. The man… well, I prefer to have him alive too. He would be a good source of information for me."

"Their crimes?" Farthow said.

"Treason, apparently," Harec said.

"I see," Farthow said. "Well, I shall set myself to providing you with some good men from the guard straight away."

"No need for such a rush," Harec said. "Why don't we all have a glass of wine? I would be very interested to hear of the goings-on in Cataling. Reports from the other cities have been sparse since the death of the king."

"With all due respect and honor, my lord," Vindrel said, "I would not feel right reclining and enjoying the pleasure of wine, and your company, without seeing to my duties."

Harec sighed. "I understand, captain. Perhaps you will share a glass with me when you apprehend your quarry?"

Vindrel bowed. "I would be honored, lord."

Farthow looked to Vindrel. "I'll collect my men and send them down to the courtyard."

"Thank you," Vindrel said with a nod. "And you, my lord." He bowed and stepped out of the balcony.

Harec watched him disappear into the hallway, then said. "Is there a man or two you can trust?"

"I trust Dem, but we'll have to let him in on things. Colby I'd want to keep in the dark."

"Very well, Dem it shall be. Any luck so far?"

Farthow handed Harec a silver coin, stamped with a large bearded head and set of crossed spears on the reverse.

Harec raised an eyebrow. "A Hviterland argent. Interesting."

"One of several."

"You have them already?" Harec fingered the coin in his hand.

"No, but I have a slave that was with them briefly. Her tongue should be loosened shortly."

"Keep her locked up and away from Vindrel. I want these fugitives delivered to *me*. Under no circumstances should they be returned to Cataling. Keep them from Vindrel at any costs, do you understand me?"

"Of course, lord. I shall see it done. I am already gathering leads."

***

Rone could hear the fire crackle in the next room and the water softly splash. A young girl pushed past the curtain holding Charlotte's clothes, folded into a high stack. Before the curtain could fall back, he caught a glimpse of alabaster flesh sliding into the iron tub, the candlelight detailing the delicate curve of a hip melding smoothly into a lower back. Rone took a step closer and peered through the remaining crack in the drapes. He heard the clearing of a throat and found the young servant, still a few years away from maidenhood, standing idly next to him, doing her best to contain Charlotte's clothes in her arms.

"What do you want?" he grunted.

"Shall I launder the traveling clothes sir, or were you expecting to have your sister wear something else now that you've arrived?" The servant's face was clean, but her clothes were covered in soot and well-worn.

"Yes on both," Rone said, finding a polite tone. He pulled a small satchel from his bag, tied in twine "Do be a dear and lay this out for the lady." He placed a stack of copper coins on the cloth satchel as he handed it to the girl. Her eyes widened at the stack of money.

"Of course, sir. Would you like to wait in the dining hall? It will take us a few minutes to draw and heat a fresh bath after the lady is done."

"No, I prefer to wait here. And don't worry about the fresh bath."

"It was her request sir, and I don't much care to return tips."

Rone grunted. He watched her walk away, then carefully moved up to the slit in the curtain again. He could see Charlotte's shoulders and back as she worked a sponge over her skin. *Of course she faces away,* he thought. He clenched his fists a few times and sat down.

The servant girl returned a few minutes later and once again disappeared behind the curtain. This time as it was pulled back Charlotte turned about in the tub. Rone looked in compulsively and caught a flash of a breast as she leaned on the side. His gaze lingered for a long moment before he saw a pair of blue eyes, burning bright despite the dim light, looking right at him. Feeling a sudden surge of embarrassment, Rone turned his eyes away, to a dusty table near the kitchen. He felt suddenly hot and wiped a bead of sweat from his forehead. *You're better than this,* he thought. *Too long. Too much time away is all.* After another few minutes Rone could hear splashing once again, and a few whispers.

"Come in here a minute Rone," he heard Charlotte say on the other side of the curtain.

"She's not decent sir," the girl said.

"Don't listen to her!" Charlotte shouted back. Rone stood up and reached for the curtain, then stepped inside. Charlotte was standing next to the tub in a long white gown overlaid with a robe of deep red. Her damp hair was pinned back, revealing a clean white neck. She spun around, and the skirt lifted up revealing her calves and ankles.

"Looks good on you," Rone said, rubbing his beard. He eyed the servant as she pulled out the stopper in the tub, letting the water flow into a closed sewer beneath the inn.

"I thought you threw away all my things," Charlotte said.

Rone frowned and shook his head slightly. He watched the servant walk back out of the tiled bathroom as the water drained.

"Did I say something bad?" Charlotte said.

"I wouldn't worry too much about it," Rone said. "As to the gown… well, I thought it would fetch a penny or two if we needed, since it's silk, so I saved it. I didn't realize how well funded we actually were when I signed on."

Charlotte smiled. It was a slightly forced smile, and her eyes still seemed to carry the same sorrow as always. "Thanks all the same. My mother gave it to me. It was supposed to be a gift for my wedding night."

Rone raised an eyebrow as the servant came back in, unsure of what she had heard. "You're welcome, I suppose."

"Will you be attending to him, or will I?" the servant girl said. She reached into the tub and replaced the stopper, then added a log to the fire beneath the tub. She began to work the pump located beside the iron tub.

"I can attend to myself, thank you," Rone said.

"I'm used to it, if you're feeling embarrassed," the girl said. "Usually doesn't do much for me. 'Course most men who come in here are older and fat. Haven't had someone like you 'round here in a while."

"It's fine," Rone said. "I need no help. Why don't you show my sister back up to our room?"

"As you wish," the servant said. "But it's not hard to find any room upstairs. Shall I launder your gear as well?"

"Not necessary," Rone said. He cracked a smile at Charlotte. "Besides, I don't have anything pretty to wear."

"You're putting your clothes in the laundry," Charlotte said sternly. "I don't want to smell that old sweaty jacket even one more day."

Rone took a long, deep breath. "Fine." He looked at the servant. "I'll leave my clothes by the door. I have a spare set of trousers in my bag anyway."

Rone watched Charlotte and the servant pass through the curtain, then he quickly stripped. He hastily piled the clothes on a chair near the curtain, then stepped up and into the bathtub. As he eased himself down, he looked to the crack, half-expecting to see a blue eye staring back at him, but all he saw was the dancing firelight from the hall. He sighed and closed his eyes.

*

A knock sounded at the door, and Charlotte paused, her needle stopped halfway through a stitch in her torn cloak.

"It's me," Rone said, muffled by the heavy oak paneling.

"Come in."

Rone swung open the door, poked in his head and looked around the room, then stepped all the way in. He tossed his leather knapsack at the foot of the bed, framed in old carved wood that had shed most of its varnish through the passing of countless guests. He was wearing a faded set of trousers and a loose shirt that was once white. After he shut and barred the door, Charlotte continued pushing the needle through the tough wool of the cloak.

"We need to get you some more clothes," Charlotte said.

Rone shrugged. "Never cared to buy cloth except as necessary; cared even less when my daily attire was provided by the guard. Where's my pistol?"

"Your pistol? How would I know?"

Rone walked up and leaned over her. She shrank back slightly as he fished under the small occasional table she sat beside. He dropped a heavy flintlock pistol, with a brass receiver and an octagonal iron barrel on the table. He stood back.

"I want you to be armed at all times. This is especially important when I'm not here. You also need to keep the door locked." He took a deep breath. "I'm not trying to be unkind to you, and I'm sorry for chastising you earlier. I was not right expecting you to understand how to act. You lack the necessary experience."

"So kind of you to condescend to me," Charlotte said. She looked out the window.

"We will need to teach you some basic skills," Rone went on, ignoring Charlotte's reaction. "Do you know how to check the prime on a flintlock?"

"Of course I do. I didn't always live behind parapets."

"I assume they are illegal where you used to live," Rone said. Charlotte glared back at him. "Show me, then."

Charlotte tucked the needle under a loop of thread. She picked up the pistol and carefully lifted the frizzen. She shook the pistol slightly to see the priming charge move around in the pan. "It's primed. Are you satisfied?"

"What's the condition of the flint?"

"Plenty of life left."

Rone nodded. "Keep that one on your person if you can."

"Why did I hire you, exactly, if you expect me to do the shooting?"

"I expect trouble," Rone said. "I plan for it. I presume you care about getting off this rock, or you wouldn't have hired me, and so if it comes to trouble, I hope you will give it your best to carry on to that purpose."

"Very well," Charlotte said. She held up the pistol and looked it over in the lamplight.

*

"Rone," Charlotte whispered. She was leaning over the edge of the bed, the quilts wrapped around her. Her hair spilled out over the pillow and hung toward the floor, close to Rone's face. The window was still open, showing a waxing moon setting in the west, blurred by fog. "Are you awake?"

"Yes."

"I can't sleep," she said softly.

"Neither can I." He sighed and turned half away from her. "I never thought I'd miss packed earth, but these floorboards make me positively nostalgic for the road. What's bothering you?"

"I don't know. I keep thinking about… I keep thinking about going back. It makes me feel sick."

"Anxiety, then. Not surprising."

"You don't worry? They'll hang you, you know."

"There are worse fates."

"I know." Charlotte turned back onto the bed and faced the ceiling.

After a few moments, Rone said, "I don't intend for us to get caught, of course."

"I'm still afraid."

"Where's your pistol?"

"Under my pillow."

"Check the prime."

"I can't see."

"Just put your finger in the pan."

Charlotte slowly tilted back the hammer and lifted the frizzen on the pistol's lock. "It's primed."

"Anyone wants to take you, at least one of them will end up with a ball through their skull. Feel better?"

"A little, I suppose."

"Anytime you're anxious, feel for that pistol. It's a good piece and the barrel is clean. Only had it misfire a few times, and I've used it plenty."

"Thanks." Charlotte leaned back to the side of the bed. "What do you do when you're scared?"

"I'm not scared. Now get some sleep. I want to find us a ship out of here tomorrow. We're going to have a bit of walking to do."

"It's a big bed, you know, if the floor is hard."

"Go to sleep."

"We slept next to each other plenty of times in the highlands."

"We're not *in* the highlands, and it's not cold." Rone turned his shoulder even further away.

Silently, Charlotte turned back and stared at the empty, black ceiling.

IV: Three Sisters

harlotte dreamt. She knew it was a dream, like she often knew, but her dreams carried their own momentum that she was powerless to change. She was always a live witness, never fully lucid and in control.

She was in the Molney homestead, where she and Rone had stopped to wait out the illness that had struck her on the road. The ruined stone walls of the abandoned farmhouse were the same, but clean-cut rafters supported a well-tended thatch roof above. She was sweeping ashes out of the hearth, which was piled with the remnants of many fires, when she realized where she was. She turned as a little girl ran in through the front door.

"Mommy! Daddy caught a rabbit for us!" The little girl, wearing a simple duck dress, ran back out of the door. Charlotte paused a moment to look up, and a strand of dark, almost black hair fell in her face. She blew it away and wiped the ash from her hands on her apron. The girl appeared a moment later, then a man appeared in the doorway. It was clearly Rone, but he looked different. His clothes were of a strange sort, better made than what she was used to, and yet the garb was also simpler, lacking buttons and buckles. His hair and beard were longer, too, and his face was fuller, but his unmistakable eyes had the same glare as always. He stood behind the little girl with his musket and a freshly killed rabbit.

"When are we having dinner?" the little girl asked excitedly, clapping her hands together.

"We'll have to let your mother tend to the skinning and such," Rone said, smiling at the little girl. "I'm going to go chop some firewood so we can get cooking. You sure do like a bit of coney, don't you?"

"Of course!" the little girl said.

Rone put the dead rabbit down on the table and walked over to Charlotte. He kissed her on the cheek. "I'm sorry I haven't patched the roof yet." She looked up and saw the straw above letting in a few sunbeams in random places.

"It's alright," Charlotte said, "It's not going to rain tonight." She felt surprised as Rone pulled her into a deep kiss. His beard tickled her and she pulled away laughing.

Rone was gone.

The rabbit on the table seemed to look at her, though she knew it logically couldn't. Charlotte could hear the little girl singing outside, in a familiar tune, though it seemed to her like she had forgotten everything about it. She wished to run outside to the little girl, but couldn't stop staring at the rabbit. The words drifted inside to her, swift like a rhyme a child makes at play:

The point of a name
Is that it's always the same
Alone, or with fame
Your name is the game
With a name you'll see
You're who you want to be

And so the raven cawed
And sat on his claws
And asked what should I be called?

I said 'you can choose
To make your own news'
He said "fine! My name is Zald!

With great effort, Charlotte pulled her gaze away from the rabbit and saw that she wasn't in the farmhouse at all. Suddenly, she was back in her old apartment in Cataling Castle. Fine furniture sat against ancient stone walls. Her heart leapt, recalling somehow in her dream the horror of that room. Her small dining table was behind her, but she did not want to turn around to look, knowing the rabbit would be there. There was something unsettling about that rabbit, and the thought of it itched her in the back of her mind.

She ran to the door. It was locked tightly like always. She shook the handle. The hinges and bolts on the outside of the heavy oak door rattled.

She shook harder. Normally, the guards would notice her by now.

"Damnit!" Her voice cracked, though she tried to yell.

"Yes, mistress?" A voice from behind her said in a calm, soothing tone.

"Ardala?" Charlotte held her hands on the door for a long, drawn-out moment. "Is that you Ardala?"

"What can I get you? Fresh water? Are you ready for tea?"

"You survived? Rone said you had been killed for sure." Charlotte still could not will herself to turn around. "Why didn't you meet me at the wall?"

"You look tired. Shall I have the guards take you to the baths?"

"Why am I here?" Charlotte said. "I shouldn't be here. I left. I escaped!" She turned around suddenly to find the space where she expected to find Ardala to be empty. Feeling a sickness overtake her, her gaze slowly slid to the right, to the small table where she had eaten virtually all of her meals with Ardala, her only friend.

There was no rabbit. In its place was a baby, tiny and bloody, with unformed features; a miscarriage.

She screamed.

Over it she heard, as if near her left ear, a familiar voice. Serpentine and far too calm, it spoke old words:

You are mine, child, whether you like it or not, though I suggest you learn to like it. While you attempt to regain my trust, I suggest you think on the poor women of the city. Who of them would not trade places with you, given the choice? You can cry if you wish, but know that ***they*** *would not.*

*

"Begging your pardon!"

Charlotte bolted up. Her mind reeled. Quickly, but not quite instinctively, she reached under a pillow and found Rone's pistol. It felt slippery in her hands, and she realized that she was sweating. Her palms, neck, and shoulders felt suddenly cold with the moisture. Hands trembling, she drew back the hammer and pushed up the frizzen. A thin coat of powder sat in the pan.

"Relax, it's just the girl from last night," Rone said. He appeared from behind the privacy screen that hid the corner privy, looping a leather belt through his trousers.

"Your laundry's come back, sir! And madam!"

Rone raised his eyebrows at Charlotte as she held out the pistol uncertainly. "Do you think she's heavily armed? Or do you want to tell the girl to stand and deliver? I can follow your lead. Let me fetch a blade."

Charlotte looked around and took in the inn room, so much smaller than her old apartments had been. She was free, but not free. Safe, but not safe. She lowered the pistol. Rone gave her a smile and laughed deeply.

"You're a heap of nonsense," Charlotte said.

"My father always said that if you don't laugh, you'll cry." Rone walked to the door and unbolted it. Charlotte quickly hid the pistol back under the pillow and got out of bed. Rone opened the door and was surprised by a stack of folded clothes being thrust into his arms.

"Here's your laundry sir, hope it's to your liking," the servant girl said.

"As long as it doesn't smell like sweat and dust, I'll be happy," Rone said, dropping the clothes on a nearby chair. "Though come to think of it, just doing that would be a hell of a job. I sweat like a horse and smell twice as bad."

"It wasn't too bad," the girl said. "We have good soap, and my ma' was here to help last night."

"Poor thing," Charlotte said, stepping up to the door, her robe wrapped around her slender body. "You must not have slept at all."

"I sleep plenty, madam. Mostly in the afternoon. Quieter then."

"Still. Here's something for your troubles," Rone said, putting on a friendly smile. He thrust a large copper coin into the girl's hand. "My name is Munin." The girl looked up at him with a smile. "Now is why don't you tell me yours?"

"It isn't much of a proper name, but I'm Missy. It's all my pa' used to call me."

"Well I think it's a lovely name, Miss Missy. Now we know each other, and we can be friends, alright?"

"Okay, but I have to go now, lots more work to do before noon. Sir."

"I have a job for you, if you fancy earning a few more of those." Rone put his hand into his pocket and shook his hand, jingling coins there.

"Okay, but don't tell Mr. Sevelny. I don't wanna get in trouble for him thinking I ain't doing my work."

"I can keep a secret if you can. All I need you to do is listen. Listen when you come in and out of the common room, or when you walk by the master of the house doing business. You do that already, don't you?"

"A little, maybe."

"Good. Listen extra carefully today."

"What should I listen for?"

"Anyone looking for a couple of slave traders – a man and a woman – or someone asking about a female slave."

"I'll do my best." The girl looked puzzled. "Why would you be looking for a female slave? You're married, ain't ya?" Missy looked to Charlotte, who forced a smile.

Rone smiled warmly. "They're old acquaintances of ours. We're looking to run into them for business purposes, but I have a feeling some other friends of ours are looking for them too. Such is the nature of this trade. Nobody likes to do it in the light of day."

Missy nodded. "Sorry, didn't mean to pry."

"Don't trouble yourself. Just keep your ears open." He began to shut the door and stopped. "Of course, if anyone is looking for me in particular, you'll let me know, won't you?"

"Of course," Missy said. She smiled and hurried down the hall. Rone shut the door as he watched her go.

"Why did you give her that name?" Charlotte said. She stood behind him, her arms wrapped around her midsection. She was frowning.

"It was the name I gave at the gate. If someone picks up our trail from there, they'll be using the name of Munin."

"If someone is looking for us, won't the innkeeper just tell him everything?"

"I checked us in under the name Melanie."

"How do you keep track of all the names?"

Rone smiled. "You'll get used to it. We should get dressed. Lots of business to attend to today." He picked up the stack of clothes and frowned.

"Something wrong?" Charlotte said, pawing through the clothes while Rone still held them.

"These clothes are known."

***

Rone pulled at the top of his jacket, feeling constricted by its high collar and tight fit. It was a piece of style unique to Veraland, a doublet meant to look like a padded jack, but with colorful blue stripes stitched over the quilted linen and a row of buttons up the front. Rone knew from experience that whatever its looks, it was not a jack or a gambeson, and wouldn't stop so much as a pocketknife in a real fight. His pleated pants, baggy enough for him to keep his spare pistol concealed in the small of his back, waved in the stiff sea breeze.

"How is the straight jacket treating you?" he said quietly to Charlotte as they walked.

"I'll admit I had forgotten how uncomfortable a corset can be when it isn't properly made," she said back. She was wearing a modest blue dress, the skirts of which fell down in neat folds to the earth. The top had a built-in ribbed corset and bright white laces over gold ruffles trimmed her bust. She twirled a light blue paper parasol above her. "If you had let me buy the green one-"

"It was too expensive. We need to preserve our coin."

"You mean *my* coin."

Rone glared at her.

"I thought you wanted us to look like a rich married couple," Charlotte said, not turning away from the glare.

"I do. And we do."

"I look like a middle-class woman trying to sneak into a salon concert."

"All the better."

"And you look like a businessman nearing middle age, absconding with a poor woman that's much too young for him."

"That's what I am."

"We don't look like a young married couple."

"We're certainly starting to argue like we're married." Rone glanced behind them and caught sight of an old grizzled man flanked by two pike-wielding men. They wore hammered steel chest-plates, far from finely made or well-cared for, with leather bindings in various states of rot. Their green pants, however, pegged them as part of the town's guard.

"Always ready to dismiss me. If I-"

Rone gripped Charlotte's arm, silencing her. She instinctively tried to pull away. "Quiet now," he whispered, "It's the man from the gate, and he's got the guard with him."

Without breaking stride, Charlotte turned her head and glanced backward. "What's he doing down here?" she whispered.

"I doubt he's doing anything out of the ordinary," Rone said, and, tightening his grip on her arm, led her to the left side of the street. They could hear the uneven gate of the old man to their right and slightly behind them, as his hard-soled boots clacked loudly on the pavement. Underneath the rhythm of footfalls was the jingling armor worn by the guards. Ahead there was a break in the tightly packed buildings and the familiar triple steeple that indicated a cathedral dedicated to the Tranquil Sisters.

"You think he's the church type?" Charlotte said, nodding slightly toward the immense church building. Rone nodded back.

As the trio closed in behind them, they could make out bits of a conversation happening between the old man and one of the guards.

"I'm telling you, he cheats," the old man said.

"Yeah?" one of the guards said back. "How'd he do that, eh?"

"He keeps an ace up his sleeve, and the spade, no less," the old man said. "Just play a few hands and you'll notice. Only one ace of spades in the deck and he's always got it." The old man spat something onto the ground.

"The captain's sneaky, but he ain't into cheating with the men. You was probably just drunk," the other guard said. His voice was gravelly, speaking to a nightlife of more than just beer and cards.

"Of course I was drunk," the old man said. "It was Tuesday, after all." They all broke into a laugh. "But that don't mean I'm wrong. I can still shoot straight as an arrow when I'm drunk."

"No, you can't," the other guard said.

"Sure as snow in Materia," the old man snorted.

"Maybe we should put it to the test," the first guard said. "We'll stand up Colby with an apple on his head and you can shoot it off." They all laughed some more.

"A winning hand for the whole table," the second guard said.

The conversation was drowned out by the tolling of bells in the triple belfries of the cathedral, ringing in a trio of harmonious pitches that made a chord.

"Those are Notsra's bells," Charlotte said, not bothering to whisper under the din.

"Will that be an open service?" Rone asked. Charlotte nodded. He grabbed her hand and pulled her across a paved courtyard ringed with grass. They glanced back to see the trio of men pausing at the intersection. Their lips were moving, but nothing was audible above the tolling bells.

Rone dragged her past three immense statues on the outer edge of a circular courtyard, each facing toward a fountain at the center. As they walked into the center of the stone circle it seemed the marble sculptures, carved in the likeness of the goddesses usually referred to as the Tranquil Sisters, seemed posed to look down on them. Years of weather below an open sky had tarnished their virginal white, and everywhere they were streaked with grey. It gave them a life-like quality, adding to the three dimensions of stone a small piece of color. Each of the statues, though they were carved with delicate smiles, seemed to, with the grey streaks running down their faces, be crying.

Their walk slowed. Other people, young and old, ambled about the courtyard, all seeming to move steadily toward the entrance to the cathedral. Charlotte stopped in her tracks.

"What is it?" Rone said. He noticed Charlotte looking up at one of the statues. The sound of the bells began to fade.

"My parents always wanted me to be a disciple of Artifia," she said. The statue that held her gaze had long hair carved so that it hung about its shoulders, and in its arms, there was the likeness of a harp. "They thought I had such a lovely voice. It never got me out of cello lessons, though."

She turned to see Rone nodding. "You do have a good voice."

"I don't think you've ever heard me sing."

"Don't think so?" He smiled, though his eyes were sad. "All the same," he said. Rone's eyes narrowed as they focused past her, back toward the street where the three men still stood. She turned her head to look again and saw another man joining them who was taller and broader of stature. He wore something close to a uniform of blue and green, complete with an officer's jacket and chord and her heart leapt as she recognized the colors.

"Cataling," she said.

Rone swallowed. "They're probably in every port on the Isle." He looked back toward the church and nodded toward it.

"You recognize him, don't you? Did you know him when you were in the guard?"

"I can't see his face."

"If you didn't recognize him, you wouldn't be staring."

"Let's go," he said, pulling her toward the ancient house of worship.

The bells sounded one more chord.

She looked back up at the statue of Artifia, her tears falling upon her stone harp. Charlotte nodded at it and then walked with Rone toward the wide double doors of the cathedral. The faint sound of the three men laughing, a deeper voice adding to them, caught her ear amidst the fading bell tones.

*

The altar of the church, though gilded and carved of wood, appeared matched to the intricate stonework and flying buttresses of the exterior. It was three-sided and three-faced, with carvings of the Tranquil sisters immortalized in careful workings of gilded relief around the outside. Each goddess faced a different third of the round church. The artisans who created the cathedral centerpiece seemed to have been determined to eliminate any flat surface, and so the details of the holy place were lost in the almost organic lines of the whole. The stained glass that ran around the outside of the round cathedral was many-hued and depicted scenes from the Canon of the Divine, with one great window for each of the twelve gods. The mix of colors made the light around the curving pews seem hazy and dream-like, but somehow by the time it fell upon the altar it had become white, adding to the cleanly air of the place. Above those visages in a higher dome, three more windows loomed, greater than all the others, depicting each goddess arrayed in light and giving their gifts with bent knee. Upon the highest point in the altar stood a silver statue of Pastorus with animals around him in honor of his month.

The congregation was seated in the pews before the facing of Nostra, leaving the other two one-third divisions of the grand circle empty save for a few silent patrons in contemplation or study. The young faces arranged below Nostra's calming visage, facing the assemblage as if on display, wore a strange mixture of emotions. Some were painted with fear and anxiety, and others seemed to be disinterested, or even bored. The boys wore white trousers and the girls wore simple long dresses of green and white. Beside them stood a priestess, wearing robes of white trimmed with muted red and cinched around the waist with a red sash. One of the younger boys at the end of the row began to pick his nose, then quickly snapped his hand back to his waist as the priestess looked his way.

"And so, let us each give what the gods compel our hearts to give, for the maintenance of mankind, worked through the divine knowledge that shall be given unto these pledges," the priestess said. She began to walk down the narrow steps from the tranquiline altar, a narrow smile parting her smooth face. In each hand, she held a brass bucket, and when she reached the bottom, she handed one to the rows of people sitting on each side. "Some may become physicians," she said as she walked back up the steps. "Some may become nurses or herbalists, but all shall serve us as trade disciples these next four years."

"One of these girls could have been me," Charlotte whispered to Rone as they watched the offering bucket moved down one of the aisles. They sat in the last peopled row, and Rone frequently looked to the church entrance away on their left. "If my maidenhood had persisted but a little longer."

"Your parents would really demand you, *you,* ply a trade?" Rone whispered back

"They certainly liked to threaten it. I think it was mostly to inspire me to keep trim and proper, and stay out of the woods."

"For all the good it did you."

Charlotte pushed her chin down and cleared her throat as the gaze of the priestess fell upon them. Quietly, she reached into her velvet purse and produced a single silver coin.

"That's a week's worth of food, you know," Rone said quietly as the bucket approached.

"We have plenty more." She dropped it into the bucket, which she could see was filled almost entirely with rough copper pennies, the scraps that the poorest of peasants produced for change, along with the larger whole cyprals that were stamped by the crown. The priestess nodded to her as she saw the gift, then another cleric, a man dressed in simple black clothes, stepped from the back and picked up the bucket.

"I'm just looking the part," Charlotte whispered to Rone, who wore a frown. "Merchants are also generous."

"I don't know what merchants you've known."

"Well, their wives are."

"Which explains why the men can afford to do so little giving." He smiled slightly. The priestess moved to a lectern centered on the altar and opened a large book. She began reading from it, slowly and with dry intonation in the way only a cleric could manage.

"Do you think they're gone by now?" Charlotte whispered.

"We can stay here awhile longer," Rone said. "You never know. This might be an interesting tale."

"Unlikely, it's the fourth canon."

"I've sat through... perhaps three sermons in my entire life."

"Do you believe in the gods? In the canon?"

"Those are two separate things," Rone said.

"You can answer both," Charlotte said.

Rone smiled as he looked at the altar. "We believe in the gods, but not... Well, not as the gods they are presented to be. They aren't the creators, nor the guardians of man... or truth, even. They betrayed the dreamer and his eternal servants, long ago, and took upon themselves an identity which they themselves created – an identity which cut them off from their true power."

"I don't understand."

"It's hard to explain. The verse and the inverse, the mundane and the magical…" Rone looked at his left hand, frowning. "The canons bind people as they try to bind the world – to make it static. This place has beauty, but there is nothing here of eternity. Just the world that is."

"A true Somniatel," Charlotte whispered. She smiled as she said, "Not just a tamed barbarian."

"As heretical as you need. The Dreamer brokers no guilt for such things."

"Well, it's as good a place as any to take a nap." Charlotte coughed and pressed her hand to her chest as she noticed a pause in the droning cadence of words from the altar and noticed the old priestess looking down upon her again with a furrowed brow.

V: The Trail

arthow handed the reins of his horse over to a stable boy and dismounted after he passed through the double-gated entryway to Masala Castle. Guards with familiar faces watched him from the house above. He caught the eye of one, a lad named Janry that he had put on a secret extra payroll to keep an eye on the guard for him, and nodded subtly. Quickly, he turned back toward the tall, wide stairs that led up to the keep doors.

The castle itself stood high above the port city of Masala, with a cliff to one side - an easily defensible fortress from a more chaotic time. Its foundations and much of its edifice were made of basalt quarried near the sea, and it appeared black beneath the grey sky. Holes in the clouds, moving swiftly toward the dry highlands to the west, cast strange shapes upon it that swirled and swayed. Flags flew proud upon the corners of its rounded towers, and the banners that hung from its front walls twisted in the crisp sea wind. Between the parapets, the shadows of soldiers moved slowly about.

As Farthow ascended the stair he heard a voice calling to him from behind. "Cap'n! Cap'n! Your woman's done sobered up!"

"Quiet, you fool!" Farthow said, turning to see Colby behind him, near one of the corners of the keep.

"Catannel's man is long gone," Colby said.

"I said quiet!" Farthow jumped the last two stairs and grabbed Colby's elbow. He dragged him toward the entrance to the outer halls. Colby shrugged off the grip and pumped his arms matching Farthow's stride. They passed through an opening in the outer walls and rushed across a dusty courtyard, their boots scraping over a floor that was as much weathered flagstones as dirt. An iron reinforced door stood ajar, a steel cuirassed guard standing beside it with a matchlock resting on his shoulder and a pike against the wall. He raised a hand to his head as Farthow passed by and nodded to Colby.

The pair descended a narrow stair, the wooden handrail worn smooth to an almost glass-like sheen. The door clanged shut above them, leaving them with only the lamplight below to guide them downward. The echoes of their footsteps shortened as they reached the bottom where the stairway opened into a low-ceilinged room, the floor made of stone. Years of dust had piled up in the corners. Another man, this one fat enough to look uncomfortable in his breastplate, stood near a gate of iron bars, chewing on something that was invisible behind his overgrown black mustache. He did not bother saluting as Farthow walked by, and Farthow did not seem to care.

They passed down a long corridor with cells branching off to each side. Some were enclosed by iron bars. Others bore banded heavy wooden doors. Another guard stood by one of these, twirling a set of keys on an iron ring. Farthow nodded to him and the guard unlocked the door. It swung outward with a slight squeak. Against the back wall, lit dimly by a small bared shaft leaning back to ground level, sat a young woman wrapped in a blanket. She was eating a bowl of soup with a wooden spoon, but dropped both when Farthow entered, pulling the blanket tighter around her and shrinking into the corner.

"Relax," Farthow said. The guard brought in a three-legged stool, and Farthow sat down on it a few steps away from the girl. Silence settled in, and Farthow smiled at her.

"I'm free," she said after a few moments.

"Doesn't look like it," Colby said with a sneering laugh.

Farthow held up his hand to silence Colby and said, "We're not returning you or taking you to market. I brought you here to help you sleep off the opium daze, and because I needed to talk to you."

"This is a prison, right?" the woman said.

"The best accommodations I could manage on short notice." Farthow pulled a silver coin from his pocket and tossed it to the feet of the girl. "Recognize that?"

Hesitantly, the girl picked it up and turned it over in her hand. "It looks like silver."

"The mark, you dummy," Colby said.

Farthow gave him a perturbed look and turned back to the girl. "Northmarch silver. A little odd for this part of the world. Where did you get coins like this?"

"I don't have any coins."

"But you did. Who gave them to you?"

"Nobody."

"There is no need to lie to me," Farthow said. "I promise, even if you do not tell me, I will not hurt you. I even have this-" He held his hand out and Colby placed a long box into it. Farthow flipped it open and removed a small pill of orange-black opium. He rolled it between his gloved fingers. "To ease the pain." He produced from the box a small opium pipe and tapped it into his palm.

The woman reached for it. Farthow quickly withdrew his hand. "Just tell me where you got the coin."

The woman drew her lips into a line. "A man and a woman. The man was tall. He had sort of yellow eyes. The woman had blue eyes. Red hair, maybe. She had it short, I think. They killed the man taking me to market."

"Were they his coins? The man taking you to market?" Farthow said.

"No. Not Marcos's. He was selling me because he was broke. He said he never would sell me, once."

"Opium?"

"Yes. Sometimes he let me have some."

"I see. What were their names? The man and the woman?"

"Munin and Daera. I don't remember which was which."

"Where were they from?"

"I don't know."

"Where were they going?"

"No idea. They turned me loose as soon as they got in the gate."

Farthow nodded. "Different business, then."

"How would I know?"

Farthow smiled. He handed the opium to the girl and laid the box and the pipe on the ground. The girl hurriedly picked it up and removed a small oil lamp from the box. Colby walked over and lit it with a match as Farthow stood up. The girl pushed the pill into the bowl of the pipe and leaned over the lamp, sighing as she drew in the narcotic vapor. Colby covered his mouth at the reek and stepped out of the cell.

"Let her leave when she wishes to," Farthow said to the guard. "But take her out through the south gate. And give her this." He handed a heavy linen bag to the guard.

"You're giving her silver?"

"It's not the coin she was given initially, but it's of equal weight. Somebody thought she should have it, so have it she shall."

"Suit yourself, sir," the guard said, and tucked the bag into his belt pouch.

"You're on your honor to do right."

"Aye, sir."

Farthow turned down the hall with Colby. "We've work to do."

"I'm thinking of the docks," Colby said.

"Me too."

*

Rone and Charlotte turned down a sloping paved street and the smell of the ocean began to fill their nostrils. The air had the dull stillness that characterized early afternoon near the ocean, when the winds began to turn from blowing out to sea to blowing back into shore.

"That smell has been a long time in the coming," Rone said. His feet fell hard against the uneven paving stones on the slope. As they turned a corner, an opening between two huddled buildings revealed a vast and imposing series of docks, freight-ways, and canals. Rone held her arm as they paused to look. "Impressive, eh?"

"It reminds me of the harbor in Fargana, only that city has a river running through it. As busy as a hill of ants."

They started down the hill. It descended quickly toward the flat walkway in front of the lattice of docks. The buildings around had grown larger and more packed together, composed more of warehouses, stockrooms, and workshops than houses. Between them and the ocean stood a forest of tall masts and rope riggings. Men jostled about in every free space on the old stone walkways, carting great boxes and barrels, and more than a few people in chains.

"Alright, that looks like it up ahead there," Rone pointed at an ancient sandstone building with a large front door facing off toward the harbor and surrounded by men. It was large enough to be a keep in its own right, though it lacked the usual defenses.

"My, it is big... Though I expected the silver seat of the west to have something a bit more..." Charlotte trailed off.

"Expensive looking?"

"Yes. Um... *current* is more the word I was looking for. This building looks a lot older than the castle, which is saying something."

"Aye, I've heard the keep has been standing in some sense since the fourth dominion and hasn't been changed for five hundred years." He stopped walking to turn and look up the hill, beyond the skyline of the twisted buildings of the city, at the massive castle that overlooked it. It appeared black at that moment, looming at the edge of a cliff over the sea. The clouds, blown swiftly over to the highlands by the winds above the marine layer, were casting frightening shadows across it that swam like a magic haze.

"If that's the case, it would have to have been built before the Harecs controlled the city," Charlotte said. "Perhaps the original keep for castle Hadelim?"

"Hadelim? Doesn't ring a bell. Hard to think of a time without a Harec ruling the Silver City."

"You know, the Harecs had an unenviable title in the south reaches of Latheria, once upon a time."

"Are there *any* titles that are unenviable?"

"Many, at least from a noble's perspective. The Harec estate was in a swamp."

Rone raised an eyebrow. "Still, I wouldn't mind the luxury."

"Somehow I think you, more than anyone I've known, *would* mind." She smiled at him. "You are much too restless to live the life of a noble." She sighed.

"You have me there," Rone said. "I had an opportunity for restful work, with the guard." He paused and looked at the sky for a moment. "Not meant to be."

"I'm sure it didn't pay as well as your current job."

Rone looked at her and shook his head. "It's not that. I haven't been paid yet, have I? No, there are some things you *have* to do. Things that are part of what you are, for better or worse." There was a short silence where Charlotte stared at him contemplatively, then Rone said, "How did the Harecs end up here, do you know?"

"Vanilla."

"An herb?"

"It was, and is to some extent, the gold and silver of the lowlands. It grows well there. They made enough over the years to buy this fief when the old lords were swept away."

They were now standing a dozen feet from the front door of the trade offices of Masala, which stood ajar with a line of people reaching out one side. Occasionally a man in a uniformed blue set of trousers would walk in or out of the empty side of the door.

"I wonder what they did to be culled. The old lords."

"Some significant heresy, I'm sure," Charlotte wore a half-smile, and Rone watched the light from the pinholes in her parasol crawl across it. Her eyes, now a bright blue, glowed in the shade with reflections of himself standing in the bright sun. A strand of copper hair picked up in the wind and blew across her nose.

Rone stared at her for a long moment before realizing how close she was standing. He took a step toward the door. "How did you know their family's history?"

"The count of Masala was a prospective suitor. It was worth my time to know."

Rone nodded and chewed his lip. "Come on." Charlotte looped her arm into Rone's and they threaded themselves through the throng into the larger inner room.

The inside of the registrar was dim, but neatly kept. The thick walls and small windows were a relic of an older style of construction within the city, much more concerned with sturdiness than comfort. That concern was well preserved within the ancient docking agency, which (as Rone reckoned) held onto much of the contraband that was confiscated on site. On each deep-set window was a set of crossed bars planted firmly in the stone, reaffirming this purpose. The ceiling was stained a deep gray, nearly black, from years of candles, lamps, and other light sources. On one side was a set of tables with a stack of books and papers piled up on it. The line of people from the outside led up to it, and a mousy clerk sat behind it scribbling onto a ledger with a ragged goose-feather pen. Rone and Charlotte could hear him conversing with the man in the front of the line as they walked by.

"Fifteen men, twelve women, three child, just like it say." The old man was holding out a dirty sheet of paper that the clerk was eyeing over.

"I assume you will be housing them on ship until tomorrow?" The clerk never looked the old man in the eye, instead focusing on the scratchy writing of his pen.

"Yar, that's the plan."

The clerk handed him a piece of paper. "Take this to the cashier next door, he'll give you a set of stamps once you pay the total due. Be mindful of them, we can't replace lost stamps, and you'll have to pay the tax twice if your slaves pull theirs off before the auction. Next." Another man with a stack of papers stood up to the table. The little man didn't seem to notice Rone and Charlotte as they walked leisurely into the next room.

The next room was darker than the first. The rear wall contained a pair of great iron doors, double-barred both inside (so Rone assumed) and out, with two padlocks. To its left was a cashier's cage, iron-shod, with an old bespectacled man writing in his ledger beside stacks of silver and gold coins just out of arm's reach. The old man from the previous room walked up to the cage and, despite his ragged exterior, produced a dirty leather purse from his pocket and began to count gold coins out on the counter while the cashier inside began stamping a set of small papers.

Charlotte pulled Rone inside an adjoining room, suddenly bright compared to the darkness of the vault antechamber, containing the makings of a small office. A young mustached man sat behind a desk in the middle of the room, looking at a stack of papers in front of him and carefully writing in a large leather tome to his left. His uniform consisted of more than the blue trousers of the guard; he had a pressed blue waistcoat with brass buttons and a matching wide-brimmed hat, topped with a white plume, which sat next to him on the desk.

"Pardon me," Charlotte said sweetly. The young man looked up at her and smiled, revealing a row of white teeth.

"How do you do, madam?" He began to stand, "and sir," he said nodding to Rone.

"Well enough for the winds," Rone said, smiling.

"Oh, we're quite well. Am I to understand you're the dock master?" Charlotte said, tilting her head to the side.

"Not quite, madam. That would be Mr. Draggle. He doesn't spend time in the office. Too much paper and not enough salt for him. He'll be out making his rounds, getting ready for the wave of ships that will come in closer to sunset. I'm the count's clerk for the seaward offices. Lieutenant Dartan Corving, at your service." He clicked the heels of his well-oiled shoes.

"I'm Phillip, and this is Halbara," Rone said naturally. A slight pause filled the air.

"Melanie," Charlotte said. Rone eyed her, frowning in disapproval for an instant. Before he could fill the silence, she added, "of the wetland Melanies. Are you of the Southerland Corvings?"

"Yes, actually. My father's estate overlooks the woods there. My wife is from here in Masala. After her brother died, gods take his soul, we moved so that she could assist her father in his import business. The good Count Harec was kind enough to accept my commission."

"I'm sure the count is happy to have someone with such a good reputation representing his interests in the sea trade," Charlotte said.

There was an awkward silence, where Charlotte tried not to let her smile fade.

"Do you need the dock master?" Dartan said. "I don't expect him in until night."

"I'm sure *you* could help us." Charlotte smiled sweetly.

"Yes, my wife and I have a need to cut our tour short, and we need passage to the Northmarch," Rone said. "Bergen, Fargana... a lesser port would do as well. We will need to travel inland."

"Let me check," Dartan said as he sat down and looked in his great book. "Let's see, port of call Fargana... not its next stop. Hmn. Well, there is a ship leaving for Golice, but it's not listed as a passenger carrier. Brought in... dry goods. Spices." He looked up at the couple. "It might not be comfortable, but it's the only thing here leaving to the Northmarch in the next week. You can ask the captain yourself about booking passage, see if he's willing."

"Thank you, sir," Rone said clicking his heels, "How shall we find him?"

"He's likely on ship. Dock seven-B. Name is..." He checked his book again, "Johnny. Odd. Only one name listed."

VI: Just Johnny

everal gaunt-looking men were stacking wooden boxes into hand wagons on the dock as Charlotte and Rone walked up to the ship. They stepped back as a young man staggered down the plank with another box.

"Who's this?" A young shirtless man wearing faded pantaloons walked up to the pair from behind a stack of boxes on the dock.

"How do you do? My name is Phillip, and this is my wife, Halbara," Rone said.

The young man stared at them and spat into the water. "You two don't look like our usual business." His jaw moved widely back and forth, working at a piece of chewing tobacco. His gaunt cheeks seemed to accentuate the motion, hiding no detail behind his thin beard.

"Are you the captain?" Charlotte asked.

"Naw. I'm Danny. First mate. Johnny's up in his quarters."

"Thanks," Rone said, pulling Charlotte a few steps onto the plank.

"What's all this about?" Danny said.

"We need passage to the Northmarch. Post haste." Charlotte heard Rone grumble beside her.

"This ain't your kind of ship, mate. Better off waiting for a state liner or something under a corporate banner."

"Normally we would, but I'm afraid time is a bit short for us," Charlotte replied.

"Suit yourselves, but don't say I didn't warn ya."

*

The Captain's quarters were dusty and dim. When Rone and Charlotte stepped inside they saw a large spectacled man sitting at a small table writing in a small book with a very ragged black pen. He towered above the back of his small chair, making him look almost comically tall. His barrel chest was pushed up against the table, leaving a fatty bulge pushing against the bottom of his tome. His jacket was hanging off the back of his chair, and his shirt was a faded grey, though Charlotte thought that it might have at one point been white. He stroked his long, black beard as he wrote. When they closed the door, he looked up at them and took off his glasses.

"What are you doing on my ship?"

Rone saw him reach down and touch a pistol in his belt. Rone felt his fingers reached for the familiar wooden stock of his own, hidden away in the back of his pants.

"We're interested in booking passage. We understand that you are going to the Northmarch," Rone said, doing his best to sound calm and polite.

"Golice, yeah," the man said, relaxing and putting his pen back into its stand, the end covered in viscous black ink. "But we don't carry people, unless you're part of the crew."

"We know there won't be much in the way of accommodations, and we're fine with that," Rone said. "We're travelers and we just need to get home quickly."

"Sorry, but I'm not in the business of travelers. Find a corporate liner, or a fleet ship." The big man put his glasses back on. Rone tossed a heavy leather sack on the table in front of him. He stopped writing once again and picked up the bag, weighing it. He looked cautiously at Rone and turned the bag out on the table. Silver and gold coins came out clinking into a small pile.

"That, and as much again," Rone said.

"So, you want to buy the ship?"

"No, we just need to get to the Northmarch." Rone said.

The captain held up one of the gold coins and looked at it closely with his spectacles, his mouth twitching as he seemed to consider it. "I still wouldn't advise it. When I say we're not in the business of hauling people, I mean it. It's really not something we should do."

"You're a pirate then?" Rone said.

"Privateer," The large man said, touching his nose. "Business is not exactly safe for ourselves; there's no way I could guarantee the safety of a gentleman or a lady."

"I make my own safety, captain," Rone said.

The captain sighed and put the coin back on the stack. "Well the sea may take ya, but I'll be damned if I don't understand risk and reward, and I'll be damned again if I don't turn away good coin. We're leaving at dawn tomorrow, provided we can get stock for our next shipment." He stood up, standing almost a half a head above Rone, and extended his hand.

"Phillip." They shook hands. The man's hand matched his stature: an immense paw that seemed to suffocate Rone's in its grip.

"They call me Big Johnny, for obvious reasons. I'm captain and majority shareholder in the good ship Parkitees." He looked to Charlotte.

"Sha-Halbara." She said, quickly correcting herself. She extended her hand. Johnny looked at her for a moment puzzled then shook her hand, taking the tips of her fingers between his own great thumb and index in an awkwardly dainty exchange.

He looked back to Rone. "Beggin' your pardon, Mister, uh..."

"Melanie, of the wetland Ravens," Charlotte cut in robotically. This time Rone softly groaned. Johnny's glasses slid down his nose as he stared at her.

"I meant *his* name," Johnny said flatly. He nodded at Rone.

"We're married," she replied. She hugged Rone's arm.

"You can't bullshit a man like me. You ain't married; least not yet. If you're eloping or whatever..." He rubbed the back of his neck. "I guess it ain't none of my business, but you can't fool an old liar like me-self. But don't worry. I can keep a secret." His half-frown turned into a wide smile, showing several gold-capped teeth.

"Thanks, we'll see to the other half of payment once we arrive," Rone said politely, dropping his air. He quickly scooped the coins into the leather satchel and turned to walk out.

"Dawn," Johnny said. His face relaxed into a flat stare. "We're not the kind to wait around. On your way out, tell Danny to set up a few bunks for ya in the high room." He smiled suddenly again, a strange glint in his eye.

"Alright," Rone said hesitantly, then opened the door for Charlotte. He raised his eyebrows at her as they exited. "Interesting fellow," he said after they stepped back out onto deck and closed the door.

The main deck, which ran over twenty paces between the captain's quarters at the rear and forecastle near the bow with a large central mast, was vacant save for a pair of deckhands busying themselves with loading supplies. Rone looked about for a few moments. The slim young man they had spoken to on the way up seemed missing on the deck and the dock.

"Excuse me," Charlotte said to a nearby sailor, busy coiling sets of ropes as he pulled them down off the naked yards. He was a tall man with messy blonde hair, wearing a shirt and pants of a faded grey, stiff and wrinkled from days at sea. "Have you seen Danny?"

The deckhand looked up from what he was doing, panting slightly from the work with the heavy rope. Though he was dirty and wet with sweat, his face was shaved and revealed a youthful handsomeness. "He sauntered off to somewhere or another in town."

"Oh-" Charlotte said.

"Just like him, too," the sailor went on, "to leave before even half the work is done. I'll probably have to do that poor sod's job, too. Be lucky to fetch myself half a pint before the night is through."

"Well, the captain wished for him to set us up a few bunks for us in the..." Charlotte thought to herself a moment. "Um, high room?"

The sailor chuckled. "Danny's not going to be too pleased with that task."

"Why is that?"

"That's the first mate's quarters." The sailor nodded toward the forecastle, which had a small door set a few steps down sunken into it. "The funny thing is, he hasn't ever slept in them since Johnny gave him the title. He's starting to think it's some kind of joke."

"Why is that?" Rone said.

The deckhand looked away for a moment in thought. "We had to use it as extra cargo space, then haul some kind of bigtime navy fellow from Golice, then we had this shipment of rare plants that had to receive exactly eight hours of sunlight a day then be put away. I think he was particularly perturbed about those."

"I suppose we could always bump elbows with the crew," Rone said. He coughed as Charlotte elbowed him in the ribs, smiling widely the whole time. "I mean... give him our sincere apologies."

The sailor laughed again. "I will. My name's Pierce, by the way." He put his hand out casually, and Rone shook it.

*

Charlotte and Rone paused for tea and wine at a shop around sunset, enjoying a bite of fresh bread and jam and relaxing midway through the long walk back to the inn. The wind coming off the ocean dried the sweat they had worked up climbing the steep slope back to the high part of town, and though they were well-dressed their hair had the crispy look of sailors. When they finally reached the inn in it was after dark.

"I'm about ready to fall into bed; the second half of that walk just went on and on," Charlotte said as they walked up the stairs toward their room. The fire in the main room down below lit the corridor dimly.

"Aye, that's the problem with walking downhill. Eventually, you have to go back *up*hill," Rone said cheerfully. "Still, the Highlands have made a climber out of you, despite yourself."

"Despite myself, what is that supposed to mean?"

"Prim, proper, polite, and protected."

"Not me!" Charlotte said through a wide grin. "I can't get you... you won't put two words together in one minute, and later you spit out the most scrumptious alliterations." Charlotte hugged his arm as he began fumbling for the big brass door key. "Prim, proper, polite, protected. You forgot politically passionate and positively pedantic. Or-"

Rone stopped her with a sudden rigidity in his touch and posture. While Charlotte was talking Rone had noticed the little girl Missy exiting a room, holding a small oil lamp. He had locked glances with her for a protracted moment before she turned away from his gaze and galloped down the stair at the other end of the hallway. The gaze had spoken volumes to the man, and though he knew he was out of his element in the city, he was not so far removed from his past experience to mistake the look on the girl's face for anything but fear and guilt.

"Yes, sometimes I fancy a bit of poetry, even if only to please myself." Rone's voice sounded cheerful, but his face was grave as he looked into Charlotte's eyes. He pressed his ear to the door for a moment and put a finger to his lips. He nodded toward the stairwell. Charlotte nodded. Quietly, she lifted her skirt and tip-toed back to the stairs.

Rone reached into his jacket and drew forth an old friend. It clicked faintly as he drew back the hammer. He reached over the top of the lock with his index finger and lifted the frizzen, feeling for a full prime. He locked eyes with Charlotte again, then watched her disappear down the stairs.

With his left hand, he turned the key; His right held the pistol at eye level. "Aye, it will be good to get some shut-eye." He pushed the door open. As it swung ajar, Rone could see a silhouette in the moonlit window. He stepped in.

"Ah, mister-" The silhouette could not finish his greeting. Rone swung the door shut. At the same time it slammed into the door frame, the butt of Rone's pistol slammed into the teeth of a very large man standing beside it. By the time his girth hit the floor Rone was upon the silhouette at the window, his left hand now clutching his knife in an overhand grip.

"Is it Munin, or Phillip?" The voice croaked as the edge of the blade pushed against his jaw. The man below sat limp.

"Speak right and live. Speak foul, and you'll dine with Grim this very night."

"It seems the girl was right to trust you. You also do not have me at as much of a disadvantage as you think." Rone glanced down to see a pistol leveled at his belly. "It's a hair-trigger."

"I'm good at my business, as it seems you are." Rone held back some pressure on the edge of the knife. Without breaking his intense gaze on the man, he trained his pistol on the man who had hidden behind the door, now lying in a heap behind him. "So, who are you?"

"My name doesn't have much relevance-" Rone pushed the blade again hard on the man's skin. "But it's Farthow, if you must have it."

"Why are you here?"

"Business, like you gathered. I'm representing a very wealthy and important man."

"In regard to what, then?"

"The girl, of course."

"I turned her loose."

"Not that girl."

Rone raised an eyebrow.

"I would make it worth your while to turn her over to me. How does five-hundred Aurals sound?"

Five-hundred ounces of gold. The price made Rone pause. His heart, already beating hard, sped up. His back felt suddenly tight and painful, leaning up against the stranger. "You could hire an army to take her for that."

"Not a very good one. And the value is in the prize, not how many men I hire to acquire it. I'd just as soon pay one than pay a hundred."

Rone eased up on the knife, bringing the muzzle of his pistol to Farthow, who remained motionless as Rone backed up.

"Who are you working for?" Rone said.

"I can't tell you that, you know."

"It matters," Rone said.

"Does it? For five hundred Aurals it ought not to."

Rone Swallowed. "Catannel? Or Harec?"

Farthow shrugged. "I can tell you it isn't Vindrel."

"Doesn't mean much." Rone licked his lips. "Can you get me off the Isle?"

"You're rusty," Farthow said. "Being desperate to leave, even without your charge? Makes me want to cut the price."

"I try not to steal anything without a way to leave safely with it."

"Bad form with the girl, then."

Rone chewed his tongue. "You could say that."

Farthow smiled. "500 Aurals and I can arrange a trip to several ports. I'll have it sitting on a ship in a chest. You can count it; I'll take the girl."

Rone took a deep breath. "Is it Harec, or Catannel?"

Farthow's eyes stared back at him, cold.

"Tell me damnit!"

"You know I can't. Just you knowing my name is enough liability."

Rone's voice raised to a scream. "Tell me who you're working-"

The door swung open once again. Rone looked away for a moment to see the man who was crumpled on the floor standing above him, also in the process of turning to look at the door. He never saw what had entered. As the big man collapsed (once again, this time against the bedpost), a slender body with long hair flying around it replaced him, holding like a club what looked to be a table leg.

In a heartbeat he felt his pistol arm being pushed up and away and felt a strike to the side of his solar plexus, knocking the wind from him. Farthow was up and out of the chair, but before Rone could level his pistol Farthow had overturned the table and leapt at the window. The move shocked Rone and he, without realizing it, held his shot, but Farthow followed through with his move, landing on the windowsill and sliding over the roof toward the street. Rone moved over to the window and looked down to see a deserted night street.

"Bastard is good."

"What was all that?" Charlotte said, panting as she moved to join Rone at the window.

"You just *had* to give us a last name." Rone eased the hammer on his pistol down and tucked it into his belt. Charlotte was breathing hard, still holding out the table leg like a sword. "But thanks for the backup, I suppose," he added, chewing his cheek. "I knew he was up, by the way.

"Do you think-" Charlotte leaned the leg-club up against the bed and breathed deep, "it was the captain, Mister Johnny?"

"Could be, but... I doubt it. Probably Corving at the shipping office." He nodded toward the window. "This fellow gave me the name Munin, too."

"So, a follow up from the west gate, then?"

"Aye, that's what I would think. Of course, it could be someone who was waiting for us all along."

"What makes you say that?"

Rone hesitated and looked into Charlotte's eyes. He looked away with a sigh. "Five hundred Aurals was what he offered for me to turn you over to him."

"What? That's three times my dowry."

Rone raised an eyebrow at her. He moved over to the large collapsed man and checked him. He was still breathing. "Part of me wants to wait till this bloke comes to and ask him some questions, not friendly-like, but I think we'd best be on our way."

Charlotte stomped. "Drat that little Missy, I paid her to tell us about things like this."

"Well, I don't trust most folks further than I can throw a coin. These two probably threw a bigger coin. But still, she did warn us, even if she didn't mean to. You can read a lot in a look."

Charlotte nodded.

A thud and a series of shouts from the common room below snapped them both to attention. "I knew he wouldn't have come alone," Rone said.

VII: In a Pinch

Charlotte followed Rone down the narrow flight of stairs. He had his backsword in his left hand, tip forward, and his pistol in his right. Charlotte held the long gun awkwardly; with their packs on, they barely fit through the stairwell, and that left no room for managing a musket. They stumbled into the kitchen to find two men wearing bright breastplates and wielding basket-hilted broadswords pushing through, with the inn-keeper's wife shouting in protest. Rone jumped the last steps and kicked a boot out as he landed. His feet connected with the shins of the first man, sending him backward and causing him to topple to the floor, which was already slick with spilled soup and food. With a hasty chop of his sword, Rone cut into the ankle of the other man, and he fell backward with a loud cry, hitting the stove and burning his forearm on a hot iron pan. With a cry, the man dropped his sword and clutched at his smoking shirt.

Charlotte charged past them, making for the door. Rone got up and stumbled on the wet floor, just managing to avoid a fall, then followed her out to the alley. Rone, smelling the acrid fuse of a matchlock musket, pulled Charlotte to the ground. They both flinched as musket fire erupted from one end of the Alley.

"Hold your fire, damn it!" A gruff voice shouted. A group of men began scrambling down the darkened corridor, drawing swords and crowding one another. Charlotte and Rone, lacking any other option, ran the opposite direction. They reached the end of the alleyway and were left with the choice of going several different ways. Rone pulled Charlotte to their right, pushing her ahead of himself.

"Hope this is the right way." Rone looked over his shoulder, but his view was restricted by his pack. He could hear the shuffling of boots echoing behind. He faced forward again only to find himself toppling over Charlotte. He rolled off of her and saw that she was pulling the leather cover off the musket and drawing back the hammer. Shadows gathered where the Alley opened up to the street.

Rone slipped his pack off his shoulders and faced the way they had come. Four men were approaching, two abreast and leaving hardly room for their elbows. The front two bore long halberds while the men behind bore swords. Rone fired his pistol, hitting one of the front two in the cheek, causing him to drop his halberd and reach for the wound. He was quickly trampled by his fellows, but one of them, realizing what had happened, stooped to help the injured man. In a smooth motion, Rone shoved the pistol into his belt and drew out a long bollock dagger for his off-hand from a sheath secreted beneath his dress jacket.

Rone beat away the blade end of a halberd with his sword. Kicking at the pole of the weapon, he stepped up and stabbed at the man's arms above his gauntlets with the point of his sword. The strike failed to do much of anything, but it did cause the man to shrink back and try to fall into his guard. Rone, being still close enough to slip past the guard, thrust his dagger down into man's thigh. It reluctantly bit through the quilting of the man's leggings and found a bit of flesh. The man flipped his pole weapon wildly in shock and Rone stepped nimbly back. Two men were up behind him, but were held back momentarily by the flipping of the blade of the halberd.

Behind him, Charlotte scrambled up to her knees and fired the musket. Smoke filled the small space, and a man cried somewhere beyond the screen. His vision blurred, Rone tucked his dagger under his forearm and pulled Charlotte to her feet by tucking his fist into her armpit. He pushed her forward through the smoke.

Three men stood at the end of the alley in the moonlight, two with pikes and one standing back with a loaded crossbow. None of them appeared injured. Rone cursed and pulled up short, feeling his feet slide under him as he tried to handle Charlotte without the use of either hand. At that moment a bolt erupted from the neck of one of the men, just above the stiff collar of his breastplate, spraying blood on the man beside him. Shocked, the soldier pawed at his gory face with a gauntleted hand, which did nothing for him. The crossbowman fired, but the bolt was far wide, clattering off the stone wall of one of the buildings after flying past Rone.

Rone slipped past Charlotte and rushed forward. The crossbowman dropped his weapon and reached for his sword. Before it could clear the scabbard, the man fell forward, his head lolling. A hooded man stood nearby, holding a long, leather-wrapped sap. Hesitating only a moment, Rone reached back for Charlotte and pulled her forward, slashing quickly at the hooded man, who leapt backward. He shouted in protest, but the words were lost in more musket fire and shouts as men spilled out into the streets on the other side of the inn. Instinctively, Rone pulled Charlotte down into a crouch as he side-stepped to their left, down a steep hill, realizing in a few tense steps that the bullet report was distant. The men were firing in the opposite direction.

The hill bottomed out into a dense marketplace, still busy after dark with people crowding watering holes and eateries. The sound of the shots had elicited a panic from those in the streets and alleys, and everywhere men and women were rushing inside as barkeeps and merchants pulled in wares and barred doors, motioning straggling patrons to hurry inside. Musicians, playing in the open air for the milling crowd, were begging for help in moving their drums and chairs. Rone sheathed his blades and lead Charlotte into the midst of the crowd.

"He's following," Charlotte said with a croak. Rone glanced back and saw the hooded man moving unhindered through the churning throng.

"I think it's the man from the room," Rone said. "Here." He pulled Charlotte hard to the left, into the middle of a crowd. "And slip the pack off." Rone put his pack down and took her musket, letting each one hang from his relaxed arms.

She followed his lead and unshouldered her pack, letting it hang in her hand from its top strap. She followed him into a deeper mass of people. Men's and women's voices filled the pressed space.

"It'll be the coca sellers on Shore Street fighting again for sure," a woman's voice said.

"Doubtful," a man said in reply. "Sounded like it was coming from outside. The sheriffs again, I'd wager."

"Just as bad," the woman said in reply.

Charlotte and Rone went along with the crowd into a quickly filling inn's common room. The barkeep was standing on the counter just inside the door, a short two-barreled flintlock in his hands, held off his shoulder but ready for action. He was, in odd contrast to his posture, smiling jovially.

"Half-priced drinks for the next keg!" he shouted. A roar from the room answered him as a boy pulled the door shut and barred it. The bartender tossed his gun to a portly woman near the kitchen entrance and hopped down.

"Not the reaction I expected," Charlotte said into Rone's ear.

Rone grunted in response, then said, "I see another dining room. Let's see if we can find a corner for a few minutes."

"Do you think we lost him?"

Rone shrugged and wiped sweat from his brow. "The door is barred. Not much else to do."

They went under a low arch into another room, darker and longer than the common room with a low ceiling of old bowing rafters. Benches and tables crowded the walls and round tables filled the middle of the long space. They found an empty stretch of bench near a far corner, far enough away from the fireplace to be drafty, and pulled themselves into it. Men and women sat scattered throughout the room, uncaring of the pair, their backpacks, or the long-barreled musket that Rone leaned up against the wall.

Very shortly after they sat down a young serving woman approached and said, "What can I whip up for you? It'll be a while before the guard clears up the fight."

"You think so?"

The woman smiled. "It was an hour last time. Was only one man they caught though. Strung up the poor sod the next day."

"You've seen this before?" Charlotte said. Rone silently glared at her.

"Ah, you usually spend time uptown, then?" the serving girl said. "We gotten a few gunfights lately." She stuck her thumb out over her shoulder. "Poppy says it's the slave trade. Bunch of fellows come in from Tyrant's Gallow with teeth. It'll all be cleared up soon."

"We don't stay out often," Rone said. "But I'm sure it will all be taken care of. And we'll have whatever the kitchen's putting on special." He pulled a silver coin from his purse and flicked it to the server.

"To drink?" The serving girl smiled and turned her head as a young man slid past, touching lightly the small of her back before crowding into a spot beside the fire. He met her glance and smile briefly before turning back to his friends.

"Ale. Two pints," Rone said, smirking. "From the cellar, please." The server shuffled away, and Rone turned his attention to Charlotte who was wringing her hands and hunching over the table.

"Are we just going to sit here?" she said.

"For the moment, yes," Rone said. He took a deep breath and rubbed his temples.

"Why?"

"Everyone else is sitting."

Charlotte narrowed her eyes at him.

Rone sighed. "We'll be able to slip out with the rest of the crowd. I hope, anyway."

"If the guard doesn't break down the door."

Rone nodded. "I'll come up with something. Till then try to look like we've been here all night." Rone glanced toward the common room as some musicians started up a dance to a loud cheer.

"Would it be too auspicious to reload?" Charlotte said, eyeing the musket.

Rone chuckled. "I don't know these people." After a pause, he shrugged and produced his pistol and powder horn. He brushed the bore and reloaded, primed his pan, then slid the pistol to Charlotte. Nobody did more than glance their way. "I'm going to track down this innkeeper and see if I can get us a room to at least change our clothes in."

*

Farthow pushed himself up against the edge of an old stone building and peered out. Behind him, Market Street had emptied, and he knew Vindrel would be leading his elite, along with the men the count had attached to him under the token supervision of Colby, down toward the normally packed entertainment center. The Old Keep way was filling now with civilian onlookers, wandering out of their boarding houses and apartments with lit lamps. They all seemed curious as to what the gunfire had been about, several minutes having now past from the shots and shouts. A few men that Farthow assumed were soldiers were milling about near the end of the street, but they were hard to make out in the partially obscured moonlight. The marine layer had swept inland and now blotted out the stars.

A slight movement to his right alerted Farthow. He saw a flash of hand signals from a man obscured beside a door landing.

Status.

Several men knew the highland hand signals Farthow had taught, but he knew only either Dem or Colby were out in the night and near at hand. Neither of them knew how to sign their name yet, so answering was a gamble. He had chosen to keep Colby out of the know for what he considered good reasons. Bringing the marksman in on things at this stage would be riskier than if Farthow had disclosed his plans from the outset.

"Nothing for it," he said quietly to himself.

He stepped out and signed, ***Status – safe. Target – hidden. Behind. Meet me at the far side.*** He pointed down the meandering avenue that was the cluster of inns around Market Street. A figure stepped out of the shadows holding a crossbow and jogged up the lane.

Dreamer, thanks for that, Farthow thought. It was Dem. He turned and ran back the other direction to meet him.

A few minutes later they were together outside a bar with its door tightly shut but the exterior lamp left lit. A boisterous sound came from within.

"Where's Gareth?" Dem asked.

"With Colby, I hope," Farthow said. "He took a blow to the head and I had to leave him behind. I think our mark is inside of Poppy's," Farthow said.

"You sure?"

"Not at all. You know where the larder door is?"

"Of course. I get out from time to time, you know."

"See if you can get in that way. There's a guardhouse a block up. I'm going to commandeer a horse and intercept Vindrel and Colby."

"What do you want me to do with her if I find her?"

"Take her back to your place."

"My house?"

"Yes. There's that alley with the sewer behind Sott's. Should take you east enough to hit the Long Circle."

Dem chewed his cheek. "Shit."

"That's generally what collects in sewers. What's your point?"

Dem shook his head and shouldered his crossbow. "I don't figure they'll listen to me, boss."

"Nonsense. You can be very persuasive if you're well-motivated. Just turn on that country charm, and they'll come around. I'm going to buy you some time and flush some people out. You'll be fine."

VIII: Streets of Silver

harlotte felt uneasy as the moments passed by and Rone had not returned. Compulsively, she put her hand into her bag and rummaged until she found the leather bag that was stuffed with her gold. An itch in her mind had made her believe that somehow, in the rush out the door of the inn, she had left it behind. There would be no getting off the Isle of Veraland without that long-hidden cache. She breathed with relief, feeling its immense weight.

Rone had proven his word to her with that bag of money, enough to buy himself whatever life he desired, though the test had been unexpected. A day out of Cataling, while still climbing into the dry highlands, he had discovered it while repacking their bags, convinced that she was struggling too much with the weight. He had nodded to her and told her to hold onto it until he earned it; Charlotte knew he could have quite simply killed her for the money and never bothered with her promise of payment by her uncle.

"Charlotte of the Plain, I presume?"

Charlotte flinched at the soft-spoken voice and looked up to see a plain-clothed man with a well-trimmed beard sitting down across from her. She reached for the pistol, folded in her lap amidst her skirts. Trying to calm herself, she eased back the hammer and pushed up the frizzen, feeling for the grit of the prime.

"My name is Dem. I am not here to return you to your husband, so please don't shoot me."

"You work with the other man, then?"

"I don't know who the other man is to you," Dem said, raising his eyebrows. "I'm just here to get you out of the cook pot, so to speak. Vindrel's company should be getting here soon, but I know of a few ways out of this particular social area."

"Those men weren't the count's?"

Dem looked at her and frowned. "It doesn't matter. We need to get you out of-" Dem flinched and cut off his words.

"You make interesting friends when I'm not looking," Rone said. He was standing behind Dem's chair, his pistol, mostly obscured by his open jacket, was pushed up against the man's neck.

Dem put his hands on the table. "I have a safe house for you, at least until you can get aboard a ship and get out of here." He turned his head to look at Rone. "You're running out of options, sir."

"You work for Harec as well?"

"I aim to keep you out of Vindrel's hands, and that should be enough."

"So that was him, and he knows we're here."

Charlotte looked at Dem. "How will you help us?"

"He won't," Rone said.

"I'll slip you out the back door and take you somewhere safe. There are a few ways to cut through to the Garden Wall that you likely don't know about."

"I have a room upstairs," Rone said. "We'll need to change our clothes."

"That can wait," Dem said. "It must wait, really." Rone stood still for an agonizing few moments. Dem turned to him and said, "I wish I could say it doesn't matter to me if you come or not, but my arse is on the line here too."

The crowd cheered as the musicians finished a song.

"Let's go," Charlotte said. "Sitting around is worse than running."

"Agreed," Rone said. He tucked the pistol back into his belt and picked up his bag. "Lead the way…" He held up his hands and raised his eyebrows questioningly.

"Dem." He gave Rone a disingenuous smile and stood up.

They followed the lanky man past the fireplace and around a corner to a small room with tables overflowing with foodstuffs. A short door stood at one end. Dem casually flipped it open and ducked in, lowering himself down a steep stair into darkness. Charlotte went next with the musket.

"I can't see anything," she said.

As Rone began to duck in, a sharp voice rang out.

"Hey! What are you doing in my larder?" It was the barkeep, and he came stomping up to Rone, picking up a small club from beside the entryway.

Without hesitation Rone kicked the man in the belly, doubling him over before he could wield his club. Rone then tipped over a table of vegetables onto the man and ducked into the cellar. A serving woman that was walking by cried out as she saw the scene and ran away. Voices in the common room answered her.

Before he shut the door Rone yelled at the barkeep, "Your kitchen is slow as shit. I ordered soup half an hour ago!" He slammed the door and looked for a latch. He found none, and so descended the stair with renewed haste. At the landing, a small stone-floored cellar spread out. A dim light cast by a small lamp illuminated the low-ceilinged room. Barrels and kegs leaned against one wall and bags of flour against another.

"That your idea of a joke?" Dem said.

"You bet," Rone said with a chuckle. "If you don't laugh, you'll cry."

Dem scoffed and moved toward the far end of the cellar. "At the very least you'll be remembered."

"And here I am usually trying to avoid that."

He stood on a barrel and pushed against the ceiling, revealing a trap door. Moonlight spilled onto the floor as Dem reached down and picked up a crossbow, then threw it up into the light. He pulled himself up and out of the cellar.

His hand stuck down. "Give me your bags."

Rone pulled his bag off and handed it to Dem, who lugged it out and set it on the street beside him. He followed with Charlotte's bag.

"The girl next," he said.

Rone ignored him. He handed his pistol to Charlotte, who, lacking anywhere else to stash it, stuffed it between her breasts. Rone then pulled himself up and out of the cellar. When he was clear, Charlotte came and stood on the keg, her arms uplifted, and Rone quickly grasped her elbows with two hands and lifted her up. Dem had already moved to the corner of the inn and was gazing away, reloading his crossbow. He looked back to Rone and held a finger to his lips, then motioned for them to come.

They both quickly shouldered their burdens and came forward. The sound of boots and voices tickled their ears as they passed out of the cover of the building. A quick glance down the side of the inn revealed men armed with long guns and pikes laying hands lightly on modestly clothed men and women as they exited a different tavern. Occupied as they were, they did not notice the trio as they slipped into another alley.

"Here," Dem said. He pointed to an opening in the alley that seemed to be beneath one of the buildings. Stairs, wet with condensation and slime, were going down into the dark.

Charlotte covered her mouth with her hand. Rone motioned her down, and she followed Dem. She had to keep her hand against the wall to keep from slipping, and she had to kick out with her feet on each step to stop herself from tripping on her skirts. At the bottom, Dem swung open a small iron gate, revealing a long open sewer that ran perpendicular to the alleyway before curving away some yards ahead. The entire thing sat some six feet below the level of the street, with small bridges and even entire buildings going overhead, blacking out sections of the path.

"Don't worry, we won't be down here long," Dem said. They followed him through a short, straight tunnel that ran under a building before revealing the moon and stars on the other side. Openings from the street cut into the walls here and there, with water and other refuse dripping from them. When they could, they walked along the dry edge, but in a few places, obstructions forced them to step quickly through a few patches of sewage. They passed two more stairs and walked along a long curve before Dem motioned them to step up and out by a short set of steps. When they reached the top of the stairs, they found themselves in an unfamiliar street, lit brightly by the silver moon that was now overhead. A long ivy-covered wall lined one side. The street was quiet, nearly soundless, and their footsteps echoed almost painfully.

"I hope you're up for a bit of a walk," Dem said. "My place is down this lane. Almost to the outer wall."

Dem turned away, and at that moment, Rone struck. He swiftly kicked at Dem's back leg, striking the back of the knee. Dem began to collapse, but even with his heavy pack, Rone was already moving to bind the man. He twisted Dem's arm, causing the crossbow to drop to the street. It released as it hit, sending a bolt flying against the ivy-covered wall with a dull thud. Rone's dagger was instantly in his right hand and against the small of Dem's back, his other arm wrapped about the man's neck.

"Stop!" Charlotte cried, fumbling the musket to the ground. "No, Rone!"

Rone did stop, but he did not remove the knife, which bit still slightly into Dem's jacket, tearing the cloth. Dem, still struggling against the hold, had his back arched and was kicking to stop himself from falling onto the blade.

"Why should I stop?" Rone's voice was cold and distant.

"He helped us."

"Only to help himself, or the count, who is his employer, I reckon. He killed for that employer little more than an hour ago, and he will kill me if he gets the chance. We have no friends here. You should know this."

"I don't care. Please."

Rone took a deep breath, but whatever thought he had brewing, whatever rebuttal he was stewing up, was lost as they heard the reverberating sound of hooves. He pulled away his dagger and struck Dem on the temple with the pommel. Dem collapsed with a groan.

"Quickly!" He grabbed Charlotte's hand and pulled her down the street. They ran with all the speed they could muster.

*

Farthow dropped off the horse and pulled Dem to a sitting position on the street. Dem was conscious, but swooning, and gripped his head with his hands.

"Are you alright man?! Open your eyes!" Farthow held up his oil lamp and saw swift blinking.

"Bastard."

Farthow smiled, then said, "Which way did they go?"

"East. Probably toward the harbor."

"Damn it."

"What's our status?"

"I caught up with Colby. They figured out independently that passage was booked on a cargo ship. Some freebooter from Golice."

"Shit."

"Yes, you reek of it."

"You and that woman's man joke at the wrong times," Dem said as he struggled to his feet.

"If you don't laugh, you'll cry."

"That's what he said."

"Sounds like a real arsehole."

Farthow led the man back to his horse. "Let's get you on and get you to a healer. A real one."

"You mean an apostate?"

"Of course. I don't want you dying of a skull bleed."

"Thoughtful, but what about our quarry?" Dem groaned as Farthow pushed him up into the saddle.

"I'll catch up to them. I think this fellow has been here before, so I have a few ideas about where to find him."

"What if you don't find him?"

"Then we'll be in a spot of trouble, won't we?" Farthow shrugged as he led the horse by the bridle, running alongside to get the beast into a slow trot. "Maybe we'll have to pluck the girl from Vindrel."

*

Charlotte dropped her bag and bent over, breathing heavily and waiting for the ache in her side to dull. They had slowed to a walk for what seemed like miles, but the escape had winded her thoroughly. She took a deep breath and caught herself nearly gagging from the smell of the sewage still clinging to the hem of her skirts. Rone, showing no signs of exertion from the flight, pounded on the heavy wooden door again.

"Damn it, Getty! I know you're in there!" he rasped. Even with the tone of a whisper, his voice carried in the empty courtyard.

A board slid back revealing a peephole. Dim light flickered in the room beyond. A small square mirror appeared, revealing deep-set dark eyes.

"I thought I was rid of you. My debt was paid with your slave."

"What slave?"

"Not too many around here know me as Getty."

Rone grumbled. "Well, you have the opportunity now to turn those tables."

The mirror shifted its angle. "Who's the girl?"

"Not important."

Charlotte looked up and met the eyes, which narrowed on her.

"So that's the rub." The mirror disappeared and the eyes themselves appeared. "I'll probably never get to collect on this debt, will I?"

Rone held his palms up in resignation.

They heard a scraping sound as the door was unbarred and opened, revealing a small room cluttered with books. A desk overflowing with papers sat against one wall, and a small passage opened into a sitting room with an iron stove. The eyes in the door belonged to a lanky older man, clean-shaven with grey hair tied back. He wore a light coat over pants, but was barefoot. He had a pistol in his right hand.

"What exactly do you need at this hour? I can't imagine it's another forgery."

"We just need to sit for a few hours. We'll be out of here before dawn."

The old man chewed his lip. "So, the guard might be busting down my door, is that it?"

"Hopefully not."

Getty sighed and walked to the sitting room. Rone put his pack down and nodded for Charlotte to follow. Getty sat down in one of four chairs. Beside it was a tall pile of books, with plenty of papers stacked between. A tea kettle sat on the stove, not yet whistling. Rone collapsed into one of the chairs and sighed.

Charlotte stood for a long moment, looking at the remaining chairs, then sat down carefully in one of them. She stared at Rone, her eyes trembling. She then buried her face in her hands and began to cry softly. Rone held out his hand to rub her back, but hesitated, let it hover for a moment, and withdrew it. She lifted her head up and wiped her tears, then fixed her face into a serious and relaxed stare.

Rone looked to Getty. "Sorry, things have been rough."

"I can tell. I have a fresh pot brewing here. You're welcome to the tea, but if you need rest, I have that extra bedroom up the stairs."

Rone shook his head. "I don't think I'll be sleeping tonight, but I'll gladly take some space to change clothes."

Getty nodded as the pot began to whistle. "That's a good idea. I didn't want to say anything, but you smell awful."

IX: A Breath

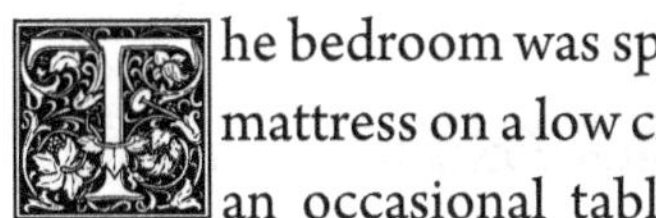he bedroom was sparsely decorated, with an old mattress on a low cracked wooden frame next to an occasional table with a single small chair. Charlotte put her bag against the door after she closed it, then put the pistol on the table. She sat on the mattress, which creaked as it sagged under her weight, and clenched her fists in an effort to get her hands to stop shaking.

"Sorry I got rattled," she said, staring into her lap. "I knew this would be dangerous. I guess I just wasn't prepared for the violence."

"Don't be sorry. It's not something I would have you get used to." Rone sat down and began loosening his shoes, the fine leather caked with mud and other things Charlotte did not want to think about.

"Are *you* used to it?"

"I thought I was," Rone said. He cracked a smile as he pushed his shoes off. "Ah, much better." He rubbed his feet through his grey socks. "Pretty things are rarely comfortable, eh?"

Charlotte smiled. "You're wrong. The finest things always look the best *and* feel the best. Of course, *these* are not the finest things." She reached behind herself and pulled on the knot, hidden under a wide ribbon, that held the built-in corset of her dress. It refused to release.

Rone stood up and unbuttoned his doublet and took it off, revealing a sweat-soaked undershirt. He saw Charlotte struggling and walked over. He leaned past her and pulled apart the knot. She felt an immediate rush as the laces up her back released.

"Thank you," she said. She leaned down to remove her soft shoes, now soaked and torn in a few places. A dull ache in her ribs replaced the release of pressure.

Rone smiled and took his shirt off as he walked back to his pack. "My apologies, but we haven't the time or space for modesty," he said. He slid his pants off and opened his pack, rummaging for his heavier clothes. Charlotte paused and looked at him. She had peeked at him impulsively as he bathed the night prior at the inn, but she had not been able to see much while hiding behind the curtain. What she saw now disturbed her.

His body was pale, drawn in shades of white like hers, but everywhere she could see his skin was mottled with discolored scars of pink and purple. Whip marks crisscrossed his back, and the evidence of smaller wounds dotted his limbs. A single long cut ran along his ribs, old and faded. And yet beneath these scars his skin was taught on a sharp physique; layers of knotted muscles were built onto a frame that looked made to endure.

She tore her eyes from him and stood up. She loosened the laces that cinched her dress at the waist and pushed it down to the ground, taking her soiled underskirts with it. Her bare breasts felt suddenly tight as the night's sweat on them chilled in the open air. She stared at the crumpled dress below her slip for a long moment, then glanced back up at Rone. She locked onto his yellow-green eyes for a moment before he turned away and worked at lacing up his pants.

Charlotte felt herself immediately begin crying again, with a shuddering sob wracking her shoulders. She fell back down to the bed and buried her face. Rone turned about and walked to her.

"Are you alright?" He said, holding his hands out but hesitating to touch her.

"I'm sorry."

"For what?"

"I'm sorry… I'm sorry that I brought you into all this."

"I'm the one who brought you here. I'm the one who dragged you across the mountains, if you'll recall. I'm the one who brought you into the city."

"You know what I mean." She looked up at him with reddened eyes. "Ardala… and now you. You're going to be killed. I know it. I should have just stayed where I was."

"No. You cannot count willful choice on your own conscience. I agreed to take you back to your home. That's my will. My choice." He knelt in front of her and placed his hands lightly, almost cautiously, on her arm. "Ardala made her own choice. I at least have the excuse of money; she didn't. Don't take that away from her."

Charlotte laid her hands on either side of Rone's neck, staring into his eyes. He hesitated for a moment, then inched away. Charlotte leaned up as he moved and pulled his head down into a kiss. She felt his hand on her hip, his fingers pressing into her flesh slightly. She let go.

She waited, her breathing shallow, then Rone turned away, falling back on his haunches. He covered his face with his hands.

"Why?"

"Because," she said, feeling fresh tears in the corners of her eyes. "Because it's my choice. Because you'll in all probability be dead soon."

"Have more faith in me than that."

"Then because I wanted to kiss a man for once in my life of my own volition."

"You shouldn't have."

"I'm tired of you telling me that."

"I'm a professional," he said, standing up.

"It's just a job, then? Just money?"

Rone sighed and shook his head. "You wouldn't understand."

She hunched over and closed her eyes, crying silently again. Charlotte felt Rone's arms wrap around her and pull her up. She laid her head on his shoulder as he hugged her.

"You're going to survive. I'll make sure of it." He looked at her. "Alright?"

"I'm not alright. I'm not *going* to be alright."

"Then just be alive, Charlotte."

He stood up, letting her arms drag around his neck, and looked down on her. His face was hard, but around his eyes a softness lingered, a squint that held back more.

Rone stepped away and retrieved his pack. "We should get dressed. That ship will leave at dawn without us."

*

Rone stepped through the small kitchen into the sitting room and launched himself backward, flinging Charlotte to the ground behind him. Sitting in one of the chairs facing him, drinking a cup of tea, was the man from the inn.

Rone scrambled, dropping his bag and trying desperately to pull his pistol or his dagger and cursing himself for thinking he was safe. He found his pistol in his belt, but as he drew, the hand of Getty settled on his arms and chest.

"No need for that! Nobody is here to shoot!" he said. A gun barrel popped out from beside Rone's hip. Charlotte was kneeling, the long gun shouldered and aimed at Farthow.

Farthow held up his left hand in a gesture of surrender. "I'm here to help! I give you my word."

"I don't believe you," Rone said.

"I know you booked passage on a Golician ship bound for the Northmarch. The captain is a man named Johnny, an old freebooter, though he will certainly claim otherwise. That ship is leaving at dawn, yes?"

Rone frowned at him.

"Tell your girl to put her gun down, by the dreamer!" Getty said.

"Don't shoot unless you need to," Rone said, glancing down at Charlotte.

"Perhaps I should give myself a more proper introduction. I am Farthow Bitterwheat, of clan Bitterwheat in the Southern Greenbacks. I give you my word that I am not here to do harm to you, Rone Stonefield. I swear by the dreamer that I will help you, and the Lady Charlotte, escape from Sarthius Catannel, if I can."

"Any man can name a clan," Rone said.

"But can any man name you, I wonder? I can draw the runes for you, but that would still require trust. I am Somniatel. That should be enough for you to know my word is true." Farthow leaned forward. "Now, I have named what I know, which means others know it. One man in particular, Vindrel, who I think you are familiar with, probably also knows it."

"How are you going to help?" Charlotte said. She lowered her gun and worked herself back to standing.

"I have a few things in mind, but you must trust me," Farthow said. He stood up and put his tea down. He held his left hand forward, palm up. "The armed man is to be feared."

"But the open hand may still carry faith," Rone said, and completed the other half of the ritual, pushing the back of his left hand against Farthow's palm. "I will trust you today. May oblivion take you if you lie."

Farthow nodded. He looked to Charlotte. "Now that the unpleasantness is behind us, let us consider our predicament."

"You have another ship for us?" Rone asked.

Farthow shook his head. "My employer cannot afford to be that overt. I think if we can get you on your own ship and get it out to sea that would be best. There might be a corporate liner going someplace else tomorrow, but I have no idea without heading down to the docks myself, which of course I cannot do."

"You have anything in mind?" Rone said.

"It'll be trouble," Farthow said.

"No different than tonight, then," Charlotte said.

Farthow cocked an eye to Charlotte. "Rumor carries that you're from the deep country and used to shooting and hunting."

"I am," Charlotte said.

Farthow smiled. "Then perhaps I have a good rifle for you. Better than that old smoothbore. Should be handy."

"A rifle?" Charlotte said.

"It's a special type of gun, technically a piece of heresy of course, used a great deal by sharpshooters and the like." Farthow walked to the corner and produced a long gun with a heavy steel barrel. "This belongs to my best man, Dem, but I can buy him another." He handed it to Charlotte. "You'll need a different sort of ball, too. I have some."

Charlotte frowned as she looked the gun over. "You said it was forbidden; why is someone working for the count allowed to keep something like that? Wouldn't the count be angry with you?"

"Who said I worked for the count?" Farthow said, raising an eyebrow.

"Rone did," Charlotte said. "And it makes sense. He's the only person in Masala who would care about retarding the plans of Sarthius Catannel."

Farthow smiled and put his hands up in resignation.

"You didn't answer my question, by the way," Charlotte said. "Does your Count condone heresy?"

Farthow chuckled softly. "What if I told you we had more valuable things than guns at our disposal?

Rone looked down with a smile. "In the world of politics, faith is nothing. Power is what matters. Heresy can be powerful."

"When we can get away with it," Farthow said. He smiled. "Of course, I make sure we always get away with it. Now, you think you can handle that?"

Charlotte nodded.

He gave a sideways look to Rone. "What about you? I've heard you may have a few hidden talents."

"Many," Rone said, "but if you mean magic, I'm afraid I'm as dull as you are."

Farthow smiled. "The talent's dwindling just like our blood, but I'm not completely watered out." He winked.

X: Glamour

The sea was on fire as the sun rose out of it, burning bright with hues of red and orange. A crewman wiped sweat out of his eyes and grumbled about the hard work of the rigging, while others busied themselves carrying crates and rolling barrels up the gangplank and onto the main deck. It was going to be a warm day. The yards were being rigged by a pair of men on the mainsail. The dingy canvas sails burned umber in the brightening sky, still furled and creaking in the morning wind. Two figures in leathers, one in a long coat and one in a cloak, walked up the gangplank to the main deck, sidestepping a few shirtless crewmen. One wore a hood, the other an oversized travel hat, flapping slightly in the wind.

"Good to see you again, Phillip. And looking right and proper this time, too. It even looks like you've traveled before!" Big Johnny walked up to the pair, sticking his pipe back into his teeth. Rone quickly stepped forward and extended a hand. Johnny reached past and slapped Rone hard on the back, causing him to cough.

"If you're not dressed for the road, you've got no business on it," Rone said, smiling from under his hat. He moved to the rail and looked out to sea.

"There are no roads where we're going, lad." Johnny leaned back against the carved rail and spat into the water. "All the same, I had a feeling a silky doublet wasn't really you. You get a sense about these things in my trade. Bright colors have a way of making men like me antsy." He narrowed his eyes.

Rone touched his nose and smiled slightly. "Brown is bright in a sea of color, captain."

"That it is." When the captain turned around, the wind coming off the land in the early sun blew the smoke from his pipe into his eyes, momentarily making him squint. He pulled his black hat lower. "You'll be happy to know we'll be leaving within the next quarter-hour, just as soon as we're done packing the fresh stores. Good, strong wind off the mainland should push us out to the northern current, and we should be into the Pelagian winds by tomorrow afternoon."

"Speed isn't too much of a worry for us. Well," Rone corrected himself, "I'd like to leave on time, but the length of the journey doesn't concern me all that much."

"It concerns me. I'm a merchant. I have ah..." The captain paused a moment and closed one eye, "deadlines to keep." Rone handed him a bag that jingled. Big Johnny immediately pocketed it.

A sailor, who Rone recognized as Pierce from the day before, walked up to the captain and handed over a leather-bound book opened to one of the middle pages. "Everything seems in order, sir. We'll be pulling up the fruit barrels shortly, and I took the liberty of acquiring several fresh barrels of water as well as more dry stock."

Without turning his head from the papers, Johnny shouted, "Quarter-hour me boys! When that sun hits the deck, I expect to be gone. Let's hope the full hold makes up for your empty pockets. Better hope none of you got the rot, because I don't pay sailors to sit sick in the cabin with fire piss!"

Some of the crew cheered and laughed, but most seemed to not even notice the captain's remark. A pack of six men stood idly by, talking to each other.

"Is venereal disease a problem with your crew?" Rone asked, laughing.

"It's a problem with every crew. Can't tell the boys where they should put their precious assets, even if some of them are a bit...rotten." He grinned down at Rone. "Thank the twelve I haven't had sick sailors spread it in the crew."

"I don't remember anyone telling me about all this when I was on a ship." Rone leaned over the rail with the captain.

"No wonder you make interesting small talk. You're a man of the sail then? No, wait, you were a company marine. You have the look of a fighter."

Rone nodded. "I wasn't a good one. Conscription has a way of taking the professional passion out of you."

"Who was it? If you don't mind me asking."

"South Sea Trading Company."

"Not even a proper warship. I'm sorry, mate."

"I'm alive. They aren't. That's enough for me."

The captain frowned with realization and looked about him at the still men on deck. "Why are you standing around?! Pull up them barrels; the wind ain't waiting for us, ya know!" The crew stood motionless; those that had been working now stopped as well to see the commotion.

"It's been a good eight years Johnny." Danny, the thin and gaunt young man from docks the day previous, now wearing a loose-fitting peasant shirt, stepped forward from a small idle crowd of men. In his hand was a pistol, aimed at Johnny. Johnny stood calmly, pursing his lips and rocking on his heels.

"Ah, Danny," Johnny said. "Put that pistol away. Your mum would squint a lemon if she were to see you trying to mutiny."

"This is serious, Johnny," Danny said. "I've stood by while you've led this crew into pointless danger for the last time. I'm doing what my father should have, and taking over controlling share of this enterprise. Be glad it's not at sea."

Johnny turned to Rone. "Sorry you didn't get to know Danny here as the ever-loyal and righteous first mate, making this betrayal all the more biting. Suffice to say," he turned back, looked Danny right in the eye, and said with a flat affect, "I'm shocked."

"You should know better than to transport fugitives."

Johnny laughed falsely. "An old conscript, is that what this is about? Or are you just sore that you have to sleep with the crew for a few more nights?"

"Try a royal kidnaper," a booming voice said. A tall and menacing man in a green jacket, with a black beard and long black hair, stepped forward to stand above them on the quarterdeck, next to the helm. In his hand was a full hilt broadsword and the other held pistol.

"Wish I could say it was good to see you again, Vindrel," Rone said.

"Every time I think it might be good to see you again, I only find you to have fallen further, Rone," the man up top said, his face expressionless.

"I've never cared what you thought of me," Rone called back.

"Royal kidnapping?" Johnny said to himself. The big man for the first time looked genuinely shocked, even scared. Footsteps thundered on the planks as pikemen and musketeers dressed in a uniform of bright green trousers and blue shirts below shining breastplates marched onto the boat from some hiding place on the docks. A few barrels fell from the plank into the water as the crew stepped back to let them pass.

"Perhaps you have not heard, Lady Charlotte," Vindrel began, sounding as cordial as he could while shouting over the sea and wind. "But the Lord King of the Isle, Eric Grasslund the twenty-third, has died, and Sarthius Catannel, your husband, the Count of Cataling, is set to succeed the throne." For a set of seconds that seemed to drag out, only the wind, whipping through the loosened sails, could be heard. "Turn the girl loose and I'll make sure you avoid the torture chamber." Vindrel pulled back the hammer on his pistol. His thick black beard obscured the features of his face, but beneath his hat, his eyes shone out as a green amber.

"A quick death then? I could just as easily have that right here." Rone looked up at Vindrel.

"Don't count on it," Vindrel said. "And it's better than you deserve."

"Why don't you just give me half your commission? That's a better bargain."

"Always joking at the wrong time. You could have had your own commission," Vindrel said, "You could have been a great spymaster – to a king, no less – but once again you are too proud to do anything on account of me."

"Well, without me you'd have no job to do out here, so I'd say I'm entitled to at least twenty percent."

"There's no bargaining your way out of this one. I have you, and the lady, whether you cooperate or not." Vindrel then called out louder, "My lady, please stop cowering behind this vagabond and come to safety. Your husband, the rightful king, is most worried for your safety."

One of the halberdiers on the deck walked toward the trio. He extended his hand toward the figure hiding behind Rone. There was a flash of movement, then he drew back a bloody stump, which he stared at in silence for a few moments before falling to his knees. As he kneeled on the deck he looked under the hood to see a pair of green eyes and a close-trimmed blonde beard that Johnny had missed and that none of the crew had thought twice about; in fact, virtually none of the crew up to that moment seemed to even remember that the figure had been standing on the deck, and those who did could have sworn that it was a small, feminine form, not a broad-shouldered man with a full beard.

"Glamour," Johnny breathed in disbelief, the lone sound that carried over the silence of the bloody moment.

It was Farthow. Crimson drops fell from the dagger in front of him.

The soldier screamed, as if suddenly realizing the horror of his injury.

Before he could react to the bloody spectacle of the shrieking, shocked soldier, Vindrel grunted at a sharp pain in the bottom of his ribs. In surprise, he pulled the trigger of his pistol. Smoke swirled as he shot, but he missed Rone wide, hitting the railing and sending wooden shards and splinters into the face of a nearby mutineer.

"They have cover from the docks!" One of the Cataling soldiers shouted. Several of the soldiers around him joined him in turning toward the docks, suddenly afraid of some hidden enemy in the jumble of tack stacked dockside.

Moments later, Farthow's hood was off and he was running through the deckhands that encircled them, slashing wildly with a broadsword and stabbing with a dagger, leaving arcs of blood where he had stood moments before. Rone at the same time ran forward, batting aside the ends of pikes with his backsword and slashing with his long dagger at wrists and necks. He put down two of the soldiers in front of him with his backsword, who swung their long battle pikes uselessly in the close quarters, before drawing his pistol and leveling it at Vindrel. Rone held the shot, watching the black-bearded man slowly slide down the wooden rail and collapse on the quarter deck near the wheel.

Johnny did not waste the moment of confusion, or spend time wondering over whatever spell Farthow had managed. He drew his cutlass and put it to work against two musketeers, who fired even as their blood splashed on the deck. Johnny was knocked down by a pikeman's knee strike before he could turn to face the men who closed from dockside. Muskets exploded all over the deck, filling the air with black smoke, but Rone and Farthow were already out of the way, hacking a path through the soldiers on either side. Those who still held their live muskets were afraid to fire on their comrades, instead trying to put to use their sidearms. Sailors who had held back from the mutiny, apparently not privy to Danny's plan, now busied themselves with the soldiers and the men surrounding Danny, fighting with blade or grappling as opportunity allowed. Some fought with what was handy – a stick here or a knife there, but already cutlasses were being pulled from the inside racks and put into ready hands.

Johnny, still floored, flinched at the shots and rolled on the deck, trying desperately to avoid the thrusts and slashes of the pikeman above him. He hit his head on the railing after rolling away from a near miss and found himself swooning. When a soldier finally readied himself for a killing blow, pulling his great spear far back past his shoulders, Johnny picked his knees up, reached into his pants, and fired a hidden pistol. The pikeman's breastplate sparked and then began dripping blood from a blackened circle under his ribs.

Within few minutes, though it felt far longer to those in the fight, the struggle on deck began to turn into a rout as mutineers and soldiers, filled with fear and unable to regroup, began to jump off the ship or back down the gangplank. Musketeers, now freed of the burden of friendly fire, unleashed a half-hearted and half-aimed volley up to the main deck, striking a single mutineer by chance but otherwise only pummeling the wood of the ship. Rone rushed forward after the volley and kicked at the gangplank. It wobbled and flexed but did not drop. A pikeman rushed up to stab him and Rone turned aside, then fired his pistol at the man. The shot hit the man high on the thigh, sending him limping backward minus his pike.

Farthow began throwing things at the retreating soldiers: small barrels, bottles, rocks, and chunks of wood – whatever was immediately handy. He knocked over one of the fruit barrels and Rone jumped over to help him push it down the gangplank. It bounced and bounded down, cracking the timber of the plank and knocking two stubborn pikemen into the bay. Three musketeers on the dock, who had failed to see the rout behind them, stopped and looked quickly at one another, their guns spent, then rushed away from the ship as Farthow continued throwing refuse.

Rone turned to look for Big Johnny. The captain stood holding a pistol to Danny, who in turn had a sword trained on him. The surrounding men had stopped to watch, and Rone could not tell who was loyal and who was a traitor.

"You know why I had to do it," Danny said. His eyes were hot with anger and fear.

"Aye, just business and all that. I don't think that'll keep you out of hell though." The captain looked to his left at the dock. "Still time to step off, my boy."

Danny shot forward with his left foot, his sword extending at what would have been a potent thrust, had the sword been a rapier and not a cutlass. Johnny, despite his size, stepped backward just as quickly, and the blow fell short. The hammer of Johnny's pistol snapped forward. The flint sparked and the pan flashed, but the gun failed to fire. Johnny held his arms out in a wide pose. "I guess you got me after all, Danny boy. Tell that pretty mum of yours I went out smiling." Danny drew back to strike the captain, and in turn Johnny, moving in a flash, drew a knife from the small of his back and rushed him.

He stopped short as a spray of blood erupted out of Danny's shoulder, blinding Johnny and causing him to stumble. He recovered quickly, faster than Danny. The big man gripped the first mate's right hand with his own free left, pushing the first mate's cutlass away harmlessly. Johnny drove his dagger home, punching it deep into Danny's chest.

The first mate's muscles went lax and he crumpled to the deck, his sword clanking against the hard oak as he reached for his chest, red death oozing between his fingers. He struggled for a few seconds, breath catching, eyes looking out to nothing, then he ceased to move. A few yards away, Rone and Farthow flinched. Farthow sheathed his blades, turned, and bowed toward the shore.

"Full of surprises," Rone said. He took a deep breath and looked to the rooftop of the closest dock house, where a small shadow stood up and disappeared, two long guns resting on its shoulder. Behind him, the mutineers that remained were holding their hands up, forced into a corner of the deck.

"You better get your lass quick, before the guard figures where the commotion's been. Don't think they'll let you get away just because those weren't Harec's men," Johnny said, cleaning the blood off of his face with a dirty cloth.

"She'll be here shortly," Rone said as he took the steps to the quarter deck.

When he arrived near the helm, what he saw was a desperate and fading Vindrel, a small pool of sticky blood beneath him. He was shoving a short ramrod into his pistol. Rone nimbly kicked the gun away and Vindrel rolled over and looked at him, gasping.

"Looks like you got me." Vindrel croaked. Rone nodded. "I knew you'd never have the balls to fight me square."

"Apparently not. Too bad I didn't get to see if you'd lost a step with your sword."

"Couldn't see if you had or not, being laid out up here, but I guess you've gained a step or two in tactics. Never would have thought with how bad you were at chess and poker"

"I do what I can." Rone kneeled beside Vindrel.

"I thought I had you."

"Every hand is a gamble, Vindy. We both know it."

"Still, this wouldn't be where I'd choose to end this game."

"The game was rigged from the start, I'm afraid," Rone said.

"Why did you take the job? If you only knew the risks-" Vindrel coughed hard again.

"I know the risks."

"Someone's gotta be making you a rich man. Who is it? Tell me before I go."

"I am a rich man. Right now, I'm wealthier than the King of the Isle. I hold his crown, for now."

"If you only knew what she really means... But who are you trading her too, eh? Datalia? Draesen Empire? I don't want to leave without knowing... it's silly, I know."

"You're a mercenary like me. In the end, we only work for ourselves."

"I'm a commissioned officer, Rone." Vindrel coughed.

"All the same."

"I couldn't ask you to do me the favor of giving me what I promised you..."

"You mean a swift death?"

Vindrel's eyes widened. "Aye."

"Sorry Vindy, I can't do that." Rone rolled Vindrel over and ripped the shirt from his back. Low on his ribs he could see the bullet wound, leaking slowly. Ignoring the painful cries from Vindrel, Rone pushed his two longest fingers in and withdrew a malformed slug. "You are a lucky man today. Your ribs stopped the slug dead." Rone pulled a wad of cloth from his pocket and shoved it into the open wound. "This will stop the bleeding till a proper surgeon can stitch you up. I'd say you have a better than even chance of living, but of course you know how bad I am at odds. This is going to hurt."

Rone picked up Vindrel and carried him on his shoulder to the gangplank, dropping him as gently as he could on the dock, which was strangely deserted after the fight. A hooded figure, wrapped in a cloak and worn clothes that revealed a feminine form, was jogging up to the boat with two muskets slung across her back. As she passed, Rone looked under her hood to see a strand of copper hair and a pair of bright blue eyes staring back at him. They trembled, reflecting the bright scene around them, and behind their familiar warmth, Rone detected a dissonance that was new and disconcerting. He felt a moment of remorse for a piece of beauty that he knew could no longer be preserved as it was.

"This isn't much like you, Rone," Vindrel croaked.

"What isn't?" Rone said, turning back to look on the wincing man who was trying to push himself back up on his elbows.

"You leaving a loose end. Why?"

"Things change. Or maybe they don't." He looked away with a sigh. "I've always left loose ends when it comes to you. Don't die, Vindy. I may never have much to wager on a game of poker with you, but I'll risk what I have if I see you again."

"Anchor's up! Let's get out of here!" Johnny's voice called out behind him. Rone could see a group of red and green-clad musketeers moving across the stone freight way toward the dock, walking slowly. With them were a few of the Cataling men, who seemed hesitant to hurry ahead.

"Time for me to go," Rone said. Vindrel looked back up at him, frowning, as if watching something terrible to bear.

"Rone..." he said, trailing off and reaching up to the empty air as Rone trotted up the gangplank. The ship began to move as the plank was hauled up behind him.

XI: Cadence

he boat rocked slightly from aft to stern, causing hanging trinkets in the captain's cabin to jingle. The slanting sunlight cutting through the dingy windows shifted across the table Charlotte shared with Rone and Farthow, who held a whiskey-soaked rag to his bleeding neck. Charlotte felt slightly queasy. She rolled the rifle lightly in her hands, remembering the two men she had shot. Though distant, their faces seemed to return in her idle thoughts.

"Something bothering you?" Rone said.

"I don't know how I should feel," Charlotte said, breaking the silence.

"About shooting those men?" Rone said.

"Do you think he was a bad man?"

"The first mate?" Farthow said. "Mutiny is a death sentence at sea. I'd say you gave him as good as he deserved."

"What about the other one?" Charlotte said. She pulled her hand through her tangled hair absent-mindedly.

"Vindrel's no worse than I am, I suppose," Rone said.

"You know him?" Farthow said.

"You were a member of the guard with him, right?" Charlotte said. "You talked about him before."

Rone nodded. "I've known him a long time. He's a stubborn man. He'll live. What about you?" He craned his neck to look more squarely at Farthow.

"If I die it's going to be an awfully slow and pitiful death." Farthow smiled and turned the rag over to another clean spot. He put fresh whiskey on it and touched it to the wound, wincing slightly. "It's starting to clot up, though I do think I'll be wearing high-collared jackets for a while."

The door swung inward and Johnny swept in, wiping sweat from his face and grumbling. He saw Farthow dabbing at his wound and said, "You owe me twenty cyprals for the whiskey. It was quite the malt, I should tell you."

"I wouldn't know; cuts don't taste anything but burning," Farthow said.

"Not my fault you didn't bother to taste it before wasting it on a cut," Johnny said. He pulled from his desk a set of logs and rolled maps, and threw them on the table.

Farthow shrugged. "Best way I know of staving off blood poisoning." He looked sideways at Johnny. "You're in good spirits for a man who just suffered a mutiny," Farthow said.

"Not just that," Johnny said. "Danny was more than just my first mate. And now I have to bury him. It should never have been this way." His face darkened as he looked over Rone and Charlotte. "Looking death in the eyes and walking away from it has a way of inspiring a certain sardonic humor. Now," his eyes narrowed as he took his own chair at the table. "Just who in the High bloody House of the Divine are you?"

"We told you our names," Rone said.

"You lied," Johnny said.

"You said it was none of your business."

"That was before I had to kill or sack half my crew and become an outlaw in one of my favorite trade hubs."

"I can remedy that," Farthow said.

"I'd appreciate the gesture – that is, I *would* if I knew who the hell *you* were as well," Johnny said.

"Farthow Bitterwheat, spy, apostate, and waster of whiskey, at your service." He nodded his head.

Johnny produced a pipe then set about looking for a match in his pockets. "Things have gotten complicated, and I need to know who I'm taking on."

Charlotte straightened up. "I am Melanie Halbara. That is all you need to know."

"Is it?" Johnny said. "Yesterday your name was Halbara Melanie."

Charlotte felt herself begin to blush and raised her chin even higher. "I believe you misheard."

"Where are you from?"

"We are… from the lowlands."

Johnny found a match in one of his many pockets and began lighting the pipe. "Not with hair like that you're not. You're from the Northmarch or I'm a slug. And this sell-sword of yours is definitely highland stock. That fellow you shot was an officer from Cataling; pity I didn't catch what he called you." He let a large smoke ring fly, then leaned forward. "Let me say, Charlotte, that rumors of the beauty of the Lady of Winter fall short of reality."

"I don't know what you are talking about," Charlotte said. She looked to Rone to see wide eyes over a blank face.

"I told you that you can't lie to a liar." Johnny laughed and smoke escaped from his nostrils. "That painting of you in Maragard doesn't do you justice." He raised an eyebrow to Rone.

Rone raised his chin and sucked in his cheeks. "My name is Rone. That should suffice for you."

Johnny grumbled and chuckled at the same time. "And I always tell people Johnny is enough to shake on. Fair enough." He spread out one of the maps. "My next question is to why we have no pursuit. Sailing off seems a bit too easy. You have something in store for me?" He laid a closed inkwell on a corner of the map to hold it down.

"Usually if something is too easy somebody has their hand in it. In this case, it was Drath Harec, who will be very grateful for your involvement, Mister..." He raised his eyebrows expectantly.

"Just Johnny, like I said." He drew on the pipe again. "Why?"

Farthow shrugged. He looked at Rone for a moment, smiled and said, "Why not?" He looked at Johnny. "Although distantly related to Count Catannel, Drath is still in succession for the throne in an eventual sort of way, and the ancient code of the Isle holds that in order for a king to be crowned there must be a queen to crown as well. Political opportunity abounds when there's no monarch to be found. There's more to it than that, of course, but I can't tell you most of it."

"Ah, the spiders of nobility, in whose twisted webs we common folk are but flies," Johnny said.

Farthow looked to Charlotte. "I had also promised to help you leave here in one piece. We had originally intended to take over your ladyship's chaperone position." Farthow bowed his head. "But not with intent to harm you, of course. If only you had gone to Dem's house..." He smiled and shook his head. "Drath will make a good show of trying to apprehend the kidnappers, but it will seem that the bandits had a ship that could mysteriously sail against the wind. Perhaps some work of sorcery. The story will tell that even the Count's best interceptors had to sail far out to sea before they were able to turn north, and unfortunately, the ship was nowhere to be found – vanished."

"So now I'll be labeled a heretic *and* an outlaw."

"You *aren't* an outlaw?" Rone said. Johnny narrowed his eyes.

"I wouldn't worry about it," Farthow said with a smile. "The dockmaster is not a fastidious record keeper, as I'm sure we shall soon find out."

Johnny looked over the map, which showed most of the North Pelagian between Veraland and the High Isles, with the divine strand, the Petty Kingdoms, and the greater parts of the mainland missing from the bottom of the chart. He pointed at an island near the southern end of a great archipelago. He glanced at Farthow "Now I'm carrying an extra man, and not the sort I like. Can you find your way from Nantien?"

"I thought we were going to Golice?" Charlotte said. She stood up straighter.

"That was before half my crew got slaughtered or run overboard," Johnny said.

"Upset that we saved your skin?" Farthow said.

"It was you that put it on the boil, you bastard," Johnny said. "But either way I'll have to dock before Golice to hire more crew. Calling what I've got a skeleton is giving too much credit to the crew and too little to bones. I also know a goodly portion of our stores were left on the docks. There'll be no room on this ship for idle hands the next few days."

"In that case, I think I can depart a bit sooner than Nantien," Farthow said. "We're not out to the open sea just yet, are we?"

"No, I was counting on the line ships being unable to rig effectively against this crosswind."

"Good," Farthow said with a smile.

"What do you mean by idle hands?" Charlotte asked. "You don't expect a woman to do the work of a deckhand, do you?"

Johnny cracked his sardonic smile once again. "I'll make it easy on you. I'm a fair man. I'll pay you a hand's wage."

"Out of what we already gave you, you mean?"

Johnny crossed his arms. "I'm a fair man. Foul too, but mostly fair."

*

The ship moved past a large cliff of white stone that descended into a pile of rocks, defying the grinding surf and remaining jagged and ugly. A wide cove opened up on the other side, filled with turquoise water and sands as pale as the rocks. The sea was calm inside the cove and sparkled with the morning sun. At the captain's barked orders, two of the sailors hurried to the bow of the ship and trimmed the foresails and jibs. The ship slowed and begin bobbing very gently.

"That's quite a sight," Rone said, squinting his eyes from beneath his wide-brimmed hat. "Pity nobody lives out here to enjoy it."

"Not much reason to be out here, anymore. Pretty views don't make up for a bad harbor and bad soil." Farthow was stripped down to his waist and was busy stuffing his clothes and other implements into a leather bag. "But it does have its uses to the Count. You may not be able to see it, but there's a path in that deep-set ravine of rocks carved out by an old creek." Farthow pointed to a dark scar in the mottled white cliffs. "You can follow that up and out and make your way to the west side of Masala. Keep it in mind if you ever need to slip back in unnoticed."

"So, you won't be going to the mainland with us then?" Charlotte asked.

"Not today. I may have to go in a bit if a particular piece of the master's business doesn't sort itself out. Till then I have other duties within the city. Shadows to hide in, eaves to drop, the usual business." Farthow slung his bag across his back, the strap running from his right shoulder to his left hip. He dropped his voice to sound just above the wind. "Before I go, keep a few things in mind. The captain knows too much. I recommend you part company when you find it convenient, perhaps Nantien. It would also be wise to keep using aliases." Farthow began putting his blades into a second tightly constructed leather bag, which had an oversized cork bottle cap on the end.

"I've known the wisdom in that since before we got here, but we'll keep traveling under other guises," Rone said.

"Make sure of it. No doubt there will be a price on your head and her body after today, and I imagine it will be quite large. Last piece of advice: beware of trickery. If it's an agent of mine or the count's, we'll bear a Masala green and maroon flag, but only trust it if there is a stripe of gold thread between the two. It's our hidden detail. Likewise, only trust messages bearing a seal with a gold, green, and maroon ribbon. That is the only way you will know it is truly from our camp. Other people may now suspect our assistance, so you must not overlook that detail."

"Thank you. You shall have me if you need me," Rone said, extending his hand.

"I'll keep you to that, Rone." The two shook hands. "I've got to get back. Thanks for the adventure of this evening and morning. A life that isn't dull is one to hold on to."

"Farewell, and thanks for everything," Charlotte said. "I will remember it, whatever my fate."

Farthow looked hard in her eyes for a moment before turning to face the turquoise cove and white cliffs.

"Almost forgot," Farthow said, turning back suddenly. He jogged up to the stair to the quarter deck. He pulled a small leather bag from his pocket and threw it to Johnny. He shouted, "The Count appreciates your burden and your discretion in all matters."

Johnny felt the weight of the bag. He shook his head. "You bunch are a heap of trouble. And cheap bastards, too."

"Remember what I told you!" With that, Farthow dove off the side of the ship and plunged into the water. Small fish leaped out of the waves as he splashed. He surfaced with his two packs floating behind him and began to swim to shore.

"Watch out!" Johnny yelled as a rope flew over the heads of Charlotte and Rone, snapping taut as one of the sails filled with air. Two sailors worked to slacken the sail, letting it fill more deeply with wind, and the boat began to rock before slowly moving away from the land. Charlotte and Rone watched Farthow reach the shore and disappear into the foliage as the ship picked up speed, heading northeast. "Once we get out into the proper channel wind, let's unfurl those mainsails and get moving!" Johnny yelled to two other sailors standing mid-deck.

"He sure was insistent about the gold thread," Charlotte said quietly to Rone.

"It's because he's sure to send word for us, otherwise he probably wouldn't have bothered," Rone said. "That's not what I wanted." He turned and walked toward the forecastle, stopping to lean on a rail and look to the north. "But we're alive and on our way. I'll gladly take on a debt for that."

"Thank you," Charlotte said. She stood beside him, watching him rather than the ocean. "You could have left me."

Rone looked at her and frowned. "I told you to have a little faith."

"I have more than a little now."

Rone smiled slightly. "Good. There's a long way left to go still. Hopefully less trouble, but if not, at least I know I've got a decent marksman at my side."

"I hired you to deal with the dirty work," Charlotte said, smiling. "The way I see it, I already ought to dock your pay."

Rone broadened his smile. "If I was just in it for the money, I'd have turned you over to Farthow."

"Why didn't you?"

Rone shrugged. "I'm weak to a pretty face, I guess."

Charlotte looked out to the sea, blushing slightly. "I won't complain about it."

End of Book I

Tyrant's Gallow

Moonsong, Book II

By
David V. Stewart

Walda

North
Pelagian
Sea

Tyrant's Gallow

Interlude II: Divinity

Claire stood at the edge of the castle chapel, staring through a clear space in one of the windows. The image of the shore beyond was blurry through the ancient glass. The sun cast on her face and the floor about her a multitude of colors. She sighed.

"You're looking rather morose."

Claire startled and then quickly dropped to a knee and bowed before the Grand Cleric, who stood before her already arrayed in his robes of office bearing two red stripes, but not yet wearing his heavy iron crown. He was a man that, had he been a commoner, would have been considered old; his hair and beard were grey and his face was lined with wrinkles. As clergy, his sixty years was well short of even retirement age.

"Apologies, master Gibson," Claire said, spreading her robes about her, covering her feet in a gesture of modesty few in Veraland would recognize. Gibson touched her hair lightly, and she looked up to see his smiling face.

"It is good to see you, Claire," he said. "I have spent too long enduring the company of seamen and temple guardians. Please rise, my friend." He held out a hand, and she took it as she stood up again. He squeezed it softly before he released it. "Yes, it is good to have the company of a friend once again."

Claire nodded. "Likewise, master. I have missed the company of the cloth."

"Come now, Claire, I am speaking of friendship, not of camaraderie, though I hope we will ever strive for the same purposes."

"Of course, my apologies."

"No more apologies and no more titles, Claire." He turned and began walking casually through the double doors into the circular castle chapel, as large as any church on the Isle, and twice as richly decorated. A large clock was set into the center altar, displaying three o'clock. "Here, in the church, we are friends, if not equals."

Claire smiled at him.

"I had a chance to drop in on your daughter some months ago. She is learning well, despite her age, as I knew she would."

"Good. Is she happy?"

"Yes, I think so. She has a small cadre of friends. They are more concerned with the boys from the art school than their own education, but they are good friends. The boys... well, they are good, too. I may arrange a courtship for Maribel with one that has a particular eye for architecture that I expect to work for the church one day."

"You know my heart too well, Gibson," Claire said. She glanced at the clock. "The count and heir apparent should be here at four if you wish to receive him."

"I do." For clergy as high as a Grand Cleric, second only to the Hand of the Divine, kings did not *command* audience. Kings were *admitted* to the cleric's presence at his discretion.

"He will be accompanied by his minister of war."

"I had anticipated this."

"Then you know that Charlotte has gone missing."

Gibson paused and turned to Claire, frowning and puzzled. "No, I did not know this." He shook his head. "War... yes, I knew of that. I was to coronate him, I thought. That would demand the lady as well."

"You arrived quickly. News travels fast. I assumed you knew everything."

"For me, it travels fast. I had not anticipated Grasslund's death, just so you know."

"I wouldn't accuse you."

Gibson nodded and looked to the ornate altar that sat at the center of the lofty room. Gilded representations of the twelve gods faced in a circle. Verbus, the god of death and words, faced the entranceway. Claire felt a shiver as she looked at the god's carved chin. His eyes were obscured by a hood.

Gibson sighed. "What will be my errand here, now? I cannot legally crown a king and not his queen. There are many words in the divine texts that can be bent, or even ignored, but not that one. Not when the nobility is already testing their relationship with the church. I must be firm."

"Perhaps we can say Charlotte was killed in her escape."

"What?" Gibson's frown deepened as he looked down on Claire.

Claire hesitated and took a deep breath. "We conclude that she was killed, then Sarthius will be free to remarry and receive the crown. The queen in the Green Isle is, at best, a figurehead."

"Your suggestion is not what shocked me. Indeed, it is a practical solution, if a bit prone to some distasteful speculation by the lesser gentry." His frown deepened. "No, you said she escaped. *Escaped.* What do you mean by this?"

Claire felt her pulse quicken as she realized her slip. "We are friends." She did not pose it as a question, but the silence turned it into one.

"You can trust me." Gibson's blue eyes burned at Claire, but their intensity came not from anger, but something else further inside. Claire thought it looked like fear or anxiety – deep an sincere.

"Charlotte of the Plain did not abide her station," Claire said. "Thrice she sent pleas to King Vegard of Hviterland, her uncle, requesting suit for annulment or divorce. I know this because Sarthius Catannel intercepted and held all these letters. Only the first was sent openly, in naïve belief Charlotte's seal would be respected."

"It should have been."

"But you know the nobility as well as I," Claire said. She collapsed into a chair beside a pew and let her brown hair fall around her face. Gibson let himself down onto a nearby bench. "I do not blame her, Gibson. I cannot. What Sarthius did... what he *does* to... others. It is very vicious. *Very* vicious."

"Will you not say more?"

"I cannot. I dare not, even if I knew everything. What I do know would turn your stomach and turn your hair white even without your years. Spend a night out of your robes in a common room in the city below. The rumors will not be far from the truth." A hand rested on her leg lightly, and she looked up to see Gibson, his eyes trembling.

"What has he done to you, Claire?"

"To me?" Claire shook her head and let out a sigh. "Not what you are thinking. He has despoiled me of my integrity, of my security, of most my worth to you and to our church, but he has not despoiled me of *that*, Gibson. I am in no danger there."

"I will quietly re-assign you."

"No!" Claire said. Her voice boomed in the hall. As the echo died, another set of doors opened, and the sounds of Gibson's attendees filled the silence. Claire spoke a soft growl, "No, that will do no good. Not for me, and not for my daughter. And not for whoever you send in to replace me in this chapel. Here I can do good. I can guide, I can push, even if it is a bit impotent. I can observe and report. And I can betray if needed. It is best to keep me here, Gibson."

Gibson nodded. "The snares of the nobility can be cruel. We view Sarthius as a useful tool, if a cruel one. I apologize for his necessity."

Claire nodded back. "So many tangles." She looked up to the altar, her eyes almost glazed. "You had a nice boy in mind for Maribel?"

"There are many boys that are nice and years yet to introduce them."

Claire smiled. The attendants began to file in, their colorful uniforms bright in the placid chapel. "Good. We are nearing the time, your grace. You will need your crown to receive the king in his dedication to you."

*

Sarthius Cattanel scratched his freshly shaven chin and examined himself in the mirror. He wore the livery of a coronation: a long plush cape enveloped his shoulders and trailed behind him on the carpet. His hose and shined shoes stood a stark black beside the white and gold of his trousers and jacket. He flicked his long fingers, and gold rings clacked together.

"You look excellent, sire," Blotella said. She stood nearby, her hands on her hips. A smile cracked her wrinkled face. "You have a good frame for a king."

"Image can have such power if you frame it right. That's the trick, though. Framing the image. Controlling who sees it, to produce the effect you desire."

Blotella looked puzzled, then bent down to adjust part of the taper of the cape. "We'll want to tack this in a bit before the actual coronation."

"I think I rather like it as it is," Sarthius said. "In fact, I intend to wear it now."

Behind him, Lord Marcus Grantell grumbled. Sarthius turned to look at his minister of war with curious, raised eyebrows.

"My apologies," Marcus said. He leaned his girth back, straining the buttons on the front of his military jacket. His black beard, flecked with grey, stood out from his chin stiff and waxed.

"I expect you to make your feelings understood, not felt," Sarthius said.

"Noted," Marcus said.

Sarthius felt a pang of frustration. Marcus was, until the coronation proper, on equal footing as a titled landowner, and he intended for Sarthius to know it. Though his estate contained only a few small villages and he was as distant from the throne as most peasants, he was still high nobility according to law.

"Well, what is your consternation about?"

"Wearing that get-up to be received by the High Cleric," Marcus said. "It sends a message that we do not need right now."

"That I am the proper king? But I am."

"*That* you are, but you are not being crowned today."

"But I should be. That is the message."

"The cleric will view you as overly ambitious. Unwilling to submit to the supremacy of the church."

"Of course he will."

Marcus pursed his lips.

Sarthius chuckled. "It is all part of the game, Marcus. We must seem dangerous for the church to view us as a powerful tool, and we must seem corruptible for them to want to control us."

Marcus nodded, chewing the inside of his lip.

"But of course, Marcus, it is *us* who will use *them*. But they mustn't think that."

"You're playing at a game the church has mastered for the better part of forty centuries."

"And the nobility has played that game with them." Sarthius turned and swept his cape, unmindful of the seamstress at his feet. "Come, let us set our benefactors on edge." Marcus hesitated to stand, and Sarthius widened his sardonic smile. "You must trust me, Marcus. Veraland shall be yours in time."

*

The ceremony – the coronation that was not – took place with nothing but proper pomp. Sarthius Catannel dressed as a king, though he was not one, and walked proudly beside his minister of war who was not a minister, since only the king could make such appointments. Marcus Grantel, standing erect in his formal jacket, was the kind of choice for a war office that only the most ambitious king would make. The Crow of the Highlands was known for his ruthlessness as much as his cunning. Rumors circulated constantly of his butchery. He had left bloodied bodies where they fell and dined of the field of battle after slaughtering the remnants of the southern Highland Clans, watching his favorite carrion birds have their much-loved supper of heretic eyes and tongues. Many enemies had he made in the southern reaches of the Isle, and not just among the farm folk that descended from the Dream worshippers of old. High Lord Bautchel had famously placed a price upon Marcus's head for three years, withdrawing it only at the behest of the now-dead King Graslund.

Only a man intending to *use* a weapon like the Crow would place Marcus Grantel in such a high position of power.

Claire turned these things over in her mind as she stood to the side of the Grand Cleric and watched the bowing and careful recitation of ancient, now nearly empty, words. Nobody acknowledged Sarthius's gesture of royalty, not even Sarthius himself. The king-that-would-be wore his smile as the ceremony passed into conventional conversation. Claire felt sick looking at that smile, and all that she imagined that it hid.

I: Nantien

The echoing thud of heavy footsteps woke Charlotte from her fitful sleep. Dreams of a great void surrounding the ship, bearing it through an ocean of dread toward a field of strange stars, faded into the reality of the sea and its constant sway. She felt the unwelcome return of the slight nausea that had plagued her since her escape from Masala.

Amid the chaotic percussion shaking the ceiling, she could hear voices, but the words were too muffled to be understood. She rose slowly from the straw mattress, rubbing her eyes and trying focus in the darkness of the small cabin. She still wore her white gown; a few light spots showed on the formerly pristine silk. She drew a blanket around herself, stood up, and cracked the door. Rone stood on the stairs outside, his arms crossed and cradling a musket. A flickering oil lamp hung on a nearby hook.

"What is it?" she said. Rone glanced at her before looking back out the door above him.

"Ship ahead. We're likely right on it to be seeing it at night and in the rain."

"Why is everyone scrambling?"

"We don't know if they are friendly or not. Is your rifle loaded?"

"Yes, I think so. You think there will be fighting?"

"As likely as not." He glanced at her again. "You should be dressed."

Charlotte turned back to the room and began hurriedly assembling her clothes by the lamplight leaking through the cracks in the door. She paused as she pulled off her gown; she imagined Rone's eyes upon her naked back and felt a strange unease. A sort of silence had settled between them since Masala, and Rone never brought up the kiss they had shared – that she had *stolen.* She stepped back toward the door and shut the last inch of it, plunging her into total darkness. By touch, she pulled on her trousers and the faded, rough shirt she had grown to hate over the past weeks.

Charlotte checked the prime on her rifle's lock with a finger, nodded to herself, and went back to the door. When she opened it, Rone was gone, so she hurried up the steps to the main deck. Outside, the small crew stood crowded toward the gunwale. A scrawny young sailor continued to howl from the crow's nest above them.

"All I can see is fire!"

"Can you see the island or not? Is it only ships?" Pierce was standing on the main deck, with hands on his hips, shirtless despite the cold mist coating every surface. The sky on the other side of the crowd glowed orange. She picked out Rone's silhouette, his wide-brimmed hat giving him away in the gloom.

"I think I see buildings. I'm not sure!" the sailor in the crow's nest called back.

A door slammed behind Charlotte and she turned to see Johnny walking out of his cabin with a large spyglass in one hand and an unbelted cutlass in the other.

"Out of the way!" he growled. Thecrowd of men parted to let him walk up to the forecastle.

"Cap'n on deck!" Pierce called, but none of the men seemed to care.

Johnny's spyglass had a massive front objective on it and telescoped out to a length too great to hold. He threw down his cutlass and rested the spyglass on a rail. Johny's immense hight forced him to lean over almost double to look into it. While Johnny scanned the horizon, Rone followed Pierce up the stairs and stood behind the captain; there was a strange sight in the distance.

"Shit. Looks like a regular battle is taking place." Big Johnny pulled away from the eyepiece and raised an eyebrow. He waved at Rone. "Come here."

Rone stepped forward and bent over to look into the spyglass, which Johnny continued to hold against the rail. Rone pulled away for a moment, squinting and blinking, before looking through it again.

Charlotte pushed her way gently through the crew, shielding her eyes from the mist. The ship rocked hard as she pulled herself up to the gunwale, and she would have fallen had Pierce not seen her slipping and grabbed her arm at the last moment. It seemed a bright fire blazed in the distance, but she couldn't tell what was burning. Charlotte could, however, hear the droning report of canons over water.

"The whole port is on fire, it looks like," Rone said, leaning back to look at Johnny. "Not so much a naval battle as a sacking, I'd say."

"I didn't ask you to look because I'm blind. Do you recognize the ships?" Johnny said. He let go of the spyglass and turned away, looking to the crow's nest with his arms out for some kind of input. The man up top didn't answer.

Rone looked back into the glass.

"Most of the ships aren't flying colors," he said. "Those that are have a yellow stripe on some kind of dark-colored field. It's hard to see."

"That's the flag of Nantien's fleet," Johnny said.

"They've been routed," Rone said. "I see a few trying to abandon the port. Most are in flames."

"What about the other ships?" Johnny asked.

Rone was silent a moment. "Those ships are galleys, and an older style, too. Draesen Imperial warships or I'm a fool."

"What?"

"Never seen one?"

Johnny grumbled. "It's been about twenty years. You sure?"

"It's the right type. I can see the shadows of oars."

Rone stood up and handed the spyglass back to Johnny. Johnny hunched down again and looked back out to the sea of fire.

Rone caught sight of Charlotte and stepped toward her. With a smile, he took his hat off and placed it on her head.

"It seems trouble comes ahead of you, as well as behind," he said, pushing up the brim of the hat to reveal Charlotte's eyes. "That's Nantien. Or was"

Charlotte looked out over the black waters, ripples of black nothing like those in her dreams, though they filled her with the same feeling. The clouds above the island reflected the battle like a dim red sunrise.

"I'll be damned," Johnny said. "I think you've got to be right. What are they doing all the way out here? Can't be a slave raid."

"That doesn't make any sense," Pierce said. "Draesen? They would have to have sailed through the entire Barrier Sea. That's a thousand leagues of hotly contested water, with Datalian Navy and corporate frigates swarming all the ports."

"Unless they came another way," Rone said with a shrug. Johnny turned around and looked at him, hotness in his gaze.

"A campaign?" the captain said. He looked away for a protracted few moments. "It could be, at that. But in the north?"

"I don't see how it could be anything else," Rone said.

"The tundra will be melting," Charlotte said, watching the fires. "They could be sailing to the Northmarch. May I look?" A memory from her distant childhood hovered on the edge of her mind, blurry and yet stark. It was an image of a strange-looking man with inhuman skin and eyes.

Rone turned back and frowned at her, but did not inquire more. He nodded to the spyglass.

Charlotte bent down and put the glass to her eye. After a few moments of searching, she caught the sight of the battle

What she saw was spectacular. A fleet of ships moved in and out of focus, drifting past each other. Cannons lit up randomly along the heavy sides of warships. Sails were on fire and withering. Entire ships were ablaze, raging as they sank. Behind the battle, she could see a port town leaning up against a large black hill, lit by dozens of fires. Flames shot up suddenly from one of the buildings on the water. She could see small shadows – people, though they looked more like ants, or fleas – running through the backdrop of yellow and red. The burning building, a fortress of some sort, suddenly grew bright. A wall collapsed, and a great black and red cloud mushroomed into the sky.

"Do you recognize the ships, too?" Rone said.

Charlotte stood back up and rubbed her eye. "I don't know anything about ships. I was hoping to see one of… them."

"A Draesen?" Rone said.

"Yes."

"We'd have to get a lot closer to see people," Rone said.

"I'm not getting any closer to see them, and I'm not sticking around to find out why they're here," Johnny said. "Hard to port!"

"You mean starboard?" Rone said. "Golice is east."

"Hard to port, I say!" He looked at Rone with a slight smile as he picked up and collapsed the massive spyglass. "You can trust me to sail. We'll be far too hard-pressed to make it to Golice undermanned and with most of our supplies sitting on the dock in Masala."

"Bergan is east, too."

"Bergan? Boy, it's been plagued for a quarter year. Haven't you heard?" Johnny looked Rone in the eye and spat off the bow. He withdrew a compass from his waistcoat and flicked it. "Turn us to two-hundred sixty degrees!" He looked over at the wheel to see that it was unmanned and roped tight. He grumbled and sighed. "I have to do bloody everything around here, eh?"

"Where are we going?" Charlotte called out as Johnny stomped down the stairs.

"Tyrant's Gallow," Johnny said. He didn't look back, but Charlotte was sure he was smiling.

*

The usual dinner Rone and Charlotte had with the captain was quiet, the only sounds for a long time being the scraping of forks on the captain's rough personal plates. The whole crew had been silent for most of the day as they left Nantien, and whatever conflict had consumed it, behind. Improving weather had not lifted the mood that hung on the ship like a layer of fog.

"Do you really want to take the ship to the lion's den?" Charlotte said once the food was almost finished.

"If it's the lion's den, then I'm a lion," Johnny said, abandoning his fork and the soft vegetables there and leaning his chair back. He drew long on his pipe, the glow from which lit his eyes in a dark red hue. He blew out a large smoke ring above him, which disappeared as it hit the cold ceiling of the cabin.

"There's no king there," Charlotte said. "No law. Rampant sorcery, heresy, and..." Johnny started to laugh. Charlotte grumbled and turned away, feeling suddenly foolish and hot in the face.

"Cannibals? Human sacrifice? Old tales for children, dear," Johnny said.

"The crew won't tell you they don't like it, but I can see and feel their mood, even if you can't."

Johnny laughed harder and fell back toward the table. "They're worried it'll be hit, too. You don't have much of a line on my men. These are the sort to mourn the Gallow, not be afraid to pull into port."

"Tyrant's Gallow has a reputation both earned and unearned," Rone said. He sat with his arms crossed and looked at Charlotte. "I've never been there, but I've known enough travelers to tell you it isn't the place of debauchery and horror you always hear tales about."

"Oh, there's plenty of debauchery," Johnny said as smoke escaped his nostrils. "It's just not *all* hookers and opium."

Rone gave the captain an appraising look, then said to Charlotte. "There are, believe it or not, great merchant lords there, men who keep a good measure of control and order over the place." Rone said.

"Oh, those are the biggest villains of all." Johnny said. "Privateers have got nothing on the plays of the rich. And when you're talking rich privateers, ah, well..." He smiled and licked his lips. "That's a dangerous lot. But it's as good as place as any in the North Pelagian to find able hands. Probably a better place to find fellas who want to buy in, since we've had so many shares open up recently. Then we'll be on to Golice."

"Buy in?" Charlotte raised an eyebrow at Johnny.

"This is a private ship, deary," Johnny said. "A lot of those mutineers back in Masala were stockholders. Get paid by the ship's profits rather than a standard salary. Very lucrative for those trying to move up in the world, if a bit higher in risk."

"Who exactly owns this ship?" Charlotte asked.

"I own thirty-six percent. A goodly portion is owned by a wealthy trader in Golice, who fronted most of the capital for the purchase. The rest is – or was, rather – owned by the crew."

"So, when you joked and said you'd pay me a deck hand's wage, you meant you'd be signing over a portion of the ship's stock, right?" Rone asked.

"You already paid enough to buy out me and the rest of the crew. I could write you out some stock if you like, but will you be hanging around the Northmarch much to be collecting dividends, I wonder?"

"I may yet," Rone said. "I don't see myself going home."

"Veraland is home, eh?" Johnny said.

"I didn't say that."

"Yes, you did." The captain laughed.

*

Charlotte stood beside Rone as the tall, mountainous island grew larger, rising from the horizon as the ship sped on toward it. Eventually, the details of the kingless port of Tyrant's Gallow fell into place. The city was massive, surrounding a wide cove full of ships. On one side, cramped and stacked grey buildings went up a rolling mountainside, and on the other gleaming white cliffs backed towers and tile roofs, the tops of the city's mansions. From a distance, the city seemed well-planned, the whole thing designed to grow up the mountain which sheltered it, like a many-terraced castle. Long docks intersected the grid of the harbor, and dozens of ships, some flying colors and others without flags, floated there lazily.

"I must admit, it's other than I expected," Charlotte said.

"What did you expect?" Johnny said through a laugh. He was wearing a wrinkled brown jacket with tassels on the shoulders, and a shirt that was close to white. His large head and beard stuck out of the poorly-tailored clothes unflatteringly, and to Charlotte, he looked quite out of character.

"Are you planning on attending a state dinner?" Rone said.

Charlotte chuckled. "If drunken thieves have a king, maybe."

"Well, the Gallow can be a fancy sort of place, and I *am* trying to find some marines interested in stock options." Johnny tugged on his jacket. "Appearances can make or break a sale."

"I'm sure," Charlotte said. "You know, I must say this city is actually quite beautiful. I expected a decrepit pirate village, lawless and on fire."

"Oh, there's probably a few pirates here, lass, but burning buildings is generally bad for business, even for them. It's buildings that have all the loot, you know."

A splash erupted on the port side, followed by a cannon report. Charlotte flinched, and Rone instinctively reached for the pistol hidden in his jacket. "Are they shooting at us?" A bunker far in front of them had a puff of smoke coming from it.

"Relax, it's just to get our attention," Johnny said. He turned around and yelled, "Get the port colors out, white field!" Two men scrambled and started running a flag up the pulleys of the mast. The wind caught it near the top, and it shot out proud: two squares of blue and two squares of black set against a white field. Two small shots sounded over the water. "Excellent," Johnny said to Rone, "Our port of call isn't on the shit list."

"What happens if it is?" Rone asked.

"We fly a different flag." Johnny said.

"They already saw the first one, though."

Johnny shrugged. "I don't make the rules. I just follow them."

"Of course, you do," Rone said.

Johnny stepped away, giving orders to a few nearby men regarding the sails and the other riggings.

"What are you thinking?" Charlotte said, noticing Rone's frown as he looked at the city. He nodded to a corner by the captain's quarters. She stepped into the shade with him.

"I'm wondering whether we stay on board or not," he said quietly. "I would normally say it would be safer to stay here, but..."

"You don't trust the captain."

"He's suffered on our account," Rone said. "There's no perfect option, as I expect that the fact that we are wanted on the Isle will be known here soon, if it isn't already. So, how do we hide from the eyes that are looking for us? Do we risk being in a place where we can't leave if they come looking? The crew here may be loyal to Johnny, but they're all pirates by my standards. I don't trust any of them."

"Well, then, we go ashore," Charlotte said.

Rone nodded. "Let's go pack. If we can leave with Johnny, we do so, if not, I'm sure we can find another ship to somewhere in the Northmarch, maybe even Hviterland itself."

II: The Gallow

he ship slowed as it approached a dock where a boy stood waiving a tall orange flag. Pierce and the other crew members threw the hawsers to a few shirtless dockhands as they closed the gap. They tied them down, and the Parkitees's crew began to pull the thick ropes back in, inching the ship closer to the dock until the hull made contact. Chains clanged as the anchor dropped and they set the gangplank down. Johnny strode down with an air of arrogance as a small bespectacled man wearing a tailored blue jacket and a matching set of pantaloons walked to the end of the dock. He was carrying a ledger and a pencil.

"Good afternoon, Mister, uh..." He looked up at Johnny.

"Johnny. Just Johnny."

"Very well, mister Just Johnny; my name is Reginald." He smiled as he extended his hand. Johnny shook it, narrowing his eyes. The little man ignored the expression and looked at his ledger. "The docking fee is six Argents, plus you owe an additional fifty-seven cyprals."

"What for, eh?"

"The cannonball and the powder to fire it. It's not our fault you forgot to fly your colors, mister Just Johnny." Without taking his eyes off the man, Johnny rustled around in the purse hanging from his belt and produced six large silver coins. They clinked as he dropped them in the little man's hand, who glanced at the varied sizes and heads effaced upon them with a smile.

"Ship name?"

"Parkitees." Johnny handed him a stack of large copper coins, equally unmatched in dimensions and design. Reginald weighed them casually before dropping them into his bag and withdrawing a handful of tiny copper cyprals.

"Excellent, sir. Can I ask the reason for your visit?"

"Oh," Johnny said, "Nothing to sell or deliver. We're here for minor re-supply and re-staffing."

"Very well, it should be fairly easy to find both. Mind that my dock is only for a week's stay at most. If you want to drop anchor for longer, you'll have to talk to someone else."

Johnny nodded to him and walked on, his hand on his long cutlass. Rone and Charlotte followed close behind him.

*

Gold Street was a long and rambling street, packed with enough people to make pulling a wagon through highly impractical. On each side, and often pushing into the common cobbled path, were awning-covered stands filled with merchants. The various types of goods seemed to be clustered together. Whether this was by decree or chance, Rone could not tell. Fishmongers were closest to the docks, along with net sellers, and as one walked further from the docks toward the motley center of town the stands began to be full of trade goods and tools, then finally finished products ready for sale. Clothing, tobacco, gunpowder, and even books liked tables near the central square of the city.

Eventually, they came to a wide thoroughfare where the paving stones of the street were at last visible amid the absence of a tightly packed crowd. They were a mottled white and gray, many old and weathered and many more newly cut, the result of a recent repair. Some of them were of granite and glittered in the mid-day sun like little jewels between darker cobbles of sandstone. The road forked; the narrower way went uphill to a procession of tightly packed buildings made of a mismatched assortment of materials and styles. Stone, brick, and wood houses with as many roofs and roof styles were clumped together. Several taller buildings jutted out like teeth in discolored gums above the line of homes on the hill.

"Here we are!" Johnny called back from a few paces in front of Rone and Charlotte.

Beyond him, the street opened up to a grand central square. Stone buildings lined the entire area, tall and imposing, with parapets and reinforced doors looking over the pavement. Charlotte's eyes widened at a dense complex of mansions that stretched up the mountain to the west. Many of the outlets of these buildings were coming directly out of a sandy white cliff, buttressed by masonry.

Johnny smiled and said, "I'm going to put up a few posts on the boards out here, then hit up the pubs and the slums. If you need anyone else from the crew, you know where to find 'em."

"The brothel?" Rone said.

"You bet!" Johnny said. "Or back on the ship once they've spent their tin." He walked up to a small wooden structure: three-sided with planks of wood covering its edifices. On all sides were nailed many sheets of paper. Most were advertisements for work or goods for sale. The gaps between these contained old words of graffiti, often carved into the wood. Some were mere statements: cryptic things like, "Fire moon piss," or the not-so-cryptic, "Janie's got the rot." Johnny began nailing up a sheet of paper that read:

*Hands needed on free-sailing vessel, mostly hauling, privateering contracts in effect (**freebooters welcome**). Inquire with the first mate or captain at the Parkitees on Dock twelve. Term pay, **Catch-and-prize pay in effect**. Stock buy-ins available (minority holdings only).*

"Alright," the captain said. "We'll have plenty signing up, I think."

"When will we be sailing?" Rone asked. "I don't want you leaving without us."

"Make sure you're back on board by dawn, the day after tomorrow. Keep in mind I have ways of finding you, at least in this ratty city, if you decide to skip out on me – I expect the other half of that payment."

Rone nodded. Johnny looked him over for a second, then smiled and strode away.

Rone turned to Charlotte, "Shall we find an inn, or would you prefer-"

"Yes," Charlotte interrupted. "I need a bath. So do you."

"When will that not be the case, I wonder?"

"When we set down somewhere civilized."

"What kind of lodgings do you want? Simple?" Rone pointed back the way they came. "civilized," he pointed up toward the stone mansions, "or queer?" He pointed off the way Johnny walked. The road was narrow and shaded, with crowded wooden buildings bending over the cobblestone walkway. It looked as though it wandered up to the old part of town crawling up the hill, with its mismatched assortment of homes and businesses.

"What's the point of wealth if you're going to spend it lodging with brigands and rogues?"

"Indeed." He looked down at her with a raised eyebrow, a slight smile on his lips.

"I didn't mean you."

"Of course," Rone said. He gestured for Charlotte to follow, and she did, grumbling softly to herself.

In the middle of the square, they encountered a great crowd. Most of the people there were simple-dressed merchants and other workers from the city. A few reeked of real wealth (literally – Rone choked on a whiff of strong perfume as he and Charlotte ambled around the crowd). As they walked the perimeter of the gathering, they could see what had garnered so much attention.

A raised wooden stage sat in the middle of the huge square, positioned to indirectly face an immense keep-like building on the west end of the open square, older and grimmer than the buildings about it. There were gallows in the middle of the stage, and stocks stood on two sides. A middle-aged bald man, portly and red-faced, his cloth looking expensive but neglected and dirty, kneeled with his head latched in a contraption very much approximating the stocks, but without hand-holes. Attached to the top of a tall frame was a blade, much like that of an ax. It was positioned to fall downward in an arc to the prisoner's neck.

A fat man wearing a large hat with a velvet robe and leggings that pinched his fat calves like sausage casings walked about the stage yelling to the crowd. A tall hooded man stood to one side near the execution device.

"Forty days!" the fat man said in a high, clear voice as the crowd jeered. "Forty days and the debt not paid. Not one Cypral, not even a seashell, was cast to his note holder for the principle, despite the contract!" He gestured at the bald man.

"What is that they've got him in?" Charlotte asked Rone in a hushed tone.

"It looks like a guillotine. It's considered humane in some places."

"Seems awful," she whispered.

"At least it looks sharp. Wouldn't want to just get half your head chopped off. Like getting tossed off a hooker half-way through a trick."

"That's disgusting," Charlotte said.

Rone chuckled softly. "If you don't laugh, you'll cry."

"It's still sick."

"Better this than what your husband does to criminals. Keep that in mind."

"Despite the guarantee of blood as collateral," the fat man on the stage continued yelling, "Despite this, he is unwilling to pay Madam Porthagan her proper due." The crowd chattered.

"I'm quite aware of all that," Charlotte whispered. "Don't make me think about it." She nodded toward the stage. "They are killing this man because he owes a debt?"

"That's what it seems like," Rone said. "Not unheard of in my line of work, though I've never seen it on display in public like this."

"However!" The fat man stopped and put his hand on his chest dramatically. "However!" he yelled again over the crowd, his voice cracking. "Madam Porthagan is not a cruel woman!" His frowned as numerous people in the assembly laughed loudly. His pitch began to rise, "She is not a woman without mercy! She is not a woman without compassion!" His voice calmed as the laughter subsided "She is merely a woman disinvested, a woman who, like any person, wishes to see her good-faith contracts fulfilled."

"Rubbish!" A man yelled loudly from the front row. "Mitha's making an example, nothing less."

The fat man on stage waved his hand in front of his face as if brushing the protestor off.

"Will anyone service this man's debt? The principle is high, very high, indeed!" The man stopped in front of the guillotine and leaned against it. "But the interest is low, so low."

"He'll never find a man to pay the principle. What's the point? Get on with it already; I came for a show!" A short fat woman shouted near the back of the crowd. A few tired laughs could be heard scattered throughout the gathering. The fat man went on like the woman hadn't spoken.

"A week's interest for a week of life, what do you say?"

"Yes, get on with it. I've wasted enough weeks listening to criers moan about it," another voice from the front rang out.

"Forty days his neck has been saved by the generosity of his fellows. Will this day be the end of Gallow's grace?" The man in the guillotine looked ragged, his beard unkempt, but he looked well-fed for having spent forty days in prison.

"Please don't!" A woman cried out from the front row. She was wearing a simple dress, which was worn and stained. Her brown hair fell greasy around her shoulders, streaked with a few strands of grey. She leaned up against the stage. "We will have the money, please!"

Rone grumbled and grabbed Charlotte's hand. "Let's get out of here. I don't want to watch this."

Charlotte resisted his pull. "You'd watch the execution, but a woman – probably that man's wife – asks for mercy, and you cringe? Some man you are."

Rone gritted his teeth. "I didn't *intend* to watch the execution either."

"How many wives have you left wailing like that?" Charlotte said, meeting Rone's eyes. He looked away quickly.

The fat man seemed not to notice the woman crying on the stage. "Perhaps today is the day after all. Ten argents!" He paused as if waiting for the crowd to gasp at this sum. "Will leave this man's head on another week. I ask again, will nobody service this man's debt?" He turned to look at a clock tower attached to the massive building behind him, the focus of the square, which read 11:59. "It seems with the end of silver, comes the end of time. In accordance with the customs of the Gold Courthouse, and in fulfillment of the terms written and stored with us, witnessed by three fellows and re-attested by a majority at the time of arrest, I proclaim the life of Mineo Hergas Gordino the Younger to be forfeit as collateral of honest debt." He nodded to the hooded man, who had stood still and silent the entire time. He walked casually over to the execution device.

"Come on!" Rone hissed in Charlotte's ear.

"Wait!" Charlotte screamed, fighting against Rone's grip. The fat man held his hand up, and the executioner stopped in his tracks. "Wait! I will pay."

"Damnit, you foolish woman," Rone said in her ear, letting her drag him forward as he held onto her arm. "You don't know what you're getting into. You put your foot in this door, and you don't know if it will come out again."

She glanced at him, her eyes narrowed.

"Silver speaks, my good lady," the fat man said from the stage. Charlotte stormed forward and threw a handful of silver coins on the stage.

"I'll pay for next week, too," she said, looking up into the fat man's face with a hard gaze. The woman who had cried out before, busy pushing her way through the crowd at the front of the stage, finally reached Charlotte and began pawing her, thanking her through a stream of tears. Charlotte recoiled from the touch, pushing the woman's hands off her and feeling suddenly very exposed as she saw the whole crowd staring.

"I'm afraid that according to the contract we cannot accept payment for interest not accrued. And alas," he began a bow, "the principle must be paid in full or not at all in the case of a third party, as the agreement requires a one-hundred percent buyout. It is all in the contract, and as a mere arbiter of such, it is out of my power. So sorry." There was a false genuineness to his words, like a well-trained actor performing one of the old dramas.

"Come off it! You just want a job for next week!" someone jeered from the crowd. Laughter erupted.

The crier stepped forward, ignoring the jeers, and smiled at the crowd. "I'm afraid there shall be no bloodshed today, beloved fellows, dukes and dames." The masked man removed the wooden stocks of the guillotine and then he pulled Mineo up by his hands, which were bound behind him, before handing the prisoner off to a nearby man at arms. The temporarily relieved prisoner looked in Charlotte's eyes and nodded before he was forced to stumble down the steps. The crowd began grumbling audibly.

"Let us hope this doesn't bog us down," Rone whispered tersely in her ear. "We can't afford to dally picking up pebbles."

"This isn't a pebble; it's a man's life!" Charlotte whispered back.

"Fear not, we shall have a treat for our honored witnesses!" The fat mat pulled a watermelon from a burlap sack sitting nearby. He began fixing the wooden stocks of the guillotine around it.

"All men's lives are but pebbles in the path of great men," Rone whispered.

"Well, I'm picking this one up," Charlotte said.

"Let's hope it doesn't give the wolves an opportunity to catch our scent." Rone's eyes were searching around the perimeter of the square, taking in the faces there.

The fat man pulled a rope and the crowd cheered as the blade of the guillotine swung down and sliced the watermelon in two. He tossed the halves into the mass of people, who began passing them around, taking out a small piece of the melon each to eat.

"Tomorrow shall be a packed day in the Gallow square, my compatriots!" he cried. "Eleven in the morning shall toll an auction of thrall, recently acquired pirates no less, and some of them are lovely young women! Help your fellows recoup their losses and acquire some help for yourself at the same time!" The fat man bowed low and a few people clapped. He gathered up the silver coins, still sitting on the stage, and tucked them into a purse hanging at his belt. As he walked off the side of the stage, he looked over at Charlotte and scowled, the pleasant façade of master of ceremonies discarded like a melon rind.

"How could you just sit there and watch a man die?" Charlotte said to Rone. Her eyes searched over his blank face.

"I *wouldn't* have chosen to watch. We did nothing to bring about that man's situation, and it looks like there will be nothing we can do to remedy it permanently. I don't like to witness the ill-fate of others, but I also know we had no part in bringing it about."

"Please, you have to help us," the woman who had cried out earlier said. Rone and Charlotte turned their attention to her as she ran her hands, which were grey from some kind of dirty work, over Charlotte. "And thank you, I can't thank you enough." Rone looked at Charlotte with a crinkle in his brow, as if saying to her without words, *I told you so.*

"It was... nothing," Charlotte stammered, looking noticeably uncomfortable, "Miss...?"

"Martelena Gordino- Mineo is my husband," tears were still streaming down her face. She began to say something else, but the words stopped in her gullet when Rone, looking hard into her eyes, held a finger up to his mouth. He nodded to the side of the stage.

They turned to look where Rone was gazing, and they saw an ostentatious woman staring at them from the back of a rickshaw on the other side of the square. Her make-up was thick and colorful, and around her neck hung a highly decorative jeweled necklace, glittering in the sun. Her dress, blood red, glinted in a thousand places as its neat pleats folded down and obscured her legs. A tight corset pushed her bosom up, displaying the pale white assets given to women of leisure. The rickshaw she sat in was no less baroque. Stiff silk details and plush velvet cushions lined the inside in a bright blue. The outside was a labyrinth of ornate carving. She put a fan up over her face, tightening her gaze on Rone, who stared back like a statue.

"Who is that?" he said.

"Mitha Porthagan," Martelena said flatly. They watched as she barked an order at two shirtless grey-skinned men who were very muscular and who possessed the yellow eyes particular to the eastern race, who began to pull her rickshaw away.

"Why doesn't she have a horse and carriage?" Charlotte asked.

"Anyone can own a horse," Rone said. The rickshaw moved off, going north up the broad avenue to the cliffs.

"My husband – lazy bastard though he is – has done nothing but right for that shrew Mitha, and she's going to take his head," Martelena said as she turned back to face them. "Ship sunk within sight of port while Mineo was doing what she demanded him do. She's bloodthirsty. All I need is a few more days, just a few days to sell our stocks in Nantien – we have piles after all the years in the business – and then we can pay her back in full."

"Nantien?" Rone.

"Yes, there's a customs house there that deals with Divine Strand stocks."

Rone took a deep breath and shared a silent look with Charlotte. "Good luck," Rone began in a polite tone. "We've got to get going. I hope everything turns out for you." Rone grabbed Charlotte's hand and she finally allowed herself to be dragged off.

"Wait!" the woman cried out, but Rone had already disappeared with Charlotte into the dispersing crowd.

III: No Strangers

one and Charlotte found a room in a place called the Bowling Inn, an orderly and clean establishment that had been designed to impress, though clearly by someone not of the aristocracy. Rather than marble tiles, it had polished floorboards. The tables and bar, well-carved and polished deeply, were of durable maple rather than an exotic hardwood. The ceiling was decorated with clouds but was too low for a house of elevated manners. These details by themselves were neither vices nor virtues, but the owner and barkeep (a middle-aged man named Dathis with receding hair who wore a simple well-laundered apron) priced his accommodations well-above what they should have fetched. As a result, his establishment was almost entirely vacant.

Rone considered it an appropriate choice as soon as Charlotte pointed these things out, and so he hired a room over her complaints. They spent the night there, much as they had before, with Rone asleep on his bedroll by the room's fireplace, facing the door.

"Do you ever get tired of being on edge?" she asked him once she had put out the lamp, and the shutters of the window were closed against the moon. "Always facing doors and looking into shadows?"

"It's normal for me. Don't worry about it. It's what you hired me for."

"That's not what I asked. I asked if you grew tired of it. Aren't you exhausted from it all?"

Rone was silent for a moment. "Yes, but I don't know if I could ever be different. All the things I've done… the messes I've been in..." He sighed. "I don't even know how many enemies I have out there."

"I'm sorry."

"I thought I was settled-in at Cataling, but it seems I just cannot turn down an adventure."

"Well, you have certainly taken me on one of those."

Rone chuckled. "Let's get some sleep."

"It should be easy, now that my bed isn't rocking back and forth."

"A hard floor or a moving mattress… hard to know which is better."

Charlotte waited a few moments, then said quietly. "It's a big bed. I won't even know you're here."

Rone didn't answer. When Charlotte woke in the morning, he was already up sitting by the open window, looking out a narrow gap in the shutters. She reached over and felt the sheets next to her, and thought maybe they had been disturbed.

At Rone's demand, they spent the entire day indoors. Charlotte whittled the time away by attempting to read from the sparse library of the inn, comprised mainly of travel memoirs and older novels which held no interest for her. Rone spent his time in the room carefully attending to his weapons. His blades seemed to have picked up flecks of rust from the sea air, and he grumbled about it as he worked them out with a smooth white whetstone.

That afternoon they dined alone on a roasted chicken in the corner of the common room after each of them had enjoyed a hot bath.

"You know," Charlotte said, holding up a piece of the chicken on a silver fork, "this is a fair bit better than that wild rabbit, but not nearly as much as I expected."

"Are you insulting my cooking, or theirs?" Rone said, frowning above a smirk.

Charlotte smiled back. "I was merely pontificating that in the context of all the bad food we've had, I expected a good meal to be a more satisfying experience."

"So, it's *my* food that was bad."

"Alright grumps, you take that how you like it."

"The rabbits *were* a bit sage-y, but good fare for how hungry we were, I thought."

"Yes, hunger," Charlotte said. "But I am finding, however odd, that a fair environment does not enhance the meal experience as much as being hungry. How about that?"

"A little less insulting. Maybe I should let you cook our rabbits from now on."

Charlotte shrugged. "I never learned how to cook. Sorry. Not necessary for someone like me."

"I thought you were from the country. You shoot like it. Do they teach you to shoot but not to eat what you kill?"

Charlotte chuckled. "Eat it, perhaps, but not cook it. Sometimes we just gave the kill away. Hunting is a pasttime. Only peasants hunt for food."

"Thanks," Rone said.

"It's not an insult. My point is, I still can't cook. I can make tea, but that's about it."

"I shall continue providing full service, then."

Rone flinched and jumped out of his chair, his hand going to his pistol, though he didn't draw it from its place within his jacket. Charlotte turned and saw Mitha Porthagan had entered the dining room, accompanied by two men armed with long guns. She wore a smirk on her face and held up a gentle hand to Rone. Behind her, the sun was in the west, and the edges of her silhouette seemed to sparkle.

She calmly approached the table, the pleats of her dress (blue that day) lifted slightly to reveal her shoes and ankles. As the door closed and the typical window light returned, Charlotte gave a small gasp. The glinting of the dress was from many tiny pearls and cut gemstones, each dangling by a filigree sewn into the satin fabric of her dress.

"May I join you?" she said in a clear, mellow voice. She didn't wait for a response. Instead, she gestured to one of her men, who quickly brought another chair to the table. She sat and stared at Charlotte, her eyes half-lidded. Charlotte frowned and stared back, taking in the lines of the woman's face, subtle around her mouth and eyes.

Mitha broke the stare to catch the eye of the innkeeper. "Wine."

Dathis nodded curtly and disappeared to a storeroom.

Mitha turned back and looked at Rone, who was still standing, his body poised for action. "Who are you?"

"I'm Halbara, and this is my husband-" Charlotte began, but stopped at a smirk from Mitha and a wave of her hand.

"No, no. I know who *you* are," Mitha said. "I have a portrait of you in my sitting room, Charlotte. I've seen that huge portrait of you in Frostmouth at least a half dozen times, too, though I prefer *my* painting as it better captures your innocence. Darus Roth always did his best iterations of you in the smaller formats. No, what I want to know is," she turned her eyes on Rone, "who is this man you have with you? And you can sit down, of course. If intended to kill you, I wouldn't risk being here myself."

Charlotte drew a blank as Rone sat down, his hand still inside his jacket. "This is... my husband..." she stammered, not wanting to speak the truth and not knowing how she should lie.

Mitha laughed. "You're not married. Even if I didn't know who you were, I would know you two aren't married. Your manners say you are noble, and you show far too much affection for your companion for him to be your husband. Nobles never marry for love. Perhaps he's your lover? Affairs make wonderful stories. And here you are, with no Sarthius Cattannel. Very interesting."

Charlotte opened her mouth to speak, but could not seem to conjure any words, which was just as well, for Dathis had returned with a set of glasses and a few dusty bottles of wine.

"So," he said, setting out the glasses on the table. "I have this bottle, which is three argents. It's a-"

"Do I look like a woman who cares about the price of a wine bottle?" Mitha said, raising her eyebrows at the innkeeper.

"Of course not," Dathis stammered. "I'll just, er..." He put the bottles down and picked one of them back up. He began working the cork out with a screw awkwardly as Mitha stared at him. It came out with a pop, and he began to fill the glasses. When they were all half-filled, he walked away with the spare bottles under his arm.

Mitha picked up a glass and took a sip. She made a face and called back to Dathis, "This port is meant to be watered down."

Dathis turned back. "Oh... yes of course. Let me just..." He dashed back toward the bar.

Mitha sighed. "At least it's a decent vintage from Rhonia." She swirled the nearly black wine around in the glass, watching it coat the freshly cleaned crystal.

The innkeeper returned and poured a small amount of water in each glass. Mitha nodded curtly, dismissing him. She turned her eyes back to Rone, who was looking at his wine glass in an almost accusatory way.

"You were about to tell me who you were."

Rone spoke, "I'm an agent of fortune."

"That's *what* you are, not *who* you are," Mitha said.

"I am who my employer needs me to be," Rone said.

"I see," Mitha said. "Who is your employer?"

"Not you," Rone said.

Mitha looked at Charlotte for a fleeting second and smirked. "Not her."

Rone twitched his eyebrow. "Her."

"You're a bad card player, sir," Mitha said. She touched her lips in thought. "What rumors do wash up on these shores... which ones shall I believe?"

"Whichever ones suit you," Rone said.

"How do you know Mineo?"

"Who?" Charlotte said, trying to place the name.

"The man from the stocks," Mitha said, raising an eyebrow.

"Um... We don't," Charlotte said, "I just... pitied him. I didn't see why he should die when just a few silver could save him."

"For today. Mineo has very little goodwill left here. Even those who pity him will eventually find their hearts heavy, but their purses much too light. Mineo is not a particularly wicked man, just a foolish one, and one who tends to be as foolish with other people's property as he is with his own. He sank a very fine ship of mine trying to run a blockade, something beyond the scope of his job and his skill as a seaman."

"Why would you not let us pay for a few more days of interest?" Charlotte felt a bit of flush on her neck as she watched the woman across from her continue to stare blankly back.

"The courthouse keeps its rules, and I keep mine. If they won't accept payment, that is their concern."

"Can we pay you directly?" Charlotte asked.

"I don't know why you would. There would be no record of it. Mineo could still be hanged next week, not that I would see to it. Giving an individual money for a debt in the public bank is generally unwise here."

"So, you are saying that you are not to be trusted with a few silver?" Charlotte said.

"A few silver is a fortune to the right people, you know."

"But to you, I can see it is not a fortune," Charlotte said. "And yet you cannot be trusted with it."

Mithu snorted softly. "Darling, I don't make a habit of trusting people without something at stake to back it up, and neither should you. And I came here for business, not flaccid insults. That should be beneath one such as you."

Mitha stood up and turned to the two armed men, who sat at a nearby table whispering. With a nod, they stood and walked back to the door.

"But I think we are not in business together just yet. Be careful whose toes you step on whilst in Tyrant's Gallow. Titles mean very, very little here, Charlotte. I look forward to our next meeting – when you are more polite."

Mitha followed her guards out the door, to where a lavish Rickshaw awaited her.

Rone stood up and said. "Let's get packing."

Charlotte nodded and stood up with him.

"Not going to second guess me?" Rone said.

"Not this time," Charlotte said. "That woman is a stomach-turner for sure. And she knows Darus Roth, which is like having the carpet pulled out from under you."

"Darus Roth?" Rone said as he walked toward the stairs.

"A... friend from when I was a child. A painter. He was employed as a house artist by my uncle, Vegard."

Rone paused on the stairs and looked back. "The King of Hviterland?"

"Didn't you know that?" Charlotte said.

"I never really kept tabs on the extended families of the elite, nor did I care too deeply to know whom Sarthius married. Originally, at least."

"Any idea where we should head?"

"To find Johnny and hopefully get off this island," Rone said. "If he hasn't already left."

"What makes you think he has?"

Rone grumbled in response.

*

They found Johnny in the third, and ugliest, pub Rone and Charlotte popped into – a dank affair called "Regget's." Johnny, due to his great height, was someone that the other innkeepers and casual drinkers had paid attention to, and so his trail for the day was easy to pick up. He was likewise easy to spot when they finally caught up to him in the crowded, dingy bar that was as dark as night inside, despite it being afternoon outside. His great hairy head stuck up from a group of bow-legged sailors like he was surrounded by children, and his face was beet red from drinking. The low hanging wooden rafters, looking near collapse due to dry rot and countless holes of unknown cause, made Johnny look more the giant he was, especially as he leaned his head this way and that to avoid hitting them. The pub's furnishings were equally neglected, made of mismatched tables and chairs, chipped glasses and plates, and nubby candles left naked on wood countertops. The floor was covered with sawdust, and Charlotte could see why, as an old woman retched in a far corner while a young man slapped her on the back.

"Dreamer, what kind of crew is he trying to hire here?" Charlotte said quietly to Rone.

"Pirates, methinks," Rone said. "Wait here."

Charlotte nodded and pushed herself against a wooden pillar beside two young and very drunk men arguing over which whore had the prettiest nipples. In other circumstances, she would have laughed, but the reeking, oppressive atmosphere of the inn made her humorless. She tried to ignore the men and watched Rone slide sideways through the milling crowd.

She clutched at her jacket and reached for the pistol Rone had given her as the crowd suddenly began pushing her backward until she pressed into the two men discussing the finer points of female anatomy for hire. Charlotte was shorter than most of the people in the pub, and she immediately lost track of Rone. She craned her neck up, trying to see what was going on as the people continued to jostle each other. The drunk men laughed as they stumbled backward.

Not knowing what else to do, she dropped to a squat and inched between the tightly-packed legs, half crawling toward where sunlight had fallen on the dust-littered floor. Heavy boots walked past her. She stood up suddenly, knocking a beer out a man's hand (who quickly quieted his temper when he caught her face), as she saw a group of armed men confronting Johnny. At their head was none other than Vindrel, the man who had pursued her since her escape from Cataling.

Charlotte choked and covered her mouth.

"What's the meaning of this?" Johnny said as two men laid hands on him, one of them holding a stout set of iron cuffs. Another man stood at attention nearby, his hand on a scabbarded sword. Johnny threw one of the men backward with a single, great arm, then used that same arm to strike the man holding the sword in the face, knocking him back into the crowd of bystanders. He then flopped onto Vindrel, taking the last man who was still holding him down with him. His fists moved wildly over Vindrel, and Charlotte saw that he got in several hearty blows before the recovered attackers seized him again. He froze as two armored men moved up beside him with raised muskets.

"As an officer of the Gold Courthouse, I am authorized and bound to take you into temporary custody to keep the peace," said the man with his hand on his sword, who was dusting himself off.

"I've done nothing against custom or law," Johnny said.

"Not here, tis true, sir," the officer said. "Other than assaulting officers of the court. We have an extradition request. Is this him?" The officer turned to regard Vindrel, who was pushing himself up with one hand, as the other was in a sling. His face was already swelling, and blood dripped from his nose.

His eyes slid over Charlotte for just a moment as one of the nearby men helped him up. The glance was enough to make her skin crawl, and she took a step back instinctively. He seemed particularly strong for a man she had shot just a fortnight past, and even Johnny's heavy blows had not suppressed his energy.

"That's him," Vindrel said, wiping blood from his mouth. "The king of Veraland demands his justice."

"Vindrel," Johnny said. He laughed and said with a slurring drawl, "He's no officer of the government. He's a bloody dream-worshipper. A sell-sword. A sorcerer, too! The king of the Green Isle is dead, damn it."

Vindrel smiled at him darkly.

The officer's voice remained even. "We'll sort it all out if that's the case. We've never turned a man over for political reasons, but we don't like to harbor criminals, either. Come with me, Mister Johnny."

Charlotte watched Johnny, now with his wrists in irons, get pulled toward the door. Their eyes met for a moment, and he frowned at her. Vindrel turned to look at the scowl, but before he could, Charlotte felt herself being pulled down toward the ground. Between the legs of two men, Charlotte watched Vindrel scan the crowd curiously before walking to the door, looking stiff but otherwise well.

It had been Rone who pulled her down. He met her eyes and kept a touched a finger to her lips. She nodded.

Slowly, the people in the tavern spread back out, conversation returning to old topics or the exciting new incident. Laughter erupted in many places.

"Shit," Rone said, helping Charlotte back up.

"The Gallow never lacks for entertainment!" said a young man, one of the ones Charlotte recognized from the earlier unsavory conversation. He slapped Rone on the shoulder and gave him a wide smile that lacked front teeth.

"Indeed, but it's best not to be part of it. Remember that, friend," Rone said, and shook the man's shoulder. The man laughed and held up a flagon, but Rone shrugged as he had no drink. The lad began to guzzle his own, and a few voices around them cheered.

Rone pulled Charlotte further away, then whispered, "This is very bad."

"So much for outrunning anyone," Charlotte said.

"You're right, and let's not panic. It won't be as bad this time," Rone said. He sighed and ran his fingers through his hair. "Vindrel doesn't have any political advantage in this port. Johnny may even be freed within the week."

"By that time, won't they find us?"

"I'm not waiting around a week to find out," Rone said. "We'll start looking for something that can get us out discreetly at dawn."

"What about Johnny?"

"What about him?" Rone said. "He's either locked up for a time or sent back to the Isle; either way, he can't help us now."

"Rone, we can't just leave him, after all that he did for us," Charlotte said.

"I think we'll have to. This isn't the kind of business where nobody eats a loss because of risk."

"But the loss of life," Charlotte said. "That's really different. Johnny could be executed."

"So could I, if we're caught. You'll just go back."

"Back?" Charlotte said. "Oh, Rone, if only you knew… I might prefer execution."

"Then we have to get out of here as soon as possible. I'm very sorry about Johnny." Rone reached out and grasped her hand, squeezing it and locking eyes with her. "We'll wait here just a little while; then we need to hurry to… whoever has all the ships' registrations."

She inched closer to him, and he put his arm lightly around her. After what felt like a long stretch, he retrieved their packs and led her out the door.

It was late afternoon. The sun dipping behind the western hills, and the clouds moving above them were already painted in shades of pale orange.

"We'd best be quick. If that central square doesn't have the ship registrations, the dock houses will have an idea who is going where," Rone said, mostly to himself. "This is just my fortune."

"Johnny's is a fair bit worse. Don't forget," Charlotte said, almost running to keep up with Rone's long strides.

"You're right, of course, but it's my luck that will hang him."

Rone stopped short, halting Charlotte with an extended arm. "Hold up." He nodded. Straight ahead, in the large square, was a gathering of armed men. They were dressed like those that arrested Johnny, and they were talking amongst themselves in a relaxed sort of way, leaning against the now empty stage.

"Here," Rone said and pulled Charlotte between two open shop tables. The shade from the west was deepening. Rone looked down and began fingering a few bolts of cloth on one of the tables.

"No discounts for the end of the day," the fat shopkeeper said from the large chair where he sat reading a book.

"Bulk?" Rone said, glancing at him, then back to where the men were gathering.

"Of course."

"What do you think, dear?" Rone said, nudging Charlotte.

"Oh," Charlotte said, tearing her eyes from the armed men and looking down at the cloth bolts. "Let me think about what we need."

A silent few moments passed.

"I don't think I see anything I want."

"I have more inside," the shopkeeper said, again not moving his eyes from his reading material.

"We have to go, I'm afraid," Rone said. "Thank you."

The fat man grunted in response, then Rone pulled Charlotte away and to one of the narrower streets that lead down to the docks.

"I could just barely hear them," Rone quietly said as they walked. "They were talking about trying to find us, I think. Luckily they didn't seem to want to try very hard."

They paused near a little alleyway that pointed straight down toward the cove and harbor.

"That might be a dock house down there," Rone said, pointing to a low bunker-like building on the edge of the water. A few men armed with pikes were standing nearby it, relaxed. "But that's a no-go, right now."

"What should we do?"

Rone looked around. "Let's find somewhere to be for a while. A room at an inn, maybe. I'll think of something."

"I know you will," Charlotte said. "I trust you to. But just to re-assure me – am I wrong to think these local men at arms aren't very concerned?"

"You're not wrong, but Vindrel is here. I don't know how he caught up to us, but he did. Again. Luckily I can guess how he'll work – always above ground, and as you said, these locals don't seem to care."

"Let's get moving, then," Charlotte said.

Rone nodded.

IV: Lords of Legend

hey took a turn past the bar where Johnny had been mobbed, into an area of town that was very between things – it was between clean and dirty, old and new, and predictable and queer. Rone found a boarding house there that had a few vacancies, including an entire room. It had no common space, and thus there were few eyes to take note of them. The owner, an old widow, seemed to care little about them besides warning them that the front door would be locked shortly after the evening bells.

When they got to their room, Rone appraised himself in a mirror. "I should have gotten to a barber," he said, feeling his beard.

"I like the beard," Charlotte said, sitting on the bed, watching the sun go down outside the window. She had a book in her arms that she had neglected to return from the bowling inn, but she was uninterested in reading it. "I can scarcely remember you clean-shaven."

"We should cut and die your hair, too," Rone said, turning to look at her.

"You've threatened that before."

"Yes, and I was stupid to think we were out of it." He sighed. "I can probably shave myself if I had a good bit of soap."

"I have a good bit of soap," Charlotte said. She got up and rummaged in one of the bags for a minute, then produced a small, misshapen piece of yellow soap. "But won't Vindrel recognize you more easily clean-shaven?"

"I'm sure he would, but it's more to avoid the guard. I'm assuming he merely described us."

"He doesn't know what I look like," Charlotte said. "He looked right at me in the bar but did nothing. It gave me an awful shiver."

"Thank the dreamer he didn't catch sight of *me*."

Charlotte stood up and stood beside Rone by the mirror. "We look like nobody special," she said, smiling slightly. "My hair even looks brown with these brown clothes."

"Me, maybe, but you... You'll always stand out. Real, true beauty always draws the eye." Rone turned and looked at her.

She gazed up at him with an almost expectant openness to her eyes. "You said you were weak to a pretty face. Did you really mean that, or were you just trying to be charming?"

"I didn't mean it," Rone said. "Pretty isn't strong enough a word. Pretty is a serving woman with slender arms and yellow hair. You?" He shook his head. "Something else entirely. Something I can't properly describe. I'm no poet."

Charlotte smiled and, to Rone's surprise, a few tears dripped from the corners of her eyes. "Thank you." She reached forward and touched his arms. "You've been cold."

"I mean to be. I'm afraid to look at you." Rone found that he was holding both of her arms, right below her shoulders. Impulsively, he closed his eyes to the blue rings of fire that were hers and kissed her lightly on the lips. He lingered for a moment, then pulled back. "I'm afraid I'll lose control."

"Maybe it's okay to."

"No, it's not right. I have dreams about you. I..." He took a steadying breath and released her.

"I have dreams about you, too," Charlotte said. "But you already knew that. Please, Rone, just tell me-"

She stopped at a knock at the door.

"Who is it?" Rone said, motioning toward his pistol. Charlotte retrieved it from the table quickly.

"Name's Horace," came a voice, muffled by the door.

"I don't know a Horace. You must have the wrong room."

"Rone, right?"

Rone growled softly.

"Just a message for you, sir. Or for Charlotte, rather. I don't-"

"From whom?"

"The Lady Mitha Porthagan, sir."

"Twice?" Charlotte said, stepping back toward the bed to find her own pistol.

"Quiet," Rone said.

"Well," said Horus from the other side of the door. "If you need me to come back, I suppose I can, but, uh..."

A folded letter appeared from beneath the door. Charlotte bent down and retrieved it. It was sealed along one of its edges with wax, stamped with an anchor emblem.

"That's the message. I'll come back in a minute to fetch you, yeah?"

"Fetch us?" Rone said. Giving in to an impulse, he unlocked the door, quickly threw it open, and grabbed the collar of the man who stood outside. The young stranger was tall, matching Rone's height, but was perhaps half as heavy, with narrow shoulders that made his jacket look awkwardly generous on his frame. He smiled nervously and held up empty hands as Rone dragged him inside, his pistol pointed to the lad's chest.

"Why are you here?" Rone said. "We already talked to Porthagan."

"She told me not to promise nothing, but I think she can keep the courthouse from finding you. They're looking for you, right? Anyway, you're invited to dinner, only nobody is supposed to see you coming."

Rone shook his head. Charlotte began opening the letter.

"You really think I'm not going to shoot you?" Rone said.

Horus smiled awkwardly. "I don't think Mitha would be sending me into danger, sir. I mean, look at me!" He gave a forced laugh.

Rone smiled at him. "Fine," he said and eased down the hammer of his pistol. He put it back in his jacket but kept one hand on his backsword, which still hung at his hip.

"It's a very kindly-worded dinner invitation," Charlotte said, reading through the letter. "Except it implies that if we don't come, something bad will happen to us." Charlotte looked at the paper again. "Here. 'I would hate to see you suffer because you didn't choose the right company. Dinner will be late for you, but my servants will be disappointed if you aren't able to attend.' Does that mean this boy will kill us if we don't go?"

Horus shook his head nervously as Rone drew his sword out a few inches. "No, no," he said, holding up his hands. "I just find people. That's it! And she just means the cook. He'll be disappointed. He loves his job, and-"

"This last bit," Charlotte said. "'I'm sorry more of your party can't join us.' She must know about Johnny already."

"The pirate, yeah. Come on," Horus said. "I can take you up a back way."

"How did you find us?" Rone said.

Horus smiled. "Well, I just asked around. That and I showed the right people the picture. Here." He withdrew a folded piece of paper from his baggy black jacket and opened it up. Inside were two charcoal drawings, slightly smudged, showing Charlotte and Rone in accurate detail. "Mitha got it from someone or other. Do you think she'll be mad I smudged it a bit?"

"Does the guard have a copy of that?" Rone said.

"Which guard?" Horus chuckled. "If you mean the Courthouse guards, then no, I don't think so. They'll be coming round soon, though. My buddy Teller words for the Gold Courthouse, and they'll be pressing their privilege to find the fugitives. That's why Mitha told me to find you straight away."

"Right, very kind of her." Rone scratched at his beard. "Mitha has ships, right?"

"A handful, yeah, but she owns stock in loads more," Horus said.

"You're not thinking of meeting with her, are you?" Charlotte said.

"She could get us off of this island," Rone said. "She found us easily enough, though I don't know who could have drawn that picture. If she wanted to ransom you, we'd likely already be fighting. And I believe that the guard will start going door to door if they're working for Vindrel."

"I'll follow you, Rone, but I don't trust her," Charlotte said.

"I don't trust her as a person, but she could be made to see the advantage of helping you. In fact, I'm sure she already does. I'll risk it. Take us, Horus."

*

The last traces of dusk had left the horizon by the time they had packed and followed Horus out of the back door of the boarding house, once again not bothering to tell the keeper of the house they had left. The narrow alleyway the thin young man led them through quickly deepened to a colorless gloom as the sky overhead turned from pale orange to deep blue. The sun, waxing, was already in the sky, providing scant silver light as they went.

"This way," Horus said, pausing at an over-large wrought-iron garden gate. Ivy covered the old brick walls, but it was all well-trimmed. Beyond the gate was what looked like a wood crawling right up to the city. He took out a large iron key and fit it into a lock, one of half a dozen linked together to keep the gate shut. They went in, and Horus closed the gate behind them, latching the lock through the iron bars.

"What sort of garden is this?" Charlotte asked as they walked into the darkened canopy of trees. Within a few steps, the night deepened and it looked as though they were in an ancient forest of menacing blackness.

"It's not a garden, it's the hunting grounds," Horus replied. "Mitha and a few of the other lords maintain it for their amusement. They even have deer and foxes shipped in for the hunt." He drew from somewhere in his baggy jacket a small lamp. It sprang to life in his hands of its own accord, illuminating the space around them in many hues before settling into a warm orange.

"How did you do that?" Rone said.

Horus smiled at him, and his thin face looked strangely inhuman in the lamplight. "What do you mean?"

"You have the spark," Rone said.

Horus shrugged. "Just a spark, though."

"That's a rare talent, lad. What my father wouldn't give to see it again, even if it is merely a spark."

"Was he a wizard? A real one?"

"No, just a spark, like you, but he forgot, somehow. It was a pain on his heart unto his death, that loss. I never understood it."

"I'd heard that Tyrant's Gallow was a city of wizards, and here we are," Charlotte said. "Walking next to one."

"Not a wizard," Horus said with a chuckle. "I can light a lamp. There are a few others around that can, too. The Church doesn't hold much sway around here, so you see it from time to time." He chuckled and paused at a stone marker on the path. There was a fork just past it. "Look over there."

A short way up the path was a wall and a small gatehouse, complete with a portcullis. An ominous and ancient stone building rose behind it, topped with a parapet and alight in many windows.

"That one belongs to Seamus Delving, in case you ever wanted to have lunch with the terror of the south sea." He glanced back at them, "He actually loves guests. He's quite the character. Tells excellent jokes. This end of the city is full of people like that if you know where to look. Lots of sailors retire here because they can buy a nice property. Nobody gives them guff about where they got their loot if they have enough of it."

"Was the city always lawless?" Charlotte asked.

"We're not lawless, miss," Horus said. "We *are* kingless, but not lawless."

"Have you ever had a king? Who wrote the laws?" Charlotte said.

"You don't need a king to write laws," Horus said. "All the laws we need, we have anyways, so why worry about a king now? Men like Delving keep it orderly enough."

"There are no kings in the mountains either," Rone said. "At least, we recognize no kingship, whatever the lowlanders say. We still have laws. The old code. It's better than a king, in my opinion."

Horus waved them forward, along the other fork, back into the strangely artificial forest.

"Now, as to whether we've ever *had* a king," he said at length. "As far as records can go, there's never been one, though the city was occupied a few times in the last thousand years or so. There is a legend if you like to hear it."

"Of course," Charlotte said.

"Well, the story that gets told around here says that many, many years ago there was a king in Tyrant's Gallow, only it wasn't called Tyrant's Gallow back then, it was called Convection because the King's family name was Convect. Anyway, this king supposedly lived in a gold palace. He was also known to consort with wizards. The island became a gathering place of sorts for them because of his tolerant attitude and our distance from the mainland."

"And now it's a gathering place for pirate princes," Charlotte said.

"Begging your pardon, but we don't tolerate pirates. Privateers, freebooters..." Horus laughed to himself, "they're a different sort. "Madam Porthagan has put out quite a few bounties on people stupid enough to prey on her ships, and it's called the Gallow for more reasons than the tyrant."

"Which you were getting to, I assume," Charlotte said.

Horus nodded. "Eventually the Church of the Twelve heard about the lavish King Convect and his cabal of dark wizards, and raised an army to put a stop to it. This was supposedly back before the start of the sixth Dominion, which meant guns and cannons were yet to be, um..."

"Canonized?" Charlotte said.

Horus laughed. "That's a good one. Yeah, there were no cannons back then, so the church couldn't just send a fleet to sit in the harbor and blast the place to smithereens. Some tales differ, but supposedly the whole affair was actually the work of the king's older half-brother, who couldn't take the throne because he was a bastard. He was supposedly angry about being forced to join the clergy and live a life of poverty."

"Poverty? Hardly." Rone laughed. "When was the last time you stepped into a church?"

"Never have, actually," Horus replied. They turned another corner and saw the end of the wood. A stone wall greeted them, and beyond it, lit by the pale moon, was the high and famous Gallow Bluffs, mottled white and grey in the night. Dots of orange light littered the cliffside above the steeples of large houses, their fronts obscured by the wall that marked the end of the lavish hunting grounds.

"Can't fault you for that," Rone said.

"This story was a long time ago," Horus said. "Maybe the church wasn't quite so rich back then."

"Once, the church taught magic, if you go back far enough. Would you believe it?"

"Yeah, I would," Horus said. "But that ain't the church in this story. The church has no real army, you know, so what really happened was an invasion by a few of the lords of the Petty Kingdoms and the Lowlands, all gone or forgotten by now, of course. The invasion force was overwhelming, but they were repelled from the harbor by the power of the wizards. They still had access to magic back then, even though it was long after the sundering of the dream-"

"Wait," Charlotte said. "Sundering of the dream?"

"When the Fay, the eternal dream, was lost to the waking world," Rone said. "And with it, the flows of the prim dried up and were lost. Magic was lost. Or almost so."

"What are you talking about?" Charlotte said.

Rone smiled to himself. "I forget sometimes."

"Forget what?" Charlotte said.

"How sheltered you were." Rone watched Charlotte frown at him. "I'll tell you the stories of the ancient world - the true history of Midgard – some other time. Or do you believe that the twelve are the beginning and ending?"

Ignoring the question, Charlotte said, "Go on, Horus."

"Yar. The wizards still had magic, and they also had many inventions they had come to develop over long years of tolerance. For ten days, the wizards fought, and many of the invading force's ships were burned. The quest was on the verge of abandonment by the parties involved, who each held a deep distrust of the other.

"One night, the king's brother, who had orchestrated the whole thing, took a single boat and rowed up to a beach outside the city. He was arrested by the king's guards but was taken to see his brother once his true identity was learned. Everyone thought he had arrived to give the king strategic information, and at first, he feigned to give it, but at the same time, he secretly poisoned the king's wine. The king was found dead the next day."

"So, the brother became king?" Charlotte asked.

"Yes, that's exactly what happened. The king's advisor notified him that, as the last surviving member of the Convect family, the crown had fallen to him, bastard or no. The advisor gave him the king's crown and clothed him in lavish robes. Servants trimmed his hair and beard. The new king was now prepared to end hostilities with the crippled fleet, but before he could even leave the palace, the admirals of the attacking force and a high priest walked in the front doors of the castle. They had found the streets empty and the wizards' machines unmanned. No guards were posted outside the palace gate. The brother, who now resembled the old king in appearance, was put in chains and dragged outside the palace.

"They hanged him there for high apostasy in front of the mixed armies of the petty lords in an otherwise deserted street. The palace was searched, and a writ of succession was found, naming 'Fontaine' to be the next legal heir to the king, should no blood relative be found. The high cleric declared it legal and stamped it. Soon it was discovered, by virtue of a lone soldier that had traveled here before, that 'Fontaine' was merely the mountain on the island. Needless to say, that man earned an ugly fate for his honesty. Frustrated by the king's will, and unable to come to a consensus on who should rule the island, the petty princes began to argue with one another. Violence broke out, and many of the armed men who came ashore died. The last prince, victorious and standing in the town square on a hill of dead men, declared himself king.

"At that time, the king's advisor approached. The petty prince soon found himself surrounded by the city's wizards, who stood on balconies and atop buildings that rung the square. They were armed with their staves, guns, and other mechanical death devices. They destroyed the prince's remaining force with their magic, ending the lives of the invading soldiers in seconds. The advisor then declared the prince a criminal, and the wizards hanged him beside the new king. The advisor sent a courier to the Hand of the Divine with the high cleric's stamped writ. After that, the island officially became ruled by the mountain. In essence, free to itself. Of course, it's probably all nonsense, and there have been other conquests since. I think we're just a hard lot to rule."

"What happened to the king's advisor?" Charlotte asked.

"He was a wise wizard and had the golden palace rebuilt into the golden courthouse, of which he became the first chairman," Horus said. "The gold from the bricks and decor of the king was melted down and used as the monetary base for a new bank in the same place. It's all legend though- even the Golden Courthouse's records have gaps and limitations due to fire and things like that. Ah, we're here."

V: The Golden Palace

They came to another wall with another iron gate, though this one had fewer locks holding the heavy chain in place. Beyond it was a wide paved street winding downhill to their right and disappearing to their left in a tangle of tall, stately buildings. On the other side of the road was something well beyond words like "estate" or "manor." It was the real golden palace of Tyrant's Gallow, a vast complex made to look like a castle, if not function as one, and though it was now night, the moonlight gathered on the structures which were all just as white as the light.

A stone wall of light-colored stone stood some twenty feet high, and the narrow parapet at the top was defended a few feet below by a row of iron barbs pointed outward. The outlet at the center was held by a double iron portcullis topped by machicolations and, Rone assumed, by a murder hole hidden between the gates. A guard armed with a musket watched them from a window in the small gatehouse.

Behind the wall, the manor itself climbed *into* the cliff behind it. Above the end of the masonry, balconies emerged from the stone itself, carved into the living rock. All of them held inner lights, and a few of them had above them small portholes from shafts cut into the rock to carry off smoke.

"This is incredible," Rone said, pausing to stare up at the high places of the mansion.

"It's been here a long time, but it wasn't quite as nice when she got her hands on it," Horus said as he made two swift gestures to the guard in the gatehouse. The guard got up stiffly, and after a few moments, the first gate ascended to allow them passage. The trio stepped into the arch, and Rone looked up to see a large circle of black iron that sealed off the murder hole. "Evening, Bart," Horus said to the grate.

"Hullo, Horus. Mind the paint in the second hallway, some of it is fresh," the man said, bowing slightly at Rone and Charlotte as he lowered the first gate back.

"Will do," Horus said. The second gate opened, and the pair walked through into a wide and well-tended courtyard. Low hedges, alive with small yellow blossoms all closing in the cool evening, lined the walkway to either side as they walked. Two white horses stood far off to one side, lazily browsing at a trough near an open stable. Blossoming trees stood near the far walls on either side, their colors muted by the night. Following Horus, Charlotte and Rone walked up the steps toward a massive set of reinforced doors covered with bas-relief.

What had first appeared to be carvings upon the doors turned out up-close to be hammered steel with a dull-colored luster in places. Large and dense, the door rang out with a deep groaning tone when Horus used the knocker, which hung from a large metal dragon head set into the right door. It had a match on the other side, and when taken as one piece, the bodies of two dragons emanated from the knockers, wings splayed wide to the arched stone door frame. Their claws clutched at the earth, and each tail crossed into the other door, eventually resting on its mate. The dragons also had a pale green hue in the raised steel, just noticeable in the lamplight. Rone mused on the color – the artist must have placed copper there before pounding the sheet of iron into its delicate shape. Despite the tension of the moment, he smiled as he regarded the artistry.

A peep-hole, unnoticed previously, suddenly opened up, revealing a set of brown eyes. A voice spoke, "Oh, it's you, Horus. Dinner will be ready soon. Those the guests?"

"They are," Horus said. The sliding of metal sounded from the other side of the door. After a moment, the door began to move inward, grinding at first over the sparse dust on the floor, then moving silently once it was well clear of the door frame. The house steward, a squat, older man with dark brown skin, dressed in a red jacket, was pulling on a circular handle as large around as his head, straining against the weight of it.

"You gonna show them up for me?" he asked with a strained voice. "She's up in the drawing-room. The high one."

"I might as well. Wouldn't want to interrupt your nap, Nom." Horus was smiling.

"It's my knees, not my eyes. You'll get old one day too, lad," the steward said.

"Only if I'm lucky. This way, friends." Horus motioned them out of the low antechamber. The hall they stepped into was almost oppressive in its magnificence, built more like a temple than a home. Pristine white floors, made of carefully fit together marble slabs with no grout, polished to a shine, filled the hall, and ran out to rooms unseen. Moonlight illuminated arched stained-glass windows reaching twenty feet above them, going into what in a typical mansion would be the second story. The combination of the many lamps in the hall and the moonlight beyond made their colors strangely bright. Rone stared at one off to his left, showing the god Ferral over his forge, which burned with red and yellow glass. In the next window over was his sister (and wife, depending on the book) Artifia, at work at a potter's wheel. As he looked around the high-walled receiving room, he saw all twelve gods arranged in their calendar order after Artifia, all the way to Verbus, the god of death and poetry, at the very end of the hall.

Rone was surprised that the merchant baron did not have a particularly exalted place for Denarthal, the god of money. He was more surprised to see the dragons painted along the walls to either side of them as they walked out of the entrance hall and into a narrower gallery. No less detailed than the front door, the gallery walls were covered with frescoes of wyrms in carefully layered paint that sparkled with some inner mineral as Horus's lamp swung in front of him. Some of the beasts were in flight, others stood upon mountains and castles, and some breathed fire of gilt paint. At the end of the gallery was a dragon examining a book, resting in a comfortable chair. The paint glistened on the curing plaster, still slightly wet.

Rone paused and stared at it.

"I rather like that new one," Horus said, holding up his lamp to the wall. "Makes me smile. Just a bit of silliness, having a dragon reading – not Mitha's usual taste."

"I don't think there's anything silly about it," Rone said. "There's a lot of symbolism in dragons, and my guess is they can read as well as you and me."

"I can't read very well," Horus said. He chuckled. "If only they were real, eh?"

"Perhaps they *were* real, once," Rone said. "Maybe they will be again, eh?"

Horus shrugged and motioned them onward.

He made more small talk as they walked down other hallways and climbed several small staircases, always moving up and further from the front door. Eventually, they reached a spiral staircase and began ascending. The stairwell started to feel small and stuffy as they walked up, and Charlotte and Rone realized that there were no longer any windows. Charlotte put her hand out and touched the cold wall, detecting no seams for stones.

"Yes, these stairs are carved out of the living rock. Quite a feat, isn't it?" Horus said. "Nobody knows how they did it so well. One of the lost arts, maybe."

As he spoke, they reached a landing, and Horus pulled open a carved wooden door. It opened up into a large room floored with a smooth white tile. Plush carpets sat beneath ornate furniture, which was arranged around a fire in a small hearth. At the end of the long room, red curtains blocked off a balcony. As the curtains flapped in the breeze, they saw the silhouette of a woman sitting in a large chair, and beyond her was sky, moon, and clouds.

On the wall hung a few paintings; one of these Rone paused at to stare. Charlotte at first did not notice he stopped moving, but her heart leapt, and she nearly choked aloud when she turned back to him. On the wall above an ornate couch was a small portrait of herself.

"It looks just like you," Rone said. "*Is* it you?"

Charlotte felt her voice stick. "It's the painting she mentioned," she said with an effort. "It's from another life." She grabbed at Rone's sleeve and pulled him onward.

Horus walked forward and stood outside the balcony, then cleared his throat.

"As requested, madam, here are the guests."

"Thank you, Horus," Mitha said as she stood up.

"Thank you," Charlotte said, smiling and nodding slightly to Horus. The messenger turned around and took a stack of paper from Mitha as she presented it to him.

"These are the paychecks for the week," Mitha said. "You can leave the night guard's in the desk in the foyer. If you could tomorrow, take the stubs to the office and pick up this week's cleared checks from the Gold House." Mitha turned to Charlotte and Rone. "Welcome to my humble abode." She extended her hand. Charlotte shook it daintily. When she presented it to Rone, he awkwardly followed suit. Her hand felt soft and well cared for, but he sensed a strength and tightness in the tendons, even as it sat lightly across his fingers, that was dissonant with her delicate image. Mitha raised her eyebrow and cracked a sardonic smirk as Rone held her hand. "I have some hot tea," she continued, "Won't you sit and have some with me? Dinner will be ready soon, and I am sure that you will find it satisfying."

"I'd rather get down to business," Rone said. "You own a good deal of ships, and stock in-"

"Not yet. We'll get there, I'm sure, but not yet. Tea first, and conversation."

"It would be a pleasure," Charlotte said flatly after a short silence.

Mitha cracked a slight smile as she turned away from them.

They followed her past the flowing red curtains to the balcony, which was a jutting section of the cliff that had been carved into a semi-circular sitting area. Even the banisters were made of living rock, polished smooth and only lightly worn by the wind and rain. A cool breeze blew across the stone, and from there, they could see the entire city Tyrant's Gallow stretching out below them as a haphazard web of lights, flowing down the hill to the mouth of the river and the harbor. Countless ships stood amid the docks with hundreds of tiny lights on them.

The height dizzied Charlotte slightly, and she leaned on Rone for support until she found herself sitting in one of the large blue upholstered chairs that sat near the rail. Rone sat beside her in an identical chair. He made to cross his legs but stopped at a quick gesture of Charlotte's hand over his lap. Mitha set herself down in a green chair that faced the other two.

Near at hand was an easel with a half-finished painting upon it, depicting the moon over a night harbor. On a nearby table were a tea set and a hot kettle. Mitha leaned back, making no effort to pour the tea.

"Will you pour me a cup, dear?" Charlotte said.

Rone gave her a curious look but complied.

"Me too," Mitha said. She smiled as Rone handed her a cup and a saucer.

"I see that you paint," Charlotte said.

"A hobby of mine. It's good to cultivate one's artistic senses."

"Judging by your hallways, they are very refined, even impressive."

"Having money helps. One day I would like to take a more direct hand in some of the decorating, but as you can see, my skills are not yet up to my standards."

"When your standards are as high as what you have on display, you must be gentle with yourself," Charlotte said, sipping the tea. "You have only been studying for... what, five years?"

"Two," Mitha said. "But I appreciate the compliment. I wish I had more time for it. Have you studied art or merely sat for it?"

"Darus Roth was my teacher, actually," Charlotte said. "I didn't have much talent for it, I think. My talent was music."

"I thought you said you were bad at it," Rone said.

"I said that I was bad at the cello," Charlotte said. "I was far better at singing and at the harpsichord, too, despite my small hands."

"I should be so lucky as to study with Darus, regardless of my talents."

"I don't think you'd be saying that in my place."

"Why is that?" Mitha said. "Is it because Darus was in love with you, or are you saying that because of something unrelated in your life, like being forced to marry that snake Sarthius?"

"Hold on," Rone said, leaning forward. "I don't care who you are; you can't talk to her that way."

Mitha smiled at him. "Rone... You're reaching for your gun. The fact that I didn't have you disarmed was a gesture you apparently did not understand."

Rone clenched his jaw.

"And were you really offended I called Catannel a snake? Charlotte's husband is quite contemptible, or would you not be extracting her from her marriage so vigorously?"

Rone leaned back down.

Mitha relaxed as well, then touched something at her leg, under the folds of her skirts: a slight, unmistakable bulge. Rone nodded at the gesture.

"I should have guessed a pirate would have a pistol hidden."

"Symmetry, my boy," Mitha said. "That's how you do proper business, but I get ahead of myself." She looked at Charlotte. "Was I wrong to assume he loved you?"

Charlotte was silent for a few moments. "No."

"You can see it so clearly in his work. It's such an ideal representation, slavishly perfect." She looked out to the night. "It must have been torture for him, looking at you all the time, but never getting to have you. And it must have been uncomfortable for you, too." She glanced back at Rone, then back out to the harbor. She sighed. "You are indeed very interesting, Charlotte, and you keep interesting company. Pirates, assassins, and spies... You would make a good queen."

Charlotte rubbed her temples. "I just want to go home."

Mitha's face warmed slightly as she looked back at Charlotte. "I know. I think it's time to dine. I'll escort you." Mitha stood up and straightened her skirts. "Rone, be a dear, and hold our lamp."

Rone frowned at her, but at a concerned look from Charlotte, obeyed. They followed Mitha into the room and back to the stairs, with Rone holding the lamp aloft for light. When they reached the bottom, she took them through another well-decorated gallery.

"How did you know my name?" Rone said. "When you sent Horus for us? And where did you procure a sketch of us?"

"All in due time, my boy," Mitha said.

Eventually, they descended another short, straight set of stairs and came to a set of reinforced doors. They were painted with wreaths of flowers, but otherwise straight and plain.

Beyond the doors was the night above a large candle-lit dining table near to a roaring open cook pit. Nearby, a young woman was playing softly at a large clavichord. The piece was gentle and introspective, with a sweet, ornamented melody above a slow bass line. Sitting around the table were several men who were busy sipping wine but stood up when they noticed Mitha stepping down into the dining area.

"Glad you all could make it," Mitha said. She turned her head toward the cook pit. "How long, Marty?"

An old, tall man turned up his head, revealing yellow eyes and sallow, grey skin – the trademarks of Draesen heritage. He smiled and said, "About two minutes to finish cooking, just to get the crust right, then another two minutes to carve up." He moved over to a spit and turned over a rack of meat that was nearly sitting on the coals.

Mitha looked back at Rone, who had one hand in his jacket, gripping his pistol. The other rested on the hilt of his backsword.

"It's alright, my friend." One of the men from the table stepped away, closer to a lamp hanging from a nearby post. He had blonde hair and a tight beard along with a bandage around his neck.

"Farthow," Rone said. "I did not expect to see you here."

"I didn't expect to be here," he said, smiling. "But alas, our mutual friend Drath Harec felt it prudent to have me accompany the great expedition of the Veraland navy. I arrived this afternoon with Vindrel."

"You could have warned us," Rone said.

"I'm sorry I couldn't manage it. Vindrel took a gamble, and I suppose it worked out for him, though not for your friend."

"There's more at stake than an unlucky privateer," Mitha said. "Have a seat, please."

"I came here hoping to hire a ship," Rone said.

"We'll get to that," Mitha said. "Please don't offend my cook by refusing to dine." She nodded toward two empty seats, near her own.

Charlotte stepped around Rone and went to one of the chairs, leaving her bodyguard to follow her. Farthow slapped Rone on the shoulder and took his seat next to him.

"Allow me to introduce you all to Charlotte and Rone," Mitha said.

"Your reputation precedes you," a dark-skinned, grey-haired man said, nodding between Farthow and Rone.

"This is Seamus Delving, a friend and a party that has a knack for knowing the interesting things that happen in this town."

"The terror of the Datala Sea," Rone said.

"Depends on who you talk to," Seamus said. "These days I mostly like to hunt and have wine with interesting people. But interesting times have a way of calling me into action."

Mitha gestured to another man. "This is my chief associate, Teal Starnly."

"Pleased to meet you," a lean, middle-aged man said.

Rone nodded to him and finally seated himself next to Charlotte.

"And here we are," Mitha said. "The wife of Sarthius Catannel, the future king of Veraland, and niece of Vegard of Hviterland, in our confidence."

"And," Charlotte paused and thought for a moment, "What do you need from me?"

"From you? Nothing, really, but we can do much *for* you. Like I said, business."

Charlotte looked at her hands, then back at Mitha. "I'm hesitant to do business with someone who executes her partners."

Delving chuckled but didn't speak.

"You mean Mineo?" Mitha sighed and leaned forward. "Many people would wish him dead in my position. He took a merchant ship I bought for him and sank it trying to run a blockade. Still, I don't really wish him to be *dead*. The truth is, I don't care whether he lives or dies; he's just a bad business partner. Unfortunately, having a soft heart attracts men like that. I enforce the contract for the sake of all the others, not because I hate Mineo."

Mitha smiled as the grey-skinned cook brought over the roast. He plopped it on a platter and began carving it. He served Mitha first, putting the thin-sliced meat on her plate along with some vegetables from a nearby pot.

"The sea's a rough business," Delving said. "Your friend Johnny understands."

"I daresay he does," Rone said. "Since he's sitting in prison, I presume."

"I was thinking of him killing his first mate. Farthow told me the story. Quite impressive. I've dealt with mutiny before – always with death. No room for mercy out on the blue. Thank you," Delving said as the cook piled meat on his plate.

"I can't argue with that. So what is this business you have in mind?"

"Your escape from the Veraland navy, of course," Mitha said.

Rone chuckled. "So, you have a ship?"

"Not one that can carry you," Mitha said. "Farthow brings word that the rest of the fleet will be attempting to block up the port by dawn. Apparently, they were delayed in Nantien."

"Admiral Dunneal decided to stop and establish dominion in Nantien," Farthow said. "Observing that it had just been sacked, but the attacking force was gone."

"Reprehensible," Rone said.

"Sensible," Delving said. "It's' what I would have done if I were him. Nantien is a rich port."

"But the Draesen leave anything worth plundering?"

"The Draesenith Empire?" Mitha said, dropping her fork. "In the North Pelagian? You must jest."

Rone shrugged. "It was them. I'm sure."

"They're going to invade somewhere in the Northmarch," Charlotte said. "They have expeditions every twenty years or so, over the Frostbacks or across the tundra during the summer melt. It's about time."

"But why did the Draesen abandon it after sacking it?" Rone said. "I figured they were looking for a strategic stronghold."

"Interesting supposition," Starnly said, rubbing his face. "Very interesting. It makes sense, though. Nantien was just a raid for supplies, then. It has no strategic use in any part of the Northmarch."

"We'll have to worry about that wild card later," Mitha said. "For now, know that I cannot spare a ship to run through a blockade against a navy so well equipped as what the Green Isle has sent. Instead, what I propose is that you take the Parkitees."

"We can't," Rone said. He ignored the fresh food on his plate. "Johnny is locked up. His crew is loyal to him. Or are you proposing we steal his ship?" He shook his head. "Don't answer that. I won't steal a man's ship, especially one who has paid so much for us already."

"I can provide the staff," Mitha said. "I can also ensure that you get past the warships, at least initially. We know a few ways to sail out of here that our opponents will not."

"We also are not planning on stealing it," said Starnly. "We'll acquire the appropriate share in stock to control it."

"Buy the stock? From whom? Johnny?" Rone said.

"Precisely."

"He'll work with us," Mitha said. "Mister Delving and I have deep connections at the courthouse, and Starnly is the best solicitor in the city. We'll be able to keep him out of the hands of Veraland indefinitely."

"We might be able to get him released when it's said and done," Starnly said. "It may take a while, but it'll be worth a good share in the ship."

"Surely you have enough ships already," Rone said.

"I'm not in the business of charity," Mitha said. "Truthfully, it's more trouble than what I will gain in a small-time private vessel. I'm more interested in keeping Charlotte out of the hands of Sarthius Catannel. A kingless Veraland is an attractive business opportunity."

"For us all," Delving said.

"The stock in the ship is in the interest of symmetry," Mitha said. "We have to all have risk and responsibility – toward each other."

"Also, my boy," Delving said, looking at Rone, "you must remember that Johnny has a crew that is not locked up. They deserve their freedom, too, yes?"

"What happens to Johnny in the meantime?" Rone said.

Delving shrugged. "The Gold Courthouse is very kind to prisoners."

Rone shook his head. "Vindrel won't leave Johnny behind."

"He will when he realizes you have slipped away and are heading east," Mitha said.

"You don't know him as well as I do. He won't let it go. He'll stay, or else come back swiftly to settle things."

"Do you have a better plan?" Farthow said. "Because this a rather good one."

"All I ask in addition," Mitha said. "Is a promissory note from the lady Charlotte toward King Vegard, her uncle."

"Of what quantity?" Charlotte said. "I can pay directly."

"It's not money I want," Mitha said. "I merely want a letter that states you are in my social debt and are thankful for me helping you."

"What good would that do?" Rone said.

"A great deal, at the right time," Mitha said. "Do we have a deal?"

Rone took a breath and looked at Charlotte intensely. "It's as good as we're likely to get."

Charlotte took a breath. "When do we leave, sunrise?"

"I'm afraid not," Mitha said. "It'll have to be tomorrow night, as we've already missed the right tide to skip outside of the blockade. You'll be taking the ship along a narrow channel, past a shallow island outside of the port. You'll hit bottom at any other tide. The sailors whom Mister Starnly will select will be able to navigate it without trouble."

"That's another day for them to catch up with us," Rone said.

Farthow laughed. "They've already caught you, Mister Stonefield. It's time for another escape. You're an expert at it, at this point."

"You can stay here tonight and tomorrow," Mitha said. "This Cataling captain won't be able to find you within the manor."

"Very well," Rone said. "It's a deal." He nodded toward Charlotte. "I assume she knows what to write."

She looked at her hands folded in her lap for a few moments, then said, "Alright. I'll write a nice letter for you, Miss Porthagan, but don't expect my uncle to care about it."

"I expect he will care a great deal," Mitha said. Once again, she looked at Rone, her narrowed eyes communicating some hidden intent about which Charlotte could only guess. "But if he doesn't, then it hasn't cost you much, has it?"

"I suppose not."

"Splendid. Now then, since most of our business is concluded, our keyboardist has a proper set of repertoire for us to enjoy. Unless you are too tired?"

Charlotte shook her head.

Mitha smiled. "Rone, would you and Farthow reconvey the details you have on the sacking of Nantien to Mister Starnly? I'm sure he'll need it in the coming weeks. A fleet of Eastern warships is a significant hazard. And I promise you won't have to miss much of the concert."

"I'll need to be going, actually," Farthow said. "My superiors on this outing will be wanting my professional advice."

VI: Entries and Episodes

he fingers of the harpsichordist blurred as she executed each flourish. She liked to hold her fingertips up mid-air before the end of each phrase, letting the penultimate chord fully speak its expectant tension before she gave the cadence its due. The movement she played was slow and somber, with but a single, highly ornamented melody and a bold set of chords in the bass range. Her brow wrinkled and she squeezed her mouth during the most active sections, letting her whole body express the dark mood of this, the middle movement of her own sonata. At last, she played a final mordent and cadenced on a broad minor chord. She let the chord breathe a few seconds in the resonate hall, lined from floor to ceiling with unfinished maple, then began the next movement.

It started with a single melody, fast, yet sorrowful. The melody entered again, transposed into an even darker mode while the first voice countered it with a series of dramatic leaps. The melody entered a third and a fourth time as the dense fugue exposed itself. The harpsichordist's face fell to a lineless relaxed beauty in her total concentration. Only her dark eyes revealed what a high price the music demanded of her.

Charlotte felt oddly comfortable watching the concert. The Harpsichordist had bowed and begun to play the ornate gilded device as soon as Charlotte sat down. She and Mitha were alone during the first notes but were quickly joined by Nom, the steward, and Marty, the cook, who sat down in incidental chairs at the back of the hall. The purity of the musician's presentation had a way of blunting the tension she felt sitting next to the brooding Mitha Porthagan.

As the fugue went on, Charlotte tracked the voices as they wove into one another in episodes of harmony and strife, occasionally breaking out in an entry of the opening subject.

"Marvelous, isn't she?" Mitha said quietly. "Her name is Joseala. She is the daughter of a freighter captain that worked for me who was lost at sea. I took pity on her and decided to pay for an education. It turns out she has quite the facility in music, as you can see."

Charlotte thought back to her own musical education experience. Her mother had been a gifted singer, she remembered, and Charlotte was encouraged to develop her voice, but her father considered a woman singing in public to be improper for a lady. Even her aptitude at the keyboard had been suppressed, and her father had forbidden her to perform in public. For the wealthy, the arts were past times; entertainment was to be hired from the middle classes.

Mitha interrupted Charlotte's thoughts again. "I was thinking of having her tour the mainland; get her some exposure. If she doesn't find some career opportunities, she might at least find a nice husband."

"Yes, she is a natural talent, and beautiful too," Charlotte said.

"So, she's got at least two things people want. I hope she finds something she wants in return." They listened to the music for a few seconds before Mitha said. "Your bodyguard."

"What about him?"

Mitha made a wordless sound, then said, "How good is he?"

"He's gotten me this far," Charlotte said. "And to me, that is a feat. Just getting me out of Cataling was a feat."

Mitha watched the harpsichordist and smiled slightly. "I think I might like to take him to bed with me tonight if that's all right with you."

"What?" Charlotte said, loud enough that the girl on stage missed a note and hesitated mid-phrase. "What did you just say?"

Mitha turned to her calmly. "I figured he has missed out on a great deal of comfort."

"No," Charlotte said. She noticed the keyboardist looking at her askance.

"No, he has hasn't missed out on sex, or no, you won't let me sleep with him?" Mitha touched her lips. "Maybe it's not your decision to make. I'll invite him up for a glass of brandy-"

"No... Just no!" Charlotte said, leaning forward with a frown.

"What if I made a trade?" Mitha said. "You let me keep your bodyguard, I send you off to Hviterland on one of my ships?"

"I can't believe…" Charlotte felt sweat bursting on her brow. She stood up over Mitha and grabbed her skirt with her fists. "And I thought you were trying to be noble!" On stage, Joseala paused and started a technical passage over again.

"I am noble, technically, and this is quite how they act," Mitha said calmly. "Which makes me wonder about you." Seeing Charlotte turn to go, Mitha reached out a hand and grabbed her arm. "Relax, girl."

Charlotte turned back to see her frowning and looking genuinely sad.

"Forgive me. I sometimes push too hard, playing my games. Please sit down."

Charlotte slowly sat back down. They watched Joseala finish her piece and clapped as she stood up and bowed. She sat back down and began a somber allemande.

"You know," Mitha said. "You can't hold onto your feelings, even if he feels the same for you, which he doesn't."

"He does," Charlotte said.

"You know it?"

Charlotte remained silent and continued to watch the performance.

"You know very well what he is," Mitha said.

"He's a hero."

"He's a *killer*."

"Just a matter of perspective, as my uncle would say."

"Vegard is a shrewd man. But I tell you, people don't change. You should see him as he is. He's a spy. An assassin. A *murderer*."

"I can only judge him as I see him. He's a good man."

"To *you,* he is, for now. I can put you on a ship within the next fortnight to take you all the way to Frostmouth. You can leave him behind. He's served his purpose. I see how hard a time you have standing up to him."

"Maybe," Charlotte said. "And maybe I'm not willing to cast people off like broken tools once they have filled their purpose."

"You'd best learn to. Catannel is cunning, or else your peril would be less."

"He's evil."

"All the worse, my dear. I pity you."

*

There was a soft knock at the door. Charlotte raised her hands from her hands, wiping tears from her cheeks, which began to feel hot with embarrassment.

"Who is it?" she called at the door, glancing at the nearly full moon in the window. How long had she been missing? She remembered a full moon from sometime in the dry highlands east of Cataling.

"It's Rone."

She suddenly remembered what Rone had made her do in Masala, and she fumbled a pistol out of her bag, spilling part of the prime as she tried to catch it.

She cursed softly to herself and pushed her cheeks to her shoulders, trying to dry them as she walked to the door. She slid back the bolt and open the door a crack, saw Rone's face dimly in the hallway. She opened the door all the way and lowered the pistol.

"Good of you to remember your defenses," he said.

"Where were you?"

"Had a bit of a talk with Starnly, about the crew, just trying to plan ahead for a few things. Nothing you need to worry about."

He stepped in, then shut the door behind him and locked it.

"Mitha had another room prepared for you," Charlotte said.

Rone gave her a puzzled look.

"You don't have to stay in here," Charlotte said.

"Do you feel safe here?"

"Yes. Do you?"

"I never feel safe. Or maybe I should say, safe compared to what?"

"I don't know."

Rone frowned. "Then I guess I don't know either."

Charlotte sighed with exacerbation. "Just go. I'll keep the door latched tight till morning."

Rone frowned again, and the flickering lamplight distorted his features, making him look older and more tired. He nodded and reached inside his jacket. He withdrew a letter and handed it to Charlotte.

"Farthow?" Charlotte said. Rone nodded. She opened the envelope and read:

To the ugly stone man:

Slipped away from my spouse again. Had to write you a letter, my love.

The Big Man will have to be at a hearing tomorrow at eleven bells. He'll be heading home with Vafty for sure.

Sorry I couldn't get to him first. Was looking for you in the wrong place.

Rest of the wooden crew inbound, maybe here the day after tomorrow for a good party, so Missy's idea is nice, except Vafty is trying to get a hold of the Big Man's rowboat. It's in the pound with the other dogs, luckily. No manners, that one.

I'll be throwing my hat into court tomorrow for the Big Man's sake. I don't think it will work.

Might be nice to find another ship for your coca.

-B

"I don't think I understand this," Charlotte said.

"Johnny's ship is impounded, and Vindrel is trying to get at it. He's got a hearing tomorrow at 11 AM, after which he'll be handed over. Sorry, Charlotte," Rone said. He looked out the window at the moon and scratched his chin.

"What option do we have?"

"Try to contract a ship from Mitha, or someone else, at great expense," Rone said. "Mitha won't have anything leaving for a few days, which will be a problem if the fleet gets any bigger, or, if I guess correctly, they start a conflict. If we try to find somebody else's ship, we could end up traveling with a criminal."

"A worse one, you mean," Charlotte said.

Rone chuckled awkwardly. "Should we get to work on that?"

Charlotte shook her head. "No. I'm not ready to throw our captain to the wolves after what he went through with us."

"That's not under our control," Rone said.

"I have something in mind."

"What is it?"

Charlotte stood up and half-smiled. "I'll tell you tomorrow."

"Why tomorrow?"

"So that you can't avoid it."

Rone shook his head. "No. Charlotte, we're moving on."

"That's my prerogative."

"You hired me to get you home safely. I intend to fulfill at least *that* part of my contract."

"Good," Charlotte said. "But you still work for me. And I'm not leaving a friend to die on my account. Not again."

"What do you mean?"

"Ardala," Charlotte said. She held her smirk, but her eyes were trembling. Tears were filling her lower lids.

"You don't know what happened to her," Rone said. "She's probably fine."

"Don't lie to yourself, Rone. You worked for Sarthius. You know what he does to traitors or those of whom he even suspects betrayal."

"We cannot undo what we have done," Rone said. "We have to keep moving, otherwise Ardala... her death will be in vain."

"What death is not in vain?" Charlotte said. "And we are already walking back into the past, don't you see? Taking me home... I can't un-marry Sarthius, Rone. I can't undo what he did to me... but I can find again some part of the peace I once had, even if all my dreams are dead and blown away like blossoms at the passing of spring. I have no illusions of a life without regrets. I don't think you do either, but I know if I have a chance of avoiding regret in the now, I will take it over trying to walk back into the past once again."

"I've already learned that you can't walk back into the past, Charlotte."

"Your people are dying. Mine are very much alive." Charlotte paused. She walked to the bed and sat down on the edge of it. Rone sat down beside her and leaned over, putting his elbows onto his knees, hanging his head.

"You were an assassin," Charlotte said.

"Among other things," Rone said. "You hadn't figured that out by now? You've seen me kill."

"Why didn't you tell me what you did before?" Charlotte said.

"You never asked."

"I guess I wanted to believe other things."

"Like what? I was just a rustic who wanted adventure?"

"That you were a good man."

Rone looked at her askance. "I wanted to be a good man. I wanted to be a good man again. I thought by helping you, I could... redeem myself. But here I am doing it all over again. I'm a criminal again."

"I thought the Somnietel lived by their own code."

"I broke the code."

Charlotte laid her hand on Rone's arm. "You decided to do a good thing for me."

"Men have died in the process of doing good for you," Rone said. "And Ardala, too, if we are being honest. And I *should* be honest and stop being such a liar. I don't see how I can be a good man like this."

Charlotte leaned over and kissed Rone on the cheek. "I think maybe you should stop worrying about being good and just be what I need you to be."

"And what do you need me to be?"

"My hero." With that, Charlotte wrapped her arms around Rone and began to weep in earnest. "I need you to save me, Rone."

Rone touched her face and lifted it toward his. He forced a smile. "You're not making it easy, you know."

Charlotte smiled through the tears. "I probably never will make it easy on you."

Rone shrugged. "Keeps life interesting."

Charlotte laid her head on Rone's shoulder, and he hesitantly wrapped an arm around her. She looked at the moon. "You know, you never asked me what it was like."

"What?"

"Being Sarthius's wife. You never asked what it was like."

"I figured you would tell me if you needed to. If it was important."

"You're lying again, Rone."

"Shit. Well, I suppose I didn't want to know. I'd rather write my own story for you."

"Still?"

"No," Rone said. "Tell me your story."

Charlotte paused and locked eyes with Rone for a moment. "How much choice have you had in your life?"

"A great deal," Rone said. "Not that I've made the most of that freedom."

"As a woman, I have no choice. Maybe peasant women can decide things for themselves, but the nobility?" She shook her head. "I think peasant girls dream of pretty weddings to hansom princes. I always knew that was a foolish fantasy. My parents didn't have a very happy marriage. My father was the brother of the king, and he had choice – he got to choose my mother. She didn't get to choose him.

"When I think about her now, I still remember her as the most beautiful woman on earth, with shining blue eyes and hair that was golden-brown; she was from Latheria, and looked so different than all of my relatives: shorter, but more elegant. I can see why my father chose her.

"You mean she looked like you," Rone said. "Minus the hair."

Charlotte smiled. "Thank you for that. She was miserable – not used to life in the country where my father's estates were. We traveled to see my uncle in Vargana, which is a busy and beautiful port, as often as my father would allow it. So, from an early age, I could see that my life would probably be similar – married to an ill-tempered man who I wouldn't know beforehand.

"So it was I ended up betrothed to Sarthius Catannel. We had only met once before our wedding, and it was when he stopped by our estate for other business. He seemed utterly disinterested in me at first. He caught me when he was leaving wrestling with one of my brothers behind the stable. I remember he gave me this strange, ugly smile. I hated it."

"I've seen that smile." Rone rubbed his hands with force. "It's a thing of emptiness."

Charlotte nodded. "I'd almost forgotten you were in the guard. I'm not used to thinking of you like that. I only saw you in uniform that one time."

"It never fit right, and I looked bad in it. It's best you forget it entirely."

"No, I don't think so. That's one thing I don't want to forget. Anyway, my father scolded us, especially me, as wrestling is very-unladylike, but he got a letter from the Count a few days later. It was a marriage proposal, and apparently quite modest. I don't know why my father cared about political alliances in Veraland, but he agreed. I had to say goodbye to everything.

"We spent a few days in the castle in Vargana before we left, and that's when I overheard my uncle, the king, berating my father."

Charlotte frowned and looked at the wall as she spoke, "'The entire Catannel family is hideous and cruel. What a waste of a beautiful daughter. And for a political attachment you *don't need,*' my uncle said. I had been hiding in the larder, eating sugar, if you can believe that.

"I can, even though I have seen you eat wild rabbit," Rone said.

"Hunger makes everything sweet." Charlotte sighed. "My father was not receptive to my uncle. 'A good king would understand the need for his vassals to gather support for themselves, and in turn their ruler,' he said.

"'A good vassal would trust his king to secure peace for his charges,' my uncle said back.

'I will do what I think is best for my family, and my daughter, unless you think your providence extends to the very bedrooms of your subjects'

'You know my objections, Brut. It is your prerogative, but I would not choose to send my daughter across the sea.' I remember that so well – a feeling that it didn't have to be like it was.

"My father exploded, though. 'Your daughter would be a princess, and you would not even need a dowry to procure security for her. I do not have such luxuries. I am *lucky* to have what you consider an ugly and cruel family take her. Who would you prefer I let take her?'

"'I will take her. She can live here, in safety and luxury, and I will arrange a suitable marriage to a proper man of northern blood,' my uncle said. My heart leapt in hope, if only for a moment. It was as if in one moment I had dreams born, fulfilled, and then burned. I loved my uncle's house, you see, just like my mother did, and I could imagine meeting a handsome knight – chivalrous and bold – and loving him.

"'To hell with you, brother, and your insults. I will do what I wish with my own family,' was the last I heard. They didn't speak to each other again that I remember. My uncle caught me a day before I left and handed me a leather bag full of gold. He said it was a dowry for me or an early inheritance, and that I should keep it hidden and for myself. And that his castle would always be my home if I wanted it."

Rone nodded toward the baggage. "I wondered how you came by it."

"I had grand ideas of what I would do with it, at one point. I thought I could… hire an escape." Charlotte looked out the window, and a tear fell over one eyelid. "But why escape? That's what you want to know now, right?"

"I can be content with just the job," Rone said. "If that is what you want. My handler didn't give me details, and I'm used to it."

"It was a beautiful wedding, Rone. It was in a cathedral, with bright blue and green uniforms and a royal guard, officiated by the high cleric of Veraland. Catannel, his aids, his castle by the sea; they were all facades, like a stiff coat of paint over rotten wood. The real Catannel's heart matches his face.

"The first thing he did when we retreated to his apartments in the castle was slap me. I was shocked, but then he gripped my throat, squeezed, and smiled, and I understood. I fought him, and he did not leave uninjured, but as I found out in the weeks to come, that was exactly what he liked. He ripped my beautiful blue dress off without care to its quality. He held me down and forced his way into me despite my screams, laughing the whole time. Nobody came to help me. He raped me, Rone."

Charlotte hid her face in her hands and began to shudder. Rone hesitated a moment, then put his arm around her.

"You can stop."

Charlotte took a breath and continued from in her hands, "I was a virgin, but the pain… it was so bad, Rone. So much worse than anything other women had told me it would be. Afterward, he left me, bloody and crying on the bed, and locked the door from the outside." Charlotte raised her head, and though her face was wet with tears, she wore a stern, determined expression. "There was but one thing I was thankful for that night, and that was the fact that Sarthius did not think to go through my things. After he left, I was able to hide the money my uncle had given me.

"I found my mother the next day and told her. All she did was pat my back and say, "It always hurts the first time, you'll get over it." I did not know how to react. Part of me was confused, though I knew deep down what I had been subjected to could never be enjoyed. Sarthius found out about what I said to my mother and punished me. He proceeded to have my door kept locked when he or his servants could not directly observe me. Nobody in my family ever came to visit me."

"I think your uncle knew," Rone said. "Since it's him who hired me."

"It is?"

"I think so, anyway," Rone said. "I can't say for sure, as I was hired through an intermediary, which is standard, but I had and inkling once you told me he was your uncle. It's a lot of money. More than your little bag by a lot."

"Is that why you never took the money and ran?"

"No."

"Good, I need to hear you say that, Rone."

Rone touched her face lightly and turned her lips toward his. He kissed her, very softly, then rubbed gently at the tear tracks on her cheeks. "If you don't want to go back to Hviterland, I'll take you wherever you want. I mean that. I have connections all through the Divine Strand. I don't need the money."

Charlotte shook her head. "No, I need to go home. And…" She sniffed softly, "he's evil. Not just to me. I couldn't satisfy him. He would often have his way with the servants or have girls from the city brought in. Somebody has to punish him. Vegard would. He will. He has the power."

"Maybe not just him," Rone said. "All men have a weakness. An arrow will kill a king as well as a beggar." Rone let his head hang. "My name is cursed for serving him, even for so short a time. I always knew something was wrong with him. You hear things – things I should have listened to but chose to disbelieve. A lot of the guards were in on it."

"They're just like him," Charlotte said.

"I hate him," Rone said. "I've spent my whole adult life being dispassionate, but I hate him. I'm so sorry he took so much from you."

Charlotte wrapped her arms around Rone's waist and pulled him closer to her on the bed. "Rone."

"I'm here," Rone said, wrapping his arms around her.

"I need you to be my hero, even if you're just in it for the money. Be a killer, but be my hero, too." They sat there for a few moments, then she said, "I'd forgotten that it can feel good to be touched."

"You still want me to go to the other room?"

"No. I want you close. I always want you close."

"I'll be close, then, but just close."

VII: Gold Courthouse

Rone woke up suddenly, snapping out of a dream in which he was lost in a forest where it was neither day nor night and everywhere he looked, he saw shades and ghosts. Some of the faces he recognized, but he lost all sense of who they belonged to as sleep left him. His pulse quickened as he realized that Charlotte was no longer beside him on the bed.

"Charlotte?" he said aloud, craning his neck to see if she was behind the privacy screen where the chamber pot sat. He could see nothing, so he pulled himself up. He still wore his clothes, though he had at least taken his boots off. After a quick look around the room, he realized he was truly alone. Breathing deeply to calm himself, he pulled on his boots, checked his pistol, and began to arm himself. When he went to strap on his sword belt, he noticed a small silver tray sitting on an occasional table.

Upon it sat an open razor, an stiff hairbrush, a small bowl of water, and a chunk of tallow soap. Rone noticed a small piece of paper and picked it up, finding a note written in an elegant hand that said:

> *You said you wanted to shave, so I asked the steward for a razor. I'm going to be brave today, but I expect to have you on hand. Meet me upstairs in the drawing-room when you are finished dressing. Wear what I bought you in Masala.*
>
> -C

Rone smiled, then set about to lighting a fire in the corner stove to heat the water.

*

"I haven't seen that face is quite a while," Charlotte said. She pulled off one of her lace-cuffed gloves and ran her palm over his cheeks. "I thought men were supposed to have rough skin." She straightened his doublet, then tightened the silk tie at the top.

"The beard helps protect it," Rone said. He looked Charlotte up and down and smiled. She was wearing a black dress, though she had pieces of delicate white lace lining the bust, hem, and sleeves. The top showed off just enough shoulder to turn a head, but not enough to be outside of formal traditions: her sleeves ended just below her elbow, leaving an expanse of skin between them and her gloves, and more lace covered where her breasts would be displayed in the top, though a crack of cleavage still peeked above. "Where did you get that outfit?"

"Mitha's wardrobe."

"She let you go through her wardrobe?"

"I told her serving maid I could."

"How deceptive of you," Rone said.

"I have a good teacher," she said. She took a sip of tea and smiled at the sky above the patio.

"So why did you want me to wear this again?" Rone said.

"Are you ready to help me be brave today?"

"You aren't brave now?"

"No," Charlotte said. "I'm terrified."

"That has nothing to do with courage." He picked up his cup of tea and took a sip. "Too much sugar," he said, though he kept drinking it. "After all you've been through getting here, you still think you're not brave?"

"I had you dragging me along. I need you to drag me again. I'm going to get Johnny out of prison,"

"How's that?" Rone said. "A prison break?"

"No, that's your area of expertise. I'm going to talk him out of prison."

"You think you can do that?"

"I'm very well-cultured, mister Stonefield, and I have a background in the art of rhetoric, as is fitting a woman of my stature."

"Alright," Rone said. "You have a plan? You hinted to as much last night."

"Yes. We're going to be Johnny's lawyers. I gathered from Mitha that this Gold Courthouse the nobles here use is very big on common law. I bet I can work out a way to get him off."

"And if you can't?"

"Then we're no worse off."

"Unless the courthouse figured out who we are, and hands us over to Vindrel."

"Would fugitives walk right into the prison?"

"No." Rone smiled at her. "Not unless they were stupid."

"Which is why they won't think we are Charlotte and Rone. They'll think we're... whoever we say we are."

Rone was silent for a moment. "I won't be much help with the talking, I think."

"Just stand there and look pretty." Again, Charlotte reached up and touched his face.

*

The Gold Courthouse was less a courthouse than a fortress, and though it was not made of gold like the old tales suggested, it earned its name as its primary concern was banking, not justice. It was like a small castle, with a tall outer wall and a fortified inner keep, but at the same time, it was open and airy, full of the bustle of people. Men and women of all social classes walked in and out freely, and the posted guards, all well-armed, were casual with their conversations. Charlotte and Rone were paid little mind as they wandered in through the front gate.

There were a few tables in the courtyard dedicated to money changing, as the island, perched as it was in the sea, received coinage from all over Deideron. The interior of the keep was well-lit by skylights and tall steel-barred windows. Far across from the entrance stood a cashier's cage, and beyond it, steel doors and a treasure room. Hallways opened up to auxiliary rooms and stairs, some labeled with different services such as "Real Estate," "Personal Loans," "Hearings," and "Common Justice."

"Are you ready?" Charlotte asked, pausing beside the sign for "Internment, Bond Guarantee, Execution."

Rone nodded and opened the door. It led from the bright central hall of the Gold Courthouse down a narrow stair to the dungeon below ground level. They stepped into an office with barred windows where a small bearded clerk sat at a desk next to a guard armed with a halberd who was leaning by a massive, iron-bound door.

"Pardon me," Rone said. "I'm here to see a client."

The short clerk immediately stood up and smiled.

"Grant Smooty, at your service," he said. He looked to Charlotte and gave a shallow bow. He looked back to Rone. "Are you an attorney?"

"Not with the Gallow, but yes," Rone said.

"We both are, actually," Charlotte said. Rone coughed to himself.

"Of course," Grant said, bowing again, "I should have known from the dress; I just seldom see women in the profession here. Pardon my ignorance."

"Think nothing of it," Charlotte said, tilting her head in response. "I am Pelna Cans, and this is Morton Lindblum." She held her gloved hand toward Rone, who smiled and nodded.

"How can I help you?" Grant said.

"I believe you are holding an employee of ours," Charlotte said. "A mister Johnny."

"Oh yeah," Grant said. "Big, huge fellow, right? He wouldn't give us a last name."

"Hmn," Rone said. "I was hoping you'd have beaten it out of him." He laughed obnoxiously. Charlotte quickly joined him, and so did the clerk.

"The truth is I don't think the fellow has one. Orphan." Charlotte gave the clerk a false sad face. "Poor thing."

Grant rubbed the back of his neck. "Well, we've got him. Fugitive contract, right? Don't remember the fellow who was on about it."

"Vindrel?" Rone said.

"Yes, that sounds right," Grant said. "Do you know him?"

"He is known *to* us," Charlotte said. "Though I've never met him."

"Well, he wants to take him off-island," Grant said. "Which means we have to hold out for a proper judge. The hearing starts in…" He looked at a small wooden clock on the wall, "An hour or so, in case nobody told you." He shrugged. "They often don't tell anybody."

"I see," Charlotte said. "I assume you will release him to us in the meantime. Providing bail guarantee, of course."

"I'm sorry madam, I can't do that. Not for maritime crimes," Grant said.

"May we at least confer with our client?" Rone asked.

"Of course. Bert!" the clerk yelled.

The guard stepped forward with a grumble. "I'm right here, boss. No need to yell."

"Send these two down," Grant said. He looked at Charlotte. "We have another prisoner downstairs – nasty little man. Let me know if he gives you any trouble. I'll deal with him if he's uncouth."

Charlotte nodded, and they followed the guard down a sloping hallway.

"He likes to spit at people," Bert said sideways. "The little fellow, I mean. Try not to get too close." He knocked thrice on the door. "Visitors for that big chap."

The sounds of metal grinding against metal echoed in the narrow stairway, then the door swung inward. Rone glanced at the door frame and the wall surrounding it, noting the vault-like barring mechanism that sent four pieces of black steel into a reinforced channel in the wall. They stepped past another armed guard into the small dungeon, though that was perhaps too harsh a word for it. It was a tidy and bright jail, lit by small, square windows, double-barred and piping in light from a ground level that was above even the ceiling. A line of steel-barred cells went down one side of the room, each with a mattress, a chamber pot, and a wooden shelf. Only two of these were occupied. One was filled by a man who lay snoring in a small patch of sunlight on the hard floor. In the closer cell was Johnny, who was staring at the ceiling.

"There you are!" Rone shouted, "I hope you remember us, we're-"

"It's you!" Johnny said, bolting upright and half-stumbling to the cell door. "I didn't even recognize you without the-"

"Pelna Cans and Morton Lindblum," Charlotte said quickly and loudly. "We were attorneys for your ships majority holder in Golice. So glad you haven't forgotten us."

Johnny stared at them with a puzzled look for a moment, his hands hanging on the iron bars. "You work for… Tommy?"

Rone waved his hand in front of his face at Johnny's breath, which reeked of whiskey and barley beer, despite him being in prison for more than a day. "Yes," Rone said, eyes wide. "We argue at the court in Golice on behalf of… Tommy."

"Oh," Johnny said. He cracked his strange grin and winked very obviously. "Yeah, good 'ol Tom, and the lawyers, always with the lawyers… that fellow."

Charlotte's eyes were bulging as she subtly tried to wave her hands and get Johnny to stop talking. Rone looked over at the end of the row to see the guard sit down at a table and begin gnawing an apple. He opened up a nearby book and started reading.

"Tom?" Rone said quietly, leaning toward the bars. "You went with Tommy?"

"It's a name," Johnny said, shrugging. "It's familiar. Tommy is a kind name. A name you call a good friend. Like Johnny, eh?"

Rone and Charlotte looked at each other in confusion.

"Bah, the guard's an idiot anyway. He doesn't listen to anything down here."

"You're going before a judge in an hour, and we're going to try to deal for your freedom," Charlotte said. "Vindrel is here, and tried to arrest you, right?"

"You're talking like a lawyer already, lass," Johnny said. "And yeah, I guess you didn't manage to kill the bastard in Masala."

"I probably saved him, actually," Rone said. "I patched him up while you were dealing with shoving off after the mutiny."

"Why would you do a thing like that?" Johnny said.

Rone chewed his cheek silently.

"He knew him from before," Charlotte said.

"I couldn't leave him to die," Rone said. "Just leave it at that for now."

"Fine, but if this fellow sees me hanged, I'm gonna throttle you," Johnny said.

"How do you aim to do that?" Rone said.

"I have an army of assassins ready to throttle those that get me hanged, in the event of… my being hanged," Johnny said.

"Right," Charlotte said.

"You don't know," Johnny said. He burped.

Charlotte shook her head. "Are you still drunk?"

"Only a little," Johnny said.

"For a big man, you don't hold your liquor well," Rone said.

"You hadn't been seeing how much liquor I was holding yesterday. I'll be right as rain in half an hour."

"He said that three hours ago," the man in the other cell said loudly, sitting up. They recognized him as Mineo, the man who nearly lost his head in the public square.

"Bah, you're just jealous," Johnny said.

"I am," Mineo said. "You know how hard it is to get a sniff in this pit? Now shut up! Some of us are trying to piddle away the hours of our day over here." His head popped up, and he raised an eyebrow to Charlotte. She tried not to return the glance and focus on Johnny. "Hey, pretty," he said.

"Pardon me," Charlotte said, then looked at Johnny again.

"How about you let me see what you've got behind all that black lace? You know I'm doomed to die."

"I should say so," Rone said. Charlotte put her hand on his chest firmly.

"C'mon, lass," Mineo said. "How about just one tit? I promise to think about it when the lights are out. What do you say, one sweet pink nipple for a dying man's pleasure?"

"Just ignore him," Johnny said. "Poor sod will be dead soon anyway."

Charlotte and Rone turned back to Johnny.

"Do you know anything about how the courts work here?" she said.

"Not really," Johnny said. "I think they just enforce contracts, near as I can tell. Common law stuff. You have to hire the court to try a criminal here."

"The clerk outside said something about arbitration and restitution," Charlotte said.

Johnny shrugged.

"Maybe we can rummage through some rule books or something upstairs," Charlotte said. He looked at Johnny and said, "Otherwise, I'll have to get creative. We'll see you in an hour. Wish us luck."

"I'm *cursing* my luck right now mister, uh, Lindgren," Johnny said as the turned to walk away.

"Lindblum!" Rone whispered back as he and Charlotte walked toward the exit. Without taking his eyes off his book, the Jailor stood up and began turning a wheel on the back of the door. Rone took one last quick look around, taking in the details and features of the underground jail before following a guard out of the door.

*

"This is the law library?" Charlotte asked, pulling out wooden bins of paper from the shelves, and pawing through them quickly. "There's nothing here but contracts."

"That's what the law is," the old bald clerk said from nearby. He was busy stamping forms with a square hunk of carved wood. He turned around to regard Charlotte for a moment. "Well, other than theft, or rape, or murder, but nobody needs to write any of that down."

"This is hopeless," Charlotte said. She eyed the clock sitting on the clerk's desk. The minute hand seemed to have jumped several spaces ahead.

"Maybe there's something I can help you with," the clerk said.

"We have a friend – a client," Rone said, "that was arrested and jailed. He has a hearing with a judge at the top of the hour."

"Well, the judge will sort it out," the old man said, writing something on a card and putting it to the side of his desk. "Of course, if you feel the need to argue, you can pull the correct contract here."

"Contract?" Charlotte said. "For an arrest?"

The old man looked at her. "Yes... well, where was he arrested?"

"In a pub, I believe," Rone said.

"Belonging to whom?" The old smiled slightly.

"I believe it was called... Reggets," Charlotte said. The old man cleared his throat. She looked down to see an open palm. She quickly pulled a silver coin from her purse and put it in his hand. He smiled as he tucked it into his jacket pocket, then stood up and walked across the crowded room.

He opened up a cabinet revealing long rows of stiff paper and began pawing through them and mumbling to himself. "Regget Harrity, Regget Harritty... ah, here he is." He pulled up a small card containing columns of scribbled words and neatly stamped dates. "Two-'C' looks to be the correct spot. He put the card down and walked to one of the bins. After a moment of rummaging, he produced a short set of printed words with a few signatures attached. He handed it to Charlotte. "This is his contract with the courthouse for arrest and security services."

Charlotte turned it over in her hand. "This is it?"

"Yes," the old man said, putting the card back in the large wooden cabinet and walking back toward his desk. "Anything the courthouse is either allowed or obligated to do is in that contract." He smiled. "Good luck, and be sure to bring that back before you go."

The door to the closet-like room opened, and Charlotte and Rone turned to see Teal Starnly, wearing a crisp grey jacket with black long pants enter, a leather satchel under his arm. "Ah, there you two are," he said. "Johnny's hearing will be in a few minutes."

"What are you doing here?" Charlotte said.

Starnly walked up and pulled the contract from her hands and glanced at it. "Thank you." He looked back at them and said, "I'm here to argue Johnny's case for you."

"You are?" Charlotte said.

He smiled. "I'm an attorney, after all. Even if the Gallow doesn't have much use for us, I prefer to flex the argument muscles from time to time." He motioned them to follow him out of the room. "I was hoping you could persuade your friend to agree to our contract. He seemed a little untrusting of me."

"I can't blame him. I don't particularly trust you, after all."

"Mister Stonefield," Starnly said, putting his hand to his chest, "I'm offended."

"Actually, it's mister Lindblum now," Rone said.

"And I'm Miss Cans," Charlotte said.

Teal chuckled. "I presume you are pretending to be lawyers?"

"Yes," Charlotte said. "In the employ of one Tom of Golice, majority shareholder of the Parkitees."

"What's his last name?" Sean said.

"I... didn't get one, I think," Charlotte said.

"Well, make one up," Starnly said as he set off again, crossing the busy central room. "You appear to be good at it. Now, my fellow solicitors, let's get to the courtroom, and please," he looked back at Charlotte, "*Do* use some of that charm on the judge." He glanced at her breasts, hidden slightly with lace, then winked at her.

"Wait," Rone said. Starnly paused and raised his eyebrows. "Do you think Vindrel could be in there?"

"Is that the fellow that caught your captain?" Sean said.

"Yes," Rone said.

"Then most certainly," Sean said. "He'll either be wanting restitution or to get ahold of your friend. Don't worry, we won't allow it."

"We'd best not go in, then," Rone said, "as long as we have you to speak for Johnny. He could recognize us."

"He won't recognize me," Charlotte said. "He's never seen me, remember? Only certain people from Cataling ever got to look at me."

"That's right, but he *will* recognize me." Rone paused and thought for a moment. "I'll catch you afterward, alright?"

"Very good," Starnly said.

VIII: Games of Chance

he inside of the courtroom was very different from those that Charlotte had experienced in her younger days. Rather than a wide hall well-lit with large windows, centered around a platform that made the judge tower over criminals and litigants alike, the courtroom at the Gold Courthouse was a small stone chamber, more like a receiving room or an office than a theater of justice. A few wooden chairs were arrayed before small desks that faced a massive walnut table heaped with papers. A few novel chandeliers that scattered light from the skylights were also present, bathing the room in a constant yet slightly too-dim glow.

Charlotte followed Teal Starnly in through the door and to a set of desks on the left side of the small room. She noticed a tall and lean man, presumably Regget, the owner of the bar, sitting at a desk in the center of the arc. He smiled at her as she walked past him. She glanced over him to a large man clad in blue and green, with a black beard and hazy yellow-green eyes, who leaned against a chair, letting his left arm, which was in a sling, rest upon the desk before him. Her heart quickened a bit as she thought twice about whether the man would recognize her. She had not explored much of Catannel's castle in Cataling, being more or less a captive during her two years there, and did not know whether the count had procured any of the many paintings that existed of her from her youth. She considered for the first time that Vindrel could indeed have seen her before, in a painting hung far outside her prison-like bedroom.

"I can't believe the pirate has lawyers," Vindrel said with a growl to a middle-aged man beside him in a similar uniform.

He glanced at Charlotte, and she shuttered inwardly. She took a shallow breath and calmed herself, feeling more confident that he didn't at least immediately recognize her. *Besides,* she thought, *He's not expecting me to just walk in here.* She smiled at him and he looked away.

"Pirates are the only men I can think of who need them," said the man sitting beside Vindrel. His accent was posh, almost exaggerated.

"Be sure to tell that to the judge," Starnly said with a smile. The posh man laughed.

"I wonder whose mistress this one is," Vindrel said, nodding toward Charlotte.

"Certainly I'll never be yours," Charlotte said, keeping hold of her voice but unable to resist the bait of the insult, "Though with a face like that I imagine you could bed any bitch in the kennel."

"I'll show you how I bed a bitch," Vindrel said, standing. "Do you know who you're talking to, woman?"

Starnly put his hand lightly on Charlotte's shoulder as if to restrain her. She stared back and Vindrel and said, her voice finally quavering, "I'm talking to a… petty little man, working for another petty little man." She took a quick, shallow breath, clenching her fists, and trying to keep her voice even. "Who King Borlond would refuse to hire as a jailor in the dirtiest dungeon holding the worst men in Golice."

Vindrel moved his right arm as if reaching for a pistol under his sling, but straightened his face and stood still as an old wooden door on the other side of the room opened up and an older man entered, dressed in a black jacket and long pants, all trimmed with gold. He had deep, dark brown skin and curly black hair, but his eyes were a pale green, and his hair had faded from black to a slate grey on the temples.

"Afternoon, gents," the man said as he crossed to the large table facing them. He put some papers down, looked up, and, noticing Charlotte, said, "And Lady." Among the documents was a small triangular nameplate, which he set at the front of the table. Upon a brass plate could be read in etching, "Charles Delving."

"Your honor," she said with a nod.

He looked back at her with a wide smile. "You must be from the mainland. We do things a bit differently here. *You* can just call me Charles, none of the 'your honor' business."

"Of course," Charlotte said, nodding again. Starnly tugged on her glove as she sat down, prompting her to follow him into the wooden chair beside his.

"Good to see you again, Teal," the judge said.

"You too, Chuck," Starnly said with a smile. "Good to see the law is treating you well."

"She treats me fairly," Chuck said with a wink. "When are you going to take the board up on that offer? Get on the other side of the bench for a change."

"Maybe during retirement," Starnly said. "Until then, I'm having far too much fun in the shipping business."

"Try not to get too rich," the judge said. "Or you'll be able to buy a house too far up the hill. You'll love the walk down, but the walk back will kill you, especially when you get to be my age." The old man pulled a set of half-glasses from his pocket and put them on, reading silently from one of the papers in his stack. "Well, let's get down to business. You two can sit any time you like," he said, looking at Vindrel and the other officer. The two men in uniform exchanged a glance and then seated themselves.

The door through which the judge had entered swung open again, and two guards came in with Johnny between them. He was in loose-fitting chains: two sets of irons locked together to accommodate his immense height and girth. One of the guards, holding an oversized brass-locked blunderbuss, motioned for Johnny to sit in a nearby chair. Johnny frowned but complied.

"Let's go through it for the record," the judge said, dipping a pen into an inkwell.

"May I have a brief consultation with my client?" Starnly said. "He still needs to sign the retainer." Starnly looked over at Charlotte and nodded slightly.

"That's right," Charlotte said, looking at Johnny. "We're prepared to cover local expenses, captain."

"Oh, of course," the judge said. "We don't want to be working for free, eh?"

"I'm a rich man," Starnly said, crossing the room to Johnny with a thick contract in his hands. "I mostly do it for fun, anyway."

Johnny stared at Charlotte for a moment after Starnly handed him the papers and a freshly dipped pen. He shrugged and signed, then initialed the other pages. Starnly smiled at Johnny and brought the contract back to his own desk, flapping the last page to dry the ink.

"Alright, where were we?" the Judge said, freshening his pen. "Oh yes… Parties present?" He pointed to Charlotte, then to each man to her right in turn.

"Pelna Cans," Charlotte said. "Representation from the court of Golice. Arguing for Johnny." The judge scrawled quickly on a paper in front of himself.

"Teal Starnly," Sean said beside her. "Representing Ashroad Shipping Incorporated, arguing for the same."

"Let's not forget representation for our dear Gallow," Charles said, scribbling. He pointed to the man in the center.

"Regget Harity," he said. "Representing myself and arguing for myself, and my property, Regget's Pub."

The officer Vindrel had brought with him cleared his throat when the judge pointed at him. "Admiral-Lord Donovan Dunneal, supreme commander of the combined fleet of the Veraland, the Green Isle, subject to his majesty King Sarthius Catannel of Cataling."

The judge looked up with a raised eyebrow. "New king is news to me." The admiral cleared his throat again, which prompted a contemptuous look from the judge. "And… who exactly are you arguing for, mister Dunneal?"

Donavan stood mute for a moment. "For justice."

"Then you'd best find a box and a street corner, admiral," the judge said. "We don't do justice here; we interpret contracts and the law." Teal chuckled, and the judge winked at him.

"Then we are arguing for the Isle," Donovan said.

"Very well," the judge said. He pointed at Vindrel.

"Vindrel Stonefield," he said. Charlotte's heart raced for a minute as she heard the name. "Chief inquisitor and minister of security to his majesty King Sarthius Catannel of Veraland. Arguing for myself, my king, and against Johnny."

The judge scribbled again and pointed to Johnny.

"Johnny. Um. Arguing for myself?"

"Johnny what?" the judge said.

"Just Johnny."

The judge looked over at Charlotte, who said, "He lacks a family name that we know of."

"Very well, Just Johnny it is," the judge said. He held up a paper slightly and read a few lines to himself. "I am Charles Delving-" The admiral cleared his throat, and the judge looked up, cocking his head. "Do you have something to say before proceedings, mister Dunneal?"

The admiral cleared his throat again. "Nothing, just a familiar name."

"He must be thinking of Seamus Delving," Charlotte said.

The judge looked over at her with a smile. "Ah, Seamus," the judge said before looking back at Donovan. "He's my little brother." The admiral cleared his throat again, almost coughing. "Yes?"

"He's…" The admiral raised his eyebrows, his face slack with shock. "Well, he's wanted for piracy."

"In Veraland, no doubt," the judge said, "but this is not the Green Isle and were you to say something like that in Datalia, I think you might be laughed out of the room. Seamus is a war hero, even if he is a privateer. And a good brother to boot." The judge chuckled, looking at his paper again, mumbling something from which only the word "manners" Charlotte could make out. He looked at Regget. "So, we had a little altercation in your pub, in which this large fellow," he pointed at Johnny, "was getting the better of this fellow." He pointed at Vindrel.

"That's right, mister Delving," Regget said. "The guard has already been paid in cash. I have a receipt if you need it. Asking for the right to recover my loss."

"Granted," the judge said. He looked at Johnny. "Any contest?"

Johnny looked back up and shrugged. "I was pummeling him if that's what you mean."

"Did you do that to his arm?" the judge asked.

"That? No, that wasn't me," Johnny said.

"Very well," the judge said. "Not contested, which surprises me. How much do you want in recompense?" He looked at Vindrel.

"Recompense?" Vindrel said. "He's a criminal!"

The judge sighed and looked at Regget, who said, "Standard fare, mister Delving. I'd say 20 argents ought to do it."

"Objections?" the judge said to Vindrel.

The admiral cleared his throat again. "Charles-"

"That's mister Delving to you," the judge said.

"But you said to call you Charles," Donovan said.

"I said *she* could call me Charles," the judge said, nodding toward Charlotte. "You can call me Mister Delving." He looked back at Charlotte. "I tell you, people from the Isle never have any manners."

"I have learned this," Charlotte said.

The admiral cleared his throat again.

"You really ought to go see a doctor about that cough, admiral," the judge said.

"We are prepared to pay mister Harity's suggested restitution, given his experience in such matters," Starnly said, "As well as reimburse him for the court costs."

"Seems pretty straightforward," the judge said.

"Mister Delving," Donovan said, his voice rising to a near shriek. "We came here expecting you to turn over to us a wanted pirate; this isn't about his assault of the inquisitor at all. He murdered soldiers of the Isle in cold blood not a fortnight ago!"

"Mister Delving," Starnly said calmly, holding up the paper Rone and Charlotte had been given by the clerk earlier, "We have a copy of the contract between the courthouse and Regget Harity. It has the standard exceptions in place for accusations of piracy." Sean stood up and pushed the paper in front of the judge. "You'll notice that in criminal or bounty pursuits, the court is to disregard accusations of piracy if the subject in question was acting within the private prize contracts of his port of call, in this case, Golice."

"I can testify to that end," Charlotte said. "Johnny has a contract with his Majesty, King Borlond Mothanan of Golice, and we assert that his actions have been within the scope of that contract." While she spoke, a door in the back opened and swung shut. Charlotte looked over for a moment and saw the familiar face of Farthow, now wearing a green jacket and maroon pants. He approached Vindrel, and, making eye contact with Charlotte, winked.

"We also assert," Starnly said, filling in the silence, "That any actions that may or may not have taken place between parties were at sea and therefore subject to private contract and maritime law."

"This is nonsense," Vindrel said, pushing himself up. "This man murdered soldiers of the Isle and his own first mate!" Farthow passed a note to Vindrel as he spoke. He looked down at it, frowning.

"What happens at sea is not the concern of the courthouse," the judge said. "Our laws end there. You can try to blast him out of the water once he leaves, but this is a free port, and I can't turn a man over on mere accusation of piracy." He cocked his head as Vindrel pushed his way past the admiral and Farthow.

"Excuse me, sir," Vindrel said. "Pressing business of the crown." He walked out the door briskly.

The admiral cleared his throat. "The actions we are talking about did not happen at sea, mister Delving, they happened on the docks at Masala."

The judge scratched his chin a moment and looked at Johnny, who shrugged.

"Mister Delving," Starnly said. "I must argue a few things. First, who was witness to this?"

"Vindrel was there himself, and injured," the admiral said.

"It's a pity he just left. We could have worked out an agreement to that right now," the judge said.

"We intend to hang the pirate," Donavan said.

"Second," Starnly said, "Mister Dunneal and Mister Stonefield are representatives of the County of Cataling, not Masala, which is under the rule of Drath Harec. Under standard rules of the court, accusations must come from those authorized to make them."

"I speak for the King of Veraland," Donavan said. "He has authority over all ports on the Green Isle.

"Charles," Charlotte said, "I'm afraid mister Donavan is not being truthful. Sarthius Catannel has not yet ascended to the throne, and will not until he can produce a wife."

"What do you mean by 'produce a wife'?" said the judge.

"This man is a party in the kidnapping of the queen!" the admiral said, pointing at Johnny.

"That's a laugh," Johnny said with a smile. "Me stealing off with the queen." He looked at the judge. "I mean, look at me, sir. Do I look like I could pull that off?"

"That's two lies, mister Dunneal," the judge said. "I'm going to have to give summary judgment for Regget and judge according to Teal's suggestions, agreeing with the argument of lack of authority."

"You would risk everyone on your island for a fat pirate?" the admiral said, leaning over the desk. "I'll have you know-"

The judge laughed. "You think I don't know about that antique fleet of yours sitting outside the harbor? I think if you put your guns to use, you'd get quite more than you bargained for in a fight with Tyrant's Gallow. We protect our own here, and there are many men here just as competent as my brother. Now, unless you have some other means of establishing authority, I'm going to send you off twenty argents heavier and mister Just Johnny free."

"I'm sure," the admiral said, breathing deeply, "that mister Bitterwheat will speak with authority for count Harec." He turned his hand as if to gesture at Farthow, only to see an empty seat right behind him. Donavan turned to see a greet coat disappearing out the door. "Farthow, get back here!" he shrieked.

The green jacket froze, then Farthow turned back into the little courtroom. "I have other business to attend to, Donny," he said, a look of annoyance on his face.

"You will address me as admiral Dunneal," he said, his voice cracking.

"I will address you as such when you are named such," Farthow replied as he strode up to the side of Donavan. "Till then, you are Donny."

"What do you say, mister... Bitterwheat?" the judge said. "Is this man a criminal?"

Fathow looked at Donavan uncomfortably for a moment. "He did have a scuffle with the Cataling guard while at dock in Masala."

"But not with the Masala guard," Charlotte said.

"No, not with the Masala guard," Farthow said.

"Is it a crime to do such?" the judge said.

"The count..." Farthow's face drooped as he glanced at Charlotte, "did allow the Cataling guard to pursue some men on the docks."

"They set up a mutiny on my ship!" Johnny said, standing up quickly. The guard standing near at hand put his hand on the large man's shoulder as if to push him down, but Johnny didn't give.

"The guard wants you to sit down, captain," Charlotte said.

Johnny looked about. "Oh," he said and flopped back into his chair.

"Well, there appears to be more to it than a little scuffle in your pub," Charles said, looking at Regget. "Life is interesting, no?"

Regget nodded, wide-eyed.

"Mister Delving," Starnly said. "I would just like to remind the court of its own policy, also stated in the contract, that transfers from in-house to out-of-country of a criminal nature can only be approved by a three-judge panel."

"Of course," the judge said. "May I keep this contract copy until tomorrow?" he held up the piece of paper Charlotte had found.

"You may file it again with the clerks at your leisure," Starnly said.

"Very well," the judge said. "I'll gather up the other angry old men, and we'll have a hearing tomorrow with the three of us. Let's say ten in the morning." He turned to one of the guards. "By the way, Gunny, you can unchain the ship. It's a criminal matter now, apparently, and we've already agreed to compensation, so no need to keep things impounded."

"Yes sir, I'll have it done within the hour," the bailiff said.

"Mister Delving!" Donavan said as the judge stood up. "It's a pirate ship. You cannot be serious!"

"You can't put a criminal claim upon property. Until ten tomorrow, sirs and madam," Charles said, taking his glasses back off. He looked back at Charlotte with a smile, "Certainly not soon enough. Keep in mind you already agreed to twenty argents if I side with you."

"I will, Charles," Charlotte said.

The judge nodded and stepped out of the room.

"We did our best," Charlotte said to Johnny as he was pulled up and led toward the door in the back.

"Tell Danny's mum I went out smiling," he said back over his shoulder.

Starnly gave Charlotte a puzzled look. She shrugged. Donavan glared at her for a protracted moment and then stomped out of the room, the hard heels of his boots clicking loudly in the small chamber.

As the door swung behind him, Farthow leaned over and said quietly. "Sorry, I couldn't lie right in front of him."

"It's alright," Charlotte said. "What did you hand to Vindrel?"

"A note from Rone," Farthow said. "Telling Vindrel to meet him in a bar. He said he'd find you when he's done."

Charlotte felt a sudden fear. "What is he planning on doing?"

"Who knows with him?" Farthow said.

"We should wait for him at Seamus's house. He'll be having tea soon."

"Good idea. I'll send him your way."

Charlotte took a deep breath, watched the door out of which Johnny had vanished for a few moments, then followed Teal and Farthow out of the room.

*

"Somehow I knew your captain would lead you to this shit-hole of an island," Vindrel said as he approached Rone's table at the back of the second floor of the pub. A large window was open to the breeze, and the distant edge of the Gold Courthouse was visible. The afternoon sun cast a harsh beam across the floor to their right, and dust and ash danced visibly as Vindrel sat down at the little table.

"Did you just guess that, or did you see the same thing we saw on our way in?" Rone took a sip of his beer. He left his back to the corner of the upper floor and frequently glanced at the well-dressed men to each side of himself.

"It just seemed like a good destination for a bad pirate and a worse spy."

"You're not a good liar," Rone said.

"You're right. I'm nothing like you."

Rone looked away casually, but not so far that Vindrel was out of his periphery. "Don't you think it's unwise of your count to send his fleet away from his homeland and unwise for you to send it *here*, having seen Nantien for yourself?" Rone smiled as a young woman appeared from the spiral stair carrying a cluster of glass mugs in each hand. She smiled back at him as she began to place beers in front of other customers.

"You know nothing of the world of nobility, Rone."

"I know more than you would think, Vinny," Rone said.

"Just like an assassin to think himself a lord. You're a tool, nothing more." Vindrel quietly regarded the waitress as she put a mug of dark ale in front of him. "But whose tool, eh?"

"I took the liberty," Rone said with a smile. "It's not Black Cliff, but I think it will suit you."

Vindrel took a long drink, his eyes fixed on Rone. "My tastes have changed."

"So have mine." Rone held up his glass. "Pale ale. Bitter is all I can stand now."

"Unsurprising."

"Change… I guess that's life, eh?"

Vindrel wiped his mouth, still staring into Rone's eyes. "You're trying to tell me you've changed?"

"It's different this time, Vinny."

"How? Enough money to finally retire?" Rone shrugged at him. "That's a laugh." Vindrel looked away for a moment with a forced smile. "It's never enough money for men like you."

"In a way, you're right." Rone reached into his jacket pocket, his eyebrows high in an expression of peace, and withdrew an old deck of cards. He placed them in the center of the table.

"What's this?" Vindrel said.

"I said I'd play you for what I have the next time I saw you."

Vindrel took another long drink, then picked up the deck. He glanced down at it, then back at Rone, as if he feared the man would disappear if he but looked away. He flipped the deck over and looked through the cards. "There are no dragons," he said.

"I used them all up cheating," Rone said. "But it makes the odds easier."

Vindrel shuffled. The old cards were notched and misshapen, not snapping back to shape after the shuffle. "What do you have to play with?"

"I'm afraid I'm a little short on funds," Rone said. "Poker is never fun with a poor man."

"What will you wager instead?"

"My life," Rone said. Vindrel paused to look at him. "The things that go with it. We can do whatever game you like; it doesn't matter to me. If you win, I'll give myself up. You can walk me right on to your ship and haul me away."

"I aim to have that prize anyway," Vindrel said. "What's to stop me from just killing you right here?"

Rone held his palms forward. "If you have it in you. You didn't all those years ago, and I don't think you have it in you now."

"Change, right?"

Rone nodded. "If I win, you turn away. You take your ships, and you leave. Go back and defend our home against the Dreasenith Empire."

"The Empire is nothing," Vindrel said.

"Will you take the wager, or not?" Rone said.

"You aren't what I want," Vindrel said. "I need the girl."

Rone chuckled. "You really don't. You can say she's dead. I'm sure it makes no difference to Catannel. Her personhood is meaningless beyond the fact that he married her. He can marry someone else."

"You said yourself I'm a bad liar," Vindrel put the cards on the table. "But, like *I* said, you don't understand nobility. She matters, or do you think Catannel would bother otherwise?"

Rone raised an eyebrow at the revelation.

"You put the girl up, and you've got a game."

"I can't do that, Vinny."

"And why is that?" Vindrel said. "Did she cut you loose already?"

"I'm the wager. Me." Rone reached out and cut the deck.

"I'll leave you room to raise that wager." Vindrel picked it back up and began dealing. "I assume you will find Denarial's high-game acceptable?" Two cards were now face down in front of Rone and Vindrel. He put two more at the center of the table, then flipped two more face-up in front of each of them.

The ten of mountains and the queen of plains sat in front of Vindrel. Rone had the knight of plains and the two of forests.

"Why this game? I already listed the stakes."

"I said I'd give you room to raise your wager." Vindrel pulled the edge of his cards off the table and looked at them. He had two queens: mountains and forests

"Yes but can you raise yours?" Rone picked up his cards and looked at them. He smiled.

"Perhaps I won't just yet," Vindrel said. "We'll let the opening hand be your suggestion, and then we can go up from there. Perhaps I will offer that you give me the girl and let you go, eh?"

Rone laughed and turned his cards over, pushing them close to the center of the table. "You can run this game however you like, Vinny." There sat the two of mountains and the eight of rivers.

Vindrel looked at Rone's hand and tried to stuff a smile. "I'll let you fold now if you like. You can just follow me back to the ship right now." Rone stared back at him, calmly. Vindrel picked up the deck and put another card face down, then added one to the center: the two of plains. "No dragons in the roost today, Rone. You'll have to win a full set. I'll raise you the girl, and I'll promise to let you escape."

"It's your game to do with as you like," Rone said with a smile. "You can see my cards."

Vindrel chuckled. "I'm trying to help you, Rone."

"If you want to help me, then fold and leave," Rone said.

"All I've done is try to help you," Vindrel said, his voice growing in volume and drawing the attention of a few nearby patrons. "Since we were boys, I've shown you nothing but mercy. I've tried to get you good, honest, work and you spit in my face."

"You and I have different ideas of honest work," Rone said. He nodded toward the table. "Go on, play. It's your game."

"You're just the same spoiled child you always were," Vindrel said. "You haven't changed." He put one more card face down and flipped the last one in the middle. It was the two of rivers. His eyes widened. His gaze went up to Rone's, who looked back calmly.

"I guess you can still fold," Rone said.

"How…" Vindrel frowned. He picked up the deck and looked through it again. Nothing was missing or added, other than the fifth suite of dragons that normally trumped the others. "How did you…"

"I've never had it in me to kill you before, Vinny," Rone said, his eyes blazing with sudden intensity, "even when you practically begged me to do it. The truth is, I don't want to kill you now, but by the will of the dreamer,

I will. It's worth it to me this time. If you force me too, I will end you. You are walking in *my* dream. It may be your game, but I control the cards." Rone downed the rest of his pale ale and stood up. He swept the cards into a pile and stuffed them into his jacket pocket.

Vindrel grabbed his arm. "You can't just walk away from this."

"I did, I can, and I will," Rone said. "We'll find out tomorrow which of us is the real liar." He shook Vindrel's grip from his arm and disappeared down the spiral staircase.

After a moment of shock, Vindrel broke his paralysis and rushed down after him, dashing toward the front double doors of the inn. When he appeared in the street, all he could see were the ambling masses of people moving among the merchants in the market. He looked around frantically, searching around the building, but Rone was gone.

"Hey, Greenman!" Vindrel turned to see the one-eyed grey-headed barkeeper. He had a pistol in one hand, hanging down. "You can't just leave without paying."

"Bastard," Vindrel said to himself, searching his pockets for coins.

IX: The Goods

harlotte had a hard time focusing, though everyone else sitting at the ornate steel table seemed relaxed and amiable. Starnly had brought her to the estate of the famous Seamus Delving. Mitha had coincidentally (or not; Charlotte had not yet decided on how-well informed the woman truly was) been at the house visiting with him.

The conversation was interesting, and Seamus's many stories of adventures both humorous and exhilarating should have cheered Charlotte. Instead, she seemed only to be able to focus on the afternoon sun finding its way through the trellis above them, irritating her eyes. She let out a sigh of relief when Rone finally appeared, the gruff guard closing the gate behind him with a clang.

"Come now," Mitha said, smiling at her, "Seamus's stories are not *that* boring."

"Let the lass have her sighs," Seamus said.

Charlotte bowed to Mitha, Starnly, and Seamus Delving, as she stood up from the little table and left them to finish their tea.

"So, like I was saying," Seamus went on, "she said she was the queen. I took her for a liar, but as it would turn out, I was just making assumptions, as she never said just who or what she was queen of..."

Seamus's voice faded as Charlotte ran forward to Rone, wrapping her arms around him in a tight hug.

"I was only gone a few minutes," Rone said with a chuckle.

"What were you doing with him? He's the enemy."

"Just a friendly conversation," he said, "and a wager."

"Wager?"

"I bet my life on a hand of cards, that he would leave and go home," Rone said. "I won."

She twisted her fingers into the fabric of his jacket. "That was stupid."

"I'm sorry." He held her hands, which were gripping his doublet iron-tight. "But I don't think he would have killed me or hauled me off, even if he won the wager."

"You don't know that," Charlotte said, shaking him with her knotted hands.

"I do."

"How?"

"He's my brother, Charlotte."

She looked up into his eyes, feeling her vision tremble and blur, then looked down at the ground.

"He's my brother. We grew up together in the dry highlands. He offered me a job in the Cataling guard when I returned to Veraland, knowing what I did... as a profession, before. He's had other chances to kill me..." Rone sighed. "He wouldn't have had it in him."

Tears were collecting in her eyes. "Don't do that again," she said. "You put us at risk."

"I promise, I didn't put you at risk. I bet my own life, not yours."

"I said you put *us* at risk," Charlotte said, pulling back to look at him. "Us. That's you and me. I need you, Rone."

Rone breathed deeply, then forced out a small laugh. "Have a little faith." He pushed his thumbs into her fists, opening them a little. "I rather like this silly jacket. It was given to me by someone I care about, so try not to destroy it."

Charlotte was crying, but she laughed anyway, collapsing as she leaned against him. He hugged her again, then said, "You were very brave today. I take it your gamble didn't work, as I don't see our captain."

"No, it didn't," Charlotte said.

"It'll be alright." He led her back toward the small table, where a servant was pouring an extra cup of tea.

"I don't think It's likely my brother will sell your friend out," Seamus said, making eye contact with Rone, then Charlotte. "We've had fleets knock on our door before. Salty privateers like myself tend to find remarkable ways to work together when pressed to it. The city is in no danger, and my brother will understand that."

"No doubt, especially if the city is filled with men like you," Rone said.

"I trust by that you mean proper gentlemen," Seamus said and winked.

"I suppose one could be a gentlemen *and* warrior." He sat down with Charlotte and took a sip of the tea. It was hot and had a pale color and flavor like the tea Mitha had served the day before. Rone looked away, watching one of the fruit trees in Seamus's courtyard wave in the afternoon breeze. "I made a play with Vindrel. If he acts like his old self, he'll have a hard time declining honor and showing up to the hearing tomorrow."

"You sound doubtful," Farthow said.

Rone looked at him. "I am. It's another gamble, and I prefer not to leave things to chance."

"Yet you played a game of chance with him," Charlotte said.

"You're right, of course. I keep things stacked in my favor, but there are always risks."

"The chance is part of what makes the play worthwhile," Mitha said. "Nothing ventured, nothing gained."

"Spoken true," Seamus said. He looked at Rone and folded his hands, smirking. "Mitha and I have selected a good crew for you. Competent sailors that men like *us* can trust."

Rone looked over at Starnly and detected a slight smile.

*

The hour of tea had ended spontaneously, with Mitha and then Seamus excusing themselves for other business. Being left alone at the table with a strange servant standing near at hand with tea kettle had felt strange, so after a minute or so, Charlotte and Rone excused themselves, telling the servant to be sure to thank Seamus for his hospitality. Farthow met them just as they were leaving through the courtyard gate.

"You got your shopping list?" Rone said to Farthow. He tapped his temple.

"Shopping, eh?" Charlotte said with a smile. "Looking for another outfit?"

"That's not quite what I had in mind," Rone said.

"Then what?" Charlotte said. They began to walk back downhill, away from the towering estates of hightown and toward the central square, the road twisting, but slowly widening. When they caught sight of the square, the central stage was occupied again, this time by what looked like a slave auction.

"The Gallow is a fine place to purchase items of less than legal status." Rone cracked a wry smile at Charlotte.

Charlotte cocked her head. "You want to get into the slave business?"

"Dreamer, no," Rone said. "I'm a man of principle. Just the smuggling business, thank you."

"I have a feeling you are already traveling with smugglers," Farthow said.

"Johnny? Trafficking? Perish the thought," Charlotte said, waving her hand at Farthow.

Rone stopped and looked down the street toward the bustling central square below. "Think we could slip back by the jail?" Rone said.

"I suppose," Farthow said. "Need to have another look?"

Rone smiled at Farthow. "Oh, I just want a word with the captain. You know, I figured I'd better clear things up with him before I fill his hull with tar."

Fathow smiled but shook his head. "Alright, they didn't catch onto you the first time."

"The Courthouse isn't looking for us," Rone said. "I get the impression they don't really care about what Vindrel wants, in an active way."

"You know, Johnny could probably give us some snappy advice on just what will sell well in Golice," Farthow said.

"You're serious, aren't you?" Charlotte said, looking up at Rone with a frown. "We don't need to smuggle. I have plenty of coin."

Rone looked ahead. "We already promised Johnny a big payout in Golice-"

"*If* he ever goes free," Charlotte said.

Rone nodded. "Yes, *if*." Charlotte watched Rone's face carefully, not liking the inward gaze he had, which refused to meet her own. "We will still need plenty of money to get you to Hviterland after we reach Golice, but there's more to it."

"What then?" Charlotte said.

Rone took a breath and stopped in the street. "There are entrenched systems devoted to avoiding detection. They are present in every city and every region. Probably even here in Tyrant's Gallow. They're involved in illicit trade, and I want to make use of the people in those systems. These are people who know how to get in and out of places discreetly. While I'm worried about getting into and out of Golice, I'm just as worried about Vargana."

"Why the concern? That's home. My uncle is the king," Charlotte said.

"The Draesenith Empire. War is brewing. I still don't know for sure who I'm working for, and there were no specifics as to how and where I was to deposit you," Rone said. "I'd walk up to the castle and give you to the king, but I could get killed on the spot. You, too, if it's not obvious who you are."

"He's got a point," Farthow said, "and I'll also remind you that although you may be family with the king, there are bound to be other factions that would be happy to gain access to Catannel's favor. The Veraland Navy is still the biggest in Deideron."

"I hadn't thought of that, I just figured we'd be home free once we made it to the Northmarch," Charlotte said. She sighed.

"I don't think we'll ever be home free until Catannel's head is on a pike," Rone said. "Mark my words, he's going to far too much trouble for one woman."

"I agree, but don't worry," Farthow said. "We'll get to the pike eventually. You mark *my* words."

"Well," Charlotte said, "we found Johnny without those entrenched systems, whatever that means."

"We got lucky. Or unlucky, depending on your perspective. His skill helped us escape, but his profession as a pirate will continue to expose us to risk for as long as we're with him – and after, possibly."

"*If* he ever gets out of lock-up," Farthow said.

Rone smiled. "Yes, *if*. He's a big man, and that's a big *if*."

"Big *ifs* don't always come with big men," Farthow said.

"They do if that big *if* has to fit into a small hole."

The two men laughed.

"What are you two planning?" Charlotte said.

"Nothing," Farthow said, "Just a couple of old men from the sticks making jokes nobody understands. Why don't you two go check in with our captain? I have some... other things I have to attend to, like changing out of this uniform."

"Good idea. It doesn't suit you at all," Rone said.

"I think he looks fine," Charlotte said.

Farthow shrugged and waved as he walked away.

*

Johnny spoke quietly. "Coca, of course, is the most valuable per pound, and pretty easy to get rid of in a hurry." He was leaning against the stone wall while sitting on the mattress of the cell. The guard had given him his pipe in exchange for a piece of silver from his personal effects, and he was busy filling the room with the smoke of fresh tobacco, which drifted slowly out the long stone shafts above and out into the street.

"It's also the easiest to blow through in a good weekend," Mineo barked. The guard against the far wall continued reading his book, seemingly uninterested. "But I can show you the best way to take it, lass." He gestured to his crotch as he lay on his back.

"Is it that easy to find a buyer?" Charlotte asked, ignoring the small bald man. She leaned closer to the bars.

"It's easy to throw overboard, or into a gutter, is what I meant," he said back, closing one eye. "This really ain't the best place to buy it, either. There's always a huge mark up by the time it gets this far north. Only grows in the jungles, you know."

"It doesn't matter," Rone said. He leaned against the bars with his arms crossed. "I just need something good to sell that will turn a modest – not insane – profit."

"You mean something to sell to criminals, right?" Johnny said. "Because you could always sell a barrel of wine to the local pub when you get there."

"I need men who prefer discretion in all things," Rone said.

"Like me. Can't say I blame you. I'm famous for my discretion." Johnny said, smiling. He stood up and moved closer to Charlotte. "In Golice, like most places, there are probably a few guilds dedicated to the black markets. Items that skipped the tariff process are always a little bit profitable if a bit banal. Technology is valuable, but only to someone who understands what he's looking at, which usually means a wizard, and wizards mean entanglement with the nobility. Or apostates." He seemed to shudder. "Most of them underground sorts aren't looking to buy things like rifles and explosives, but to sell."

"Wizards? Are you serious?" Charlotte asked.

"I'm a wizard," Mineo said. "I can show you." He started to cackle slowly.

"Of course. You've never met one?" Johnny pushed his head into the bars and opened his eyes wide. "They could turn you to ash with a glance!" Johnny's face turned from grim to strangely happy.

"There are no wizards who can do all that anymore," Rone said. "It's all gone out of the world."

"Have *you* met one?" Johnny asked, raising an eyebrow at Rone, who stood statue-like with his arms crossed.

"Maybe I am one," Rone said.

"Preposterous!" Johnny said, looking away and pulling back from the bars. "Now, what were we talking about?"

"Drugs," Rone said. "By which I mean the sorts that are illicit according to either custom or law."

"Right," Johnny said. "Like I was saying, Coca and opium are always a good, profitable way to find the absolute scum of the earth. Just don't try to sell your dope to the wrong person, or-" He drew his thumb across his neck.

"Who do we sell it to in Golice?" Charlotte asked.

"I don't know." Johnny shrugged.

"You don't?" Charlotte said.

"How would I know that?" Johnny said.

"You're a smuggler?" She scratched her head in confusion.

"I'm a privateer," Johnny said.

"That doesn't include smuggling?" Charlotte said.

"Not in Golice." Johnny sat back down on the bed.

"But you smuggle things elsewhere," Charlotte said.

Johnny smiled at her and leaned back again. He drew on his pipe. "You ever hear the expression, 'Don't piss in your own pond?' My ship and its private contracts are registered in Golice."

"I'm sure we'll figure it out," Rone said to Charlotte. "I don't want to raise our profile by asking around, but I'm sure we can manage once we get there."

"How are you going to get it past the customs house and the inspector at the dock?" Johnny said.

"Kiester it!" Mineo yelled.

"Sharp ears on that one," Johnny said, staring at the little man, now sprawled on the floor of his cell.

"I figured we would use your hidden smuggling bays in the hold." Rone smiled.

Big Johnny stared at him in wonder for a moment. He closed one eye. "How did you know about those?"

"I didn't. I just assumed you had some," Rone said. "You also answered another question for me. So much for not pissing in your own pond."

"What are you smuggling?" Charlotte said.

"Bah," Johnny said. "I shouldn't tell you."

"Rifles or explosives, I would wager," Rone said. "Since he doesn't know the drug guilds."

"Those are for a royal contract, I'll have you know. Totally legal." Johnny crossed his arms.

"Not from the church's perspective. Things can get nasty during an inquisition."

"Not like I'll be smuggling anything any time soon."

"We're working on that," Charlotte said.

"For a hefty cut of my stock." Johnny shook his head.

"I thought there were plenty of shares open now," Rone said.

"Yeah, but I hadn't planned on selling to Mitha Porthagan. Gods! I can't have her knowing what kind of things I get into."

Rone paused for a moment and looked at the ceiling. "I hope your secret is as safe with us as ours is with you."

"How secret?" Johnny said looking over at Mineo. A soft snore seemed to be emanating from him. He looked back at Rone. "You're a sly bastard I'll give you that. Coca or opium is right easy to find here. They just sell the stuff by the box at the market, though I have to warn you," he took a few puffs on his pipe, trying to bring the tobacco back to life, "if you want in the drug business you're gonna get raped on the price anywhere above the thirtieth parallel."

"We'll make this our last run, then," Rone said, smiling.

*

Though illicit materials were easy to find in the Gallow, they were located in places that indicated to some degree the danger associated with them. In the case of drugs, the most significant concentration of sellers was in Lowtown, a cluster of tenements and slums between the harbor and the western rise of modest suburbs and country shops. It was subject to flooding and to the passage and pooling of sewage from the lower quarters.

Everything there was washed in a perpetual grey; even the wooden eaves of the leaning houses had faded to a non-color from decades of neglect. Even so, there was a sense of energy emanating from the residents of the poorest quarter of the city. They guarded their old houses, swept their steps, and children played with each other in the streets, or at least the clean parts of them.

Rone walked through the dejected stalls of the market, manned by hard merchants wearing armor and carrying pikes and blunderbusses. Stacks of unprocessed coca leaves littered one stall, with a small sign hanging in front that read, "Great for a smoke- or hire your own chemist." A lean man with a short brown beard sat behind reading a small, tattered book.

"Do you know any reasonable chemists in town?" Rone asked.

"If I did, you think I would be selling the leaves?" The man didn't look up from his book. "Big mistake on the last order, this is. You can still smoke 'em to get a buzz, or chew 'em for a bit of energy, but that ain't too fashionable these days."

Rone walked on without saying goodbye. The next table had a series of tiny barrels, inconsistent with each other's shape but averaging about twelve inches in height. One was open and a well-dressed man with an outrageous purple hat, complete with a bleached white peacock plume, was bent over the table. Rone angled his head to see the man snort some of the pale powder on a metal tray up his nose. He rose quickly, rubbing face.

"Outstanding!" He said, "How much for an ounce?"

"I can do about, ah... Six argents," said a large, deeply tanned, and overweight man behind the table as he scratched his thick, black beard. Rone thought he looked Datalian.

"Splendid." The over-dressed man counted out six silver coins and handed them to the man behind the table. The dealer used a spoon to carefully measure out a pile of the white powder onto a small scale. The over-dressed man handed him a small but highly decorated wooden box. When the scale balanced, he pushed the powder into the box and fastened the lid.

"Pleasure doing business with you." The Datalian saw Rone as the rich man moved away. "What can I do you for?"

"Looking to buy." Rone walked up to the table and looked around. The fat man threw the coins into a chest, then closed it and put his foot on it.

"Of course. You want a sample, I presume," the Datalian said.

"How many ounces do you pack in one of those barrels?" Rone asked, ignoring the question.

"I don't usually sell that much around here. You looking to travel?"

"How many?"

"Two pounds plus an ounce, give or take. I don't recommend trying to sell this stuff on the street, wherever you're going, stranger."

"Why are you so concerned?"

"Don't want to sell a man his death warrant," the Datalian said.

"It's for a private party. Would that satisfy you?"

"It's your skin, son. One barrel coming up." he walked to the end of the table and picked up one of the small barrels.

"Three."

"Three? You in the business? I don't think I know you."

"That doesn't matter, and you *don't* know me. I'll give you three aurals apiece for them."

"They're worth at least four."

"Three apiece and you can buy yourself a house in this town, with enough left over for a nicer shirt."

The Datalian looked him up and down. "Alright, then. Nine aurals for the lot."

"I want to see you measure it." Rone stood still, his arms crossed in front of him.

"You're serious." The large man seemed perplexed, but pried open a barrel anyway and began measuring it out onto the scale an ounce at a time.

*

"I don't think it would be a proper deal without opium," Rone said. He shuffled one of the small barrels to his other arm. "We'll just get a few pounds," he said, motioning for Charlotte to follow him inside the darkened house. Its porch had a leaning roof, nearly ready to collapse.

"How do you know they sell opium?" Charlotte said.

"The smell," Rone said. "Not quite so bad as the smell of it burning, but it's still there."

Charlotte puckered up her nose and did detect something rather unique, though not altogether bad. It was a wet, oily smell, almost like drying rubber.

Inside was another packed shop full of locked boxes, barrels, and other paraphernalia. There was no open guard, just a big, squat man who held a double-barreled blunderbuss lightly in one arm.

Charlotte was shocked at how expensive the strange, almost crystalline, yellow-orange substance was. Four pounds of the stuff had set her back six aurals, and all of it fit into two tiny paper-wrapped satchels. Rone hadn't bothered to haggle.

"Expensive," Charlotte said, laying the bundles inside of Rone's shoulder bag.

"It was a great price," Rone said. "We'll triple what we just paid, and the local dealers will still make another thirty percent on that. I daresay we'll have a few extra coins when we get to the end of this mess."

"As long as you're sure about this," Charlotte said.

"After all that, you're just grubbing smack dealers!" A familiar voice accosted them. They looked up the road to see Martelena Gordino stomping toward them. She had lost the innocent, sad countenance of when they had first met her and instead looked fierce and disheveled.

"Misses Gordino," Charlotte said politely.

"You probably could have bailed him out with all the money you dropped on that junk."

"It is not my obligation to do so, even if I could," Charlotte said, turning up her chin.

"You work for her, don't you?"

"Our business, whether with Mitha or not, is our own. *Stay out.*"

"You are! You're working for that whore!"

"I can see why your husband is not eager to leave the dungeon," Charlotte said.

"You're lucky I'm not carrying a gun!" Martelena moved closer to Charlotte, her hands curled into fists.

"I'm quite certain I've killed more men than you," Charlotte said. "Do not mistake a moment of mercy as weakness." Charlotte turned her back to the woman and strode away quickly. Martelena stood in the middle of the street, her jaw slack. Rone watched her for a moment, smiled at her, then turn to catch up with Charlotte.

"That was good," he said, falling into step with her. "You're becoming a regular brigand."

"It's just a conversation I didn't want to have. I'm a coward, really."

"I'm proud of you."

*

The opium was neatly packed into its own small barrel, lying under an oil cloth next to the coca and the cache of rifles onboard the now unchained Parkitees. As they left the hold, they saw the new members of the crew bustling in and out of the cabin, negotiating sleeping and storage arrangements. Pierce, the unofficial first mate turned interim captain, seemed able to settle most of these disputes amicably. Business was getting on, even if it wasn't business as usual.

The sun set in the west during Rone and Charlotte's trek uphill to Mitha's estate, casting the mostly grey city into shades of orange and red. The people they passed were all in a hurry as the clock rang out at six o'clock, broadcasting the final half-hour of business at the Gold Courthouse for the day. The men at the gate and the door of Mitha's estate were amicable, now that they recognized the pair, but there were no dinner plans; Mitha was conspicuously absent, tending to "important interpersonal matters."

Rone and Charlotte took the opportunity to recline in their bedroom, enjoying a late meal of duck and fruit brought to them by Nom the steward, as formally as ever. When they were done, Charlotte decided to seek a bath, excited to have two in as many days.

"There are two baths, dear," she said to him as she folded her white gown and placed it among her other things.

"Not to be too foul," Rone said, busing up the dishes. "but I think I shall enjoy some time to myself in the privy. The ale this afternoon doesn't seem to be agreeing with me."

"Suit yourself," Charlotte said. "I'm sure you'll be able to have one later as well." She opened up the bedroom door, and Rone stood up and rushed over to her. He grabbed her around the waist and pulled her into a hard kiss. She resisted first, in surprise, then softened to it. She opened her eyes wide as she pulled away. "What was that about?"

He looked down for a moment, then went to Charlotte's things and retrieved a pistol. "Don't forget it."

He listened for her to walk down the hall, then set to work quickly, dressing for the task ahead. He slipped on a pair of fingerless gloves, and with a ball of twine, he tied the sleeves of his faded grey shirt down tight over them. Likewise, he drew his pants and his jacket at his midsection tightly against his body. His hood lay lightly around his shoulders. His moccasins, old friends now seldom used, he slipped over his feet. They were thin and tight, and he could feel the wood floor as if he were barefoot. On top of all these clothes, he carefully put on his baggy finery and doublet. He found his wide-brimmed hat and put the ornate pen from a nearby desk in it. *Not a perfect illusion, but it'll do for now,* he thought.

The door swung open, and Charlotte slipped in. She stopped when she saw Rone standing up, fully dressed. "I… forgot to bring a robe," she said, her face cast into a frown. She still held her pistol in one hand.

"Just going to head out to get a few more supplies," Rone said, smiling weakly.

"I thought you needed to use the privy."

"Things went faster than expected."

"I'll come with you." She smiled at him. He didn't react.

"You don't need to come with me, stay here and enjoy Mitha's hospitality," he said, smiling back.

Charlotte's smile dropped. "What are you really doing, Rone? Tell me."

"I need to meet someone."

"Horseshit." She moved within an inch of his face and stared at him.

"Just-" His voice failed, and he looked away. He relaxed his shoulders. "I just need to take care of something. I was going to pack up our things and leave some instructions; I don't want to put you at risk."

"We talked about this, Rone. Putting yourself at risk puts *us* at risk. You're my bodyguard, my guide, my agent." She stopped and looked into his eyes urgently. "And I love you."

"It's nothing I can't handle," he said, shrinking from her stare.

"I'm coming with you."

"You can't. Where I'm going, you can't follow. It's something I have to do alone."

"Or nearly alone. Farthow's in on it, isn't he? I knew you two were planning something. Well, now I am, too."

X: Into the Dark

arthow was waiting outside the gate as they appeared, dressed like a middle-class merchant and standing beside a few large sacks.

"I thought you said you were leaving her behind?" he said when he saw Charlotte wearing her fine dress with her backpack over her shoulders.

"I thought I was," Rone said.

"Here, got you some treats," Farthow said and pitched a heavy sack to Rone. Rone opened up the cinched top and looked inside, then nodded.

"So, what exactly are we planning?" Charlotte said.

"Already planned," Rone said.

"You didn't tell her?" Farthow said

"I didn't want to risk it. Mitha's walls might have ears."

"Fair is fair. I guess we can explain along the way." He smiled as he set off down the street with them.

*

The bell tolled eight times in the old clock tower overlooking the city square. Charlotte walked stiffly beside Rone, listening to him softly remind her of what she was to do. There were still many people in the square, some stopping to peruse items of necessity or convenience from the few vendors still perched about. Most of the shops were closing for the day, with the street vendors holding onto the last minutes of daylight in their little hand carts. Other groups of people were forming for social engagements at the ring of inns and pubs that faced the Gold Courthouse.

There was a little temporary textile stand that stood across from the Gold Courthouse with a cluster of women standing around it, chatting and looking over the last items remaining. Charlotte stopped a moment to look at a piece of cloth spread across a table in front. The merchant, a middle-aged bespectacled man, was busy throwing all of his bolts of fabric into his mule-drawn wagon.

"How much is this?"

"Twenty cyprals for the rest of the bolt," the vendor said, stopping his task to look at her.

"I only need two yards," she said.

"Alright, fifteen, but leave the dowel behind." She produced a few large coins from her bag, and the vendor swept them into his pocket. He finished his packing and lowered the wooden doors of the kiosk, then began to lead his mule off. Charlotte rejoined Rone as they walked by the row of vendors packing up around the perimeter of the square.

Rone walked with heavy feet. The clack of his hard heels rang out as a high-pitched snare on the flat cobblestones. Occasionally, he looked off to his left at the castle that the city called a courthouse. As they walked, one step made a low melodious tom sound, and he squeezed Charlotte's arm. They slowly turned down a narrow lane. A tall blonde man, wearing an apron, was sitting beside the entrance to a small restaurant smoking a pipe. As they approached, he looked at Charlotte and said, "Fancy a pinch and a drink? Early evening special." He nodded toward the open door. Charlotte returned the nod and walked past him.

Every few steps, Rone stepped loudly in the center of the street, his hard heels sounding out the same deep tom sound. Finally, he found what he was looking for, which was an iron grate lying flat in the street. A small amount of water flowed into it from up the hill.

"This is it," he said.

"Are you sure this is a sewer and not just for rain drainage?"

"Yes, I can smell it faintly. This is as good a chance as we've got." He looked up and down the street. The restaurateur stood with his back to them, still smoking. The street in the other direction was vacant. Rone bent down and began prying the heavy bared grill from its place using a small flattened metal bar from his bag. Charlotte looked down the street to either side. Suddenly a couple appeared from the direction of the courthouse. She recognized the man instantly as the clerk they had met outside the dungeon.

When he looked down the alley, all he saw was a middle-class woman attempting to fold a very large and unwieldy length of cloth. He looked for a moment, wondering where he had seen her face, before greeting the blonde man and walking into the little eatery. The blonde man turned around and saw Charlotte walking back up the street toward him.

"Sure you won't consider a stop in? I'll treat you if you like." He smiled widely.

"No thank you, I need to get going."

*

Rone dropped down into the sewer. He heard Charlotte push the grate above him closed. The smell, which was faint above, hit him immediately in the narrow tunnel, and he quickly stuffed his hat into his bag and tied his wet cloth around his mouth and nose. He then pulled on his hood and drew it tight onto his head. He breathed freely for a few moments, trying not to wretch. *Just a few moments, and you'll lose sensitivity to the smell,* he told himself.

He removed a small cloth bag from his larger leather one and sat it lightly, almost cautiously, on a dry brick nearby. He crouched down and began removing his outer clothes, stuffing them into his leather bag. He was left standing in his brown shirt and black pants, tied close to his body with twine in various spots. He cinched up the leather bag and slung it and the smaller bag over his shoulders.

He had to crouch to walk through the filthy tunnel. He placed his feet lightly each time to avoid the sound of splashing in the muck. In his mind, he wondered if his moccasins, aiding him in so many infiltrations in the past, would be salvageable after he dragged them through a mile of waste. *Good shoes are like a good friend. Hard to find, reliable, and hard to throw away.*

He counted his paces as he walked along, noting to himself where he passed landmarks above. *Fifty paces, restaurant. Seventy-five paces, cloth shop to my left.* He knew when he had reached the courthouse, not only by the count of his steps, but by the sewer splitting off to the right, left, and down.

Dungeon is down, he reminded himself.

Before him lay a slope so severe, it was nearly a shear drop. Slivers of dim moonlight from a sewer grate a few feet behind him cast themselves upon the smooth stone of the descending shaft. The bottom was a black abyss. He tied a rope to a loose brick protruding from the archway, tested it, and then used it to slide down into the darkness below him.

The passage he had just left seemed very dim above him, and he wondered if it was some trick of his eyes that he perceived light at all. He reached out and touched the wall and felt his way, as near as he could tell, north toward where he reckoned the dungeon to be. He hoped that the careful memories he had made when visiting Johny would lead him true.

He still had his small oil lamp, as well as some extra matches in his pocket he could use if he got desperate, but he wasn't there yet. He needed to save those things for later. Rone's senses began to sharpen as he went down.

The passage went on until he felt it open to his left and perceived a dim light in that direction. He followed it. Suddenly, the light grew bright, and he squinted, trying to rectify it with the darkness of the last few minutes. About twenty paces away, he could see firelight being cast down into the sewer through a grate. He could hear a sloshing sound as waste temporarily blocked out the light, falling in front of him. He had grown used to the smell of the sewer, but fresh remnants carried their own stink, and he stifled a cough. He crawled to just in front of the grate and listened to a few voices.

"How does it feel to dump out my shit?" a familiar voice said.

"It feels like being a free man, earning coin," a voice said back. "Thank you for at least crapping in the bucket. You don't know how many people here shit all over the floor thinking I'll come in and clean it up."

"Haha! You don't?" said the first voice.

"Not until they're dead, which means I got the last laugh, or they've paid up, and we *do* charge extra for soiling the cells."

"What is there to eat today?"

"Same shit as always."

Rone pulled from a pocket a small mirror attached to a thick copper rod. He pulled on the rod, and it extended as a series of small nesting metal tubes, like the barrels of a tiny spyglass. He pushed it up through the bars of the grate and saw in it a reflection of the small dungeon lit by dim lamps and candles. The first voice belonged to, he could now verify, Mineo Gordino, who hung his arms out of the bars of his cell as another man, short and slouching with wispy grey hair on the top of his head, pushed a plate of no-colored slop under a gap in the bars.

"Shit food, shit company, shitty shit," Mineo said, picking up the plate and shoveling the food into his mouth.

"I'm the only company you get. You really ought to be nicer to me. If you break my heart, I might forget to feed you or empty your bucket."

"Bah, I've got this fat chap at the end to talk to," Mineo said, gesturing behind himself. Rone turned the mirror and could faintly see Johnny at the other end of the room, sitting on his mattress and eating quietly.

"He'll be out tomorrow," the old man said. "One way or the other."

"They hanging you, boss?" Mineo said to Johnny.

Johnny looked up. "Not tomorrow. Maybe the next day. Maybe the judges will side with me and set me free."

"What are you in for?" Mineo said. "Can't have been too bad, I saw your lawyers."

"He's got lawyers?" the old man said.

"Yeah," Mineo said. "And one of them's a girl, a right pretty young one. I bet she's got a scut to kill for too. Nice and tight."

"Oh, I *wish* she were here," Johnny said with a laugh.

"Me too," Mineo said. "I'd grease her up with some of this slop and tend to her back door, if you catch my meaning."

"You're disgusting," the old man said. "How'd you ever get a woman to marry you?"

"Doing what I just said," Mineo said. "You got to find the right type. The kind that like it up the arse will do just about anything for you, and like it."

"Actually, I changed my mind," Johnny said. "I wish the other lawyer was here."

"I figured he was more your speed," Mineo said. "You being a sailor and all. I bet he's got a big dick, too, to fill an arse like yours."

"Because he would cut your tongue out," Johnny said.

"That's something, Minny," the old man said. "You're so filthy you're making the sailor blush!"

"What happened to the other fella that was in here?" Mineo asked. "The big ugly southern dandy?"

"Francis?" The old man scratched his head. "Got sold as bond for his debt. They sent him down to market in Masala."

"Shit," Mineo said. "He was at least interesting to talk to."

"Did he have soft hands?" the old man asked.

"What the fuck is that supposed to mean?" Mineo said.

"Ha! Nothing, 'cept what you think. I'd miss him too if I were a man like you. You ain't the only sailor in the room." The old man blew Mineo a kiss. He sat down at a little table right above the grate and across from the small group of cells and began eating a hunk of cheese.

Rone thought about how he could throw a weighted garrote around the man's neck at that moment and have himself light, likely the keys, and if not those, all the time he needed to pick a lock. That would be a loss of life, though and would defeat part of the point of his little mission. *It was so much simpler back then,* he thought to himself, shaking his head.

"I swear Jim when I get out of here-" Mineo began.

"You'll what?" the old man interrupted. "You'll thank your lucky stars somebody bought out your worthless maggoty ass. Gods know I wouldn't spare a penny for an old cheat like you."

"Fuck you, Jim."

"I know it's not going to do you well, being cooped up in there alone without poor Francis to reach through the bars and help you relax."

Mineo pushed the cleaned plate forcefully through the bottom of his cell door. Jim got up and picked up the plate, then walked down the row and picked up Johnny's. He pulled the lamp off the wall on his way back, then banged three times on the steel door at the far side of the room. A guard opened a small window at the top, looked in, then Rone heard the bolts sliding before the door opened outward.

"See you tomorrow, renegade," Jim said mockingly. "Do avoid breaking your neck trying to suck your own cock while I'm gone, I'd hate to be out of a job."

So that jailor doesn't carry keys at all, Rone thought.

The light from the torch faded as Jim walked away, and the door closed, leaving the little prison almost totally dark. The only light was the small beams that escaped through the edge of the door or the peep-hole. Rone waited a few minutes, leaning himself against the sharp bricks that lined the tunnel to take the tension off his thigh muscles. Mineo began to whistle in the darkness.

Bah! This creature never shuts up.

Rone leaned up and looked through the small bars of the sewer. Mineo was directly across from him, laying back-down in his cell again. He could see Johnny far down at the other end. He had misremembered where the sewer grate was, and he realized he would be unable from where he was to pass Johnny the pieces of equipment necessary to free him. Rone sighed.

"Mineo," Rone whispered. Mineo continued his whistling etude. "Mineo," Rone said again, rasping. The etude evolved into a sonata, the melody floating high and modulating freely. "Mineo Gordino, shut the fuck up!"

Rone said at last, bringing his voice into tone. Mineo stopped.

"Johnny, can you hear me?" Rone said, unable to see Johnny's cell without the help of the mirror.

"I can now," Johnny said. "What are you doing here?"

"Who's there?" Mineo said aloud.

"Quiet!" Rone whispered. "I'm here to get you out. Both of you, I guess."

"Really?" Mineo said aloud, then whispered, "Really?"

"Yeah." Rone thought quickly. "Your wife couldn't get your stocks sold, so I'm going to break you out of here."

"So, she found out they're all junk huh? Shit," Mineo said. "Where are you?"

"I'm in the sewer," Rone said.

Mineo snorted. "You know you're standing in my shit, mate."

Maybe I should think about this some more, Rone thought.

Rone removed from his pocket a small open-wick oil lamp made of brass. He opened up the top and felt the soaked wick, then spun a little rough wheel pushed by springs onto a small section of flint. Sparks leapt up, but the wick didn't catch fire. He tried a few more times, but still, the lamp did not spring to life.

Rone heard a snap and felt an empty spot where the flint was supposed to sit.

"Hold on," he said aloud.

He crouched down, into the recent muck, and felt around for the fallen flint. He had to suppress a gag several times, but for all his searching with his bare fingers, he could not seem to find the flint.

He withdrew his pistol from his bag, quickly emptied the pan into the sewer, and tried to use its flint on the wheel of the little lamp. Sparks flew, but again, it did not light. Rone rechecked the contraption. He grunted aloud when realized that the wick was indeed soaked, but with water as well as oil. Somehow, he had not kept it dry on the way to the courthouse dungeon.

Rone took a deep breath, wiped his fingers carefully on a spot of his pants, then fished in a pocket. He found his few extra matches there, and they felt dry enough to use. He stood back up and, by the dim light of the dungeon, struck the first match. It erupted and died without bringing the wood of the matchstick to life.

Rone tried another. This one caught flame, but died before he could get the wick hot enough to light while wet.

The next match didn't spark. A dud.

He had one last match. He held it up in front of his face. It was just barely visible. "Of course my plan hinges on one thing that cannot seem to work, and I'm losing all the time in the world."

"What?" Mineo said.

"Dreamer, if ever you indeed hear prayers in your realm beyond time, let this one work," Rone whispered.

He struck the match, and it came to life. Quickly and carefully, Rone put it up to the wick. He could almost see the fibers beginning to light when the flame began to die.

"Please," Rone said, concentrating all his thought on the single match, now just a strand of tiny warm coals. "Please," he whispered again.

As if hearing his wish, or perhaps responding to the rush of air across the hot wood, the match caught fire again, then the wick hissed and caught light.

"Thanks," Rone said. He pushed the lamp through the grate and looked around again with his mirror in the flickering light. Johnny was standing at the end of the row, squinting. Rone checked the sides of the grate and determined the old iron was indeed set in the stone. He grabbed the bars and tested them. They rattled slightly, but the mortar was still holding firm.

"You here to break me out or just give me a little light?" Mineo whispered.

"Patience, son," Rone said. "You will need the light in a moment. I need you to do exactly as I say."

"Trusting strangers standing in piss and shit? Why the fuck not?"

"What do you need me to do?" Johnny whispered.

"Hold on for a minute." Rone pushed a small cylinder through the bars and held it on the floor with tense fingers. "Mineo, I'm going to try to roll this toward you. I need you to catch it. Be careful with it. Okay?"

"Okay," Mineo said.

Rone pushed on the small cylinder, and the tension of his fingers launched it toward Mineo's cell. It bounced on a few uneven places on the floor then clanged against the bottom of the cell door. Rone held his breath.

"Got it. Hey, what is this?" Mineo said. He shook it next to his ear.

"For the sake of the Dreamer don't shake it, it's explosive," Rone said. Mineo held it away from himself and eyed it suspiciously. "Roll it down the way to Johnny."

"You gonna blow the lock?" Johnny said.

"That's the idea," Rone said.

"Why should that bastard get out and not me?" Mineo said.

"I have another one for you," Rone said. "Just roll that one down to Johnny, coordination is critical."

"Fine," Mineo said. Rone peered down the lane between the cells as Mineo reached through the bars and rolled the cylinder down toward Johnny. It bounced about tremendously from the pitch, and Rone held a gasp, but Johnny was able to reach through his cell door and retrieve it.

"Get ready for the other one," Rone said. He pulled the second cylinder, which Farthow had purchased as a back-up, out the bag, and repeated what he did with the first. Mineo caught it before it hit the bars this time.

"What do I do with it?" Mineo said.

"There is a lid on it, carefully unscrew it," Rone said. Mineo unscrewed the container, and another smaller brown cylinder, a tiny knife, a few matches, and a fuse fell out. Johnny did the same. "Do you know where the keyhole to your cell door is?"

"Of course," Johnny said.

"Not in the dark," Mineo said.

"You've been here over a month, and you still don't know where the locks are?" Rone reached down for a minute and rubbed his forehead. *This man was a smuggler?* "Find it!"

"Okay, I think I found it," Mineo said.

"Check to see if the explosive fits," Rone said.

"Which one's the explosive?" Mineo whispered.

"The one that isn't the knife, match or fuse." Rone began to sweat, his frustration bringing forth what the warm rot of the sewer could not.

"Okay," Mineo said.

"Aright, I need you to use the knife to poke a hole in the top. Put the fuse in. Make sure the stiff end of the fuse goes in first."

"Okay," Mineo said.

"Got it," Johnny said.

"Put it in the keyhole of the lock," Rone said.

"Done," Johnny said.

"It doesn't fit," Mineo said.

"Why didn't you tell me?" Rone whispered angrily.

"You only told me to check. You didn't tell me it needed to fit."

"Hold on. Someone's coming. Hide that stuff!" Rone pulled his small lamp back down into the sewer and Mineo dove onto the bedroll, hiding the small explosive beneath himself. Johnny quickly pocketed the cylinder and matches, then leaned against his mattress.

XI: Down and Out

harlotte walked calmly, along with the few remaining people in the square, toward High Town. Occasionally, she could feel the clink of metal in her bag or feel a hard bulge bump against her leg. She smoked a small meerschaum pipe Farthow had handed her. It was the type she knew to be fashionable with ladies of the middle class in Veraland. Smoking was, however, a habit that for women had not permeated the Northmarch, and she was unaccustomed to the techniques involved, coughing harshly whenever she drew in a bit too much smoke. She did her best to stifle these impulses, wanting to draw as little attention to herself as possible.

She saw the shop she was told to look for after Rone dropped down into the sewer. The nursery had closed and locked its shutters, and the lights inside were out. The rows of plants on the large patio were now gone, save for a few exotic potted palms that were too large for a thief without a wagon to abscond with. She quietly reached into her bag and felt for the bomb with the next shortest fuse. She pulled out the heavy iron ball and touched the fuse to her lit pipe. She carefully pushed it into one of the palm pots, its fuse glowing and burning down slowly.

One to go, then to turn back when the action happens. She turned the last corner and saw the back door to Doughan's pub. She pulled the final iron bomb out of her bag, lit the fuse and threw it casually into a barrel standing a few feet from the door, then turned quickly and walked back in the direction of the Gold Courthouse, nervous sweat beading her face.

*

The peephole of the door opened, casting pale torchlight into the little prison. A guard put his face up to it.

"You asleep already Mineo? I ain't been hearing you whistle, you alright?" The guard said, peering in.

"I was asleep. Now I'm awake, thanks to you," Mineo said. A low-pitched boom sounded through the lockup.

"Hey sarge, you gotta get up here!" A voice said from behind the guard. Sounds of footsteps could be heard beyond the door.

"Go to sleep! Both of you!" The Guard slammed the peephole shut.

"What's going on?" Mineo whispered.

"Our diversion. Now, we need to hurry!" Rone put the little lamp back up. "Use the knife to shave down the sides of the explosive. Try to cut as little off as possible. And be careful, or it could explode and kill you." Mineo kneeled and began shaving down the little stick. Johnny already had his in the lock. "Hurry up!"

"I'm going as fast as I can, considering I could die at any moment from this shit," Mineo said.

"Die in here or on stage. Your choice." Rone busied himself with his own explosives. He set a few more of the sticks in the stone around the grate, inserting into each a fuse. He held them against the bars in a few places with balls of wet clay.

"Okay," Mineo said.

"Did you put it in the lock?"

"Of course," Mineo said.

"Johnny?" Rone said.

"Ready to go when you are, lad," Johnny said.

"Okay, get ready to light the fuse. Once you light it, back as far away from the door as possible. And cover your face."

Mineo struck a match. It quickly died. Rone held his breath, looking over to see Johnny cradling a small, burning match. Mineo struck another. Sparks leapt out from the fuse. Rone didn't have time to see if Johnny followed suit. He quickly held up the flame of the lamp and lit his own. He dropped back down into the sewer and scrambled behind a bend. He put his fingers in his ears.

A few seconds later, the first explosive detonated, tearing apart the lock on Mineo's cell and flinging the steel door open. The second occurred, and the barred door to Johnny's cell flung itself against the wall, clanging loud enough to match the sound of the explosions. Then the sewer grate was obliterated, along with all the stone surrounding it. Rone dashed back down the tunnel and began pulling rocks away, holding his lamp in one hand. The room was dense with smoke, like an impenetrable fog.

"Get it in here, you fools!" Rone screamed, no longer caring about stealth.

"What did you say?" Mineo called back, staggering through the smoke.

Drat, I forgot to tell the idiot to plug his ears! Rone said. He stood up in the room and gestured for Mineo to follow him down.

"Why aren't we going out the door?" Mineo said, pointing down the length of the dungeon.

"Because there are guards that way!"

"What?!" Mineo swayed in confusion.

Johnny appeared out of the smoke and grabbed Mineo by the collar. "Just follow the man, gods!" He marched both of them to the smoking sewer entrance and threw Mineo into the darkness before getting on his back and sliding in himself.

Big Johnny, having to stay nearly bent to the floor to stop his head from being knocked about by errant stones, kept a hand on Mineo's back as he followed Rone down the low-ceilinged sewer way. He tried desperately to get the smuggler to move beyond a plodding stagger, but Minneo was tottering like a drunk goat. Finally, Rone stopped at an intersection and lit another fuse with his small lamp. He wildly exaggerated the motion of putting his fingers in his ears and Mineo, finally understanding, imitated him. Another explosion rocked the stone as the sewer behind them collapsed.

*

Charlotte nearly fell with sudden fear as the first bomb went off, rocking the back wall of the courthouse. She fell in step with a group of people running out of the restaurants and public houses to see the commotion. Some looked frightened, others merely curious, and many now held arms. The small herd, gaining members as it went downhill, was flushing the onlookers down to the back of the square and the Gold Courthouse.

She saw a group of guards assemble outside the front door of the fortress-like building, looking confused. She slid past the other people, working her way over to them, and cried out.

"The back of the building, somebody was using a bomb at the back of the building!"

Without discussion of the strange woman's sudden appearance, the guards barked to each other quickly.

"The vault! Get Sarge up here, you two walk around to see what's happening," the leader for the moment yelled to the others. Two of the men jogged off, one holding his halberd at the ready and the other clutching a blunderbuss. Charlotte slipped back into the mass of bodies and began jogging against the crowd in the direction of where Rone had entered the sewer. A minute or so later, the next bomb exploded, lighting the awning of the nursery on fire.

Please be alright. Please! she thought.

*

Mineo and Johnny followed Rone down a few twists and turns until they finally reached Rone's rope. Rone pointed upward and handed the rope to Mineo. The fat sailor tugged on it, trying to pull himself up, but was never able to get his elbows past a slight bend.

Too weak and too fat to climb a rope. How this man was a sailor I will never know, Rone thought to himself. Johnny grabbed the man's legs and began to push up, groaning with the effort. Mineo made it a few feet past the shoulders of Johnny, and then the rope snapped the stone protrusion to which it was tied, causing Mineo to tumble down onto Johnny.

"Son of a Bitch!" Johnny said, pushing the fat man off of him. The rope fell limply at their feet. Mineo looked over and shrugged.

"How are we supposed to get out now?" Rone said. He clenched his hands into fists and hit his temples with them.

"I don't know. You didn't think of this?" Mineo said.

"I devised an exit route. I didn't, however, take *you* into account," Rone said.

"What's that supposed to mean?" Mineo's face, for the first time, took on an appearance of offense.

Rone threw up his hands. "A fat, foul-mouthed, ungrateful, idiotic, sailor who can't climb a damn rope!"

"I wasn't sure who you were talking about there for a minute," Johnny said, rubbing his back as he staggered to his feet.

"Yeah, why would you expect a sailor to have a clean mouth?" Mineo said.

"Now we're trapped down here," Rone said.

"No, we're not," Mineo said.

"Eh," Johnny said. "I've seen worse places to die."

"We're not trapped," Mineo seemed calm, even nonchalant.

"I'm not sure I have," Rone said to Johnny. "I'd prefer for the last thing I smell to be wildflowers, not shit."

"Fellas," Mineo said. "We're not trapped."

"You know a way out?" Rone said.

"The sewers empty into the ocean, we can just go out that way," Mineo said.

"Of course," Johnny said. "Why didn't you just say that?"

"You didn't ask," Mineo said.

"How do we find our way there?" Rone said. "These shit-pipes aren't exactly easy to navigate. I don't even know which way is North."

"It's easy, you walk downhill. You aren't very bright, are you?" Mineo put his hands on his hips. Rone squeezed his hands into fists again but controlled the urge to hit him. A cacophony of footsteps and voices sounded out above them. Rone pulled a small roll of paper from his bag and wrote on it quickly with a piece of charcoal he produced from inside his glove. "I thought we needed to hurry," Mineo said.

Ignoring him, Rone finished, rolled up the paper, and tied a small piece of twine around it. He jumped against the wall and pushed off, propelling himself upward. He managed just to reach a small grate, about the size of his head, and push the roll of paper into it before tumbling to the ground. He landed hard and felt a sharp pain in his ankle. He bent down to feel it for a moment.

"Nice trick," Johnny said. He reached up high and felt to the same opening with his hand. "How about next time you just ask for a little help?"

Rone laughed. For some reason, at the bottom of a waste-filled tunnel in the darkness, surrounded by enemies, it seemed like the funniest thing he could imagine. He bent over, took a breath, then motioned both of them to follow. They dashed down the way they came, Rone's little lamp casting light in front of them.

*

Charlotte waited above the grate. There was still a frantic crowd in the center of the city, and a person would occasionally go running past her in either direction. As they did, she would move down one lane of the intersection or the other, hoping to seem innocuous. No guards had made their way up to where she was. Rone had yet to emerge from the appointed sewer grate, and the street was quiet. As time plodded forward, she began to wonder if it was because Rone had already been caught at the courthouse.

In the silence of the night, the worry began to nag at her, and her imagination invented many endings to the story, none of which were pleasing. A terrible sense of loneliness crept into her, along with a dread that it was she that had crafted Rone's doom. *If I had left it alone – if I never put my foot out that door – he would be safe and in my arms.* She took a deep breath, buried her fear, and put her worry aside.

The minutes ticked by as the noise from the square began to die down. A couple of young men, carrying muskets but dressed plainly otherwise, appeared around the corner, meandering up toward her.

"Yar, those explosions were for real," the shorter of the two said. "I can't tell what they was trying to hit, or if they had some kind of vendetta against the whole square."

"Ted's nursery is wrecked," the other said in a deep voice.

"Nah, all the plants are inside. His awning's ruined, though, and those palms were worth a few argents."

"Yeah, good thinking of him. Do you think they were really trying to get in the vault?"

"Who knows? Nobody's ever gotten in before. Don't see how that should change now." The shorter of the two noticed Charlotte standing in front of him. "Evening ma'am. You waiting for someone?"

"My husband heard some noise from the square and went down to check on our shop," she said.

"Oh yeah?" the shorter man replied. "Which shop is yours?"

Charlotte's brain raced. "My husband sells... textiles, just off the square proper."

"Oh, so you're Gunter's wife?" The short man cracked a wide smile through his young but stubbled face. "I never knew that bloke was married. Funny how the little things slip by. Our uncle Samuel runs a gun shop next door. He sent us down there to see what's up."

"Is everything alright?" She asked.

"Things are dying down. Your shop is fine. Courthouse guards are bloody serious about something, though," the shorter man said again.

"Then if you'll excuse me, I need to see to my husband."

"Sure thing. Tell Gunter I said hello!" The pair continued walking up the lane as Charlotte rushed past them, pulling up her skirt to free her feet.

I will not suffer despair without a look for myself, she thought.

Around the corner, Farthow appeared, dressed plainly. She ran toward him.

"He's not at the other grate," Farthow said, "though I think I've drawn the guards away from this one."

"He's not here either," Charlotte said, swallowing hard.

*

After what seemed like hours stumbling through the dark of the tight and twisting sewer, they came upon a widening of the tunnels. There was there even a semblance of light, though it seemed to illuminate nothing but the sheen of the muck surrounding their feet. The arched tunnel would have been big enough for all of them to run, but the very slippery substances underfoot demanded a more cautious approach. The opening of the sewer way also meant a slowing of the passage of waste, and Rone's mask, soaked in water before to deaden the stench, was now drying out at the same time the sewer contents were piling up. He held his little lamp aloft, but the floor seemed to be little more than wet blackness. *Probably better if I don't see it,* he thought to himself, trying not to choke from the smell.

Mineo staggered next to him, pushed along by Johnny's massive hands, which picked him back up whenever he stumbled. Rone was sure he would have vomited, had there been anything left in his stomach to throw up. As it was, only an occasional hack or gag would escape him. After a few minutes in the broader tunnel, the dim light started to become substantial and less of an illusion bleached out by Rone's small hand lamp. At last, in the distance, they could see pale glow bleeding between the bars of a large vertical grate. Rone quickened his pace, allowing Mineo and Johnny to fall behind for the moment. Beyond the tunnel's exit was another silvery reflection, rippling and moving chaotically – the ocean.

The end of the tunnel was closed off by an iron gate, rusty and overgrown with green slime. A heavy chain, slightly less rusted, was wrapped around the gate's closure and the surrounding iron bars. A padlock hung down on the outside, gently rapping against the iron bars as the wind howled outside. Past the gate was a small stone ledge, and a narrow stairway leading up to the right, looking as ancient as the gate itself. Beyond the shelf, all that was visible was the ocean in the cove, gathering the moonlight in many small waves.

Rone reached through the bars and grasped the padlock, testing it to see if it was both locked and secure. The lock wouldn't budge. He stepped up and felt the hinges of the gate, which were caked in rust. He rattled the gate door, hoping that the inclusions of rust would break the old hinge, but it stood fast. When he stopped, he heard the rattle echoing loudly down the corridor behind him, and he became suddenly aware of the silence he was disturbing. He pulled the padlock in past the bars and examined it carefully.

Mineo, huffing and staggering, jogged up behind him, Johnny close behind. "What's the problem?" His voice echoed loudly.

"Shhhh!" Rone hissed. That sound echoed too. "Keep your voice down, the open end of this tunnel is amplifying us," he whispered.

Mineo looked over Rone's shoulder. "Why don't you just blow it up like we did on the last lock?" he said quietly.

"I don't have any more explosives."

"Any gunpowder?"

"Yes, but we're whispering for a reason," Rone said. "By now, they've realized you're both missing and that you went out the sewer. They might be inclined to look for us here." Rone pulled a small flat canvas satchel from his pocket and unfolded it on a nearby stone. Inside were a variety of steel implements.

"What are those?" Mineo asked.

"Tools of the trade," Johnny said, watching Rone.

Rone selected a piece of flat metal and small tension rod, curved at the end, and began working on the lock. He felt the tumblers and springs through the tips of his pick, working carefully and swiftly. After just a few moments, each tumbler was locked in place, and he turned the whole mechanism. The lock fell open, and Rone replaced his tools. He set the padlock down silently and began removing the chain, doing his best to be stealthy, though the clinking of the many links on the old iron bars was unavoidable.

At last, the chain was off. The gate began to move in response to a hard push. The ancient and rusty hinges began to squeal loudly, and Rone winced at their report. He tucked his tools back into the long pocket of his pants and stepped out onto the windy precipice, feeling sudden relief from the oppressive smell of the sewer. Mineo and Johnny (ducking under the low arch) followed him out to the small ledge.

The wind, mighty at the top of the cliff, blew up under Rone's hood and scattered Johnny's hair around wildly. Below them was a great fall, ending in spires of twisted rock a few dozen feet below them. When Rone poked his head over the edge, the crashing of the waves against these sharp teeth grew to a roar. He became aware that the sound of the sea was nearly non-existent in the small tunnel, and he wondered if anyone about would have been able to hear them anyway. The moon was visible, still rising barely above the outcropping that surrounded the tunnel's exit, some ten feet higher than the ledge.

"So, we're facing west," Rone said. "The harbor will be south of here, then."

Rone pulled the gate closed and started wrapping the chain back through the bars.

"Why are you doing that?" Mineo asked, no longer whispering.

"Never hurts to cover your tracks; keep people guessing as to where you've been and when. Besides, what if someone was following through the sewers, eh?" Rone clamped the lock back onto the chain and started up the old crumbling stair. As he reached the top, he stopped in his tracks, his head just poking above the level masonry above the sewer exit. Two men sat on the crumbling stones about ten feet from the landing, their backs to Rone. In front of them was a waning campfire they had built in a dry gutter. The pair were sitting close together to shield the flames from the wind off the ocean.

Sparse houses and stone buildings, all with darkened windows and ill-tended yards, littered the landscape behind them. The two men wore steel breastplates and simple helms, and each had a blue feather protruding from it, like the guards from the little jail. As they talked to each other, one fidgeted with a blunderbuss. The other leaned on a long halberd.

"What is it?" Mineo asked. Rone quickly reached down and put his hand over the former prisoner's mouth. Johnny peeked up his head cautiously, and Rone looked down to see the sailor standing a few steps below him. The two men at the fire continued, oblivious, and Rone realized that he was holding his breath. Mineo inched himself around Rone, taking in the view for himself.

"That captain I understand. Men will stick up for their captain in a pinch, but why would anyone bust old Mineo out of jail?" one asked.

"Don't know, he don't have many friends. I would think it would be a fine... ah," the other man snapped his fingers then pointed at the first. "Diversion. Yeah. This is when I'd try to bust the vault. You know, if I were a thief."

"There's no way to break into that vault anyhow unless you were a wizard or something."

"There are wizards in the world. Somebody managed to break the prison all apart. I bet a wizard had a hand in it."

"Yeah, but they didn't bust the door, did they? And the one in the vault is twice as big and thrice as thick." The guard took off his helm and wiped his face with a rag, then replaced it. "I don't think we'll see the old bastard or the captain again."

"You mean we're wasting our time out here?"

"Better than working." They both laughed.

Mineo ducked back down and whispered to Rone and Johnny, "The one on the left is Hitch. The stupid one on the right is named Mel. They're both right cruel."

"They were fine to me," Johnny said.

"You weren't there long enough to get hungry," Mineo said. Rone looked at the man's gut, which spilled over his worn belt. "You got a wire or knife? We can off 'em real quick and get out of here."

"We're not killing them," Rone said.

"Why? I thought you were trying to help me escape."

"We are – I am," he corrected himself. "But nobody dies tonight." Rone turned around and looked over the edge again, watching the waves beat against the rocks.

"Whoa, lad, you're not thinking of jumping, are you?" Johnny said.

"We might have to," Rone said, silently counting the waves, waiting for a large one to cover the rocks.

"You're stupider than you look," Mineo said. "Let's at least try to sneak by."

Rone took a breath to calm himself. "Alright." He stood up slowly and silently walked to the top of the stair again. Hitch and Mel seemed to be enjoying each other's company still. Johnny, despite his size, seemed limber and capable of stealth. Mineo was the variable, and Rone wondered if the clumsy man would be able to tread silently even in the wind. Rone crept to the landing and motioned Mineo and Johnny to follow. He spied a line of bushes running behind a house to their right, and without any other options, began to make his way to it, moving slowly behind the guards.

XII: The Business

anic began to set into Charlotte's throat, clogging her breath and spinning her head as her heart raced. She walked briskly back toward the grate Rone had used to enter the sewer, suddenly fearing that he had emerged and found her absent. She tripped suddenly and almost fell, sliding her feet apart on the smooth stone and flinging her hands out for balance. Farthow caught her from behind, leaving her face pointed at the rough cobblestones. With her head hanging downward, she saw something.

"What's this?" she said to herself, bending down to the little gutter.

"Sorry, what?" Farthow asked.

In between the bars of the grate, no more than six inches tall, sat a small piece of paper, with a small knot of twine around it. Charlotte unrolled the little bit of paper and read it.

"I'll never curse luck again when I trip!" She handed the note to Farthow, who read it quickly.

"He's going out a different way," he said. "Where the sewer empties. The cove to the East."

Charlotte picked up her skirts and hurried toward the harbor, Farthow following closely.

*

Rone focused on his body, relaxing what he could while he held his foot aloft, though his muscles resisted with a rigid tension. He set his toe down, slowly transferring his weight to it as it came to rest fully on the ground. In his mind, Rone wondered why he was bothering, given Mineo, who probably had as little practice in sneaking and stalking as he did running blockades. Then there was Johnny, whose weight was as likely to crack the old paving stones as not, no matter how softly he tread.

Still, it's best not to double up the noise, Rone thought. One of the men from the courthouse threw another small twig on the little fire.

"Can't wait for summer to get here. Cold down here at night," Mel said. "And my jack ain't too good for staying warm."

"It's cold up here in the summer too. Sea wind does that. Even the people who can own a house don't want one up here." Hitch took his helmet off and set it down, then began scratching his scalp and scraggly beard. "Dry sweat is the worst."

Rone continued tip-toeing across the patchy grass toward the line of wild bushes, Mineo behind him and Johnny in the rear. He heard a crack and turned back to find Mineo frozen, his foot pressing down on a wooden piece of debris. The men continued talking.

"You should really think about a rag under that helmet," Mel said. Rone continued tip-toeing.

"But then it doesn't fit as well. The leather's already too thick."

"I swear I get a rash on my forehead without a rag on my-" Mel suddenly stopped. Rone looked over to see the man looking back at him from the reflection of Hitch's shiny helmet. Mel turned quickly, and without even standing up, swung his halberd in a wide angle toward Rone. Rone jumped and looked down to see the blur of the steel spearhead under his feet. Mel was on his feet quickly, and Hitch was scrambling for his blunderbuss. Mineo stood shocked, his eyes open as wide as a fish's. Johnny rushed past him.

Rone dove to his left and missed another swinging strike from Mel, just as Johnny approached from behind, reaching under the man's arms and pressing his palms to the back of the guard's head, locking both of his shoulder joints. Hitch shouldered his heavy blunderbuss and cranked back the over-large hammer, leveling the muzzle at Mineo. Rone, breaking out of a roll, kicked the gun at the stock, knocking it into Hitch's chin. The muzzle fell forward as Hitch dropped the gun barrel-first into the dirt. A few small balls of shot rolled out of the end of the gun as Rone stood up and pushed Mineo back onto the stairs. He reached for the familiar handle of his sword and felt a twinge of panic when he realized he had left it wrapped up and sticking out of his bag. His pistol, likewise, was still stowe.

Mel, unable to free his arms from Johnny's nelson, pushed the blunt end of his pole between his legs, let go, then kicked the butt of the halberd up into Johnny's crotch. The captain staggered back, winded from the strike, then fell onto his back, his head hanging over the edge of the masonry, just as Mel picked his weapon back up.

Rone dodged a quick stab from Mel's halberd and turned to see Hitch picking his gun up again. "Johnny, the stairs!" he yelled. Johnny groaned in reply and rolled himself down the first stairs, his belt buckle rattling on the old stone.

Ignoring the stairs and the large man blocking them, Rone dove over the side of the cliff, feeling debris and rocks kick into his feet and legs as the blunderbuss roared, flinging dirt up from where Rone had just been standing. He landed on Mineo, and both of them nearly fell over the edge. They scrambled up quickly.

"I guess it's the ocean after all," Rone said. "No time to count."

"Son of a bitch," Johnny groaned, pulling himself off the bottom stairs and struggling to stand.

"Just jump," Rone shouted.

"What?" Mineo reeled in confusion as Rone grabbed his collar and threw him over the edge. Rone looked down to see him splash just past the rocks. He turned to Johnny, who pushed away his grip and jumped half-heartedly off the precipice, stumbling at the end, which sent his arms flailing as he tumbled. Rone looked over to see another splash. *Thank the dreamer,* he thought, then turned to see Mel coming down the stairs, his halberd held out as far as his grip would allow.

Rone turned back to the sea, took a deep breath, and leapt. His thoughts raced during the descent, and it seemed as though he had a long time to ponder many things while the shiny blackness below slowly moved up toward him.

He considered whether he should try to enter on a slim profile, feet first, or slow his landing on his back. *Feet first. I could break a bone from this height on the water, whether there's rock below or not.* He considered how he could get back to safety. *Swim. Nothing for it.* He wondered if he had lived a good life. *I can do better.* His last thought filled him with a fear of death, something he had not experienced in a long time. He splashed down, feeling his body plunge into black water. He felt his feet hit a boulder below him, the hard, sharp shells of barnacles tearing the bottom of his moccasins. As he bent his knees to pad the blow, he felt one of the carapaces scrape through the leather and into his right foot painfully. He pushed off and held his breath, swimming forward and trying to get back to the turbulent surface at the same time.

His head emerged, and he took a deep breath. He looked around for Mineo, who was franticly trying to keep his head above water and reach the rocks. *He can't swim either. Why should I be surprised?*

"We'd best get on with it, lad," Johnny said. Rone turned around to see the tall sailor's head bobbing a dozen paces beyond him. "There's still a gun up there!"

He looked up to the ledge above him to see the two men, now rather small figures in the pale moonlight, looking down at the water. He realized the rocks on the south end of the tiny bay they had leapt into were in the shadow of the moon's light, and there might be hope in avoiding sight. He swam over toward Mineo, putting his arm around his chest and pulling him away from the rocks with a strong scissor kick. Johnny watched him and followed his line, swimming laterally toward the shadow of the cliff.

"Got to stay away from the rocks, we'll get battered to death there!" Rone shouted into Mineo's ear. Mineo coughed and sputtered in response. Rone pulled him through the shadow, hoping that they were unseen by the men above. He thought that Hitch would have reloaded by now, and though the blunderbuss had little in terms of range, he knew a stray piece of shot could still hurt. After a few dozen feet, Mineo began to relax and kick a little bit with Rone.

The three of them exited the shadow and began swimming in the moonlight around a large outcropping of rock that enclosed the southern portion of the small cove. Rone paused and put his hand to his ear, but was unable to hear any report of the two men over the sound of the ocean. Southward there ran a long stretch of rocky shore, and Rone wondered where he'd be able to pull Mineo back onto land. His legs were already getting tired, and his foot was stinging and burning.

"Gonna be a long swim," Johnny shouted over the banging of the waves on the rocks.

"Longer for me than for you," Rone said back.

"Let me know if you need some help with the lubber," Johnny said.

Mineo gargled in protest, his voice croaking as if he was trying to speak.

"I will," Rone said, kicking hard to try to catch up to Johnny as they pushed their way out of the rising humps of the waves. "Are you hurt?"

"Getting kicked in the balls fills you with all kinds of feelings," Johhny said. "Your back hurts, you need to shit… but I'll live. You?"

"Think I sprained an ankle and cut open the other foot," Rone said. "Luckily, we're not having to run anywhere right now."

"How bad is the cut?" Johnny said.

"I can't see," Rone said. "It hurts pretty bad. Why?"

"Just thinking about sharks," Johnny said.

*

Pierce was drunk. Charlotte had found him inside Johnny's quarters, looking over manifests and leaving the rest of the crew outside to drink grog, the removal of the ships impoundment (by an iron chain) having driven the crew to celebration even in the absence of their captain (*or perhaps because of it,* Charlotte thought).

It seemed impossible to explain to pierce the situation. His response to each statement was things like, "The bloke is in jail!" and he only became fully cognizant of her intent as she and Farthow attempted to push the longboat off the main deck.

Once he realized what they were doing, he was quick to join them but slow to give any real help. The boat was in the water before he started to give instructions on how to manage the pullies that launched the craft.

Pierce handled the ropes and rudder well enough, but he seemed to mumble curses constantly. Charlotte sat at the bow, still in her dress, looking out around the shore as they carefully worked their way north. Unlike most companion boats, the boat for the Parkitees, nicknamed "Bertha" by the crew, was more than a lifeboat with a few oars. It had a small mast, which could be removed and laid flat while it was on the ship, a rudder, and a sail. Pierce, despite his stupor, was still able to rig the sail, and it currently sat across the mast at an angle catching a crosswind.

"Where are we going again?" Pierce asked, leaning on the rudder and looking slightly sick as the waves bobbed the boat up and down.

"We're looking for the exit to a sewer," Charlotte said.

"Just follow the shore around north and east," Farthow said. "Could be a cave or a drain, or-"

"Or a river of shit, eh?" Pierce laughed and took another swig from a whiskey bottle he had refused to leave behind.

A flash of something white in the distance made Charlotte stop and squint. "Do you have a glass?"

"I'm not sharing. Get your own whiskey!" Pierce said, smiling broadly.

"I meant a spyglass," Charlotte said.

"I have one," Farthow said and pulled a brass-barreled spyglass from his inner jacket pocket. Charlotte looked out in the distance as she extended the objective and saw the white splash again. She quickly held the glass up to her eye and focused the image. Charlotte saw another small splash, then a whitecap with two heads coming up from it. She could see arms waving. Great, big, long arms. *Johnny,* she thought. Looking past him, she could see a wet hood attached to a swimmer that seemed to be having a hard time swimming. Struggling beside him was a man that was bald, his head a white dot in the moonlight. As she focused, she realized that it had to be Mineo.

"Over there!" She said, pointing to a cluster of sharp rocks.

Pierce straightened up and squinted. "Can't sail in there. Wind gets funny in a little cove like that."

"Then row."

"Why don't you?"

"A lady doesn't row." She crossed her arms.

"A lady doesn't dig convicts out of the sewer, either." Pierce laughed at himself.

"One of those is your captain," Charlotte said.

"Yeah, and I'm liable to get it," Pierce said and took a sip of whiskey.

"I'll row," Farthow said, pulling up the pitted wooden oars from the bottom of the boat.

"Sounds good to me." Pierce yanked on a rope and pulled up the sail. "I'll man the rudder."

"You realize we don't need it with the oars, right?" Farthow said, looking over his shoulders as he dipped them into the water.

Pierce stared off for a minute. "I knew that."

*

Rone found that Keeping Mineo afloat was a monstrous challenge, despite taking turns with Johnny. His legs ached, and Mineo was no longer able to help propel them. He seemed surprisingly un-buoyant in the saltwater. He felt the man pull him down, and both their heads dipped below the waves. Rone kicked furiously to bring them up again.

"Just lay on your back!" Rone shouted at the near-drowning man next to him.

"I can't," Mineo gasped. "I'll sink!"

"No, you won't!" They dipped below the waves again, and Rone suddenly felt devoid of strength. He considered letting Mineo go but was pulled up by a pair of large hands before he could give it more than a fleeting thought. Johnny now swam beside him, tugging one of Mineo's arms while Rone dragged on the other.

Exhaustion was setting in, and each kick was slower than the last. Rone turned his head and was able to look in front of them with one eye. He saw a boat and began to panic. Treading water, he looked for a place he could drag his burden, but rocks and the plumes of angry waves were all he could see.

"We might have to leave him," Rone said.

Johnny ignored him and continued to move forward. Rone relented and pushed onward, giving his best effort to help the captain with Minneo.

"Rone! Johnny! Can you hear me?" a familiar voice said, barely above the hissing of the sea. Rone turned to look at the boat and saw a slender body on the bow, and long hair, a dark grey in the moonlight. He felt a return of hope and began kicking furiously toward the boat. As it approached, he could recognize Charlotte's familiar profile, though her face was in shadow. Johnny and Rone reached the boat at the same time, and Charlotte reached over and grabbed each of their free arms as they touched the side.

"Never mind us," Johnny said. "Get this poor sod here off of me." Johnny dragged Mineo again by the collar, up toward the boat. The drowning man seemed to get some life back into himself, though he coughed still, and latched onto the side. The boat began to tip toward him.

"Whoa, don't knock us over!" Pierce instinctively fell against the opposite bout.

"With Pierce," Farthow said, moving to the side and grabbing ahold of Mineo. He strained but failed to lift the fat man even half-way out of the water.

"Hold on a minute," Rone said, turning loose of Mineo and swimming to the other side. He reached into the water and slung a wet bag onto the little deck and grabbed the side with both hands. "Come here, Charlotte." Charlotte moved over to help him. "Don't worry about me. Don't let go, Mineo!" The boat was now tipping toward Rone. "Pierce, get over there and pull him up! Johnny, you push the bastard out."

"I'm the captain, I thought I was supposed to give the orders," Johnny said.

"Then just do whatever the hell you want," Rone said.

"Fine." Johnny ducked below the water and grabbed hold of Mineo's legs. He began kicking hard, pushing the man up as Farthow and Pierce pulled up on one of his arms each. Mineo man finally tumbled over the side of the boat. It rocked a few times, then slowly settled. He gasped as if he had never breathed before.

"Ok, don't move, stay on that side," Rone said. He tensed his tired back muscles and pulled himself up and out of the water, turned his palms onto the railing and pushed himself all the way up, so his waist was against the upper edge of the boat. Rone wearily pulled one leg into the boat, then the other, which were heavy with wet cloth. He sighed. "Let's get Johnny up."

"If there's one thing I can do, it's get in a boat," Johnny said. He was working his way up the other side, resting on his folded arms and trying to push his body the rest of the way in. "Little help," he said grunting. Farthow grabbed the collar of Johnny's shirt and pulled. When Johnny flopped into the middle of the deck, the large boat dipped in the water wildly from port to starboard.

"Gods, the smell!" Pierce said, scrunching up his face.

"Sorry, I had hoped the water would have washed most of it off. Some seems to have stuck," Rone said, lying down and dropping his head to the deck in a sudden need for rest.

Charlotte smiled. "And now you've got it all over my nice dress." Charlotte looked at the gasping sailors, who didn't seem to react. She sighed and moved above Rone, pushing his wet hair out of his face. "You must be tired."

"I just dragged a fat man through a mile and a half of ocean," Rone said. "A surprisingly unbuoyant fat man. I'm ready for anything."

"Always with the sarcasm. At least I know you're alright," Charlotte said.

"And no sharks," Johnny said, poking at Rone. "You're a lucky charm, even if you're a heap of bad luck."

Charlotte smiled and looked into Rone's eyes. "I'm a little disappointed, though. You said nothing about how sailors shouldn't complain about the smell of ass, or that you're surprised he can smell anything through the whiskey-"

"My whiskey!" Johnny said, seeing the bottle rolling around up near the rudder. He dove toward it, rocking the boat, and held it up in the moonlight. Only a small amount remained at the bottom.

"Aw, you spilled it!" Pierce said.

"You been drinking my highland sweets," Johnny said, holding the bottle to his chest and pointing at Pierce . "There will be consequences for this, mark my words!" He quickly started drinking down what remained before choking. He dropped the bottle, and Pierce picked it up and finished it off, then gave a grunt.

"What's wrong?" Charlotte moved over to Johnny as he coughed violently.

"It was seawater!" He leaned over the side of the boat and vomited suddenly. One the other side, Pierce looked like he would do the same, but was perhaps held back only by how little he had swallowed.

"Must have gotten filled in all the rocking," Pierce said, and groaned painfully.

Farthow inched himself up on his elbows to watch. "I guess I'll be rowing us back as well."

"I'll row," Charlotte said.

Pierce held his head above the side for a moment, still fighting the vomit. "I thought you said," he coughed, "That ladies don't row?" He leaned back over the side and started retching.

"I can do it, I guess. I still have a little more powder in the horn," Rone said, sitting up.

"Sit down." Charlotte put her hand on Rone's chest and pushed him down onto the bench seat on the bow side of the mast.

"I'm fine rowing. It's a good back workout," Farthow said, using one of the paddles to try to bring the boat about. "We'll be back in the wind in no time."

They moved out into the open water and turned the boat south. Charlotte and Rone loosed the drawn sail and let the cross-wind pull them back toward the harbor.

"Thank you," Mineo said, looking up at Charlotte as she looped the rope around itself. He looked tired and humble, more like the man in the guillotine and less like the man making lewd comments in the prison.

"I didn't do anything. Well, except save your life just now." She sat down and held onto the rudder. "I guess that *is* quite a bit. You're welcome, though you should thank Rone."

"I get the feeling he didn't care much for getting me out," Mineo said.

"I still don't care much," Rone said.

"Well I don't give a *shit* for getting you out!" Johnny said, suddenly roused from his stupor. His scowl broke into a strange smile, and he laughed.

Rone joined in the laughter. "But all the same, I guess I feel alright about it. It can be my good deed for the week." He sat down and began shivering as he finally noticed the cold wind blowing through his wet clothes. "I think every shirt I own is wet now. And my poor shoes," he looked down at his moccasins, cut to ribbons and hanging in tatters from his feet.

"What happened to your foot!" Charlotte said, pulling his leg up and wiping away the blood and torn leather on his sole.

"Damn Barnacles. At least I cut my foot in the water and not in the sewer," Rone said.

"I'm telling you, I'm damn shocked we didn't attract sharks," Johnny said.

"They don't come out at night," Mineo said.

"Damn, son, you *are* a lubber," Johnny said. "Sharks are always sharks. They never sleep. In fact, if they stop swimming, they die."

While Charlotte began tying the wound with a makeshift bandage, Rone opened his bag and looked at the clothes Charlotte had bought him in Masala, which he had worn over his current gear, to see if they had survived the sewer. He had managed to keep them clean, but they were soaked with seawater.

As if sensing his thoughts, Charlotte said, "We're going straight to the ship now, so you won't need them to sneak around town." She wrapped her arms around Rone, pulling him into the heat of her body, ignoring the smell.

"Tell me," Mineo said, still lying down. "What was the explosive we used to break the lock and bars in the dungeon?"

"I forgot," Rone said.

"Bullshit."

"What does it matter?" Rone asked.

"It wasn't gunpowder. I know that much," Mineo cast an odd glare at them as if he was a thief studying a mark.

"He's a wizard, you know!" Johnny leaned against the side of the boat. He looked cheerful despite the stains of vomit on his grey shirt.

"Just another tool of the trade." Rone cracked a slight smile.

Farthow laughed. "It is indeed. I hope you stocked up."

"What trade?" Mineo cocked an excited half-smile.

"We just call it the business," Farthow said. Rone joined him in laughter.

Sitting in the boat with Charlotte's arms wrapped around him and a free wind in his face, Rone knew he could no longer call it merely "business."

XIII: Shoals

one and Charlotte watched as Pierce and a few deckhands pulled Bertha back onto the starboard side of the mid-deck using the pulleys. Other sailors dashed between the forecastle and mast, trying to prepare the sails while still more (many with grog in hand) hauled supplies up from the dock. Preparations were being made for a swift departure, as it was plain that the operators of the Gold Courthouse would eventually remember that one of the fugitives had a ship at dock. Johnny sent a lone runner to gather up what could be found of the crew off-ship before disappearing into his quarters, cursing about the smell of the sewer.

"What do we do with him now?" Charlotte asked quietly to Rone as she nodded toward Mineo. He lay against a rail with a cup of grog, his soaked beard dripping beneath a deep scowl.

Rone sat on a box, carefully removing the tattered remains of his moccasins and his torn shirt, shivering in the sea breeze. "Is that our responsibility? We saved him from execution; he can find his own way now."

"Can he stay in town? I would think he would get locked up again as soon as he was found. Too bad Fathow's already gone."

"I don't think Farthow would have the time or inclination to keep him safe. It's up to Mineo where he goes now. We certainly can't take him with us."

"We could. We could get Johnny to hire him as a hand. We can't just save him, then leave him to die."

"That is a terrible idea," Rone said. "The man is weak as a noodle and heavy as clay, and he can't swim. He's a terrible sailor; how he managed to command a vessel is beyond me. And I don't think he endeared himself to our dear captain during the escape."

"I suppose you are right. It's not our responsibility anymore, is it?"

"It wasn't ours to begin with. We've done more than our good deed for the week."

"Oh Rone, your foot is much worse than you led on," Charlotte said, bending down and picking up the now naked sole. In the lamplight, she could finally see the long, jagged gash that ran down the arch of his foot to his heel. Fresh blood was there, weeping out as she squeezed the wound shut.

"Ah! What are you doing, woman?"

"I think we're going to have to stitch it up. It's wide."

Rone pulled his foot up with some effort to look at the wound. He gave a slightly disgusted look. "I think you're right." He grimaced as he pulled at the skin to examine the inside.

"I'll see who in the crew has some experience with surgery." Charlotte stood up and looked around at the chaos.

"I can do it myself if you just fetch me a needle and thread."

"You've impressed me enough already today," Charlotte said. "You don't have to sew your own flesh up to make me think you're more of a man."

"It's not that," Rone said. "I just don't trust-"

Charlotte didn't listen to the rest, but ran off toward Johnny's cabin, dragging her wet skirts behind her.

She returned a few moments later with Johnny himself, who was shirtless, his hair sticking out in wild directions from the water and wind.

"Mate, you're in great luck," he said, pulling up Rone's foot to look at the sole. Rone winced as he poked near the wound. "Good and clean, I say. No reason to heat up a poker."

"I said I could do it myself," Rone said.

"Let's get you inside where I can see better." Johnny grabbed two nearby crew members, and they helped him pick up Rone and shuffle him over to the captain's quarters, where they plopped him down in one of the chairs.

"You've done this?" Charlotte said.

Johnny moved quickly about the cabin, grabbing various items. "You don't run a warship without learning a thing or two about treating injuries. Light another lamp, will you? I want to see what I'm doing."

"Any more whiskey?" Rone said. "To clean the wound."

Johnny laughed at him. "I always keep a few extra bottles of the good stuff around. Hopefully, Pierce didn't loot my whole stock. Not the best behaved first mate I've had."

"Certainly not the worst," Rone said. "If I remember Masala right."

Johnny's face went downcast for a moment. "Aye, Danny. He was a good lad, till the end there. No matter, I *do* have some." Johnny reached into some hidden space behind his bed and retrieved a large corked bottle of nearly clear liquid. "I keep the good stuff hidden well enough, I suppose."

Johnny pulled up Rone's foot and, ignoring all the wincing from his patient, doused the wound with water and booze, and then cleaned out the clots and scabs with a coarse bandana.

"Do you have to be so rough?" Charlotte said.

"He's a tough bastard," Johnny said. "Most men are crying for their mum about now." He pushed harder into the wound with the cloth, removing more clots, then doused the wound again. The liquor brought up fresh blood, which Johnny wiped away quickly with another rag. "Besides, quicker is better. More pain for less time is always a bit more tolerable than the other way around. You ever have an itch you can't scratch?"

"Charlotte," Rone grunted. "In your bag is my medicine satchel. Do you remember what it looks like?"

"No."

"I haven't used it since the mountains. It's black, about the size of two hands. Fetch it, please."

"Alright," Charlotte said. "Is that it?"

"We'll need hot water, too."

"I have a stove here," Johnny said.

"I'll be right back," Charlotte said and stepped out the door.

"Good thinking," Johnny said. "No reason a lady should have to watch this."

Rone nodded, and Johnny threaded a large, curved needle. "Best to be accurate rather than quick, captain."

Johnny smiled. "I'm both."

He had finished the ugly business by the time Charlotte returned. Though there were still spots of weeping blood, but the wound was closed and his foot looked otherwise whole.

"This is it, I think," Charlotte said, and handed Rone the small bag.

Inside were numerous small vials and pockets filled with dried herbs.

"If you had opium in there, we probably should have started with that," Johnny said, washing his hands and arms in a nearby basin.

"No opium in here. We do have a few pounds hidden in the hold, though," Rone said. "This is just old medicine."

"Magic?" Johnny said with a raised eyebrow.

"Maybe," Rone said with a chuckle. "But if so, it's weak. In the old days, you could brew a potion that would close the worst wounds of battle or chase away deadly poison. Now? Well, we'll see."

"Feel free to use my stove," Johnny said. "I need to get this ship out to sea. Now, I think. They'll eventually look for me here, and I'd like to be gone when they do."

"Mitha's men know a way out. I'm not sure which ones, though."

"I'll figure it out," Johnny said. He pulled a jacket from a pile of clothes near his desk and threw it around his bare barrel-chest. "And thanks for getting me out."

"I'm the reason you were there."

"Right," Johnny said, pausing at the door. "I guess you owe me double, then, Ha!"

He walked out and slammed the door behind him. Even through the dense wood, Rone and Charlotte could hear him barking orders frantically.

Rone hopped over to another chair by Johnny's small stove. It was a cast-iron piece clearly meant to do little more than heat up water for tea or coffee. Rone dipped out a cup from the water barrel nearby, then put it onto the stove. Using the flame from a lamp, he lit the few pieces of coal in the bottom chamber. When the coals began to smoke, he opened up the flue on the iron stack leading outside.

Charlotte pulled a chair beside him and laid the medicine parcel out on his lap.

"Are you serious about the magic?" Charlotte said.

"For now, I'm just trying to dull the pain a bit." The cabin rocked slightly. "We're shoving off. Good." Rone began holding some of the vials up to the light, inspecting their contents, then using a small silver measuring spoon to put tiny portions of the substances into the water. He hesitated on one vial, full of a fine brown powder.

"What's that?"

"Something precious. And dangerous."

"A kind of drug?"

Rone shrugged. He sighed and carefully put in a few grains. He closed his eyes and began mumbling as he stirred it all into the steaming water.

When he stopped muttering, Charlotte said, "Prayer?"

"In a way," Rone said. "An incantation. A memory."

"Of what?"

"The prim," Rone said. "The fathomless infinity that we are all born from - that this *world* was made from." He sighed again. He tapped the side of his head. "Everything has become so straight, we've almost lost it, but it's still there, in our memories."

"You talked like this before, in the mountains. When you healed me of my fever."

"What do you remember?"

"You and me."

"I mean, what did you remember when the fever was on you, and I gave you the medicine?"

"The same. You and me, but we were different." Charlotte leaned against him as he steadily stirred and began to mutter softly again. "We lived there, in that little house. We were married. We had a daughter."

"Is that why you love me?" He began incanting again.

Charlotte was silent for a few moments. "I feel like there has never been a moment when I didn't love you. It's like a dream I can't remember, or can only remember pieces of, where you weren't a stranger. We always knew each other. Always loved each other."

Rone stopped stirring and picked up the cup of hot water. The inside had a strange, semi-translucent color of orange that gathered the light around it. He blew the steam off the top and waited a moment.

"It sounds like madness, doesn't it?" Charlotte said.

"It sounds that way," Rone said. "But I believe it." He took a sip of the potion. "I believe it," he repeated. "Vindrel and I always had one profound disagreement – that the Dreamer existed. He's a follower of the gods, now. Your twelve gods. Ever have I rejected them as false upstarts, but my faith in the true god of eternity is rather new, I realize." He took a deep drought of the potion. "This magic is real, however small. This world is not yet totally mundane, at least. I can feel it, can you?"

"I don't… I don't know."

"We're touching a kind of dream." He shook his head. "The way it should have been. I'm so wicked, Charlotte. How can you love me?"

Charlotte reached forward and touched Rone's smooth face, where tears were starting to form in his eyes. "All *I* know is a good man."

"I love you. Dreamer help me, I do, and I can't figure out what to do about it."

"Just take me forward," Charlotte said. She looked around. "How will we get you out of here when you can't walk?"

Rone swallowed the rest of the potion. "Just give me a few minutes. Then the pain will be gone, and I'll be able to move a bit."

*

Rone hobbled out of the cabin, helped only a little by Charlotte, who couldn't reasonably take much of his weight on her shoulders. The Parkitees had already cleared the docks, and the deckhands were busy trying to rig the sails to get her moving in earnest. Rone collapsed onto a crate near the stairs up to the poop.

"Where are we going?" he shouted.

Big Johnny's face appeared over the top rail. "Not that way," he said, pointing to starboard.

Even in the dead night, Rone could see the dots of lights and the great shadows of ships floating out past the shallows.

"Mitha's man knows a way around them," Johnny said. "Why don't you head down to the quarters and take it easy? We've got this."

"I'd miss all the action."

"Action is what I aim to avoid."

"All the same."

"Suit yourself, but I'd take a wink if I were you."

Rone shook his head. "Charlotte, can you fetch my boots?"

"No."

"What?" Rone said, shooting her an incredulous look.

"You're staying off of that foot."

"I don't think that's up to you."

"I can still go throw them into the ocean. Now let me take you down to bed. You need to rest."

"I don't think so."

"I do."

"Are you going to drag me there?"

Charlotte gave him a cold look, then stomped away.

"Mighty Nautus, what did you say to her?" Johnny said, stepping past him as he went down the stairs and back toward the captain's cabin.

"I told her I loved her," Rone said.

Johnny laughed. "Bad move. Now she owns you, you poor bastard."

All Rone could do was shake his head in reply.

Charlotte did return a minute or so later with a thick wool blanket, which she draped around Rone.

"There, now at least you and your stubborn…" Her face scrunched up, then she said with some effort, "*Arse* won't get chill."

Rone laughed.

"Laugh all you want," Charlotte said. She tried to hold a stern face, but a smile slipped in for a moment.

"Now *I'm* going to go change. Don't get any ideas about sneaking in to peek at me."

She turned away, stopped halfway down the deck, nearly causing a sailor to bowl her over, looked back once, then went on.

The ship leaned to port for a few seconds, then righted. They were indeed not heading out to sea, but to the cove and the cliffs that hemmed edged the city. Rone pulled the blanket more tightly around himself as the wind kicked up, running slightly cross to the deck. The ship slowly turned to a few barrier islands near the cove. A lighthouse was perched on some rocks in the distance.

Johnny re-emerged with a spyglass, cursing softly to himself, but smiling.

"Problem?" Rone said.

"No, not really, just a bit… Nervous, I suppose."

"I'm nervous, too, if that is any consolation."

"Eh, you're always too cool on things," Johnny said. "I got a feeling this isn't going to work."

"What's the plan?"

"We're going to cut through the shoals. Apparently, there is a dip in them that is just deep enough to get a ship along, if the wind is good enough. Mitha's man," Johnny thrust a thumb over his shoulder toward the wheel, "Jasonick says he's done it before. The tide is still a little low, but he says we can make it."

"You trust him?"

"I don't see any reason he would wreck a ship he's on," Johnny said. "But still… I've had this ship a long time. Say a prayer, won't you? To whatever god you follow. One of them has got to be listening."

Johnny padded back up top. Rone watched the shadows of the Veraland fleet as the Parkitees picked up speed. It ran straight north, far closer to the mottled cliffs of Tyrant's Gallow than any ship of such size should be able to manage, but somehow it sailed on. They got so close to the cliffs at one point that Rone could hear the waves breaking on the rocks and could feel the wind off the cliffs buffeting the ship, making one or another of the sails snap.

"Kill the lights!" Johnny shouted. Crewman rushed around and extinguished the few lamps, leaving only the waxing moon to light the deck.

They entered a narrow way, between two jagged rock formations a hundred yards from shore. The ship cleared them with ease, then Rone, standing to see ahead, spied the actual danger.

The lighthouse was closer now, but Rone could see it sat on a narrow island. The white foam of the waves revealed a series of shoals, some just below the water, that stretched between the island and shore, as well as between several other rocky islets, sticking up like old stumps.

"They're signaling!" A voice said. Rone looked up to see one of the new crewmen leaning out of the crow's nest. He stood, wincing on his injured foot and looking over starboard. Several of the ships in the distance were now using light signals, flashing large lanterns toward one another.

"Let them," Johnny said. "We'll be far out of range of any pursuit soon enough. If we don't wreck my poor ship."

Rone was so focused on the signals, trying to make sense of their almost familiar code, that he didn't notice charlotte sneak up behind him.

"I found a few dry effects for you," she said.

Rone turned to look at her and smiled. "Thanks. And my boots?"

Charlotte frowned and licked her lips. "I'll help you inside so you can change."

Just then, the lighthouse went dark.

"A little help from our friends!" Johnny shouted. "Easy!"

"I'll change in a moment," Rone said, limping up toward the forecastle. "We might have a shipwreck right now. Then I'm going to want my feet bare." Rone ascended the stair, using the rail to stay off of his injured foot.

"What is that?" Charlotte said when she reached the top.

"Just wait."

The sails went taught, and the ship rocked as the rudder worked against the momentum, turning the ship a little to their right. The bow shot up a moment, then crashed back down, sending water spraying up over the rails. Charlotte grabbed hold of Rone for support, and he, in turn, held onto one of the rigging dowels that was near at hand. A few idle sailors had the same idea as them and had come up top. They cheered as the spray enveloped them.

The ship leaned to starboard and made a small but desperate turn. The bow went up again as the Parkitees buffeted against a buried shoal, then the floor vibrated as the bottom of the hull scrapped something. The momentum was strong enough, however, and the bow crashed down again with anther spectacular splash. The ship lurched and repeated its bob one last time before beginning to even out.

The ship was now in full sail. The barrier islands were further away from the big island's shore, which was also now lower and made of beaches of dark sand, almost shiny in the wet moonlight. The Parkitees had made its escape. It was now separated from its enemies by distance as well as line of sight.

Rone hobbled back down the stairs. He could no longer see anything beyond the barrier islands besides the infinite night.

"This is just how I like it to be," Johnny said to him. He had returned to the main deck and was sitting on a stool, looking cheerful and tired at the same time as he packed a pipe. "The wind at our back and the ocean in front of us."

"There's also a couple of hundred guns at our backs, too, captain," Rone said.

"If they saw us."

"I'm sure they did."

"If they can find us," Johnny said. He put the pipe in his teeth and felt in the pockets of his jacket, looking for a match.

"They'll certainly try."

"Captain… Is that the pipe you had with you in jail?" Charlotte said.

"Of course," Johnny said, smiling. "I wouldn't leave one my truest possessions behind."

"I was just thinking about where it's been," Charlotte said. She gave Johnny an apologetic, open-faced smile.

Johnny frowned and took the pipe out of his teeth. He looked at it almost scornfully before craning his head around. "Pierce! I have a present for you!"

"I have one," Charlotte said and removed the pipe she had tried to smoke earlier in the night from one of her trouser pockets. "I've never gotten the hang of it."

"Thank you," Johnny said, taking the small meerschaum pipe. "I'll give it back, as long as you won't be needing it."

"It was Farthow's as far as I know. I can always steal Rone's if I wish."

Rone chuckled. He looked at Charlotte. "I think I will get off of this foot and have a rest after all. The medicine is not sitting well, and the sea is not helping matters."

"Are you alright?"

"I think I will be. Just need to close my eyes for a few minutes, that's all."

*

Rone watched the shore. It seemed to be changing. Slowly and subtly, the beaches and rock formations moved. The shape of the land shifted. As he watched, he realized he was on a hill that was growing. It was covered in green grass. The wind rolled over it, and he saw that the grass was moving like the water. Waves began in the infinite bright blue below him, then continued over the grass to where he stood.

He turned from the Ocean and saw a vast, empty plain, with a forest in the distance. It began as suddenly as the water ended with wet sand, and like the shore, it changed its shape slowly. Rone began to realize that if he focused on one area, or one tree, that focus of his vision would remain fixed, but he could see the other shapes changing in his peripheral vision.

There was a hill above him now, he realized, that had grown up when he wasn't looking. At the top of it was a tree. Feeling an impulse to go to it, he began walking.

He winced. The pain in his foot was nearly unbearable. He focused on the pain, and it intensified. He couldn't stop walking, though, and so he continued plodding up the hill, grunting against the pain in his foot. The pain got worse with each step until he reached the shade of the tree.

It was a massive thing, reminding him of a yew, but it twisted away in all directions with many large trunks like an ancient oak. As he collapsed, he realized he was hot, and the shade gave him relief.

He looked down at his bare foot to see a jagged and ugly stitched-up wound there. He reached down and touched it lightly. It was tender, pulsing with pain wherever he touched it.

"What? Who is it this time?"

Rone pushed himself back up to his feet, looking around himself quickly to see to whom the raspy voice belonged.

"Above you, silly!"

Rone looked up to see an exceptionally large raven perched on a tree limb above him. It appraised him with a cocking head and dark, intelligent eyes.

"Who are you?" Rone said.

"I asked first."

"I suppose you did. Why should I tell you?"

"Because I can turn you to ash, is that a good enough reason?"

"You?"

"No, dummy, my friend the dragon. Of course, me!"

"How?"

"Don't tempt me, silly creature. Now tell me your name!"

Rone looked around at the empty plains surrounding him. "Where am I?"

The raven laughed. "Where? Where?! You really are quite dull, but... Perhaps you are not dull, just silly. Since you won't give me a name, I'm going to call you... hmn, yes... let's see..."

"My name is Rone."

The raven hopped down from its perch, landing on the turf. It began to hop around Rone, rocking and laughing. "Too late!" it said. "I have already named you Juxtatopicaladad!"

"It doesn't work that way."

"In my tree, it does."

"I'm not *in* your tree. I'm below it."

The raven hopped up on one of the lowest branches, sitting at eye-level with Rone. "Juxtatopicaladad the fool. An excellent name. My name is Zald."

"What is this place?"

"Ah, that's a better question. Getting some idea yet?"

"I'm dreaming, aren't I?"

"Yes, and so am I."

Rone eased himself back down to the ground. "I don't remember you, I'm sorry."

"I would be offended, Juxtatopicaladad, but I don't remember you either."

"Am I dead? I don't remember how I got this." Rone pointed to his wound. "Maybe it went bad and killed me."

The bird stood still, seeming to contemplate him with his unknowable black eyes. "No, not dead. Why don't you get rid of that scratch, eh?"

Rone stared back at the bird. "How?"

"Too long away, methinks," Zald said. "You can't remember that either?"

Rone shrugged. "If I ever knew." He stared at his wound for a few moments, then back up at the bird. "How is this tree here?"

"It's my tree, so it's always here." The raven gave a strange croak, almost like it was sighing. It hopped down to the ground. "You have the spark, just focus. It should be easy."

"I don't-"

"Bah!" Zald interrupted. "Let it never be said I am unkind, especially to Juxtatopicaladad." The bird hopped onto Rone's thigh, then leaned down as if to inspect the wound. It rocked and breathed out. Rone flinched as he saw fire seem to leap from the raven's open beak.

The bird flapped back up into the tree. "Yes, Zald is ever merciful, especially to Juxtatopicaladad."

Rone looked down at his foot. The wound was gone, and in its place was no scar or deformity. It was as if his foot had never been hurt.

"Thank you," he said.

"Bah, thanks are for nothing. You owe me a fresh kill. You are a mankiller, yes?"

Rone tried to remember exactly who and what he was. He looked up at the Raven. "I'm a damn good one."

"Well, you owe me a meal. A fresh, dead, man. Yes! Both eyes! Be ready to give it up."

Rone laughed. "You'll have to come and collect it."

"I will. Ah, but we have made a bond, oh unwitting Juxtatopicaladad, the fool." The raven cackled maniacally. "And a bond I shall indeed hold you to. Farewell!"

The huge bird flew off from the tree into the sunlight. As it flew away, it seemed to grow rather than diminish in size.

XIV: Greyskins

one opened his eyes. Though the cabin was dark, there was enough light leaking in around him to confirm that day had come.

He made to sit up but found that he couldn't. He looked to his left and saw that Charlotte was lying against him, her head on his arm, which was numb. He tried to pull it away without waking her, but she woke up as soon as he moved it an inch, shooting up off the bed and flailing her arms about as if searching for something.

"It's just me," Rone said. She paused and looked at him in surprise, her hair a wild tangle of red hiding most of her face. "I appreciate you looking for your pistol, though." The night before began to come back to him.

Rone swung his legs out and stood up without thinking. He walked across the room to where his backsword hung with his belt. He picked it up and slid it out, then smiled as he saw no rust. There was only a few beads of errant water unable to find the steel through the coating of tallow he had put on it. He shook the water off, then turned over the scabbard, shaking out a few more drops of water.

"Rone," Charlotte said, standing up and trying to smooth out her hair.

Rone looked at her and saw that she was wearing only her white shift. He smiled.

"Your foot," she said, walking over to him.

He picked up his foot and looked at his arch. A long, thin thread weaved its way through his skin, but the wound was closed. Not just closed – it looked almost like the wound had never been. Only the thread and a narrow pink scar gave a hint as to what had been there. He laughed in amazement, put down his sword, and sat on the small bed. He pulled his foot up higher.

"It looks better," she said.

"Not just better," Rone said. "Almost totally healed." Rone got a small knife from his pack and cut the knot on the thread. With a grunt, he tried to pull the stitching clean of his skin. It wouldn't budge. "Well, this presents a challenge."

"Here," Charlotte said. She took his knife and carefully cut one of the stitches, then, with some effort, pulled the small length of thread through the skin. It came out bloodstained.

Rone took a deep breath.

"Did that hurt?"

"Very uncomfortable," Rone said.

Charlotte continued until she had removed all the thread a piece at a time. Rone wiggled his toes. A few drops of fresh blood collected in some places, which he wiped away with a cloth.

"I guess that medicine really was magic," Charlotte said.

Rone turned his head to her, frowning contemplatively. "Maybe. Maybe it was something else that was magic."

"What do you mean?"

"I had a dream. I met a raven…" He shook his head and laughed softly. "Impossible to explain. I think it was like your dream in the mountains. Something divine…" Rone frowned. "My people once held such dreams as sacred, but I think we'll have to consider it later. There's a lot of moving feet outside."

*

Rone quickly understood the sudden motion of the crew. A pervasive tension hung on the men of the Parkitees because several ships were trailing them.

Rone hopped up to the poop deck and found Johnny there with Pierce and a dark-skinned man dressed in a grey wool jacket and tricornered hat.

"I guess we didn't slip them," Rone said.

"No, but in open water, they'll have a hard time catching us," Johnny said.

"The ships of the line, maybe," said the dark-skinned man. "But that's not all they have."

"Jasonick?" Rone said.

The dark-skinned man nodded to him. "They've been gaining slowly since dawn. There's three, it looks like."

Rone scratched his chin, itching already with the first of his beard re-growing. "Might want to have anyone with marine experience get their guns out."

"We have plenty," Jasonick said. "All of us have *some* experience in battle."

"I hope it don't come to that," Johnny said, pushing back his hat to scratch his oily head. His eyes looked worn and almost swollen. "But we best be prepared. I'll go unlock the stuff."

"Unlock?" Rone asked.

"I know better than to leave my precious arms unattended when I walk ashore," Johnny said. "And a good thing I did, too, considering the party of drunk sailors we had on the ship last night."

"I was going to ask what you intended to do about that," Rone said.

"You'd earn a lashing for a comment like that on the wrong ship, lad," Johnny said with a smile.

"Oh, I know it," Rone said.

"I'll worry about dockings once we get clear of that fleet." Johnny nodded off to the southwest, at the shadows floating in the water.

"How's the cannon on this ship?" Jasonick said.

"Thirty-four guns, some six pounds, some eight. We also have a gun we call the long nine we like to fire off the bow."

"Are you sure you're in the business of taking prize? That's an awfully weak complement." Rone said.

"It ain't how many you load, it's how you use 'em," Johnny said. "The Parkitees, when properly manned, is quite a force to be reckoned with, I'll have you know."

"It had better be," Rone said. "They're fast out there, but don't think they aren't carrying a sizeable number of canons and marines."

*

By midday, the ships had gained a considerable amount of water on the Parkitees. There were now three in full pursuit, a lead ship that was larger than the other two but riding high in the water. A fourth ship, larger than the others, had fallen back and was now almost out of sight.

Johnny sat smoking in a wooden chair near the wheel, which a very hung-over Pierce held steady. The captain held his hat low, but his bloodshot eyes were open in a stare that was determined to deny his need for rest. He nursed a cup of coffee, long gone cold.

"Take a look for me, won't ya?" Johnny said Rone, holding up his telescope. "Looking across miles of water whilst on a bobbing ship doesn't sound too fancy to me at the moment."

Rone took the spyglass and kneeled, resting it on the rail. He scanned the water behind them and quickly found the set of ships and masts, hazy but large in the captain's massive glass. "They're each of them gunships. Two decks of cannon, it looks like. Perhaps sixty guns each."

"Well, we're still a few hours ahead," Johnny said. He pulled a flask from his pants pocket and unscrewed it, then stared at it a few seconds, eyeing it up and down. He smelled the opening, made a sour face, and then put the flask away. "At least if I got shot in the head today, I wouldn't know the difference."

"The tallest mast is flying green and blue," Rone said, still hunched over. He stood up and looked over at Johnny. "It's Dunneal, then. Or Vindrel, if he broke his promise."

"Promise?" Johnny said.

"He lost a card game with me."

"You had him, and you didn't just shoot him?"

Rone chuckled in response.

"Pierce!" Johnny shouted, still seated. He pulled a compass from his jacket pocket.

"Aye, sir!" Pierce shouted faintly from the wheel.

"Turn us to one-hundred degrees!"

"That's partially into the wind."

"I know that, but we aren't outrunning the bastards going with the wind. Let's see if they can sail as well as us before we turn to give them a fight."

*

The ships were getting larger by mid-afternoon, and they continued to gain even going with a slight crosswind. The lead ship was indeed one of Catannel's, a three-mast warship that lacked reinforced sides, made for speed rather than pure power. The vessels that had joined it were also flying green jacks, but their second flags were maroon and yellow - ships committed by other fiefdoms in early homage to Catannel.

"They're going to intercept soon, captain," Jasonick said, looking up from his own spyglass. Johnny leaned against a rail, still looking sick and tired.

"It seems they got our number. Steady as she goes, Pierce!" Johnny shouted back over his shoulder.

"Aye, captain!" Pierce shouted back.

"Shouldn't we turn a little more into the wind?" Rone asked. "If we have our broadside to them, we could get a few shots in before they close, then they'll have a hard time turning about to continue the pursuit."

"You think we'll have to turn and fight?" Charlotte said. She had returned to deck wearing Rone's large hat and now sat on a barrel, drinking tea out of a tin cup.

"Relax," Johnny said. "There should be a continental current a few miles south. If we can catch it before them, we should be alright. Their displacement will hold them back no matter how much sailing power they have."

"You think that'll be enough?" Rone said, watching the little fleet in pursuit.

"We better hope it is," Johnny said seriously.

"Captain! Captain!" The sailor in the crow's nest shouted.

"You need to take a piss or what? I told you to bring up a bucket!" Johnny shouted back.

"Dead ahead, sir! One o'clock!"

"That's not dead ahead, now is it?!" Johnny shouted back at him. He walked over to stand beside the wheel, then leaned over and looked through his spyglass. "Looks like we found a different set of friends," he said, handing the glass over to Rone. Jasonick was already scanning with his own.

Rone saw a few silhouettes in the distance. He wasn't sure if they were floating low, or were still appearing above the horizon, but their masts looked large. One of them was broadside to them, and it had the tale-tell high forecastle and poop of a Draesen galley. "Looks like about seven of them. No oars are down."

"No sails, either," Jasonick said. "They're just floating."

"Why?" Charlotte asked.

"I don't know," Rone leaned down and looked at her. "They could be waiting, or they may have rigged up a foresail or the like. Or they could be resting the slaves."

"The Bergen peninsula isn't too far south of us," Jasonick said. "Maybe they're just waiting for the rest of them."

"Pierce !" Johnny yelled across the ship. "Move us to one-hundred and ten degrees."

"Are you sure!?" he yelled back.

"I'm the bloody captain, of course I'm sure! Pull us to a hundred and ten degrees." Johnny pointed at two sailors, resting against a nearby rail. "Let's trim up and pull the crossbeams accordingly."

"When I suggested we pull further into the wind, I didn't presume it would be into a fleet of warships," Rone said.

"It told you. If there is one thing you can trust me on, it's sailing a ship." Johnny laughed as the boat lurched to starboard, the sails flapping loudly. "Load the cannon and prime your arms!"

"I'll gather the marines up, sir," Jasonick said. "It's going to be a fight!"

Two sailors standing on the main deck grunted in a vicious approval.

"The Gallow wasn't a bad place for labor after all," Rone said.

*

"He put everyone to post too soon," Rone said softly to Charlotte as they watched the dedicated marines assembling on deck. The Draesen ships grew closer, pushed on by countless oars manned by slaves.

Mitha and Delving's marines were a motley bunch. Some were old and grizzled, clearly experienced with piracy. Less experienced men, a few of them young enough to have served as cabin boys on bigger corporate ships, clutched their guns to their chest and sweated even in the cold wind.

"What do you mean?" Charlotte said.

"Johnny's given them far too long to think about the battle. They'll be pissing themselves with the first volley."

They turned toward the ominous group of galleys in the distance. The Parkitees surged forward, its speed renewed by a shift of wind to their rear. Even so, as the distance closed between the Parkitees and the small fleet of Draesen Empire warships, so did the gap between the Veraland ships and the Parkitees. Tensions were as taught as the sails.

One man and then another would compulsively check his flint or fiddle with the hammer of his pistol, or loosen a cutlass or tighten his belt. A few men held old matchlock arquebuses taken from the ship's official weapons cache, though it was apparent they had not been subject to much inspection or maintenance.

"Old guns," Charlotte said.

"I was thinking the same."

"Will they work? Or are they just for looks?"

"They're for looks. Inquisitors are omnipresent in the Divine Strand. There's a certain reliability to lighting a gun with a match, but it won't matter much. If the hooks are coming out, you're only getting one shot either way before everything goes full melee."

"It seems like everyone ignores the law."

"As much as they can," Rone said. "But you shouldn't underestimate the church."

Pierce stood on the rear deck behind the wheel, looking much the captain with his feather cap and rifle. Meanwhile, Johnny's booming voice could still be heard below on the cannon deck, muffled but with a strange echo from the water. Charlotte pushed herself closer to Rone, feeling his arm wrap around her waist. She gripped her rifle tightly and fell into the tense dance of the marines: shifting her weight from one leg to the other, checking her prime time and again.

The ships grew larger on both sides. It was apparent they would reach the Draesen craft first. Dark figures, the numerous warriors of that ancient and strange empire, were moving on their decks. Rone had seen them before, even fought them, but he guessed he might be the only one. He prayed silently for courage for the men. The race of the East would terrify any normal-sized man.

"This is going to be bad, isn't it?" Charlotte said quietly.

"Well," Rone said, "Johnny hasn't spoken about any plan, but if he does have one, I wouldn't expect it to include too much fighting, given the circumstances."

"But there will be some, right?"

"Without a doubt. Just stay down as much as you can, and it will be fine."

"Will it?"

"I'll make sure."

They were interrupted by Johnny running up from the cannon deck with a large piece of cloth in his arms. "I almost forgot!" he said. He ran over to the central mast and, with the help of another man, began running the cloth up a rope. When it reached the top, a large green jack unfurled. On the field, a blue square sat, with a yellow circle within.

"Cataling colors?" Rone called out.

"You'll see," Johnny said. "Don't forget to haul up sails after the first cannon shot!" He yelled over his shoulder to Pierce, who stood holding the wheel above.

"Do you just have a box of different flags sitting in your hold?" Charlotte said.

"Yup!" With that, Johnny ducked back into the door and ran down the stairs to the cannon deck.

The sailors up top began to murmur to themselves as the galleys in front of them grew larger at the same time as the gunships behind them spread out into a "V," the smaller, lighter ships moving east and west to cut off any chance of escape. They were perched now between an anvil that was the Draesenith Empire and a rapidly closing hammer.

"We should just haul up and go about," one man, clutching an old matchlock, said. "They may be Isle ships, but they're still from Diederon. Might be a clutch of mercy there."

"I hear ya," his neighbor, holding a similar gun, said. "I hear if they don't want you as a slave, the grey skins will run a spike up your ass and through your mouth, then leave you to die."

"It don't kill you?" the first said.

"Not for days."

"That's enough, you two," Pierce shouted down from above. "Nobody's going to have to fall on anybody's mercy today. Look alive, and we'll come through this just fine."

A splash went up a few hundred yards behind them. The Veraland ships were closing fast and were ready to light up the cannons in their bows in a test of range, and perhaps, a warning. The smaller gunships to the east remained well out of firing range but trimmed their sails as the Parkitees drew nearer to the line of Draesen ships. A few more canons fired, but the ships were still too far away from each other.

The battle, like an invisible beast growling in the stomach of all of them, was hungry for its beginning but remained angrily un-satiated while the Parkitees rolled its straight and windward course toward doom. Rone picked up Johnny's spyglass, left sitting on a barrel nearby, oddly forgotten, and stepped lithely up the stairs to the poop deck. Charlotte followed close behind.

He stared back toward the fleet of the Veraland, taking in the different ships. The lead ship, flying proudly the same flag as the Parkitees (though it's jack was much larger), stood out at the front of the formation, with smaller ships from Masala, Griffing, Sandy Cape, and one from Darfeld that had caught up over the course of the day flanking it.

The lead ship was longer and leaner than what Rone thought of as a typical ship of the line. Its three tall masts urged the ship on to a speed that rivaled that of a clipper, but it was much more heavily armed. He also thought of how heavy their ship was loaded (the Parkitees was, after all, still a shipping vessel), wondering if perhaps they had been willing to throw some cargo overboard, they might have outrun the Veraland fleet.

Rone began to scan the flagship, noting her usual riggings and her steep bow and long body, flanked by gun bays, though only the long guns in the bow were showing. On the front deck, he also saw something that piqued his interest: a large bearded man leaning against the bow rail and looking back with his own spyglass. The ship was still too distant to make out his identity for certain, but he didn't need every detail to know that Vindrel had not kept up his end of the wager.

That'll teach me to hold a gambler to his word, he thought to himself. Rone bowed his head and said a silent prayer. *Dreamer, Lord of the Dragons of Eternity... I named you once, "Lord of Luck," and I shall do so again. Bind my brother to his promise. I have played the game and won, so let me keep my winning this day. Let my dream prevail.*

"It's him, isn't it?" Charlotte said from beside him.

"How did you know?" Rone said.

"You're an easy read," Charlotte said.

Rone sighed. "He's still trying to play cards like before, I suppose. He doesn't know that he doesn't know. It's his flaw. He still thinks he has a card in the deck for me." He stepped away from the aft rail and handed the spyglass to Pierce.

"What do you mean?" Pierce asked as he put the spyglass up to his own eye. After a moment, he said, "Looks like our friend from the docks."

"And the courthouse," Charlotte said.

"He seems to have survived to punish us for our mercy after all," Pierce said. "Well, *your* mercy."

"I wasn't ready to let the man die back then. If it turns out badly, I apologize," Rone said.

"Don't, sir," Pierce said. "I can't fault a man for saving his brother."

"Where did you hear that?" Rone said.

"Men talk," Pierce said.

Rone nodded and walked briskly down the stairs to the main deck, feeling a few prickles of pain in his now healed foot where the stitches had been. Charlotte followed him down and up the other stairs to the bow, where a few marines huddled beneath the foresail. Beyond them, at the other end of an expanse of rippling blue that seemed distant and yet far too close, the Empire ships approached swiftly. Their oars were down, dipping into the water, pushing them forward against the wind.

As they got closer, the details of the shadowy fleet became more concrete. Each ship had deep carvings along their top rails and on their masts. The top few feet of their hulls along the bow were covered in long iron spikes meant to devastate the broad side of a ship during a ram.

The marines began to talk in hushed voices as the details of the enemy became clearer. The Draesenith warriors were huge men with flat grey skin and high pates, long flat faces, and dark eyes that seemed to glitter. They began to howl in a horrid song as they drew nearer, clanging broadswords onto large wooden shields in time with each other, pounding out a steady beat that matched the turning of the oars.

Many of the Draesen held longbows, though they looked somewhat diminished in their great hands. As they closed the distance, flames leaped up from behind the rails like a river of pitch had been lit on fire. The soldiers of the Dreasenith Empire stood still, unaffected and unafraid of the flames.

After a maddeningly tense few minutes of waiting, a shot from the gun deck of the Parkitees set all the actors in the scene into motion. The ship vibrated as the cannon on her bow, the "long nine" Johnny had mentioned, erupted and sent a ball hurtling forward behind a wall of dark smoke. The front of the foremost galley, now pulling just to starboard in preparation for an attack, exploded in a cloud of splinters as the cannonball pierced its iron armor and ripped into its hull. Rone was surprised by the power of the load, flinching as it fired, but also surprised at how high it struck the ship. It was a first shot that was unlikely to sink their enemy, being wholly contained in the top half of the boat.

As they got closer, he could see that the gun deck, stationed above the rows of slaves at the oars, was open to the air. A cannon had fallen through the floor into the midst of the slaves, and their oars stuck out of the water and away from the boat. The galley began to turn as a result, pointing its bow to the Parkitees and also leaving its remaining broadside cannons unused. The ship to its starboard side began to turn as well, angling itself toward the Parkitees in a similar manner, though this one clearly did it with intent. The oars dipped into the water, and the ship moved forward as if it meant to ram them. Another cannon on the Parkitees lit up, and the front of the new galley shuttered under the impact.

Behind Rone, the men jumped into action, and quickly raised the sails. The Parkitees slowed, the iron bow of the enemy closing, but it remained moving forward with its momentum. Rone understood why in a moment, as the marines of both Empire ships moved forward with longbows. Each arrow had a patch of burning pitch attached near its head, and they passed these through the row of flame on their deck. Rone grabbed Charlotte's arm and pulled her down the stairs as the arrows were unleashed, falling and sticking into various places of the ship. Fire caught in a few barrels and leapt onto the shirt of one sailor, but none of the flaming arrows hit the sails.

Suddenly, the door beside Charlotte and Rone burst open, and a familiar face poked out.

"Good gods!" Mineo said, his dazed eyes glaring about at the battle. Rone grabbed his arm and pulled him down into the shadow of the forecastle as a few more flaming arrows zipped past, one lodging itself into the top of the wooden door just above their heads.

"What in the nine worlds are you still doing here!" Rone shouted at him. "I thought you'd be sent off back in the Gallow."

Mineo winced and squinted. "Well, *I* thought I was sleeping off a hangover. Where are we?"

"In the middle of a fight, that's where!" Charlotte said from beneath the staircase.

"Still better than being home with my wife," Mineo said with a shrug.

"Dreamer!" Rone said. "You're a fool if I've ever met one!"

Charlotte darted back up the stair before Rone could stop her and leveled her rifle at the ship on the port side. She shot along with the other marines on deck, who had somehow managed to avoid all of the arrow fire. A few men on board the Eastern ship went down with a shriek, and Charlotte darted back down the stair to reload, horn in hand.

The Parkitees began floating past the ship on its port side, and the spikes lacing the front of the galley scratched across the rails, sending splinters flying in every direction. A few brave Draesen warriors jumped off the bow of their ship onto the deck of the Parkitees, or swung over on a rigging rope, pikes in hand. They landed among the men of the Parkitees like giants, all of them standing a head taller than the sailors. Only Johnny himself, who was as good as half-giant, would have been able to look any of them in the eye. Rone leaned his musket down and drew his sword and pistol. The canons of the Parkitees fired from the broadside, and more wooden shards exploded from the hull of the attacker.

Rone ran at the first colossal pikeman in front of him, parrying the long downward thrust of the mail-armored Draesen with his backsword, forcing the point into the hard oak of the deck. He then stood on the pike with his left foot. The enemy unhanded his weapon and let it drop to the deck with a loud clack.

The Draesen stepped back with surprise and drew his own curved sword from a scabbard at his hip, scowling at Rone as he did so. The marine slashed wildly, never able to fully connect as Rone moved around him in circles. Rone, at last, stepped nimbly past his opponent during a hard overhand slash and struck him in the back of his neck with the tip of his backsword. The warrior collapsed in a spray of blood, grasping at the wound below his ear. He began to scream in his strange language, but Rone had already moved on.

He stepped forward to the next grey-skinned man, who already had a long scimitar drawn and held it forward in a right-foot leaning stance. Rone suddenly longed for a more substantial weapon than his trusted backsword as the warrior attacked. He had experience in battle and displayed it with a series of well-aimed and controlled thrusts while he kept strictly to a balanced fighting style.

Rone shuffled around him in circles, keeping his weight forward on his right foot, ready for the killing thrust if he saw an opening. Rone parried and dodged with calm precision, but was reminded of his limitations every time he tried to step past the giant's outer arc and was treated to a shield bash or whirling cut. Rone understood that the swordsman was, with the strokes of his blade, pushing him into a corner of the railing. The guns in the deck below them roared to life again, pushing the Parkitees away and crushing the hull at the front of the galley. Its iron-spiked bow began to droop as the ship drifted away, chunks of wood and stray boards falling into the sea.

Another flurry of arrows rained down, this time from the crippled ship off the Parkitees's starboard. Rone quickly turned his body to miss one, and his opposition closed in with a slash that cut his shirt and narrowly missed the flesh of his ribcage. Rone jumped back and saw Charlotte being attacked by a pikeman. She kept him at a distance by parrying his mocking blows with her rifle as he tried to push past and put the single-edged spear to use. Rone threw himself to his left and shot his pistol, not nearly so much aiming as hoping, at Charlotte's attacker, who collapsed in a grunt as the ball hit his leg. A nearby marine saw the Draesen bend down and took advantage of the wound. He moved past the blade of the spear and smashed the Draesen's clavicle with a cutlass, spraying the deck with fresh blood.

Rone's adversary had not let up, however, and he swung down on Rone with a powerful overhand stroke. In a fit of confusion, shock, and fear, Rone threw up his left hand, and the scimitar hit the stock of his pistol a few inches from his knuckles. Rone fell to his knees with the force of the blow, crying out as his wrist twisted with the impact. His opponent pulled back for the killing blow but found his blade stuck in the tight-grained wood of the pistol. Before he could adjust position and free himself, Rone was pulling the off-balance warrior down onto the tip of his sword. It split the rings of the Draesen's mail coif and entered his neck. Rone rolled with his opponent's immense weight, pushing him down on the deck. With a gasp, the Draesen closed his eyes and went limp.

Rone looked around to see a few dying fires from the arrows, which seemed unable to coax the old and well-treated oak slats of the deck to flame. Seawater was being dumped on the few bits of fire that managed to survive. The Parkitees was pulling away from the two ships, though the impact had significantly slowed her inertia. The cannons on the starboard side lit up again, pelting the already crippled Draesen ship with fresh lead, all of the impacts high above the watertight hull, as the few enemy marines on the Parkitees's deck scrambled to get back on board their own ship.

Charlotte shuddered as one sailor, a thin and short man, probably a boy among the race of giants, made a running leap to return home and fell short, his hands flailing wildly for purchase among the shredded remains of the galley hull before he fell into the sea. The sailors of the Parkitees scrambled to the ropes and began loosening the sails. As they filled with the wind the ship sprang back to life, surging off past the two galleys.

Rone, astonished, realized that despite their damage, they had almost totally avoided cannon fire. He snapped back to the moment at the cries of an unfamiliar marine nearby, clutching at a wound on his leg. Blood was surging up between his fingers. Rone quickly tore the man's sleeve off and wrapped it tightly around the leg wound, making a quick tourniquet. He stood up and could finally see just what Johnny's plan had been. The small fleet of the Draesenith Empire now blocked Vindrel, along with the rest of the Veraland ships, from continuing their pursuit. Already ships flying green were breaking their formation to engage the galleys, and the flagship was forcing a hard turn to avoid the two galleys the Parkitees had sped past. Those Draesen ships, though crippled, were now moving to engage the new threat, the warriors packing the decks screaming a new song.

The two smaller ships that had moved east to block the Parkitees's retreat were well wide of the Empire ships, but Rone watched as they turned hard about to assist their comrades, the green and red jack of Masala flying high up above their mainsails.

Johnny emerged from the gun deck, covered in soot, but smiling. "Well, that's as close as they come. Was there any fighting up top?"

"A little," Rone answered, "but it was nothing we couldn't handle. One significant injury. We're going to have to fix some railing, though." He looked over to see Mineo push himself up, debris and shards of wood falling away. He had apparently remained where Rone had placed him throughout the entire fight.

"Aww," Johnny said, looking at the starboard deck rails, which lay in pieces on the deck proper. "Where am I going to lean over and vomit when I get seasick?"

The cannon fire continued behind them, but within minutes relaxation and a sense of relief seemed to permeate the crew. The battle was behind them, and the wind was in their sails. The sounds of cannons began to fade into to the sounds of the sea itself. Johnny went into his quarters and returned with a full bottle of whiskey.

"To long life between the hammer and the anvil!" he shouted, then took a long drink. The crew that was still assembled above decks cheered in response. Mineo walked over and held out his hand as if expecting the captain to share. Johnny jerked the bottle toward himself and took another swig. "Get your own!" The men laughed.

"It's grog for you," Pierce said from up top, "Never try to drink the captain's whiskey."

"I'll deal with you soon enough!" Johhny said, "I'm missing a bottle of Drachman Sour, thanks to you!" He raised his middle finger to the first mate.

Charlotte pushed herself under Rone's arm and leaned against him. He sighed deeply, letting go of the tension of the moment and leaning on her. He looked down to see her smiling back as if the bloody struggle minutes before had never happened.

"Now, pitch these stowaways overboard!" Johnny yelled, kicking a nearby corpse. Laughter answered him. Rone walked over and picked up the Dreasen's long scimitar, thinking of how much trouble the man had given him. His dead opponent stared back at him with blank, yellow eyes.

Charlotte gently rubbed his back. He felt the steel, which was keen and smooth, with a forging pattern like the grain of a piece of wood. Suddenly, he felt something else from the steel, something imperceptible, and he threw it down.

"It doesn't feel right," he said. "I don't want it."

He pulled his pistol from his belt and looked at it. The small stock was broken apart, and the handle would no longer contain the lock and barrel. He pulled the broken stock off and tossed it to the side, then stuffed the rest of the gun in his belt.

A few of the marines busied themselves with the robbing of the bodies. Armor, clothes, bags, and weapons were laid in a heap as each bloody body was stripped down, then picked up by its hands and feet and thrown unceremoniously overboard.

"Shouldn't we say something?" Charlotte whispered into Rone's ear.

"Like what?" he whispered back.

"Last rites? A prayer? Don't these men deserve a proper blessing and burial?"

"A Draesen burial is something we can't give them, nor would I ever pray to their gods – they're cursed. Silence and a burial at sea are the best we can offer, I think."

"Perhaps I can say a prayer to Verbus?"

"It couldn't hurt," Rone said. "But if they were living, they would be enraged. They believe the soul returns to the body. That is no mercy!"

"You're a strange man, Rone."

"You're the only one questioning their burial. It's *you* that's strange."

"Don't try to turn this around on me, you scoundrel," she said, a smile cracking her ash-greyed face. "You are a very, very strange man, but I still love you. And I know you love me." She stood on her toes and kissed his jaw. His face, taught from the tension of a fight, relaxed at the touch.

"It makes it complicated."

"You'll have to deal with it."

Rone wiped some grit from her face with his thumb and sighed.

"What is it?"

"I think your importance in all this might have dropped somewhat. War is here."

"Lucky for me, my partner is a fierce warrior."

"Partner?"

"Well, I can't very well keep calling you my bodyguard, or my servant, can I?"

"Suit yourself," Rone said, raising his eyebrows in a kind of faux disregard.

"I'm starting to do just that," Charlotte said and hugged him around his waist.

End of Book II

ABOUT THE AUTHOR

David Van Dyke Stewart is an author, musician, YouTuber, and educator who currently lives in rural California with his wife and children.

He is the author of *Muramasa: Blood Drinker, Water of Awakening,* the *Needle Ash* series, the *Moonsong* series, and *The Crown of Sight,* as well as numerous novellas, essays, and short stories. He is also the primary performer in the music project *David V. Stewart's Zul.*

You can find his YouTube channel at http://www.youtube.com/rpmfidel where he creates content on music education, literary analysis, movie analysis, philosophy, and logic.

Sign up to his mailing list at http://dvspress.com/list for a free book and advance access to future projects. You can email any questions or concerns to stu@dvspress.com.

Be sure to check http://davidvstewart.com and http://dvspress.com for news and free samples of all his books.

CPSIA information can be obtained
at www.ICGtesting.com
Printed in the USA
BVHW010654311220
596645BV00014B/85